READER'S DIGEST

CONDENSED BOOKS

FIRST EDITION

Published by

THE READER'S DIGEST ASSOCIATION LIMITED
25 Berkeley Square, London W1X 6AB.

THE READER'S DIGEST ASSOCIATION SOUTH AFRICA (PTY) LTD.
Nedbank Centre, Strand Street, Cape Town

Typeset in 10 on $11\frac{1}{2}$ pt. Highland Lumitype Roman
and printed in Great Britain by Petty & Sons Ltd., Leeds
and Carlisle Web Offset Ltd., Carlisle

Original cover design by Jeffery Matthews A.R.C.A.

For information as to ownership
of copyright in the material in this book see last page

ISBN 0 340 19183 X

READER'S DIGEST
CONDENSED BOOKS

COLLECTOR'S LIBRARY
EDITION

In this volume

COLLISION
by Spencer Dunmore (p.9)

The jam-packed airspace above our cities is haunted by the nightmare of collision. It is totally dependent upon sophisticated safety devices and rigid international traffic control regulations. But the most cunning device, the strictest regulation, both are subject ultimately to human fallibility . . . and to the million-to-one chance against which no one can guard. This, then, is a novel about human fallibility, about love and hate, about mistaken pride and divided loyalties. It is also a novel about that million-to-one chance, and how it was that no one was on guard against it.

WILD GOOSE, BROTHER GOOSE
by Mel Ellis (p.117)

Among birds the Canada goose is an aristocrat; strong, beautiful, and – some would say – wise. This is the sensitively-written story of two years in the life of one such bird, his adventures and incredible journeys across many thousands of miles. Based on the author's keen personal observations, it tells movingly of the gander's devotion to his mate, his care of their fledgelings, his triumphant survival in the face of guns, traps, tornadoes and starvation. It is a book to fascinate any nature lover, young or old.

THE PROPERTY OF A GENTLEMAN

by Catherine Gaskin
(p.179)

Strangers were not welcome at Thirlbeck. Yet when Joanna came to the old house to appraise its valuable antiques, she stayed on—in love with the house, its history, and its heir. For all her love, Joanna was aware of some bizarre mystery surrounding Thirlbeck, in particular the uneasy presence of a Spanish girl long dead . . . Once again the unrivalled Catherine Gaskin tells a compelling story rich in romance and subtle intrigue.

I CAN JUMP PUDDLES

by Alan Marshall
(p. 349)

For those who had legs that worked, legs were all very well and good. But for those who didn't, arms —and courage—were fine things to be blessed with. So Alan Marshall's father believed, and so he taught his son. For young Alan childhood became a running battle against the handicap of polio. He refused to admit himself a cripple. And now, as he looks back on those years, he reveals not only the struggle and the pain but also an extraordinary, unexpected gaiety.

GO IN AND SINK!

by Douglas Reeman
(p.433)

Lieutenant Commander Marshall was a tired man: three years of war had taken their toll. But now it was 1943, and his new command vital to Allied

plans. The British had captured a German U-Boat intact, ready for battle. Marshall's task was to captain her in a deadly masquerade, striking against any target that might pave the way to invasion. It was a duty he could not refuse.

Published by Peter Davies, London

Collision

A CONDENSATION OF THE BOOK BY

SPENCER DUNMORE

Illustrated by Cecil Vieweg

"*Suddenly the barometric pressure soared. As if someone had pressed a button, the winds abruptly shifted. Hail thrashed the earth, and the sky became a battleground . . .*"

Three aircraft enter the turbulence over Toronto simultaneously: a charter Boeing 707, on its way from Gander; a Douglas DC-8 coming in from Los Angeles; and a lightweight Aeronca flown by an inexperienced, but enthusiastic pilot, Henry Peel.

Are the weather conditions the cause of the catastrophe to come, or does the blame rest with the pilots, each distracted by personal problems of his own making?

This is Spencer Dunmore's most ambitious novel to date, a novel about planes and people—pilots, passengers and crew, wives who wait and wonder—all under pressure, the incessant pressure that forces them to the point of *collision*.

CHAPTER ONE

The right main landing-gear of a Boeing 747 of Anglo-World Airways cut Lee Chan's general store in half.

The incident took place a few minutes before midnight. The shop was closed but Lee Chan had remained to work on his accounts.

It was raining hard but through the drumming on his sheet-steel roof Lee Chan heard the approaching aircraft. He took no notice. Aircraft were always flying over his shop on their way to the International Airport, bringing traders and tourists to the coast of Africa.

He continued to work. Then he looked up, frowning. The aircraft was uncommonly loud. The roof was shuddering. Lee Chan shook his head, annoyed. Aeroplanes should not be permitted to make such a din so late at night.

Then the 747's undercarriage sliced through the shop timber and corrugated-iron structure like a razor through butter. A slow motion film would have shown the building staggering, bending and finally collapsing.

Dazed but unhurt, Lee Chan stood in the wreckage of his shop and watched as the 747 hit the ground a thousand yards beyond— five miles short of the runway at the International Airport.

The plane touched down in tolerably good landing attitude even though most of its right undercarriage had been shorn off. The

huge machine veered wildly to one side and the nose gear and left main unit crumpled and snapped. Skidding, the Boeing's wings and engine took the weight and the punishment. Metal buckled and ripped. One entire JT9D engine unit went bouncing between two shacks. Another skidded and vanished with an explosion of steam into a river.

Blindly, like a suicidal beast, the plane plunged across the scrub, scything a path through bushes and trees. Three-quarters of a mile later it came to a stop.

The 364 passengers, 15 cabin crew and 3 flight members were shaken but unhurt.

There was a minimum of panic among the passengers. Most were benumbed and stared stupidly as crew members dashed through the 747's cavernous hull, exhorting everyone to escape via the chutes and the emergency exits.

"Hurry! Please hurry! She might catch fire!"

Everyone, it seemed, came to their senses simultaneously. There was a scrambling. Shoving. Clutching. A woman slipped and fell.

A child screamed. At the exits there was cowardice—and courage too: standing back and permitting the old or the young to jump out first.

At last the enormous jet was empty. She didn't burn. Mute and still, she lay in the dirt, her engines scattered, her ribs exposed. Heavy raindrops hit them with odd, ringing thuds.

"I say, it's raining," observed a tall man. He sounded surprised although he was already drenched; a woman opened her umbrella; it struck a portly man as hilarious. He laughed unrestrainedly.

The passengers gathered in confused little groups. Members of the crew hurried among them. No need for further alarm. Yes, everyone was safe. A few cuts and contusions were apparently the worst that anyone had suffered. Transportation would be arriving very soon to take them to the airport. And yes, Anglo-World Airways was extremely sorry about the whole thing but, no, it couldn't be said at this time precisely what caused it or what the Corporation might be prepared to do about it.

A tractor materialized through the deluge. Its driver, cowled like a monk, asked in sing-song English if there was some assistance he might be.

"Aye," said a man with a Lancashire accent. "Do you have any petrol? We've run out."

Then the official traffic began to arrive, sirens wailing, lights blinking.

ROGER T. THORNE dabbed at his forehead with a handkerchief. A plump man, he was Anglo-World's local manager—a job that under normal circumstances was only moderately demanding. Suddenly, however, the world's news agencies wanted to talk to him; the local papers wanted to photograph him.

All very flattering of course, but Thorne knew the drill. No statements to the Press until Head Office in London gave the nod. A crash had to be handled like the public relations dynamite it was. The Corporation's reputation and the ticket-buying decisions of who knows how many people were at stake.

"Be helpful to the Press," the Procedure Manual advised, "but do not permit them to interview members of the crew. Confine your remarks to facts. Do not reveal the names of any passengers."

It was easier said than done, Thorne had discovered. A reporter after information was like a shark who has tasted blood.

He scowled at the buzzer on his desk.

"A Mr. Parrone on line one. He's with Reuter's."

Thorne sighed. "Just give him the statement I dictated to you. And tell him we have no more information at the present time. Then hang up." He looked at the man sitting opposite him, a man in a dark blue uniform spattered with white mud. "The media will be hounding me now, absolutely hounding me."

"I'm sorry to cause you so much trouble," murmured the man.

"No trouble, old man. After all, it wasn't *intentional*."

"No, it wasn't intentional."

"Are you feeling all right, old man? You look a bit pale."

"I often get pale when I crash-land 747's."

"I . . . yes, quite."

Thorne sniffed. Sarcastic sod, this Beatty. No need for it. Didn't help the situation one bloody iota.

The buzzer again. "London on line one."

Thorne cleared his throat and reached for the telephone.

FOR THE FIRST TIME in ten years Frank Beatty regretted having given up smoking. He was tempted to reach for the cigarettes on Thorne's desk—but no, they would unquestionably taste frightful.

He rubbed his eyes. Why did his mind persist in dwelling on trivialities? Didn't he have critically important things to think out? Wasn't his entire future in the balance?

A tall, spare man in his late forties, Beatty had a face that an aunt had once described as "patrician"—the result of high cheekbones, a prominent, though well-formed nose and lines of unusual severity framing his regular features. At Anglo-World he was considered somewhat reserved and caustic. The truth was that he was shy, and he tended to over-compensate for his shyness by speaking directly and sometimes curtly. Only a few of his intimates knew that he possessed a lively sense of humour. He looked younger than his years; only in the sunlight was it noticeable that his thick hair contained as much grey as blond.

They're going to crucify you, he thought. They have no choice. There are no extenuating circumstances. You were in command and you flew the bloody aeroplane into the ground. It's that simple. What isn't so simple is, *why*. He didn't know. The events were curiously blurred and foggy.

But Diane will be an absolute brick, he thought. The soul of loyalty. Not for an instant will she suspect that any of this might have been my fault. But what of Vincent? Would the boys at school make fun of him?

Beatty shook his head. I wish I had been killed, he thought. Oblivion seemed infinitely preferable to a future full of questions and sidelong glances. There's Beatty. Flew a 747 into the deck. Good man in his day, but . . . .

Beatty had wanted to be an airman since he was eight years old. He learnt the fundamentals of flying ten years later on the Downs at Dunstable, strapped into the hard tin seat of a glider. When the war came he flew Tiger Moths, Oxfords, Ansons and Wellingtons, and he applied for a permanent commission when the war ended. He stayed in the air force half a dozen years, flying coal to Berlin and paratroops to Salisbury Plain.

In the early fifties he presented himself and his log-book (a wondrously worn affair detailing some six thousand hours aloft) to Anglo-World Airways. The Corporation accepted him as a probationary pilot at £625 per annum plus £99 Daily Allowance. He worked hard and progressed to first-officer rank. Seven years ago he had made the leap up to captain at £10,000 a year. He had arrived at the peak.

And now this.

Thorne was talking earnestly to London, assuring them that everything was being handled the Corporation way. By now, Beatty reflected, in the minds of the powers-that-be, he would have become part of the wreckage that the authorities would examine and eventually cart away.

"Captain Beatty. The Chairman wants to speak to you."

Beatty took the telephone. "Hullo, sir. Beatty here."

The Chairman seemed undismayed by the fact that a ten-million-pound aeroplane had been written off. He said that he was most frightfully sorry to hear what had happened but he was gratified to learn that no one had been seriously hurt.

"Have you been in touch with your wife, Captain?"

"Yes sir, I spoke to her on the telephone."

"Excellent. I'm sure she must have been relieved to hear from you. I believe you are coming back to London tomorrow morning."

"Yes sir."

"Good, good. Well, the important thing is that everyone is safe. What you should do now is to get a good night's rest. You'll feel as right as rain after a good night's rest."

"Yes sir," said Beatty. "Good-bye, sir. Thank you."

He handed the telephone back to Thorne. A kindly man, the Chairman, to telephone him halfway around the world. Or was it written into his contract, to telephone the surviving captains of Corporation crashes?

Beatty massaged his right wrist. It ached. Tomorrow he would be flown back to London. To the questions. You've got to think up some bloody answers, he told himself. *You've got to remember.*

IT WAS EASY to remember the departure from New York. Utterly normal. After the pre-flight routine checks, Anglo-World 712 was ready to roll.

Beatty, and Oscar Dowling, the first officer, sat side by side in the forward seats. Between them, before them and above them were the dials, levers and switches that controlled the entire

14

aircraft. Behind the two pilots, facing to starboard, sat Milden, the flight engineer.

Cleared for take-off, the 747 began its roll, three hundred tons propelled by the power of air being compressed, expanded by fuel combustion, then ejected in a furious stream to the rear.

Quickly the enormous machine picked up speed, although from the lofty height of the flight deck, the pace still seemed lethargic. A light pressure on the rudder pedal corrected a tendency to wander from the runway's centre line. Time to coax the whole colossal contraption into the air. The white runway strips became a single line. A gentle easing back on the control column, and the rumbling of the main gear ceased. Airborne.

The jet thrust her nose up through haze and scattered cloud into the clean sunshine. Effortlessly the JT9D engines propelled her to her cruising altitude.

Now the aircraft was controlled by a complex of computers, accelerometers and gyroscopes collectively known as the Inertial Navigation System ("the little black boxes" to the flight crew who did little more now than supervise the workings of the system).

Beatty stifled a yawn. No time for dozing. He watched the control column moving gently in obedience to the nagging demands of the little black boxes. Insulting, the sheer efficiency of the things. The truth was that the little black boxes could fly a smoother, more accurate path than any human pilot. And they could land the 747 by itself, superbly. But sometimes the boxes went wrong. Then the humans had to come in and sort out the mess; they still had their uses.

Beatty pretended not to notice the glances from Dowling. He had flown with him before. Nice enough chap, but appallingly loquacious. Give him the slightest encouragement and he would chat the rest of the way to Africa. Beatty preferred a quiet, contemplative trip.

Dowling's face was a series of jolly but rather over-fed curves, bubbling out of his wilting collar. He was a year or two older than Beatty, a veteran of three decades of flying, a superb craftsman. At his age he should have been a captain. No one seemed to know why he wasn't. Perhaps it was simply his girth. Or his garrulity.

The clouds began to thin. Now the Atlantic could be seen, restless, merciless. As he often did, Beatty spared a thought for the doughty souls of the twenties and thirties who had attempted to span the ocean in their underpowered and overloaded crates. Somewhere in the waters below a sixty-three-year-old lady of noble birth had gone to her death, dressed in a bright blue suede flying suit. Aboard her aircraft she had been carrying half a dozen hat boxes containing the millinery she intended to wear on her triumphal tour of North America as the first woman to fly the Atlantic. Something had gone wrong; they never found a trace of her, her aircraft or her hat boxes.

The big jet sped on, becoming lighter at a rate of four hundred and seventy pounds per minute as the engines thirstily consumed fuel. The passengers ate, watched a film, then ate again. A man made an indecent proposition to a stewardess. Two dinners were spilled in laps. One hold-all crammed with holiday funds was lost. And found. It was a normal trip.

An hour from the African coast Beatty told his passengers that the weather ahead was not good. "It's been raining on and off all day," he said, "the temperature is ninety-seven degrees Fahrenheit with a humidity of ninety-four. A trifle sticky, I'm afraid. We expect to be parked in front of the terminal building in fifty-eight minutes."

He released the intercom button on his mike, glad to have the tiresome little PA duty done. He disliked talking to invisible people who didn't respond. But hearing the captain's voice was said to be good for the passengers' peace of mind.

In the early jet days their peace of mind was assured by personal visits from the great man. But during one trip across the Atlantic, an auto-pilot had become disengaged. The captain was in the passenger cabin and the first officer, engrossed in a book, didn't notice the problem until the jet snapped suddenly into a dive. The captain managed to get back to the flight deck. Together he and the first officer coaxed the machine out of its plunge. And only just in time. Tossing waves were said to have slapped the undersides of the wings as it levelled out. From then on, captains were required to remain on the flight deck, leaving only for calls of nature.

Another weather report: rain, torrential at times, visibility ranging from five hundred yards to two miles.

Beatty's eyes prickled with fatigue. Why was it that sometimes one could sleep like a top in a strange bed and at other times it was impossible? He had gone to bed at midnight, leaving a message with the desk to call him at 6:00 a.m. But it was already 6:00 a.m. in London where Beatty had last slept. As far as his body was concerned, the new day had already begun. When he rose at six he hadn't slept a minute. He had felt groggy and slightly dizzy, but he had to go to work. After this trip there would be thirty-six hours of recuperation in which his body could sort out whether it was day or night.

Now the clouds were thick. The airport was reporting visibility down to half a mile. The controller was instructed, "Anglo-World Seven One Two, continue on heading one niner fife until you intercept the ILS for runway one six. Over."

"Tell the passengers we'll probably be encountering some turbulence," Beatty said to Dowling.

The 747 rocked and swayed in the clouds as it was slowed with flaps and air-brakes. Beatty watched the ILS dial. The vertical needle indicated direction, the horizontal needle the angle of descent. Both were bang-on.

"Undercarriage please."

"Gear down, sir."

Still nothing to be seen outside but swirling, dank greyness that smeared wet fingers over the windscreen.

"Middle marker."

"Roger."

"Altitude is . . ."

Beatty didn't hear the altitude. Other matters were capturing his attention. The ILS needles were wandering, stating with dreadful clarity that the aircraft was pitching and tumbling through the murk. His hands moved to wrest control from the auto-pilot. Not an instant to lose. But there was a gap somewhere. Moments seemed to drift by. Voices were low and languid. Lights kept flashing, although the flashing was somehow lethargic. The control column was exerting back-pressure, but it was a gentle, undemanding kind of pressure. Beatty saw Dowling turn, hands reaching, clutching. The noises faded, then returned, amplified until they were deafening, stupefying.

He saw the building, dead ahead.

Suddenly the noise ceased. The ground swept up at him. He felt the wrenching, twisting thump of impact. He was aware that his mouth had opened. But no words came.

CHAPTER TWO

A few minutes after 8:00 p.m., a DC-8 in the eye-catching red and gold livery of TranState Airlines touched down at Toronto International Airport. The passengers disembarked, followed by the crew and the captain. Of average height, he moved in an easy, fluid way. The dark blue TranState uniform flattered his trim frame. He had a pleasant face, good-natured rather than handsome, blue eyes, a strong, well-formed jaw and dark brown hair touched by grey at the temples. His name was Charles Vaughan.

"In my entirely unhumble opinion," Walt Przeczek said to Vaughan, "your average airport has as much gorgeous stuff walking around it as your average Playboy Club."

He looked around the terminal building, smiling at females of every age. An astonishingly high proportion of them smiled back.

Walt Przeczek was a large man, over six feet in height, ugly and yet with overwhelming charm. He was also a TranState captain, although junior to Vaughan. At a few hours' notice he had been asked to fly co-pilot for Vaughan to Chicago, Toronto and New York; the scheduled first officer was down with the 'flu. The arrangement suited both men; they were old friends and had flown together dozens of times; now they lived within five miles of one another in the San Bernardino mountains near Los Angeles.

Together they made for the TranState office. There, they heard for the first time about Beatty's crash.

"Did anyone get out?" It was the first, urgent question.

"They all did," said Adler, the company's Toronto traffic manager.

"What happened?"

Adler shrugged. "All I heard, the guy undershot and hit a store. I just hope that he has got something good and solid to blame. Spoiler malfunction or a runaway stabilizer. Something. And I hope he can prove it. If not, he's in one hell of a lot of trouble."

Vaughan agreed. Investigating committees seemed only too eager to heap Everests of blame upon the captains of crashed airliners, especially it seemed, those who weren't alive to defend themselves.

18

He handed Adler the flight documents, way-bills and passenger manifest that represented the official existence of Flight Twelve. The flight was due to leave on the last leg of the trip, from Toronto to New York, in fifty-one minutes.

Adler reported that there would be forty-three passengers joining at Toronto. Vaughan nodded. That would put him well over the magic sixty-two per cent occupancy figure, the point at which TranState started making aviation pay.

According to Met, the east coast had been hit by severe thunderstorms earlier in the day. There would be moderate to severe turbulence en route, but the worst should be over by the time Flight Twelve reached New York.

Light rain was falling when Vaughan and Przeczek walked out to the DC-8 and commenced their routine external inspection. It was Przeczek who observed the jet fuel on the underside of the left wing. He and Vaughan examined it together. All wings of jet liners tended to leak, but it was a question of degree. How much was acceptable?

"Better get in touch with Dispatch," said Vaughan. "Tell them there could be a delay. I'm talking to Maintenance."

Irwin, the chief mechanic, said there was a gunk that would do the trick. "No sweat, captain. If it were a big leak, we'd have to strip the wing. They'll probably do that when you get back to LA. But in the meantime the gunk'll do just fine."

"What happens when the gunk sets? Does it get dry and hard?"

"I guess so. It's a sort of plastic, you know."

"What happens if the wing flexes more than usual in flight? In turbulence, say."

Irwin pondered for a moment. "Reckon the leak could open up again," he admitted. "But I never heard of it. Always worked just great."

Vaughan walked slowly back to the office. "I'm sorry," he told Adler. "I'm cancelling. We've got a leak."

Adler clicked his tongue as he studied the passenger manifest. He seemed to be silently counting the money TranState was going to lose.

"Can I use your phone?" Vaughan asked.

"Be my guest."

In three minutes, Vaughan was explaining the situation to the company's Flight Director in Los Angeles. "Maintenance can only provide a temporary plastic filler to plug the leak."

"And does Maintenance say the stuff will be satisfactory for the trip to New York?" The Flight Director had a terse, incisive way of expressing himself.

"Yes, sir, but there's turbulence and the wing is going to flex more than on an average flight. If it does, and if that stuff has dried and hardened, then the leak will open up again."

"Yes, but if Maintenance—"

"Maintenance isn't flying the aircraft, sir, I am."

"If you'll permit me to get a word in edgewise, Captain—*if* Maintenance says the leak is minor, then my advice would be to make the flight."

Vaughan felt irritation bubbling within him. "To a guy in a hangar, a leak can easily be classified as 'minor'. But it can look as major as hell to another man thirty thousand feet up in the air. I'm cancelling the flight, sir."

When the conversation ended, Vaughan felt drained. The Flight Director had urged him to think of the inconvenience to the passengers, the damage to the company's reputation, the expense of re-scheduling. But Vaughan was stubborn. He knew he was right to cancel the flight.

Adler went off to inform the passengers while Vaughan completed the Flight Cancellation documents. Under "Reason for Cancellation Decision" he wrote: "Moderate to severe turbulence was to be expected en route (see Met report attached). This turbulence made temporary repair of wing leak a safety hazard. In my opinion the leak could not be classified as 'minor' and the possible danger to the aircraft and passengers was completely unacceptable. (Signed) C. J. Vaughan, Capt."

But no matter how carefully he phrased the thing, there would be trouble. Cancellations were about as popular at TranState as FAA inspectors. On countless occasions, TranState aircraft had flown when other lines had opted to stay put. Management was fond of reminding employees that the only way to make a profit was to keep flying. In the five years since he had become a captain, Vaughan had cancelled only a dozen flights. In each case the circumstances were such that management couldn't complain. But this time the whole thing was open to interpretation. He

20

decided to write down the complete sequence of events for the inevitable company inquiry.

He was engrossed in this task when Przeczek came bursting into the office, grinning delightedly. "Great news, buddy. I happened to bump into a bevy of luscious ladies from Air Canada. They've invited us to a party in Toronto somewhere. One of them is getting married or divorced or something."

Vaughan smiled despairingly. "Can't you ever stop bumping into strange women? Count me out."

"You're coming, Charles."

"Walt, it's definitely no. Absolutely, irrevocably no!"

THE ROOM was packed. And noisy. And infernally hot. Vaughan put up with it for a couple of hours. Someone trod on his foot; someone else spilled a gin-and-something down his tunic front. A young man called him "sir" which depressed him a little. He wondered what had happened to Walt as he edged towards the door.

"Are you Martin?" A girl was asking the question, a girl with very fair hair that fell straight to her shoulders.

Vaughan shook his head. "I'm not Martin. Sorry."

"I haven't met him yet, you see."

"Nor me," said Vaughan.

"Then you must know Peggy."

"Peggy?"

"She's the one who's marrying Martin." The girl frowned, puzzled. "Are you at the right party, for goodness sake?"

Vaughan chuckled. "You might say I was invited by proxy. I don't know anyone here, except the screwball I came with and he's vanished."

"She's invited too many guests," said the girl. She had an intriguingly husky quality to her voice. "Typical Peggy. Always overdoing everything. Peggy and I were stews together for Air Canada. What line are you with?"

"TranState. Out of Los Angeles."

"Do you like flying?"

"It's better than working for a living."

She smiled. She had heard the adage before. Her teeth were white and even except for the front left incisor which angled

slightly away from its mate. Curiously, the imperfection failed to detract from her looks.

"You're not a stew any more?"

"No," she said. "I quit when I realized waitresses on the ground were making more money. But I like flying. So I took up gliding."

"Gliding?"

"We have a little club about forty miles out of town." She reached into a brown leather handbag and withdrew a billfold. The licence, issued by the Canadian Department of Transport, was made out to PRINGLE, Rosalie.

Vaughan said: "I've never flown in a glider."

"If you're willing to part with four dollars, we can fix you up with an introductory flight."

"I might take you up on that, Rosalie."

"Isn't that a hideous name? Everyone calls me Lee." She smiled again, "Do you live in LA?"

"About eighty miles outside the city. Up in the mountains. A little place called Blue Jay."

"Sounds nice."

"I like it." *Why didn't you say; "We like it?"* He asked her: "Do you live in Toronto?"

"Yes. The west end. Near High Park. Do you like Toronto?"

"Sure do. Good places to eat. Two or three theatres. You can walk around without getting mugged. And there's usually some real fine jazz in town."

She looked up. "You like jazz?"

"Uh huh."

"Me too."

"No kidding. Most people who like jazz—I mean, *really* dig it— are men."

"Typical male." She shook her head reprovingly.

"I apologize. Who do you like on trumpet?"

She grinned. "Testing me, huh? O.K. I dig Miles Davis, Clark Terry and Maynard Ferguson. By the way," she added, "Stan Getz is in town—at the Colonial."

"I just had an idea," said Vaughan.

WHEN VAUGHAN landed at Los Angeles he was requested to report to the Chief Pilot at 9:00 a.m. two days hence. It meant a ninety minute drive into the city during his off-duty period. The corporate needle was at work.

His white Cougar sat baking in the sun in the parking lot where he had left it three days before. At that time, he reflected as he eased himself into the driver's seat, you were in pretty good standing with the company. And you weren't an adulterer.

He started the engine. I'm honestly sorry, Susan, he told his wife silently. I didn't want to hurt you. I really didn't *mean* to do what I did. In daylight the whole thing seemed inconceivable.

He drove along Century Boulevard then turned north, accelerating into the bunched, speeding traffic of the Harbor Freeway. After the orderly patterns of aerial traffic, the freeways always seemed terrifying.

He dreaded the confrontation with Susan. Would she *know*, the instant he walked into the house? Would the guilt in his eyes blurt out the whole sordid story as surely as words?

But it wasn't sordid. What happened was wrong; there could be no denying that. It wasn't sordid, however. But how could he convey the fact to Susan? Should he even try?

He edged across the lanes as the Route 10 exit neared. Was all this really happening to *him*? Square old Chuck Vaughan? The guy whose idea of a big time was to curl up with a Budweiser and the *Journal of the American Aviation Historical Society*? He was the

23

one who had shaken his innocent head at the pilots who maintained discreet little pads in Chicago and Atlanta and Montreal. Now he was an ageing Lothario, just like the others, and just as despicable.

You're nearly old enough to be her father, he thought. But you conveniently neglected to mention that fact. She told you she was twenty-four. Did you figure she'd take you for thirty? Thirty-five tops? But the fact that Lee was almost sixteen years his junior proved to have a curious elasticity.

The traffic began to thin. The mountains were near. Blue Jay was 6,000 feet above sea level, way above the smog. Vaughan had bought the cottage almost ten years before, soon after Janet's birth, as a weekend escape from the apartment in Inglewood. Then, as tensions in the city mounted, the decision was made. The cottage became a home. Huddled against the hillside, it had doubled in size, sprouting bedrooms, patios, sun-decks.

He sped up the mountain road, his tyres squealing round the tortuous curves. He far exceeded the 40 m.p.h. speed limit as if craving to hasten the moment of confrontation—and yet his stomach churned in apprehension.

Six-year-old Lynn met him on the driveway. The Carters' cat had had kittens. Could she have one? Vaughan said he would think about it. Lynn sighed and nodded. She had guessed that would be the response.

"Hi, Chuck."

Susan was in the doorway, jeans and check shirt in becoming contrast to her rather dainty features. She wore just a touch of make-up. With her short dark hair, she could still turn heads on Wilshire Boulevard. "Good trip?"

He smiled. "Fine." He kissed her. As if nothing had happened, nothing had changed. It was easy. Damnably easy.

CHAPTER THREE

Captain Fisher, Chief Pilot for Anglo-World Airways, stoked his pipe, slowly, methodically. Sometimes the act of getting his pipe operational helped to solve problems. This time it did not help a bit. What faced him was a vile job and there was no getting out of it. For so many years, Beatty had been an excellent fellow in every way. But, dash it all, he had flown the thing into the ground when it was apparently in good working order. It was true that conditions were poor. Torrential rain could affect the glide path and localizer beams. But every airline pilot knew of such problems and was ready for them.

The first officer, Dowling, had been of little help. Busy with his check-lists and instruments, he had been unaware of any problem until instants before the aircraft hit the shop.

Fisher relit his pipe. Should Beatty's superb record be taken into consideration? No, of course not. Beatty was paid superbly to handle aircraft superbly. In return, a masterful performance was expected at all times. He had spoken of extreme fatigue. But the Corporation rules were straightforward: a pilot had to ground himself if for any reason he felt physically unfit for flying. No excuse could be found there.

A knock on the door. Miss Abbott announced that Captain Beatty had arrived. Fisher didn't respond for a moment. If only the aircraft had had something wrong with it. Something blameable. Damn! He had bitten through his pipe stem.

"Ask Captain Beatty to come in, please."

"THEY WERE really very nice about it," Frank Beatty told his wife. "Very reasonable, actually. But the fact remains that I have now joined the ranks of the unemployed."

"They are rotters," Diane declared, her fists clenched. "After all the years you've given them."

"I've hardly *given* them any years," said Beatty. "They bought them, at a pretty high price. Besides, they had no choice but to let me go." He smiled wryly. "I don't suppose it's any consolation but they permitted me to resign under my own steam. They didn't have to do that."

Diane wasn't placated. "It was the least they could do."

Beatty smiled again. Diane was frightfully worked up about it. Understandable, of course. The question was: why wasn't *he* frightfully worked up? He reminded himself: It isn't some other poor soul they're sacking. And your licence is revoked for three months. You are grounded. What do you have to say about that?

The worst had happened, yet nothing had changed. The world still tottered on.

25

Diane asked: "Are you going to talk to the Association about it?"

"I don't think so. I haven't been denied any rights. I can't honestly say I've been unfairly treated or victimized. The company did what it felt was necessary."

"Why do you defend them after what they've done to you?"

"I'm not defending them. Let's suppose A-W kept me on as a captain, and I had another crash. Imagine the headlines. BEATTY PRANGS AGAIN. After that, how much confidence would the travelling public have in Anglo-World?"

"It's horrid and unfair."

He took her hand and held it between both of his. By degrees her anger evaporated. Then she became the comforter. Everything was going to be all right, she told him. There were hundreds of other airlines. Scores of them would jump at the opportunity of obtaining a captain with his experience and skill. In the long run it would all turn out to be a blessing in disguise. She suggested a drink. He agreed. The whisky tasted good. Possibly, he thought, this is the first step to a brand new career as a hopeless alcoholic.

Vincent came in, mumbled hello and dashed upstairs. Beatty wondered whether he would succeed in getting his son to cut his long hair before his return to school. He would be at home until early September—until twenty-nine days before licence reinstatement. Funny, Beatty thought, how he had worried over Vincent's reaction to the crash. But there had scarcely been a reaction: just a kind of mild annoyance that Father had done something not terribly bright, like taking the wrong turn off the M1. The kid was so unbelievably secure.

"Another one, darling?"

"Why not?"

Why not indeed. He watched her as she poured the drinks. She was taller than most women, slightly over five feet ten. She carried her height with a grace that Beatty had first noticed at a Corporation Christmas dance.

A navigator named Kellaway had brought her. Shortly before midnight, he went off to replenish drinks, leaving her alone. Beatty crossed the floor as the band groaned into action. A clearing of throat. Would she care to dance? Yes, it seemed she wouldn't mind at all. To the laboured strains of "Moonglow", he cleared his throat again and asked if she might care to have a spot of dinner one night? Absurdly, he added that he was sure Kellaway wouldn't mind. Happily, she was amused rather than irked. She would love to have dinner with him, even if Kellaway *did* object.

Seven months later they were married. No flutter-brained kids, they; he was thirty-six; she was twenty-eight. Twelve years later, Diane still carried herself well, her features unremarkable but pleasant. Beatty loved her and considered himself lucky to have found her. But it never crossed his mind to tell her.

"I was talking to mother," Diane said. "She's frightfully sorry about it."

"And your father?"

"He said it . . . it was a shame, or something."

"He was right. It is a shame or something."

Beatty's own parents had died more than ten years before. They had hated his flying. Medicine, they said, was the profession; the world needed doctors and accorded them respect and magnificent livings. You were right, Beatty thought. I won't let Vincent make the same mistake; the hirsute little rock-'n'-roller will do what I say . . . .

He smiled to himself. The whisky was working well.

HE AWOKE. Why? He listened. Nothing. He lay still. It was half-past four. The vulnerable hour.

You're grounded, he heard himself say. Chances are that you'll never fly for an airline again. You'll keep on applying and they'll keep on turning you down. You can hardly blame them, can you? You crashed. And you're nearly fifty. *Fifty.* Most pilots have had it by the time they reach fifty.

What then? A job in an office? Selling cars? Instructing? Damn it! If it hadn't been for that bloody crash-landing you could have expected more than ten years of airline flying before reaching mandatory retirement age.

Ten more years. A lifetime.

Fear lay on his stomach like a cold hand. His heart pounded. Loud, panicky. In a moment it would disturb Diane.

Why did I survive the crash? He stared at the ceiling and its mottled pattern of shadows. Why couldn't I have been the one casualty? It would have been so much simpler and neater. Diane would have found herself a moderately rich woman with the

27

insurance proceeds. And I wouldn't have had to face an utterly bloody future.

To make matters worse, he still didn't know why the crash happened. Uncertainty nagged at him like a toothache. Something had caused it. There was always a reason.

"Darling, are you awake?" Diane spoke softly, sleepily.

He didn't answer. In a few moments he felt her relax. She slept.

He left the house at eight, wearing his track garb. He told Diane he would be back for breakfast in thirty minutes. He headed for his usual route: the path beside the river, then over the bridge, through the wood and back by the railway lines.

It was a fine morning after an overnight shower. The world smelt fresh and good. Beatty set himself an easy pace. He enjoyed jogging; it had been a part of his life since an A-W doctor had observed an increase of seven pounds in six months.

His body seemed particularly well balanced today, everything pulling and pushing and pumping in splendid concert. He reached the wooden bridge. Hardly breathing hard. Lungs like a lad of eighteen! With constitution to match!

Cinders crunched softly beneath his shoes. Still he breathed easily. Optimism now warmed him. He *would* get back into flying. Others had bounced back from adversity, hadn't they? Take Bader; smashed up a Bristol Bulldog doing fancy aerobatics at Woodley; lost both legs in the process. Did he let that minor inconvenience prevent him barging his way back into the RAF and subsequently shooting down twenty or more Jerries? No, indeed.

Dash it all, airlines *need* experienced people like me, Beatty thought. I have lots to offer. It may not be easy to become re-established but I shall do it. I shall keep on trying until I do.

He was aware of the sun as he ran. It was strong and it came splashing down through the trees above him. The branches kept interrupting the light. It fell on his face and then vanished, like the flickering light from the old film projector. An instant of glare. An instant of gloom. Glare. Gloom. Light. Darkness. Black. White. Blackwhiteblackwhite. . . . Black.

HE HAD no recollection of falling.

"Did you hurt yourself, young man?" A man with white hair was speaking to him.

"No," said Beatty. He rubbed his eyes. "I don't think so."

"I'm relieved to hear it," said the man. "Would you like me to help you to your feet?"

"Help me? No . . . no, thank you." An absurd question.

The man's features were slightly blurred. And why was it necessary to hold onto a tree in order to pull himself up? The coarse black bark seemed to pulsate beneath his hands.

"If you are certain you are all right, I shall be on my way."

"What?" Beatty had momentarily forgotten the man's presence. "Yes, of course, thank you. I tripped. I'm O.K. now."

He watched the old man walk back towards the river. Decent of him to stop. Must have thought I'd dropped dead. Must have tripped. He took half a dozen deep breaths, then attempted a gentle trot. But it was no use. He had been robbed of his strength. He had to walk, slowly.

Diane asked what had happened.

"I fell down," he told her.

"Are you all right?"

"Perfectly."

"I was getting worried. You've been gone over an hour."

"Don't be ridiculous," he snapped.

She frowned, stung by his tone. "I'm not being ridiculous, Frank. It's after nine. Did you go a different way?"

"No," he said. "But I went around twice."

She smiled, everything was explained.

He went upstairs to change. All the clocks in the house said the same unbelievable thing. It was an hour and ten minutes since he left the house. And, despite his explanation to Diane, he knew he had travelled the course only once. Forty-five minutes had been lost somewhere. Evaporated. Vanished.

He was suddenly clammy with fear. Had he fallen and knocked himself out? But if he had knocked himself out, why didn't his head ache? Why no cuts or bruises?

Diane called up the stairs, asking if he would hurry; breakfast was ready.

"Be there in a mo!"

All very casual. Not-a-care-in-the-world Beatty. He changed into a sports shirt and slacks and went downstairs. He sniffed appreciatively at the bacon and eggs. But he had no appetite.

CHAPTER FOUR

Vaughan closed the telephone door behind him. He assembled a small heap of change. He wanted no itemized credit-card calls on monthly statements. Evidence for the prosecution.

"Operator. Can I help you?"

"I want to call Toronto, Canada."

He waited, betting that the phone would be slammed in his ear the moment he identified himself.

But she most likely wouldn't be in. She was an attractive girl, wasn't she? Why wouldn't she be out having a good time? One thing was for sure: she wouldn't have been spending the last three weeks waiting to hear from one Charles Vaughan. Chances are, he thought, she won't even remember me.

"That'll be sixty cents for the first three minutes."

Vaughan injected the coins. Soon the dull, far-off sound of the ringing could be heard.

"Hello."

One word. And he could picture her face in every detail (after twenty-one days of trying to reassemble the parts of his memory).

"Lee?"

"Yes. Chuck?"

"Yes."

"Chuck!" She laughed in her open way. "Where are you calling from? Are you in town?"

"No, Buffalo."

"That's not far. Are you coming to Toronto? How long have you got? It's good to hear your voice again, you know that?"

It disintegrated, the whole silly assemblage of apologies and explanations, reasons and protestations.

"I'll rent a car," he said. "How long does it take to get to Toronto from here?"

"Hour and a half to two hours. Take the Peace Bridge and just follow the Queen Elizabeth signs to Toronto. But hurry."

FROSTY MARTINIS. Good gin in cheap, thick glasses. Posters for art shows and bullfights. A jungle of plants, tumbling over shelves and tables. Teak and junk furniture in equal proportions. Matisse prints and two earnest original oils. A highway STOP sign over the bed. The warmth of her, her vibrancy, lingered in every corner of the little apartment.

White skin against black velvet cushions. The soft down on her arm. Her hair falling against her breasts. The touch of her long fingers on his back pressing insistently, urgently. Flesh against flesh. Tastes of ultimate pleasure.

They lay in silence. Vaughan dozed momentarily. He awoke and kissed her.

"You're marvellous," he said.

She kissed his nose. "You're O.K. yourself."

She stood up suddenly and walked into the living-room. A moment later the sound of piano, bass and drums filled the apartment. Oscar Peterson. Lee had not only a beautiful face and a magnificent body, but also splendid taste in music. And she was a glider pilot. What a girl! Vaughan found himself thinking how great it would have been had they met thirteen years before. He checked himself; Lee would have been only eleven years old.

She returned with two glasses of cold beer.

"You quit your job with Air Canada," he said. "So what do you do now?"

"Work for an advertising agency. I do copy for toilet paper and the things girl copy-writers usually get to work on. But one day I'd like to do an ad for a tractor or a Boeing 747. Something durable."

"Do you have family?"

"My parents are divorced. My mother lives in Brampton, not too far from Toronto. My father lives in Calgary. I was married once."

"You were?" He was surprised; he wasn't sure why.

"I was eighteen," she said. "He was twenty-one. A nice looking weakling. Cute curly hair but no backbone. I despised him after six months. Horrible, isn't it, how you can change?"

Vaughan glanced at her. "I'm married," he said.

"Of course you are," she said quietly. "And you have children."

"Two. I'm also forty years old or I will be in a few weeks."

"So?"

"So I thought I should tell you. Don't you care?"

"What, about your being forty or being married?"

"About either."

32

"They're truths," she said. "Facts. I'm quite a realistic person. I know you and I aren't going to come to anything. It's impossible." She looked up at him. "I want to tell you something, Chuck. I didn't think I'd ever see you again. I had promised myself that if you called me, I would tell you to get lost."

"Why?"

"Because you were obviously married although you hadn't told me then. So you were a lousy prospect. But all my good intentions flew out the window the moment I heard your voice. The very moment."

"Imagine that," said Vaughan.

IT WAS A sentence, a term to be served. Ninety days of enforced idleness, of petty irritability, of bitter, unreasoning thoughts. Ninety days of avoiding neighbours and tradesmen, of envying the crews of every aircraft that passed over the house. Flying was a part of Beatty; without it he was incomplete, only partly alive.

Vincent had returned to school, his hair uncut. The leaves turned. The weather cooled. Sluggishly the days passed. Diane, splendid Diane, was courageous. She ignored Beatty's savage moods. She pretended not to hear his insults. She went about her work as if he were not in the house.

During the second-to-last week, Oscar Dowling telephoned.

"Oscar Dowling, old man." His voice evoked memories of catastrophe, of questions. "How are you, Frank?"

"I'm well," said Beatty. "Taking it easy, you know."

"Jolly good. Envy you, old man."

Beatty frowned. Did Dowling imagine that he was doing a good turn, cheering up the black sheep?

Dowling said, "Look, this is absolutely none of my business, old man, but I thought I'd give you a tinkle about it anyway." He cleared his throat. "A chap I used to know during the war is starting up a new line and he thought I might be interested. I wasn't—well, you know, I'm a bit of a fixture at A-W now. But I thought of you."

"I see," said Beatty. Flatly, noncommittally. No point in getting eager, not yet.

"His name is Amory. A Canadian. Used to run Provincial Airways till the big boys bought him out. Made a good thing of it, I understand. And now he's decided to start a charter business over here. If I know old Don he'll make a success of it. Bit of a rough diamond, of course, but a good type when you get to know him. Anyway, he's in the market for some crews so I thought I'd tell you about it."

"It was thoughtful of you," Beatty said. "I'm much obliged."

"Don't mention it, old man."

"Of course, I have feelers out with several lines, but nothing has been signed and sealed as yet. So no harm in having a chat with your Mr . . ."

"Amory."

"Yes. Amory. Where can I get in touch with him?"

"He's at the Savoy. Nothing but the best for old Don. I took the liberty of mentioning your name already, so he's expecting to hear from you."

AMORY WAS A craggy-faced man in his fifties with broad shoulders and gigantic hands. He greeted Beatty at the door of his suite wearing a striped bathrobe. His feet were bare; his thinning hair was rumpled; he needed a shave. "Eaten lunch yet?" Beatty said he had.

"I haven't. You mind if I eat while we talk?"

"Not at all."

Amory telephoned room service and ordered a steak and two pots of coffee. "So you're the guy who piled up with old Ossie Dowling," he chuckled throatily.

"Yes sir, the actual circumstances—"

"I know all about the circumstances." His smile was surprisingly warm. "I don't waste my time talking to people until I've done some checking. You were with A-W a long time."

"Twenty years."

"When do you get your licence back?"

"Next week."

"You figure you did everything possible to prevent the crash?"

"Yes, I think so, sir. And the fact that my licence was revoked for only ninety days is an indication, I believe, of how doubtful the airline's decision was."

"Old Ossie thinks highly of you. Did he tell you what I'm planning?"

"Yes, sir, a charter operation."

"That's right. There's a lot of business around. I've already got some lined up. May have to do some sub-contracting; depends how soon we can get things rolling on our own. You think you'd be interested to come and work for me?"

"I. . . . I think I might, sir. I'd have to consider . . ."

"Not too sure about it?"

"It's just that . . . there are a couple of other companies . . ."

Amory raised a hand as if to express complete understanding.

"Sure, after flying for Anglo-World for twenty years, a little charter operation seems like real small potatoes."

"It's not exactly that, sir."

"Lots of prestige, I guess, working for A-W. And now there's a wild man from the Colonies with no offices, nothing but a whole lot of talk. I know how you feel. But remember, I've been a pretty successful guy in my time. In the end you might wind up farther ahead than if you'd stuck with A-W. Then again," he smiled, "it could turn out to be a real stinkin' bust."

When Beatty left the hotel an hour later he was simultaneously elated and alarmed. It was marvellous to think that he might be flying again in a mere matter of days. But for whom? And for how long? The job might last only a few months. And it would mean flying in the right-hand seat for a "while" according to Amory. Back to co-pilot on a 707 after being captain on a 747. Marvellous, he thought bitterly, what a bloody success story. ·

He walked along the Strand. In Trafalgar Square the inevitable tourists were feeding the inevitable pigeons. The sun appeared and played on damp stone lions. Deep in thought, Beatty strolled up Charing Cross Road. It became warm. He took off his raincoat and carried it on his arm.

He had told Amory that he wanted until Friday to think the offer over.

But was there really anything to think over? Letters from the airlines had been arriving in a steady stream, all with basically the same message inside. Thank you, Mr. Beatty, but no thank you. The simple truth was that he was branded. You've no choice, chum, not if you want to fly. All right. Nothing to be ashamed of, flying for a smaller line. Lots of chaps spent their entire careers doing it.

As he walked, his enthusiasm grew. Yes, it was going to be all right. Amory would succeed brilliantly with his UK charter company just as he had succeeded in Canada. And everyone involved would prosper.

He turned up Coventry Street. Cheerful now, he strolled in a leisurely manner—something he realized he hadn't done for ages. He sat on a bench in Leicester Square, a gentleman of leisure savouring the warmth of the autumn sun. Good old Amory; good old Oscar Dowling.

It will be a breeze to convert back to 707s, he thought. He spent a few enjoyable moments, trying to recall the exact positions of the instruments on the panel: ASI, Machmeter, compass comparator, horizon switch . . . .

He seemed to doze. The instrument panel became rubbery, the dials went floating away; wandering, bumping into one another.

Pressure. Something was crushing his shoulder. Something heavy, insistent. He opened his eyes. An empty cigarette packet, a dead match, yesterday's evening paper.

"Go home and sleep it off, chum."

"What?"

A burning pain seared through his skull. The light of the sun hurt his eyes.

"Come on, now, let's not have any trouble with you."

Beatty discerned a policeman, a young fellow with a kindly face. "Trouble?" He moved his shoulder but the policeman's hand remained. "What do you mean, officer?"

The policeman stooped lower. "Now you've 'ad one or two too many sir, 'aven't you?" His tone was less assured.

Beatty snapped, "I haven't been drinking, for God's sake."

"Are you ill then, sir?"

"My head hurts like hell."

"I'll call for an ambulance."

"No!" Beatty shook his head. "I'm all right now, Constable. I must have fallen asleep."

The policeman nodded gravely. "You were almost on the ground, sir, you were lolling half off the bench. I really did think you'd had a couple too many. But . . . if not, I beg pardon."

Beatty swallowed. His stomach churned. "It was good of you to be concerned, Constable. I'm all right now."

Reluctantly the policeman moved off. Beatty stood up. For a

frightening instant, the world revolved. He caught hold of the bench arm and steadied himself. A deep breath and he began to walk. His legs felt oddly disconnected, as if they belonged to someone else. Sweat beaded his forehead. He longed to collapse but no, damn it, he wouldn't give in. Nothing the matter, he kept telling himself. All that happened was that I fell asleep and my head lolled forward which made me feel a bit sick. Then he remembered the man with the white hair in the wood.

Was he going mad?

CHAPTER FIVE

Henry Peel had an almost overwhelming desire to smile. But a guy had to look serious when he was embarking on his very first flying lesson, even though it was unbelievably gratifying to be in the pilot's seat of a Piper Cherokee after all those years of waiting. Henry Peel was nineteen.

"You got to be comfortable and relaxed."

"I am . . . really."

"O.K. Put your hand over the dash. Feel the grip? Grab it and pull yourself forward until your feet are nicely set on the rudder pedals. That's better. You're not driving a sports car."

The instructor's name was Joe Machin. His face was weathered like old stone; he looked old enough to have been fighting over the Western Front with Billy Bishop. His mouth was set in a long-suffering pout of disappointment at the ineptitude of his pupils. But his voice was gentle.

"See, the wheel moves the ailerons out there on the wings. One goes up, the other goes down. Pull the wheel back and it raises the elevator on the tail and the aircraft goes up. Push it forward; the elevator is depressed. Down she goes. Whole idea of flying an airplane is to keep her balanced. Kind of like a bicycle."

Henry nodded gravely as if absorbing brand-new information. In fact however, he knew it all by heart. He had read it a thousand times. For as long as he could remember, Henry had wanted nothing in the world more than the opportunity to fly.

"We'll take a little ride around," said Machin. "See how you like it."

"I'll like it," said Henry fervently. And the smile popped on to his lips like a nervous twitch.

Expertly, Machin's fingers danced over the instrument panel. "See the ignition switch? Just turn it to the right, through the two magneto settings to ignition. Now push her. O.K."

The machine trembled as the engine heaved, caught and sent the propeller hurtling into motion. Machin called the tower, and received permission to taxi.

"The brake's right there under the dash," Machin told Henry. "Press the button to release it and away we go. No need to hang on to the wheel; the steering's done with your feet. Try it."

For a moment it seemed impossible; Henry found himself reaching for the control yoke. Then he discovered that steering by feet was easy.

"O.K.," said Machin. "Just ease off the throttle a little as you get near the runway. And always make sure your door's latched. It's tough to do in the air. Now ask the tower if we can go."

He showed Henry how to apply pressure on the right rudder pedal during the take-off run in order to correct a tendency to swing to the left, how to ease back on the yoke to get the nose-wheel off the ground. "See, she just floats off herself. Up she goes."

At 3,000 feet over Southern Ontario, Henry took control of an aircraft in flight for the first time. He noted the time; he would record it later. Machin told him to fly straight and level, to try to keep the horizon in the same place.

It was a delicious hour; it escaped in great chunks, ten and fifteen minutes at a time. "Fantastic," said Henry when they landed.

"You want to get your licence?" Machin asked as they walked back to the office.

"More than anything," said Henry. "You think I'll be able to?"

"Sure. You have a good feeling for the controls. You figure on making a career in aviation?"

"I might; I don't know. I just know I want to fly."

Machin nodded his grizzled head. "Wednesday at 8:00 a.m.?"

"I'll be here," Henry said.

FOR MOST PILOTS it would have been a drag: a late Saturday-night trip into Toronto with a lay-over until Monday afternoon. For Vaughan it could hardly have been better.

Sunday dawned bright and mild. Lee's little MG whisked them to Brockton, a small field with a single hangar, a club house and an assortment of gliders leaning sideways into the wind. Two Piper Cubs, for towing the gliders, were the only powered aircraft in evidence. The club members, ranging in age from sixteen to sixty, comprised a congenial group and talked endlessly of cumulus clouds "popping" and "rates of sink".

Shortly after two, Vaughan strapped himself into the front seat of a metal Blanik. Lee climbed into the rear seat. The transparent canopy closed over their heads, and the tow-line was fastened beneath the sailplane's nose. A youthful Air Canada second officer named Larry who flew tow-planes on weekends, wormed the Cub forward. Then, a burst of throttle, a jerk as the line took the strain and the grass flattened behind the Cub's whirling propeller.

As the Blanik started its roll, Lee eased the stick forward to get the tail off the ground and balance the sailplane on its central wheel. For a few yards, the wingman ran alongside, supporting one wing. He let go. A moment's wobble, then, almost immediately, the rumbling of the wheel ceased. Airborne.

"We get off before the tow-plane," said Lee, "but we have to stay close to the ground or we'll drag his tail up and he'll be in trouble."

Vaughan nodded, his eyes on the rocketing ground just inches away and the Cub careering along the bumpy grass strip. Then up, into the sparkling fall sunshine, obediently following the Cub, always turning in a wider arc to keep the tow-line taut. Lee flew well, with the smooth assurance of the natural pilot. What a girl, he thought.

At 2,000 feet she asked him to release the tow-line. The umbilical line went snaking away behind the turning Cub. Suddenly it was quiet but for the sighing of the wind against the canopy.

"Like it?"

"Great," he assured her.

She found a modest thermal which won them four hundred and fifty feet. Vaughan tried the controls and promptly lost the thermal.

"Keep turning tightly," she told him.

But it was too late. Laughing at his incompetence, they turned gently over the flat countryside, in perfect peace. They landed ten minutes later, side-slipping in to a gentle touchdown. The Blanik

rolled for only a few yards before settling onto one wing-tip. Vaughan unfastened his harness, twisted round in the narrow seat and kissed her. She squirmed, laughing, aware of interested on-lookers.

They drove to Niagara-on-the-Lake, saw a Shaw play and ate at The Pillar and the Post. They talked; there was so much to tell each other: likes, dislikes, memories, fears, hopes. The words tumbled out and the hours slipped by, filled with a marvellous intensity. That night there seemed to be another dimension to being alive. And only they were privy to its secret.

"YOUR AVERAGE adult male," said Walt Przeczek, "needs a change of female every now and again."

Vaughan wished Walt would keep his voice lower in the airport coffee shop. "So you think everyone should be hopping into bed with everyone else?"

"Why not? If they want to, it'd be a hell of a lot less hypocritical if nothing else."

Suddenly Vaughan was saying. "I met a girl in Toronto. She's only twenty-four. I'm far too old for her. And, hell, I'm married—*happily*, that's the crazy thing about it. But, still, I can't get her out of my mind."

"Is she a good lay?"

Vaughan stared, feeling the heat of anger in his cheeks. "What sort of a question is that?"

"A perfectly valid question," said Przeczek mildly. "I've been through this, you know. And I want to help you, Chuck. Tell me, when you think of her, do you remember all those deep, philo-sophical discussions the two of you have had, or do you remember scrambling around in the sack with her?"

"I'm going," snapped Vaughan.

Walt Przeczek grasped his arm. His voice was low now, sincere. "I'm telling you the truth, Chuck. I'm giving you the benefit of a lot of painful experience. I'm as ashamed as hell about most of it. Deceive Sue if you have to, Chuck, but don't deceive yourself. Enjoy it. But don't rate it as any more important than it really is. . . ."

Vaughan's anger boiled over, "Go to hell!" He strode angrily out of the coffee shop.

Walt Przeczek sighed. It was impossible to be honest with some guys. Poor old Chuck. Why was it that it was always the sweet guys got hurt the most?

DR. T. ROYDON GOODALL arranged his pen, calendar and appointment book in a perfectly straight line along the far edge of the desk. He often reflected that his passion for tidiness was in all probability a subconscious reaction to the extreme untidiness of most of his patients' lives.

Although short and distinctly overweight, Dr. Goodall was as neat as his desk. His white shirt was crisp, his grey tie boasted a superbly symmetrical gully below the knot, his face was clean-shaven, and the remnants of his dark hair were brushed smoothly across his skull.

Mrs. Latham buzzed. "Mr. Carter," she announced.

Carter. New Patient. Telephoned yesterday for the first appointment.

He rose and crossed to the door. Through the refracted glass-panel he was able to have a leisurely look at Mr. Carter without Mr. Carter's knowledge. Dr. Goodall frowned. There was something familiar about him. He opened the door and asked Mr. Carter to enter.

They exchanged good mornings. Carter spoke well, firmly, but he seemed ill at ease. He wore a good-quality blazer and striped silk tie. His hair was well trimmed. One might take him for a military type in mufti, Dr. Goodall reflected. And, by George, there *was* something familiar about him.

"You are aware that I'm a psychiatrist, Mr. Carter? I mention it only because people have been known to come and see me in regard to everything from gallstones to gout."

Mr. Carter's smile was brief. "I know you're a psychiatrist. I looked you up in the medical directory."

"I see."

"You don't remember me, do you?" Carter asked.

Dr. Goodall shrugged, smiling vaguely.

"At school I used to call you Hoke but I can't remember why."

"Good Lord! Frank Beatty! I should have known you at once. How extraordinarily nice to see you."

Then he frowned. Why was Frank calling himself James Carter?

Were the police after him? A slight squeakiness affected Dr. Goodall's voice as he asked Frank about the name Carter.

"I'll explain it in a minute, Hoke. It's quite simple."

"I'm sure it is." Dr. Goodall smiled in what he hoped was a casual way. But apprehension had formed a lump in his stomach. Most probably here for a loan, he thought with distaste.

"And Hoke, have no fear. I'm not here for a loan."

"I didn't think for a moment . . ."

"The fact of the matter is, I'm here because I need your professional services, or rather, I think I need them."

"I see." Dr. Goodall's apprehension began to dissolve. "Perhaps we ought to start with a spot of personal background. Often very helpful. You went into the RAF, didn't you? You were jolly keen on aeroplanes."

"You remember, do you? Yes, I was in the RAF for a few years."

"And what do you do now?"

"Now? I'm . . . a commercial traveller."

"A salesman."

"What? Oh yes. That's right, a salesman."

"What do you sell?"

"Aircraft parts, and systems . . . electronics, that sort of thing."

"Interesting. Are you married, Frank? Sorry, Mr. Carter?"

"Yes, and I have a son of twelve. Hoke, will you be a friend and put me down on your records as James Carter?"

Dr. Goodall had been considering the question for several minutes. No law stated that a chap had to demand proof of identity from private patients.

On the other hand, in a Court of Law, a chap could hardly claim that he didn't know the true identity of a patient who had been a close chum at school . . . .

Frank said, "The reason I want to use a pseudonym, Hoke, is my employers. They're rather a sticky lot. If there's nothing wrong with me, I'd rather they never knew I had been to see you. If there is something wrong, it won't matter much because I probably won't be able to continue working for them. You see the pickle I'm in, don't you?"

"Of course," said Dr. Goodall, relieved that Frank had provided a good reason. He placed his fingertips together. "Perhaps you should tell me about your . . . problem."

Frank nodded. "I'm afraid I may be heading for some sort of mental breakdown."

"What makes you say that?"

"A couple of times I seem to have . . . well, faded away. I've woken up to find that I've been *out*. Once I was jogging. I found that I had fallen down. And yesterday I almost fell off a bench in Leicester Square. A policeman thought I was drunk!"

"Well, one does tend to doze more, Frank, the older one gets."

"It's more than a doze, Hoke. It's sort of . . . *cutting-off*."

"Have you consulted your family doctor?"

"No."

"Your wife?"

"No. She knows nothing about it. I don't want to worry her needlessly."

"I understand." Dr. Goodall nodded thoughtfully. "Naturally, I'll do whatever I can, Frank. First, I think I'll quickly check your heart, lungs, blood pressure, that sort of thing. Odd, how frequently a problem in one location is associated with a symptom in another . . . ."

AMORY ANSWERED the telephone with a characteristic "Yup?"

"It's Frank Beatty, Mr. Amory."

"Sure. How are you? And what's the good word?"

"Fine, sir. I would, er, like to take you up on your offer . . . if you still want me, that is."

Amory's heavy chuckle sounded metallic over the telephone.

"You decided in our favour, eh? When can you start?"

"Whenever you want me, sir."

"How about tomorrow morning?"

"First-rate."

"O.K. Gatwick. Nine a.m. I've got an office up on the second floor—only you call it the first floor. You'll find it."

"Yes, sir. Thanks very much."

"See you," was the breezy farewell.

Beatty hung up the telephone. He grinned. So that was settled. He hailed a taxi. "Sloane Square, please."

What made everything splendid was that Hoke had failed to find anything wrong with him. Indeed he had remarked upon his apparent normality and good health. My guess, Beatty told himself, is that the whole thing will turn out to be some idiotic virus and that it's already gone for ever.

Admittedly, Hoke didn't have time to delve very deeply. Another appointment had been set for the following week; and there was talk of some tests; Hoke hadn't gone into details. But Beatty was convinced that all was well; he had never felt better.

He met Diane at the entrance to Peter Jones. She wore a bright green coat that she had just bought. It suited her admirably.

"Do you like it?" She asked. "Really?"

"You look gorgeous," he told her. "And, by the way, in case I haven't mentioned it for a while, I love you."

She glowed. "You haven't mentioned it for about ten years." She said. "Your business must have gone well. Are you going with Amory?"

"I start tomorrow morning. So tonight we celebrate. The old man's working again. It's dinner at the Café Royal for us!"

"Frank, that's terribly extravagant!" She laughed, drawing close to him as they walked.

It was a moment of happiness without reservation after three bleak months. Frank would be flying again.

BEATTY SPENT three hours at the controls of one of Amory's Boeing 707s. A pilot named Williams flew with him, first in the left-hand seat, then in the co-pilot's position. Williams was an Australian, an excellent pilot and Amory's senior man.

"You seem to remember the thing pretty good," Williams observed as Beatty performed a faultless engine-failure procedure.

Beatty nodded, smiling. He had done more than three thousand hours in 707s. He had a high regard for the superbly designed aircraft.

This particular 707 had seen a good deal of service. According to Williams, Amory had purchased it from a French company. The aircraft had been repainted in pale grey with maroon trim with the legend AMORY INTERNATIONAL on the fuselage, and the main cabin had been redecorated. Only the flight deck revealed the machine's age. The crew's seats were worn; the metal of the control column was dented; paint had been rubbed from switches and levers by years of contact. The aircraft had been flying almost continuously for thirteen years.

"Did Mr. Amory buy his three aircraft from the same company?" Beatty asked.

Williams shook his head. "The other two came straight from the States. They're good aircraft, all of them. Amory knows what he's doing when he's buying aeroplanes."

Beatty agreed. The 707 handled well. Aircraft were as individual as people.

Most pilots agreed that no aircraft in the world had a thoroughly good cockpit layout. Since there was no attempt at standardization among manufacturers, important levers might operate forward in one machine, backward in another; even the same model might differ if different airlines had ordered them. Each line had its own ideas of what constituted the correct arrangement of instruments and switches.

Amory was waiting on the ramp. "How did you like her?"

"She's no chicken," Beatty said, "but she seems sound in wind and body."

Amory grinned. "Good to be flying again?"

"Marvellous."

"Good. You'll be flying co-pilot with Mr. Williams here for your first few trips. It's Athens for you on Saturday. O.K?"

"O.K, sir," said Beatty with enthusiasm.

CHAPTER SIX

It was a surprise birthday party for Vaughan. The house was full of people.

"For your fortieth birthday!" someone yelled. "Don't forget that, old-timer. It's not just a run-of-the-mill birthday!"

Everyone chuckled. The ploy had succeeded. The catering firm had delivered the food on time to the Arlens; the liquor and mixes had arrived as planned at the Gregorys.

"You're a lucky man, Chuck," Maureen Biggin said between nibbles at a bacon and chicken liver hors d'oeuvre, "Susan went to a lot of work arranging this. You men never realize just how much."

Peter McIlvray said, "When I got to be forty I didn't have a party. I had a *wake* in honour of the sudden and untimely death of my youth!"

46

Soon the guests stopped talking about Charles Vaughan and his birthday; they drifted to the familiar topics of politics, and the price of food and property. The bottles emptied and the guests finally departed.

Vaughan, mellow and pleasantly tired, latched the front door and went back into the living room to find Susan sitting with an almost full glass beside the window that overlooked the lake.

"A wonderful party," he told her. "You were a doll to go to all that trouble." He leant down and kissed her cheek.

"I arranged the party," said Susan, still gazing at the lake, "because I thought you would be grateful."

"I am grateful. Of course I'm grateful . . ."

"It's really rather funny," she said, turning to him. "I went to all this trouble because I felt frightened and insecure. I thought this might solve my problem. And now, because of what I did, I've consumed enough alcohol to face the thing that was bothering me in the first place. That's funny, isn't it, Chuck?"

"Very," said Vaughan but he felt the heat rising in his face.

"I *know*," she said.

"Know? Know what?"

"Please don't insult my intelligence by denying it. You're seeing another woman. You have been for some time. I know it. So there's no point in trying to deny it."

"Susan. . . ." He looked at her. The glow from the coffee-table lamp highlighted her cheekbones. Only a slight fullness beneath the chin suggested that this wasn't the profile of a girl in her early twenties. He groped for words. He wanted to apologize but he couldn't.

She said, "Who is she? No, on second thoughts I don't want to know her name. Just tell me where it's been happening."

"Toronto," he said.

"For how long?"

He shrugged. "I don't know. . . . A few weeks."

"I know it's been much longer than that. Did you really think I was unaware that anything was going on?"

"Why didn't you say something sooner?"

She drank deeply of the whisky. "I guess for the same reason that someone with a suspicious pain doesn't go to the doctor right away. You hope the trouble will go away by itself. And I thought

I could help make it go away by doing things for you, like arranging this stupid party."

"It was a good party."

"I don't know how long I might have gone on saying nothing. Months, maybe years. I guess some women never say anything."

"I'm sorry," he said. "I didn't mean it to happen." Numbly, he watched a power boat streak across the lake, its light probing the darkness ahead like some great antenna.

"Do you love her?"

"What do you mean?"

"You know perfectly well what I mean." Susan reached for the Scotch bottle on the coffee table. With a slightly unsteady hand she poured another drink and banged the bottle on the table as if demanding his response. "Well?"

"I don't love her the way I love you."

She turned and laughed in his face. "That's for sure."

It was a nightmare. He rubbed the flesh above his eyebrows. His fingers seemed to burn into his skull. "I was telling the truth," he said, "when I told you I didn't mean it to happen."

"But it damn well did happen, didn't it? So what are you going to do about it?"

"I'll . . . I'll give her up."

"Why didn't you give her up months ago?"

"I tried."

"But you couldn't quite make it."

"No . . ."

"She must be some dish. Tell me about her. Blonde? Brunette? Nice legs?"

"Please, Susan . . ." He leant towards her—but she shrank away.

"No, I don't want you near me," she said. "It sounds like a cliché but I don't want you to touch me."

"I'm sincerely sorry."

"You keep saying that. But I'm a hell of a lot sorrier than you."

The telephone rang. Vaughan took it.

"Captain Vaughan?"

"Speaking."

"It's Mangione, Captain, from the office. I'm sorry to have to tell you, but there's been an accident. It was Captain Przeczek."

"God. Is he. . . .?"

"Yeah. I don't think there were any survivors."

"Have you told his wife?"

"No. We thought, maybe, as you and he were friends . . . ."

"All right," said Vaughan. "I'll tell her."

"Thanks, Captain."

Vaughan hung up. He turned to Susan. "It's Walt Przeczek," he said. "He crashed. He's dead."

"Oh no," she said softly.

"I've got to tell May."

"I understand," she said, nodding in an almost mechanical way, her eyes bright with tears. "Poor Walt . . . . and May."

Hours of anger and agony began. Hours in which tiny worlds were smashed for ever. May wanted to know precisely what had happened. The official word came shortly before dawn. After an apparently normal lift-off from runway 32 of a mid-Western city the aircraft had suddenly plunged vertically into the highway leading into the city.

"They killed him," May declared, shaking her head helplessly.

Vaughan knew the airport well. If an aircraft flew straight out after taking off from runway 32 it would find itself over the city's swankiest sub-division—which had been developed some years after siting the municipal airport. The residents of the sub-division objected to the noise and they had pull at City Hall. Soon the Federal word was transmitted to all pilots using runway 32. Turn left to 290 degrees as soon as practicable after lift-off; intercept Brewer Beacon, then make another left turn at 2,500 feet to intercept Markton Beacon. The manoeuvres guided the aircraft around the sub-division; they were not difficult provided everything was working properly, and the weather was reasonable. But something had gone wrong with Walt Przeczek's aircraft in foggy, wet conditions.

"He told me about that stinking runway, Chuck," May said. "He knew he was going to run into trouble one day . . ." She began to sob silently. Susan tried to comfort her. Vaughan watched the pale light creeping along the walls of the neighbouring houses. Soon it would be the new day, the day that Walt and his passengers would never see. God, but it was hard to believe him dead. What went wrong? What did he think in those last horrific mini-seconds? Did his life hurtle past his eyes like a movie in a runaway projector? Or did he believe to the very last that he was going to get out of it?

There was, it seemed, a useful device attached to the brains of pilots that refused to accept inevitable death. Vaughan had heard tapes from flight recorders recovered from wrecks; the voices were calm and confident up to the moment of impact. No screams. No prayers. Only an occasional apology, in mild tones, for having done something inexcusably stupid.

"Hi."

Vaughan turned. It was six-year-old John, tousled from sleeping. Delighted to see Uncle Chuck and Auntie Sue. Wanting to know why his mother was up and about before him. Before anyone could respond, he pattered into the kitchen.

"Why?" May said. "Why, Chuck?"

"God knows."

"He hurt me often. But he was a good and gentle man the rest of the time. And I loved him very much. I'm going to miss him like hell."

"I'm going to miss him too," Vaughan said. "I know how you feel."

She looked at him and shook her head. "No, you don't, Chuck, you don't know at all."

TAKE-OFFS weren't too hard, in Henry Peel's limited experience; landings, however, were quite another matter. While the aircraft would float good-naturedly into the air given sufficient power and enough runway she seemed positively cantankerous when the time came to return to *terra firma*.

Joe Machin was patient. "People get up-tight about landings," he said, "but all you're doing is slowing her up until she can't stay in the air any more. You fly straight down the runway two or three feet up, then cut the power and keep on pulling up the nose when she starts to settle."

Henry nodded soberly. He knew the theory inside out. The problem lay in converting theory into action. Since taking up flying, he had discovered that air is seldom still, rarely reliable. Trees, buildings and hills create treacherous currents close to the ground, lying in wait for the unwary like icy patches on city streets. And, he had learned, aircraft could be wilful, like spirited animals.

They loved to wander off to the left or right when they thought you weren't paying attention.

In Machin's hands the Cherokee was docile and obedient, settling onto the runway with an obsequious little sigh from her two main wheels. When Henry landed, the same machine wallowed into the ground in a semi-drunken manner; from the bounding cockpit it sounded as if the landing-gear consisted of a thousand metal components tied together by iron chains.

"You're getting the hang of it," said Machin, chewing his gum with determination after a particularly bumpy arrival.

"I don't think I am."

"Sure. Just practice. Let's go round again."

Henry eased the throttle forward. The aircraft rolled; the runway began to unwind. It was a moment that never ceased to thrill. He, Henry Peel, was at the controls of an aircraft rushing at breakneck speed. Right foot on the rudder pedal to keep her heading straight. Gentle heave back on the yoke.

At once the Cherokee soared. Her left wing dropped a few degrees. Henry applied right aileron control. But too much. Up; down; at last she was level. Three hundred feet. Flaps up: lever to the floor. Fuel pump to Off; fuel pressure still O.K.

A glance over the side. Two kids standing outside a store, ignoring the Piper. Why weren't they staring up, envying him.

"Always keep an eye out for other traffic," Machin said. "I'll bet Lindbergh looked for traffic all the way across the Atlantic."

"Right," said Henry. He eased the Cherokee's nose down and looked from left to right. Nothing to be seen but flat land dotted with patches of snow.

Machin pointed. "Two o'clock," he said.

Henry automatically looked at his watch. He cursed himself. Holy cow, you're a bloody *groundling* through and through! Two o'clock meant off the right beam a bit. You had to imagine the nose as the hand of a clock pointing to twelve.

"See her?"

"Well . . ." Henry stared.

"She's turned off," Machin said "A One-Fifty."

"Right," said Henry. He had caught not a glimpse of the other aircraft. He thought of those stories he had read about sharp-eyed heroes in Camels spotting enemy Albatrosses five miles away and ten thousand feet below. They must have had infra-red eyesight.

Machin indicated the left. Henry nodded. It was time to turn into the crosswind leg of the circuit. Check speed. Damn! Too fast! He felt nervous sweat on his body. Please behave, he begged the Cherokee.

"Watch your height," Machin murmured.

Jeepers! Two hundred feet too high! Throttle lever back. He was flying the downwind leg of his circuit, parallel to the runway on which he would land. In a moment it would be time to turn onto the base leg.

"Landing checks," said Machin with a yawn.

Landing checks. What were they? For a moment his brain seized solid. Ah yes. Fuel. Left tank. Almost full. Fuel pump on. Carburettor heat on. Reduction in revs. No ice. Count to five but keep looking out for traffic. And listen to Machin suggesting, in a slightly bored voice, that it might be nice to let the tower know his intentions.

So many things to do. He grabbed for the mike fastened to the window post, dropped it, fumbled for it and gabbled the message: turning left base for a touch-and-go on Runway Zero Six.

Now he was too close. He would have to turn onto final at once. But he was still travelling at well over one hundred miles per hour. If only the bloody aeroplane would stop for a moment and let a guy catch his breath.

At last Henry got the nose of the Cherokee pointed at the runway. One notch of flap. Two. Trim nose up some more. Speed: ninety-five. Too fast. Nose up more. But now the runway had vanished behind the nose. Was this the time to abandon the landing attempt and do an overshoot?

Ah, the runway reappeared. Speed eighty-five. Not bad. Control column back. Power off. Nose up. The runway unrolled beneath him, a mile-long carpet of grey concrete. Keep your eyes on a spot forty or fifty yards ahead, Machin had said again and again. The speed dropped but the Cherokee began to wander off to the left. Rudder, thought Henry desperately. Use some rudder.

But the Cherokee had already landed. On one main wheel. It bounced to the other. Then onto the nose wheel. At last, shaking herself, she ran along on all three wheels.

"Oh God," said Henry.

"I've seen worse," said Machin.

"Honestly?"

"Sure," said Machin, "Though not without some blood."

BEATTY DISCOVERED that charter flying had a character all its own.
For one thing, it was maximum capacity business all the time. As
for charter passengers, they were a breed apart, consistently
good-natured and noisy, given to visiting and making friends
throughout the aircraft. (Sometimes it was necessary to discourage
them by dipping the aircraft a few times, announcing that
turbulence was being encountered and instructing all passengers to
return to their seats and fasten their safety belts.)

Charter passengers were also infinitely more philosophical about
delays than their scheduled brethren. The reason was simple:
charter flights were holiday flights. An hour or two made little
difference. Day after day they trooped aboard Amory's aircraft:
members of social clubs, athletic clubs, church clubs, servicemen's
clubs. And almost without fail, they burst into spontaneous
applause at journey's end.

Because Amory's 707s usually flew to airfields where the
company had no service facilities, they carried a substantial
inventory of spare parts. They also carried a fourth crew member,
a flight engineer who, unlike the majority of flight engineers, was
a qualified aviation mechanic who could tackle major repair jobs.

Like most organizations, the Amory company seemed to take on
some of the characteristics of the head man. There was a brash,
pioneering air about everything. There were times when not one
member of the crew had ever seen the destination before; often,
when briefed they were unsure just where it was. Amory kept
promising to get stationery printed with the company name but
did not.

Supplies of company cheques ran out one week; Amory paid the
staff in cash. Schedules became badly scrambled; shortly before
Christmas Beatty found that he was supposed to fly to Nice and
Montreal on the same morning. More than once, Amory himself
flew as second officer; no one had the nerve to ask him if his
licence was still valid.

When Diane asked her husband how he enjoyed his new job, he
said truthfully, that he had never enjoyed flying more.

HOKE SEEMED a little testy. "Frank, I do wish you'd try not to cancel appointments at half an hour's notice. It's really not playing the game. This is the third one in a row."

Beatty couldn't help smiling into the telephone. Hoke's tone was so plaintive. "I apologize, old man, but it's this job of mine. I have to go out of the country unexpectedly at times."

"I see."

"Besides, I've been feeling so much better, Hoke."

"Quite so. But I do think those tests we talked about are advisable. I'm going to make an appointment with a hospital lab. Now, do you wish to make it in the name of Carter?"

"Yes, I suppose so."

"When will you be back in this country?"

"Next week. Thursday."

"I'll make the appointment for Friday. Now do be a good fellow and keep it. It could be important."

TWO HOURS after the take-off from Gatwick, the intercom signal buzzed. A stewardess reported a problem. One of her passengers had gone berserk; he was convinced the aircraft would crash.

"Shall I see what I can do?" Beatty asked Hallman, the captain.

Hallman nodded, relieved. "Good show."

Beatty eased himself out of the right-hand seat and put on his tunic and cap. Full uniform often helped in this sort of situation.

He opened the flight-deck door. The troublemaker stood at the rear of the cabin, his legs apart, his arms folded tightly over his chest. He was about twenty-five, thin and sallow-faced. His eyes bulged with terror. He was screaming that the plane would crash at any moment. Occupants of the rear seats now stood jammed in the centre aisle, frightened and confused.

"His name is Birdlett," the stew told Beatty. "I can't do a thing with him."

"Is his wife on board?"

"No; he's travelling alone."

"Damn." Beatty drew a deep breath and made his way along the packed aisle until he stood a few feet from Birdlett. The man was trembling. Sweat poured down his grey-toned face.

"Everything's all right, old man," said Beatty in what he hoped was a conversational tone.

"We're all doomed!"

Beatty smiled. "I can assure you we're not." He took a pace forward. Birdlett swung wildly. Beatty ducked, but the blow caught him on the shoulder. He plunged forward, trying to pin Birdlett's arms. A thin, bony fist cracked into his cheek. Angered, he hit back. He clutched at Birdlett. Both men went down, Birdlett's head cracking against the toilet door. Clumsily they scuffled in the confined space.

Now there were dozens of hands, eagerly helping. Beatty rescued his cap from the floor.

"Are you all right, Mr. Beatty?"

Beatty nodded at the stew.

"He hit you."

"Not too seriously."

They tied Birdlett down on a crew seat, using the belt extensions normally reserved for corpulent passengers. A policeman named Forbes was given guard duty over him until the aircraft landed.

Beatty returned to the flight deck. He closed the door behind him. Then he passed out.

It was easily explained. A nasty scuffle. Vicious blows from a deranged passenger. A shock to the system. Passing out wasn't all that surprising when you thought about it. So said the crew. So said the doctor at the airport.

BRISK FINGERS cleansed the skin with alcohol and saline jelly. A solution of pyroxylin in acetone formed tiny transparent patches of secondary skin which secured the electrodes in position. Each electrode was the terminal for a wire leading to a control panel.

"Not nearly as complicated as the aeroplane systems you deal with, Mr. Carter, but quite interesting. We can learn quite a lot about the brain if we can study its electrical discharges. So we attach the electrodes to various areas of the scalp. When you are fully plugged in, so to speak, we can measure the impulses." The hospital technician chattered on . . . .

"PLEASE SIT down, Frank."

"You mean Carter, don't you, old man?"

"What? Oh yes, of course, Carter." Hoke didn't smile. He rubbed his chin as if it ached. "How have you been feeling?"

56

"On top line, except for a silly little incident. I got into a scuffle. A chap hit me. See the bruise? I sort of flaked out afterwards, but I don't think that counts as a *spell*, do you?"

"Possibly not. But you feel quite well now?"

"Perfectly. Don't look so disappointed, Hoke. Surely you have other patients."

Hoke appeared not to have heard the remark. "I have the results of your EEG, Frank. Mind you, they are not absolutely conclusive but they do indicate strongly—" he cleared his throat—"an abnormality."

Beatty felt his insides chill and contract. "An abnormality? What sort of abnormality?"

"This really isn't my field, Frank. It's a neurological rather than psychiatric problem. It's my understanding, however, that this type of condition can frequently be treated very successfully, although there's a great deal that isn't yet known about it."

Beatty said, "What is the condition called?"

The chubby little man looked haggard. "It's a form of epilepsy, Frank."

"God."

Hoke began to talk rapidly. "People think epilepsy means frightful, uncontrollable fits. But it isn't always like that Frank. And it's not in your case. I believe you have a mild case of psycho-motor or temporal lobe epilepsy. It's characterized by short losses of consciousness such as you have been experiencing . . . ."

"You're sure, Hoke? There's no doubt at all?"

"I don't think so, Frank. But I want you to see a neurologist . . . ."

"Bloody incredible." Beatty shook his head as if unable to comprehend the truth. *Why me, for God's sake?* "If I do nothing will the attacks continue?" he asked.

"I have no way of knowing. Frank please. . . . I'm a psychiatrist."

"Yes, but you're a doctor too. I bet you got jolly good marks in epilepsy classes, didn't you?"

"Frank. . . ."

"Tell me all about it, Hoke. I'm really interested. It's nice to know what's happening to one's brain, I always say."

Hoke frowned unhappily. "Well, the medical term is cerebral dysrhythmia. It's the result of disturbances in the electrical discharges from the brain. The attacks are usually triggered by such things as changes in the chemical balance of the blood, by hypo-glycaemia—which is a very low glucose level in the blood; by exhaustion, or psychological stresses; sometimes by something as innocent as a stroboscopically flashing light."

"Which," Beatty said, "might be caused by running under a long line of trees on a sunny day."

"What? Yes, I suppose so. Treatment varies, Frank. Pheno-barbitone and phenytoin are often used successfully, I believe. Mind you, there can be side effects if the dosage is heavy: drowsiness, lethargy, that sort of thing."

A minor inconvenience for an airline pilot.

"But, Frank" said Hoke earnestly, "people under this sort of treatment usually manage awfully well. Often their friends have no idea that there's anything wrong with them."

"Except when they do odd things such as cutting off ears and posting them to girl-friends."

"Pardon?"

"That's what Van Gogh did and he was an epileptic. I read it in a book at an airport waiting for the weather to clear. Funny, I never thought for a moment. . . ."

Funny as hell.

Beatty walked for three hours. Along Oxford Street and through Hyde Park, along Piccadilly, down to Trafalgar Square, along the Strand. He had Hoke's prescription ("For Mr. J. Carter") filled at a chemist's shop. "To be taken four times a day or as required." He walked on, to find himself at last somewhere east of the City. It was raining now in a sullen and insistent manner. He had a cup of tea in a grubby little café and swallowed one of Hoke's pills.

"Anything to eat, mister?" A doleful black man.

"No, thanks." The black man shrugged.

Don't look so glum, Beatty told him silently. You're not an epileptic. He rested his fingertips against his forehead. Inside, he thought, the electricity is operating properly. But for how long? Odd to think of the thing lurking in one's head, waiting for the right moment to strike. Nice of it to pick the moment when one was bringing in a jet to land. . . .

Anger surged within him. But it was impotent anger. There was nothing to strike; the enemy was invisible, lurking deep within the —what had Hoke called it?—ah yes, the cerebrum.

58

His licence would be permanently revoked the instant the authorities knew of his condition. He would no longer have a profession. You can claim insurance against the loss of your licence on medical grounds he told himself, but you can't live on it for ever. You have to find another line of work. Think positively: there are thousands of ways for a chap to make a living.

He ordered more tea.

Whenever he thought of employment on the ground he saw herds of grey-faced, cheerless people streaming out of underground stations, piling into office buildings that looked like colossal coffins on their ends. Always hurrying and pushing. Worrying about being late. Fretting their lives away.

I want to keep on flying, he said, as if he had only himself to persuade. It's a hell of a life when you think of it, hard, unrelenting work all the way. But I want no other.

Rain dribbled disconsolately down the café window.

Beatty recalled that he was due for his next medical in three weeks. During that time he was scheduled to fly about a dozen trips, all as co-pilot; therefore any landings and take-offs he performed would be under the supervision of the captain in command. Hell, there really wasn't any danger, was there? Even in the unlikely event that he began to feel whoozy while actually flying, the captain could take over at once. That was one of the reasons for having two pilots, wasn't it?

Just a few more trips. It wasn't much to ask. Then he would go to his medical. The doctor would discover that all was not on top line. Beatty would express surprise. No need to mention Hoke. No need to admit to any symptoms. No need to do a bloody thing except stand still to be stamped UNFIT.

He drained the tea cup. God, how he would enjoy those last trips.

MR. COX disappeared into the attic. Below, balanced on the steps on the top landing, his wife heard a crash. For an anxious moment Mrs. Cox thought the object was Mr. Cox. Then she heard him triumphantly announce that he had found them. "Gawd, but they're dusty," he added.

A moment later he reappeared, his blue serge waistcoat sporting patches as grey as his moustache. He passed the suitcases down to her, one at a time. They were indeed dusty—but, Mrs. Cox reckoned, since they had been up in the attic since the summer of forty-eight, the year before Joycie went off to live in Canada, it was hardly surprising.

When he had successfully negotiated the steps, Mr. Cox examined the cases. He was relieved to find them sound; at his time of life, he didn't want to be buying expensive new luggage.

"They'll see us to Toronto and back all right," he affirmed.

His wife giggled girlishly. "I can't hardly believe we're really going, I really can't."

"Course we're going," said Mr. Cox, as if a transatlantic trip were the most usual thing in the world.

Mr. and Mrs. Cox were due to fly to Toronto via Amory International in four months and two days.

CHAPTER SEVEN

Vaughan watched Lee as she slid the meat out of the crab legs. She tackled the job in the total way she did everything. Recently she had purchased a guitar; now she practised as much as five hours a day. Lee hurled herself into the business of being alive.

She dipped the last morsel of crab into the drawn butter. "Heavenly." She wiped her fingers on the damp cloth supplied. "Is it on my face? I feel as if I've been wallowing in the stuff."

"A smidgin right there." He touched the corner of her mouth.

She thanked him then looked at him for a moment, steadily. "My antenna tells me you have something to say, Chuck."

"Your antenna could be wrong."

"Could be. But isn't."

The waiter materialized. Vaughan ordered coffee and Hennessey.

"Nothing's wrong," he said.

"I didn't say anything was wrong. I just said you have something on your mind."

"I haven't."

"O.K." A gentle little shrug.

God, she couldn't have been fairer, couldn't have made it easier for him to tell her. It was simple enough. Secret revealed: wife irked; decision in her favour; the kids; the end. Uttering the words had become as unthinkable as thrusting a knife into her heart.

He seemed to be suspended in a kind of maddening limbo, wanting her yet wishing he had the courage to break with her.

The waiter appeared with the coffee and cognac and the conversation became politely automatic. Then, her eyes roaming his face as if committing every feature to memory, she said, "Your wife knows, doesn't she?"

He turned the cognac in his glass and nodded.

"Why didn't you say so?"

"I couldn't. I don't know why. It was impossible."

Her eyes glistened. "I knew it had to happen. I mean it was inevitable, wasn't it? I just hoped it might last a bit longer."

"I'm sorry," he said inadequately.

"Poor Chuck." She smiled, her lips trembling. "He has to apologize to two women. It must have been rough for you. I guess she was bloody sore about it."

"Yes, she was sore."

Her eyes searched his face again. "I don't blame her," she said. "I'd be bloody sore too if I were in her position." Her tone became falsely bright and businesslike. "What happens now? Is this it? End of the line? That sounds like a song title, doesn't it? The next move is up to you, Chuck. Hell, more song titles. I can't stop it." She poured too much cream into her coffee. "We both knew it wasn't going to last for ever. You know, that would make a pretty good title too. Maybe this is the beginning of a new career for me. Sad song specialist."

Vaughan heard himself saying: "I don't want it to end, Lee. Somehow I just can't imagine life without you."

"You're not playing fair, Chuck. You're saying dangerous things. The sort of things that build up a girl's hopes."

"I'm being honest," he said. "I won't let you go."

"Please don't say things you don't mean."

"I'm not." He took her hand. "I don't know what the hell I'm going to do. I don't know what's going to happen. But I do know I love you and I'm not going to give you up."

A GREY-HAIRED, innocuous-looking couple named Hardcastle walked out of a Toronto department store. Mr. Hardcastle carried two large cans of paint. He planned to start painting the spare bedroom the very next morning. It would not be very long before his sister would be occupying the room; she was booked on a charter flight from Gatwick to Toronto.

Mr. Hardcastle hadn't seen his sister for more than twenty years. He hoped she would like the room. He and his wife, after more than an hour of wondering, had selected a pale shade of pink. It didn't strike either of them as strange that they should take so much trouble to select a colour for someone who had been blind since birth.

ACCORDING TO flight-deck etiquette it was an unforgiveable *faux pas*. Captains bestowed the privilege of landings and take-offs upon their co-pilots; a co-pilot was never expected to ask. But as the English coast came into view, Beatty asked Williams for the landing.

Williams smiled, puzzled. "Any particular reason?"

"I'm due for my medical tomorrow," Beatty told him. "This may be my last chance."

"Do you think you'll fail your medical?"

"I hope not. But there's always the chance." A bloody enormous chance, he thought.

Had Beatty not been a former 747 captain, he would have been ticked off for being cheeky. Instead, Williams nodded. "She's all yours."

"Thanks very much. Good of you."

Auto-pilot off. Beatty wanted to fly her, feel the life of her through the controls. He settled himself, time to concentrate completely. No matter how skilled and experienced, a pilot could never permit himself to relax during a landing; too much could happen too rapidly.

The ether was full of chattering voices: voices from other aircraft reporting positions, intentions; voices from the ground requesting descents to certain heights, turns to certain headings. The nearer the airport, the more complex the patterns. Somewhere in the grey sky were Lord knows how many jets, arriving, departing, climbing, descending. *Hurtling*. The men on the ground had to keep them in their proper places, safely apart.

"Clear to descend. Advise established inbound on ILS."

Checks of seat-belt and no-smoking signs, altimeters, speed brakes, pneumatic pressures, ADF, VOR.

Beatty glanced at the ILS dial to ensure that the tiny failure-flag hadn't appeared. Pilots had been known to fly to their deaths faithfully following the directions of an instrument that had failed and was trying desperately to tell him so.

"Flaps fifty," Beatty reported. "Runway in sight."

The aircraft was docile as she approached the concrete strip. The ground rolled beneath him: damp, shiny fields, a road packed with Dinky-toy traffic, tiny houses, ant-like people. A steady, progressive descent of 100 tons of machinery and humanity at 700 feet per minute.

Beatty relished the challenge of every landing. This one, he decided, would be a triumph with which to terminate his career. The passengers would never know the precise moment they ceased to fly.

He mentally computed height, distance and speed. Now the ground was rushing at him. This was the moment. Ease back on the yoke. The runway levelled. Power down. He felt the aircraft's tendency to wander to the left because a strong wind was pressing on her flank. He made her resist by angling her nose and lowering one wing a degree or two.

Speed fell off; her wheels could no longer resist the force of gravity. They touched the runway. Barely a bump. The nose plopped down, the wheel smack on the centre line.

"Reverse thrust, please."

The 707 slowed. She was behaving like a lady, accepting the reverse thrust without pitching and bouncing as was her occasional habit. Beatty waited until the speed was down to 50 knots before cancelling the reverse thrust. The brakes and tyres weren't unduly worked.

He parked the aircraft at the terminal, applying the brakes as the parking pointer touched the windshield, signifying that the main exit was in line with the ramp.

Williams said: "Good luck with your medical."

"Thanks very much. Thanks for the landing too."

"Don't mention it. It was a dandy."

As he collected his gear Beatty looked around the flight deck. It was cramped and ugly. But there was nothing quite like it and he would miss it dreadfully.

So long, he said silently.

THIRTY-SIX HOURS later, Frank Beatty swung his car out of a parking space near Baker Street and drove off smiling. He felt like a prisoner granted a reprieve on the morning of his execution. *He had passed* his medical; he was *officially* fit to fly.

Admittedly, he had lied to the doctor. When asked about his general state of health, he had reported no problems. *(If they're going to ground me, let them find out for themselves.)* The doctor had accepted the statement without demur. Heart, lungs, hearing, vision; all had been tested and found satisfactory. Not given a clue to make him think otherwise, he had passed Beatty as fit.

Lots of chaps lie at medicals. He felt the box of pills in his pocket. They would keep him out of trouble. Good old Hoke.

The sun broke through the overcast as he drove along Oxford Street. He beamed up at it. Life had plunged him into the depths and then, just as rapidly, hurled him to the heights. He had telephoned Mr. Amory himself.

"Passed your medical O.K?"

"Yes sir."

"Glad to hear it. I just bought a couple more aircraft. Need captains. Interested in stepping up in the world?"

"Hell, yes! Er, that is . . ."

Amory had chuckled in his throaty way. "That's O.K, feller, I know how you feel. I got to be made captain myself once. I goofed. Did a perfect landing at Toronto. It was a hazy day, though, and for some reason or other I came down on the runway at Downsview instead of Malton. The two fields are pretty close, you know. Anyway, my employers came to the conclusion they could get along just fine without my services. And I'm sorry to say, have. Well, so much for ancient history. You're hereby promoted to the dizzy rank of captain in Amory International Airways. We'll talk about dough the next time you're in my office."

"Right, sir. And thank you very much indeed."

Beatty then telephoned Diane on whom he had vented his angry frustration that very morning.

"You sound better," she had said. "I gather you passed your medical."

"Yes. Er, sorry I was a bit of a bear this morning."

"Don't mention it. I'm used to it by now, just like any well-behaved airline pilot's wife."

He had grinned. "I would appreciate it, madam, if you would have a modicum of respect for my rank. Be so good as to address me as 'captain' from this moment on."

Diane had shrieked with delight.

He felt marvellous. Never better. And intensely grateful to Amory and Hoke.

ON THE MORNING of April 19, after ten hours and twelve minutes of dual instruction, Henry Peel flew solo. It was a brief flight: take-off, turn to the left, downwind leg, another left turn to base leg, then one more left turn onto final.

Joe Machin stood beside the runway chewing gum. He looked bored but he was nervous. You could never tell what a kid might do the first time he got up in an aircraft by himself.

Thump.

Henry was down. And if his first solo landing was something slightly less than perfection, it had at least deposited him on the runway the right way up and facing in the right direction. And that, in Joe Machin's experience, was considerably better than the way many a first solo had ended up. He sent Henry off to do a few more circuits.

FOURTEEN MINUTES after Henry Peel touched down on his first solo landing, a man in Santa Ana named Earl Gasparac told his wife about the trip he had arranged. New York by TranState, then Providence, Boston and Portland, Maine, by car.

"After Portland," he announced "we head over towards New Hampshire and Vermont—and then New York State and a little joint called. . . ."

"Utica!" she cried, delighted.

They laughed. Mrs. Gasparac had been born in Utica thirty-one years before, but it was almost ten years since she had been back east.

For this trip Earl Gasparac would have to borrow heavily from the Credit Union. His salary as a repairman for the telephone company, while adequate, had its limitations. But the trip couldn't be delayed. Dr. Malcolm had made it horribly. clear: if Mrs. Gasparac didn't make the trip before the end of summer, she would never make it at all.

A WOMAN IN Des Moines, Iowa, named Lillian Dumont counted the money she had been stealing from her husband and from her employer, Associated Security Services, manufacturers of Ever-Watchful Television Equipment for Stores and Offices. It amounted to nearly $17,000. Amazing, she thought, how little bits out of Petty Cash, housekeeping and the savings account can mount up.

CHAPTER EIGHT

The visit to May was an ordeal. She was still in semi-shock. There was so much to say and yet there were no words. Talk was little more than a respite from silence.

May and Susan made tentative plans for shopping expeditions, bridge parties and picnics for the kids, knowing that none of them would take place.

When it was time to leave, Vaughan and Susan said they would come again soon, guilty with the relief they felt at parting.

Susan was silent for a couple of miles. Then she said, "You're still seeing that girl in Canada."

He lied. Too easily. "No, it's all over. I told you."

"I don't believe you."

"It's true."

She turned away from him and huddled against the passenger door. Her shoulders jerked spasmodically. Vaughan pictured her eyes full of bitter tears, her mouth trembling. She hated him. And he didn't blame her. He wanted to take her in his arms and tell her, convince her, that everything was going to be all right. She *deserved* to hear it.

His hands tightened on the steering-wheel. He drove faster. Was there still time to salvage the wreck of his marriage and make amends? Was there still time to be forgiven? All he had to do was call Lee and tell her good-bye. That was all. He swallowed, remembering the time he had stopped at the phone booth on Wilshire Boulevard, determined to end it all there and then. But even as he had lifted the receiver he seemed to hear her voice and see her face. Hopelessly he had let the receiver drop back onto its cradle.

Why in God's name, he wondered, did I have to tell Lee there might be some sort of permanent relationship? What right did I have to say that? None! Zero!

"Stop at the grocery store," said Susan, "if you don't mind. I have to get a loaf."

Vaughan nodded. No matter what the crisis, the domestic machinery still had to function.

It was a strange part of the Vaughan's lives, full of silences, full of television, magazines and books. When he was off duty, Vaughan took long walks alone, gazing for hours at the lake and wondering how to put his life back in order. Inevitably the situation touched Janet and Lynn. They reacted to the tension between their parents with the sure instinct of the young and took their mother's part. Yet, through it all, the family still somehow functioned as a unit. The annual trip to Disneyland took place and Lynn's birthday was celebrated as usual by dinner at the Fox and Hounds. There was even brave talk of a summer vacation. Sometimes there was laughter; but it tended to stop in mid-flight as if reality had cut it short.

In early May they drove to Carmel to visit Susan's parents. "We've got to," she said. "It's been more than three months. They'll think something's wrong." Vaughan was of the opinion that a visit would remove all doubt but he kept silent.

The Jearards' house overlooked the Pacific; it was a pleasant, tranquil spot. Harold Jearard was a retired steel mill vice-president, a slim, stooped man with tired eyes and a wry sense of humour. Susan's mother was plump and warm and a superb cook.

The visit turned out to be remarkably successful. In the company of her parents Susan seemed to soften, as if calling a silent truce. There were strolls along the cliffs, visits to boutiques, a movie. When Sunday came, Vaughan prepared for the return drive in a relaxed mood, glad that the visit had been made. Soon after breakfast he asked Susan what time she wanted to leave.

"I'm not leaving," she said.

He looked up from his packing. "What?"

"I'm not leaving," she said. She avoided his eyes. "I'm staying here. So are Janet and Lynn. You know why."

He shrugged helplessly. "What about their school?"

"There are schools in Carmel. If necessary they can transfer here. Besides, they're due for vacations soon."

Vaughan shook his head. Why was his first reaction to wonder about the girls' school?

"I told you, Susan, it's all over."

"Please don't lie to me."

"I mean it."

"Yes, I know you do, Chuck, when you're with me." There was the hint of a sad smile on her lips. "I think you're sincere when you say such things to me. But you haven't been able to make them happen, have you? I'm sorry for you. But it's up to you to work the problem out." She turned and crossed to the door. "You'd better come up," she called to her parents. "We may as well get this over with."

And then her parents were in the room. For ghastly moments there was silence. No one looked directly at anyone else.

At last Susan said: "I've told Charles that I'm staying here with the girls. They'll lose a bit of school but I really don't give a damn."

Suddenly all eyes were on Vaughan. He felt like an actor who had missed his cue. He looked at them. Susan's father wore an expression of mild regret, her mother, bewildered, was close to tears.

"I'm sorry," he said. "It's embarrassing for you and for me. I don't know why Susan had to bring you into this. It's between her and me."

Mrs. Jearard said something which became sobs. Mr. Jearard said, "Susan, why don't you take your mother into her room and give her a glass of water or something."

Vaughan swallowed. He felt slightly sick. Was this nightmare really happening?

When the door had closed, Mr. Jearard said, "I agree that Susan should not have brought us into this. It simply makes the situation more painful. All of us, I think, would have felt better if we had pretended that you had to return for business reasons."

"I suppose you know why she did it," said Vaughan. He tossed socks into his bag. The sooner he left the better.

"I think I understand something of the ordeal you're going through," Mr. Jearard said, "Of course, I deplore what it is doing to my daughter's happiness, but I doubt that you went looking for the problem you found."

"Maybe if I was the sort who looked, I'd be able to get out a hell of a lot easier."

"I think you're absolutely right, Chuck. You try to avoid hurting. And by doing so, you hurt more. But now, I suggest, is the time to hurt. Because I truly am convinced that you are far better to stay with Susan than go with . . . let's say anyone else. There are also the children to consider. And me. I'm very fond of you. I would be most upset to lose you as a son-in-law."

Vaughan smiled. "Nice of you to say so."

"I mean it. And you mustn't think for a moment that Susan or her mother will fail to forgive you. Of course they will. Indeed, they will probably think the higher of you."

"Higher?"

"Certainly. The prodigal son syndrome."

"I doubt it applies in this sort of situation."

"Oh, but I can assure you it does," said Mr. Jearard. "And I can assure you of something else. You will recover from the blow of giving up . . . *her*. Indeed, you will relish her memory the more keenly for it. A morsel or two of memory is good for a man as he approaches middle age. Believe me, I know."

DR. GOODALL munched a lunchtime sandwich as he listened to Sibelius on the FM radio. The buzzer sounded. He sighed long-sufferingly. Would Mrs. Latham never learn that lunchtime was sacred? Then he remembered: Mrs. Latham was on holiday; Mrs. Whateverhernamewas had taken her place.

"It's Mr. Carter. I told him you were having your dinner—" Dr. Goodall winced—"but he said it was very important."

"Carter, you say?" Oh Lord. Frank Beatty. "All right, put him on."

Frank's voice had a jovial quality that was oddly mechanical.

"Hullo, old man, awfully sorry to disturb your lunch. The fact of the matter is, I need a few more of those pills, Hoke, so be a good chap and reach for your pad, will you?"

"Pills?"

"The ones you prescribed. They're just the job. Not a hint of a spell since I started taking them." Frank spoke rapidly, as if he had learnt the sentences by heart.

"You mustn't think those pills are a cure," Hoke cautioned. "All they do is tend to nullify the symptoms; you see . . . ." He sighed. "Frank, as I explained to you at some length, your condition is outside my field. I recommended a man. . . . You haven't seen him."

"I will, Hoke. But I've been travelling all over the place."

"Your employer still knows nothing of your condition?"

"No, I haven't passed on the good news yet, Hoke. I have a few sales to wrap up before I do so. You see, they'll remove me from the scene the moment they know what's wrong with me. Now be a good chap. . . ."

MRS. LATHAM felt better the instant the jet's wheels touched the runway. She could cease eyeing the neatly folded paper bag in the seat pocket before her and gaze through the window instead.

Everything looked grey and drab after the dazzling sunshine of Bermuda. A typical English spring day, but she was rather pleased. It would have been irksome to have returned from a costly two-week holiday only to be told that it had been just as sunny and hot at home.

She disembarked and passed through Customs and through the terminal building heading for the railway ticket office. Then she stopped dead.

"Why, Mr. Carter!"

"No, you're mistaken. My name's not Carter."

"And with that he dashed off," Mrs. Latham told Dr. Goodall the following morning.

"Possibly you were mistaken."

"No. It was definitely Mr. Carter."

Dr. Goodall shrugged. "Perhaps it was him, then. I understand he travels a great deal." He glanced at his watch and his appointment book. He faced a busy day.

Mrs. Latham smiled. "Travels a great deal?" She paused a moment for dramatic effect. "I imagine he does. He's an airline pilot."

Dr. Goodall stared. "He can't be."

"He had the uniform, the cap, everything. He was walking along with two other pilots. It was definitely Mr. Carter."

"Good God," said Dr. Goodall softly. "Some commercial traveller!" He rubbed his chin, frowning. "What airline, did you notice?"

70

"It was a blue uniform with a peaked cap."

"I think they all wear that." Dr. Goodall leant back in his chair. "He never intimated for a moment that he was . . . flying."

"We've got to tell his employers," said Mrs. Latham.

"No. It would be quite unethical."

"But this is different . . ."

Dr. Goodall shook his head with vigour. "What passes between a physician and his patient is sacrosanct, privileged. A principle is a principle. But we must tell Mr., er, Carter in the most forcible manner that we have discovered his secret and that he must, er, I think the expression is 'ground' himself."

"You're right there," said Mrs. Latham, "but the crafty beggar hasn't given us an address or a phone number. There's nothing in your file. I can't think where you planned to send the bill."

Dr. Goodall shrugged apologetically. "He told me he was . . . mobile."

It took Dr. Goodall more than an hour of telephoning airlines before he reached Amory International and was told that Frank Beatty was in Rome and would be back in London on Wednesday.

"Please ask him to telephone Dr. Goodall. It's rather important."

"Certainly, Doctor," said a most agreeable girl.

But Frank didn't call on Wednesday. Or Thursday. Or Friday. Hoke rang Amory International once more. Frank telephoned a week later.

"Hullo, Hoke. I understand you've been calling me."

His offhand tone wasn't convincing. Hoke felt the warmth of righteous anger in his plump cheeks. Dash it all, couldn't Frank realize what a wretchedly invidious position he was putting a chum in?

"So it was your nurse at the airport."

"Yes. Good God, Frank . . . you're a *pilot*, of all things."

"As far as your files are concerned, I'm a commercial traveller named Carter. You're not involved, Hoke. That was the whole idea. I used a false name for that very reason."

"Frank, it's absolutely out of the question for you to keep flying. Suppose you had an attack . . ."

"Hoke, listen to me." Frank sounded patient and good-humoured. "There's no danger at all because I'm not doing any landings or take-offs. I'm giving them all to my first officers. And

71

the amusing thing is, I've told each to keep quiet about it because he's the only one getting such privileged treatment. So you see, there's really no danger."

"But if your employers knew . . ."

"They will soon enough, Hoke. Airline pilots have to take regular medicals. I just want to keep on flying as long as possible. I happen to enjoy it enormously."

"I know you do, Frank, but . . . I consider it my duty to instruct you to . . . er, ground yourself immediately."

"Are you going to tell Amory about me?"

"No. It's up to you, Frank. When will you tell them?"

"Soon, Hoke, Soon."

THE MAN FROM THE Medical Defence Union said, "I take it you have advised your patient to resign his position."

"In the strongest possible terms," Hoke said. "But he's reluctant. Do you think I should tell his employers?"

"Under the circumstances, yes, quite definitely yes."

Unhappily, Hoke said, "I was taught that information given one during treatment was privileged."

"True," said the MDU man, "but from time to time we are faced with situations such as yours in which physicians have a moral duty or even *legal* duty to break secrecy in order to prevent foreseeable harm to others. My advice to you, Doctor, is to inform your patient that if he fails to tell his employers the truth, you will be obliged to do so."

Hoke thanked the man. He would write Frank a letter. Put the whole thing to him in a straightforward manner; tell him that he had a week or so (possibly two) to advise Amory; a deadline; if by that time, etc. . . . He would get on to it first thing in the morning.

HENRY PEEL taxied to the ramp. He parked with care, lining up his wingtip with that of the next aircraft on the line. Brake on. Radio off. Mixture to Lean. The propeller slowed and gurgled to a halt. Ignition to Off. Master Switch to Off. He mopped his dripping brow.

The man in the right-hand seat scribbled something on his clipboard, then sniffed and unlatched the door. He was halfway out before he looked back at Henry. "I guess you passed," he said.

Henry felt a shameful tear spring to his eye. He had done it; he had actually done it. He was a licensed pilot. Within the hour he was on the telephone to a man in St. Catherines who had a dainty little yellow Aeronca for sale.

LEE ARRIVED AT Brockton shortly before noon on a bright Sunday morning. She turned her green MG into the members' parking lot, got out, and strolled towards the flight line. The day promised good soaring, but it was still too early; the cumulus clouds which provided the essential up-currents of air would not be "popping" until afternoon.

She sat in the long grass beyond the landing strip. The sun was warm and it was good to be alone. It was time for rumination. To cut free or become more and more entangled.

Larry, the Air Canada second officer who doubled as a club tow-pilot, interrupted her thoughts. What was she doing all by herself?

"Thinking," she said. "Wondering why we don't spend all our lives soaring. It's only when we come down to earth that things get nasty."

He smiled. "Very philosophical aren't we? Are you flying today?"

"I will when the thermals pick up."

"The cu are beginning. Look."

Tiny white clouds were indeed appearing against the blue, like balls of cotton.

"Larry, take me up to five thousand, will you?"

"Five? It's above club limits."

"I don't care. Will you take me?"

"Sure."

The wind had freshened. It nudged the slender sailplanes as they sat waiting in their lopsided way; ailerons and elevators sighed lazily, moving against safety locks, signalling that they wanted to be free.

Someone held the Blanik's nose down while Lee clambered into the cockpit, bulky in her parachute which was mandatory for solo flights. She sorted out the harness straps; two for the shoulders, two lap-straps, all meeting in a buckle at the waist. It felt good when they were snugly adjusted; you became part of the aircraft, a comrade of all the other components. She tested the controls: all

O.K. The canopy closed over her. The world tilted as a handler raised the grounded wing.

Minutes later she was in the air, her eyes fixed on the Cub, anticipating its turns. Her movements on the stick and rudder were smooth and instinctive. Up, up, while the grass and trees moved around her like some colossal roundabout.

At 5,000 feet Larry sought the elusive up-current of warm air. His wing waggled. Success! Time to release. Lee leant forward and tugged on the lever. The line went wriggling away. The noise of the Cub receded.

She was on her own. She was the first to attempt any serious soaring that day and she smiled. For the moment she had the sky to herself. She was the queen soaring, turning, her slim craft sparkling in the sun. Still she climbed: six thousand, seven, eight, almost nine. It was delightful. Utterly peaceful. Her mind wandered. A sailplane was a good vantage point from which to study your life. You saw it in perspective.

She thought about Charles Vaughan.

There was a chance—a real chance—that he might leave his wife and children for her. Would that solve all her problems? Or would it simply create a whole batch of new problems?

He's a wonderful guy, the nicest, gentlest man in the whole crummy world. If there is such a thing as love, this has to be it. But I have to give him up.

It wasn't a noble decision. She acknowledged the fact. Indeed it was a selfish decision. She refused to settle for a future jeopardized even before it began. It wouldn't work. The odds were stacked too high. She had been leading up to the decision for weeks. Now it was definite. She would write him a letter, explaining everything. . . .

Suddenly she noticed the altimeter. She had descended almost three thousand feet. Her thermal had long since abandoned her and she had drifted God knows how many miles from the field. O.K, no need for panic. There's the lake to the north. The wind was blowing from the west, so you've strayed to the east. O.K, just keep heading west, you're bound to find the field sooner or later. Make it sooner, please, she thought.

"Anyway," she said aloud, her voice assuming an odd tonal quality in the enclosed cockpit, "I can always put her down in a field. No sweat, girl." All she had to do was look out for power lines and barbed-wire fences. The sailplane could alight in a few yards.

Now the altimeter indicated 2,000 feet. None of the fields below looked familiar. She eased back on the stick and pulled the nose up more, "stretching the glide". The Blanik's speed hovered around the stall mark.

Then Lee smiled. Two gliders at ten o'clock! And presumably right over the field. It was only a hop, skip, and a jump away. She could see the orange hangar and the windsock. "I'm coming straight in!" she chortled. "So anyone else had better get out of the way!"

But her progress was painfully slow. God, how the wind must have picked up. And then, as if she had drawn a diagram of the distance and measured the speed and the rate of sink and the strength of the wind, she knew without a doubt that she wouldn't make it.

"O.K.," she said, swallowing, "then I must put her down. Now."

But below, it was all fences and sheds. Biting her lip, Lee turned. No; power lines. Could she get under them?

"Make your mind up," she said. "You haven't got all day."

There it was—a little strip of ploughed land, just beyond the road. The wind was blowing across her path, but this was no time to be choosy about wind direction. With her hand on the spoiler lever she angled the nose to the left. She felt the Blanik's side sway as the wind pressed against her.

"That's it," she said. "Between the trees, over the road and you've got it made."

Her approach was good. There was no reason why she shouldn't have made a safe landing—except for the wires stretching between the tall elms. She couldn't see them; but they caught her wing as she banked. There was a snapping, a screeching, a crumpling. The Blanik swerved. Lee saw the white lines of the road rushing up at her. Her hands and feet still moved the controls in a futile attempt to straighten out in time.

But there was no more time. As the wing thudded into the road, she heard the squeal of brakes.

THIRTY-SEVEN MILES away, Henry Peel touched down on his private landing field: eight hundred feet of the family farm that had been carefully levelled. The yellow Aeronca bounced gently, then settled down. With a burst of throttle, Henry turned and taxied to his hangar, formerly an implement barn.

His parents were waiting for him there, shaking their heads and saying they never thought they'd see the day when a member of the family would be flying his own aeroplane.

CHAPTER NINE

It had drizzled all day. On the way to Gatwick, Diane said she hoped the weather would improve for Vincent's holidays—he was due in two days. Beatty said he wished he could be there.

"Gosh no," said Diane, "it would be too much of a shock for the poor lad if he came and found his father there."

Beatty smiled. "Actually I don't think he was too keen on it when I was at home more or less permanently. I was too much competition for your attention."

"Flatterer." She grinned. "Will you have time to ring the Baxters in Toronto? Bobby's mother is always asking when you're going to see them."

"Bobby and I weren't particularly compatible when they lived next door. I don't know why his mother thinks we'll be great chums simply because he's moved to Canada. Just tell her I keep hoping to go to Toronto but never seem to."

"I'm not a very good liar," Diane said.

I am, he thought. I've become an expert. But how long can I keep it up? Until the next medical? For six months? A year?

Diane's private log book was open and her pen poised. "What time will you be leaving Toronto?"

"Twenty hours forty."

"When do you get to Belfast?"

"Eight in the morning your time."

"And you're off to Lisbon that afternoon?"

"Correct. And home Thursday evening. With luck."

Over the years Diane had filled several small notebooks with particulars of her husband's journeyings. Strictly speaking it wasn't necessary; his whereabouts could always be known by telephoning the line. But she preferred to keep her own records, mentally flying with him wherever he went.

At the terminal building, he stopped and took his bag from the back seat. Diane took the wheel.

"Drive carefully," he told her. "It's a bit slippery in spots."

She nodded. "You drive carefully too."

He stooped and kissed her through the car's open window. She touched his cheek; her fingertips were cool and soft.

"Have a nice trip. Don't forget to put your wheels down." It was her stock farewell.

Beatty gripped her hand for a moment, then he let go and watched her as she put the Rover in gear and drove away.

Jordan, the flight engineer, met him in Dispatch.

"Sorry, number four's U/S. Temperature."

"Damn," said Beatty. "How long?"

"Don't know yet. Could be the thermostat spring."

"O.K. Keep me posted, will you?"

"Roger." He headed for the ramp, a stocky, vaguely untidy figure, his cap set at a jaunty angle. A good engineer, Jordan; he would get the recalcitrant engine working if anyone could.

Beatty joined Webb, the navigator; together they examined the charts giving the wind and weather patterns over the North Atlantic and checked on the available levels and routes. The North Atlantic was heavily travelled; thus each aircraft was allotted a block of airspace and, in theory, it should never be less than 120 miles from the next aircraft. In practice it occasionally worked out to be rather less.

MR. AND MRS. FREDERICK COX found themselves a window seat in the cafeteria. Over tea they watched the aeroplanes landing and taking off. It was deliciously exciting to think that soon they would be inside one of those glistening monsters high over the Atlantic. Neither had ever flown before.

A thin, young man, wearing cowboy boots and faded jeans sat a dozen feet away. Len Sparrow was twenty and was on his way to spend three weeks with a married brother who lived in Ontario. As he lit a Camel he caught a hazy reflection of himself in the glass door. It pleased him. The lean, lone stranger. The silent man with a secret. He would have been deeply hurt to know that the few people who noticed him saw an undernourished, nervous-looking youth in desperate need of a haircut and a shampoo.

THE BAGGAGE CHECKERS received their instructions: a delay on Amory Flight 1010; tell the passengers an hour. The checkers sighed. Passengers seemed to think that they were responsible for delays.

As a rule Miss Hardcastle was a patient individual—you learn patience when you have been blind since birth. But today, waiting in the Gatwick terminal for the Amory flight to Toronto, she had a quite absurd desire to stand up and shout, "Oh, do hurry up, will you!"

She felt the wallet in her handbag; the passport, ticket and travellers' cheques were safe. An amiable young lady from the airline had found this seat and had assured Miss Hardcastle that she would return the moment the flight was called to guide her through the formalities and to her seat on the aircraft. It was like being a celebrity.

Miss Hardcastle amused herself by listening to the airport noises, then she heard someone sit down beside her. Someone light-sounding. And smelling rather delightful. Obviously the someone had commendable taste. Was she as pretty as her presence suggested?

Had Miss Hardcastle asked Len Sparrow, she would have received an enthusiastically affirmative reply. Seated a few feet away, he studied the girl's profile. She was unquestionably a bit of all right. Len lit another Camel. Our paths have crossed, girl. No use fightin' fate. This thing is bigger than both of us.

BEATTY TOLD Amory that the No. 4 temperature problem had been solved, but now trouble was being experienced with the transponder, the "secondary radar" system which enables ground controllers to identify individual aircraft on their radar screens.

Amory scowled at the rain through the office window. "We've got to get that flight off the ground, Frank." He punched the palm of his left hand. "That transponder could just as well have gone U/S in the air as on the ground. You simply advise ground control, right?"

"Right." Beatty nodded. "And that's what you'd like me to do."

"Correct."

"I'm the one who stands to lose my licence for taking off in an aircraft I know to be improperly equipped."

"I know that," said Amory. "But it's important that this flight goes. If you hold it up any longer, you'll compound the problem. Belfast, then Lisbon. I can't afford to let that happen, Frank. I mean that. Literally."

"Is a few hours really going to make that much difference?"

Amory rubbed his eyes. "I'm afraid so." He sounded tired and dispirited. "To tell you the truth, Frank, I'm out on a financial limb. Just bought new aircraft. New crews to fly them. Bigger payroll. I'm over-extended. It's going to be all right in a little while. There's a lot of business lined up and the new aircraft will more than pay for themselves, in time. You see, time's the bloody problem. What I'm saying is, I can't afford any more problems, not now, not until the heat's off."

Beatty felt embarrassed. "I'm very sorry to hear you have problems, sir."

Amory shrugged. "It's business, Frank. I don't know why I don't keep out of it. Balancing payrolls and bills and contracts and interest payments. It's a dumb way to live. The trouble is you feel like Napoleon when you win!" He laughed. "So what I'd like you to do is to load your aeroplane up with passengers and get the hell over to Toronto."

"I'd be less than honest if I didn't tell you that I'm reluctant to fly without a transponder. There's an element of risk."

"Of course there is," said Amory. "But you're a hell of a good pilot, Frank. Sure, we cut down the risks with radar and all the nav-aids but equipment fails; machines break down. And so we rely on the pilot to get us out of the mess. Usually he does."

Beatty smiled, shaking his head. "After that, how can I refuse?"

"Thanks, Frank," said Amory. "You won't regret this."

I hope not, Beatty thought.

THE VOICE over the PA was bright and cheerful.

"Amory International apologizes for the delay in the departure of Flight 1010; that flight is now ready for boarding. . . ."

Miss Hardcastle was already on her way through Passport Control, the briskly courteous hand of the Amory official steering her.

Len Sparrow eased himself out of the chair. The pretty girl was gathering her belongings too. Could it be that she was catching the Amory flight too? Strewth, he thought.

"THE TRANSPONDER is U/S," Beatty told Corfield, his first officer for the trip. "But we're going anyway."

"Roger," said Corfield, an uncommonly cheerful individual.

Beatty ran his eye over the instrument panel. The aircraft was one of Amory's new acquisitions, a 707-32B; it was in excellent condition. He rolled up his shirt sleeves and loosened his tie. Only actors in aviation epics and models for airline advertisements wore tunics and caps on the flight deck.

The light on the interphone glowed.

"Passengers all loaded, sir." The girl had a soft Scots accent. "Doors and chutes are secured."

"Thank you." He turned to Corfield. "Stand by for engine start."

CHAPTER TEN

Vaughan walked from room to empty room. The windows were latched and the television sets and radios and electric blankets were unplugged. He wrote notes for the milkman and the paperman. No deliveries until further notice, thanks. Outside, he met the postman.

"Hi there, Mr. Vaughan. Where to this time?"

"New York."

"Can't say as I envy you. Just one for you today. Have a good trip."

Vaughan took the envelope. The childish scrawl was Janet's. She was having a nice vacation in Carmel but she missed him and wished he would finish his work and come and stay with them and Lynn threw up in a store and Grandpa caught a cold.

Vaughan replaced the letter in its envelope. His eyes had suddenly become prickly and irritated.

As he backed the Cougar down the driveway, he knew he had to end the affair. He loved Susan and the kids. And he missed them. Alone, he was only half alive. He put the car into drive and sped away.

GRANT HOBBS was also driving to the airport at that moment. For some years Hobbs had made a prosperous living by sending invoices to companies all over the United States. The invoices covered listings in various business directories—which were never published.

Hobbs was moving—something he found it necessary to do from time to time. The fact of the matter was, he had had the post-office box number in LA too long already. By now there would be outraged letters on the way to the postmaster informing him that his post office was being used for fraudulent purposes. It always happened eventually. But in the meantime a remarkably high percentage of the companies invoiced had sent in their cheques. And Hobbs had cashed them. The trick lay in knowing when to move on.

Hobbs was heading east for a vacation. Later he would set up operations in the Hartford area, although he regretted leaving the Coast; the weather agreed with him.

IN SANTA ANA, Earl Gasparac poured a second cup of coffee for his wife. She had had a bad night; the pain must have been savage; he could see the evidence around her mouth and eyes. Her smile didn't fool him. Neither did her eager chatter about the trip back East to see all the old places again.

Earl felt seething anger within him, anger at a fate that could condemn an innocent to a slow, lingering death. How could anyone believe in *anything*?

TRANSTATE'S FLIGHT PLANNING DEPARTMENT was full of teletype machines that clattered and telephones that jangled. Captains called the Department to ascertain the serviceability of their aeroplanes, weather conditions, availability of radar and radar aids, etc.

"Er, Captain, I'm Garten."

Vaughan turned. Garten was a young man with a bland, ingenuous face, corn-coloured hair, and an anxious-to-please look in his eyes.

Vaughan nodded, "How are you?" He knew he sounded terse and disinterested. "How long have you been with TranState?"

"Two months, sir. I finished the course last Friday."

"And this is your first line ride?"

"Yes, sir."

Vaughan nodded again, mechanically. He wanted to welcome

the young pilot to the line; it was the nice thing to do; today, however, he seemed incapable of doing anything nice.

He studied the Met charts with Cutshall, the navigator. Conditions looked good. Thunderstorms were brewing east of the Mississippi but it was hard to predict just how severe they might turn out to be.

"Anything reported en route?"

"A Northwest flight reported some CAT at thirty thousand."

Calm air turbulence could be thoroughly unpleasant and dangerous. Vaughan decided to request air-traffic control to route him at a minimum of 35,000 feet—flight level 350.

Garten was making notes of the conditions at Chicago, Toronto and New York and calculating the amount of fuel required for the trip—an amount that had to include reserves for emergencies.

It always made sense to carry as much fuel as possible. A famous case in point was the four-engined airliner that took off from a field in Africa bound for the United States with scheduled refuelling stops at the Azores and Gander, Newfoundland. The first stop was made without a hitch but before reaching the midway point between the Azores and Newfoundland, a radio message reported that dense fog had closed the Newfoundland airport. They headed back to the Azores. But now came another shock. A radio message from the Azores regretted heavy fog there also. The nearest fog-free airport was Casablanca.

The hours passed. The fuel gauge needle edged towards Empty. When the aircraft made a safe landing at Casablanca it was found that only a gallon or two still sloshed around in the tanks. And Casablanca was the point from which the passengers had embarked many hours before.

The moral was: always pump in as much fuel as you can lift; you can never tell when it may come in handy.

In the Crew Lounge, the cabin crew awaited Vaughan: six girls in pale blue trouser suits. Vaughan recognized three of the girls, including Jane Meade, the chief stew for the trip.

"Mr. Garten will be the first officer and Mr. Cutshall is our navigator," he said. "I think the trip will be pretty smooth to Chicago. After that we might run into some rough stuff."

As he spoke, he found himself wondering whether the girls knew his wife was living apart from him and that he had a mistress in

Toronto. Had they been giggling about him before he entered the lounge? Anger flared in his cheeks.

Testily he insisted that the girls demonstrate their knowledge of emergency procedures. When two of the new girls became flustered and made mistakes, Vaughan told Jane to ensure that the girls studied their manuals before flight time. "I don't want amateurs in my crew."

Jane coloured but said nothing.

Outside the lounge, Vaughan was immediately contrite. For God's sake, he thought, why take it out on those kids? In all probability the stews knew nothing about Lee and Susan. But he couldn't go back, and apologizing would only make a bad situation infinitely worse. Better the girls thought of him as a martinet than a mental case.

Garten said, "Shall I do the external now, sir?"

Vaughan nodded. "I'll come with you. I could use some fresh air."

Garten smiled nervously. Vaughan thought: he thinks I don't trust him. I'm doing a great job of instilling confidence in the crew.

The DC-8 was connected to the terminal building by the umbilical-like tube through which the passengers would shortly enter. It was cool beneath the broad, swept-back wings. Vaughan looked up at the engine pods that dangled on their slender mountings. Nothing appeared to be loose or leaking. He inspected the aircraft's tyres, each of which cost roughly $250 and was good only for about seventy-five landings. Plenty of tread left, no nails or sharp stones embedded in the rubber. The fuselage smelt of metal and fuel and a number of other unidentifiable substances created the smell peculiar to aeroplanes. He saw Garten peering studiously at the underside wing. "You figure she's safe to fly, Garten?"

"Yes, sir."

"Captain Vaughan?" Vaughan turned. Wills, one of the Flight Planning men, was calling him from the office doorway. "Air Canada's on the phone for you Captain."

Vaughan went inside and took the telephone.

A girl said, "This is the Air Canada office here at LAX. We've received a telex from Toronto."

"Toronto?" Vaughan caught his breath.

"Yes, Captain. They asked us to pass on the message."

Vaughan listened. When it was over he asked the girl to repeat it. This time the words had to mean something different. But they didn't.

"LEE HURT IN GLIDER MISHAP. IN ST. MICHAEL'S HOSPITAL, HAMILTON. SORRY. LARRY."

Larry. The tow-plane pilot.

"That's it, sir."

"O.K., thank you."

It seemed to take an hour for the long-distance operator to put him through. At last a woman's voice announced, "St. Michael's."

"I'm inquiring about a patient named Lee—no, Rosalie Pringle."

"Pringle. Mrs. Pringle is in Intensive Care, sir."

His fingers tightened on the phone. "Look, ma'am, I'm calling from Los Angeles, California . . ."

"I'm sorry. The line to ICU is busy at the moment."

"I'll call back," said Vaughan. His mouth was dry and bitter.

MISS HARDCASTLE had been led aboard Amory Flight 1010 ahead of the other passengers. The stewardess found her a seat beside a window and immediately in front of a toilet. Soon other passengers came clattering along. A young girl's voice said hello—followed at once by the inevitable intake of air. It was, Miss Hardcastle supposed, a bit of a shock to discover that one is talking to a blind person. She suggested that the girl take the window seat; it was after all, completely wasted on someone unable to see out.

The girl's name was Julie and she said she was pleased to sit next to the window. She told Miss Hardcastle she was going to Canada to visit an aunt and uncle and decide whether to emigrate. Soon the two of them were chatting like old friends, blissfully unaware of the irritation boiling within the occupant of the aisle seat.

In Len Sparrow's opinion, fate had delivered him a low blow. When the flight had been called he had slipped into the queue right behind the bird with the nice profile. But when he got inside, he found the girl changing places and he was stuck next to an old blind bint with dark glasses. What a turn-up!

Mr. and Mrs. Cox held hands during the take-off. It all seemed rather frantic, that enormous contraption hurling itself headlong at the London-to-Brighton railway line, but with a great heave, it went zooming up—almost vertically, it seemed. Mr. Cox realized that he had been holding his breath since the beginning of the run. He heard his wife say, "Well, I never" several times. He patted her hand and smiled at her. She smiled back, definitely a bit on the forced side.

FLYING THE ATLANTIC was not particularly demanding. It was largely a matter of guiding the aircraft to the correct altitude and heading, then handing it over to the automatic pilot. Thereafter the job was handled by gyros and accelerometers. At 35,000 feet there was little for the pilot to look at. The clouds lay far below. The ocean, when it was visible, looked like a grey motionless pond. In theory a pilot at that altitude can see about two hundred miles. In practice the sky is rarely clear enough to see more than a few score miles. It is a problem for jet pilots, for the speed of their aircraft makes their eyes a poor safeguard against mid-air collisions. Before a speck of dirt on the windscreen is identified as an approaching aircraft, it may be too late. Jets, not noted for their nimbleness, need distance to change direction. Distance means time—and that is precisely what they do not have when another aircraft is dead ahead. . . .

"Captain?"

Beatty turned. Jordan, the engineer, stood behind him.

"Yes?"

"Troubles, I'm afraid. That bloody temperature in number four."

THE DC-8 STREAKED UPWARD; the sprawling city of Los Angeles seemed to shrink beneath its trembling wings. Despite the twenty-one square feet of window on three sides of the flight deck, the crew could see little but sky. The nose section blotted out their view until 35,000 feet when the aircraft reached cruising altitude and levelled off.

Climb-out completed. Auto-pilot on. The DC-8 had consumed nearly 10,000 pounds of fuel. At cruising speed, it would burn kerosene at approximately 12,000 pounds per hour. The computer announced that the aircraft was travelling at a ground speed of 478 knots and would arrive at the next checkpoint in eight minutes. At the navigator's table, Cutshall methodically entered the figures on the company's route sheets.

The sun was brilliant, sparkling on wisps of cloud, even managing to reflect a fraction of its brilliance against the black anti-glare panel painted on the nose immediately before the windshield.

It was superb weather. CAVU—ceiling and visibility unlimited. Far below, the Rockies slid away, the colossal peaks and valleys no more than sandcastles on a beach. Ahead lay the endless prairies that had seen convoys of covered waggons groaning westward, measuring their progress in miles per day. Hurtling eastward, the DC-8 gobbled up the miles, one every six seconds.

Jane came in, taking orders for coffee. Vaughan shook his head, not looking at her. I'll talk to her later, he thought. She'll understand. He noticed Garten glancing at him from the right-hand seat. He seemed a little apprehensive, which wasn't too surprising. The poor guy had probably been told that Vaughan was all right. Now he's probably wondering how the others can be worse.

What about Lee? What the hell did *hurt* mean? Did she break a leg? Get a black eye? *In Intensive Care?* What did that mean?

Is this a punishment?

Vaughan winced and glanced at the panel clock. In an hour and a half they would be landing at O'Hare. He would call the hospital again from there.

He stared ahead through the $2\frac{1}{2}$-inch thick windshield. The sky was losing its clarity. The horizon had become fuzzy. Below, the ground was becoming progressively muted as the stratum of moisture particles settled.

He turned to Garten. "You want to take her into O'Hare?"

Garten beamed. "Sure thing, Captain, thanks."

"O.K. I'm your co-pilot now. She's all yours."

"REDUCING NUMBER FOUR'S power won't help," said Jordan. "The oil's cooled by the bloody fuel anyway. I'm just about a hundred per cent sure it's the gauge. But I can't be sure until we get on the ground."

"So we shut it down."

"'Fraid so, skipper."

Beatty nodded. Gander was 890 miles ahead. He told Corfield to advise them of the problem. "But we're not declaring an emergency," he said. "Piece of cake getting there on three engines."

Thank the Lord, Gander was in Canadian territory Beatty thought.

Collision

If the landing were made on a British or American field, an emergency would be mandatory and fire engines and ambulances and other expensive vehicles would be called out. All very comforting of course, but hardly necessary in this case.

The passengers were unaware of any problem. There was no sensation of sudden power loss as the fourth engine was cut off. And no tell-tale stationary propeller stood guard before the stilled engine.

Beatty cleared his throat as he pressed the PA button on his headset. "This is the captain speaking. I'm sorry to have to tell you that we'll be making an unscheduled stop in Gander, Newfoundland in slightly more than an hour. A minor problem has occurred, nothing to get the slightest bit alarmed about, but we want to look at it. No extra charge for letting you have a quick visit to Newfoundland; all part of the Amory service." He groaned to himself; he really wasn't good at this sort of thing.

One hour later the 707 touched down, incurring landing fees of approximately $1,000 plus some $300 for such necessities as steps and ground power.

At that moment, TransState Flight 738 was 2,114 miles away, approaching Des Moines, Iowa.

JORDAN CUT A shim out of a small piece of aluminium. It was, he pointed out with pride, worth about two pence, but it would do the work of the thermostat spring that had been causing all the trouble. The crew ran up the engines; everything checked out. Beatty ordered the aircraft's tanks refilled. Everything was under control.

Five minutes later he was clinging to the towel dispenser in the washroom. His limbs were as heavy as lead. He gasped in air. The room began to revolve, then steadied itself like an aircraft coming out of a spin. Everything O.K. in a minute, Beatty thought.

It was. Strength travelled slowly along every nerve and through every bone. He felt weak but steady. You're all right now, he said to himself.

But the truth was, he felt sick and wobbly. Why, he wondered, didn't the pills work this time? Did he need a stronger variety?

He shook his head, pained by his own delusions. You've had it, he told himself. Grounded. But here? In Newfoundland? If he grounded himself the flight would be held up until Amory could send a replacement. Which would mean that the flight would be even more horrendously off schedule and the passengers would have to be fed and probably accommodated too. It would be another major slap in the pocket book for old Amory, the only chap willing to offer him another chance.

But I won't be doing him any favour if I smash up, Beatty thought.

He shook his head. He wouldn't fly. He would take another pill and play at co-pilot. If he dropped dead it wouldn't make any difference. Corfield was a thoroughly competent chap.

He felt better. He would telephone Amory from Toronto and explain the situation. Amory could replace him far more readily in Toronto than here in Newfoundland.

The passengers filed back to the aircraft, thankful to be on their way. But Len Sparrow was irked that the old bint hadn't let go of the bird with the profile for an instant. Poor kid, she hadn't even managed a glance in his direction. That's life, baby. You had your chance.

As the crew strapped themselves in, Beatty turned to Corfield. "You're the skipper. Take us to Toronto, there's a good fellow."

CHAPTER ELEVEN

It was sultry in Chicago, the air still and heavy with warm, clammy moisture. Vaughan eased himself out of the captain's seat. "See you back here in twenty minutes."

The terminal building was thronged with irritable people laden with baggage or children. Was it July 4th? A holiday? Vaughan couldn't remember the date. He swore as he looked for a telephone that was free. He stationed himself behind a stocky man in a crumpled tropical suit who was explaining to someone that the business had gone to the competition simply because of nepotism and not because the account had been poorly serviced. Hanging up the phone, the man looked drained and weary.

He glanced at Vaughan's uniform. "Sure wish I could fly aeroplanes for a living."

"It's better than working for a living," said Vaughan automatically, and reached for the phone. He slipped the dime into the

slot and told the operator his credit-card number and the number
of the hospital in Hamilton.

The hospital switchboard answered. He was, he explained, calling
regarding the condition of a patient named Rosalie Pringle.

"One moment please." Then, "Are you the gentleman who called
from California?"

"That's right. Now I'm calling from Chicago, Illinois."

Pause. "Are you a relative?"

"Yes. An uncle."

"I see." Another pause. Then: "Sir, I'm not supposed to reveal
information of . . . but as you're calling from so far . . . Sir,
Mrs. Pringle passed away at three-twenty-five."

"Three-twenty-five," he said.

"Yes, sir."

"Thank you."

He hung up while the PA crackled something about Memphis
and New Orleans. Dazed he inserted a dime as he searched for the
note bearing the Carmel number. Be in, he begged, please be in.

Susan's father answered. "I have to talk to Susan," Vaughan
said.

Mr. Jearard sensed the urgency in his voice. "Very well, Chuck.
Hold on."

Somewhere in the house a TV set was playing. Cackles and
screeches and canned laughter.

"Yes?" Crisp. Curt.

"She's dead, Susan."

Silence.

"Susan?"

"Yes, I'm here." Her voice softened. "I'm sorry, Chuck . . . I
don't know what to say. What . . . what happened?"

"It was an accident in a glider. She crashed, I guess."

"I'm sorry." She added, "Yes, I am sorry because she was
young and . . . I mean it, but . . . how are you?"

"I'm . . ." He thought, rubbing his forehead with his hand. "I'm
kind of stunned. I don't know really how I am. Do you understand?"

"Of course I do. Where are you calling from Chuck?"

"O'Hare. I'm due out in a few minutes. Toronto, then New York.
I'm coming back to the Coast tomorrow, Susan. Will you . . . ?"

"Do you want us to be there?"

"Of course I do. Please come home. I'll be getting in around six, LA time. I can be home around eight, eight-thirty."

"We'll be there," she said.

"I know it's . . . crazy, my calling you . . . to tell you about . . . you know what I mean."

Susan said, "I don't think it's crazy at all, Chuck." She sounded as if her eyes were full of tears. "In a way it's . . . rather lovely that you called me. I don't know if I'm supposed to react that way, but I am."

"I'm glad. Thank you."

She said, "Don't fly, Chuck. They can get someone else."

"Not at such short notice. Besides, I'm O.K. Really. Don't worry. Give my love to the girls, and see you tomorrow."

"Yes," she said. "Good-bye."

"Good-bye."

Vaughan walked to a bench and sat down. Had he just had a totally unbelievable conversation with Susan? He stared at the headline of a *Tribune* someone had dropped. No mention of Lee, just a lot of unimportant, meaningless words.

"Cap'n Vaughan, sir?"

Vaughan looked up. Garten stood there, perspiring freely.

"It's thirteen forty-five, sir."

"What?" Vaughan stared at his watch. "Sorry," he said. "I didn't realize it was so late." It would be necessary, he thought numbly, to complete a Reason For Delayed Departure form.

"I've completed the external, sir."

Vaughan nodded. "Good. So let's go."

GRANT HOBBS habitually travelled Economy despite the fact that the income from his invoice enterprise exceeded $100,000 a year. He appreciated the anonymity of Economy, since his only desire was to pass among his fellows as uneventfully as possible. Flying scared him.

When he boarded TranState Flight 738 in Los Angeles he had checked out the emergency exits. Survival was, after all, largely a matter of planning ahead.

On re-entering the DC-8 at Chicago, Hobbs again checked the exit. He then opened his book, but before he could start to read, a bright red head appeared over the seat-back and an equally bright voice declared that he didn't need to worry about the emergency exits, these airplanes were safe as houses.

"Thank you very much for your information," mumbled Mr. Hobbs.

Lillian Dumont turned to the front, a smile on her lips. In a few minutes she would be on her way to Toronto, she thought, for the Big Adventure. She knew no one there, but she had heard that it was groovy. She held her purse tightly. It contained $16,821.37, thanks to Associated Security's petty cash, housekeeping, and the savings account. She had left a note for Herman saying it was a shame but she found him a drag and that went for his mother too.

Half a dozen rows forward, Earl Gasparac was helping his wife with her seatbelt. She was smiling and chatting, but it was obvious that she was going through hell. There should be a medal, Earl Gasparac thought bitterly, for people who suffer uncomplainingly.

Briskly the stewardesses strode down the aisle. All seatbelts were fastened, the emergency chutes secure, the doors fastened and latched. TranState Flight 738 was ready for departure. It was twenty-two minutes behind schedule.

THERE WERE 27,304 aircraft flying in the skies over North America when TranState Flight 738 took off from Chicago. One was Amory International Flight 1010 which was crossing the border between Maine and New Brunswick. Another was Henry Peel's tiny Aeronca. He had just made a low pass over the farmhouse; now he was zooming away into the sky at full throttle. The earth was shrinking like a gigantic balloon with a puncture.

He flew to Niagara Falls. Utterly content, he circled the huge waterfall, his wingtip slicing the rising mist. Below, the streets were jammed with cars. Henry looked down with amused pity.

He felt the urge to wander. Was there any happiness greater in the world than being at the controls of your very own aircraft? Perhaps he should get a bigger aircraft and try to break a record or two. LONE EAGLET HENRY PEEL LANDS IN PARIS TO TUMULTUOUS RECEPTION. He grinned. You're nuts, he told himself. But it was delicious to think in those terms. Practically speaking, he would have to brush up on his navigation and learn how to use the ADF and VOR and all those other things.

The diminutive Welland airport appeared through the summer

haze. Henry eased back the throttle and a few minutes later he touched down in a professional three-pointer.

He refuelled, then took off, heading north, following the ship canal towards Lake Ontario. The air was bumpy which was usual at this time of year, Henry had learned. His little machine bounced and swayed as it cut through the up-currents.

Henry hadn't taken the time to check on the weather at Welland. If he had, he might have headed for home.

THERE WAS A tightness around the eyes and throat. A few minutes earlier, Beatty had taken another pill. I'll be all right in a minute, he kept telling himself. But he knew it was pointless. Montreal below. He glanced at his watch. In less than an hour the trip would be over. Right now Corfield was in command. And he was doing a perfectly competent job.

The navigator, Webb, had news of the weather. "Toronto is reporting thunderstorm activity, severe in spots. At the moment it's not affecting the field itself but they think it will before we get there."

"Roger," said Corfield. "Let's have another check in fifteen minutes, shall we?"

Ahead, ground and sky merged in haze. Typical summer conditions for this part of the world: moisture and heat—with cooler air on the way to stir up trouble.

Beatty reflected that from now on the air and its restless movements would merely be of academic interest to him. He would never again have to see and feel it as an airman does: the ever-mobile masses of air roaming over the earth, umpteen billion tons of it, cold, warm, moist, dry, sometimes tranquil, sometimes angry. An airman learns to know and respect the air just as a sailor discovers the vagaries of the sea. It is the seventh sense, the one that takes over when the instruments fail. Beatty frowned. He didn't like the look of the weather ahead.

TRANSTATE FLIGHT 738 was already feeling the turbulence in the air. Invisible fists struck at her as she sped by. Her passengers were drawn to the rather disquieting sight of her huge wings flexing as they took the jolts. None of them knew that the wing was capable of "flapping" as much as nine feet without damage.

92

"Seatbelt sign please," Vaughan told Garten. "And look after the PA will you? Tell them we're encountering turbulence."

Vaughan scanned the instrument panel. Speed, altitude, course, temperatures, pressures: all O.K. But it was getting bumpier by the minute. Behind the dials, needles shivered and vibrated.

Lee, I can't believe you're dead. I can't, I can't.

The ground had almost vanished beneath a blanket of haze. Lake Erie was ahead. Detroit lay beneath a layer of brown-tinted air that looked incapable of sustaining any form of life.

"The stuff's building over there," he said to Garten, pointing.

Before them, the sky was dominated by gigantic, blue-black clouds piling themselves one upon the other as if attempting to build a wall before Flight 738 reached them.

IT HAD BEEN a sweltering day in the northeastern United States and the adjoining Canadian Provinces. The air was heavy with saturated heat. But, according to the news media, relief was on the way in the form of a cold front edging down from the north.

Because cold air is heavier than warm air, the front clung to the earth as it moved. It was an invisible wedge that pried the warm, damp air from the surface of the ground and sent it rolling skyward on the back of even cooler air that came piling in behind.

The warm humid air kept rising. Soon it found itself ten, fifteen, even twenty thousand feet high. And suddenly the air became cold. Like steam from a kettle, the moisture in the air underwent a rapid transformation. It became visible: tiny droplets of water that formed clouds. Cumulus. Cumulonimbus. And, far below, the invasion by the cool air continued, thrusting even more warm, moisture-laden air into such great altitudes that the water particles promptly froze. Quickly the ice crystals grew, nourished by moist air from below, until they were so heavy that even the strongest up-current could no longer sustain them. Down they went, billions of them, at speeds ranging from sixty to one hundred and twenty miles per hour. They were an avalanche that smashed its way down, dragging waves of frigid air in its wake.

It was the storm's catalyst. Now the winds began their battle. Suddenly the barometric pressure soared. As if someone had pressed a button, the winds abruptly shifted. Hail thrashed the earth, and the sky became a battleground. Up-draughts and down-draughts fought in deadly proximity, creating windshears like guillotines that were capable of slicing an aeroplane's wing from its body.

"OH LORD," said Henry Peel loudly and distinctly.

He gulped, frozen in horror at the sight. The clouds were enormous. Blue-black. He hadn't noticed them forming. He had been looking over the lake, thinking of it as the Atlantic, imagining himself flying it, a famous hero. . . .

The sun disappeared. It was night. Henry tore his dark glasses off and dropped them on the floor. Never had he experienced such utter, complete loneliness. No one could help him. He had no radio, no means of contacting anyone until he landed. *If* he landed. He clasped a hand over his mouth. I may be dead in a few minutes, he thought.

The storm clouds had formed a huge, mobile wall bent on forcing him out over the lake, but he couldn't let it. He had to turn inland. Ten o'clock direction. Over there, the sky seemed a bit lighter. With a morsel of luck he might find somewhere to land.

He pushed the stick forward. The tiny aircraft bounced and tilted, bravely pushing its way through the hostile air. He passed over the shoreline with its ribbon of busy highway. The ground was still dry. The storm hadn't really begun, but he could feel its anger already.

No field in sight. Where the hell was he? Why hadn't he paid attention? Wandering around the bloody sky like a hobo. . . .

He flew across rows of houses and roads on which people walked, their feet sensibly planted on good, solid earth. It was densely built-up. Nowhere to land. Good God, he thought, it must be Toronto. There was no other city of this size in the area. How he had wandered. "You idiot."

The first drops of rain hit the windshield. Almost simultaneously a giant hand grabbed the Aeronca. Up it went. Madly. Suicidally.

Henry opened his mouth as if to protest. Nothing, absolutely nothing, he did made the slightest difference. Stick fully forward. Rudder pedals hard left, then right. Throttle forward. Back. All futile. The Aeronca still zoomed upward, almost vertical, bouncing on a torrent of boiling air. The ground vanished. Above was nothing but blue-blackness.

It was the end. It had to be. Henry felt his body banging against the side of the cockpit. Something hit him on the head. In a moment of semi-light, he saw his sunglasses pinned to the roof of the cockpit. Henry was sure he wasn't upside down. But, upon numbed reflection, he wasn't sure of anything. He had thought the air to be his friend, his companion in adventure; now it was doing its level best to kill him.

With the realization that he was utterly helpless came a kind of calm. He could do nothing but sit there and wait for the end. In all probability the aircraft would shortly come to pieces. A thousand bits would flutter down to the ground. He would be one.

CHAPTER TWELVE

"It's going to be all right," Frederick Cox assured his wife, patting her hand that had become a fist. "A few air-pockets, that's all. Nothing to get het up about."

She groaned. "Fred, make him put this thing on the ground."

"Make who?"

"The driver."

"Can't do that, old girl. He's got his hands full up there, you know. We don't want to interfere with his work, do we?"

Len Sparrow was thinking what a godsend this rough weather would have been if only he had been sitting in the right seat! A bit of the old strong-silent-comforter would have worked wonders. No, don't mind a bit if you want to put your head on my shoulder. You go on and. . . . Without the slightest warning Len Sparrow's lunch came up. He heard the girl say, "Oh, you poor little chap!" Aggrieved, ashamed, he rushed for the toilet.

VAUGHAN TOOK A deep breath as he gazed at the enormous thunderheads. Toronto was reporting bands of thunderstorms, moderate to severe, heavy rain and hail, and winds gusting up to fifty knots.

"We'd like to orbit until the worst of this stuff has gone through."

"Roger, TranState 738. Stand by, please." A minute later, the controller called again, advising the flight to orbit the Ash beacon where the storm was not active.

Soon the aircraft's path became smoother. Vaughan pressed the

PA button. "This is the captain speaking, ladies and gentlemen. I'm sorry to have to tell you that we're going to be a few minutes late landing at Toronto. They're experiencing some rough weather at the airport, but it should be through the area shortly. We apologize for the delay, but we think you'd rather be a few minutes late than . . ."

Than what? Dead? Like Lee?

He winced. No, he hadn't intended to say that. He thumbed the PA button again. "Er, we'll let you know just as soon as we have clearance to land. Thank you."

Lake Ontario turned smoothly below.

The radar operator frowned. Was that an echo? It vanished, reappeared, then vanished again. The operator shook his head. It was impossible to sort things out properly with storms all around. If that was an echo, then it would be from a small aircraft, judging by its size. But no small aircraft were in the vicinity—at least none had announced their presence on the Toronto Advisory frequency.

THE VOICE from Toronto control battled with the static. "Amory Ten-Ten, you are clear to descend to and maintain 15,000. Over."

Beatty repeated the instructions to Corfield who was guiding the 707 between towering thunderheads. The aircraft descending at a rate of 2,000 feet per minute slicing through the turbulent air. "What are your intentions?" Beatty asked. Corfield thought a moment. "The visibility is almost down to minimum on the ground. The storms are severe. I heard a couple of aircraft saying they intended to wait it out. I say we should do the same."

Beatty said, "Thunderstorms can go on for a hell of a long time in this part of the world and we're badly behind schedule."

"I realize that, sir," Corfield said, reddening. "But if conditions make it dangerous . . ."

"Don't you think we should plan on landing until it becomes absolutely obvious that we can't?"

Corfield swallowed. "I don't feel I have sufficient experience in conditions like this, sir. I'd rather you took control."

Beatty nodded. "Very well."

Corfield abruptly raised his hands from the yoke as if it had become too hot to hold and stared ahead, rigidly.

Beatty smiled to himself. The poor blighter was probably thinking fierce thoughts about captains who give a chap a command and then take it away again on a whim. He sympathized and silently told Corfield: We've all had to go through it, old chap.

Toronto said, "Amory Ten-Ten, we're not reading your transponder squawk." Which, thought Beatty, is hardly surprising. He made a show of switching to the back-up transponder. Predictably, the ground controller reported a continued lack of response on his radar screen. His task was now to make sure which of the flickering dots on his screen was the Amory 707.

"Turn on a heading of three three zero . . . O.K., Amory Ten-Ten, we have you identified now. Please advise your intentions."

"Landing Toronto."

"Roger, Stand by."

Beatty scratched the tip of his nose. He felt well and was absolutely confident of his ability to land the aircraft. "Let's have the preliminary check-list, shall we?"

One by one the aircraft's systems were checked. No problems—except for the unserviceable transponder. Even that was no longer a problem; Toronto radar had identified the Amory flight. The flickering dot on the screens now had an identity.

IF HENRY PEEL had been asked to state how long he had been tossed by the storm, he might have said half an hour, even forty-five minutes. In fact, it was less than three minutes.

For much of that merciless interlude he was upside down. At one point he emerged from a wall of cloud as if propelled through a door. The Aeronca was spinning. Henry saw a blur of sky. Then, without warning, it was dark again. Dark and wet and lonely.

The instruments had gone mad, so he had no way of determining his altitude. But gradually, it seemed, it was becoming cold. Rain pelted the windshield, immediately followed by hail that caked his tiny world with a layer of frost. Moments later the frost melted and flew away in jagged chunks. There was no sign of the ground. Was this, Henry wondered, the end of the world?

Suddenly, gloriously, he was free. He could see the earth below. "Good God. I'm out of it," he said.

He came to the conclusion that he was remarkably cold. He looked at the altimeter. He was at 17,000 feet.

His consciousness was swimming. He could hear his own voice instructing himself to shove the stick forward. You are flaking out from oxygen starvation, his voice explained. If you don't do something about it, you will die. And yet it was a shame to leave. Up near the heavens the colours were soft and the sounds sweet. Then his eyes began to focus on something.

He blinked. Good God. It was a layer of cloud. Hurtling at him. It looked solid enough to shatter the Aeronca. But then he realized that he was through the layer of cloud and more and more layers.

Reality returned with each breath of denser air. One by one the facts of his situation thrust themselves upon him.

He was diving. Rapidly. The joystick pumped against his hand and Henry discovered that the engine was blasting away at full throttle.

He pulled the throttle back to idle.

THE TINY AERONCA was suddenly there, mere feet away: a flimsy thing, wobbling in the air. Inside, clearly visible, sat a young man in a bright check shirt. His face was turned towards the hurtling 707. He looked disbelieving.

Corfield uttered a strangled croak of a warning.

Beatty had already jammed on aileron and rudder. But there was so little time. In a fragment of an instant, the jet had consumed the space between the two machines. The Aeronca loomed in the windshield, insanely huge and close. And then it was gone.

In the passenger cabin, Len Sparrow had just emerged from the toilet. He was closing the door, when, without warning, everything tipped over. He was tossed back into the toilet to sprawl dazed on the seat.

"We're crashing," gasped Mrs. Cox as pillows and blankets tumbled from the overhead racks.

"No . . . quite normal manoeuvre just before landing," her husband muttered bravely.

THE 707 PLUMMETED. "Give me a hand, man!"

Corfield nodded jerkily, his eyes bright with horror. His hands gripped the yoke. Together the two pilots fought to force the 707 back to level flight before it smashed into Lake Ontario. Layers of cloud rushed past. Somewhere a radio voice was yelling something in agitated tones. Jordan called out altitudes.

Beatty didn't know whether he had hit the Aeronca. Would a frail little thing like that make any sort of impact? Why was the stupid plane *there*, then?

"Easy. Don't force her."

Corfield was pulling on the yoke too energetically.

Oh my God, thought Beatty, I think we might make it. He saw the waters of the lake tipping, then straightening.

"Bloody marvellous!" yelled Corfield, beaming. He patted the instrument panel as if it were a faithful hound.

Beatty smiled. Reprieved again! How many lives did he have left now? "Are the bloody wings still on?"

Corfield elaborately gazed out of the windows. "All wings present and accounted for, sir. Better luck next time."

"What's that din?" Webb said.

"Shut off the undercart horn, will you?"

It screeched at the crew like a cantankerous old fishwife telling them that the undercarriage was still retracted although they had brought the aircraft down almost to ground level.

The control column heaved against Beatty's hand. Up a bit, old girl. We need a spot of height.

"Would someone go and see how the passengers are coping? Tell them it was a near miss. . . . Near missmissmissmissmiss . . ."

The dials on the instrument panel began to move like amoeba beneath a microscope. Beatty had time to think: God, I'm having another attack, and mumble, "Take over," to Corfield and then the world became a blur of lights and shadows and dull, insistent sounds.

CHARLES VAUGHAN seemed to be talking to Walt Przeczek.

"I'm trying to be honest," he was saying. "I'm aware of a shifting of the balance in my emotions. A little while ago I could think only of that sweet girl, dead. But now I'm able to realize that I haven't seen my children in a long time and I've missed them. I've missed Susan, too."

"So it was lucky for you that the broad in Toronto got killed."

"No, it was a tragedy."

"Sure it was. But it was fortunate, in a way. You're grieving for the girl and yet you're grateful because fate has stepped in and dragged you out of a situation you couldn't handle."

"Yes, I admit it," said Vaughan. "I'm as ashamed as hell of it, but I can't deny it."

Walt Przeczek was chuckling. "In your own fumbling way, buddy, you're a genius. You could start a whole new trend. One minute you're the all-American son-of-a-bitch, the next you're someone to comfort because you've suffered a great loss! Beautiful!"

THE CONTROLLER'S face was ashen. His radarscope had become a nightmare. The bright green blips—each representing a jet packed with humanity—were like wilful little creatures bent on self-destruction.

Frantically he tried to create a perspective of the situation and what it would be in ten seconds and thirty seconds. The errant blip on the left side of the screen had to be Amory. But what had caused it to dive? Now it was streaking out across the lake. And climbing.

"*Mother of God!* Amory Ten-Ten, make an immediate left turn!"

HE'S HAD A bloody heart attack, Corfield thought. He gazed appalled at Beatty's mouth and its pathetic attempts to form sounds.

Then Jordan snapped, "Control is calling us!"

"What?" Precious, irreplaceable seconds slipped by.

The controller's voice cut through the static again. "TranState, 738, make an immediate right turn! *Immediate!*"

VAUGHAN HEARD the controller's order. But for an instant he didn't react. The words of the controller had somehow become part of what Lee was saying. Her voice was sharp and urgent. And he wanted somehow to tell her that there was meaning in it all, that it wasn't just a mindless sexual ritual; there was significance in what had happened. . . .

An instant. Then he was thrusting control yoke and rudder hard over, hurling the machine towards a gigantic wall of cloud.

"TranState 738, turning ninety to the right." The cloud enfolded them. A second later, they were in the sunlight.

And then Amory Flight 1010 hit them. Simultaneously, scores of people saw different things happen.

Grant Hobbs saw a row of seats rise as if lifted by giant hands. An instant later a shuddering bang exploded out of the walls of the aircraft as a second wing suddenly materialized beneath that of the DC-8. Absurdly Hobbs thought that the aircraft had become a biplane. Then, frantically, he reached for the emergency exit handle.

Jane Meade, the chief stewardess, checked herself from screaming. The DC-8 seemed to have halted in mid-flight and was coming to pieces before her eyes. The deck had reared up and broken; the seats spilled passengers who were not strapped in; those that were tried to free themselves.

Earl Gasparac saw the sides of the aircraft bend and buckle, he clutched at his wife and buried her head in his chest.

An emergency exit suddenly opened beside Lillian Dumont. Shocked, she saw Grant Hobbs, for an infinitesimal fragment of time, suspended in mid-air—a few feet from the aircraft. His thin face wore an expression of mild surprise. Then he vanished, a charcoal-grey blur.

Lillian screamed as a tidal wave of air grabbed her. Her seatbelt held her securely, but her purse, snatched by the boiling-yet-icy gale, rocketed away from the aircraft.

Aboard the Amory aircraft, the passengers were already strapped in their seats. It was fortunate, for the impact caused them to half-rise towards the roof that was abruptly crumpling in upon them.

There was an appalling eruption of sound, a grinding and smashing, as the aircraft shuddered and squealed in pain from every stringer and spar.

Mr. Cox looked up to see the underside of another aeroplane. It was a dreadful-looking tangle of metal, and incongruously, baggage. The impact had opened up the DC-8's luggage compartment and a flimsy nightdress fluttered by.

"Good gracious," exclaimed Miss Hardcastle "Whatever has happened?"

"I think we . . . hit another aeroplane." Julie looked up through her window to find an enormous shimmering mass of metal bearing bright red letters spelling TranState.

CORFIELD realized something appalling.

The instruction to turn right had been given to a TranState aircraft, not to Amory 1010. He had obeyed the wrong orders. He had turned right instead of left.

He was to blame.

CHAPTER THIRTEEN

The floor of the DC-8's flight deck heaved and broke in a confusion of metal, wires, switches and levers. Part of the nose broke away and an icy hurricane tore through the flight deck.

Vaughan felt the wind tearing at his earphones. He looked down at the torn wing of the Boeing 707. It looked close enough to touch.

A mid-air. It had happened to him.

But why was the aircraft still flying? Why wasn't everything exploding and burning and tumbling?

Cutshall, the navigator, was crouching beside him. Vaughan leant back out of the wind. "Check the damage!"

Cutshall nodded. Vaughan turned back to the controls. The control yoke was loose, like a broken limb. He dared not move the thrust levers.

He swallowed. His brain reasoned: of course the controls are useless; the linkages of the hydraulic-boost system run through the floor beams, under the flight deck. How could they be expected to work? Icy fingers grabbed at his intestines. He had no controls. He was powerless. In a moment the whole thing would come apart.

DAZED, GROGGY, Beatty thought the aircraft had hit something on the ground. He kept seeing a West African village store cut in half by the right main landing-gear unit of an Anglo-World 747.

"Mid-air," Corfield was croaking. "We've had a mid-air."

Beatty struggled with his consciousness. "What did you say?"

"We hit another bloody aeroplane! Look behind you."

Then, through the side window he saw the unbelievable sight of the 707's wing snuggling up to the DC-8's wing, the tips almost touching. The metal was torn and folded back. Fuel poured out in a wind-battered mist.

"He hit us," said Webb, the navigator.

"No, we hit him?" said Jordan.

The flight-deck roof semi-collapsed; buckled, broken, it sagged over the heads of the crew. The bulkhead at the rear of the flight deck had disappeared and Beatty turned and saw the terrified faces of the passengers. Then he heard the voice of the TranState pilot on the VHF radio.

BY SHEER MIRACULOUS chance, the two aircraft had been travelling in almost exactly the same direction and at similar speeds when they collided. This saved them from instant destruction.

Angled upward a degree or two, the 707 had thudded into the belly of the DC-8, her roof slithering along the underside of the other. Like voracious predators, the jetliners bit through metal, cables, tubes, longerons, bulkheads. Metal plating crumpled and fluttered away. A section of the 707's wing folded and snapped amid a haze of escaping fuel. Joined by a tangle of tortured metal, the two splendid aircraft had become one.

They had become a monster. An aeronautical aberration that remained in the air only because its wings were still capable of creating power from the speeding air and fuel continued to pour to the engines that still functioned.

But the monster was inefficient because its two sets of wings did not meet the air at precisely the same angle; and it lacked stability because damage to its tail and sides spoiled the smooth flow of air. Like a ship without a keel, it wobbled, on the point of tumbling.

The monster staggered towards the shore. For the moment the pilots were little more than passengers. Still struggling to grasp the enormity of their predicament, they dared not attempt more than tiny, exploratory movements of the controls.

The passenger cabin of the DC-8 had become a nightmare. The wind, gulped in through the torn nose, swept into the hull, hurling anything movable down the length of the cabin.

A section of metal panelling smashed into Earl Gasparac's forehead. A million lights burst before him, then went out.

Jane Meade managed to drag an injured girl to an unoccupied row of seats. She kept repeating that everything was going to be all right, wondering whether she was really talking to the girl or to herself.

Earl Gasparac was only dimly conscious of the icy wind that

105

battered his face. But he could feel his wife's fingers pressing insistently on the side of his head. He knew he was cut badly; but his wife knew what to do; she had been a nurse for a dozen years.

"I HAVE NO AILERON or elevator control," Vaughan reported.

"How about rudder?" asked the controller. He sounded calm and matter-of-fact.

"Negative, jammed."

"Roger. Your controls, Amory?"

Beatty said, "Our controls seem to be working, after a fashion." He and Corfield had the control yoke hard over the left, compensating for the missing wing section. It was odd to think that the TranState pilot was only a few feet away, inside that aluminium cocoon that couldn't be seen from the flight deck.

"Amory to TranState. We seem to be temporarily wedded. If you have any ideas on how we might get this thing down, let's hear them."

The American answered at once. "Negative, Amory. She's all yours. All I can do is sit and watch."

There was so much to decide, and so little time. The airport, shrouded in fitful rain showers, was only a few miles distant.

Jordan said, "Ready to dump fuel, sir."

"Roger," said Beatty.

The speed was now below 240 knots. Both knew only too well the appalling probability of everything suddenly becoming a bonfire in the sky. What, Beatty wondered, is the stalling speed of two crashed jetliners?

Why was the thing still flying? Beatty felt the sweat trickling over his forehead. The monster was appallingly unstable; it wobbled through the air like a top-heavy tightrope-walker. The turbulent air kept trying to tip the whole contraption off balance and send it tumbling out of the sky.

"Amory to TranState. I'm just aiming it at the airport and I plan to plonk it down as rapidly as I can."

"Roger, Amory. We can maybe help you with a little power if necessary. I haven't tried the engines yet but they may be O.K."

"I'll let you know if we need more power."

Ground control reported all runways clear for emergency landing. There was not, however, time to foam them.

106

"Anything else we can do?" asked the controller.

Webb said flatly, "Ask him if he knows a good prayer."

"Shut your bloody mouth!" snapped Corfield.

"Go aft," Beatty told Webb. "Tell the crew to prepare the passengers for crash-landing."

The speed was falling off. Gently he edged the nose down. To apply more power was dangerous: it was liable to free the DC-8 and send it tumbling to the ground.

He felt dizzy from the effort of holding the controls hard over. The monster had had enough of this idiotic game. It was tired of pretending to be an aeroplane.

Beatty pressed the PA button. "This is the captain speaking. I don't have to tell you what has happened. I *am* telling you, however, that we have control of the aircraft and we are heading straight in for landing. But it could be rough, so please obey the instructions the cabin crew give you. Thank you."

What, he wondered, am I thanking them for? For not storming the flight deck and lynching him for being criminally dangerous?

He called the TranState pilot. "I think my undercarriage and flaps will still work. I'm going to leave them until the last possible moment, though."

"I understand," said the American. "If we try it before, we might stall out, uh?"

"Exactly. She's frightfully wobbly even now." For the first time, it occurred to Beatty that their conversation was being taped, every word recorded for posterity and the accident investigators.

The rain stopped in the typically sudden manner of a North American summer storm. A patch of blue sky appeared.

Heading in from the lake the jets appeared to be in the tightest formation in the history of aviation.

In the control tower, binoculars were suddenly in short supply. One controller hastily loaded his camera with film. On the field emergency vehicles cruised warily along deserted runways, their crews watching and wondering, a curious tension apparent everywhere.

"We have you in sight," the ground controller announced. "You are cleared for a straight-in approach to runway three two."

"Good," said Vaughan, "because we sure as hell can't do a circuit of the field."

"The wind," said the controller levelly, as if this were a normal, everyday landing, "is two eight degrees at twenty knots."

"Roger," said Vaughan. "O.K, Amory?"

"Piece of cake," came the Englishman's voice.

Vaughan gazed ahead. It was weird to see the runway and be powerless to control the approach. Now his flying resembled his life: he was no longer directly in control of anything any more.

Suddenly the Englishman's voice cut through his ruminations.

"We're sinking too fast! Have to have some more power!"

"O.K." Vaughan's hand was on the thrust levers. His heart pounded. The surge of power could tear the two aircraft apart. Gingerly he pushed the levers forward.

It took time. Three seconds, four, five. Rows of houses wobbled nearer.

Then, with a terrifying heave, the engines began to deliver more power. Metal groaned and stretched. The monster tottered, trying to tear itself in two.

Vaughan said aloud, "Hang in there, baby. For God's sake, hang in there. Please."

A pungent smell seeped up from the shattered electrical and radio compartment beneath the flight deck. Garten had emptied a portable extinguisher into it, but still it smoked. Hydraulic fluid sloshed over the floor; the hurricane still screamed in through the torn nose.

Jane Meade appeared between the two pilots, hair plastered flatly across her grimy forehead. She reported that the passengers were in crash-landing positions.

"How are they?"

"Pretty good," she yelled. "But it's as draughty as hell back there. Mind if we close the window?"

Vaughan smiled. "Good girl," he said.

"Still there, old boy?" The British voice sounded as if it were taking orders for whiskies and soda.

"Affirmative. But only just."

"Good show. I think we might bleed off a little of that power now, don't you?"

"O.K." He's one hell of a fine pilot, Vaughan thought. Somehow he's bringing this monster in on a reasonable facsimile of a final landing approach.

EARL GASPARAC realized that he was dying. He was content. He managed to squeeze his wife's hand.

She looked down at him, her eyes gentle, brimming with love, without speaking she was able to tell him that she knew he was happy. And she understood why.

Len Sparrow came to his senses. Where was he? Everything was rattling. Then he remembered. He was in the toilet in the jet. What had happened to it? It looked squashed. He reached for the door. The handle turned but the door wouldn't budge. He was trapped.

Mr. Cox grasped his wife's hand and braced himself. "In case we don't get out of this, er, in one piece, if you know what I mean, I just want to say. . . . I've always loved you, old girl."

She nodded. "Me too, Fred. You've been a good husband and father. I couldn't have asked for better."

"Good of you to say so, old girl."

"And," said Mrs. Cox, "that business with George Harris didn't mean anything at all, really."

"Course it didn't," said Mr. Cox comfortingly. Then his eyes grew big. Had he heard a-right? What business with George Harris?

THE NEARER TO touchdown, the more viciously the monster fought, twisting, nosing, one instant dipping a torn, trembling wing, the next skidding like an overloaded truck on an icy road.

Beatty felt weak. I mustn't pass out, he thought. The runway was dead ahead.

"Fifteen hundred feet," said Corfield.

Beatty thumbed the transmit button. "TranState, let's peel off some more power, shall we?"

"Sure thing," came the reply.

Beatty grinned wryly. Both he and the American were trying to sound quite unconcerned by the catastrophe and neither man was fooling the other.

Beatty blinked as the airfield blurred for an instant. Just sweat in the eye, thank God. Suddenly the window panel at his left shoulder began to vibrate, shivering as if terrified by the imminent return to earth.

Corfield's hands were on the flap and undercarriage levers. Beatty nodded. "Now!"

He grimaced as the monster bucked and swung. Oh God, he

thought, only half the flaps are working. Controls hard over and forward. Power off on one side.

The ground tilted and swayed. The strip of dark grey concrete swept towards him, white stripes flickered below. He thought: when the speed drops off another few knots, the wing will suddenly drop. The poor thing can't do anything else. And when it does, we'll be cartwheeling all over the aerodrome. He corrected the wing even before it began to drop.

Corfield thought he had gone mad; he tried to cancel out the control movements.

Beatty shook his head. "We've got to," he explained as the ground whirled past. "I know I'm right."

The monster wobbled threateningly. And then its wheels touched the concrete. The tyres held for approximately five seconds. An instant later the nose wheel and the right main undercarriage unit collapsed.

The monster slewed off the runway in an explosion of dirt and turf. Simultaneously, the TranState DC-8 tore herself free, thrusting her nose forward as the 707 dipped. For a fragment of time, the two aircraft were bridged by tubing, cables and wires. Then they separated.

The DC-8 hit the ground. A wing snapped cleanly and spun sideways as if flicked away by a giant finger. The 707 skidded in a virtually straight line over the sodden grass, shedding fuselage while fuel cascaded from the torn wing tanks. There was nothing that either pilot could do. The tools of control were now just so much more weight to charge the relentless impetus.

Inside the two aircraft, passengers and crew members huddled in their seats, stupefied by the merciless battering and din. Muscles turned to jelly under the pounding. A billion drummers were hitting a billion cymbals.

And then, suddenly, miraculously, the world was quiet.

THE DAMP WIND pulled at the clothes of the mourners. Dr. T. Roydon Goodall shivered. He had felt sick at heart ever since he had read the appalling news of the crash at Toronto.

"MAJOR AERIAL DISASTER . . . DEATH IN THE SKIES . . . BRITISH AND U.S. JET AIRLINERS COLLIDE." He had scanned the story for the name he intuitively knew was there.

"The British aircraft was a 707 charter belonging to Amory International, piloted by Captain F. N. Beatty, 49, of Royston, Herts."

Now, cold and miserable, he stood amid a hundred strangers at the graveside and watched as the service ended and the minister spoke to the widow and her son.

The flowers on the grave fluttered desperately in the wind. Hoke observed a man in a pilot's uniform speaking to the widow. Someone said it was the pilot of the American jet. He was tanned, a pleasant looking individual, and his name was Vaughan, if Hoke remembered the papers correctly. He had spoken of Beatty's "amazing piloting" in managing to coax the two airliners back to the ground.

Hoke shivered. He imagined Frank's aircraft smashing across the field on its belly, fire gobbling at the torn wings, the crew hurling open doors and hatches, inflatable escape chutes prancing out like great, dangling tongues, passengers and crew slithering down them to land in piles in the mud. And then the frenzy to run from the flames.

"Everyone made good their escape from the 707 on landing," *The Times* reported, "except for Captain Beatty and a passenger, twenty-year-old Leonard Sparrow of Streatham, who had become trapped in the wreckage and was overlooked by the other members of the crew. Captain Beatty, without regard for his own safety, remained inside the burning, smoke-filled hull in order to help Mr. Sparrow escape. Mr. Sparrow is in satisfactory condition in Toronto General Hospital."

The papers rued the fact that Captain Beatty didn't make his escape at the same time. "He returned to the interior of the hull, presumably searching for more passengers." They had no inkling that Captain Beatty would undoubtedly have remained in the burning aircraft even if there had been no one to rescue, thought Hoke.

The papers had no definitive information as to why the two machines collided. One account hinted at "electronic problems, possibly caused by storm conditions." Another speculated that a third aircraft might have been involved. A "full-scale investigation" was being initiated by the Canadian authorities.

What would it uncover? Hoke didn't know; he didn't care. The reason for Frank's death seemed unimportant now; only the fact of it mattered.

The cars moved away. Only a handful of people remained. His hands in his overcoat pockets, Hoke walked slowly along the gravel path. On the way he passed two men in airline uniform. One said that Frank Beatty was a good pilot, a damned good pilot.

ADVERTISEMENT:

FOR SALE: Aeronca 7AC-468. Clean. No reasonable offer refused. Apply: H. Peel, R.R. 3, Filden, Ontario.

Spencer Dunmore

Spencer Dunmore, born in London and educated in Yorkshire, is married and lives in Canada, where he is an advertising executive during the day, an author in the evenings and a private pilot at the weekends. Collision *is based partly on his own experiences as a pilot, and partly on his researches, as he explains here:*

My novel is founded on fact, or rather a series of facts, dating back to the first mid-air collision between airliners on scheduled flights which took place more than half a century ago. A DH 18 of Daimler Airways and a Farman Goliath of Grands Exprès Aèriens were flying north of Paris—and navigating by the elementary means of following a main road. Unfortunately, they were following it in opposite directions.

Today, when navigation has become electronic, such collisions should never take place—in theory. The main problems are that the number of aircraft has grown at an incredible rate; equipment sometimes fails; human beings occasionally err; and private aircraft—often with inexperienced pilots at the controls—roam more or less at will. The result: hundreds of "near-misses" are reported every year; hundreds more go unreported. And from time to time everyone's luck runs out and a collision takes place—usually with appalling carnage.

But not always. People *can* survive mid-airs. On a perfectly clear day in the 1950s, a DC-3 crew suddenly found they had a private aircraft astride their fuselage. Damaged but still airworthy, the DC-plus-Cessna combination landed safely. The tiny airport at Sandwich, Illinois, was the scene of a similar incident some years later when a Cessna 150 flew into the rear of a Fairchild 24, and both interlocked aeroplanes made a safe, if bumpy, landing. During a World War II raid on Hamburg, a B-17 climbed abruptly, hit the underside of another and interlocked. Eleven crew-members parachuted, but the pilots of the upper Boeing managed to steer both bombers to a successful crash-landing.

The ability of the Boeing 707 to fly *sans* major portions of wing was dramatically demonstrated when a 707 collided with a Constellation over Carmel, New York. It lost a phenomenal thirty feet of the port wing plus one engine, yet the captain succeeded in setting his aircraft down safely—as did the pilot of the Constellation. All praise to the awesome skill of the airmen involved.

Wild Goose, Brother Goose

A CONDENSATION OF THE BOOK BY

Mel Ellis

ILLUSTRATED BY JOHN SCHOENHERR

Published by Robert Hale, London

It was spring and the Canadas were winging north towards the great breeding grounds. On their long journey which passed over the grass flats and spreading ponds of Wisconsin, one of the ganders tarried and took for himself a mate whose wings had been pinioned by man so that she could not fly. On the bright clear days that followed, when the migrant flocks that had touched down lifted off again, the gander longed to go with them. Many times he was tempted, and many times he left, but he always came back . . . .

With the keen eyes of a born naturalist, the author saw all this happen. The couple's love, loyalty and amazing courage inspired him to write this story. It is a story that will set you thinking about the ways of civilization as well as those of nature.

HE CAME out of a tumultuous Wisconsin sky onto the man-made ponds which floated a captive flock of his own kind, and while waiting out the storm, took one of the geese as his mate. When the skies cleared and his wild flock lifted, he went with them, and when she did not follow, he came back clamouring for her to lift, ride the wind, come to the north to build her nest.

She ran along the dike, wings flailing; but the long feathers furnishing the ultimate needed thrust had been lost in the pinioning of her right wing.

Until dark, and even after, the gander winged low over her, back and forth, clamouring. Then, when it was obvious she was not going to follow, he stretched the webs of his feet, braked with his wings and surfed along the water to settle beside her.

They spent the night together, but the next morning he rose again to the clamour of a passing flock, and insisting that she follow, went down the sky until even she, with an eye for scanning horizons and an ear for hearing worms burrow, could no longer see or hear him.

She waddled out of the water and sat disconsolate on the bank, her neck tucked in and her feathers so ruffled she looked ill. He had taken her and now he had gone, and this was not in the code of the wild goose, which mates for life and sometimes, for one or the other, beyond the days of living. When a gander of the captive flock came importantly over, she ignored his compliments. When he put out his long neck to offer her a billful of bright coontail moss from the pond, she thrust out at him. He gathered in his

117

pride and went back among the flock, seeing if there was yet one he might want and who would want him.

There were many geese on the clustering ponds of the Silver Sun Trout Ranch, which was, among other things, a ranch where people paid to come and fish. The geese, all made flightless soon after birth, were there so that people might have some illusion of being in the north country, where trout caught rising flies instead of pellets of meat and cereal flashed from hoppers by electrically timed devices. For generations these geese had been earthbound. Sometimes still they clamoured when the skies from dawn to dusk were etched with passing flocks, but with each passing generation the will to freedom was lost in fine feeding, until the days of longing to be airborne had become only minutes of mourning.

The mated goose kept an eye on the sky. She was sure that at any minute the gander would reappear to claim her forever.

All day pairs of geese broke away from the flock to go off and establish their territories where barrels had been put down for their nests in an orchard or among a grove of birches. But the mated goose sat alone on the water, though the spoons and flies of the fishermen fell close. People made remarks about how lonely she looked out there, but it is not the way of Canada geese to take love lightly. If there was to be any frivolity, let it be among the mallard ducks, who stole hens shamelessly from one another with much fighting and raucous quacking. Canada geese courted with quiet dignity. The gander protected the goose on the nest and guarded the goslings even after they were flight-borne and until they went off to form alliances of their own.

Now when darkness came, the goose stood on one leg and put her bill into the feathery nest of her wing, but her whole being was tuned to his voice, which, though briefly heard, would be instantly recognized as long as she lived.

So she passed the night. The goose flock resting on the water and the mated pairs around the barrels were mostly silent. Only the ducks quarrelled in the dark.

Morning came, and as storm clouds dropped away, the day was suddenly bright. The goose put down her leg and tilted an inch to come square. She stretched one leg and wing, then the other. She ruffled her feathers, shook vigorously and walked to the water. She stepped off the bank, paddled along the pond's surface a little way and lowered her bill to skim and lift a morning drink. Then bowing gracefully, she dipped her head into the water and up to let a silver stream run down her neck and back. Bath finished, she shook, and the spray from her feathers showered like diamonds.

The rest of the flock was loud now with impatience, and even the mated pairs walked away from their barrels towards a hard-packed circle where corn was spread. It was feeding time.

Right on the chiming of the hatchery clock, the diminutive fore-man, Tom Rank, stepped from the long, green warehouse where the food was stored. He carried two yellow plastic pails from which corn spilled as he walked. Though foreman of the ranch for nearly twenty years, he had never got over the excitement of feeding time. He liked to hear the geese honk and the ducks clamour, and watch the excitement of it infect even the songbirds, so that the cardinals whistled piercingly above the bugling of the geese back near the fence with its grapevines and bittersweet, its nightshade and wild cucumber.

Now Tom's eyes swept out over the six ponds to where the single goose sat alone. He whistled, thinking she might come to feed; but she turned and swam slowly the other way. Tom scattered the corn, whistled once more and hurried off to check in the men who were arriving for work.

John Mackenna, the ranch owner, saw the lone goose too. He had come out of the big, white house to stand on the shaded porch and watch nostalgically. He'd seen his flock grow from a single wild pair, and for many years the job of feeding had been his. He often came from his office to watch the men at their chores, feeling a need to leave his paperwork for a moment and return mentally to that place at which he'd started.

The flock gobbled the corn quickly, drank from the ponds and then drifted off the water to eat grass. Some mated couples went to the barrels to see about nest building, and a few birds not yet mated began bobbing and weaving in the courtship dance. This aroused the other geese, even the yearling non-breeders, into emulating them. But Mack noticed that the deserted one stayed aloof on the pond. Under other circumstances, he might have slid a skiff into the pond, driven her to a dike and gently coaxed her behind wire, to see if she was injured or sick. But now he turned away.

Gradually the flock, full of new green grass snipped from under

119

the fencing where the ranch ponies could not reach, drifted back to water, and those not ready to set up housekeeping bunched together in a feathery flotilla and let the breeze drift them.

It wasn't yet summer, but the sun was warm. The hatchery help was waiting for the yellow trout eggs spread on trays to hatch, and for the helpless fry to fall through the screens to lie waiting for strength from their yolk sacs. Chattering sparrows were carrying goose feathers to eaves, and the crows, usually so noisy, came and went with a shadowy black stealth to their eggs in a nest in the fence-like oak. Epaulets flashed as the boundary quarrels of the red-winged blackbirds erupted into aerial combat; cock robins screamed hysterically at one another among the apple trees; and mallard drakes raided their brothers' harems and were in turn cuckolded when their backs were turned.

But the geese entered placidly into a creative partnership with nature, and there was no evidence of discontent except for the lone goose. Only once did she cry out. When a hawk came sailing so high in the sky no man might see, she caught the wingbeat in her eye and for a second thought *he* had returned. But hope guttered, and she looked down again at the water dejectedly.

So noon came. The sun was so hot on the shore that violets were opening, plump apple buds showed prematurely pink, and newly dried dragonflies flashed jewelled wings. In the unseasonable warmth even the mallards quieted, and the air hummed with soothing insect sounds.

Then, during the quiet, the call came—distant, but high and carrying as the sound of a silver horn. The lonesome goose raised her head and tried frantically to lift. Some of the other geese answered the call. As Mack, hearing the geese, came out to watch, the lone goose stopped trying to fly and cried out with longing.

There was a speck on the horizon. It grew larger until the goose heard the powerful beat of the gander's wings and saw him bend his neck to look upon her. He did not come directly down, for once he knew she was waiting, there were other considerations.

He was a *wild* goose. Except in an emergency, he would never land near trees lest they be hiding a predator. The ranch sheds, the trucks and men, all meant incredible danger.

Instead he called to her again to come, to follow him north a thousand miles to a wild river where there were spits of gravel and broad flats of grass and where the moose came and sometimes the wolves, but man rarely, if ever.

The goose tried until her wings were dragging. She tried until the pond glistened with bubbles and the frightened trout went to the bottom. She tried until her bill came open and her breath was hot. Then she put out her neck and lay flat and could not even answer when he called. As the ranchmen watched, he circled lower and lower until he could plane along the water to come close to her. He did not touch her. She lifted her head, and he bowed a few times. She drank some water, and as mated geese do, he took water too. They swam to the far shore, and she started towards the trees to lead him to the grazing grounds, but when he refused to follow, she went back to him, and they made hardly audible noises as they swam together like a royal couple on parade, back and forth, so the unmated males—there were too many ganders for the geese—would see that they were a pair.

Once again she swam to shore and started up towards the orchard, but he still would not risk going among the trees, where danger might conceal itself. A wild goose must have places where a fox cannot hide and even a mink might find it hard to get close without being seen. Delta country was his kind of land, or wheat fields cut to stubble and stretching to Saskatchewan horizons, or big water flat to the farthest seeing. He could not abide cramped areas with trees, as a wolf cannot abide farmlands, nor a moose high mountains, nor a wild goat broad valleys. He must know about every moving thing within range of his eyes. When he would not follow, she swam again with him to the centre of the pond.

Mack went over to Tom Rank. "You'd better get that goose into a pen, or that gander will take her down the creek to the river, and next winter she'll freeze in the ice there."

Rank went to the pond. The wild gander swam nervously to the far shore, his head high, wanting to fly but waiting for the goose to loft first. "You're a wild one," Tom said. He often talked to the geese, just as Mack once had. He went to the tiny skiff on the bank, slid it into the water, and paddling, started to force the goose and the gander against the shore. The gander stood it until the skiff was coming straight at him. Then, clamouring loudly, he lifted into the sky.

The goose managed to skid along the surface with a wild

wasting of energy, but when Rank expertly slid the boat parallel to her, she had to land. He beached the skiff, and spreading his arms, began to drive her towards a wire enclosure beside a small shed. Overhead the gander climbed a hundred yards and began circling, calling down for the goose to come before the man could kill her.

At the pen the goose would have eluded the foreman, but he was expecting this. He rushed her through the open door and quickly swung it shut. The goose walked up and down behind the wire, raising and lowering her head to find some way out of the enclosure, while the gander circled and called. Rank went for corn, and the captive flock, nervous now, began to add to the clamour of the wild one above them.

While Tom was scattering corn for the goose, the gander flew so far he was only a speck in the sky, but when Tom went to put the pail away, the gander dropped down into the pond and swam anxiously in every direction.

Mack joined Rank, who asked, "Do you think he'll go, or will he stay for the summer?"

"It would be better if he left, but I think he'll stay," Mack said.

"Then perhaps we'd better leave her out after all."

"You know what would happen. They'd go overland to the river, and a flightless bird doesn't have a chance there. Isn't it better if she has a little heartbreak now and lives, rather than going with him to die?"

Rank looked thoughtfully out to where the gander was swimming. He said, "Maybe. I honestly don't know." He didn't have to be told why Mack was prescribing longing in the beginning rather than heartbreak in the end, for John Mackenna had had his own heartbreak, and it had made him bitter. Rank did not ask again that the goose be let out, because sometimes, since his wife had died, Mack did not take kindly to suggestions.

Marcia had been dead nearly five years, but she'd lived long enough to see the trout ranch grow from a dream into reality. She'd seen muddy waters seep out of the earth to fill the craters the huge draglines had dug. She'd seen the silt settle and the sun shine straight down through ten feet of water to where you could see a silver dime on the blue clay bottom. She'd seen the pair of ponies come to be bred so there'd be mounts for the customers'

122

children. She'd seen the first pair of geese grow into a flock, and that it was a slave flock never occurred to her.

Tom Rank had been Mack's first full-time employee, and those early days had been feverish with activity. Together they had planned, and then like boys they'd go to the house for Marcia's approval.

Evenings, Rank would go home to his own family in a house he had bought on an abandoned farm a few miles from the ranch, and Mack and Marcia would sit on their porch, where they could look out over the spread and consider ways to better soil conditions, improve water resources, overcome the limitations of men and machines.

It had been a gigantic do-it-yourself project, involving earthen dams, concrete spillways, cedar and spruce windbreaks, stone or sod banks, beds of daffodils, tulips, iris and tiger lilies, corners for wild flowers, grapevines, kennels, ponies, ducks and geese, and a long, cool stone hatchery where millions of eggs could turn into millions of trout.

Marcia had lived to see Tom Rank made foreman over a score of helpers, to see the mortage burned and to see on her husband's face the glow of satisfaction from a dream realized.

Then came the day he was called to the doctor's office. Mack could still remember the man's exact words: "It's cancer. I'm not going to try to fool you, John. It looks ominous."

In the years since Marcia's death, women had slid in and out of Mack's life, and though Tom hoped that one might come to live in the house where Mack rattled around alone, none had. Tom felt Mack's decision to keep the geese apart was partly because of his bitterness. Perhaps, Tom reasoned, Mack did not want to be reminded of the urgency of love.

The sun lowered, and as it slipped below the horizon, eddies of cool air came up from the creek. The gander flew over the pen in search of the goose, who had been making muted, plaintive sounds. He swooped low but saw that she was behind wire, and he swiftly rose on a long slant, so high there was bright daylight all around him and he could see the sun. He circled until the ponds and forests and the pen where the goose waited were shrouded in night.

It wasn't until fullest dark that he angled down without a sound.

A hundred yards above the pen, he slipped like a skimming stone, to brake at the last moment and come down to the packed earth inside the enclosure.

She came over to him, and in the dark they stood together.

NO ONE saw the gander leave at dawn. The goose did not call for him to stay but merely crouched down on her webs and watched him lift. He flew to the far pond.

Rank saw him there, and after feeding the flock and the goose behind the wire, went to the far pond and scattered some corn along the shore, hoping the gander would come over to eat.

But the gander, fearing the corn might be a trap, picked at what grass he could reach without going ashore and nipped tendrils of plants growing in the water. He even found little stones for his gizzard along the shoreline. When the ranch help began to arrive for work, he lifted into the air and flew a quarter of a mile to where the Rose River moved placidly in its shallow valley.

He sat on the water for a long time, drifting with the current, and then, satisfied that he was alone, edged towards shore and started feeding. Geese were in the sky again, riding the wind, and sometimes he called out to them, because a goose alone is like a man lost. But though they called back and sometimes dropped down to see what was so enticing as to tempt a lone goose to stay behind, they never stopped. Once the gander winged from the water and joined a V of more than a hundred birds. Tucking himself onto the tail end of the formation, he flew until the ponds were so far behind they looked like drops of water on a green leaf. Then, with a little cry, he left them and turned back.

Some of the flying geese, especially those few who had not found ganders, called out an invitation to come along to a summer of fulfilment in the northern lands of little trees. But they did not cry with the persistence of flocks southbound in fall.

Fall flocks, more than half of them youngsters, bayed like beagles at every green field, every resting flock, every marshy bay, even at duck gangs. Sometimes in the fall, young snow geese and specklebellies, having lost their parents to guns, joined the great Canadas. It was laughable to see the smaller birds wing frantically to stay with the formations and to hear their excited yelps in contrast to the clarion bugling of the Canadas.

But now in the spring the snows and blues and white-fronted geese had consolidated their flocks, and so far as the Canadas were concerned, there was no time for checking out stubble, grass flats or spreading ponds, because each goose had a date with the destiny he'd been hatched for. When the big gander dropped back, the others did not waver but drove north and a little west, pausing only to eat and rest, and relentlessly counted progress on the big rivers and lakes which swept beneath them.

The gander dropped lower and lower. Turning, he came to the Rose River, and flying at treetop level, went all the way back to where he'd been sitting when the flock went by. He ate again, then climbed onto an old muskrat house, and lifting a leg, leaned a little to rest. Sandpipers ran the shore, and rails toured the pads of lilies only days out of the water and still so freshly green it was hard to believe they would ever be leathery enough to hold a bullfrog on top and hoard enough insects on their undersides to feed a sunfish.

When the sun was directly overhead, the gander put down his leg, and after ruffling his feathers, shook vigorously so each fell precisely into place and he was smooth as a velvet goose. Then he walked down off the heap of rotting moss and frightened a muskrat which had been critically eyeing the structure as if to decide whether it was worth repairing or whether he should start a new house in some other place.

Diving, the muskrat splashed loudly, and the gander gave an involuntary cry. Then he slid out into the current, turned into the wind and lifted. He flew to the ranch and came silently over the goose's pen. Neither uttered a sound; it was as though they had come to some understanding and there was no further need to discuss it.

Having checked to see that she was safe, he glided down onto the far pond. Tom's corn was still there, glinting yellow along the bank. The gander swam slowly towards it, looking warily over every blade of grass on the bank. Finally he picked up a kernel, toyed with it, then dropped it. He picked up another and felt it with his tongue before swallowing it. Then he ate six kernels swiftly and swam back to the centre of the pond.

That evening he was still on the far pond, and Tom Rank came down to talk to him, because the sound of a persistent, calm human voice can sometimes dispel fear in wild things. "So, you're going to stay," Tom said. "Why don't you go join Duchess? No one is going to hurt you. I think you've mated with her, so I'll call you Duke."

Duke fitted because he was a beautifully arrogant bird. His throat scarf of white reached around on either side almost to the top of his black head and was like a badge of distinction. He was big for a second-year gander, perhaps ten pounds, stood well over three feet and could stretch his neck until he came to a height of four feet. His white bib washed away to grey beneath, and his back feathers were like the smooth steel of chain mail.

While Rank talked, Duke swam nervously, turning his head from left to right so that he always had the man in his eye.

"I won't bother you," Rank said. "You still have corn. Take it easy, easy, easy. . . ." The gander stopped swimming to eye the soft-spoken man.

Finally Rank went back to his chores, and Duke swam back to the middle of the pond to wait for sunset. As soon as it was dark, he flew silently to the pen and dropped down beside Duchess. He put out his long neck and touched her across the back, and she settled softly, flat to the ground, waiting for him.

So the pattern was established: Duke lived out each day along the river or eating corn by the far pond, but at night he came to Duchess. And it must have been enough for them, because she never probed the wire again to see if there was a way of escaping, and he did not lift to follow the passing flocks.

They had been living together for about two weeks when John Mackenna came from the house one warm night to walk through the orchard and smell the fragrant apple blossoms, white in the light of the stars. He was amazed at how the night could soften the harsh realities of day. As he went down the gravel path, past the pen which held Duchess, he stopped in surprise: a large shadow lifted with a ripping of air to loft above the building and fly smoothly west to the river.

Mack, who rarely laughed these days, did so now softly. So in the night the wild gander came to his mate. Mack stopped by the wire. Looking over the top, he said, "Make the most of it, old girl, because when the snow gets deep, he'll go."

The goose bobbed her head as geese sometimes do when people

talk to them, and Mack, hearing the swish of the gander's wings above, turned back to the house.

Next morning was Saturday, and with high-school boys to augment the regular help, Tom Rank turned Duchess free to graze on the greens that are necessary for a Canada's health. He drove her past the ponies' pasture to a narrow field lush with short grass, and sat on a stone fence under a billowing white cloud of plum blossoms. Duchess wandered down the field with her head held high. Then she called out, stopped, and turning her head to scan all the sky, called again.

Down on the river Duke heard the call, lifted into the air and passed over her at a height of a hundred feet. Satisfied now, Duchess began grazing. Since Tom remained quiet, Duke finally glided down to the far end of the narrow field. Duchess started running, but then slowed to a walk, and stretching her neck low, weaved slightly as she came towards him. Coming close, Duke presented her with grass. Then they grazed together. When Tom Rank got up and came to the end of the field, Duke flew back to the river, and Duchess went willingly back to her pen.

Satisfied that they were really mated, Rank carried a barrel to her enclosure and set it in a corner against the shed. Duchess went at once to examine it. She pecked at the nail heads along the bottom and tried the iron rim at the top with her bill. After repeated inspections, she picked up a twig and placed it in the barrel.

When Duke came that night, he too inspected every crack and nail hole in the old barrel. At last he bobbed as though in approval and came over to pay court again to Duchess.

Gradually a nest took shape in the barrel, but the geese in the orchard already had goslings before Duchess presented Duke with her first egg. He inspected it much as he had the barrel, but once he had accepted it as theirs, he became a sentinel. No longer did he court her at length but took her swiftly and then stood guard, his long neck extended, his bright eyes investigating a toad's hop, an owl's patrol, a bat's swift winging, a nighthawk's mutter of wings—every sound and movement down to dew splatting from an eave to the barrel.

After the fifth egg had been laid and during the pre-dawn dark, which is blacker than all the rest of the night, a little wind which had been blowing went away, and such a silence came as brings

127

all wild things awake. In the kennel the dogs uncurled and lifted their ears. In the pasture the ponies, sleeping on three legs, stood foursquare. Mallard ducks chucked softly, and in their pens cock pheasants stretched their necks. Duchess put down a leg and came erect. Then in a little while all these creatures except Duke came into harmony with the weather change, and ruffling, curling, leaning or twisting, went back to sleep.

But Duke's bright eye was focused on the darkest place under the shed overhang. There was something there in the shadow, silent as fur. The gander was so delicately tuned to the earth that he had an acute perception of things neither truly seen nor heard, and though he could not identify the danger, he knew it was there.

Then the thing moved one paw after the other, as lightly and softly as the touch of milkweed silk. Duke braced himself and waited. When the feathery sound of sleep was around again, the mink moved swiftly out of the shadow, towards the eggs. Duke coiled his neck like a snake, and his flint-hard bill darted like an arrow to break the mink's neck. The mink struck at the same instant, and its sharp teeth put a half-moon across Duke's cheek. Then the mink writhed briefly and was dead.

Duchess walked over, and the geese talked in low tones. Duke grasped the mink and shook it as though to kill it again, and Duchess bowed approval and then invited him back into the shadow. But he remained on guard, because what was between them now was more than life. There was death too.

When Tom found the mink in the morning, he saw that Duchess was sitting on her eggs. And now Duke left the river often during daylight, to fly low so that his sharp eye could probe into the shadowy barrel and he could know that all went well.

One warm morning the goslings, armed with sharp egg openers on the ends of their tiny bills, began cracking their shells. During the course of that day and night, four of them emerged limp and wet, to dry out on the feathers with which the nest was lined and look at the world they'd been born into. One infertile egg did not hatch, and Duchess rolled it out of the barrel with her bill.

The next Saturday Tom was sick, so Mack took the four downy goslings, all females, and their mother to the narrow field, where Duke joined them. While the five grazed, the gander stood tall and still as a statue, watching for danger.

And danger came, swift as a storm wind. In one instant the scene was one of pastoral peace; in the next a whirlwind of death was sweeping down on the geese. Mack jumped up shouting, but there was no stopping the liver-and-white hunting dog that had scented the geese. The pup, never yet restrained or taught manners, swerved around Mack, and with every sinew pulsing, charged into the goose family.

Duke met the attack head on, spreading his powerful wings wide, flailing the dog with their bony-hard undersides. But the pup's jaws had already closed across Duchess's neck, and she throttled herself and broke her own bones in her wild winging to escape. The dog loosed his grip and turned on Duke. But before he could lash out, blood was running into his eyes, and terrified by the gander's attack, he turned, yelping back to his kennel.

It was too late for Duchess. She lay ruffled on the grass, her neck at a grotesque angle from her beautiful body. The frightened goslings gathered around the gander, and Mack knelt beside the dead goose, while Duke led his goslings to a safe distance. When Duchess didn't follow, he made little noises in his throat for her to come.

Mack got up and went to the fence at the end of the field so that Duke might come back and find out about her. Duke finally walked over, took a few of Duchess's feathers between his bill and tugged gently. Then he lifted his head, mourned once in a low, plaintive tone, and turning, walked away with the goslings in tow.

Mack did not try to stop them. They walked to the end of the green field and down through the tall grass of a hayfield to the creek, silvery over a bottom of stony jewels, and out into the little current which floated Duke and his goslings under a white footbridge, through a concrete culvert and down through willow and dogwood to the Rose River.

RAISING goslings required no special effort on Duke's part, for the Canada gander always helps raise his young. Duke kept his family safe and together and led them finally to a bay full of water greens, by a beach with gravel for their gizzards. John Mackenna came to visit them often, and though Duke swam his goslings into the rushes on these occasions, Mack could count them and be assured of their survival.

129

The goslings mushroomed into geese that summer. Their down became feathers, and the feathers lengthened to long, graceful fronds. When the fronds were strong enough for skittering across the water in half flight, Duke took to leaving his family at intervals. He always flew to the trout ranch and came in low over the shed where Duchess had been penned. Then he dipped down to the pond where he had taken her for a mate, and his wing tips almost touched his shadow when he flew the length of the field where she had died. Mack and Tom Rank wondered if he *had* to revisit the ranch; if there was something within him which could neither be denied nor understood, so that down all the flyways of his life he would always remember and want to return.

When the goslings learned to fly, they came with him on his morning and evening flights, and Duke always led them across the ranch.

So the long, warm days shortened and cooled. One night the grass was laid over by a silvery frost. Duke was restless, and the youngsters perhaps caught the urgency from him, or from the lessening light, or from some ancient timing device. The daily flights took them farther afield, and the youngsters talked incessantly, until sometimes when heard from afar they sounded like hounds hunting the skyways. When the first wild packs came trumpeting out of the north, Duke called to them, and they called back, but the gander did not guide his flock up to the others, nor did any of them drop down. They knew where they were going: they were headed for Heron Marsh.

Now the maples on the hill were crimson and the river willows tawny. At the ranch the oaks turned auburn and the birches were golden. The need in Duke to go was as strong as the need he felt to stay and fly over the places of remembering. He called out to the flocks which some days passed in endless procession. Yet he waited, and the crimson leaves of the maple turned brown and went spinning. The birches were stripped bare, and a cold rain turned to snow. The youngsters, strong now and with feathers as sleek and steely grey as Duke's, were wild with the need to go. Their entreaty to every passing flock was an almost incessant clamour.

Then one morning Duke lifted, and after a low swing over the ranch, began his ascent. The four young geese honked approval as they lifted higher and higher to the stronger winds, and when an updraught sent them soaring, the youngsters whooped. They spread their wing tips like fingers and beat the air rhythmically. Each air pocket was an adventure into which they plunged with the gaiety of children on a roller coaster. When a gust thrust them precipitously forward, they haronked with unbounded joy.

Behind them were the cries of many geese, so Duke slowed the wingbeat until a flock of more than a hundred drew alongside, and he and his brood dropped into a slot on the abbreviated side of the lopsided V. Flying in the wing-tip vortex of the birds ahead, they moved easily at a speed which would take them hundreds of miles in a day. Beneath, the earth slid north until the trout ranch ponds were the merest pinpricks of light and the Rose River a thread of dull silver. Duke turned his head once to look back and call out faintly—and then the place was gone.

On the ground Mack and Rank had watched until the flock was a far-off speck in the sky. Then Rank asked, "Do you think he'll come back?"

"I doubt it," Mack said. "It was a freak thing that he came here in the first place. First off, he should have been mated weeks before he got this far north. Second, if a storm hadn't put the flock down, he'd never have met the goose. Third, it was a miracle that *she* wasn't already mated. And even then the call to go north should have been stronger than the need to stay."

"How much do we really know about the Canadas' mating habits?" Rank asked.

"Well," Mack said, "the experts used to think that Canada geese remained celibate if they lost their mates. Now they know that not all of them do."

"It's nice to think," Rank said, "that they mate for life and that maybe the survivor is even celibate afterwards."

"Nice, but not very practical. I've got a theory, and I've heard one or two biologists come up with the same one, that with hunting taking a terrific annual toll, celibacy is such a risk to the survival of the species that it has been abandoned."

The two men could hear the soft sounds of ducks talking and the occasional low plaint of a goose. Soon all the birds would be put into the poultry house where they wintered.

"Maybe Duke's even glad to be free," Rank said.

"Well, he'll have other problems once the hunting season opens. They shoot geese by the tens of thousands every year. It's almost managed mayhem. Before the winter is over the poor old guy will probably wish he had been born anything but a goose."

"I hope he makes it," Rank said.

THE GREAT goose flock arrowed south, and like children come to a party, Duke's youngsters were infected with the gaiety of the gang and gabbled incessantly. Duke remained silent, flying expertly in the slipstream pocket of the goose ahead and making a place for the daughter who followed behind. Several times he turned his head as though looking back, but his wings never missed a beat.

On his first flight Duke had been as excited as the first-year geese were now. But today he did not join in the wild honking when Lake Winnebago slid into view and the flock could look down on the smouldering city of Oshkosh, stretching concrete tentacles to Fond du Lac and lesser huddles of houses. When an aeroplane heading for Minneapolis cast a shadow over the flock and some of the birds slid out of line, he kept the rhythm.

He had seen it all before: smoking chimneys; cars on winding trails; trains curling like snakes along twin rails; poison clouds marking cities farther down the line of flight than they could see. A clutter. No plan, nor any pattern. Houses strewn like hailstones; roads wrapping around onto themselves. It was no world of his or of any wild thing.

The first thin layer of night came like a grey veil, and then over southern Wisconsin the V tipped forward like an aeroplane during descent, and each bird slowed tempo. The earth pulled at them, and they were glad to give in, to lower along with scores of flocks converging from northerly directions. Some flocks had come nonstop all the way from Lake Superior, from a country where trees grew right out of the rocks and the rivers ran swiftly out of the hills.

From the earth came the first welcoming haronk, then another and another, until there was an incessant babble of sound, and the descending flocks could see long ribbons of geese literally hiding the waters of the canals; wide swaths of grey-black birds covering the green fields; long furrows of geese moving restlessly between rows of cornstalks—thousands upon thousands of them.

133

The V in which Duke and his daughters were flying levelled off abruptly. Birds had to brake with their wings to keep from running over one another. Then the geese began to spill wind from their wings, sideslipping expertly.

Down sharply now like kites which have lost the wind. Sideways; straight; sideways again. Scattering. Plummeting. The ground looms and the geese brake hard to set themselves gently to earth. Now preen feathers gone awry. Stretch long necks. Walk and unlimber legs. Stand alert and listen. Look all around. The flocks quieting gradually in the deepening dark.

Geese feeding, drinking, running water over their backs. Shelled corn bright even in darkness along the road. Corn on cobs hanging from specially bred short stalks so geese can reach them. Winter wheat. Long strips of lawn grass. Thick stands of cattails. Round reeds smooth as pencils. Tattered pads and brown, wrinkled seeds of lilies. Paradise.

Once this land, known as Heron Marsh, was a seventeen-mile-long lake, five miles wide. Coal barges and excursion boats plied it. Fishermen set lines and nets. Duck hunters built clubhouses on its shores. But few geese came.

The waters were held in the lake by a dam, but farmers said it put water up into their fields. Investors laying claim to lake-bottom land joined the farmers. The dam was destroyed, the waters bled away, and the lake became a marsh filled with rough, tough marsh grass.

Only small wild things like rabbits and jays, skunks, a few frogs and a casting of grasshoppers lived there.

It was a sea of infertility in summer and a white waste of snow in winter. Finally a few men bought it up for pennies and cut the rasping hay to use in packing wine and dishes.

But there were some who envisioned what it might be. A feud began between the men who wanted packing hay and those who wanted a place where all wild things could come. In the end the conservationists won. A new dam was built so water levels might be controlled, and instead of a lake, there were puddles and ponds and canals and long, wide, wet marshes.

The geese came, only a few at first, then more and more, until tens of thousands knew its precise location. With the geese came the ducks, cranes and herons, blackbirds and bright-eyed marsh wrens, gallinules and coots, rails and snipes, plovers and chicka- dees, hawks and sometimes eagles—until there was no place on the continent except the Florida Everglades which so teemed with birds. Deer came too, and raccoons, opossums, foxes, mink and rabbits, and so many muskrats that men left their regular jobs to get permits to trap them. Bullheads, pike and perch came, and carp and minnows for the kingfishers and coons.

The government made one half of this wildlife reservoir into a national refuge, while the other half was to be managed by the state for hunters. A speaker came from Washington to dedicate the refuge and he vowed: "No man shall ever carry a gun on these acres. This is ours to keep in trust." It was a noble speech, and the man meant it, but he was naïve.

THIS WAS the place, then, the trap, if you will, where Duke and his daughters grazed. They soon had full crops, and when they swam to where the corn was, they had room for only a few kernels. So they swam to a muskrat house and decided to make camp. All five climbed from the water to the roof of the house, which was still being built, and when the muskrats came back with moss in their teeth and cattails dragging behind them, Duke put out his wedge-shaped head and warned them off. The muskrats moved along and started another house.

Duke lifted a leg and locked the other, and putting his beak to his feathers, rested. But the youngsters could not sleep for excite- ment. They swam and drank and ate green tendrils, until at last they slept, floating on the water.

Next morning a golden haze filtered the sunlight to begin an Indian-summer day, with frogs back up from the mud, and turtles on their logs. Duke stretched before coming down off the musk- rat house for a swim, a bath and a drink. Then he led the goslings to where he could see a drift of corn just dumped by a growling truck. As the vehicle progressed, it winnowed geese into the air, but they dropped right back into the ruts along its route. When Duke's daughters saw such a prosperity of corn, they haronked and walked past him to eat greedily.

Now that the first excitement of the staging area was over, Duke and his daughters lolled all morning like holiday-makers at a summer resort. That afternoon they ate more corn and sipped water.

Finally Duke's daughters became restless, so he lifted, and they followed him east to where the hills were higher. Here they could ride small thermal lifts. They flew many miles to where a field of winter wheat stretched down to the water. Duke circled the surrounding area. Then he guided the youngsters to the centre of the flat field, where he could see danger from any direction. While the daughters snipped short stems of wheat, he stood motionless; then after the youngsters had eaten, the largest of them stood guard while Duke ate.

The sun was low when Duke and his daughters lifted again, and it was twilight when they came back to Heron Marsh.

But on this evening there was a feeling of uneasiness there, and Duke complained about it. Other geese felt it too, and they gabbled softly. As darkness deepened, noises from around the perimeter of the marsh intruded to the places where the geese were sleeping in what was now a crisp night of brilliant starlight. The hunting season had begun.

There were lights along all the roads. Small aeroplanes buzzed over. A gun went off and dogs barked. Sometimes shrill shouting came down into the marsh as exuberant hunters built bonfires beside the road. Game wardens drove along the back roads, and deputy sheriffs drove along the highway to catch speeders. A few cars were hopelessly stuck in ditches, and one, overflowing with hunters, was wrapped around a tree. An ambulance came wailing out from the town of Beaver Dam, and the sound seemed to the geese to go on for ever, far off, then closer, then departing but still heard on and on—a thin scream in the night.

An army gathered all night, five-deep, twenty-deep; and across southern and central Wisconsin other hunters picked any point of vantage where a tired goose might try for a landing. The land bristled with guns, and fields and marshes and knolls were armed camps.

The hunters' blinds encircling the refuge were placed every one hundred yards, so there was little chance a low-flying goose could get through the barrage. Perhaps the geese had a feeling of being surrounded and cut off from escape, because throughout the night they moved restlessly. At intervals one or another distraught bird would raise its voice, and then a ripple of consternation would run through the whole flock.

An hour before dawn, men of the first firing line—selected at a drawing held by the state—were issued armbands to show that they were of the elite and privileged to take the first shots when the geese came out. Guns in one hand and thermos flasks in the other, they positioned themselves right in the refuge itself.

In the blinds they poured coffee into plastic cups and let the steam warm their faces, conversing in low tones, as though to keep secret their hiding places. The last loop of the human noose had been drawn tight, and the geese began to call out nervously.

Some of the men remembered that goose hunting was once such a sport that they had spent days building concealments and with nearly frozen fingers made decoys to entice a passing flock. In those days the Canada goose was a trophy bird, and if one was killed, it was a credit to the hunter for having outwitted it. Not many men hunted Canadas then, because few would learn skills like the call which could make a lead goose turn its flock towards the hunters.

These old-timers, each time they participated in a mass attack, swore they would never come back. But some kept coming, because there were no other places to hunt and they could not get the need to hunt out of their blood. Perhaps they always hoped it wouldn't be quite as terrible as it always was.

Hunters on the state side of the marsh, where hunting was legal but no geese lived, frightened whole rafts of ducks from the water; they went hurtling across the bending grasses to the federal side of the marsh. Herons, bitterns and cranes squawked in alarm as they lifted to look for less crowded acres. Blackbirds churned up out of the cattails, then swirled back down again. Coots deserted open water for the reeds. Raccoons scurried to their hollow trees. Deer ran from the willow bluffs onto farm fields, only to be frightened back into the bluffs again.

And still the hunters came—from hotels, motels and homes in Oshkosh, Fond du Lac, Milwaukee, in twenty, thirty, forty towns— wanting to be the first to kill a goose. There were traffic jams on dirt lanes; cars jammed farmers' yards; gates were left open, and cattle strayed; wire fences were cut, and sheep wandered down the roads.

Then came the first streak of light in the east and with it an explosion of guns.

A game warden said, "Damn them! It isn't time yet!" But soon the east broke open into a long, pink crater, and then no living thing—furred or feathered—was safe at Heron Marsh.

As was their habit, the geese began flying at dawn. Lead swept the marsh, and armadas of geese fell like flies caught in a lethal spray. Birds with broken wings plummeted. Some with body shots set their wings and sailed down to burst their breasts on the hard ground; some came down like rags; others turned end over end. Distraught geese followed fallen mates straight into the guns. For fifteen minutes shots crackled like fire running through a forest. Then the great mass of geese settled back into the refuge, and except for the mournful cries of widows and widowers, the flock was mostly silent.

The blackbirds and ducks stayed down, and the usually imperturbable wrens sat as though shocked into silence. Even the men themselves were silent as witnesses to a funeral. It took them twenty minutes to regain their composure after the assault. Then some tried to call the geese out by blowing on goose calls. But no goose accepted the invitation. The calls sounded almost hilariously human.

The wounded geese tried to fathom wings that wouldn't work, legs that dangled, the burning of breasts, necks or thighs. Some crawled into the reeds and stretched their necks and died.

Duke and his daughters had come down off the muskrat house and swam about nervously. The gander had not taken his family into the air. He only watched and listened, and though he could not understand the danger, he knew from where the firing came. Like most of the Canadas, he knew now that to cross a given line would precipitate an explosion. The flocks settled for what they had, ate the corn and grass, drank from the canals, and slept.

The hunters, angered at the reluctance of the geese to come out and be killed, began shouting to one another about how poor hunting was. The first cars began stringing down off the high places to head towards home.

In the afternoon a breeze came up, and half a dozen flocks lifted on it and tried to cross the firing line. But hunters still waited, and

138

some geese were killed and others wounded. The rest came back.

When the sun set, car lights came on. Horns sounded raucously, and the army of hunters began moving away. That night there were telephone calls to the refuge manager, the state conservation commissioners and the governor about the geese being so well fed they would not come out to be shot. What good was it for a man to spend money for a hunting licence when the hunting was being sabotaged? Some even called their congressmen in Washington.

Hundreds of thousands of hunters in the state added up to a lot of votes, and money paid by them for hunting and fishing licences virtually financed the state's conservation efforts. The three-dollar federal duck stamp annually brought in hundreds of thousands of dollars. The politicians were concerned.

But next day the trucks rolled again from the warehouses, and corn was spilled for geese to eat, and except for foolish first-year birds and a few looking for their mates, the hunters had nothing to shoot at. When night came not twenty geese had been killed out of the tens of thousands in the refuge. Some hunters angrily vowed to invade the refuge if the feeding did not stop.

The pressure on the refuge manager became intolerable. Investors had paid exorbitant prices for farms on which to rent goose blinds. Wealthy hunters with frontage on the marsh had invited important guests for an exciting hunt. Thousands of workers were there for their two- or three-week holidays. Hundreds had given up beer and bowling to buy shotguns, hunting coats, boots. When the crowds dwindled, the restaurant owners felt the pinch, motel owners put up vacancy signs, and garage owners added their voices to the clamour. So one day a call came through to the marsh manager: "Stop feeding the geese!"

Although no trucks rolled the next day, there still was an abundance of food. But when no corn was spread on the second, third and fourth days, the armada of geese, now one hundred and twenty thousand, became hungrier every hour.

On the sixth day they began going out. Clawing for altitude, some of the birds got through. But once past the first firing line, they had to contend with the hunters on private lands. They were shot at from hills, along roads and in fields. Still they kept filtering out of the marsh to find food.

Duke felt the pinch. Though the four youngsters complained

loudly, he did not try to cross the firing line. He led the family to grass in back bays, to puddles, knolls and ridges, finding them acorns, snails and worms. It wasn't enough, but it kept up their strength.

That night a south wind brought unseasonably warm weather, and by morning the cold ground breathed up a solid covering of fog. Hunters were completely hidden, and the birds felt a false sense of security; they started going out.

Duke decided to make a run for the green field they had visited the day before the shooting started. He stayed close to the ground to sight on familiar landmarks, and with his family, came winging into the firing line hardly a hundred feet high. They heard the sizzle of lead cutting through them even before they heard the gun blast. One youngster's leg was hit and dangled, and another youngster called out as pellets lodged against her breastbone.

Duke turned, and they sailed back into the refuge. But thousands of other geese, hoping to get through, came over the line, where hunters now kept up an incessant barrage. Families were wiped out as hundreds of geese were knocked from the sky, but in the low overcast the hunters never knew they had fallen.

Duke decided to try again. But this time he first gained altitude, and when he moved out of the marsh, he was so high that the hunters below did not know he had led his flock over them. Duke angled away from the sounds of guns and wounded geese, higher and higher, to where the fog began to thin. Then they broke through into brilliant sunlight, and the fog lay below, shining white. Other flocks had come up here too.

Duke flew a wide circle, slowing his pace for the two wounded ones. When the sun had melted the fog beneath, they followed a river south until, near a village, Duke could see a green field. He started his descent, and the youngsters gabbled anxiously at the sight of the lush winter wheat. Down, down . . . just topping the trees to slide around and into the wind for a mid-field landing.

At the last instant Duke saw the danger. He called out a warning and beat frantically to climb back to safety. But the youngsters had not noticed the disturbed earth around the camouflaged trap-door. When it flew back and guns came out, they were already on the ground.

The young goose with the wounded leg had trouble getting into

the air, and she died first. Then the goose with pellets by her
breastbone caught a charge of number two shot full in the breast
and sailed off to land in high grass near the river. A third goose was
hit in the fleshy part of her thigh but managed to climb. While
one of the hunters ran to where the second goose was threshing in
the grass, Duke brought his two remaining daughters up to altitude. When they turned north, he could see the man beating the
dying goose with a stick until she lay still and only her wings
quivered a little.

Duke scanned the river for a place to dip for waterweeds to fill
his shrinking crop. Twice he went low, only to spot hunters hidden in the rushes, and honking with alarm, he climbed back to
three thousand feet. Going north to avoid Milwaukee, he then
turned east and came to Lake Michigan. Below he could see waves
breaking, to send white foam skimming onto the sand. A boat
moved ponderously ahead of a tassel of black smoke, and a tug
ploughed blue water. There were rafts of ducks, and their presence
signalled safety. Tired now because of his long fast, and with
the wounded one complaining, he let down until the three geese
were bobbing on the waves.

It was restful on the water. There was an almost hypnotic
rhythm to the lifting and falling waves. Here, far from land, there
was no danger; but neither was there any food. The ducks dived
thirty feet to the bottom for molluscs, and then on the way up
snipped greens from a submerged weed bed. But the geese did
not know how to dive. They were primarily land birds, even
though they had webbed feet and water-resistant feathers.

Ducks and geese are loath to mingle, but when Duke saw the
ducks eating, he swam his daughters among them and scavenged
for vegetation which floated to the surface. The ducks sometimes
uprooted whole plants. It was fine feeding for the three geese,
and they followed the ducks, eating until their crops were full.
Then, for no apparent reason, the ducks all began to walk on the
water, with their stubby wings beating a tattoo. Seconds after they
were airborne, the flock disappeared over the horizon.

Duke and his youngsters rested, but they did not sleep. The sun
went down, and then the wind strengthened until the geese were
riding a galloping sea. When it was full dark, Duke permitted the
waves to take them ashore. On the sand, ne stood for several

141

minutes listening, but there was no sound except the wash of waves. The youngster with the pellets in her thigh sank down and picked at the sand for bits of gravel in it. The other goose walked along the shore looking for other bits to grind her food.

Duke stayed on guard for an hour. When it was black dark and the stars glinted like flint chips off the waves, he began to eat gravel. Then, turning into the wind, the three settled down. The wind whipped little sand barriers around them, and they slept comfortably and without fear.

In the morning the wounded one couldn't walk. Where she had tried to bite away the pain on her thigh, the flesh had turned green. Followed by his one unmarked daughter, Duke went into the water and waited. Several times the wounded goose scrambled to her one good leg, only to go careening over. Her efforts to get into the water caught the attention of a woman in a beach house. She called her husband, and he came running with his gun. Duke and the able daughter took to the air. The wounded one flopped along until a charge from the gun blasted her into the sand. The man proudly displayed the goose to his wife, as if he'd shot a trophy.

At a thousand feet, the other two headed back for the marsh. At least they'd find something there to live on, if only wire grass or a small fish. Coming near the marsh, Duke made a swift descent. It was a mistake.

With the first blast, his one remaining daughter went flopping from the sky. Instead of climbing to get out of range, the gander followed her down. He felt pellets pound his breast. Then he was past the firing line and gliding down.

He drank even before he had planed to a halt in a ditch. Then, after climbing the bank, he picked at the place where the pellets had penetrated. He pecked free two pellets just beneath the skin, but four others, the size of apple seeds, had buried themselves too deeply to be dug out. Except for a few tiny drops on his grey breast, there was almost no bleeding.

He spent the night alternately searching for food and sleeping. At dawn he was awakened by the crackle of guns running like fire again around the perimeter of the marsh. There was an intense burning in his breast. He crept onto an old muskrat house and sat soaking up sun; but as the day progressed a film came over his eyes. From time to time he walked weakly to the edge of the house to drink. The burning spread to his entire body.

When night came, Duke was too sick to go for water. He laid out his long neck, as a dying goose does, and in the morning he was all but dead. He lifted his head but could not hold it erect, so he stretched it so far forward that it brought him off balance and he tumbled into the water. He drank, hearing the guns and the cries of geese as though from a great distance. Listlessly he paddled to the bank and nibbled grass. Once a goose, searching for her mate, swam up to him, looked him over and swam on.

At sunset he went back to the muskrat house but was unable to climb onto it. He swam feebly into an inlet, and on a cattail wand which had been laid over by the wind, he rested his head.

ABRUPTLY the shooting ceased. The season had ended, and stillness settled over the marsh. After spending the night barely conscious on the water, Duke revived enough the next morning to pull himself to the top of the muskrat house. Around him, geese were uncommonly quiet. Only the widows and the widowers flew from place to place looking. When every flock had been visited, they flew back to the place they had last seen their mates and started searching anew. A few might go on searching to the end of their days: every time their flock came to a new place of strange birds, they would go through the entire gaggle.

Duke was beyond caring. Burning with fever, he only moved to take water and then back to where he could lie with his neck stretched before him. Three days and nights slipped away. He lost so much weight that his breastbone was a sharp protrusion parting the feathers to left and right. On the fourth day he should have died, but the strong heart which can send a Canada goose a thousand miles through wind-ripped skies kept beating; and finally he began winning the battle for life.

On the fifth morning Duke awakened clear of eye but so weak that he had to push with webs and wings to get into the water. He nibbled at some moss, closed his eyes and rested. When he opened them again, he spotted a vivid green patch of duckweed among the rushes. Head low, he skimmed the tiny plants up with his bill and swallowed them. He ate two snails and some shreds of green still floating where a muskrat had feasted.

The marsh manager had ordered that feeding be resumed, and by nightfall Duke had found enough strength to swim to the islands where the corn had been dumped. But he did not gorge, because something within him warned him to eat sparingly.

All night he heard geese calling and wings cutting the air. By morning the water had iced over, and all that was left of the great goose gathering were scattered flocks strung along the river where currents had kept it open. Duke filled his crop with corn and then walked slowly to the river, where water was a black cut in the bright ice. There he joined a small gathering of geese. He was warm in the sun, but the temperature was dropping steadily. That night the last of the geese left, and in the morning Duke could find no open water. He ate the frost which whitened the dried grass and then ran, beating his wings frantically. But he was not strong enough to fly, and in the end he went tumbling like a big, broken toy.

So he walked, looking for water. Sometimes he called out plaintively for his goslings or his goose. Towards evening he came to a protected place where muskrats had opened an air hole. He drank and then slept.

That night big snowflakes fell softly as breast feathers. The wind drove the snow into drifts, and Duke had to stand and shake himself often to keep from being covered. The snow stopped falling at dawn, but now the marsh was desolate. Only its iced veins glistened. Its islands were impassable snow hummocks with skeletons of reaching trees. The marshes were dry bones of cattails rattling. No furred or feathered thing moved in the shadow and shine of wind-carved drifts. Most tragic of all, the corn had been covered. The gander started to trek south, keeping to ditches and canals, until there was a ploughed field swept clean of snow.

He walked between the frozen furrows. Small puddles furnished him water, but there was no food. He tried to fly again in a frenzy of winging, but though his feet came off the ground, he was not strong enough to stay airborne. So he rested, and while resting, heard a far-off gabble of geese. He had never heard their language; they were not of his kind. Yet he knew they were geese, and where there were geese there would be food, so he walked past the pits where the gunners had waited.

It was like coming across a battlefield after a war: red hulls of spent shotgun shells; a mitten hanging on the barbs of a fence; filter ends of discarded cigarettes; the shine of a discarded thermos flask. The gabble of the geese was louder now, but Duke stopped. The sound was coming from a group of buildings, and buildings meant danger.

Still it was also near buildings that he had found Duchess, and a thin calling of remembered things ran through him. He had come a little closer when the banging of a door startled him. He turned back towards the marsh, but he heard a hard-running dog. In a thrust of legs and wings Duke got into the air. However, his wings carried him only a little way, and then the black dog was on him. Barking frantically, he merely held Duke to the ground with his front feet.

A boy came running and said to the dog, "O.K., Buck," When the dog got up, the boy bent down, and clasping both arms tightly around the gander and holding the long neck with strong, sure fingers, lifted him from the ground. With the dog jumping alongside, the boy carried Duke to a low shed, within which Duke could hear gabbling, and opening the door, went inside. He put Duke to the ground carefully, and releasing him in one swift movement, stepped back.

Duke rushed forward, wings flailing, straight for the shed's one window, but the wire mesh across it threw him back. Seeing the boy, he threw himself again towards the light and once again went over backward.

The boy quickly stepped out and closed the door. Once he was gone, Duke sat quietly looking at the huge geese around him. They were like no geese he had ever seen. They had comblike crests on their heads, their rumps touched the ground and they were so wide and fat that they waddled awkwardly from side to side when they walked. Now the geese gathered in a group, their bright eyes looking Duke up and down. Duke went back to the low window, but though it admitted filtered sunlight, it was too grimy to see through. He walked back and forth in front of it, neck craning to see if there might not be some way out.

Finally in the evening, when a dim bulb near the roof of the shed cast a glow, he came down to crouch on his webs. Outside there were farm noises: the clump of boots, the clatter of milk pails, the harsh bark of a dog and the more muted sounds of human voices. As the tame geese clamoured, the shed door opened abruptly and the boy came in, closing the door behind him. He poured water into a large, shallow pan and spread corn. The tame geese clumsily jostled one another for the corn, but Duke stayed by the window. The tame geese fed and drank, and then Duke went over to the feeding spot; but the corn was gone. He sipped water, looking warily at his strange bedfellows, and then walked gracefully back to his place by the window and settled down.

So the place beneath the window became Duke's place. When it was feeding time again, he moved in among the tame ones to get corn, but they drove him off, and he walked away because this was their territory and he did not know what their feeding rules were. But the next time, after the boy brought corn, Duke struck out at a goose, and his thrust, though weak, was like a lance compared to the others' feeble fumbling. The goose fell back, and the others watched while he picked up kernels swiftly until his crop was swelling. Then he drank and went back to his place.

So the days passed, and Duke knew winter was hard on the land. Sometimes the tame geese challenged him, but not often. With the return of strength came the ability to bash the brains from any of the tame ones with a single blow, and a few hard body thrusts had taught those who would question his right to feed and rest here to mind their own business.

Imprisoned as he was, he remembered the winters spent in the south, where there were always greens and fresh water and a whole wide, wild sky to go riding the wind on. But while the yearning for freedom was a part of him, so also was a wisdom rare in birds—the ability to adapt to whatever life might bring, which kept him eating and growing stronger of wing. A bird or animal of lesser intelligence might have pined away. It happens with species that lack the ability to tolerate man and can't sustain a freedom of spirit while physically confined.

Perhaps memories of other days sustained him, and he lived in the green fields of his dreams. He must have remembered them; else how could a goose come each year to the very hummock upon which it nested the year before? How, in a sky with roadways around the world, could he each year find the right lane back to a precise island where corn is spread? He must have remembered, else why couldn't he forget his mate and his four goslings?

If a goose can remember where a river bends, how can he forget blue water and the way it can caress feathers in silvery streams; the freshness of the wind singing through his feathers as the pack goes barking down the sky in the miracle of migration? Perhaps Duke dreamed of the time when he found the courage to land in the darkening night beside his mate, and of the night when, on velvet paws, the mink had come. The scar from that encounter was still a bright slash across his cheek. . . .

Perhaps it was because he could remember—a capability which is a prerequisite of hope—that he learned to tolerate even the boy when he came with the corn, watching him but not fleeing to throw himself against the window. Perhaps . . . perhaps. . . .

And then one day he felt spring. It was in his heart first, and it came as a trickle of water across his webs as melting snow sent small rivers between the boards to muddy the floor of the shed. It made Duke increasingly nervous. From as far away as South America birds would be coming back to their nesting grounds. Soon the geese would be back on Heron Marsh, and then after resting and feeding, they would go on north. Some days, when the wind was right, the grey, paper skies would be pencilled from horizon to horizon. When the last flock was a faint scribble on a faraway sky, would he be left behind?

The tame geese were mating, but he watched without interest. Then one day a female without a gander broke away and came over to make herself available. She bowed and scraped and chucked deep in her throat and then squatted in front of him. Duke lifted his head higher and walked a few careful steps to one side, but she came again and again, and at night she even left the tame ones to sleep near him. He became occupied less with dreaming than with avoiding the advances of the goose.

Then one night he heard the wild geese. The last light had just left the window when the clarion call of a lowering flock came from far out over the marsh. Duke ran to the door, honking as though they might hear him and come. When the wild flock was silent, he walked back to his place by the window, came up on one leg and put his head into a wing. Through the night he awoke intermittently and cocked his head to listen. But there was only the wind in the bare branches of the box elders, and once a sparrow in the eaves chirped in his sleep, and once the big goose which

had been paying him court gabbled and then stopped abruptly as though her own voice had awakened her from a dream.

But in the morning more flocks roamed the sky. He heard them plainly as some passed directly overhead, and he was beside himself with the need to fly.

Meanwhile the fat goose still pursued him, but Duke could not accept a tame mate. One morning, when he was straining to hear the honking of a far-off flock and she pressed towards him, he turned in rage, attacked with a fierceness that sent feathers flying and drove her across the enclosure to the wall.

When he regained his composure and walked away, the entire flock started after him with angry babbling, drove him to the ground and hammered at him with their bills. He would have died there beneath their beaks and feet and wings except at that moment the boy came in and sent them scattering.

Duke lay still for a moment and then lifted his head. There was blood on his white scarf, and his feathers were awry, but when he stood strongly square, he shook like a dog, and his feathers fell straight and into place.

The boy had left the door open, and the tame geese quickly crossed the threshold. Duke started to follow, but the boy closed the door and advanced on him. In his hand he held a pair of heavy shears. Duke opened his wings, prepared to make a run for it, but the boy pinned him to the mud, wrapped an arm around his body, and with fingers of the same hand, held his neck.

Once he had the gander immobilized, the boy opened the door and stepped out into the light. A man Duke had sometimes seen came from the barn. The boy spoke to the man and handed him the heavy shears. Then, with his free hand, the boy took Duke's right wing and fanned out the flight feathers. The man stepped to one side so he could cut the feathers and make the gander earthbound, but the rasping sound of the shears as they separated shook the gander. With a convulsive thrust of wings, neck and legs, he freed himself from the boy's arms and ran across the muddy yard. The black dog came out of nowhere and pursued him, but this time the gander was strong; before the dog could bring him down, he had lifted and was flying almost straight up.

On the ground below, the man and boy stood watching and they marvelled that a heavy goose could ascend at such an angle.

Duke didn't level off until he was a thousand feet high and realized that he was free. A wild haronk strained from his throat, and he wheeled on the wind again and again until he had circled the farmyard a half-dozen times while the man and boy watched.

Then he flew straight until he was only a speck out over the marsh, and the man went back to the barn, and the boy went into the house, and the tame geese waddled around importantly, inspecting nesting boxes and bowing and making inane noises to one another.

Once over the marsh, the gander flew to where two of his goslings had died and came low over the field but did not land in it. Then he flew east and through the haze which held Milwaukee and followed the beach north to where the third gosling had been killed. Once again he dropped low but did not land. He turned inland and flew along the route he had taken on the fateful day he had been wounded and came to the spot where the fourth gosling had died. From there he flew to the centre of the refuge, where many geese were gathered. He landed and swam to the muskrat house on which he himself had nearly died. Then, standing with head high, he looked out over the vast land where the first green spears of spring were streaking the dead brown of winter.

NEXT DAY winter came back. The marsh froze and even the rivers were bridged over. The geese, a wildly winging cloud, lifted in such frenzy that villagers and farmers came from their beds to windows to watch the mass exodus. Duke lifted with them to fly south but came back and let down, skidding along glare ice to come to a thumping halt against a ditch bank. Again the great marsh seemed deserted, and most of the day, like a ghost goose, Duke wandered from ditch to ditch, complaining in querulous tones. But that night, when the moon's red glow changed to a white shine, he went aloft and winged north to the Silver Sun Trout Ranch.

A dozen times he circled the frozen ponds and called out. In the house Mack turned out the light and drew back the curtains, hoping to see Duke's shadow against the moon, and Tom Rank, about to drive home, turned down the window of his car and leaned out. Neither of them doubted that it was Duke, though they could not but wonder what brought him back on a night of biting cold.

Finally Mack turned the lights back on, and Tom started his car down the drive. The gander saw Tom's headlights, and lowering to treetop level, followed them. Then, when the car turned in at Tom's farm and the lights were turned off, the gander flew south towards Heron.

Along the streets and in the houses they heard his cry; and many of the earthbound were envious of the gander's freedom. How could they know that such a routine thing as night makes even the hawk a prisoner; or that life, even for Duke, was a web of restraints, since he was compelled by some unfathomable urge to fly the roadless night sky, calling out for things that should long have been forgotten?

Turning away from Heron, Duke flew to the streaming river of white light that was the Madison–Milwaukee highway. Through an open window a truck driver heard, and he relaxed the grip with which he'd been fighting the wheel all winter, knowing that the goose call prophesied balmy days of easy driving. From city to city Duke flew. Boys leaving a basketball game tried to look skyward past the blinding streetlights. In a river cottage an old man heard him and put his hand on the head of an old dog and remembered Rock Prairie days before the geese had been herded so hunters could shoot them like chickens. He did not feel sorry for the geese but for the hunters, because he considered hunting a sport graced by a specific code. He looked at the gun on the wall, remembering sunrises in marsh and field, and was sad because there were so few places now where a man might find such solitude.

In Sheboygan a woman who had forgotten to take in the wash had kicked over the basket of frozen clothes; then she heard the gander and his promise of warm breezes, and laughing at herself, took the clothes in for another washing. And when Duke passed over a prison, men stared through barred windows, hoping for a glimpse of this wild, free-flying bird—a symbol of hope.

THEN Duke came back to the marsh. Next day a flock of geese came there, ruffling their feathers against the cold, and settled down to wait. By noon a rift had opened in the river, and the next night flocks of arriving geese had turned the ice grey.

But Duke stayed aloof, a solitary goose, sitting on a muskrat

151

house or flying around the perimeter of the marsh. Occasionally he flew up alongside a formation, and they would make room for him in the spearhead, but he always flew on ahead—alone. He was strong now, stronger than he had ever been. He had come to the prime of a Canada's life, when he should have been standing sentry for a flock, making decisions about what fields to land on, where to camp for a night.

Once a flock of fifty invited him to join, and an unattached female swam over to make herself available, but he ignored her. When she pressed her suit, he turned on her and drove her back to the flock. There was always consternation among other geese when Duke turned on a female. They uttered sharp little sounds of indignation, but their disapproval did not disturb the gander. When a yearning female had been sent packing, Duke always swam back to the muskrat house where he had almost died, and perched there.

Each day more geese came. The marsh grass sprouted back even faster than the geese could snip the blades. With such a wealth around them, they could have stayed; but this was the enigma of Canadas: though they might accept the handouts of humans while travelling, there was a need to nest far away from man's prying eyes.

One day, fifteen hundred miles north, the ice in the Saskatchewan River creaked and groaned and finally broke up, as it did in a hundred other streams. Across Canada from the Pacific to the Atlantic there was monumental movement. How the geese on Heron knew is a mystery. But know they did that it was safe to fly north because there would be grass in abundance by the time they got there. So the flocks lifted, pointed north and disappeared.

Several times Duke rose with them, but always he came back to the marsh. By the time the oak buds had unfurled, he was a lone goose amid thousands of ducks, swirls of red-winged blackbirds, coots, gallinules, rails, marsh wrens—the biggest bird except for the blue herons and, once, an eagle.

Why had he stayed? He was by nature a flocking bird. Canada geese are swayed by some desires—the choice of this lake or that; this field or the next one, this leader or another. So apparently Duke had a choice. His was not to go north, but to stay here on the marsh where his goslings had left him. Whatever his underlying reason, he became a surly gander. If he came upon a nesting duck, he drove her into the air, and when she tried to land to warm her eggs, flew at her with neck outstretched. He chased the muskrats off their feed beds and swam swiftly after them, whereupon they would dive, and Duke would sit, head high, waiting for them to surface so he could chase them again.

The weather turned sultry. The sun came up red-eyed every morning and sank in a haze of heat each evening. Mosquitoes lifted in clouds to passing pressures, ponds warmed and turned bronze, and the deer stayed in the brakes belly-deep in water. Duke felt the threat like a fever in his bones. It can happen in Wisconsin in late May or early June. Suddenly it is brazen summer, and the earth is not ready for such heat, and elemental forces are at odds. Hawks stayed in the high trees because the air was stagnant. Appetites diminished, and a raccoon was satisfied with a half-dozen crayfish when it usually ate two dozen. Frogs could not lift their measured beat into a choir of voices. That evening the sun splashed blood-red on every cloud, and in the night even the crickets were quiet.

Next day the brazen sky was cloudless until late afternoon. Then over the horizon lifted the first jagged edges of a storm, until the west was a mountain range of cloud peaks, with sunrays putting an edge of snowy brilliance on the tumbling tops. Weather broadcasts brought sharp warnings through crackling static. Mothers herded children to basements. Fishermen retreated to shore. The massed winds, marshalling rain and hail, moved swiftly to the drums of thunder. Police and fire forces went on alert. Wisconsin waited.

The tornado was born full-blown; no ordinary little funnel with a whiplashing tail but a storm nearly a mile wide; with two other tornadoes to the rear, on either side, like outriders. It moved nearly fifty miles an hour, and winds whirled with it a hundred miles in every direction. The great funnel arched far forward, and the vortex was lost twenty thousand feet high in the clouds.

With a flick of its tail it flattened five farmhouses and lifted four trucks, stacking them side by side in a marsh near Beaver Dam. Picking up a cow, it set her down in a strange pasture, where she went on grazing as though nothing had happened. Then, with a whining roar heard for fifty miles, it dipped over the southern half of Heron Marsh, and Duke saw a waterspout as the tornado sucked up the sloughs and all their denizens. Populated with frogs and fish, mallards, songbirds and a mink, sticks and stones and one boat, the funnel headed for the federal end of the marsh.

As the fury of the winds hit him, Duke saw the boat crash down on end in a mudbank. Fish rained around him. He tried to fly to the safety of the rushes, but in seconds he was caught up in the vortex, helplessly lifted higher and higher. Below, the marsh whirled. Lightning slashed and edge winds shunted him closer and closer to the centre of the funnel. He dropped like a stone into the eye of the tornado, but a hundred feet from the ground, the winds wrapped around him again, and he went sailing.

Higher and higher the tornado lifted, and Duke went with it past Oshkosh and Appleton, up to ten thousand, then fifteen thousand feet. Rain froze now on his feathers. Twisting, turning, he was lofted to eighteen thousand feet, where the temperature was fifteen degrees. . . . Twenty thousand feet, and the air grew thinner. . . . Then finally the tornado had come so high there was not enough atmosphere to sustain it, and the force was shattered like glass, with winds going off in every direction. The gander felt himself falling. He tried to fly, but having been so long without sufficient oxygen, he lost consciousness and turned slowly end over end.

However, he hadn't stopped breathing, and at twelve thousand feet his lungs were giving oxygen back into his blood. At eight thousand feet he opened his eyes. At three thousand feet he tried his wings and managed to divert his fall into a slide. At a thousand feet he flew, but with a lurch, his right wing damaged.

On front winds of the storm, he flew fifty miles in thirty minutes, and then a thousand feet ahead he saw a chain of lakes. Tipping earthward, he began a slant. With a slight stagger at the end of each wingbeat, he ploughed down onto a lake and swam over to a slough to recover.

The wild ride had so dissociated him that it was dark before he became oriented. Then he discovered that he was among pencil reeds in a bay of cold, crystal-clear water hemmed in by a rocky shore. At sunrise he began to forage, but this was no fertile place a goose would ever come to but a glacial lake, void of floating weeds. He had to be satisfied with a few snails, a couple of caddis-worms and a water-lily leaf.

After hours of searching for food, he took to the air, skittering like an aeroplane with a faltering engine. Michigan's Upper Peninsula slid south beneath him and then Sault Ste. Marie. Gradually he learned to compensate for the damaged primary feathers on his right wing by holding back with the left. He spent two days flying north, coming down occasionally to rest and try to feed, but to a goose, the wilderness he found was a wasteland of infertility. He kept going until he had crossed the fifty-fourth parallel, and beneath him flowed the Winisk River on its way to Hudson Bay. He looked down and knew that this was it—goose country.

THE WINISK, a river of many moods, flows through the land of the Cree and the Ojibwa, a land of little sticks, in that remote northwest corner of Ontario where there are trees only along the river and death waits for human mistakes. But the place is a sanctuary for geese. Below the Winisk's rapids and roaring falls, between the lakes, are wide mud flats covered with the velvet green of new grass, and here the Canadas nest.

All the way to the salty bay were gathering places for the geese, and as he flew Duke could hear their quiet gabble, see ganders standing guard near females already incubating eggs. He landed at the confluence of the Winisk and a tributary, and let the swift current carry him for a mile to where it lost its force between wide banks. Then he swam ashore and began to graze. Just before that dim time which is a summer night in the north, he flew to a bar for gravel. Then, at the edge of the water, he rested.

An Indian saw him there the next morning. He guided his canoe to where a line throbbed from a willow limb, and pulling on it, flopped a thirty-pound sturgeon to the shore. The Indian tied one end of a rope to the sturgeon, another to a tag alder bush, and threw the fish back into the water so it would stay alive until the plane made its weekly pickup. Then the Indian shot his canoe against the current to round a bend in the river.

Duke could now so compensate for the damaged feathers that the lurch was barely discernible. He made a tour of inspection and found an Indian camp on the high ground of a peninsula.

As he went aloft the next morning, he circled downstream over

155

two white men by a tent. Both looked up, and both immediately noticed the slightly lurching flight, though not one man in a hundred would have detected anything wrong with the gander.

Duke flew back to where he'd spent the night, swam to the bank and lazily began an inspection of the shore. He turned stones, probed the mud and sent a school of small brook trout shimmying from a trickling creek down to the river. He stood eye to eye with a fox until the little animal whimpered and went running. He ate succulent grass, then swam out and dipped to run water over his feathers and try to preen the broken feathers so they'd lie straight.

A week went by, and during his times aloft Duke noticed that the two white men were gradually moving towards the flatland where he headquartered. Then one afternoon he saw their canoe crossing the river, and Duke left the grass flat to make way for them and moved downstream to another flatland of short grass.

Towards evening he came back. The men had set up camp, and a thread of smoke from their fire was spreading a bluish haze through the trees. He was surprised to see a quantity of corn sharply bright on the flat. He remembered vividly the corn feasts at Heron and that corn was a comforting source of energy such as no amount of grass could provide. But he was wary and flew to the farthest upstream end of the flat to put down. One man said to the other, "He's a wise one."

When the sun was well up the next morning, Duke flew downstream and saw that the corn was still there. He came low, looking for a trap. Lifting a little, he flew over the tent, but the men were not there, and he could not find even their canoe. Staying well out from shore, he flew up the river with eyes prying such hiding places as he remembered hunters used. He could find nothing.

Making a wide swing, he came so low his wing tips almost brushed the mud. Then he abruptly lifted to see if his lowering flight had triggered any hiding thing into making a move. But there was nothing. From two hundred feet up he spilled air from his wings to come tumbling straight down to the bait. On the ground he stood with head high for a full minute, like a stone goose.

Then he tilted his head to look at the corn. From his throat came a trembling sound so soft his neck feathers barely moved. He lowered his head and delicately picked up a piece of corn. Then he turned the kernel on his tongue as if to see if within the corn

156

itself there might not be some threat. Finally satisfied, he swallow-ed, and with the corn a kernel of satisfaction in his crop, began to feed. He took a step towards more corn, and the webbing of his right foot came down on a lightly covered trigger which detonated devices buried in the mud. The twin explosions set him back on his tail feathers. He saw a net lift, but before he could move, it shot up in an arc to come down over him. In spite of every precaution, he had walked into a trap set by men who, during years of study, had come to know the Canada goose better than the Canada goose knows itself.

He was so stunned that he neither fought the net nor saw the canoe come streaking out of its hiding place in a thrust of red willow and stunted poplar. Only when the two men were standing over him did he begin to fight back. But he was quickly and humanely subdued by strong arms and hands. The men were biol-ogists adept at trapping everything from moose and bears down to birds no larger than a man's thumb.

While one man held Duke, another fastened a yellow plastic collar to the goose's outstretched neck. They examined his broken flight feathers, took a blood sample with a small syringe, put him in a bag and hung him on a scale for weighing. They took a couple of lice from his breast feathers, fingered the mink scar on his cheek, plucked one tail and one wing feather. Then, while one man wrote in a notebook, the other took the gander to the edge of the water and gently put him down.

Duke could not believe he was free. The men backed away, and he watched them. Then he exploded and propelled himself with his wings across the water. But he did not fly. He spread himself on the river, and lying low as though hiding, let the current take him, until the two men on the shore were indistinct in the distance. Two miles downstream he climbed on an outcropping rock. Standing above the river, he looked down and saw his reflection —a great grey goose wearing a ridiculous yellow collar. He moved his head up and down, and the plastic crackled. He tried to curl his neck back in the comfortable fashion of a contented goose, but he could not. He stood on one leg and with the claws of the other web scratched to dislodge the neckband. For the better part of two hours he fought the collar, complaining morosely, until he was the picture of dejection.

It was two days before Duke was reconciled enough to the collar to take to the air. In flight it was less troublesome because his long neck was always stretched straight out, and when he came to a meadow where there was a scattering of other Canadas, he noticed that some of them were also wearing collars. If they were irritated by the mark by which men followed their flights across the continent, they gave no sign. In a puddle Duke also noticed a swimming fuzz of ducklings; instead of being golden brown, they were vividly pink. The biologists had injected colouring into each egg of a duck's clutch.

If misery loves company, Duke was an exception. He took no comfort in the fact that other Canadas were marked. Instead he looked for a place to sulk unseen. He flew to a tributary stream of the Winisk and a wide place held in by low rocks. There was food here, though it was not plentiful, but there were no other geese. The rock outcropping was a natural haven for the dens of wolves, foxes and wolverines. As Duke swam aimlessly about in the middle of the stream, a pair of wolves lay watching him from the top of a small bluff, while their five youngsters wrestled at the mouth of a cave a hundred feet away. The male wolf was black, while the female, though dark across the back, shaded away to almost white on her underside. They had just fed on the last of a moose calf, so their interest in Duke was purely curious, though they had both eaten wounded or flightless moulting geese in the past.

Duke drank, and the water had the fresh taste of a stream so young it had not travelled far enough to pick up flavours from roots or rocks. Then he walked from the water to inspect the meadow.

The wolves used this flat to move out across the tundra. Duke could see their trail clearly, but what didn't register with him was how it sharply deviated in one place to bypass an old, rusty trap some Indian had long forgotten.

Having satisfied himself that there was enough grass, Duke went back to the water and drifted out. In the two days since the biologists had demeaned him by affixing the collar, he had hardly slept. Each time he tried to curl his head back to a wing pocket, the plastic crackled and wrinkled. Gradually, however, the collar had been shaping itself to the contours of his neck. Now, warmed by the sun, it had softened, and he tucked his head beneath a wing

158

and slept. When he awakened, the sun was loafing along the horizon. There would be no real night, but this did not disturb Duke, since geese, like cats, can nap.

Duke lofted and began circling. He saw a moose, a pair of ptarmigans, and one goldeneye drake resting on the water beneath a hole in a hollow tree where a hen was obviously warming eggs. He discovered the wolf family almost at once. The male wolf had just come back from a hunting trip and was regurgitating a partially digested hare, and the young were crowding each other ferociously to get a fair share. Duke was not concerned. Ordinary precaution would keep the wolves' teeth from his throat.

He came down and went ashore. While he grazed, the elder wolves lay side by side, ears erect, looking down from their promontory. It amused them to watch Duke step gracefully along, but they had no designs on him. In fact, they welcomed him as a watchdog. His eyes were far-seeing, and he flew a daily patrol, scouting out the country to see if any alien thing had moved in while he slept.

So for Duke the days passed in a somnolence of eating, drinking, swimming, washing, preening . . . and only rarely now did he try to dislodge the collar.

The wolf pups grew larger each day and made exploratory trips down to the water and Duke's meadow. Though it does not seem possible, Duke began to exhibit a proprietary interest in them. Perhaps it was because he was by heritage a family bird: tame geese have been known to become guardians to kittens and have fought to keep the rest of the flock from killing them. In any case, when the pups ventured too far out onto the meadow, Duke would haronk sharply, and the pups would flop back on their haunches and look with lively interest across the meadow to where the goose stood.

Meanwhile the meadow grass kept growing, and toughening in the process. So Duke took to following the wolves' trail, because along its edges there were always tender new sprouts. Many times he took the little detour around the trap, now completely camouflaged by grass. Then one day when he was coming along the trail, he heard an aeroplane's drone. It was the fish plane come to pick up sturgeon at Indians' camps along the river and en route to check out likely places for wolf packs so government trappers might put

160

out poison baits before the caribou came. It flew down so low that the prop wash flattened the grass. The engine roar was so loud that Duke's feathers flattened in fear. Sure the big bird was aimed to pounce on him, he ran down the wolf trail to get into the air, and where the trail turned to go around the trap, he went straight ahead. Snap—the rusty jaws closed over two toes, and he was caught.

His momentum carried him, the trap and the rotting log toggle to which it was wired, off the ground, but the great weight brought him crashing back, while the pilot, unaware of his predicament and satisfied that there were only wolf pups among the rocks, lifted the plane and headed for the Winisk.

Duke sat trembling, and then he panicked. Thrashing the air with his wings, he dragged the trap and toggle across the meadow dangerously close to the wolves' den. The pups sat in a row on the edge of the flat ground and watched. Unaware of them Duke fought the trap with all his strength, gasping with his beak agape.

As the fight went out of him, the pups came close. Duke saw them, and if he'd once felt fatherly, now that was gone. They were the enemy. He hissed at them, knowing that if the old wolves came back, he would surely die.

The biggest and bravest of the pups got a wing tip between its teeth and started pulling. Encouraged, another playfully nipped at the goose's tail, while a third went around for a muzzleful of feathers on the other side.

Duke struck out with his wings, and the pups went tumbling backward. Then, with little growls and snarls, they rushed in again. Duke met them with a thrust of wings, but now it was a game to them, and the instant he was quiet, they came charging in.

In an attempt to keep his flight feathers from being destroyed, Duke tucked in his wings. The biggest pup sprang for his neck and would have got his needle-sharp teeth in the jugular except for the plastic collar. The pup's jaws closed on the collar, and he savagely shook his head. Another pup closed in; he too got a mouthful of plastic, and the gander was yanked about in a tug-of-war. Then the plastic, warmed by the sun and his overheated body, expanded, and Duke slid his head out of the noose. The pups, growling, tried to wrest the collar from each other.

Duke put up his head to see both adult wolves standing near

161

the den. As the adult wolves started towards him, Duke made a mighty effort and lifted. The rotting toggle broke, and he managed to get a few feet into the air with the chain and wire dangling beneath. One of the pups, fascinated by the swinging chain, made a dive for it. For a second the pup was suspended in the air like a furry pendulum. His weight slipped the jaws of the trap from the gander's toes, and the pup fell back with the trap on top of him, while Duke went off at a wild, winging slant for the open water.

Though his foot was not seriously hurt, he was in a state of shock. Only his feather ends quivered as the adult wolves stood at the water's edge to watch him. Then the male wolf started swimming towards the gander, who was paddling feebly, almost unconscious. It was the goldeneye drake who saved him. Thinking the wolf had designs on his hen, the goldeneye turned his head for a quick look to see that she hadn't come out of her hollow tree, and then, with a guttural quack of warning, splatted along the surface and into the air.

The warning stirred a response in Duke. He began frantically beating the water with his wings and scooted downstream, while the wolf, turning, swam slowly back to shore.

DUKE revived quickly. His wings were not damaged seriously, and when his fatigue began to dissipate, he drank and then took to the air. The wolves looked up when his shadow came across their rocks, and the adults, red tongues hanging, seemed to be giving him a grin. However, in Duke's life it was a dreadfully close brush with death, and he knew he would never come back here again.

He flew with the Winisk to the tidal flats of Hudson Bay. Here he rested, listening to the gabbling of yearling blue-goose and snow-goose flocks, as the birds incessantly traded grazing places. Here, before many weeks would pass, tens of thousands of geese from the eastern Arctic and sub-Arctic would gather to wait for a north wind to send them south. It was a staging area, and already the non-breeders had come, and these ebbed and flowed in endless procession with the tide.

It was an unsettling place for a mature gander, and the old restlessness came over him, until one night when the sun had gone for its brief nap below the horizon, he climbed on a brisk north wind and headed south. In six days of flying and resting and feeding, he re-entered the United States, crossed Michigan's Upper Peninsula and came back to Wisconsin.

He went straight to the Silver Sun Trout Ranch and came down on the farthest pond. Hardly had he preened himself when Tom Rank and John Mackenna came to the shore with a pail of corn. They stood at a distance so the gander could feed.

"He looks rough," Rank said. "Wonder what happened?"

"Storm, maybe. Could be he got caught in the big tornado."

Duke rested and fed at the ranch for three days and then headed south again. At Heron Marsh he flew to where each of his daughters had died and then came back to stay at the muskrat house where he himself had almost perished.

One brilliant morning Duke found another goose. He had taken to the air shortly after sunrise to fly the perimeter of the marsh. Then, instead of coming back, he followed the river south. He was flying low across a lake when he heard a haronk. He scrambled for altitude to get a better look and spotted the floating lone goose. He flew over, circled her several times and then glided down to skim along the water. When he was a few feet away, he stopped to look her over.

The female made soft sounds of joy at having been discovered by one of her kind. She had been alone since the great mass of geese had continued their journey north. Victim of a gunner, she had taken several pellets, and now one wing curved back on itself. The wound had healed, but there was no possibility that she would ever fly again.

Duke made no advances, but neither did he leave. They swam together until dusk, and then Duke lifted and called to the female to follow. She ran on the water but could not rise. When she did not come, Duke headed back for the marsh.

For a week Duke spent his nights on the old muskrat house but his days swimming and feeding with the goose at the lake.

On the morning of the eighth day, the lake lay smooth as a sheet of cellophane, and Duke took the goose to weeds he had sighted from the air. They had almost filled their crops when he heard the ominous growl of an approaching motor. The boat came from the mouth of the river and pointed straight at them, leaving a wake curling away on either side. Duke uttered a warning and began swimming swiftly for the shore. The goose hurried along behind him, and Duke ran on the water to get into the air. The goose ran too, but she could not lift. When the boat was about to crash over her, she swung hard to the left and it went by. The goose swam hurriedly towards the marshy shore, but the boat swung in a wide circle and came back. Duke, flying above it, clamoured loudly; this was a strange manœuvre for a wild gander, since he had not mated with the goose.

The crippled goose walked high on the water, her wings flailing to give her speed, and again she was just barely able, at the last moment, to swing left with a hard push from her one good wing and get out of the way of the boat. Duke, in a rage, bent his head and hissed. But the two men in the boat waved at him as though they were enjoying some kind of game.

By the time the boat had skidded around to make another run, the goose was at the edge of the marsh. She swam swiftly among the reeds where the boat could not follow her and disappeared. From the air Duke could see her follow the muskrat trails deeper and deeper into the slough.

Twice more the boat circled, and then giving up the chase, headed back towards the mouth of the river. When the roar of the motor had faded, Duke came down beside the goose, and while she slept from exhaustion, he remained alert and on guard. All that day he kept a sharp lookout and fed only when she was full and could guard.

So it was that he accepted the minimum responsibilities of Canada-goose society. He did not search out tender grasses for her, nor touch her with his bill, nor try to drive her before him. He only stood guard. But he stayed that night and the next, and on the third day he discovered that the moult had made him flightless. Resigned to weeks of virtual imprisonment, he spent hours spreading oil from the sac at his tail to his feathers, since he could not go aloft to dry them out. They made a partially submerged log their headquarters, and when not floating and feeding, they stood there with webs in the water.

The summer passed, and one September day they saw the first flock of returning geese, and Duke remembered the corn on the marsh. When he took to the air it was with a sure beat of powerful

new feathers. When the goose could not follow, Duke came back. Then he swam across the lake with her in tow and started into the mouth of the river.

They swam all day and most of the night against the current and then rested in the marshes. After they had eaten, they went back into the current, and so they came to a small bay below the city of Heron. Here Duke waited for dark. That night they followed the river into the city and swam through it until they reached a dam. They rested below it until the sounds of the city dimmed. Then, while the people slept, they came up a green bank, walked across the concrete road and went down the other side. By the time the city awakened next morning, they were a mile up the river and into Heron Marsh.

They rested and fed before swimming to the north end of the marsh, where the geese and the corn would be concentrated. Every day geese trickled in from the north until there were more than a hundred thousand geese on the marsh. And each day Duke and the goose could feel fat coating their muscles and adding to their reserves of strength.

Then, inevitably, the hunters came. Geese died by the thousands, but Duke made no attempt to leave the marsh even when the daily ration of corn was cut off. Instead, he led the crippled goose back to where springs promoted an extra growth of grass, and though they often went hungry, they did not starve.

As abruptly as the shooting had started, it stopped. The government had decreed that Wisconsin hunters had taken their quota of Canadas. There had to be some left for those waiting in southern Illinois, Kentucky, Tennessee . . . all the way south to Louisiana and Florida.

Then the trucks came out again with corn, and Duke led the crippled goose to the feeding islands, where they lived in luxury. Nevertheless Duke was restless. Within him was the memory of another autumn when he had been unable to flee before the ice of winter trapped him, and there had been days without food or water. But mild autumn weather held the land well beyond the time for winter. And there was plenty of corn.

Then came a night of sharp cold, and in the morning some of the ditches had a skim of ice. Duke tried to get the goose into the air, but she would not even try her wings now. Finally Duke settled

166

back down beside her and folded in his neck until his bill was resting almost on his breast.

That night it snowed, a soft fall of big flakes, and in the morning the cuts of open water were black in the stainless white surroundings. After the pair had fed, Duke led the goose to the river. They slipped into the water and the gander swam north against the current. The pair came to the northernmost boundaries of the marsh, and here, on a frozen hummock of rushes, they spent the night. By morning the ice on the riverbanks had widened, and the only open cut was where the current ran swiftly. But Duke breasted the current, and the goose followed. They didn't look back. Their way was north.

NORTHERN lights built icy colonnades in the sky, and cresting, spilled colour—only to gather at the horizon and build again, shaft on shaft. Beneath the display the geese rested. A muskrat came across the ice to peer at them curiously, and a great horned owl lowered on velvet wings but discreetly decided to forego the pleasure of a goose dinner. They were a splendid pair, each cocked on one leg on the white hummock: big birds with feathers so neatly and firmly interlocked they looked like armoured geese impervious to tooth or talon, wind or snow.

It was an illusion, because they could shiver like any other creature when they had to go without food. This night they were warm. The days of feeding stood them in good stead, and even next morning, though they were hungry, it was no pressing hunger of great need.

But there was nothing here for them to eat. They walked to the open cut of water, and swimming, the gander headed north through flat marsh country looking for any green morsel. At a turn in the river, they found a surprising lode. Muskrats had been working all night to fill their stomachs, and fragments of vegetation floated on the current. There was enough for both.

Duke decided to camp there. But next morning there were no greens because the muskrats had moved downstream. So Duke began the trek north again—under bridges, between bone-bare trees, down flat marshes, while the stream grew smaller and the open water narrowed, and they lived on greens left floating by the muskrats.

Then finally they came to the end of open water. The river had dwindled to a tiny creek, and stretching before them was a snaking, narrow ribbon of ice. They sat together on the ice edge and sometimes made tracks to the banks and dug with their bills through the light snow to see if there might be some green thing to fill the emptiness they felt.

Next morning they followed the frozen creek into a dense little forest of small straight poplars. Here, in a marsh pocket, the stream ended. They left the ice and started walking through the woods, bearing north. The snow was soft beneath their webs, and they moved at least as fast as they had been able to swim against the river current.

On a knoll they broke out of the trees, and before them sprawled farm buildings. Duke stopped, every nerve tingling with fear. Then he turned and walked back into the trees. Beneath an oak he began probing and found an acorn.

He did not offer it to the goose as he would have if they had been mates, but swallowed it himself, and then, using his bill like a miniature snowplough, uncovered another. He looked over at the goose, but instead of picking it up and laying it at her feet, he only backed away so she could walk over and eat it. Then both of them cruised back and forth looking for acorns.

When dusk came, the goose would have settled next to the trunk of the tree for the night, but it was such an alien place for a Canada that the gander started with every mouse sound. It was one thing to hide here during daylight hours and another to stay when darkness gave them cover under which to leave.

The goose however was reluctant to go. Her crop was full, her webs were sore from the ice, and wary though she was of the closeness of the trees, sleep seemed desirable. The gander did not drive her. He walked a little way and waited, and when she did not come, he walked a little farther. When he was almost out of sight in the gloom, she got to her feet and followed. They walked all night, and by daybreak they were exhausted. The goose lagged often, and Duke had to pause for her to catch up. That day they rested in a small grassy marsh. When night came, they were hungry, but there was only snow, so they ate some, and it revived them enough to continue.

At dawn, bedraggled and swiftly weakening, they stumbled

onto a tiny spring which trickled out of a grove of young poplars, an oasis in a frightening world. The goose honked excitedly as she stretched herself full length, letting the water run down her throat, while Duke, though as thirsty as she was, stood guard. When she had had enough, he went to the water and skimmed it with dignity. Then both began eating moss from the stones and snipping the few grass blades kept green by the spring. It was no banquet, and though Duke tried to remain alert, he caught himself sleeping often during the afternoon.

That night the goose was again reluctant to move, but something was driving Duke. He walked away a half-dozen times before she finally got off her webs to follow slowly. The fat they had hoarded on the marsh had been absorbed now; still they moved, and always on the North Star, through lands which were becoming increasingly rugged.

It was midnight and a thin slice of moon had just come out through the clouds when Duke detected the creeping shadow of a fox, and in the same instant smelled his rank odour. With a low, sharp warning for the goose, he swung to face the fox, his head down and wings spread slightly. But the fox moved just beyond the range of the gander's beak, looking for a way to break through Duke's defences and get a throat hold. He circled, but Duke turned with the fox, so the animal decided to concentrate on the goose.

She made no move to defend herself, but Duke walked between them. Around and around they went, the fox with his ears laid back, stepping carefully, the gander sometimes hissing; two superb antagonists fencing for a weakness in one another.

Then the fox attacked. Duke's neck coiled and shot forward. He hit hard with his beak, and the bony wings flailed the fox's body. The fox went over backward and then fled.

Duke walked sedately back to the goose, and after preening what feathers had gone awry, he started the northward march again. The goose faltered often now. Sometimes she went down on her webs and refused to move, and Duke halted to let her recover.

That morning there was no water or food as they made camp by a hedgerow. A hundred times the goose and the gander probed the snow in front of where each squatted, as though by some miracle they had overlooked a morsel. But there was nothing, and they had to be satisfied to eat snow, which began to burn their tongues as though it were hot instead of cold.

That night, coming out from among the trees, they saw ahead what seemed an endless brown sea of grass high above the snow, an impenetrable wall to the faltering Canadas. The goose refused to broach it. She sat as though at last she had come to the place where she had decided to die.

Duke rested with her, and then ran into the wind and took to the air. The goose called out for him to come back so she would not have to die alone, but he made a circle and flew north to land on a large river. After drinking, he flew back to where the goose sat. She honked her joy at seeing his shadow against the stars. He landed and started to walk around the fringe of the dense stand of grass, and now the goose followed. It was daybreak before they came to the river Duke had visited. They went into the river and let the current take them while they drank and ran the refreshing water over their bodies. Then they preened. With every feather in its proper place they were waterproofed and perfectly insulated against the cold.

They started out again and came to a dam festooned with great overhangs of ice, where the water crashed into the river in eddies of foam. At the edge of the rough water the Canadas clambered up a steep bank. They walked around the dam to the edge of a frozen lake and slept the rest of the day among the bulrushes. That night they followed the shoreline back to the river, but they still had not reached open water.

They stopped to rest, but when Duke moved out, the goose looked wearily after him and refused to move. Duke came back, as he had so often, but she put out her neck and laid it low on the snow in the manner of a goose which has been hurt and is hiding. A dozen times the gander came back, and then in a flurry of rage, rapped her sharply with his bill.

She jumped to her feet, haronking, and they started north again under the starlight, waddling now like tame geese, coming down heavily with each step and swaying awkwardly from side to side as though their own weight were too much to bear.

Duke felt the snow getting mushy beneath his webs, and in his excitement at the feel of it, left the goose far behind. Then he was floating, and the water was warm around his webs and cool trickling down his long throat. When the goose came up, she was so excited she haronked, and Duke looked around, alarmed lest she had drawn some danger to them. After they had sported in the water awhile, Duke swam north and the goose followed.

At a shallow rapids they probed the bottom but found only a few molluscs and caddisworms. Ahead now a small town loomed. When they had swum closer, they found they had another dam to bypass. Duke toured the banks looking for some way to go around it, and daylight caught them there. A group of small boys saw them and came to the concrete banks with stones to throw. One hit the goose, and Duke took to the air, protesting. He flew above the goose in circles as the boys drove her from one end of the pool to the other until the school bell sent them on their way and saved the goose.

But word had already got around that there were two geese below the dam, and people gathered in little groups, speculating on why the pair was wintering so far north in Wisconsin. Some got their cameras and took pictures.

Duke swam nervously in circles around the goose. A man took bread from a brown paper sack and threw it to the water. Hungry as he was, Duke let it float on past, but the goose swiftly intercepted and gobbled it. After school the boys came back to throw stones again, but a man in uniform scattered them.

Just before dark a woman came to the embankment and carefully poured corn from a coffee can on a low rock. When it was full dark, Duke swam the goose over to the corn, and they ate every kernel. It was a fresh grip on life for both of them, and they could feel their returning strength as they preened feathers into place. When all but a few of the town's lights had winked out, they climbed the bank of the dam, and together they walked down the main street—two wild geese in the middle of the road, from streetlight to streetlight, on past the post office, the drugstore, the grocery store—all the way back to the open water.

The current was so strong that they had to paddle frantically. As daylight neared they came to another river, and Duke swam excitedly into this new waterway. Like a salmon come back to the stream of its birth, the gander, by taste or smell or some sixth sense, knew that this waterway was the one. It was a stream of no great momentum, and on it they made good time until the open water diminished and then disappeared beneath ice, and on every side there was flat, frozen marsh.

But Duke showed no hesitation now. He pushed himself up onto the marsh and began walking. He must have known that he was near, and he hurried. The goose fell behind, but Duke took to the air and flew low until he came to the creek. The goose hurried after him, and both swam up the creek.

Now Duke could see the roofs of the house and the hatchery. Although he had been composed during the long trip, he haronked loudly, and from where the geese wintered, he heard a chorus of answers. If he wasn't home, this was the closest thing to it.

WHEN Rank came with corn, Duke did not take to the air but only backed off to the far side of the creek. After Rank had spread out the kernels, he walked away, and the goose began greedily to eat. Duke, though as emaciated as she, waited until she had glutted herself and then swam over to eat with the restraint a well-fed goose might display.

Rank stood back so as not to disturb the pair and marvelled at what was obviously a miracle. He took it as an omen, and he couldn't wait to tell Mack, hoping it would provide his employer with the impetus he needed to turn a corner in his life and leave the lonely days behind.

Though John Mackenna had escorted various women since his wife's death, of late he had been seeing more and more of a widow, Sarah Greenlee—a striking woman with dark eyes and high colour. She was with him when Mack drove into the yard, and Rank, with a note of triumph in his voice, told them that Duke was back and had brought a goose.

Mack took Sarah's hand to show her the way, and in the fading light they watched as the exhausted goose, her crippled wing plain to see, slept floating on the creek while the gander, head high, cast a wary eye towards them. In the cold the woman moved closer to the man, but he did not put an arm around her. If Mack was impressed, it was not because the gander had brought a goose, but because they had crossed this land in winter, swimming, and on foot.

"Incredible!" he said as they turned away and started towards the house. "There is no place they could have come from except Heron Marsh. Imagine! Across all that ice and snow!"

That evening Mack told Sarah about how the gander kept gravitating back to this place, where he had lost his mate, and Sarah wisely let him talk.

Next morning Mack spent several hours watching the pair from a distance with binoculars and then sought out Rank in the hatchery. "They aren't mated," he announced.

The foreman said, "Impossible!"

"It's a fact," Mack replied. "He doesn't treat her like he would if they were mated."

"Then they will be soon enough," the foreman said.

"I suppose so. Soon as the weather breaks," Mack said.

So the two men watched, and there was hardly a day that the goose did not offer herself, but the gander did not take her.

March melted off into April, and water began running in the ditches. Songbirds came back, and then one day there was a cut of open water, and a giant black snapping turtle groped lethargically from the mud towards the light. Spring kept backing winter north. The soil quickened, pushing forth pale, fragile flowers, and in the tangled brown of dead grasses there was a tint of green.

One day Rank turned the pinioned geese out of their quarters, and they went in a wild, winging rush for the ponds, clamouring their joy at being free. The pair at the creek heard them, and both came to higher ground where they could see the flock.

The goose started towards the liberated flock, and when the gander failed to follow, she stopped and turned to look at him. He bobbed his head but made no move to follow. She came back. Standing together, they watched the pinioned geese flail the water in their exuberance. Once again the goose ran towards them. Once again she stopped when the gander failed to follow. Duke took a few steps in her direction, and then, dipping his head and talking softly, turned to go back to the creek.

Now, with wings beating the air, the impatient goose rushed to join the flock, and that afternoon she took a mate. Next day the first northbound flock of geese crossed high above the ranch. Duke lifted and followed.

Rank and Mackenna watched him go. They stood until he was a speck and then nothing in the sky. Then Tom went back to the hatchery, and Mack went into the house.

Day after day both men looked to the sky, waiting. Blue herons

173

came. An eagle. An osprey pair looked down. Red-tailed hawks hunted the meadow. Black-capped night herons were silhouetted against the moon. Egrets stopped briefly, and all manner of wide-winged birds. But not Duke.

Summer came, and the crippled goose walked goslings to the water. Fall came, and the leaves fell, and the geese moved across the sky again on their way south, but no gander dropped out of a passing flock to visit.

Then it was winter, but when Rank drove home after work, the only light in the big, white house was the one in the tiny office. Sarah came to the ranch less often and then not at all. And if Duke had died or been killed, then it was his ghost Tom and Mack heard on moonlight nights, when sometimes there was a clear, cold fluting from the sky. But perhaps it was only a trick of the wind, because they never saw the gander again.

Mel Ellis

Wildlife writer and conservationist, Mel Ellis started out in the 1920s as a hunter, and his knowledge and admiration of Canada geese came the hard way—by hunting them over thousands of miles from north Canada to Mexico. "The wild goose is the wariest bird there is." he says.

Over the years, however, his passion for hunting has been replaced by a passion for protecting wildlife. On their fifteen-acre wooded oasis at On-Little-Lakes, Big Bend, Wisconsin, he and Mrs. Ellis run what is, in effect, a private wildfowl sanctuary. Both tame and wild migratory birds revel on the ponds, or feed in a "bush pantry" off special shrubs and grasses that the Ellises planted. "We're just off the Great Lakes flyway," he says, "so we get many species." Here lived wild Duke and tame Duchess, the two birds who inspired *Wild Goose, Brother Goose*.

Ellis is a hardworking writer, putting in several hours a day at the typewriter in their old converted farmhouse overlooking the ponds. He has published more than a dozen books, plus hundreds of articles in *National Geographic* and other important magazines. He also writes a nationwide syndicated newspaper column called, "The Good Earth Crusade". In between, he combs countless publications for ecology facts to use in his work.

"I'm optimistic about the environment problem," he says. "Technology, which has been blamed, will save us in the end. The will to survive is just as strong in man as it is in the wild goose."

THE
PROPERTY
OF A
GENTLEMAN

A condensation of the book by
Catherine Gaskin

·

Illustrated by
Ben Wohlberg

·

Published by Collins, London

Joanna Roswell was young, beautiful, and had a promising career as an antiques expert in one of the world's great auction houses. Yet something was missing from her life. Then comes the invitation to accompany Gerald Stanton to Thirlbeck, ancestral home of the earls of Askew. They hope they'll be asked to arrange a discreet sale of whatever antiques might be housed in the decaying old manor. Once there, Joanna finds priceless treasures. She also discovers that it is easy to believe in ghosts.

Against her will, Joanna becomes deeply enmeshed in the lives of the two men who stand in the path of Thirlbeck's rich but deadly legacy—Robert Birkett, the present earl, and his reluctant heir, the disturbingly intent Nat Birkett.

In this, her finest novel, Catherine Gaskin weaves a rich tapestry of romance and mystery. A gripping tale from the author of *Edge of Glass*, *Fiona*, and *A Falcon for a Queen*.

About half of the ninety-three passengers, those in the tail section, on the flight out of Zurich bound for Paris and London survived when the plane ploughed into a mountainside shortly after takeoff. Among those killed were an antique dealer from London by the name of Vanessa Roswell, and a man, presumed to be Dutch, whose body no one claimed and whose passport the authorities, after close examination, found to be forged.

Within hours of the crash, Joanna, the daughter of Vanessa Roswell, and a friend, Gerald Stanton, were on their way to Zurich, with the desperate unspoken hope that Vanessa might be among the survivors. Before he left London, Gerald Stanton managed the difficult feat of reaching by telephone a remote hacienda in the mountains of Mexico, to summon Vanessa Roswell's husband to Zurich. He arrived the day after the crash. Her body had already been identified, so he went to a hotel to which the police directed him. There he found, sitting in silence before a fire in a private sitting room, Gerald Stanton and a young woman. A beautiful young woman, he thought, gauging her with his painter's eye, although her face now wore the numbed expression of shock and grief. She looked at him without recognition. That was not surprising; she hadn't seen him for twenty-seven years.

"Joanna," he said quietly. "I'm Jonathan—your father, Jonathan Roswell."

BUT IT was not my father, Jonathan Roswell, whom Gerald and I discussed at lunch one day more than two weeks after the Zurich crash. It was, rather, the man we were going to visit, Robert Birkett.

"When a year in jail, Joanna, is for manslaughter of one's wife and son—as it was for Robert—it must be a particular sort of hell."

Gerald drew slowly on his cigarette, not at all hurried by the thought that we still had a long way to travel that afternoon. He had deliberately sought out this well-recommended restaurant far off the motorway, had had his martini to the exact degree of dryness and chill his cultivated palate demanded, had had his wine with lunch. Because I was driving I restricted myself to a glass of sherry.

"Robert's father and grandfather were typical English eccentrics," Gerald continued. "They were recluses and autocrats; their estate, Thirlbeck, must have seemed like their own kingdom, so isolated and remote. Robert quarrelled with his father. Then he committed the heresy of joining the International Brigade during the Spanish Civil War. While in Spain he married an aristocratic girl whose family, of course, fought on the other side—with Franco. She was a Catholic, naturally. Robert returned to Thirlbeck only for his father's funeral. He was actually on his way back there when the accident happened. So he attended his father's funeral and then the funeral of his wife and son. Afterwards they charged him with manslaughter—said he'd been drinking and lost control of the car. A year's sentence."

"And I suppose he's kept to the pattern himself—a recluse in his own isolated world ever since." I said it absently, thinking of the journey ahead.

Gerald stubbed out his cigarette and added to my impatience by pausing to light another. I realized I was fussing, worrying about small things. After all, this was a restaurant, not Hardy's, the auction house that was the centre of both our lives. In Hardy's one was not permitted to smoke in the public rooms. But Gerald smoked incessantly at other times; he was in his late sixties, and a lifelong devotion to good wine and food had produced only a pleasing roundness of face and the slightest thickening at the waist.

I suppose if I had to name my closest friend, I would have named him. I was twenty-seven. It was nice to have a friend who had never even remotely threatened to become a lover.

"Quite the contrary," Gerald answered. "Robert got out of jail just after the war started in 1939 and immediately enlisted. He was antiestablishment before anyone heard the word. Nothing would persuade him to take a commission. Perhaps he intended to serve out the war anonymously. But he wasn't born to be anonymous. He won a Military Cross at Dunkirk and a Victoria Cross in the Western Desert. When it was all over he made an effort to disappear. But people like Robert find it difficult to disappear."

"What happened?"

Gerald frowned a little. "I know he went back to Thirlbeck, and I think he stuck it out there for perhaps six months. Then he left, and so far as I know he's never been back. He began to travel. I'd known him at school—at Eton. Whenever I encountered him in later years he always was just back from some odd spot like Yucatán—or sailing round Cape Horn. I don't think he ever had a permanent home—always rented villas. He never married again. That might have been too permanent also. But he probably has had a dozen-odd mistresses—some rich, some famous, some both. All of them beautiful, those that I've seen. He could always attract women, could Robert. He has style as well as charm. You'll see."

Outside, the bright April morning had darkened to a rain-threatened afternoon. "Odd," I said. "I don't remember ever hearing of him. And I'm not too stodgy to look at gossip columns."

Gerald shrugged. "Well, he's in his early sixties now—he's not one of the *young* beautiful people. And in the last few years it's been common knowledge that he's short of money, probably broke. He doesn't buy jewellery for the beautiful ladies any longer, nor give parties. He may yet become a recluse. By necessity, not by choice."

"Unless he decides on a sale and then lives off the proceeds."

Gerald's lips tightened just a trifle. "My dear Joanna, I really am surprised that by now you do not display more discretion. There is not yet even the whisper of a sale. All we know is that he is financially embarrassed, that he returned, hardly a week ago, to a house he has not seen since 1945, and that he has invited me to visit. In this business we go anywhere we're invited socially—and keep our eyes open. And then, perhaps I'm wrong, but Robert gave me the impression of a fearful man needing . . . help. I believe that is why he asked me to come." He gave me his smile of restrained affection. "And that is why I asked you to come with me. We all have need of our friends, Jo."

Gerald paid the bill and then wandered off to the gents' in a leisurely fashion. I went out to the car, emptied the ashtray, studied the map, and cursed myself for being a fool. Was I going to spend my life emptying ashtrays, because that was what they had taught me at Hardy's? But they'd also taught me a reverence for people like Gerald, who seemed to know far more than I could ever hope to. So I was willing to empty ashtrays and chauffeur his stately Daimler just for the experience of being with him, of going over a house and seeing his discerning eye scan a library or a ceramics collection, while I made notes. I was privileged, and I knew it.

As I waited I swung the driving mirror down and combed my hair. The face I saw always seemed to belong to a stranger. Was it because I tried to please too many people too often, never letting my own personality come through? Twenty-seven. Not old, but not so young either. I worked more determinedly at my hair. Was all my passion, were all my young years to be spent authenticating pieces of ceramics, my specialty at Hardy's? Then I saw Gerald strolling towards the car, and like a dutiful girl guide I rushed to open the door for him. I did it before I could stop myself. Damn it! Hadn't I any blood in my veins besides what Hardy's put there?

But Hardy's was in my blood, whether I liked it or not. There had not been the slightest thought of refusal when Gerald had suggested that I join him on this visit to Thirlbeck, home of Robert Birkett, eighteenth Earl of Askew, where we might find treasures or perhaps—in Gerald's favourite phrase—a load of old rubbish.

GERALD had told me to take the turnoff from the motorway at Penrith. I thought there might be a stream of cars heading for the Lake District this Friday afternoon, but it was spring, still cold, and the traffic was thin. A slashing rain closed the horizons; Gerald dozed, and I was left to my thoughts.

Gerald probably had been my mother's closest and oldest friend. They had met soon after I was born, when she was trying to set up in business in Kensington; he had taught her much of what she came to know about antiques, introduced her to other dealers,

182

and kept a friendly eye on her rather chaotic business methods. He had watched her indulgently through a series of love affairs and comforted her when they inevitably ended. He'd never lectured or tried to change her. She had been a beautiful, passionate woman, and in a world that too often contains dull, safe people, Gerald had prized her. For what he had done for Vanessa I loved Gerald. Now it seemed almost as if I had, with her death, slipped into her place, though I was unlike her in so many ways.

Gerald had, of course, been my introduction to Hardy's—that and the fact that Vanessa had been there every week, viewing, attending the sales, bidding when something interested her. Some of her buys had been inspired, some good, some bordered on mad extravagance. This quality in my mother had been well known and, I thought, hadn't helped when I went for my interview with the directors of Hardy's. My chances hinged on whether they believed I might have Vanessa's brilliance without her hasty excesses. Other things did help; I was the right age then—eighteen. Better, in their eyes, to have too little education than too much of the wrong kind. They would teach me what I needed to know.

I had come through the interview, Gerald carefully absenting himself, and had taken my place on the front counter, as everyone who worked for Hardy's did for some period. Except for the beginner's salary it was wonderful. I had everything going for me— my beautiful, flamboyant mother giving me an airy little wave as she ascended the great staircase to the salerooms; there was Gerald, who was my friend and mentor; and there was also the fact that I was the daughter of Jonathan Roswell, some of whose paintings were even then beginning to bring very respectable prices in the salerooms. After a year on the front counter someone decided that my aptitude might lie in ceramics. For the next few years I saw less of Vanessa because I had taken a flat on my own. I went on working, growing up, and somehow waiting for something to happen—perhaps waiting to become identifiably my own self.

The rain was drifting off into mist. I enjoyed the power and smoothness in the big car. Smoothness was Gerald's whole life-style, and on it he spent what was necessary of his considerable fortune.

He had money for a way of life that had thrown him into the company of people who trusted Hardy's with the sale of their most valued possessions, people who didn't want publicity for such sales. At Hardy's their treasures would be discreetly marked with the obscure designation THE PROPERTY OF A GENTLEMAN, or some other kindly shield. Of course, all was recorded—the price, the owner's name, the buyer, and if the object had ever passed through Hardy's before—all of it there in the leather-bound daybooks kept since Hardy's had opened in St. James's two hundred years ago. And how much of the information in those books—and more—Gerald literally carried in his head!

This venture today had been brought about by Gerald's long-reaching contacts. And I was along because he had wanted me with him, and because I was only two days back from Mexico, and the shock of my mother's death and the spell of the man who was my father were still upon me.

When, in Switzerland, Jonathan had turned to me after the funeral and said, "Will you come back to Mexico with me—for a few weeks of sun and quiet, Jo?" it had been Gerald who pushed me towards the decision. "You should go, Jo. I'll make it all right with Hardy's."

I looked at the stranger who was my father, who was proposing that I learn to know him after twenty-seven years, and I answered with a nod. I had not regretted the decision.

It had been what he promised—quiet, remote, an almost peasant style of life lived by the numerous descendants of a family who had been granted huge acreage and licensed to mine its silver by Spanish kings. Their sprawling hacienda was nearly in ruins. Jonathan had stumbled across it twenty years ago and had asked to rent one of the dilapidated outbuildings as a studio and living quarters. He had lived as a member of the family ever since, paying for expensive items like electricity, transport, and the food they couldn't grow themselves. They didn't consider his paintings true pictures at all, and so they didn't take his work seriously. What they did take seriously was his concern for them, his efforts to keep their way of life going, even though the silver mines had long since passed from their control. As his daughter I was regarded with curiosity and veneration. At first I found it uncomfortable, and in the end succumbed—to the place, to the gentle people, to the atmosphere of life centuries ago.

I could remember standing beside him, staring up at the great stone sixteenth-century aqueduct which still fed the hacienda its water. "How clear the air is—and the light's so harsh."

"A painter's light, Jo. I see all I need in it—bright, fierce colours and black shadows. This landscape says everything I want to say." And it was there that he had become one of the foremost abstractionist painters in the world. "I'll never leave here," he added. "They'll bury me with their family, Jo—there beside the chapel."

Somehow, in that short time, I knew at last why he and Vanessa had parted. Impossible to imagine her in this setting. Impossible to imagine him anywhere else. He had been right to ask me to come; now I had a father whom I'd begun to understand.

Then back to London and, with my bags hardly unpacked, Gerald's phone call; he wanted me to come with him to visit Thirlbeck and had gotten the permission of my director. I visited Hardy's, and everyone was kind and said nice things about Vanessa. I wandered upstairs to the largest of the salerooms, where they were auctioning English pictures. The room was packed, and the prices were running high; dealers murmured deprecating remarks about what other dealers bought. It was very far from the clear, calm silence of Mexico. I was back to my old world, but something in it had changed.

Afterwards I went and gave my routine donation of blood at St. Giles Hospital. Then at home I cooked some chops for supper, and sat and willed the telephone to ring with a call from Harry Peers, but no call came. Harry had sent three long, extravagant cables to Mexico, but no message waited for me here. I began to repack for this trip with Gerald, a kind of hurting ache in my throat at the thought of Harry Peers. Gerald said Harry had flown unannounced to Switzerland on the day I left with my father for Mexico and had just missed me. That was Harry. In the end I finally telephoned his flat, and his manservant told me that Mr. Peers was out of the country; he didn't know when he would be back. So I would wait, and sometime he would phone. I wished I could feel angry with him, but I couldn't. I could either accept him as he was or do without him. I didn't want to do without him.

GERALD's voice came to me over the soft clicking of the windscreen wipers. I had thought he was asleep.

"It's wonderful how the excitement comes back. I was beginning to think I was too old for this business." Because of his age Gerald now worked only in an advisory capacity, and he was, therefore, free to indulge his passion—the quiet search for what was still unknown and undocumented. As if he knew I would bridge his thoughts he continued. "I can't find a record of Thirlbeck's contents anywhere. It must be the only house of any size in England which hasn't been photographed and written up. They must have been eccentrics with a vengeance, those Birketts." Then he added, "Robert won't be expecting you, but he will accept you. He is charming, always, with women."

Gerald continued in a low tone, as if his words were almost for himself. "All those years—and a house unvisited, unrecorded. What shall we find, I wonder? Of course, there *is* something—something so superlative that even the Birketts haven't been able to hide its existence. But who would ever buy it? No one in his right mind. Still, what an auction La Española would make. . . ." His voice trailed off into a sigh. I kept the pace, driving steadily at seventy, and asked no questions. "I hope the place isn't too run down," he said a minute or so later. "I hope there's ice for the drinks."

We edged towards Thirlbeck by miles of those tortuous, magical roads of the Lake Country; the mountains humped about us, fantastic shapes, like a strung-out menagerie of child-drawn animals marching along the skyline—not high mountains, really, but the rises and descents so sheer that they seemed to tower above us.

"Theatrical," was Gerald's comment. "We'll have to remember to call them fells," he said, nodding at the mountains. "And the small lakes are tarns. Well, we shall make mistakes, but then, here all visitors are contemptible tourists. I know an art dealer—odd sort—who comes up here every year for fell walking. I took the trouble to telephone him before we left. He's heard of Thirlbeck, of course, but he doesn't *know* anything about it. It's just a name on a map, in a valley that's almost completely bounded by the national park. My friend once wrote and asked to come onto the estate. He got a less than polite letter warning him of legal action if he tried it. When they say trespassers will be prosecuted they *mean* it. Oh, Jo, I wish we'd *get* there; it's been a long day. I've never much cared for the Lake District. Too violent. Too much rain."

"And this is my first time here. Funny, I really don't know England at all. It's shameful, but on holidays I always shot off to

Paris and Rome and Madrid to look at museums and churches."
The thought came sharply, unexpectedly. "Gerald, have I spent too
much of my life with my nose pasted against the display cases in
museums? I'm twenty-seven—don't laugh! It sounds young to you.
But quite suddenly I'm beginning to feel that I've missed out on
something. And I haven't really any idea what it is."

"Why don't you marry Harry Peers? You could have the Metropolitan Museum *and* a suite at the top of the Hotel Pierre. You
could *buy* those little pieces of Chinese porcelain, instead of just
looking at them. Perhaps Harry can give you all the worlds you
think you might have missed."

"What's wrong about that idea, Gerald, is that Harry hasn't asked
me to marry him. But yes, I think I would if he finally decided that
I was right. Because he'd want it to be for good—and forever. His
values are still working-class. He'd never gamble on marriage the
way he does in the property market."

"Well, then, he's a bit of a fool, something I didn't think I'd ever
say of Harry Peers. If he won't gamble on you, Jo, he *is* a fool."

I smiled. "Gerald, you're kind. That will make reading his doings
in the gossip columns a little easier."

Perhaps I was thinking too much of Harry, but then the bend in
the road at that particular point was very sharp. I was almost on
top of the other car before I saw it and applied the brakes sharply.
"Sorry," I said to Gerald. "But he's absolutely crawling along."

"Yes. . . . It would have been a pity."

"What would have been a pity?"

"If you'd run into the back of a . . . well, I'd guess it could be
about a 1931 Bentley. Beautiful condition, isn't it?"

I dropped back. We were within ten miles of Kesmere, the town
closest to Thirlbeck, and for all I knew, there wouldn't be a stretch
of road on which it would be safe to pass before then. The bends
were sharp and numerous. I sighed; it would soon be dusk.

Then the Bentley, a convertible with the top down, pulled over
to the side and stopped. I saw the driver signalling me to pass with
an impatient gesture. I had the impression of a youngish man with
careless, tow-coloured hair. I saluted to thank him, and drove on.

We went about two miles farther, dropping down almost to the
floor of the valley, and once again I had to touch the brakes quickly.
Both of us had almost missed it—a break in the high stone wall we

187

had been following for about half a mile and, between crumbling stone pillars unpleasantly topped by barbed wire, a strong pair of galvanized iron-mesh gates. Behind the wall, which was also spiked with barbed wire, were the ruins of a gatehouse. A bleak, rather crudely lettered sign hung on the gates.

THIRLBECK
STRICTLY PRIVATE
TRESPASSERS WILL BE PROSECUTED

I looked at Gerald. "This is it?" The road beyond the gatehouse seemed barely more than a half-overgrown track, rising at an impossibly steep angle between hand-cut stone walls.

"Has to be." Gerald drew a deep breath. "Good grief—do you suppose this is the *main* entrance?" He was fumbling in his jacket pocket. "Must say his directions weren't very explicit. . . . Where's that letter?"

I was out of the car by now, and Gerald had wound down his window. "This has to be his back door," I said. I was rattling the chain and lock that secured the gates and looking beyond them to the ruined lodge, which must once have been quite beautiful. Then I saw, propped against its side wall, the rusted remains of heavy wrought-iron gates, a tracery of design through them, and what might be part of a crest. "I hope his front door is more welcoming. We'll have to go on, Gerald. I'm sorry."

He had found the letter. "Yes—he says go through Kesmere and take the right. . . . Oh, well, we'll ask when we get there."

I took one last look at the road and saw that its paving had been hand laid, as were the walls. There was a kind of lordliness in that, a memory, even, of the days when labour had been so cheap; and now the weeds grew through the stones, and the noble emblem on the great gates had rusted into anonymity.

FOR all its splendour, the Bentley had a noisy engine; I heard it coming before it rounded the last bend. It stopped in front of the big gates, and the man got out. He looked less young, less sporty now. He wasn't old or even middle-aged, but it was a tired face, a thin, straight-cut mouth, and weather wrinkles about the grey eyes. He had heavy brows, darker than his tow-coloured hair. He was wearing a thick sweater and stained corduroy pants.

"Do you need help?" It was said rather brusquely, as if he didn't want to waste any time on pleasantries.

Gerald answered. "Lord Askew is expecting us. We—"

"Lord Askew is *expecting* you." He didn't attempt to disguise his sarcasm. "Lord Askew hasn't been here since who knows when."

"You're misinformed." Gerald's tone grew terse. "Lord Askew is in residence, and we are expected this evening. His note says 'go through Kesmere', but we thought this might be a shorter way."

Now the man rounded the car to speak, and I saw a strange softening of that strained face as he looked at Gerald. They were such an odd contrast: the one with the whiff of the farmyard about him and yet driving that elegant Bentley, and Gerald in his London suit. Still, they recognized the basic honesty in each other.

"You know he's here, then? It's hardly been a week."

"He asked me here. I might presume to say I am a friend."

"A friend. I'm surprised to hear he has a friend in England. Well, no matter. I might be able to help you. This road isn't easy, but it is the shorter way by about twelve miles. Saves you going into Kesmere and looping back."

"But the place is padlocked," Gerald said.

"I rent a piece of land from Askew. I need access and have a key." Gerald brightened. "Well, then, let's get on."

The man turned to me. "You used to driving steepish inclines?"

"I've driven mountain roads—I take it all carefully."

"Better watch it up there. It's slippery in places. I wouldn't want the responsibility of sending you over the side of a fell." With this, he brought out a bunch of keys.

I was back in the car, the engine turning over. I didn't want the man to change his mind. "Thank you," I said as he swung the gates open for us and we drew level with him. "How far?"

"About three miles. Over the rise and down again."

We went on, and the dim green beauty would have forced silence on us even if we had not been so tired. There were moss-covered rocks within a grove of larch trees, and everywhere the sound of rushing water, as though a stream accompanied us all the way. The rain had stopped, and a flash of the last of the sun came through the trees. It was a scene from an oriental watercolour—the mossy, green stillness; the rocks, each seemingly placed with its own significance. A thousand men could have taken a thousand

189

years to create it. And it had grown here, naturally, in this remotest part of England.

The shock was all the harsher when we emerged from the larch grove and topped the rise. Here was the roof of heaven. We were almost among the clouds. The fells slipped down into a green pasture, then to the dark beauty of a long, slender tarn. And those unbelievable stone walls marched relentlessly up the sides, into the heights—put there time out of mind to mark one man's land from another's, to keep sheep from straying. How could men have built such straight lines over the roughness of a mountainside, with nothing to guide them but their eyes?

In all this secret place there was only the intensity of the terrain, the sheep grazing by the tarn, and the narrow, stone-lined road winding on forever. I was taking the pace very gently on the steep grade. About a mile down beyond the crest a copse of white birches straddled the road. As we descended into the copse we were in the shadow cast by the opposite fells. Suddenly, in spite of the car heater, it was cold.

Then I saw it—a tall white wraith of a dog who stood for an instant beneath the birches and then took flight straight across our path. I slammed on the brakes. Whether it was weeds beneath our wheels or just the suddenness of the braking, the car slipped sickeningly sideways, sliding too fast down the slope towards the next bend, the wheels locked in a skid. I corrected as much as I could, easing my foot off the brake, doing a kind of manic steering. We grazed the wall with the back fender, and I heard stones topple. Then we were straight again; I put my foot very gently on the brake, and we came to a halt. Without a word to Gerald I turned and looked back; the dog had crossed the road and was almost lost among the birches, the long, high stride like a deer in flight.

It was a time before Gerald spoke. "Jo! What possessed you? Is there something wrong with the car?"

I turned to face him. "You didn't see it—the dog? It took off from the trees straight in front of us! I would have crashed right into it!"

"The dog? *What* dog? I didn't see a dog."

"Gerald, it was a very large dog, a whitish dog with long legs. You had to have seen it!"

He took a cigarette from his case and lit it. The trembling of his

190

hands told me that he did not believe me; he had seen nothing. "I must have nodded off, Jo, dear. No, I missed the dog. Let's get on, then, shall we? It's getting dark. It can't be much farther."

The words were spoken with infinite kindness. He was prepared to give me the benefit of the doubt or at least not question me further. But it was impossible to believe that so close to the end of the journey, in such a place as this, he had nodded off in sleep. My eyes had seen what his had not. That also was hard to believe.

We went on, and very soon the house became visible about another mile away. As the mist reached us and moved before us the house kept appearing, vanishing, and reappearing—a stone pile, a formidable and strangely beautiful outline in the settling dusk. I wished Gerald would speak; I thought perhaps I was imagining this also.

He did, and his words reflected my own sense of unease, but at least he saw what I did. "I would feel better if there was even a light," he said. "I suppose they *do* have electricity."

"It isn't quite dark yet."

"It feels dark."

The valley floor widened as we drew nearer the house; here were meadows where cattle grazed. Around the house itself was a parkland of ancient trees flushed with the first green of spring. The tarn drifted off into a slim, dark finger close to the walls of a dark and tangled outer garden. Farther on, in what was meant to be the formal garden, daffodils now held sway, thousands of them, rampant, wild, thin little things, growing weaker with the years. Quite abruptly we reached a wide gravelled area, weed infested, in front of the house. Half-obliterated paths led off towards the lake and a forest of untamed rhododendrons. "Well," Gerald said, "this has to be Thirlbeck. And . . . yes, it *is* worth seeing!"

It was a magnificent piece of domestic Tudor architecture, loosely wedded to a rough stone peel tower that must have been some centuries older. The house would have been built in Elizabeth's reign, I guessed, when the noblemen, beginning to feel some security, no longer enclosed themselves in castles and fortresses. It was a house of windows, in those times a sign of wealth—tall, mullioned windows, thrusting out in square bays and rising a full two storeys. It was beautifully proportioned; its builder had borne in mind that its origins were firmly rooted in that crumbling stone

192

tower which must have been the refuge of the whole manor at the times of the border raiders. There was still a strong sense of the wildness of Scotland even in this graceful structure.

"And to think it's been here so long, and no one seems to know about it—or care," I said softly.

As we sat, feasting our eyes, a door opened. A light shone on the steps, and suddenly what seemed like a dozen enormous shapes came bounding towards the car with a silent, deadly kind of speed. Within seconds the great white hounds were all about us—not really more than eight, I thought, though they seemed more. They were the largest dogs I had ever seen—at least three feet high at their shoulders; they stared at us—huge heads on long necks, deeply whiskered brows, with hairy, bristly faces and little beards. Long, thin tails curled over those powerful but slender backs.

Gerald said faintly, "One might have expected it. These, without doubt, are the hounds of the Birketts."

We didn't move, and the dogs stood motionless, their eyes fixed intently on us. It seemed an interminable time before a tall lean man with faintly hunched shoulders started down the steps. As he drew near, Gerald rolled down the window a few inches.

"Is it safe, Robert?"

The man bent to our level. "The dogs? My dear Gerald, they're gamboling puppies. I'm glad you made it before dark. I saw your lights up on the edge of the fell. The drive over Brantwick in the dark is not for the timid. How are you, Gerald? Good of you to come. Come in—come in! No, really, the dogs are all right. Here, let me help you with the bags. You're both staying, of course."

He was, as Gerald had promised, completely charming. I slid from the car, and even in the fading light I was aware of his curious combination of silver hair, which must once have been very blond, with a rather dark complexion and brows. An incredibly handsome face. The eyes were light—grey or green—I couldn't tell.

"Gerald seems not about to introduce us. I'm Robert Birkett."

"Joanna Roswell, Lord Askew," I answered. "I work at Hardy's, and I often drive Mr. Stanton—"

I stopped because he had put the suitcases down and was staring at me with strange intentness. "You said Roswell? Are you related to the artist Jonathan Roswell?"

"His daughter. You know him, Lord Askew?"

193

"I used to. But—well, it must be close to thirty years since I last saw him. Of course, he's become famous since then." I smiled now, pleased. So few people seemed to have met my father. He answered my smile. "And your mother—" He stopped abruptly. "How clumsy of me. Please forgive me. She died in that plane crash. I was shocked to read her name in the list. Forgive me," he repeated.

He bent to pick up the cases, and I sensed real distress at what he thought was his blunder. "Well, then," he said quickly, "welcome to Thirlbeck." As Gerald emerged warily from the car Lord Askew called to the hounds. "Ulf, Eldir, Thor, Odin—mind yourselves now!" They moved back obediently.

We followed him towards the house. The double doors had now been opened wide and more lights turned on. I knew, without being able to see her face, that the woman standing in the doorway was beautiful. She carried the assurance of beauty. A sharp wind blowing from the tarn moulded her long, thin pale dress about her body. Her long hair was dark, with a sheen of blue. She was like something from those birch woods, a creature of black and white, with hands whose incredible grace and form I could already see and marvel at.

We had mounted the steps, and Lord Askew paused. "Carlota, may I introduce Miss Joanna Roswell. Miss Roswell, this is the Condesa de Ávila. And this, Carlota, is my friend, Gerald Stanton."

Gerald was gazing at her, enchanted. She smiled, familiar with the effect she had had on him. "Please . . . you must both be tired after that fierce drive." Her speech was almost accentless, with but a trace of Spanish. She moved before us into the great hall. Her dress, high-waisted and long-sleeved, low-cut on a beautiful bosom, was pale champagne in colour. Several of the dogs flanked her silently, seeming for these moments like creatures from a mediaeval tapestry.

The hall was splendid, almost bare of furnishings, but warm with the richness of the intricately carved panelling which reached the full two storeys. The staircase, which split at a landing, went off on two arms to an upper gallery. There was the scent of flowers from a large jar filled with daffodils on a long oak table. There was the brightness of two fires burning in opposite chimneys. There was little else—a few tall, carved oak chairs, one silken rug. And this graceful creature gesturing towards an open door. "Here is a fire

194

and the drinks. Roberto remembers that you like martinis, Mr. Stanton."

I was conscious of two things as I followed: that Gerald had said all Robert Birkett's mistresses had been beautiful, and that the great white dog that had appeared like a phantom in front of the car at the birch copse, the dog that Gerald had not seen, belonged to the family of these great hounds.

CHAPTER TWO

IT WAS grandeur, and the beginning of decay. We sat in the library, and Gerald had his martini exactly as he liked it; the condesa was expert at that. But my heart ached over the ominous stain of damp in the plaster over one corner of the huge room. Save for the fireplace wall and the great oblong windowed alcove, the room was lined with mahogany bookcases with faceted glass fronts, behind which was the dull gleam of gold-stamped bindings. Under the windows were ugly iron radiators, which gave out a faint heat. The chintz covers of the chairs and sofas were thin to the point of shredding, the flowered patterns of fifty years ago badly faded.

I was not part of the conversation; I roamed the room, glass in hand. There was a single tall prunus jar on top of one section of the bookcases, and I was trying to get a closer look at the plum-blossom design, but it was lost high in shadows. I moved slowly around the perimeter of the room and saw, with a sense of sickening disappointment, that in the damp corner the pale vellum bindings of the books were horribly stained. I wondered if they would survive handling. Lord Askew must have watched my progress. "They're all locked, I'm afraid. I must ask where the keys are." He shrugged. "Perhaps no one knows anymore."

A lifting of Gerald's eyebrows told me to mind my own business. But, of course, this *was* our business. The library held more than books. Crowded between the decaying sofas and armchairs, arranged with no eye to displaying them to advantage, were some of the most beautiful pieces of furniture I had ever seen. Mainly French, I thought—Louis XIV and Louis XV—marquetry tables, writing tables, two magnificent bowfront commodes placed awkwardly back to back, some carved gilt chairs with rough string tied across the fronts so that no one would inadvertently sit on them. They stood about like pieces in some fantasy furniture shop, unrelated, a collector's dream, but a guardian's nightmare when one remembered the fatal combination of the invading damp, and the heat from the big iron radiators. The sale of almost any single piece, I guessed, would have brought the money to find and fix the place where the moisture seeped through the wall. Under our feet, as a cushion for the great dogs who lay about, were rugs, most of them Persian. But the big main one before the fire, the one in imminent danger from the spluttering sparks, was surely Aubusson.

I began to be impatient. What else was in this house? And why had no one known that these pieces—a superb collection—were here? But then, given Gerald's story of the Askew family and the isolation of this valley, what might not have come to it unknown and unmarked? I began to realize more fully the implications of Askew's invitation to Gerald, and the thought was enough to drive out all fatigue. I returned now to my seat near the fire, more anxious to listen to the talk.

The firelight lovingly played over the carved wood of the mantel and reached to the outstretched forms of the dogs on each side of Lord Askew's chair. They seemed extraordinarily content, as if in the presence of their master. Yet Askew had returned only a week ago, and surely this great pack could not have travelled the world with him. I mused on them as the talk went on about me. I still wasn't included, but suddenly, like the dogs, I felt content just to be here.

It was strange, then, to see the condesa shiver and lean further towards the fire. Askew also noticed the gesture and was on his feet at once, laying more split logs on the fire. He smiled. "My poor Carlota, it seems a long way from the sun, doesn't it?"

He said nothing more, but she seemed warmed by his words. The look which passed between them was its own communication. She had to love him to be here with him, this far from the sun. She was about forty, I guessed, but she had the smooth grooming of the international beauty whose age is difficult to tell.

The door opened then, and a man said, "Mrs. Tolson wishes to tell you, my lord, that the rooms are ready. She's put the young lady in the Spanish Woman's room."

I glanced at the condesa, wondering if this was some kind of insolent gibe offered to her. But neither she nor Askew reacted with any sign of outrage. Evidently the Spanish Woman referred to was not she, and all of them understood that.

"Has she, indeed?" Askew said. "Not the coziest place, is it?"

"Can't be helped, my lord," the man answered. "It's the driest— at short notice." He didn't look in the least like a servant, with his flannel trousers and a tweed jacket. He was tall, with stooped shoulders, and very powerfully built. He had a mass of dark hair thickly frosted with grey. It was difficult to see his eyes behind his heavy pebble glasses, and his long, dark, rather melancholy face seemed closed against the coming of strangers. I judged him to be a few years older than the earl, but he seemed rocklike and monumental by contrast. "I've got the fires going," the man continued, "and there's three hot-water bottles in the bed. Be comfortable enough, I should say. I've put the young lady's bag there, and Mr. Stanton's is in his room. Anything else, my lord?"

It was the most curious mixture of familiarity and deference. That he was the man in charge of this establishment there was no doubt; that he respected the titular owner was not open to question either.

Lord Askew gestured with his glass. "Nothing, Tolson, nothing. You've managed very well, as always. Thank you."

The man stepped back, closing the door without another word.

"That was George Tolson. You'll get used to him—Cumberland independence and all. The place couldn't have held together without him all these years. He's been steward and handyman and bookkeeper all in one. He believes I never should have left, but my coming back makes problems. More fires, more hot water. He's never been a butler, though he's trying his best now. . . ." Askew paused, and in that instant his eyes seemed to go beyond the house, to the lake and the surrounding fells and dales.

"There must have been Tolsons here as long as there have been Birketts. Two of his sons have tenancies of land within this valley, two more have farms at Thirldale, just beyond the gates. That's about the area of the original estate. We've sold off a lot of other land. . . . I wish the entail would allow me to sell to the Tolsons; they deserve to own the land they farm." He nodded, as if reinforcing his own words. "The Tolsons are strong men, all of them, intelligent and competent. Tough, as farmers here have to be. George Tolson and his brother, Edward, were just a few years ahead of me.

197

My father sensed the good material he had, and he saw that they both got to the grammar school in Kesmere. Edward went on to become a solicitor—my father got him articled to a London firm. He was more than a success. Handled all the estate business until he died about two years ago. But George Tolson never had any idea of leaving Thirlbeck. He's become quite a patriarch over the years— I swear he must have chosen all the wives for his sons. If he did, he showed eminently good sense. They're a clannish lot; they've kept this valley just about totally closed off. That's the way my father wanted it, that's the way he trained Tolson. I've sometimes thought how much better it would have been for my father and Thirlbeck if Tolson had been his son. . . ." He brought his lips together in a wry smile, switching the subject off.

And then the noises began—a heavy metallic clanging. Gerald and I straightened and glanced at Askew. He gestured to dismiss the sound. "That will be Tolson closing the metal shutters he's had put on the windows on this floor. Part of his idea of security. One of his sons, Ted, fitted them. He is a very handy mechanic as well as a farmer. The Tolsons are almost self-sufficient. One of the granddaughters lives here in the house, and others have come in to help since we arrived. Carlota thinks—"

Suddenly Askew rose, and the dogs all scrambled to their feet. It was like seeing an army come alive. He had evidently decided against telling us what the condesa thought about Tolson and his family. "Shall we go up, then? Give you a chance to get settled before dinner." Then he looked down at the condesa. "You stay, my love. No need to leave the fire. I won't be long."

She stretched her slender body in the big chair, and the shining black hair fell forward, an incredibly sensuous movement. "Will you pour me a whisky before you go, Roberto—please?"

She accepted it from him with a charming smile, and then her eyes were drawn back to the fire, as if it were a substitute sun.

GERALD and Askew went ahead into the hall. At the landing, where the two arms of the staircase branched, they waited for me.

"Mostly sixteenth century—except for the peel tower, which might go back to the twelfth," Askew was explaining. "The townspeople used to come out here to the tower for protection from the border raiders. Very feudal. The Birketts exploited their power in every way possible, I'm afraid. The title dates from Elizabeth's time, and the first earl built this house. Modern conveniences were introduced about fifty years ago—electricity, bathrooms, and the heating, which never really has worked. But it's better than outright freezing. I'm afraid the whole place needs a complete overhaul, but it won't be done in my time. If it is *ever* done. . . ."

"What will happen to it?" I couldn't bear Askew's detached tone.

He shrugged. "I expect it will fall down when there isn't money to keep it together and when the Tolsons' ingenuity and energy is exhausted. Perhaps the National Trust will want to preserve it. I haven't offered it, and I don't know if there's enough money to endow it or that I care to spend that much on it. Perhaps you can end up giving too much to a mere building. Well, it doesn't concern me greatly. Shall we go on?"

He had treasure all about him, a truly great inheritance, and he didn't care. For this, I felt myself almost hating him as he led the way up to the gallery, then to Gerald's room. It was comfortable—in its masculine, red-plush Victorian style—rather than imposing; and it was stuffy. The fire must have burned there all day. "I thought you'd find it warmer than most we have to offer, Gerald. Bathroom's through here. Miss Roswell, I think Tolson means you to use this bathroom, too—there's a door from the passage."

Gerald waved airily. "Jo will manage, Robert. At Hardy's we bring them up to manage. And she's been *very* well brought up."

I felt my anger at Askew extend to Gerald also. He didn't have to make me appear such an earnest child. And yet, I supposed that was how I often did appear. When Askew gestured to show me to my own room I followed silently.

We came out on the gallery above the hall again. Askew paused. "Let me see. . . . Yes, this is it. I haven't had time since we returned to see all the rooms." He opened the door and waited for me to precede him. But the involuntary stiffening of his body warned me that something had disturbed him. "I hadn't remembered it quite like this," he said, as if he were talking to himself.

It seemed an immense room, its size increased by the fact that only one light burned there—an absurdly modern lamp perched on a stool by the bed. The shadows, therefore, were black and deep, and the glow from the leaping flames of two opposite fireplaces didn't bridge the darkness between them.

"Can you stand it? Perhaps I should ask Tolson . . ."

"Please, don't." I moved past him, fascinated by the room's sombre magnificence. A huge four-poster bed, hung with dark blue velvet curtains, hardly impinged on its space. There was a long oak stretcher table in the big rectangle of bay windows, and a straight-backed chair at one end. A tapestry-covered chair stood before one of the fireplaces, with a footstool beside it, and a carved oak chest flanked the second fireplace. A few pieces of blue Delftware were the room's only ornaments; the biggest piece, a deep bowl, had been placed in the middle of the table. I moved towards it, and quite distinctly came the sad-sweet smell of last summer's roses. The bowl was full of petals, and I couldn't stop myself from running my hand through them.

It did not seem like a place just disturbed from a period of long neglect. The wax polish on the table shone lustrously, and the Delft pieces had been recently dusted.

"I suppose Tolson's right. It's dry enough. The chimney probably has a common flue with one of the chimneys in the hall, and Tolson keeps fires there all year round. There are some closets. . . ." He was opening wide doors in the panelling on each side of one of the fireplaces. In the dimness I hadn't noticed the carved wooden knobs indicating the doors. "Shelves this side—hanging on this side." He shrugged. "Well, it will have to do, though I wish Tolson could have managed something a bit less forbidding."

"I like it, Lord Askew."

He glanced at me curiously. "Do you? Shall I draw the curtains? It would make it cozier."

"No, thank you. One gets enough of drawn curtains in London."

We moved towards the windows at the same time. I realized now that this room was directly over the library and shared the same oblong bay of leaded glass windows that faced out across the lake. The rain had cleared, and an icy moonlight struck obliquely through. "Look," I said, "there's snow on the mountain."

"That's Great Birkeld—the highest around here. It catches all the weather. Quite often you can't see it for days at a time because of clouds. The word changeable must have been invented for this country—mist, bright sun, pelting rain, snow, clear moonlight. Heaven knows how the people stand it. I couldn't. . . ."

Three of the dogs had now crossed the room to join him. He

200

stood staring out at the tarn, and the moonlight turned his hair to bright silver. I literally saw a gust of wind ripple along the surface of the lake and heard its moan about the building.

"Mr. Tolson called it the Spanish Woman's room. Why is that?"

Askew fidgeted for a while without attempting a reply. He checked the closet again, as if he were counting the hangers, lighted the candle on the mantel and carried it to the oak chest. "The Spanish Woman . . ." He took a deep breath. "The Spanish Woman was the second countess of Askew. It was a kind of derogatory term given to her in this household where anyone both Catholic and Spanish was not welcome. Her husband, the second earl, was also Catholic—many of the landowners still were Catholic or were changing from Catholic to Protestant and back again according to who was on the throne. But this was Elizabeth's reign, and so the Protestants were in power. The second earl was accused of plotting to put Mary, Queen of Scots, on the throne, and he lost his head on Tower Hill. He was a relic of the old faith, rather a fanatic, I'd judge. Before he inherited the title he spent some years in Spain—at the court of Philip the Second—where he married a Spanish bride. It may have been love, but more likely it was politics. She was a noblewoman, distantly related to Philip, and, of course, Philip hoped to bring England back to Catholicism. He was already preparing to send the Armada. It would be a great help to have a Catholic nobleman and ally here in Cumberland. And if Philip should successfully invade—or if Elizabeth should die and leave Mary the throne—the earl would have become one of the premier earls of England, instead of a minor border lord. Then, too, his Spanish bride came with a dowry and a promise of large wealth to follow. She joined her husband here just before he was arrested and taken off for trial. In the little time they had spent together she had become pregnant with a possible Catholic heir. Her husband's brother, who would have succeeded if the marriage had been without issue, was Protestant.

"Stories were spun about her over the years, how many true, one doesn't know. It seems that her brother-in-law sent her own servants away, and she was left entirely alone—no friend but a young English serving boy who had been with her husband on his travels and who spoke a little Spanish. There must have been precious little comfort or kindness for her. One imagines—I've imagined—how frightened she must have been, wondering if Elizabeth's commissioners were riding north to question her or if the next mouthful of food was poisoned. They say that for distraction she took to walking high and far on the Brantwick road."

Suddenly he turned and motioned to me. "Look at the tarn down there—innocent, isn't it? Well, she drowned in the tarn. Some were prepared to swear that she had been murdered by her brother-in-law. Poor, lost, lonely little Spanish Woman."

It was the first time I really liked him. As he spoke I knew that the Spanish Woman was a real person to him, not a dry family legend. He pictured her growing heavy with child, a political pawn, longing for the sound of her own language, the dry heat of the Spanish plains. She must have written her sad letters at the table here, sat in that chair by the fire—the chair with the footstool that suggested she had been a small woman. Then I shook my head; I was falling into the earl's mood. It was impossible that no one had disturbed the arrangement of this room in all these years, that that had really been her chair.

Beside me Askew stirred, as if waking from a dream. "You'll be all right here? Perhaps I shouldn't have told you—"

"I'm glad you did. She has to have some friends, doesn't she—the Spanish Woman?"

His smile thanked me for sharing his dream, and I was lost to that smile, as I was sure many women had been. I began to understand very well the presence of his own Spanish woman, the modern beauty who had followed him to this remote, cold world. It would be easy enough to follow Robert Birkett if he asked it.

"Come, dogs." They rose as one and went with him.

TOLSON hadn't become so much the butler that he attempted to unpack for guests. I sorted my clothes between the two closets. One had a wooden rod on which padded hangers rested, and at the back were stout oak pegs which served as hooks, probably there from the time the room and the closets had been panelled.

I wasn't without a sense of clothes—no daughter of Vanessa's could have been. I even had a touch of her flamboyance in that respect, which Harry Peers always found amusing and unexpected. The long skirt I put on was of brilliant orange quilted cotton, and I wore it with a yellow high-necked sweater. Tied about my waist was a long black sash I had bought for a few pounds in one of Hardy's auctions of Victorian costumes. I also wore the amber brooch which had been in Vanessa's handbag on the day of the plane crash. I wore it for her, and with love—the gold and amber had seemed so much a part of Vanessa's personality. "It shall be yours one day, my pet," she had promised.

The gong sounded for dinner, and I combed my hair quickly and added a little more pale lipstick. It wasn't a beautiful face in the mirror, not beautiful the way Vanessa's had been or in the classic mould of that Spanish beauty downstairs at the library fire. "A twentieth-century face you've got, Jo," Harry had once said. From someone, perhaps my father, I had received the blessing of dark brows and lashes, looking odd with the light-coloured eyes, neither green nor grey nor blue, and the blonde hair. From Vanessa came the mouth, but wider than hers and curving—perhaps to my detriment—to every mood. I made a grimace in the mirror for bothering about what couldn't be changed, and hurried downstairs.

THE dining room was not crowded as the library had been. There was another long oak table, which could only have fitted into a house of this size—Jacobean, I guessed—with a dozen or so chairs which matched it. There were two long sideboards on which the red pilot lights of electric hot trays shone eerily, some beautiful gilt-framed mirrors, and some very ordinary Chinese vases. Once more, all the dogs were grouped about the fire.

Dinner was, unexpectedly, very good. There was onion soup, hot garlic bread, chicken in a sauce that only a serious cook could make, the sort of pastry one saw on the trays of the most expensive restaurants, and a beautiful German wine poured into engraved glasses. I hardly spoke through the whole meal; I was hungry, and the food was delicious. I said so with no trace of false politeness.

"Tolson's granddaughter does most of it," Askew said. "Jessica. She's a natural cook and brilliant, too. Won a scholarship to Cambridge. She didn't take it, though I'm not sure why. Undoubtedly she's her grandfather's pet. He says she just prefers to stay here. She's quite high-strung. . . . I suppose they're afraid of what will happen to her out in the world. Tolson said she was quite seriously ill about three years ago. A pretty little thing, she is. Must be going on twenty now."

The condesa smiled. "Roberto, she will marry someone her formidable grandfather approves of, and live very close by. Wherever one goes in this house, there she is—"

"She helps with the work," Askew interrupted. "A great deal, as far as I can see. Why shouldn't she be around?"

"Housework on the top of the peel tower? I've seen her there."

"I wish you hadn't. The peel tower isn't safe. But then a bright, imaginative child probably has romantic fantasies."

"She is not a child, Roberto," the condesa said quietly. "Highstrung, brilliant—a wonderful cook? Yes. A child? No."

He shrugged, as if to end talk of Jessica, and turned to the dogs. "Extraordinary lot, aren't they?"

"More than that," Gerald said. "I almost had Joanna turn the car around when they appeared. It's hardly . . . well, it's hardly *decent*, my dear Robert. So many of them, and so huge!"

"Don't blame me. They're Tolson's dogs, but since the instant I arrived they unaccountably attached themselves to me. There have always been Irish wolfhounds at Thirlbeck. Somehow Tolson managed to feed and keep alive one breeding pair during the war."

Gerald leaned forward. "There's something particularly important about them?"

"I don't really know." He seemed embarrassed. "Tradition has it that there have always been wolfhounds here. They're a very ancient breed, said to be the largest dog in the world, and famed in Celtic literature for bringing down enormous stags."

"Do they always stay together?" I asked. "None of them ever goes off alone?"

"Not that I've noticed. Always seem to be eight sticking by me."

Then I was aware that his look hadn't been one of embarrassment but of unease. He was gentle with the hounds and offhandedly affectionate. He wasn't afraid of them, but I had the feeling that he wished they weren't there, which was the same feeling I experienced when he had said they never went off alone. I shivered, and hoped that no one had noticed. One of these dogs, I would swear, had dashed across the road before my eyes at the birch copse that evening, nearly causing me to crash.

"I don't know why Tolson bothers with metal shutters," Gerald said. "These dogs would seem better security than armed guards."

"I would not interfere with his arrangements," Askew replied.

"Nor would I, Robert." Gerald beamed over his wineglass. He was at his best at this time of evening, with good food and drinks inside him. His pleasant well-preserved face glowed. All he needed now was a little Mozart.

The wine had brought other thoughts to the condesa. "Roberto tells me your father lives in Mexico," she said to me. "He is fortunate—always the sun. And there is quite amusing society in Acapulco. Does your father go there in the season?"

I almost laughed. "No, never. He lives in a very remote hacienda south of Taxco. He never leaves it, if he can help it."

She shuddered delicately at the thought. "Never?"

"His health's no good in damp places, and sea level in Mexico is very humid."

"I remember he didn't like damp places," Askew said slowly. "He still has that weak chest, then? It rained so much when he was here, and he was trying to paint and not succeeding at all."

"He was here? *Here*—at Thirlbeck?"

"Of course. That's when I knew him." He looked at me in puzzled surprise. "He and Vanessa rented that lodge by the gate where you came in. It wasn't a ruin at that time, though the roof did leak. I would have fixed it if they had been going to stay on. But it wasn't right for either of them—for different reasons. They left with the first snow, and I left soon after." He looked directly at me. "They never told you they were here?"

I shook my head. "All my mother said was that they had rented a cottage in the Lake District the summer the war ended."

"Odd. Well, we had all survived a war, and we were rather heady with the triumph of that simple fact. We were reckless with what remained of the wine cellar my father laid down. I was grateful to them for being here then—it was my one attempt to live at Thirlbeck, and they were good friends, though they were both quite a lot younger than I. They made my attempt bearable, even if in the end it didn't work out."

I couldn't help seeking Gerald's eyes across the table. His rosy face had become almost pallid; I hoped I hadn't betrayed the same shock while Askew was speaking. Gerald and I had thought of Thirlbeck as uncharted ground, and already we had seen treasures here. And Vanessa, whom we both believed we knew so well, had once spent a summer and autumn among these lovely things. In

205

those days, even with limited knowledge, she would have recognized the best of the pieces—who could have forgotten them? Yet she had said nothing of this place—nothing.

WE WENT to the drawing room for coffee. By now I think both Gerald and I had come almost to expect what we found—a room only a little less crowded than the library, herding together beautiful pieces without any thought of display. I ran my finger over the dusty tops of a few of them—commodes, pier tables, gilt wood and tapestry chairs with the same rough string tied across them to prevent their use. A few sofas and chairs, covered in the same faded chintz as those in the library, were there to be sat on. The rest of the contents of the room—if it ever came to auction—would make one of the most exciting sales of fine French furniture Hardy's had ever mounted. I could have cried with impatience at the elaborate game we all played—no one mentioning even the smallest of the magnificent pieces while we drank coffee from inexpensive earthenware cups.

I looked again around the room and realized what was missing from the whole house. While there were beautiful mirrors, there were no pictures, not even portraits of ancestors. Their total absence made me think that in some other room with metal shutters there would be frames and frames stacked against the walls, and among them there might be just one picture that came up to the quality of the pieces we saw about us here.

There was a restlessness in the room, as if we were all holding back from saying what we most wanted to say. Gerald and the condesa were seated on a sofa, talking of nothing that much interested them. The condesa was stitching an intricate petit point design. Askew smiled a little as he stood beside me at the coffee service, and nodded towards the condesa. "Unexpected, isn't it? I always see her as the sort who should be carrying skis or skindiving equipment—and she is expert in both those sports. But whatever part of the world she is in, out comes the tapestry, and you can be sure that every man in the room will eventually gravitate to watch the progress of the work. But how demure she looks, doesn't she? Like a girl in a convent."

"Yes," I said lamely. I was feeling a small jealousy of her, but hoped it didn't show. Why did I suppose she was rich as well as

206

beautiful? Because she had that carelessly elegant look that is only produced by a great deal of time and money?

Askew refilled my cup, attending to me as if he thought I had been neglected. As he poured he said, "So they teach you well at Hardy's, do they?"

"They do their best," I said carefully. Was he expecting that I would be the one to break the silence about the furniture? "They try to find out what you might be good at—if anything. You spend your time on the front counter answering questions and, when someone brings something in for a valuation, phoning for the experts to come in from the various departments. Sometimes the oddest pieces turn up. You learn what you can by handling, seeing, listening."

He nodded. "What do *you* handle mostly—pictures?"

"Ceramics. What I'd really like to do is oriental ceramics, but that's very specialist. I suppose everyone in ceramics ends up by going back to the oriental things. Oh . . . I'm sorry."

"Sorry? Why?"

"I'm talking shop. Gerald thinks it's the worst form of bad manners. Fishing, he says . . . trying to smell out if someone might be persuaded to put something up for sale."

He laughed aloud, a spontaneous sound that caused Gerald and the condesa to raise their heads, and a faint flush appeared on the condesa's pale olive skin. She didn't much like me, I thought, and it made me feel better about my own burst of jealousy of her.

"Gerald, your protégée here has just told me she's been fishing and that you wouldn't approve. Shall we make her fishing worthwhile? Do you think she'd like to see La Española?"

Gerald was trying to control his excitement. "It *is* here, then?"

"Of course. Where else would it be? It will stay here now as long as it exists or the house exists. But I can't help wondering if the curse will finally leave La Española when this house tumbles before the bulldozers or gives up to the weather."

The condesa gestured impatiently. "Roberto, you make too much of this silly superstition. If you were determined, it could be sold tomorrow." She slipped the embroidery frame into its bag. "Come, show Mr. Stanton. If it is never to leave this house, it may be his only chance." She had neatly cut me out by making this showing of what they called La Española for Gerald's pleasure, not for mine.

Askew led us to another room which opened directly off the great hall, opposite the dining room. This one was panelled in linen-fold—wood beautifully carved to resemble linen scrolls. Against one wall, shelves had been built, on most of which were thick boxes—not books—bound in red leather, with dates stamped in gold that had dulled with the years. Probably estate records, I thought. At some date in this century the binding had stopped and inexpensive box files filled the lower shelves.

"Just a minute," Askew said. He left us and went to open a green baize door under the staircase, revealing what seemed to be a service passage. "Tolson, are you there?" We heard their voices, and a minute later Askew was back with us. I had a brief glimpse of Tolson's figure in the passage, and I thought there was disapproval in the stare he gave us.

The room was long, lighted only by a single lamp on a large, carved desk. "This is really Tolson's room," Askew said. "He does most of his work here." He nodded towards another desk—a humble, rather battered rolltop. While he spoke he felt for a spot at the side of the carved mantel; then he went and touched another place in the panelling itself.

"Such elementary precautions," he said, "but Tolson insists on them. I had to have him turn the alarm system off." He had opened a small door in the panelling, and he fumbled within the cavity. A light came on, showing a velvet-lined interior behind a thick glass screen. Wordlessly the three of us moved closer.

It was a blue-white diamond, roughly octahedral in shape, about an inch and a half at its widest part. It was touched at four points by simple cage grips and strung on a gold chain of medium weight. Only its natural planes had been polished, and the stone itself was relatively uncut. Still, with only these large surfaces revealed, the refraction of light from its heart, the inner facets, was of extraordinary brilliance. It seemed too big to be a gemstone. There was something almost crude in its size, and yet it lay there so quietly, so innocently, on its black velvet cushion. Askew swung open the glass screen. He lifted the massive thing on its chain and swung it gently. The light sprang from it as from a living flame.

"La Española—the Spanish Woman," he said softly. "When the countess came to Thirlbeck from Philip's court she and the jewel she brought as part of her dowry were called the same thing. How

208

barbaric she must have thought the manners of this household."

Gerald leaned closer. "May I . . . ?" Askew slipped the gold chain over his hand, and Gerald carried it to the desk, where the light fell directly upon it. "I wondered if I would ever see it again," he mused, turning the great stone in his fingers. "I remember when, in the thirties, your father sent it to Hardy's and there were no buyers." Gerald's eyes never left the stone.

"He was right to try to get rid of it, but it wasn't the time to sell, and the reputation of the wretched thing went before it."

"You might have had it cut into small stones and disposed of. None of the buyers would have known they were getting part of the reputation of La Española." Gerald glanced up inquiringly at Askew. "Somewhere about two hundred carats, isn't it?"

"The last jeweller who examined it gave it a few more, but he made no offer. That was after the Terpolini affair, and the publicity had been enormous. So here it lies in its primitive little cave, uninsured, because I can't afford the insurance. It would be absurdly easy to steal, except that no one wants to touch it."

"Two hundred carats," Gerald mused. "Worth . . . well, four or five thousand pounds a carat. There's a million pounds, and its value is rising every day. And no one wants to *steal* it?"

"That's about it, Gerald." Now Askew touched it, his long fingers slightly reluctant in the movement. "The Spanish Woman brought it to the Birketts, and it seems she means to keep it forever."

"How so?" I was now spellbound by the sight of the gem.

"Philip the Second wanted to send her to her English husband with something substantial as evidence of good faith. He had the stone polished just a little and mounted virtually in its rough state. That, of course, makes it more valuable now. It's ready for all that a modern cutter can take from it. Well, it might have been intended for her husband and his family, but she never let it go—the little Spanish girl. About seventeen, they think she was when she came here. Old enough for those times, I suppose. Then Elizabeth's men beheaded her husband, and she was alone. She was in mortal danger, and she must have known it."

His voice now had taken on the distant tone it had had upstairs. "The story goes that in calm weather she would have the serving boy, who had been her husband's favourite, row her on the tarn. He must have grown attached to her. They say she wore the jewel

always, a kind of talisman because it had come from Philip. She waited endlessly for word from him—instructions as to what she must do, where she must go; but I can't help thinking she hoped to be summoned back to Spain. So far as we know, Philip sent no word. She just waited—waited to know if her child would be a boy and therefore third earl of Askew, displacing her Protestant brother-in-law. The brother-in-law, another Robert Birkett by name, evidently intended that the child should never be born."

It was odd, how detached he sounded, as if he weren't speaking of his own family. "They say that when she was out on the tarn he rowed after her, taking a younger brother with him. The Spanish Woman was not to survive, but no one knows precisely what happened, of course. They must have beaten the boy first and then the Spanish Woman. They couldn't let her drown and the jewel go with her. She must have struggled fiercely, but the thing was finally taken from her neck. Afterwards someone whispered that he had heard the Spanish Woman's voice shouting what sounded like the motto of the Birketts—probably she reverted to Latin, the only language she had in common with anyone here. It's as wild and aggressive a motto as any untamed border lord would wish—"

"The motto?" I asked.

"*Caveat raptor*—roughly, 'Who seizes, beware.' Did she mean the jewel, her life, the life of her child? Did she even say it? Her body was never recovered, and the new earl had the jewel. He simply said she had not worn it that day. No one believed that part of it, and they began to believe that the boy had survived, a witness and perhaps the origin of the stories that began to fly about."

Askew shrugged. "The story fattened, and a curse became attached to the jewel, especially when the earl broke his neck after a drunken tumble on the stairs. He had been, they said, displaying the jewel to one of Elizabeth's council members."

Askew leaned back against the desk. "His brother, the fourth earl, died peacefully in his bed, but not before the jewel, along with anything else portable, had been taken from the house by border raiders. The odd thing was that the leader of the raid never got beyond this valley. His horse stumbled, and rolled on him. There seemed no reason for it. He was left there to die, and none of his party would touch the jewel. There was blood from his pierced lungs on La Española when it came back to Thirlbeck."

211

Now I could make myself touch it. Somehow I had expected it to feel warm, as if it had just left the throat of the Spanish Woman. "Could they really have abandoned something like this with a dying man?"

"So they say. They must have begun to believe the motto and the curse. The Spanish Woman, whom they wanted to forget, was a permanent legend. A stone monument was placed near the tarn by someone who wished her passage to be marked. But as many times as the earl removed it, it reappeared—or another like it. He began to see that he could not lay the ghost, and so he left her monument alone to let the grass grow up around it.

"And La Española stayed on. There were several attempts on it over the years—none successful. There was a serious attempt in the twenties, but the thieves took the way out of the valley that you came in by today. At the worst bend, where the road cuts through the birch copse, they went out of control. Their car crashed and burned, and they with it. The diamond, of course, survived. After that my father lodged it in a safe-deposit vault in Manchester. It was there three years before there was an attempt, by tunnelling, on the vaults. The thieves' tunnel collapsed, killing them all. La Española came out covered with dirt, and shining just as ever. We brought it back to Thirlbeck then. The Manchester bank wasn't anxious to have it again. I made only one effort to sell it after that. And that was when the Terpolini affair burst on the world."

"Terpolini?" I said. "The opera singer? Isn't she dead?"

Askew looked at me. "I keep forgetting you're so much younger. No, not dead, but she might as well be. She was at the height of a very sensational career, and everything she did was news. She was the mistress of the oilman, Georgiadas. He was—still is—strongly superstitious, but he believed then that the gods looked with particular favour on him. Until he encountered La Española. I had sold it to him subject to expert examination, and Tolson brought it to Milan. It was everything they had hoped for. It was to be cut, but Constanzia Terpolini asked to wear it just as it is, uncut, when she opened the season at La Scala. The papers were full of the story; she was photographed, in costume, wearing it. But the next day papers were full of the story of her fall down that long flight of stairs in the last act of *Turandot*. They had to

212

bring down the curtain. She never saw another curtain go up. A fractured spine, which paralyzed her from the neck down. On the same day, Georgiadas's only son was lost in a sailing accident off Crete. That was the day the gods really turned their backs on Georgiadas. Soon after, he had La Española returned to me, and Tolson brought it back to Thirlbeck."

The lines in Askew's face appeared sharper now. "What's the capital gains tax now, Gerald?" he asked. "Thirty per cent? I could live quite a long time on what was left if I could sell it—if La Española were not drenched in superstition and greed. And so my unfortunate heir will have to scratch about for the death duties on something *he* won't be able to sell or insure either."

Carlota spoke. "If you had only the will, Roberto, to find someone to cut it in Amsterdam, it could be sold. The Birketts would be rid of La Española at last, with no auction, no publicity."

Askew gathered up the gem and ended one of La Española's few moments of exposure to light and admiration. "And will you fly with me to Amsterdam, Carlota? Will you find the cutter who will touch it?" He snapped the panel shut. "I think we might just leave La Española in peace." He turned back to us. "I do, however, have one other thing that could stand beside La Española in importance and value. What would you say to a Rembrandt, Gerald?"

"A Rembrandt?" Gerald looked across at me, warning me to stay quiet, as a charge of excitement ran between us. I felt my mouth go dry. And I wondered again if Vanessa had known of this also.

"A legacy which has come to us in a perfectly ordinary fashion, Gerald. Did you know that my grandfather was only a cousin to the fifteenth earl? He never expected to inherit, but the Birketts seem to be unfortunate in losing their direct descendants. My grandfather had been a prosperous farmer, with an interest in some small mines, and he ran a few coasters out of Whitehaven. He liked to travel with them himself and often went over to the Continent— even more after he had met Margeretha van Huygens, the only child of a rich burgomaster in Rotterdam. They married. And naturally, on the death of her parents, she inherited everything. All the French furniture that the van Huygenses had picked up after the French Revolution, when fleeing émigrés had to sell good pieces cheaply. With the furniture came a collection of Dutch pictures—most of them pretty dull scenes of cows and windmills. We

213

don't know how the van Huygenses acquired the Rembrandt. But in my grandmother's day Rembrandt wasn't in fashion, and it must have hung at Thirlbeck in a dark passage. . . . It *is* possible, isn't it, Gerald, that a Rembrandt could exist that has never been catalogued?" Askew asked.

"It's entirely possible, Robert. There is no central registry of works of art, no record of when they are sold or to whom. Even the museums don't have to tell us what they buy and sell or what they pay. It's a state of chaos which would send the normal businessman mad. Yet we live with it, because there is a general unwillingness to admit that art is big business."

Askew said, "I've had Tolson bring it out of the room where he stored all the pictures at the beginning of the war." He began to lead us across the long room. In its darkness we could see the dull outlines of a picture that hung on the farthest wall.

I thought Gerald walked with a kind of stiffness, as if the same cramping excitement I was feeling had gripped him also. If what Askew said was true, this remote house would suddenly witness the coming and going of experts to authenticate the picture, photos of it would appear on the desks of museum directors, and it would arrive at last in the special high-security rooms on the top floor of Hardy's. Television lights would go on in the great saleroom, and the world's press would gather. If the buyer was foreign, there would be the usual appeal for a fund to save it for the nation, and Robert Birkett would be condemned for selling away a national treasure. No wonder Gerald walked warily.

He stopped. "I can't see it, Robert. Aren't there lights?"

Askew pressed a switch, but that only activated the modern extension-arm lamp perched on the rolltop desk. The sconces on the wall remained dark. "Damn!" he said. "I was stupid to let Tolson hang it there—I forgot about light. Well, perhaps we can tilt this one?"

"No, don't," Gerald said. "I don't want my first sight of it spoiled. We'll look at it tomorrow morning." His tone was curiously flat.

Suddenly the excitement was gone. I was more than ever conscious that I was tired and chilled. We said good night to the condesa and Askew, and I could feel them staring after us as we went up the stairs. When we reached the gallery Askew said something, and the condesa's voice rose in sharp protest. As I glanced down

214

she had already started up, but at the landing she turned to take the other arm of the staircase leading to the opposite wing of the house. By the time we reached Gerald's door she had vanished into the shadows.

"Can I come in for a moment, Gerald?"

He nodded, as if he had known I would say that.

"IT'S NO use asking, Jo. I *don't know* why Vanessa never said anything. She must have had a very good reason, but we'll never know what it was—not now." He pulled on his cigarette wearily, but I had to talk.

"Perhaps he *asked* her not to. Yes, that would be it. From what I've been hearing, the Birketts all seem a bit touched to me—at least *he* is. Their secrecy about the house, keeping a Rembrandt hidden away. Do you suppose it really is a Rembrandt?"

"My dear Jo, I haven't seen it. There's no reason why it shouldn't be—the van Huygenses could have been of the same family as Constantijn Huygens, who wrote about Rembrandt in his autobiography. Pictures and furniture do get passed on, just taken for granted by the family."

He sat, half hidden behind the haze of cigarette smoke. "A Rembrandt . . . I wonder . . ."

"I don't much like Lord Askew, Gerald—or at least I keep changing my opinion of him. He hates this place, doesn't he? He doesn't care if it falls down. I almost felt he could sell his own grandmother—after all, it was her furniture and pictures."

"And now they're his, to do with as he will. Never forget it, Jo. It's his property. It doesn't matter if we like our clients."

I shrugged. "Of course it doesn't matter. So what if the house does fall down? It is just one of England's least known architectural treasures, stuffed with wonderful furniture—and it *would* cost the price of a Rembrandt to preserve. Who *would* want it, after all?" I wondered why I was arguing with myself, and moved towards the door. "Good night, Gerald. I hope you sleep well."

"Nothing, dear Jo, would keep me awake tonight."

I suddenly thought that I had never seen Gerald look old before. The idea frightened me. I couldn't lose him now—not just after losing Vanessa. I think I would have kissed him then, but for the fact that he might have guessed what was in my mind.

215

I was back in the Spanish Woman's room after bathing in a marble tub of Edwardian proportions when I realized that my handbag and my only cigarettes were downstairs. I had managed to cut down to ten cigarettes a day, but the last and best of them was something I looked forward to. It was after midnight by now—too late to disturb Gerald to ask for his. I went downstairs, hesitating just a little at the thought of the dogs, but there was no sign of them. The lights in the drawing room were still on, and I found my handbag.

I was halfway across the hall when I saw her. She stood in the shadow thrown by the stairs, a girl of perhaps eighteen or nineteen, with a shower of silvery-blonde hair framing a face of childlike delicacy. She seemed very tiny in her short skirt and plain blouse, and she had the porcelain look of a figurine—a complexion which glowed even in the shadows, and red lips that curved upward in an almost fixed half smile. She regarded me calmly, with neither curiosity nor surprise. I knew then this was Jessica, Tolson's granddaughter. I moved towards her, meaning to speak some greeting and wondering why it was I, and not this slender girl, who should feel discomforted. I just caught myself on the verge of explaining my presence here at that hour.

It was then that the door to the room which housed La Española was flung open and a sharp, angry voice reached me.

"—had enough of it! Askew, if I see one of those dogs on my land again—whether it's the land I rent from you or my own—I'll shoot it. I'm a farmer. I need my lambs. I'm damned if I'll have them slaughtered as playthings for your bloody dogs."

"Nat, you haven't a shred of proof that these dogs are responsible for your dead lambs. In any case, I think it's a matter to be taken up with Tolson. They are not *my* dogs."

"They stopped being Tolson's the minute you set foot here—by what magic I'll never fathom. So it's you I'm warning."

"What of those eagles of yours, Nat? Don't they—"

Askew was cut short. "Shows what you know about golden eagles! They almost never kill lambs."

After a pause Askew spoke again. "I accept your warning, Nat. Now won't you stay and have a drink with me? There are things we should talk about."

He was cut off again. "Some other time. I've things to see to now.

216

When you feel like it, come to *my* house. It'll be a long day before I sit comfortably in this hellish house."

The door closed in almost a slam, and I saw the angry face under the tow-coloured hair. He was wearing the same clothes as when he opened the gates for us. But if he remembered me, he gave no sign of it. His glance swept past me and on to the girl.

"Nat," she said, also ignoring my presence, "you've a right here as much as he has. This house is yours—"

"Oh, hush, Jess," he said impatiently. They turned and started down the passage that opened under the stairs. I caught the last of his words as the green baize door swung closed. "Be a good girl and make me a cup of tea. I've got to go look at some ewes. . . ." There was a homely acceptance between them that excluded the world of run-down grandeur on this side of the door. They would drink their tea in the kitchen, and his voice would probably lose its anger as he sat with this porcelain creature, who seemed to know him so well. Unreasonably, I felt troubled by the exclusion.

"Oh . . . there you are." I turned and looked at Askew. He stood gripping the door frame, his lips trying to force a smile but producing something that barely covered a grimace of pain. He didn't seem to think it strange that I was there, in my dressing gown. "Do me a favour, please? Go into the dining room and bring me a brandy? It should be in one of the sideboards. A large one."

I found the brandy easily enough and carried it back to him. It didn't seem possible that the exchange I had overheard could have produced such a reaction. He was stretched in a chair behind the large desk, as if trying to straighten his body from cramp. But then, almost at once, he doubled over, clutching his stomach, his eyes closed.

"Lord Askew, are you ill? Shall I call . . . ?" Whom would I call?

He opened his eyes and reached for the brandy. While he took the first long swallow, my fingers held the glass also; his hand felt terribly cold on mine, but his palm was sweating. He straightened and leaned back in the chair. I withdrew my hand.

"Not supposed to do this. Terribly bad for me, the doctors say. I've got some tablets upstairs, but it's a long way to go."

"If you tell me where, I'll get them."

He shook his head. "No, I'll get there eventually. And in the meantime the brandy gives me relief. They tell me I'm burning

217

out what's left of my stomach, but what's the choice? To live and enjoy—or not to live at all?" Then suddenly he seemed to focus fully on my face. "Oh, don't look so stricken! It's an ulcer. It kicks up from time to time. Tonight is one of the times."

"I'm sorry. Sorry that you are ill. That the man who just left is in trouble about his lambs. That you're in trouble about your dogs. I'm sorry for both of you."

He took a large gulp of brandy and made a grimace. "Do you know who he was—the righteous farmer with the dead lambs?"

"No, but he let us in at the other end of the valley."

"He is a cousin very many times removed. Nat Birkett by name. He is also my heir!"

"Your heir? But you really don't know him. I heard you—"

"I know, I know. But he's next in line. This last week is the first time we've met. And it hasn't been a happy occasion. The title and the entailed part of the estate—the nucleus of the land here in the valley, the Tolson farms, the house—they go to Nat Birkett, whatever we both might wish otherwise. Of course, he doesn't want them. A pretty sorry inheritance. But I thought he'd come here tonight as a friendly gesture, and now I find it's about his stupid lambs." He gave a half laugh which ended in a gasp of pain.

"You shouldn't be talking to me like this. What's between you and Nat Birkett is your business. It can't possibly be mine—"

"You are right, Miss Roswell. It isn't your business." At the same instant she spoke I became aware of her presence in the doorway. I didn't know how long she had been there.

I smelled her perfume, watched the graceful sway of her body in a robe of amber silk as she went to Askew. "Roberto!" Her voice shook a little, a mixture of anguish and anger. "Why do you do it?" She took the brandy glass from him, then felt for the pulse at his wrist. "Why?" she repeated. "You'll kill yourself with this madness."

His face was white, and beaded with sweat. He made a weary gesture. "Carlota—don't!"

She turned and looked at me. "Go," she said very simply.

And I went.

I HAD my cigarette by one of the dying fires, thinking of what I had seen and learned that day. But I was very tired, and when I got into bed I felt the warmth of the hot-water bottles gratefully,

218

and I was asleep almost at once. I hadn't drawn the curtains, so I awoke, startled, to the sense of a changed atmosphere. The straight, cold, direct rays of the moon were gone, and I heard the wind moan in the chimneys. What else did I hear? What did I think I saw? Was it the sound of stiff petticoats moving, or was it simply mice behind the panelling? Did I actually see a small dark shape seated in her chair, hear the sigh of loneliness? No—both fires had died now to a bed of embers, giving little light. I saw nothing, I heard nothing. It was no more than a dream imperfectly remembered. If the little Spanish Woman was there, I did not feel she resented my presence. Perhaps she only wanted recognition. I slept again, easily and deeply.

CHAPTER THREE

She was in the room before I was properly awake; there was the faintest rattle of the spoon on the saucer as she put the tray on the long table in the window bay, and I opened my eyes to the sight of that tiny figure silhouetted against the blaze of morning light. She turned to me at once.

"Hello. I'm Jessica Tolson. I expect Lord Askew told you I live here and help my grandparents." She spoke with cheerful familiarity; not for her the reserve of her grandfather, though her voice was light and whispery, almost on the edge of excitement. "I've put the tea tray over here. It's never very comfortable having things to eat in bed, is it? At least I don't think so. I hope you like the bread—I bake it myself. Do you like this room?"

I wasn't fully awake, but I struggled to answer—to find something to stem this rush of words. "Yes, I do. Very much."

"This is my favourite room at Thirlbeck." She was bending now and scooping the faded rose petals from the big Delft bowl, smelling them, and letting them flutter down again. "I often come up here to read or study. I like to sit in the window, where I can see the tarn. I've written poems about it—how it looks in each season. It's not very good poetry, but it will get better."

I knew then whose hand had kept this room so immaculate, who had gathered the rose petals of last summer and let their scent linger on here. "I build up the fires in the winter and sit here and imagine how it must have been when she had this room."

"She—the Spanish Woman?"

"Oh, of course. They say that after the Spanish Woman died no one wanted to use it, and it was shut up for a long time. I expect they wanted to forget about her." She seemed to take it for granted that I knew the whole story.

"I've slept here just to see what it was like. But, then, I've tried most of the rooms in the house. This is the best."

She spoke of the place as if it were her own, and I suppose it often must have seemed that way. No one had lived here but her grandparents since she was born. She had never set eyes on the present earl until this past week. She was moving around the room now, touching things with loving familiarity. Her eyes quickly skipped over my toilet things lying on the big chest, alien things to her, and possibly resented. She was like a piece of quicksilver, whispery, her eyes large and Dresden blue, her cheeks touched with the faint pink flush of a painted doll. And the colour was her own—nothing artificial. She was just slightly fey, I thought, for she couldn't resist this chance of an audience. Brilliant, too, Askew had said, but she hadn't accepted the scholarship at Cambridge. It seemed to me that she walked the delicate line of nervous tension, which threatened to spill over on the wrong side.

And then she was around near the bed and on her way to the door. "Well, do drink your tea before it gets cold."

"Mr. Stanton—"

"Oh, I've taken tea to Mr. Stanton. What a sweet man!" Her air of sophisticated judgment infuriated me. What business had she making comment on Gerald? And then I felt like laughing, because I recognized the jealousy in my reaction.

"Breakfast will be ready when you come down. Just help yourself. . . ." She bestowed an enchanting, unreal smile upon me and closed the door very softly.

I lay back on my pillow, forgetting for the moment how badly I wanted the tea and reaching for a cigarette instead, something I rarely did at this time of the day. I could laugh a bit, but it really wasn't funny to be trapped for some days between the two opposites of ideal beauty—this tiny, perfect English rose and the haunting, dynamic presence of the Spanish aristocrat.

I flung back the bedclothes. Better try this maddening little girl's tea and bread; the tray gave me no reassurance that she ever made mistakes. The teapot was kept hot by a knitted cosy, and the wafer-thin slices of bread tasted like something everyone had forgotten how to make fifty years ago. And this girl-child wrote poetry as well. I scowled at the morning-blue surface of the tarn—not the best beginning to the day.

GERALD greeted me in a rather subdued way when I entered the dining room; he was eating a piece of toast with a very thin scraping of butter on it.

"Would you like anything else?" I said as I lifted the lids off the silver dishes. "You can have bacon, kidney, sausage—three kinds of eggs."

"Thank you, this is enough." His tone was unusually remote.

I turned to him swiftly. "Didn't you sleep well?"

"Well enough, I suppose. Yesterday was a long day. Perhaps we were overambitious. Should have taken two days to come up."

I sat opposite him. "You're missing something in this sausage."

"Cumberland sausage. They make a thing of it up here."

"I suppose you were awake enough to see the fairy child who brought the tea?"

He brightened a little. "Yes, lovely little creature."

"She's spoiled and is certainly her grandfather's pet. Likes to think *she* owns Thirlbeck, too."

For the first time that morning he smiled fully. "Jo, you sound rather like the condesa. Little Jess hasn't many friends among the women here."

"All right," I answered, "so I'm jealous."

"That's better. Always better when you face the truth."

"The truth is she could put on a drawstring bodice and a Bopeep hat and she'd be the ideal model for a porcelain shepherdess. Not really my taste in china."

"She drew my bath for me. I think she's charming."

"That leaves the condesa and me to our own opinions. And where," I said, "are Lord Askew and the condesa? Do you know?"

"Robert's been and gone. The condesa, being a Spaniard, probably doesn't like to rise before eleven." He snapped a piece of toast in two. "And I've finally remembered about the condesa. She's the daughter of a Spanish nobleman and was involved in some scandal. She took up with another man, and there was no

221

prospect for a divorce from her Spanish husband. And when *that* relationship fell through she was on the international circuit, with barely enough money to keep her afloat, I imagine. Cut off from her family, to whom, naturally, she is a disgrace. She must be about thirty-five to thirty-seven." He was giving her the benefit of a few years, I thought, but I did not object. "Her relationship with Robert can't be of very long standing. She wasn't with him when I met him in Venice last spring. She can't like it here. It's not her sort of place."

"Perhaps she loves him," I said. "It may be that simple."

"It may be that she is forty," he answered with unusual ruthlessness. "Or more. And perhaps she is growing a little afraid. She would have come here with Robert to prevent losing him. Naturally, she can never marry again, not so long as her husband is alive."

"Now that she's seen what is here—will she ever let him go?"

"Will it be her choice? I think that since the death of his wife and son he hasn't allowed himself to become completely committed to anyone or anything. But, well, there comes a time. Perhaps he might be willing to settle with the condesa for the rest of his life. A man grows tired of endless pursuit. In fact, a man just grows tired."

He stopped. Tolson stood at the door. "Miss Roswell. There's a telephone call for you—a Mr. Peers."

I smiled, not able to help myself. Harry did that to me.

"If you will take it in Lord Askew's study, Miss Roswell—I'll show you."

"Yes. Yes, I know. We were there last night," and I hurried across the hall ahead of him.

I waited for his steps to fade away before I picked up the phone and spoke. "Harry?"

"Fine one you are! Leaving me stranded—alone—all weekend. Didn't you know I'd be rushing back to hold your hand?"

"Liar! You never rushed anywhere to hold my hand. You just happened to come back. Had a good time?"

"A good time? It was business, luv, not a good time."

"Since when has business ever stopped your good time?"

He laughed, and made no more protests. "Well, it was profitable. I'll be able to afford to take you to dinner a few more times. What

I'd like to know is when that will be. You're up there in those damned lakes. I once knew a chap—he went up there and never came back. Dangerous, I call it. My old mum would never let me go up there."

"Harry, you fool. If only I could believe you sometimes."

"Honest, luv, cross my heart and hope—and all the rest of it. So when are you coming back from Lord Whatsit's?"

"Perhaps tomorrow. How did you know I was here?"

"Listen, luv, when Harry Peers wants to know something there's always a way. Found out you were with Gerald Stanton. So then I found out where he was headed."

"But it's the weekend. Hardy's isn't open."

"I roused a director from his bed to inquire about Mr. Stanton." I sucked in my breath. "I wish you hadn't."

"Cool it, Jo. I didn't mention your name. And the same director thinks I may buy something quite big in a sale that's coming up. Which I might. He didn't mind talking—not at all."

"Harry, you're dreadful."

"You mean it?"

"No. You're wonderful!"

"*That's* my girl. And how is that madman, the noble Lord Askew? What's he trying to sell—that bloody great diamond? Does he still have it?"

"It's right here in this room."

For once he had no immediate reply. Then slowly, "You mean *there*—in the room with you? Did you see it? What's it look like?"

"Fabulous, Harry. It's like a—a mountain of light."

"Two hundred-odd carats. Always wanted something like that."

"You wouldn't want this one." All at once I felt a coldness about me, and I knew that I believed the stories about La Española.

"Who says I wouldn't? I'll bet I could make a tidy profit by the time it was cut into a few decent-sized hunks. Is he selling? Is that why you and Stanton are there?"

"I don't know how you know so much about La Española, but *you* ought to know that I can't discuss business with you. So far as I know, Gerald is paying a social call, and I am driving him."

"Luv, I don't believe you. But I like a girl who can keep her trap shut." His tone changed. "Are you all right, Jo?" I knew he was talking about Vanessa's death. "I just missed you in Switzerland,

and I didn't like to bust in, in Mexico—not when you were just getting to know your dad. It went all right with him, did it?"

"Yes; Harry. It was—it was very good."

"Glad to hear it. Nice to find a dad at your age, and one that won't breathe down your neck either. I'll miss your mother, though, Jo. She was my sort, Vanessa was. Smashing girl."

"I know." There was a tightness in my throat.

"All right then, luv. Take care. Try to stay dry up there, and don't fall down a mountain. See you."

"When?" I couldn't help saying it even though he hated to be pinned down.

"Oh—soon. Bye, Jo." I heard the dull buzzing of the disengaged line, and I felt more lonely than at any other time since Vanessa died. Harry had slipped away from me once more. And with this emptiness upon me I believed I loved him. But I didn't think he loved me. Love had been beaten out of him as he had pushed and shoved his way to the top. His women were the decorations of his success; no particular woman, it seemed, was essential to him. He was offhandedly fond of me and in these last weeks unusually attentive and kind.

I replaced the receiver slowly, hearing Harry's flirtatious mockery, seeing his half-ugly face with its strong eyebrows crooked in amusement, his brown eyes quick and knowing.

I was remembering, as I too often did, the first time I had felt those eyes fastened on mine. It had been my first exposure, too, to his cocky good humour. I had been walking from the bus stop in Piccadilly to Hardy's, noting the changes in the windows of the art dealers which lined the street. This day there had been a new pair of Chinese vases of an early dynasty, and I looked much closer. I was rooted, entranced by the pale green colour, the long, tapering necks, their perfect proportion to the flare of the base. And then, behind me, Harry's voice, unknown until that moment.

"What a beautiful pair"—I turned, and his grown-up urchin's face was grinning at me, his eyes just a little above the level of mine—"of legs," he finished.

And then he walked on with me, talking about the Chinese vases with a certain degree of expertise. I made some stumbling replies, and then, to my great shock, he mounted the steps of Hardy's with me. Wondering what to do with him, I paused at the front counter

224

to say something to Mr. Arrowsmith, the man who had presided there for more than twenty years. Meanwhile the young man—not really so young, in his thirties—continued up the great staircase to the salerooms, saluting me with an impudent wave of his hand. It was a gesture that for all the world reminded me of Vanessa.

Mr. Arrowsmith acknowledged him with a smile.

"Mr. Arrowsmith, who's that?"

"Who's that? But you came in with him, Jo."

"I'm still asking who he is."

"That, my dear, is Mr. Harry Peers. Clever young devil. Jumped up from nothing, and now he's a millionaire, they say. His hobby is spotting good buys at Hardy's. I'm surprised you haven't seen him in here before."

I was remembering all this now, as I began to move slowly away from the telephone, pausing about the middle of the room. Lord Askew's study looked so different as the morning light poured in the long windows on each side of the painting. With the same cold excitement I'd felt the night before, I stayed on to look at the picture. I stared, and a face came more and more to life—the painted face of a man with an ugly, bulbous nose, careless hair, and eyes that registered suffering. He had painted his own face so many times in his life, in great adornment. Now here he was in his old age, revealing himself in the splendid beauty of his plainness. Rembrandt van Rijn, son of a miller, painter of Leiden and Amsterdam, thrown from poverty to riches to bankruptcy—all of it looked from the portrait without self-pity or compassion. It was painted in the dark tones of his later years, but it also wore the dirt of the years since it was painted. The signature was there, almost obscured, and the date 1669.

"Ah, you're here before us, Jo." I turned to see Gerald and Askew coming into the room.

"It's almost as hard to see as last night," I said. "It happens to be in the shadow between these two windows."

Askew sighed. "Tolson seems to have picked the worst place in the house to hang it. But he insisted because of security."

"Move it onto a chair facing the light," Gerald said.

It wasn't a large canvas—about three feet by two. I propped it against the back of the chair directly facing one of the windows, and Gerald went around to look at it.

225

I glanced at Askew. At this moment, for all his sophistication, he was eagerly watching Gerald's face. When the waiting became too much he said, "Well, what do you think?"

Gerald spoke slowly. "Remarkable—very remarkable. An unrecorded self-portrait, but signed and dated. Would there be any provenance—any record of its being bought or when it was bought?"

Askew gestured helplessly to the wall stacked with the filing boxes. "That's full of family papers—several hundred years of them. There may be something relating to Grandmother van Huygens' possessions. Dutch bourgeois families are pretty careful about such things. Perhaps Jo wouldn't mind looking, but is it really needed? It's signed and dated."

"Yes," Gerald said. "Any scrap of provenance would be very significant—"

"Excuse me, my lord."

Startled, we all looked up. None of us had been aware of Tolson's appearance at the open door of the study, but I sensed that he had been standing there for some time, listening as keenly as Askew to what Gerald was saying.

"What is it, Tolson?"

"It's Mr. Nat Birkett, my lord. He would like to have a word with you. I've put him in the library."

"Damn! I'm busy now, Tolson. Ask him if he can come back."

"I should see him, if you can, my lord. It's about the dogs."

"Not again! We've been through all that."

"It isn't about *our* dogs, my lord. He's found the one who's been after the sheep. I think he's come to apologize. Not easy to ask a man to come back again to do that, my lord."

I was astonished to hear the tone of pleading in Tolson's voice. Evidently Askew recognized it also. He shrugged. "Very well, I'll come. Can't have Nat Birkett forced to grovel."

Askew strode from the room, and we waited for Tolson to close the door after him, but the great round-shouldered figure stayed where it was. "Is there anything I can do, Mr. Stanton?"

"Do?" Gerald looked bewildered. "Why—I don't believe so."

"Well, sir, perhaps you would like the picture hung up again."

"No, not for the moment, thank you. I'll just look at it a little longer. If you don't mind."

226

"Very well, Mr. Stanton." The door closed gently.

I turned at once to Gerald. "What's the matter? The picture's all right, isn't it? I mean . . ."

He didn't even glance at me. His eyes were fixed on the painting, and his face was as grave as I had ever seen it.

"Remarkable," he said again. "A wonderful piece of work. But I don't think it was painted by Rembrandt."

"Oh. . . ." I felt the excitement leave me and a dull disappointment take its place—a sense of outrage, too, that I had been so completely taken in by the picture. "But it's *signed*."

"Yes, Jo, but I have a feeling that I'm looking at a photograph of Rembrandt. Everything is here, and yet it isn't the real thing. I hope to heaven our people will come up here and tell me that I'm wrong. But if I'm right, then we're looking at the best piece of forgery I've ever seen." He shook his head, a gesture of sadness and wonder. "Yes—remarkable. Very remarkable indeed."

We stayed looking at the painting for some time, Gerald's face unhappy and pensive. Finally he shrugged. "It's no use, Jo. We'll have to bring Lutterworth up here to examine it. In the meantime what am I going to say to Robert? He believes it's the painting his grandmother brought from Holland, I'm sure of that. But I just don't think that at the time it came here anyone would have been bothering to forge Rembrandts. As recently as the 1820s and '30s, Rembrandts sold for as little as twenty pounds. But I don't need to remind you of what has happened in the last ten years. When the Metropolitan Museum bought *Aristotle Contemplating the Bust of Homer* for over two million dollars the rush was really on. Anyone who owned a Rembrandt was rich."

"Then if this is a forgery, you think it's a recent forgery?"

"Has to be." He shook his head. "I'd love to know who's good enough to have done it. Remember van Meegeren? He painted Vermeers that Vermeer had never thought of. It would have to have been someone of his quality."

"But *how*, Gerald? And when? Has someone stolen the original and replaced it with this?"

He shook his head. "I don't want to know. And it could be that I'm wrong. Perhaps you could try looking through some of those papers anyway."

"Gerald, that's a lifework."

"Oh, just make a game of it. Anything, so I won't have to tell Robert here and now what I think. Time enough to break his heart later, when we're sure. We'll leave tomorrow, and I'll tell him I'm sending Lutterworth for an opinion. And, Jo, you had better forget you've ever seen Thirlbeck." He stiffened suddenly. "Yes?"

It wasn't to me he spoke, but Tolson, again standing by the door, which we had not heard open. "Mr. Stanton, Lord Askew would like you and Miss Roswell to join him in the library. Shall I replace the picture?"

I wondered if he was so possessive of everything at Thirlbeck, and then again wondered why he should not be. After all, he had tended it alone for so many years that we—and I included Askew in this—were interlopers in *his* treasure house. Gerald and I must seem to him even worse—the appraisers who descended on his kingdom to put a price on everything, a price that valued beauty but not the devotion which had preserved it.

He was beside us already, lifting the picture and rehanging it on its hook. "There," he muttered. "Out of harm's way now."

The sound of the condesa's laughter greeted us in the library. She hardly turned at our entrance, calling a good-morning and then giving her attention once more to Nat Birkett. He stood in front of the fire, wearing the desperate air of a man who finds himself with a glass of champagne in his hand at eleven o'clock in the morning and wonders why he is where he is.

Askew gestured to us with a bottle. "Champagne? Carlota's tastes run to it at this time every morning. When Vanessa and Jonathan were here we drank all there was in the cellars." He was now holding a glass towards me. "Jonathan said it reminded him of the sun. . . . Is that what you feel, Carlota?"

"I do feel gayer," she admitted. "But poor Mr. Birkett here thinks all this is a waste of time, I'm afraid. He'd really rather be getting on with his farming." The words had no sense of sarcasm.

"It's a good thing to remind farmers that they should take a few minutes for . . . well, for this." He gestured to include the room, the champagne bottle, and even, I thought, the condesa herself. She looked this morning exactly like someone one saw in a glossy magazine; her pale cream slacks and cashmere sweater, her shoes and needlework bag were the badges of understated wealth and

228

taste; if she was, as Gerald said, short of money, I wouldn't have minded being short of money in the same way. Nat Birkett's eyes were on her appreciatively, and she was enjoying that.

Then he looked at me. "You managed to find your way last night, then? Perhaps I shouldn't have sent you over the Brantwick road."

"Managed perfectly," Gerald said quickly. "We were grateful to you for saving us so many miles." Again I felt my skin creeping as I thought of the dog I had seen and Gerald had not. . . .

"It was a great help," I said. "And spectacular views. Formidable country, though. I wouldn't like to be lost up there."

He looked at me more closely. "You'd be surprised how many experienced walkers do just that. The trails lead them up near the top of the fells, and sometimes the temptation to see what the private land of our valley looks like is too great. A few times we've had searchers out for days looking for walkers. People won't believe how quickly the weather changes. They panic, take any way down they can, to where the paths aren't marked. There are signs along the wall telling people it's dangerous and to keep out. But one or two will always ignore a sign. This year we're getting volunteers from the district to see that no one does stray across to this side."

"Do you really need to have volunteers?" Askew asked.

For the first time Nat Birkett's face relaxed. "We've got that pair of golden eagles nesting up there on a crag of Brantwick—this is only the second pair to nest in the Lake District for more than two hundred years—and if they're scared off the nest, the young won't hatch. Then perhaps they'll not continue to return to this valley to breed. If it kills me, I'll see that no one gets near that nest—either for the eggs or just out of curiosity."

His voice grew louder. "I'm so damn sick of what's happened to this country—overrun with people and their cars and their infernal plastic picnic litter. Places where heather and ling used to grow are nothing but impacted subsoil now. . . . If I have to use a gun, I'll keep them away from that nest until the young can fly!" I wondered what there was in the life of this young man which made him both attractive and yet too blunt, angry almost.

He had stopped, aware of the silence about him. "Well, I'm assuming too much. It isn't my valley, but with your permission, Lord

230

Askew, I'll organize these watches. And now I think I'd better go—"

"Wait awhile, Nat," Askew said. "Have another drink. There is rather a lot I'd like to talk to you about—certain legal matters. But as to the rest—of course, you must do as you wish. The Tolsons, I imagine, will cooperate. Anything for golden eagles, Nat." Askew's air of faint amusement changed suddenly, his features twisted with a kind of distress. "Yes, I wish you *would* do it! There isn't much left in England to protect from the developers, and I'm for doing whatever can be done."

Nat Birkett was already at the door. "I'll fix it with Tolson, then. Good-bye."

In a few moments the motor of a Land-Rover parked in the gravel circle was started. From where I stood I could see Jessica come running from the house as the vehicle began to move. It stopped, and she leaned her arms along the open window, talking. I could see Nat Birkett nodding, his face settled into a look of determined patience. She held him there perhaps three minutes and then stepped back. At once the Land-Rover roared into life, sending the gravel flying from under the wheels. But there was a smile on Jessica's face as she turned back towards the house.

We were silent until the condesa spoke. "That is a rather handsome young man, Roberto. What a pity he is so gauche."

"Gauche? In his own world he functions very efficiently. He's a hardworking farmer, and it must seem unbelievably frivolous to him to drink champagne at this time of day. He has no particular reason to like me, since I'm saddling him with an unwelcome inheritance—"

"He doesn't want to be Lord Askew?" She smiled at the simplicity of a person who didn't want a useful social title.

"Why should he? There's no money with it. Just this house, out of which I'll probably have sold anything of value, and this valley. The mines and quarries are worked out. Some land was sold at the time my father died, for death duties. And then, after the war, when the income from the land wouldn't support my idle, roving life, I instructed Tolson to sell what he had to. I didn't want any of the details—just the money. For that I don't doubt Nat despises me." Askew took a long drink from his glass of champagne.

"He comes of quite a different breed. He lives in a house, carefully preserved, which has been handed down for several hundred

231

years. Not a grand house, but I'd bet it's a damn sight pleasanter to live in than this pile. He's in debt a bit—what farmer isn't? But he owns far more than his indebtedness. That will all change, though, when he has to find the death duties for Thirlbeck."

"And the estate is entailed," Gerald ventured.

"The *original* estate is entailed. What was added after the creation of the earldom is not. It's complicated, Gerald. All I know is that I can't sell certain farms the Tolsons rent, land in this valley, or some land lying towards Kesmere. The rest Tolson has been selling piecemeal as I've asked for more money. So Nat Birkett will inherit a very shrunken estate. And who in his right mind would want this house?"

Without thinking I spoke. "I would." I recognized the statement as the exact opposite of what I had said to Gerald last night.

Askew smiled at me, disregarding Gerald's frown, and went to refill his glass. "We weren't meant to be here—my grandfather, my father, and myself. Remember, my grandfather was a farmer and a merchant landed suddenly with an unexpected title. He was a reformer in his day—all kinds of new ideas about land drainage and reclamation. When he took his seat in the House of Lords he thought it was going to be a platform for his ideas—a better deal for the farmer, rather than the landowner. But he never finished his maiden speech; he was howled down. Whenever he walked the corridors of the House after that, some wit or other would set up the cry of *Baa aa* after him. Not a noble lord at all. Just a farmer. So his son never went near the House. Neither have I. Of course, if Nat Birkett chooses to go, there'll be more respect for him. These days the man who really knows what farming is about is listened to." He moved towards us. "Well, let's fill up the glasses again."

The condesa delicately tossed a cigarette into the fire. "And Nat Birkett has a wife?" she said. "The future Countess of Askew? And children?"

"He has two thriving, beautiful sons, Tolson tells me. He had a sweet, charming wife. The ideal wife for a good farmer who was going to become an earl. Only she died. And do you know where? Right here in this house. She had a heart condition—serious, but not so serious, they thought, as to cause her death except in rather extraordinary circumstances. But she died in one of the upstairs

232

rooms here. No one even knew she was in the house. And this place being what it is, they didn't find her until she'd been dead for almost a day, they think."

Now I heard his voice as it had sounded when he had looked over the wind-riffled tarn and talked of the Spanish Woman. "Poor little lost girl," he said.

LUNCH was an awkward meal during which Gerald uneasily skirted the subject of the Rembrandt, but Askew seemed so sure it was a Rembrandt that he felt no need to talk about it either. Only when Gerald mentioned leaving the next afternoon did Askew take any real notice.

"So soon, Gerald? Why not stay on a few days? You're looking far too much like a city gent."

Gerald set down his coffee cup. "I'd better ask it now, Robert. Do you want to sell the contents of this house?"

"Well, I thought just the picture . . ."

"There is some very valuable furniture here, Robert." He hoped, I thought, to turn Askew's mind away from the painting, to show him that there were other things of value, so that the disappointment, if it came, would be tempered. "It's worth more than you can afford to pay in insurance on it," Gerald said bluntly. Then, as complete silence answered him, he looked around, shaking his head a little. "It seems so wasted, somehow. Almost lonely." This was totally unlike Gerald, who loved beautiful things but was not sentimental about them.

It was a long time before Askew responded. "Lonely . . . It's always been lonely." He wasn't talking about the furniture. "This place has always felt like some enormous hotel with no guests. If I could sell it—house and all—I'd gladly do it. As it is, yes, I suppose I'd better sell what I can. *You* tell me."

Gerald's face coloured slightly. "Well, I thought that was what you had in mind—to liquidate what you can and enjoy the proceeds. After all, it will lessen the death duties on Nat Birkett. No one can tax him on what's been spent."

"So what will you do, Gerald?" Askew said it almost as if he were grateful to Gerald for thrusting the decision on him. Perhaps mostly for this kind of help he had invited Gerald to Thirlbeck.

"Jo and I will leave tomorrow after lunch. I'd like to look at the

233

rest of the paintings before I go. There could be others of interest among them. And then I'll arrange for some of our people to come up here. They will have to take an inventory of every item, and you, Robert, must stay here at least long enough to tell us exactly what it is you want us to handle." He glanced apologetically at the condesa. "We must have your absolute authority for each article."

We sat for a while over coffee, and Gerald went on about his plans to set in motion what would be a great auction. "You're aware of our scale of commissions for selling, Robert?"

"Commissions? Oh, yes, there has to be commission, of course!"

"I'd just like to be sure you know it," Gerald said. "On lots up to five hundred pounds it's fifteen per cent; from five hundred to ten thousand pounds it's twelve and a half per cent. Over ten thousand pounds it drops to ten per cent." He glanced around him. "There are a great many items here which will, in my opinion, bring far more than ten thousand pounds. You may set a reserve price, and if, at auction, the item does not reach that price, we, the house, buy it back in for you."

He was reciting this almost by rote; this scale of charges was printed in every catalogue Hardy's issued. It was one way the great auction houses were more attractive than the private dealers in modern paintings. A dealer's commission on living artists and on those who, dead or alive, were bound to him by contract was often forty, and sometimes fifty, per cent.

Askew twisted his cigarette into the saucer of the coffee cup. "Whatever your arrangements, Gerald, I might as well let it all go. There aren't many fond memories attached to this place." He looked across at the condesa. "We'll have some days in the sun, won't we, Carlota?"

His answer was her hand extended to him. "Let us go for a walk, Roberto. Yes, there will be days in the sun. . . ."

They were gone, and Gerald produced his notebook and was writing quickly, muttering to himself. In my imagination I saw the place stripped of what was preserved here, of all but what was too massive to move. The beauty of the house would shine through then, but it would be a house deprived of most of its history. For the first time in my life I felt a disloyalty to Hardy's. I began to understand the jealous possessiveness of Tolson and Jessica. And then, at that moment, I thought I began to understand Vanessa. It

234

she had seen all this and said nothing, her reasons and feelings might have been what I was now experiencing. Once again I switched to dislike of that man, Robert Birkett, Earl of Askew, walking in the fitful spring sunshine with his mistress, planning their lives in a place where the sun always shone.

FINALLY Gerald had finished with his notes. "I'm going up for a nap, Jo. You'll make some sort of start on that load of papers in the study, will you? Not that you'll discover anything in a few hours, but it will, at least for now, keep Robert quiet about the painting." I watched him go up the stairs, moving quite heavily. It was unlike Gerald to retire in the afternoon, but then this day had been unusually trying.

Before I took the circular ladder from the library to begin my task in the study, I climbed up and inspected the prunus jar that I had seen last night on the top of the bookcases. But when I held it in my hand I saw that it was the sort of jar turned out by the thousand in Hong Kong. I shrugged and put it back in its place. Well, what family didn't collect junk along with treasures? As I climbed down the ladder I looked again into the bookcases and noted the volumes—many titles in Latin, some in Greek, books on botany and anthropology, and there, in faded green leather, a set of the works of Darwin, possibly a valuable first edition. This family had had its scholars, as well as its farmers. What a mixed, odd lot they were. Suddenly I felt more enthusiasm for the task Gerald had set me.

The enormity of it, though, struck me again when I wheeled the ladder into place under the wall of filing boxes in the study. I didn't even glance at the picture in its dark place at the other end of the room; that was for Gerald and the experts to worry about. I climbed the ladder and began staring at the dates on the boxes. When would Askew's Dutch grandmother have come to Thirlbeck? I allowed for Askew's age, and then gave fifty to sixty years earlier for the birth of his grandfather. When would he have married? At about the age of thirty—in 1880 or 1882? I took down a box marked 1880 and pulled on its red strings to open it, the dust tickling my nose. I noticed with annoyance that the first few papers were for the year 1883. They were brittle to the touch and brown at the edges—sheets with accounts, then a surveyor's drawing of some acreage. Then something written in Dutch, I thought, something that looked like a recipe, with one absurd word at the bottom in English—gooseberries. The prudent Dutch housewife putting down the store of jams for the winter? There might have been two hundred separate sheets of paper in that box. I looked despairingly at the boxes reaching over my head to the ceiling. I sighed, and sneezed loudly.

"God bless. . . ." It was Jessica, standing in the doorway. "Can I help you?" She seemed even smaller than before and like a bright butterfly in this dim room, wearing a rather childish yellow sweater that looked as if it had been left over from school.

"Well, I don't know." I wondered why she made me so uncomfortable, as if I had been caught prying. "Lord Askew and Mr. Stanton thought I might find some references to the picture. But the papers don't seem to follow the dates on the boxes."

"No, they don't," she replied cheerfully. "You'll never get through them all this afternoon, will you?" So she already knew that Gerald and I would be leaving tomorrow. "What sort of paper are you looking for? I've been through a lot of the boxes myself—just for fun."

"Well, anything that might relate to the pictures the earl's grandmother brought over from Holland. There might have been a list of some kind . . . anything about when the family might have acquired them."

She was already shaking her head. "Is it important?"

"Quite important. When something is to be sold it helps if there are details of its history. We call it provenance."

Her face grew blank. "I don't remember seeing anything of the sort." She took a few steps towards me. "Lord Askew shouldn't sell what's here. It doesn't really belong to him—it has to be kept." The blankness was suddenly gone, replaced by a passion which made her soft voice shrill

"Jessica!" Tolson had heard her voice and had come to the door. Then he saw me perched on the ladder. His eyes seemed to darken behind the heavy glasses. "Is there something I can do for you, Miss Roswell?"

I found myself explaining once again why I was there. His face remained impassive, and Jessica broke in before he could speak. "I've told her there's nothing. I would have found it, wouldn't I,

Grandfather? I've been through almost every box that's there."

"Hush, Jess, hush. Don't excite yourself." His tone was deliberately calm. "I expect none of us ever paid much attention to what's in those boxes. But it's far too big a task to be done in a few hours. Perhaps after tomorrow you and I, Jess, could start to look. Now I think your grandmother would like some help preparing tea. Lord Askew and the condesa have driven into Kesmere." He looked up at me. "Jessica will bring a tray to the library in about twenty minutes. Perhaps you might be good enough to inform Mr. Stanton?"

I climbed down the ladder as he turned back to Jessica. "Go, now, there's a good girl." The tone was gentle, more full of emotion than I could have believed possible. There was the sound of her light running steps in the hall and the unoiled squeaking of the service door.

"I'll carry the tray to Mr. Stanton," I said. "If that's all right. He's a little tired and might like to rest until dinner."

"Of course, whatever you say, Miss Roswell." His voice was indifferent, utterly changed from a few seconds ago. He was about to turn when I halted him. I had to ask him.

"Wait, please, Mr. Tolson. You—well, you probably remember my mother."

"Your mother?" He repeated the words as if I were a fool.

"Yes, my mother, Vanessa Roswell. She and my father, Jonathan Roswell, were here for some months just after the war. They had the lodge at the other end of the valley, across Brantwick." I was using the name as if I had known it all my life.

"Yes, I do recall. What about it?"

"Oh, just . . ." He made it impossibly difficult. "Well, I wondered how much you remembered of them. Lord Askew said they were often here with him. It was before I was born—I never knew they were on the Birkett estate."

"What do you expect me to tell you?" he demanded. "I don't remember every little thing. It was the end of the war, and things were very difficult—rations hard to get. Mr. Roswell used to drive the Bentley that Nat Birkett has now, and it used too much petrol. Lord Askew used to give him *our* coupons. And then they had cream and eggs and even meat—from the lambs and bullocks we slaughtered. I had a terrible time accounting for it all with the

Ministry of Food. The earl didn't seem to understand about such things."

I sighed. "I'm sorry to have revived unpleasant memories. You didn't much care to have my mother and father here, did you?"

"They just came here and asked to rent the North Lodge because they saw it was empty. Out of the blue, like a couple of gypsies. Lord Askew was present at the time, and he said that they could rent it. It wasn't strictly legal. The Ministry of Defence had requisitioned the whole house and the North Lodge during the war, but they never came to use it. They hadn't derequisitioned it at that time, but Lord Askew insisted that we could go ahead without permission. . . . Then, when the cold weather came, the Roswells went off without paying the electricity bill. Lord Askew had even wanted to give them the Bentley, but Mr. Roswell said he couldn't afford to run it. They just went off the way they came—like gypsies."

Yes, it sounded like Vanessa—not to pay the electricity bill. It sounded like my father, too, who had a passion for old cars, a passion that he could now afford to indulge. The Bentley would have been a joy he must have hated to leave behind. And he had said nothing about that, either.

Tolson stood there frowning, remembering, no doubt, the electricity bill and all the wine and champagne that had been drunk that summer and autumn. Gypsies . . . And Tolson's values were so deeply rooted in loyalty to place and family. In his fashion Askew had turned into a gypsy, too. Did Tolson blame Vanessa and my father for that? Well, he surely would never say so.

"Was the house like this when my mother was here?"

"Like this? Like what?"

"All the furniture about? All the good pieces?"

"Why don't you ask her, Miss Roswell?"

I drew in my breath. Hard to believe the whole world didn't know that Vanessa Roswell was dead. "She died a few weeks ago," I said.

"I'm sorry." It was not an offer of sympathy, just barely polite.

"But was it like this?"

"I really don't remember. It was a long time ago. I had put most of the furniture into one room when the requisition order came from the ministry. Who knows what strangers will do; some people get a few drinks and start putting holes in things. Your mother might have seen the pieces that were too big to move. She spent a good deal of time here. She didn't like the lodge very much. Mr. Roswell was . . . artistic, wasn't he? He painted. Terrible daubs, I seem to remember. He actually gave Lord Askew one—as if he thought he would hang it."

"Were the other paintings hung then, Mr. Tolson?"

"Others? What others?"

"There were more than the—the Rembrandt. Lord Askew said his grandmother brought over a lot of Dutch pictures. Perhaps I should look at them. My father's picture might be among them. I would like to see it."

"I don't remember seeing it after Lord Askew left. Perhaps he got rid of it. But the other pictures are—are put away. In safety. And I can't remember whether your mother saw them. Why should I? She came and went. It wasn't important."

Without another word he turned and walked out. Unbelievingly I listened to the sighing squeal of the green baize door. It didn't seem possible that anyone could be so deliberately rude. Tolson was a law unto himself. He cared for nothing beyond Thirlbeck. And he had been one of the few people my mother had not charmed. I wondered if she had cared—or even noticed. She appeared not to have thought anything at Thirlbeck important enough to speak of later.

And that was what was wrong.

It was while I was having tea with Gerald in his room that the next shock came. I had just reported on the muddle of the papers in the study and seen Gerald's shrug of acceptance. "Well, I didn't think you'd turn up anything in a few minutes. I continue to hope, though, that somewhere there exists an inventory of Margeretha van Huygens' dowry. If she was the sort of house-wife I imagine her to be, there would even be a list of linen."

I had been wandering around as he talked, looking at the things that Robert Birkett's father had gathered into this, the room to which, Robert had told us, he had retreated in the last years of his life. There were a few photographs in faded brown tints. I moved on.

And then I saw it. "What's *this* . . . ?"

"I wondered when you'd come to it," Gerald said. "Aren't they charming? Almost certainly by Nicholas Hilliard, I'd say, and most likely he made the frames also, since he was a goldsmith as well as a miniaturist."

Four tiny oval portraits had been gathered into a group, the loops above them pinned to a background of faded crimson velvet. Each miniature, not more than two inches high, encircled by an intricately worked gold frame surmounted by a golden bow studded with small diamonds, was obviously meant to be worn with a chain or pinned to a gown. A man and three fair children, two girls and a boy. They all wore the ruffs of the Tudor period, and the quality of each portrait was extraordinarily high. Gerald's guess of Hilliard as the artist could very well be right. "Who are they?"

"I asked Jessica. They're the third earl of Askew—I suppose that makes him the villain of the ill-fated Spanish Woman's story—and his children."

"One miniature's missing." There was space for a fifth, and it was possible to see a faint oval of slightly darker red on the exposed velvet.

"The countess, I suppose. Jessica didn't know what had become of it. It has been that way as long as she can remember."

"Yes. . . ." I was suddenly impatient. "If you've finished, I think I'd better take the tea things down. Are you going to rest a little longer, or would you like to take a walk?"

He shook his head, his eyebrows raised questioningly, indicating with a glance the rain that pelted against the window. The spring day had changed again. "Not now."

"All right. See you before dinner."

I left the tray on the long table in the hall—I didn't quite possess the courage to penetrate into Tolson's domain behind the baize door—and hurried back to the Spanish Woman's room. I went to the closet, and I took from my handbag another of the things, along with the amber brooch, that had been in Vanessa's handbag, found among the scattered wreckage on that mountainside. I had carried it with me to Mexico and looked at it often. There was something about the tiny, perfectly painted face that had reminded me of Vanessa, and this Tudor lady had the same rather wild red-gold hair. I had imagined that Vanessa discovered

240

the miniature during her stay in Switzerland, but I had not shown it to anyone. The contents of her handbag had been too evocative of pain to discuss. I had simply kept it with me, thankful that these few things had survived.

I sat down at the table and studied the miniature. The bag had been thrown from the plane with sufficient force to tear the leather on one side. Inside, zipped in an inner compartment, the miniature had had the protection of its soft surroundings and a little leather pouch which must have been made for it. But still, the impact had broken off one side of the delicate filigree of the gold frame, and the glass had cracked diagonally across its face. I put the fragment of the frame where it belonged and stared at it. I knew now that Vanessa had not bought it on her trip to Switzerland or anywhere else. In every respect it was the companion piece to the miniatures in Gerald's room. If I were to carry it there, it would fit perfectly into the vacant space in the grouping. Attached to the little diamond-studded loop was a small white tag, held there by a piece of fine red string, identical to the price tags Vanessa used for small items in her shop. And a number—the price, I had supposed—scrawled in Vanessa's writing on the tag.

Had she taken it from here? Had she really stolen this, and even Tolson had not dared to accuse her to me? "Gypsies," he had said. Had he been implying that she had been light-fingered as well? And had she, after all these years, been hoping to sell it out of England, where there was less chance of its identity and its real owner being discovered? I didn't believe what I was now thinking, and yet what else was I to believe?

The wind moaned softly in the chimneys, and an icy draught from the ill-fitting windows found me. I shivered in the last light of the April day. And then a sudden uproar among the pack of wolf-hounds somewhere below told me that Robert Birkett had returned to Thirlbeck.

I put the miniature back in its pouch, wishing I had a more secure hiding place than my own handbag for it. From that moment I knew I didn't quite trust the little golden-haired girl who slipped through these rooms on soft feet. If I stayed at Thirlbeck much longer, I was certain that Jessica would find it, and I couldn't bear that Vanessa's long-held secret should now, at this time, be violated.

It is strange how quickly one becomes used to the unusual. Gerald and I went through the ritual of drinks in the library before dinner, dinner itself, and coffee in the drawing room, and our eyes hardly ever strayed to what was exhibited before us. Gerald's afternoon rest had seemed to restore him. He referred to the auction only in general terms; the painting was never mentioned. It was a quiet evening, even a dull one; the condesa stitched at her needlework, we listened to the news on the radio, and went up to bed much earlier than the night before. At his door Gerald said, "Good night, dear Jo. Sleep well."

"Sleep well. . . ." And once again I felt the urge to kiss him, to offer some thanks for what he had been to me. But I was not Vanessa, who would have done it spontaneously, so I moved on.

After my bath I sat by the fire for some time, savouring the last of the day's ten cigarettes. I was drowsy from wine, well fed, and comfortable in this room that at first had overwhelmed by its size. In this mellow mood even the Hilliard miniature in Vanessa's handbag had an innocent explanation. She had discovered it somewhere and known where it truly belonged. If she had ever completed that flight to London, she would have been in touch with Askew, and the miniature would have been returned to its proper place. I stubbed out the butt of the cigarette and went to stand by the windows. Once more the scene had changed. The rain was gone, the wind had died. Everything was still. Just the caps of Brantwick and Great Birkeld were now mist-shrouded; even as I watched, the mist moved higher on those two great shapes that dominated this enclosed world. In any other part of England I would have guessed that the morning would be fair and clear, but I had learned not to predict such a thing for this country. I turned back to bed, leaving the curtains undrawn, liking what the moonlight did to the room.

And if in the chair I thought I saw the same shadow as the night before—the small, quiet shadow, perhaps of a young woman heavy with child—then it disturbed me no more than it had before. If Thirlbeck had a ghost, she had no malice for those who wished her well. Soon I was easily and deeply asleep.

It was all the more of a shock, then, to wake as if an arm had tugged me rudely from sleep. I lay for a second frozen with fright. A look around the room revealed nothing unusual, but the sense of urgency persisted. I could never describe the force that impelled me from the bed. There was no sound in all the great house. But something was wrong.

I flung on my robe and, by instinct, groped my way to Gerald's door. Without knocking I went in.

The bedside light was on, and Gerald lay against the headboard as if he had struggled to prop himself up. The pallor of his face was shocking, and the sound of his heavy breathing reached me across the room.

"Gerald, what is it?" I was bending over him, feeling inexpertly for his pulse.

An expression of relief and hope flooded his eyes. "Pain, Jo. Rather bad, I'm afraid. Chest—and down the left arm. Very tight."

I had by now placed pillows behind his head. "If I help, do you think you can push yourself up a bit? It would be easier to breathe." His weight was more than I thought, but I got him almost upright and wedged the pillows so that he wouldn't slip. "Gerald, you must have a doctor at once." I looked at the clock on the mantel. It was two twenty. "I'll have to go and rouse someone. Don't try to move."

"Jo . . . ?" The whisper reached me as I neared the door. I turned back. "How did you know . . . ?"

I shook my head. "I don't know. Some—something wakened me." I had almost said "someone." "Stay quiet, please, Gerald."

Outside I paused on the gallery, wondering what to do, where to go first. Tolson or Jessica would be the best—they would know which doctor to call; but where, beyond that baize door, would I find them? Then suddenly I saw in the moonlight a sight which almost froze my blood. Onto the gallery across the hall from me, their huge white shapes well defined against the dark panelling, had come the whole pack of wolfhounds. They lined up against the railing, in near silence, and stood there, watching, waiting.

For a moment I couldn't make myself move, and then the urgency of Gerald's situation reasserted itself. I *had* to go for help. Would the dogs let me do that? I tried to remember the names Askew had called them. Strange names, names that belonged to the Viking ancestors of these dogs. "Thor—Ulf—Eldir—Odin." My whisper sounded loud in the stillness. I began to walk slowly along the gallery to the head of the stairs. The hounds moved also.

243

We started down each arm of the stairs at about the same time, but then they went quickly and were waiting on the landing for me. I felt my mouth go dry with fright as I made a very slow and deliberate descent towards that waiting pack.

And then I was among them. There was no growl. Why? No sign of threat. I realized that if they were to bark, Gerald might interpret their ear-splitting chorus as an attack on me, and the shock might be more than he could bear.

"Shush . . . Thor, Ulf. Come now. . . . Come now."

They were all moving with me down the stairs, some ahead, some behind, their big paws and nails making scratching sounds on the wood. We reached the bottom of the stairs, and I made to turn for the baize door. Still there was no sound from them. Then I thought there might be a quicker way to summon help. The telephone by Tolson's desk had a small push-button system on it; I could probably reach Tolson easily using it. I turned slowly and made my way, surrounded by the dogs, to the study door.

As I touched the knob Tolson's alarm system was triggered. Bells sounded everywhere. I stood petrified, the sweat trickling down my arms. Lights began to come on, from the gallery above, from the passage when Tolson swung open the door. But in that time the strangest of all the strange things which had happened since we had entered Thirlbeck occurred. Instead of adding their own chorus to the ringing of the alarm, the dogs, as if moved by one reflex, squatted down around me, those odd whiskery faces almost smiling at me and their long tails beating the floor with pleasure. None of their heads turned as Askew appeared on the gallery or as Tolson paused, rooted in the doorway.

Though the dogs were like a loving circle of protection about me I thought once more of the great white hound who had been seen by me—and only by me—on the slope of Brantwick, and I was sick with fear and bewilderment.

CHAPTER FOUR

WE FOLLOWED the flashing blue light of the ambulance along the road that led to Kesmere, I seated beside Askew in his sports Mercedes, my teeth clamped together to keep them from chattering with cold and tension. I kept watching the blue light, somehow

believing that as long as it kept flashing, Gerald would still live. At the South Lodge a man stood by to open the gates for us. About a mile farther along the valley, we passed a house set back on a slope, where lights burned at a lower window.

"Nat Birkett's up," Askew said. "Either going to bed late or getting up early. It might be a calf being born. . . ."

We didn't speak again until we reached Kesmere Hospital. We saw Gerald only briefly as he was wheeled to a room, but I was cheered by the smile he managed to give us. He was attended by a man of about Askew's own age, Dr. Alan Murray. "He's a very good doctor," Askew said reassuringly. "He looks after the Tolson family."

We sat together in the waiting room, and I broke my rule and smoked one after another of Askew's cigarettes. A nurse came in and gave us some tea; she stayed to arrange magazines on the table and offer remarks about the weather. She stared at Askew. I watched her colour when he spoke to her; in his sixties he was handsome enough to cause a woman to do that.

Then Dr. Murray came back. I jumped to my feet. "How—"

He gestured me to sit again. "Well, now, things aren't at all bad. We've got a good little cardiac unit here. Quite new. Mr. Stanton is all right. You're not his daughter, are you?"

"No, he's a very old friend. We work together."

"He's doing well. It was quite a mild attack—or at least that's what the cardiogram is saying now. We'll keep him here awhile— do a workup on him, and it's imperative that he rest."

"Would there be better treatment in London, Alan?" Askew asked. "I don't mean to be offensive, but a lot of us regard him as rather important. And a lot of us"—now he was looking at me— "love him."

"He'll get everything he needs here, and fresh air as well. Probably better nursing. The journey back to London by ambulance wouldn't help him one bit—not screaming down that motorway, breathing diesel fumes. I'll let you know if he needs a specialist from London. I promise you I won't hesitate about that. But until he's completely fit to travel, he's better here."

"Can I see him?"

He shook his head. "He's dozed off. We've sedated him."

"I'll wait, then. I want him to know I'm here."

246

"It may be hours before he wakes. You aren't going to keep Robert waiting with you? We old men need our sleep."

"No, of course not. There's just the question of how I'll get back."

Askew got to his feet. "Here are the keys to my Mercedes. Dr. Murray'll run me back. Won't you, Alan? Not too far out of your way." He smiled down at me. "Tell Gerald that Thirlbeck is his home for as long as he cares to use it. And I will gladly stay on to keep him company. I hope you will, too. You're good for him. Oh, here . . ." He put his cigarette case in my hand. "You'll be needing these."

For the first time I was grateful to Askew. He had understood that I could not have left before Gerald woke; the time was still too close to Vanessa's death. I would wait.

One of the nurses let me sit near the windowed area of the Intensive Care Unit. From there I could see Gerald's every movement. I was watching the second that his eyes flickered open. I went and touched the arm of the nurse on duty. "Can I . . . ?" I said.

She nodded. "Be very quiet. Don't excite him."

And then I did what I should have done before. I bent by the bed and kissed him. He smiled faintly. "Knew you'd fix it, Jo."

It was beyond all the canons of my time, my generation, but I no longer wanted to play it cool. I pushed back a lank piece of hair from his forehead. "I love you, Gerald," I whispered.

And then, obeying the beckoning of the nurse, I left.

I went out into the air, to Askew's car. Against all that I had thought about the changeability of the weather here, the morning had dawned as calm and fair as the radiant night had promised.

THE gates at the South Lodge were firmly locked, and no one came to open them when I sounded the horn. Smoke rose from the chimney of the lodge, a building very much like the derelict one over beyond Brantwick, except that this one was in immaculate condition. Here the wrought-iron gates with the Birkett crest had been preserved—no doubt by the same Tolson son who was so skillful at making metal shutters. They were formidably high, beautifully worked, and painted a glossy black. The face that Thirlbeck showed to those who ventured on this dead-end road was prosperous enough, and hostile. On the wall beside the gates was another starkly painted notice.

247

Here was an enticing, beckoning fairy-tale world to which admission was forbidden. I rattled those closed gates in frustration and returned to the car to wait until one of the Tolsons turned up. It was Sunday morning, but in a farmer's life the chores were there to be done as always.

The thought of farming brought to mind Nat Birkett. His house was there, visible on the slope about a mile back; if he had a key to the North Lodge gates, then he surely had one to these. I turned the car; better to do something than sit and wait.

Nat Birkett lived in a rather beautiful house, I thought. It was called Southdales and made of the stone and slate of the Lake Country—blues, purples, dull greens, and greys. It was two-storeyed, quite low, with dormer windows on the upper floor. The vines and climbing roses that twisted about its length were just beginning to put out leaf, and they gave it the homeliness of a house that had never aspired to grandeur. I began to understand Nat Birkett a little more—he, in his independence, possessing this and good farming acres as well, what would he want of Thirlbeck?

He came out quickly to meet me. "Is there trouble? Can I help?"

For the first time since I had discovered Gerald ill I could have wept with relief. It seemed that Nat Birkett would shoulder all my worries. "Yes, there was some trouble. You can help, possibly. I'm locked out of Thirlbeck. I thought you would probably have a key to this gate."

"Yes, of course." Then he looked at me closely. "What's happened? You look awful. . . . Come in."

I found myself in a kitchen which felt as if it had been inhabited for a thousand years and that all the domestic life of the house flowed from it. There was a beautiful dark oak hutch displaying blue china; red striped curtains at the windows, and two rocking chairs before a brick chimneypiece. There was an electric stove and a big refrigerator and a new sink surrounded by old oak cupboards. In the middle stood a table which was worthy of Thirlbeck itself and a set of beautiful Windsor chairs. I had rarely been in a room of such charm and warmth. I found myself seated in

248

one of the rocking chairs, nursing a steaming hot mug of coffee into which Nat Birkett had splashed some brandy. He was rapidly making slices of toast as he listened to me talk.

"Bad shock," he said. He placed the buttered toast on an oak table stool between us and dropped into the opposite chair. "You'd better eat. You must be famished. I'll be cooking some bacon and eggs for the boys in a few minutes, and you can have some of that."

After a night of cigarette smoking I had thought I couldn't eat, but because of the atmosphere of this house, and Nat Birkett himself, I felt it was now safe to lay down the night's burdens. I ate like a hungry child, licking the dripping butter from my fingers and holding out the mug for more coffee and brandy.

"You don't have brandy for breakfast every day, do you?"

"No," he said. "But I don't have champagne at eleven either." We laughed at the memory of it; it seemed much farther away than yesterday. "I felt a right fool, I'll tell you. That elegant pair, Askew and his beautiful condesa, really put me off. I've handled champagne glasses before—I'm not quite an oaf—but I suddenly felt as if the damn thing was going to break in my hand. And then you and Stanton came in, and I felt even worse. The experts up from London—art dealers. You looked as cool as the condesa, only a bit more useful. And I must still have faintly smelled of the cow byre."

I gulped the coffee. "I don't look like that now, though?"

He shook his head. "No, you don't. You look . . . well, human. As if something got out of you that had been locked up."

Without meaning to I found myself talking about Vanessa, about the way the wreckage had looked in the snow. "It's all been so unreal. Then last night I was terrified I was going to lose Gerald. . . ." To this man, a stranger, the words were spilling out as if they had thawed from some frozen place at my centre—the jumbled mosaic of Vanessa's life; the acquaintance with my father, which had quickly become a friendship; even a little of my peregrinations all over Europe to look at works of art, but somehow missing myself on the way. I think I even talked about Harry Peers —wondering if Harry saw me as the cool creature of Nat Birkett's description. All this spilled out in the half hour or so that I sat with Nat Birkett, and the sun grew stronger at the windows and a collie scratched at the door to be admitted, taking his place without question near the hearth.

"You know," he said at last, "you need a couple of weeks walking on the fells. Get yourself a pair of decent walking boots—not fancy gear—and a parka, and get up on the fells and walk. Walk until you want to drop. You'll be too tired to think. Just don't get too high, and stay on the trails."

"You think I'm going to remain here?"

"You should. Stanton needs you with him."

"Yes, I suppose you're right. But someone at Hardy's has to know at once what's happened to Gerald. I should telephone . . ."

"Time enough," he said. "No one's out of bed at this hour on a Sunday morning. Might as well have breakfast while you're here. Judging from the elephant noises above, the boys will be down in a few minutes."

"You were up early yourself—or to bed late." I told him about seeing the lights on the way to the hospital.

He grinned. "I'd like to pretend I had a roaring night out. But I didn't. A heifer had a hard time calving—" He was interrupted by a rumbling noise on the stairs. The kitchen door was flung open, and two young boys stopped dead as their eyes fell on me.

"Strawberry had her calf," Nat said. "And this is Miss Roswell. She's staying at Thirlbeck and got locked out."

"Jo is my name," I said. "What are yours?"

The older one straightened himself. "I'm Thomas. He's Richard." And then he added with complete seriousness, "We thought there might be a Harry, but Mother died."

"Shall we call the new calf Harry?" the younger one asked.

"You'd have to call her Henrietta," Nat replied. "No, I don't think you should call her Henrietta. We might sell her one day. And then Harry would be gone. You wouldn't like that."

"No, that's right." Thomas looked expectantly towards the stove. "Shall we start breakfast? It's almost time for church. Richard's lost his Sunday tie. . . . I gave him one of my old ones." The talk flowed on, and I was accepted. They were beautiful, these boys, as Askew had said. The older was about ten years, the younger about eight, and they had that soft, rosy bloom that healthy children wear. Their badly combed, still-damp hair was a wheat-coloured blond. They looked like their father, but I knew that their mother must have had intensely blue eyes and a spiky fringe of lashes. Each knew his appointed tasks as Nat got out the frying

250

pan. The eggs and sausages and bacon came out of the refrigerator, the table was set, the bread ready for the toaster.

At last the younger came close to me, patting the collie as he spoke, a gesture that protected his shy eagerness. "You're staying for breakfast, aren't you, Jo? I've laid your place."

We all sat down, and I ate as much as the boys did, and more than Nat. I watched him as he moved from stove to table, and the eggs were dished straight from the pan. "Sorry about all this," he said. "But breakfast is done to a tight schedule. . . . Thomas, elbows off the table."

"Dad, here's Mr. Tolson, coming up the drive."

"Then you're late. Put your jackets on." Nat gave a last-minute twitch to Richard's tie and straightened his socks. "There—out you get."

"Dad, you're not going to come?" Thomas said.

"Thomas, being up half the night to bring a calf into the world is as much the Lord's work as going to church."

"Can I *not* go sometimes?"

"When you're older you can decide that yourself. Until then you'll go with Mr. Tolson—and me, when I decide to go."

The door opened and Tolson stood there, clad in a severe grey suit that looked out of place on his big body. His hair had been greased in an attempt to tame it, without much success. He just stared at me. Jessica came to the door behind him.

"Miss Roswell . . ." His tone was a rumble of displeasure. "I was surprised to see Lord Askew's car here."

"You'd locked her out, Tolson," Nat said.

"There's a phone, isn't there?" Jessica observed. She looked like a spun-sugar fairy, in a pink suit which she managed to make look elegant even though it wasn't expensive. Sensibly, she wore no ornament; she knew enough not to gild the lily.

"Yes, there's a phone. But I invited Jo to breakfast." Nat cut off Jessica, as if to tell her to mind her own business. "Well," he said to Tolson, "you've had quite a night over at Thirlbeck."

"Very unfortunate. But Lord Askew says Mr. Stanton is doing well. Will you be leaving today, Miss Roswell, as planned?"

"I don't know. Lord Askew thinks it would be better if I stayed."

As Tolson's dark eyes bore in on me through the pebble lenses my resentment grew. This man dominated too much at Thirlbeck;

251

he was its guardian, not its owner. If I couldn't outface this man, for Gerald's sake and my own, then I might as well crawl back into my niche at Hardy's. "I will make that decision when I have consulted Mr. Stanton's colleagues," I said crisply. "But I think you may take it that I won't be leaving at once."

"Well, *that's* nice," Jessica said sharply. "Grandfather, we'll be late. Thomas, Richard." Tolson stood looking at me for a moment longer, and for the first time I sensed a sort of helplessness in him. Something in his carefully planned world had been upset. In that moment his strength seemed diminished and my own grew.

"I shall need to get into Thirlbeck, Mr. Tolson," I said. "Would you be good enough to lend me a key?"

"A key?" His head went up like that of an old lion whose territory had been challenged. "That won't be necessary, Miss Roswell. My daughter-in-law, Jessica's mother, is now back at the South Lodge. All you have to do is sound your horn. Good morning, Nat. I'll see you when I bring the boys back from church."

"You might not," Nat replied. "I'll probably be in bed. But I'll be over in the afternoon to discuss putting up some new fencing."

"In that case," Tolson said as he turned to go, "Thomas and Richard can have their lunch with us. My wife will have cold food ready for you to bring back for supper." Then he was gone.

I waited until the sound of Tolson's car had died away. "They seem to have arranged things very nicely. Do you always let them run your affairs like that?"

"I suppose it does look that way." He shrugged. "It's difficult to see how *not* to do it. And it works. Things were in a pretty bad state after Patsy died. The Tolsons have provided a continuity for Thomas and Richard that no outsider could have given them. In every crisis that's arisen one or another of them has been here to help. Jessica's mother comes up every day and does some cooking and cleaning. As the Tolsons see it, they're simply beginning a little early a service that they'd normally be giving to the earl of Askew. The boys have friends in the younger Tolson grandchildren, mothers of a sort in the Tolson wives. Things could be worse. I go along because they've made it easy for me."

"And that includes taking your sons to church every Sunday?"

"It includes about everything. Tolson has strong ideas about how my sons should be brought up. Church is one of them. School

252

is another. Tolson doesn't think the Kesmere grammar school is fitting for the sons of the future earl of Askew. He's offered to finance sending them to prep school, using income from the Birkett estate, with Askew's permission, of course. I gave him a flat no. He really can't believe how much I loathe the idea of moving into the niche that's all carved out for me."

I was standing by the window while he talked, staying very quiet because I did not want the flow of words to stop. There was the anguish of a lonely man in them, a man who had surrendered a part of a cherished independence so that his children would have a family. I saw the two rosy faces of those children, and I couldn't blame him. And then, coldly, I wondered if Tolson had already selected the woman that Nat Birkett should marry.

"I didn't realize how well you could see Thirlbeck from up here. That peel tower, and the tarn." The sunlight had made the lake a shimmering cloth of gold behind the buildings—the England of storybooks it seemed now to be, and no one could have guessed the dark spots of its history. "Will you go and live there, Nat?"

"Live there! Never."

"Then what will happen to it?"

"I'll worry about that when I have to." He paused, and poured himself more coffee, banging the pot angrily on the table. "I suppose all women are soft about things like that. They see a great pile of stones, and just because it's got a bit of history they think it's got to go on forever. Tolson got to Patsy that way. He began to get her over there . . . any excuse at all. He wanted her to think of it as her home. It was insidious, the way he planted things in her mind. He meant it for the best, of course, but it turned out for the worst. She actually died there, my Patsy, in that wretched place."

He rose to pour two glasses of brandy and carried both to the window where I stood.

"Here, drink this, and then go back and get some sleep. And try to forget all this nonsense I've talked. It gets too much at times—when I'm tired and I realize the boys are growing up. I've seen her stand there where you've been standing—she didn't look like you, though. And she didn't act like you. She was unsophisticated and given to dreaming. I suppose most people would have said she was sweet, and let it go at that. But she was generous as well. Oh, hell, what's the use of trying to describe someone you've loved?"

253

He moved away from me and poured more brandy. "I wonder if I'm getting drunk? Well, I'll be sober enough when I go to pick up the boys. Setting a good example, Tolson always calls it. You're right! I *do* let them run my affairs, simply because I haven't the strength to think for myself." He cupped the glass between both hands. "I'm smothering under it. They cook my food, do my laundry, clean my house—try to make it seem as if Patsy hadn't died. But they can't give her back to me. And there's Jessica. . . . My, I *am* drunk. . . ."

I put down my glass. "I'd better go now."

He didn't hear me. I had grown cold at the mention of Jessica's name, as if the sun and the brandy hadn't touched me. For a moment I stood and looked at him, and remembered some of the things that had spilled from me earlier. And now he had talked of his loneliness and the pressing sense of the future being shaped in a way he didn't want. Would we be able to forgive each other for the things we had spoken? Or would we despise each other for the weaknesses confessed?

"Good-bye, Nat." I don't think he even looked up as I went. Outside, the first cloud had appeared at the ridge of Great Birkeld.

CHAPTER FIVE

I FELL into the routine of the next days and weeks with a strange ease, as if I had somehow been waiting for this pause in my life.

Later that same day phone calls were made to Hardy's; the managing director, Anthony Gower, asked me to stay on at Thirlbeck. He had already been contacted by Lord Askew, who wanted me to stay. I was to telephone daily reports to Hardy's and make certain Gerald had every attention he needed. My time, he implied, was of far less importance than Gerald's comfort.

Then, from a public telephone box in Kesmere, I talked again with Mr. Gower. This time his correct, pleasant voice had a faint note of excitement. I told him what Gerald and I had seen in the few rooms of Thirlbeck which were open to us and that it was Askew's intention that it should all go to auction at Hardy's. But nothing was to be done until Gerald was completely recovered, lest he become involved and overstrain himself. I said nothing for the moment about the Rembrandt.

I also telephoned Gerald's manservant, Jeffries. I had a difficult five minutes calming his first panic. Jeffries had been with Gerald more than thirty years; he and his wife entered Gerald's service when Gerald's wife had been living. With the deaths of those two women they had grown closer, the remains of what had once been a family unit. "Mr. Stanton really *is* all right, Jeffries, and he would like you to come up here. I'd be grateful if you could drive my car up. Then you could take over the Daimler. Lord Askew would like you to stay on here until Mr. Stanton is able to leave, so you should pack suitable clothes for you both."

I asked him to go to my flat and bring some extra clothes for me also; I would telephone the owner of the ground-floor flat, who had a key. Jeffries was the one man I could have asked this favour of; he was the sort who could buy an entire wardrobe for a woman, once given her size. I told him I would telephone the garage about my car. "You remember it, Jeffries? It's a Mini."

"A *Mini?*" He cleared his throat. "I do seem to recall it, Miss Roswell." He didn't recall it with any pleasure.

"I'll expect you late tomorrow, then?"

"First thing in the morning, Miss Roswell." It would have been useless trying to dissuade him; he wouldn't rest until he saw Gerald.

I went then to the hospital, but I was only allowed to see Gerald for a few minutes the first day. Dr. Murray said that he would probably be out of the Intensive Care Unit within forty-eight hours. The condesa came with Askew and blew Gerald an airy kiss through the glass which separated them, and I realized I was jealous because Gerald looked so pleased. He was washed and shaved, and the colour of life had returned to his face. I was suddenly able to laugh at my jealousy and exult in the feeling of something won back from death.

I had arranged to meet Jeffries in Kesmere the next morning. As he pulled his long, grey-suited figure from my red Mini he was already registering disapproval of everything he saw. He couldn't see anything of merit outside London.

"How is Mr. Stanton?" was his greeting.

"I've telephoned the hospital. Doing very well, they say."

"We'll go at once, then."

"Jeffries, I don't think you should. You look tired yourself, and you probably need breakfast. It won't," I added as he started to shake his head, "do any good for Mr. Stanton to see you looking tired after such a long drive. He'll start to worry about *you.*"

He submitted reluctantly, and we went and ordered bacon and eggs in a café that did a large trade with fell walkers. Jeffries was supremely out of place and seemed happy that he so obviously was. He had a highly developed snobbism from long service to a rich man, and yet he had remained kind. He asked if the Daimler was running well. I thought of his long night on the motorway in my poor Mini and laughed. "Beautifully. Not a rattle in her."

He relaxed a little after he had eaten. "What sort of people are they—who take care of Lord Askew?"

"The Tolsons—good people, Jeffries. But not . . ." I didn't know how to express it. "Well, Mr. Tolson has been a kind of steward for the estate, and all his family work for it as well as for themselves. They're not actually help. It's more *their* home than Lord Askew's."

"Most irregular," he said.

"I don't think you'll find it irregular when you meet them."

Nor did he; he made a point of driving round to the stable yard, which now housed only farm machinery, and entering through the back door. I went along with him. Before unloading Gerald's and his own bags, he carried in the large red suitcase he had packed for me. Tolson and Jeffries confronted each other in the kitchen. Mrs. Tolson was seated at the table, mixing a batter, and Jessica, wearing a neat skirt and blouse, came in from an adjoining pantry. Jeffries took one swift look at the family, the spotless, old-fashioned kitchen, and his approval was instant.

"My name is Jeffries," he announced. "I am Mr. Stanton's man. I expect to take care of him while he's here and, of course, to take over any of the extra duties which Mr. Stanton's and Miss Roswell's presence may involve. I am used to cooking, polishing and dusting, cleaning silver, and valeting. I also drive Mr. Stanton and clean his car. Anything I can do for Lord Askew in that direction I shall be happy to do. I'll take up Miss Roswell's bag first, and then, if you'd be good enough to show me where my quarters are, and if I might locate an ironing board . . . I understand Lord Askew doesn't travel with a valet. . . ."

There was a tradition of service—of how the world should be ordered—which made these people instantly recognizable to each other, as disparate as they were. I knew what was going on between them, but I was not part of it. So I turned away and walked back to the stable yard, where the Mini and the Daimler were parked. Then, for the first time since Gerald became ill, I found I was brushing tears away from my eyes. The Mini, which I remembered as perpetually dirty, was transformed. It had been washed and polished, the ashtrays emptied; the shelf which usually held half a year's accumulated rubbish had been tidied. It was the innate reaction of an extremely tidy man to a car which he would drive, for however short a time. I felt somehow shamed as I looked at it.

THERE was Harry Peers on the phone from London. "Why didn't you tell me, you idiot? I'd have come up. Listen, do those hicks up there know how to take care of him?"

"He's all *right*, Harry. He really is all right."

"Don't trust that lot myself. They know how to look after animals better than people."

"He's being very well looked after, Harry." I was beginning to grow tired of making that statement.

"Are *you* being well looked after, luv?"

"How well is that supposed to be?"

"As well as your Harry would look after you. I'm waiting for you to come back, Jo. Don't make it too long."

And then there was the vacant dial tone on the telephone after he had hung up. I suppose it was part of Harry—that habit of never letting anyone else finish a conversation.

I thought of Harry and how he would have disapproved as I took Nat Birkett's advice the next day about fitting myself out with walking boots and a parka. I had been to see Gerald quite early, and although he had made a marked improvement I knew that it would be weeks, not days, that I would stay at Thirlbeck. I felt self-conscious in the shop, not really knowing what to ask for. I was looking through the racks when Nat touched me on the shoulder. "Saw you through the window. You're in the wrong place, you know."

"But they said this was the best shop."

"I meant you're looking at the wrong stuff. Those things might look all right in Bond Street, but they don't keep the cold out up on the fells. You need a padded parka with hood and zips like this, with plenty of pockets. Here—this your size?" He jerked down a

257

yellowish one from a hanger. "Yes, that'll do." Then I found myself, under his supervision, trying walking boots that laced firmly about the ankles, worn over two pairs of heavy socks.

"Am I supposed to *walk* in these?"

"You will, once you hit the right stride. They could save you breaking an ankle." We were outside, Nat carrying the boots, and I wearing the new, stiff parka rather self-consciously.

"We'll break it in, shall we?" Nat said.

"How?"

"Take some wine and sandwiches and go to the coast. That'll get some mustard on it and put some sand in the pockets." We were walking towards the small town square and our cars. "I'll just telephone the farm. Suddenly, I feel like a holiday."

I sat in the high passenger seat of the Bentley and stared down those who stared at me. I was glad when Nat came back, his arms loaded with paper packages. "I've been causing some gossip, I think," I said to him. "People have been wondering what Nat Birkett picked up in a spanking new parka."

"Let them. Do them good. Everyone here wants to know your business." The ancient Bentley made a lot of noise as Nat manoeuvered it out of the parking space. "Needs a bit of work," he shouted. "Damn thing takes more time than she's worth. . . . Don't know why I bother." The top was full of holes, he said, and so it was kept down permanently. I found myself zipping up the parka as we passed the outskirts of the town. Nat roared at me, "Cold?"

"No." But I was. I was also exhilarated, riding so high in the world, feeling the stream of air flowing about my face.

We headed west over a series of passes through the mountains. After an hour the scent of the salt wind came to us, and we turned into a dirt track leading towards the dunes and stopped at an empty shed, almost roofless.

"This is far enough. I know the man who owns the place. He never uses it—the land isn't much good for farming. A little sheep grazing, but really only for summer. I've often thought I'd like to buy this bit so that the boys and I could fix up the byre as a kind of beach hut. But somehow there's always something else to spend the money on." He looked at the place more speculatively. "Really ought to, though. It's necessary for me to spend time alone with the boys. I can't let them grow up completely with the Tolsons."

258

He led us through the dunes at a place where a brook trickled down to the Irish Sea. Then we walked about a mile to a small beach that glistened between two headlands. We sat and ate hunks of bread with pieces of cheese and ham, and tried to smear on butter and mustard with plastic knives. I got both butter and mustard on the new parka, and Nat said it looked better. With our backs against a boulder we drank very good red wine, passing the bottle back and forth to each other because the paper cups spoiled the taste. Afterwards we walked along the beach, and Nat showed me how to make my way up a small cliff face, using the new boots.

As we climbed he gathered the little flowers and plants that grew in the crannies of the rocks, giving them their names—thrift, scurvy grass, bloody cranesbill. Marvellous names, I thought, and tried to remember them. I tried to memorize, too, the birds he named—the terns, guillemots, kittiwakes—but only the gulls and their haunting, piercing cry were familiar. Then suddenly Nat said, "We'll have to move, or we'll be stranded here. The tide's coming in." We went back down the rock face with careful ease. But there was a sense of haste as we packed together the remains of the picnic, for drops of rain had begun to fall. By the time we reached the car it was a downpour.

He showed me how to adjust the hood of the parka so that it covered almost everything but my eyes, and then he took an old cloth cap and loose oilskin from under the seat. As he climbed in he said, "This is one of the times when I know what a fool I am to be bothering with a kid's toy like this Bentley. The Land-Rover is a damn sight more efficient and comfortable. But after Patsy's death Tolson sort of thrust it on me, as if I needed something to play with. Well, keep your head tucked down. It's going to be a long, wet, cold drive."

It was all of that. And it was worse, because Nat's mood seemed to have changed as quickly as the rain had come down. He didn't talk during the drive, and he said a perfunctory good-bye in Kesmere, stopped beside my Mini. He had probably taken me to a place where he and Patsy had often picnicked, and with me it hadn't been worth the journey. As I got into the Mini he suddenly said, "Here—take these." In my hand were the little rock plants he had gathered, and the feathers of dune grasses. I didn't know whether he gave them to me as a gift or because he simply didn't

259

want them himself. That night in the Spanish Woman's room I laid them carefully in a newspaper and put them away in my big suitcase. Then I shook the sand out of the pockets of the parka.

In the next few days I eased myself into the stiffness of the new walking boots. In spite of the heavy layers of socks they raised blisters in a few miles' hike. Tenderfoot, I told myself, as I soaked in a mustard bath that Jeffries had insisted on my taking. Jeffries knew all about such things as mustard baths and when to have brandy after a long walk. He'd have it poured and waiting for me in the Spanish Woman's room. Jeffries loved the Spanish Woman's room as, by this time, he loved every part of Thirlbeck. "It's a marvellous house, isn't it, Miss Roswell? And those pieces downstairs— they'd make you want to weep to see them all bundled together like that. But still, I suppose Mr. Tolson's right. He has to look after them in the only way he can. Actually his security is quite good, considering it's a homemade job." Jeffries didn't, however, like the dogs, and he was puzzled, as I was, that they had begun to hover around me whenever Askew was away. "Ugly-looking brutes, aren't they, Miss Roswell? When I saw you setting off for a walk yesterday and all eight of them trailing you I wondered if you'd be safe."

"I think I couldn't be safer."

He had looked doubtful, but then brightened as another thought came. "Well, Mr. Stanton will be out in less than a week if all goes well. Remarkable recovery. He'll live to be ninety." I had the feeling that if Gerald did do that, Jeffries would feel obliged to live long enough to take care of him. "Wonderful people, the Tolsons. There aren't many like them now. Perhaps there's something to be said for living in the country and keeping your roots. That little Jessica—very clever, she is. Can turn her hand to almost anything. It'll be a lucky man who marries her."

The ragged edges of life at Thirlbeck became smoother with Jeffries' presence. In his total devotion to Gerald he wanted to serve Gerald's friends. If he was not at the hospital, he took on any task at Thirlbeck. "I like to be busy," he said when Askew demurred about him doing too much. Then he added quietly, "One likes to be needed, my lord." And so he waited on table, pressed clothes, vied with Jessica in producing beautiful food; he baked and iced a triumphant birthday cake for a Tolson grandchild.

The condesa had an ability to amuse and charm Gerald, and she used it unsparingly. She had a knack for finding books and magazines which would interest him. She would even read aloud to him sometimes, making wry comments on English manners, which delighted Gerald. The flowers that arrived from friends in London were handed over to her for arranging, and she brought vases from Thirlbeck to replace the hospital vases, which Gerald loathed. When she sensed he was tiring she would sit quietly in the room, busy at her needlework. Jeffries openly adored her. "A really elegant lady," was his comment. "What a pity she can't marry Lord Askew."

I found my own rather solitary place in the world of Thirlbeck in those days. There was the daily visit to Gerald and a report to Hardy's. After that, at first, I drove far afield of Thirlbeck, doing the obvious things—Wordsworth's tiny cottage at Grasmere, the haunting ruins of ancient castles, the druidic circles of stones that had stood, their purpose unrecorded, from prehistory. At Askew's insistence Tolson had given me keys to the two gates of the Thirlbeck valley, so I could come and go as I pleased. But as the days passed I found myself turning back to Thirlbeck after the morning visit to Gerald. I walked the road over Brantwick, through the larch grove, to the ruin of the lodge where Vanessa and Jonathan had lived that summer and autumn. I stood often in the copse of birches where the first evening the great white hound had appeared, but I never saw it again.

I found the stone marker that Askew had talked about. Half hidden by the tall, reedy grass, it was set in the marshy area that ran down towards the lake. It was a rough-hewn stone, about three feet high, tapered slightly, giving it the air of an obelisk. I brushed the grass aside and deciphered the clumsily chiselled letters, almost obliterated by weather. JUANA. And then, beneath this, THE SPANISHE WOMAN. I traced the lettering with my fingers, wondering if this had been made by the boy who had been with her when she died. Juana . . . I wondered if Vanessa had ever seen this.

The ruined chapel and the burial ground of the Birketts was totally unexpected. It lay to the east of the house. I found it by following a path to a copse of beeches, elms, and oaks planted more closely than through the rest of the park. The walls of the

261

roofless chapel had almost disappeared under ivy and briars; little sapling trees were gaining height among the graves, and one, a slender young birch, had even raised itself within the chapel. There were enough headstones here to account for many generations of Birketts. A stone wall kept the sheep out; the little iron gate sagged, but still held its place. It looked as if some work had recently been done on the hinges; Tolson, no doubt, had qualms about letting the sheep graze the graves of the Birkett family.

IN THE brilliant sunshine of one early afternoon I followed a sheep trod that wound steeply upward on the rough, heathery slopes of Great Birkeld and experienced the shock of seeing clouds quickly rolling down from the top, the mist descending rapidly, the trail ahead and below blotted out, the tarn obliterated, the sheep wall I had taken as my landmark gone. I understood at last the danger Nat Birkett had warned me about, and I remembered, too, that I had told no one what direction I was taking.

Now that I could no longer see the trail, every step was in question. Had it gone up here, down there? Was this a fork or some blind turning that might take me towards the dangerous rocky slope? Sounds came to me out of the mist—the faint bleat of sheep in the distance, the rasping sound of my own breathing—all thrown back and distorted by the white wall of vapour. I had definitely lost the sheep trod. This was spongy moor grass, hollows filled with dark peat and little pools of water. In the next hour I'd not found the trail again, and I was exhausted. I stepped beyond the shelter of a boulder, and my foot touched the edge of the rockfall; a few pebbles were dislodged, and I listened to them rattle and bounce on their terrible journey to the bottom. I froze then, edged back a little, holding on to the boulder as if to save my life. I sat down on the wet ground, prepared to wait for the mist to lift. After a time I grew light-headed with cold, with hunger; and sleep—that deadly sleep—began to seem a pleasant alternative. How cold did it become up here before dawn? I wondered. A kind of dreadful calm settled on me; I could begin to acknowledge that what I might be waiting for was not the mist to lift or for the rescuers to come, but for death itself.

I first heard it as a kind of far-off howl, unbelievably eerie and desolate. Was it near, or something coming from the floor of the valley and thrown back by the mist? It seemed to come from every direction. Then, very suddenly, I knew it was quite close, the sound of small rocks disturbed, the sound of feet on grass. I screamed as something wetter than the mist touched my face, and then, at once, they were all around me. Sobbing, I put out my hand and touched the whiskery faces. "Thor . . . Ulf . . . Odin . . ." I found myself clinging about the neck of one of them. Several of those rough tongues licked my face. One of the pack thrust his great head under my arm, as if to urge me back on my feet. I got up slowly; one stayed beside me, the others went off into the mist— they might have been only feet away, but I could no longer see them. Their voices called to each other and to me at intervals, indicating the direction. With my hand firmly on the collar of the dog who had stayed with me, I started down.

I don't know how long that journey lasted. I was nudged and pushed and pulled—up a little here, down at another point. I never knew if we got back on the sheep trod. They were smelling and sniffing their ways, hoarse barks of encouragement and guidance coming from the invisible leaders.

At a place where the land began to level out, the bottomland soil of the dale, the mist grew thinner. I saw the sheen of water, and the dogs led me to the trail that circled the tarn. They all clustered about me then, the whole pack, as if to convey that their task was over. Then they strung out again, the leader ahead, the last one at my side all the way back to Thirlbeck.

When we reached the house the dogs left me at once to search for Askew. As I leaned over the balustrade of the gallery I saw him open the library door to admit them in reply to Thor's insistent scratching. I could hear his voice. "Well . . . where have you been? I've never known you lot to wander off before." I was glad they could not answer; I myself could never speak of how they had come to find me on the mountain that afternoon.

NAT Birkett noticed the cuts and scratches on my hands. He found me, after my visit to Gerald, about to look for lunch in the same café where Jeffries and I had eaten breakfast. I felt his hand on my wrist. "Well, then—I didn't see you," he said, turning my palm upward. "Were you stuck somewhere and couldn't get down?"

"More or less."

"Come and tell me. I know a rather cozier place than this café." He led me across the town square to a very small pub called The Drover's Rest. Inside, there was an instant greeting from the landlord. "Morning, Nat, what'll it be?"

Nat looked at me. "Would you like beer? It's local. Very good."

We sat over beer and a cheese salad, and great slabs of bread almost as good as Jessica's. "Gerald's coming out of the hospital tomorrow," I said. "I expect I'll be going back to London soon. With Jeffries here, I'm really not needed. I've been doing just a bit of paper sorting at Thirlbeck and driving around. . . ."

"And walking," he said. "And getting into trouble, by the looks of it."

I told him a little of what had happened, but nothing about the dogs. I simply said I had found my way down by a sheep wall.

"I never imagined you'd go off the valley floor, or I'd have insisted you have a compass." He thrust out his legs and looked as if he were trying to keep his patience. "Damn it, Jo! You could have broken your neck."

"I would have been a lot of trouble, wouldn't I?"

"You should stay in the city where you belong."

"I'll see that I do in future."

He took a drink of his beer. "All right—all right. But I've every reason to be annoyed. You've been a fool, and you must know it. Now, if you've got any time to spare, we can put you to work watching the crag where the eagles are nesting. I've put up a sort of shelter—just enough to keep the rain off. The thing is that no one, not even the watchers, must go near the nest."

"What do you do if someone tries?"

"Well, if they've come over from the other side of Brantwick, you would drive back and rouse any of the Tolsons. They'd telephone me. But if people have climbed in by the estate wall, you could easily stop and challenge them. It *is* private property."

We sat over our beer, and ordered some more, and Nat's talk drifted to his farm. He went on and on about his flocks and herds until finally he put down his beer and took my hand in his, tracing the scratches and deeper cuts. "You know, I'm awfully glad you didn't tumble down Great Birkeld and break your silly neck. And I've been talking like an idiot—about things that you probably don't care a damn for. I can't talk about old silver and paintings, Jo. It's hard for me even to imagine the world you live in. I thought, when you left Southdales that morning, that I had bored you to death with my stupid rambling—and here I am doing it again."

"And here I am listening. You listened to me, too, Nat."

"Yes, I remember. But afterwards I wondered if you really had been there or if it was some drunken dream. You really don't belong at Southdales. Thirlbeck is your sort of place." He shrugged and dropped my hand. "I imagine the hay is sticking out all over me." Then he laughed suddenly at his own gloomy words. "Well, I'll walk you to your car, and then I have to come back here to see a man with a couple of good calves. He wants too much for them, but if I get enough whisky into him, he might drop his price." He was helping me on with my parka. "Farmer's talk, Jo."

"We talk shop, too. It's different shop, that's all. Don't bother to come with me. When shall I take my turn eagle-watching?"

"Would two to five in the afternoons be all right?"

I said it would, and left him. It was true. I didn't belong here, and he didn't belong anywhere else. There was a kind of amazing innocence in him that wouldn't have survived long beyond this world of his. Then I began to imagine him meeting my father and how very well Nat would have understood and respected my father's need for the lost, remote world of his hacienda.

GERALD came back to Thirlbeck, and life took up yet another rhythm. The days were mostly sunny, and garden furniture of a bygone age—teak benches and chairs, a handsome teak table—appeared in an open space which gave a view along the length of the tarn. Drinks were set out there on days when the weather permitted. Gerald's conversation was brisk and sharp, but he still returned to his room after lunch and didn't reappear until before dinner. Askew and the condesa looked forward to his coming; Thirlbeck oppressed her, I thought, and she wanted talk of other places, something Gerald could well supply.

I began to take my turn, as I had promised Nat, at the shelter below the crag where the eagles nested. My eyes ached sometimes from looking through the binoculars, but the hours never seemed long. I was supposed to watch on every side of the crag

265

for the approach of strangers, but often I found myself just watching the flight of the eagles. I learned to anticipate, to love, that heart-stopping moment when one or the other soared above the crag and then swooped in a dive to earth. The eagles became for me a manifestation of all that was free, free to soar, to mate, and to nest—wild things that needed a territory as big as this valley and peace to nurture their fledglings. I grew to feel about those two birds as I felt about the house itself—that once it vanished something quite irreplaceable would have gone.

I was now spending several hours a day working on the boxes in the study, looking for any paper relating to the Rembrandt. Perched on the ladder, my hands smeared with dust and cobwebs, I scanned the brittle brown papers, but despaired of finding what Gerald hoped for. Indeed, there was almost a malevolent disarray about the contents of the boxes. Some would begin with the date stamped on the cover and then skip ten years. Others would bear no relation to the date on the box at all. It seemed utterly useless, but I persisted because Gerald had asked it.

Curiously, Gerald was in no particular hurry to return to London, nor was Askew impatient to leave. Both of them seemed to have fallen into their own pattern at Thirlbeck. Perhaps Gerald was more tired than he had known. Perhaps Askew was beginning to face without fear his own past in this house; he even took his turn at the eagle watch and became almost as zealous as Nat Birkett. Only the condesa chafed under the restrictions of life at Thirlbeck. She did not openly complain, but at times I sensed a growing desperation in her. I thought that she feared Askew's seeming contentment in his surroundings; it might be difficult to pry him loose. Yet she sat at her needlework with the quiet grace of a woman who has schooled herself in the art of waiting.

The telephone calls from Harry continued, but they were brief and less frequent. And then there came one during which he said he was going to Australia. "Just for a day or two, luv."

"Don't be ridiculous, Harry. No one goes to Australia for a day or two. What are you going to do there?"

"Mind your own business, luv. That way I'll never be able to blame you for talking out of school and letting some other bloke in on what Harry's already got his eye on. Back in a week. See you—that is, unless you've decided to retire up there."

266

"No, we'll be leaving in a few days."

"That's good. Someone else might slip into your spot."

"What spot?"

"Your spot at Hardy's, stupid. Well, keep your eye on Gerald. Worth having around, he is. Bye, luv."

"Harry . . . ?" But he was gone, already a world away from me.

Tolson had long ago, at Askew's insistence, produced the keys to the bookcases in the library. I searched there, too—for a diary, anything that might list the possessions of Margeretha van Huygens. In the mornings the sun came into that room—with the metal shutters thrown back it was a cheerful place, the jumble of furniture even making it seem cozy. I enjoyed sitting on the ladder, taking down books. There were a few that I began to suspect could be of more than usual interest—books in manuscript, with stately Latin phrases, illuminated, some of them. I had a sense, as I touched them, that they had been handled fairly recently. They were dusty, but the dust had not been undisturbed for years. Perhaps Jessica had also enjoyed these treasures, trying out her Latin on them. As I carefully turned the pages I wondered if I should talk to Gerald about them, or to Askew. Something held me back. I was beginning to think that, while all seemed right on the surface, much at Thirlbeck could be very wrong.

I found the Book of Hours on the top shelf of a case whose lock yielded only after I had eased its stiffness with fine sewing-machine oil. The dust inside this case was heavy and undisturbed. The Book of Hours had fallen, or been pushed, behind taller volumes. It was tiny and exquisite, this *Horae*, illuminating with those curiously mediaeval figures the seven canonical offices of the day. My memory spelled them out as I turned the beautiful hand-wrought pages—matins, prime, terce, sext, none, vespers, compline. So beautifully executed, this book could have been made for a princess. I could not, from my very small knowledge of such things, know for what historic personage such a book had been designed. But it once had been given, and the name of the giver, or the receiver, was written in a faded but readable script: Juana Fernández de Córdoba, Mendoza, Soto y Alvarez.

And then an ancient, brittle sheet slipped out and, along with it, a page which held Vanessa's writing.

I don't remember how long I sat on top of that ladder. I do remember staring out at the lake and back at the two sheets of paper. Finally, carefully closing the bookcase, I climbed down the ladder and left the study. When I reached the Spanish Woman's room it was more than ever a sanctuary to me.

I sat at the long table in the window alcove and spread out the two pages. One was fine parchment, yellowed, with a flowing script in Spanish. The other was ordinary modern notepaper on which, in her scrawling hand, Vanessa had copied the Spanish words. Someone had written a translation beneath:

> And this do we send unto you, beloved cousin, our likeness, by the hand of Domenico Theotokopoulos, a mirror of conscience, to keep close, in faith and in trust, until the day of the final victory and the eternal union in Christ and our Holy Mother Church.
>
> I, the King,
Felipe

I looked in awe at the signature on the yellowed parchment— that of Philip II, using the majestic title, "I, the King," as all sovereigns of Spain had done in the days of her power and glory. I knew quite surely that this scrap of parchment had been sent to the Spanish Woman to hold her loyalty to the political mission on which she had been sent, a pawn in Philip's hand.

But the vital importance of the message was in that other name, the name of an ordinary painter known not to have been greatly favoured by the king, but obviously used by him for this special commission. The portrait must have been quite small or it never could have reached the Spanish Woman in secret. Domenico Theotokopoulos—the name he had been called in official documents. To the world, who would now pay almost unimaginable sums for one of his pictures, he was known simply as El Greco.

I grew weak at the thought that one of *his* canvases might exist in this house and that Vanessa *had* come across this slip of parchment in the Spanish Woman's cherished book. Vanessa had found it, copied it, and had it translated. And told no one.

I looked wildly around the room and wondered about all the rooms in this great house in which I had never set foot. I thought of the locked door which guarded the pictures of Margeretha van Huygens. Was it possible that among them, alien to those Dutch landscapes and still lifes, there existed a small portrait of a Spanish

268

Hapsburg face, the face of Philip, arch-enemy of Elizabethan England? I doubted it. *If* the portrait existed, it would be in the place where the Spanish Woman had hidden it.

I looked out on the calm, golden mirror of the tarn. The Spanish Woman had taken to her death in that tarn the knowledge of a greater treasure than the enormous jewel she wore at her neck.

THAT was the day at Thirlbeck when I opened doors I never had opened before. Until now good manners—perhaps misplaced, considering the job I held—had kept me from prying. Now I drew back curtains, lifted dust sheets. I opened chests and met only the softness of old curtains or bedcovers. There were no pictures and few mirrors. In some rooms I saw fingerprints in the dust, a trail of footprints on the oak floors. I seemed to follow a trail that someone laid before me. It could have been Jessica, who walked the rooms of this house with loving familiarity; it could have been someone whose curiosity had been greater than mine.

But when I opened the door of a room in the wing opposite the one I slept in, I realized that wherever I had gone in that house the perfume that was so strong in this room had been with me—this flowery scent the condesa used. On the room she inhabited she had indelibly stamped her personality. Her amber silk gown lay across a chair, a table with a swinging mirror was strewn with silver-topped bottles and jars. There were flowers and foliage in a big vase, arranged with the careless grace that the condesa had made into high art. And the perfume. I began to think that the perfume wasn't in each room because the condesa had been there before me. She could not have been everywhere, nor so recently. It was the strength of her personality, not her perfume, that was so pervasive. It had impregnated these walls as if she had been here forever, not just a few weeks.

But now I was realizing I had no business looking in her room or in the one Askew used, and I didn't linger.

The house, which from the front appeared to be two storeys, grew to three at the centre. There was a cluster of low-ceilinged attic rooms with half windows that looked over the roofs of Thirlbeck. Here was the litter of generations—old trunks, bedsteads, a croquet set. The narrow corridors all came back to a steep stair, which must have led down to the wing on the rear of the house which the Tolsons inhabited. I turned back. This, too, was territory I could not invade, and there nagged the thought that somewhere in their rooms might be the portrait of Philip II of Spain.

That night my sleep was fitful. The sense of the closeness of the Spanish Woman pressed on me; I woke to the faint noises that the room always held and to the familiar shadow that had no substance. It was not fear I felt, but something tugged at me with overriding urgency.

Unable to sleep, I lit a candle and took it to the long table. Then I brought the Book of Hours and turned its pages, feeling the faith of a young Spanish girl, who must have held this among her dearest possessions. But where had she hidden the portrait of the man whose words must have been almost as sacred to her as the text in this hauntingly beautiful book? Juana Fernández de Córdoba, Mendoza, Soto y Alvarez, the name written in her careful script. They had taken her life and the life of her child; they had tried to take away her identity, but they had not succeeded. She had lived in legend as none of the Birketts had lived; her presence now seemed a cogent reality. I turned to something she had written at the back of her book, words I couldn't understand but which must have been important to her to have written them here. Was it a message she meant to leave? The condesa could possibly have translated them, but I had no intention of showing this to her.

I slept there in the chair, and woke to the sound of a vehicle on the road that led up the valley to Brantwick. The eastern light was glowing over the top of the mountain, and that had been Nat Birkett's Land-Rover taking him to his watch at the shelter.

IT WAS chill in the dawn when I walked to find him. But it was a morning of great radiance, the trees, the grass beaded with moisture. Yet I was weary of this place; I longed to be free of the thoughts of Vanessa's odd connection with it; I wanted to talk to Gerald about Vanessa. But he could not be worried now by such things. So I walked out in the dawn to talk to Nat Birkett, still almost a stranger.

The shelter was a kind of three-sided hut, with the open side facing away from the crag where the eagles nested; the crag was watched through a long cut in the opposite side, with a shelf where the watcher rested his elbows during the long sessions

270

holding the binoculars. A little Sterno stove was for making tea, and a few biscuit tins stored the provisions.

Nat, followed by his collie, came to meet me. "I've been missing you, Jo. Have you done any more stupid things like climbing Great Birkeld? There's water for coffee on."

He had put his arm around my shoulders in a way that was warmly companionable, and I was instantly conscious that this was not enough. All at once I wanted much more than absentminded affection from Nat Birkett. "I followed you," I said. "I heard the Land-Rover and knew it was you coming up here."

I shivered even with the warmth of his body close to me. "You're cold," he said. "I'll make the coffee."

The night had been long. I could feel my eyes swollen from lack of sleep; the worries of Thirlbeck and Vanessa's connection were back with me, and now this added new dimension of being acutely, painfully aware of Nat Birkett. "Any brandy?" I said.

"Just so happens . . ." He brought out a flask. "Do you make a habit of vigils? You always seem to be wandering in the dawn."

I ignored the question. The mug of coffee laced with brandy was comforting between my hands. "Anything to eat?" He passed over a meat pasty. And then I was talking about my disquieting thoughts. "Nat, do you believe that the Spanish Woman really brought bad luck to the Birketts?"

"The Birketts aren't unlucky. It's the earls of Askew who are unlucky. You take an ordinary but clever man of business like Askew's grandfather. He becomes earl of Askew, and everything goes wrong. He has only one son who survives, and *he's* a bit off his head—enough to make him retreat into Thirlbeck and never see a soul. Then he quarrels with *his* only child. That child dashes off to the Spanish Civil War, marries a Spanish girl—and a Catholic—and they all begin to think that the Spanish Woman is returning to take Thirlbeck back again."

I sucked in my breath. "I never thought of that!"

"*They* did. You'd think almost four hundred years hadn't passed since the Armada. Then she has a son, and, of course, the earldom would go to a Catholic. But it never did. That unlucky Askew manages to kill them both just before they ever reach Thirlbeck, when they were almost in sight of it. There's something that hangs on in that place. No wonder he's stayed away."

271

"Nat, sooner or later *you* will be the earl of Askew. What will you do with Thirlbeck?"

"Tear it down if I have the money."

"Nat—*no!*"

"Why not? Who wants it?"

"Who—who? I can't say who. But people want it, Nat. They *need* it. They pour out from the cities, from concrete housing developments. They drive hellish distances to *see* something different. They would come to Thirlbeck to see something built four hundred years ago, something that no one could afford to build today. It's a dream, Nat, and they want it preserved."

"Why? They don't even know what they're looking at."

"Nat!" I was pleading desperately. "Thirlbeck is as unique as golden eagles. If you lose this pair of eagles, perhaps in a hundred years or so another pair may come back to nest—there's always the hope. Once you tear down Thirlbeck, it's gone forever."

Suddenly his mug of coffee turned over and the liquid ran onto the ground. He went and gazed out the long viewing space in the wall. In time, after minutes, he came back, sitting on the ground close to me. "Jo, you ask me to preserve Thirlbeck. I owe it nothing. Do you know how Patsy died?"

"They said—yes, they said she died at Thirlbeck. Oh, Nat, I'm sorry. I shouldn't—" His face was in torment.

"But do you know where and how she was found? I'll bet no one told you that. It was agreed between the Tolsons and me that it was an inexplicable accident. When the person you love most dearly in the world is gone you don't have feelings of revenge—not against people like the Tolsons. And nothing will bring Patsy back. So we just let it go."

He picked up the mug and placed it among the biscuit tins, as if he were trying to decide whether he should say more. Then he sighed. "She just simply disappeared. Her car was still at Southdales; she couldn't have gone too far. We didn't even know she was gone until she failed to meet the school bus. It was Richard's first year at school, and she always met him. I telephoned around, but no one had seen her. Every farmer around here searched—any place it was possible for her to be. I thought I'd go out of my mind that night. It was November and bitterly cold. If she were out, I just knew she couldn't survive. We organized a search for

272

the next morning. It was a hellish day, so long, and yet it got dark so quickly. When the light was gone Tolson suggested a search of Thirlbeck itself. We had no reason to suppose she was there—Jessica was at the house all the day Patsy disappeared, and she said no one had come. But she also said she'd been in the vegetable garden for a while. The thing that made Tolson suggest it, really, was that La Española was gone from its safe, though the alarm system was still connected and working."

"Nat, I'm sorry. Please, no more. I shouldn't have said anything."

"Be quiet and let me talk, will you?" He was hunched on the ground beside me, his arms wrapped about his knees, his chin thrust down towards them. "She had a heart condition from having had rheumatic fever in childhood. She was often breathless; small things made her tired. We went to London to a consultant, and he said they could operate in about six to eight weeks. You have to wait for the really good guys unless it's an outright emergency. So we came home, and we were waiting for her to be called back to London. . . .

"We found her, Jo, eventually, in the Spanish Woman's room. She was lying against the door as if she had exhausted herself utterly by banging and calling. Those old fastenings on the windows are very stiff, so she broke some of the diamond panes of glass. But she wasn't seen or heard. Tolson and I had to break the lock of the door to get in. Ted Tolson said afterwards that the whole mechanism had jammed; it was the lock put in when the place was built. Patsy had made it worse, he thought, by trying to turn the key to free it. It was jammed tighter. Well, those things didn't concern me at the time. All I knew was that Patsy had died there, cold and alone and frightened. She just couldn't take the state of panic she must have gone into. Dr. Murray said she died that first night. She lay there, my little Patsy. And she had La Española in her hand."

"Nat! La Española . . . *why?*"

"Why? We'll never know. She'd been encouraged to go to that house, to get familiar with it, as if it were already hers. Tolson encouraged it. The way he encouraged her to come and look at La Española, to take it, handle it. He thought she should not be afraid of it—of those stupid stories they tell about it."

"Did he teach her how the alarm system worked?"

273

Nat shrugged. "He *said* he did. Oh, what the hell! Who knows about the why of it? Patsy must have walked to Thirlbeck, used the duplicate key to the South Lodge gate I always left in the house. I blame myself for not checking at once to see if the key was still at Southdales. But there she was at Thirlbeck—dead. Even before I lifted her, Tolson and I had agreed that we would say nothing about La Española. I just couldn't have Patsy's death surrounded by the horrible publicity it would have brought. And then there was the question I never really asked, but it was there, all the same. How *could* Patsy have been in the house and no one know it?"

"Nat, why on earth didn't she switch on the light? Why didn't she light a candle or the fire? There's always a basket of wood."

He shook his head. "There *was* no light. That was something Ted put in afterwards. The way he fixed the lock—afterwards. Yes, there was a candle and a basket of wood. But she had no matches." This explained his rather fanatical preaching about always being careful, about the need for proper clothes and compasses. I felt the anguish of his thousand regrets.

"The dogs. Didn't they try to suggest that she was there?"

"The police had brought their own tracker dogs, and they told Tolson to keep the wolfhounds shut up because they might start fights. So we put them in the stable, where they howled their heads off. Another mistake, I suppose.

"After that," Nat continued, "the Tolsons sort of closed ranks around me. But when Tolson and I look at each other the question is still there. Why did we let it happen? We never speak about it. I can't talk about Patsy."

"You're talking now. About Patsy and the Tolsons. Do you understand what that means, Nat?"

"I think I do, Jo. Finally I'm talking. To you. For three years I've felt like an old man. I've acted like one. Then one morning you appeared at my door, sat in the chair that Patsy used to sit in, and I didn't mind seeing that. In fact, I liked it so much I got drunk in astonishment. I felt like a kid, and I was trying to cover it up. Well, I'm not going to cover it up anymore. Kiss me, Jo."

At first I wasn't sure I liked the way he kissed me. It was hungry, almost greedy and hurting. For Nat Birkett there had been nothing for more than three years.

274

"Jo . . ." he said. "I'll stop in a minute."

"Don't . . ." I moved closer to him.

"You're crazy and so am I. You're going back to London and your fancy young tycoon, and that will be that. What's all that stuff about gathering rosebuds while you may? You're not a rosebud, Jo. On both of us the thorns stand out an inch each side. But we are what we are. Jo, I wish you weren't going."

"I know I must go. I'm all wrong for your sort of life, Nat. As wrong as you'd be for mine. But kiss me again—with all the thorns. Or are they nettles? They say they don't sting if you have the courage to grab them hard enough."

But this time it was easier, gentler, his lips dwelling on mine. And then to my shock I felt my own deep hunger, which I had not recognized as being there unsatisfied. I heard my own voice. "Yes, I wish . . . I wish, too, Nat."

There are many places to make love. A forest of larches and birches a little after dawn is one of them. Not so different or unique. Lovers have done such things for centuries. But for me it felt as if it were the first time.

IT WASN'T that we heard anything. There was no sound, no movement. There was just the sense of another presence, and Nat's collie standing alert, ears up. Then he was gone like a flash through the wood, and we saw a figure among the trees, a slight, fairylike figure with spun-gold hair, like a wraith of the mist. She and the collie were running together, back towards Thirlbeck.

Nat crashed his fist down. "Will they never let me alone? That Jessica under my feet every time I turn around. Don't they understand I loathe the sight of her? Tolson still tries to pretend none of it happened. I suppose he's terrified she may say too much one day, or something may happen again."

"*Again?* Nat, what are you talking about?"

He took his time about lighting cigarettes for us both. I noticed his hands trembled a little. Then he rolled over and rested on his elbows, looking into my face. "I'm talking, Jo, as I shouldn't talk. But now that I've begun I can't stop.

"Jessica—who really knows what happened between her and Patsy? Did Jessica find her looking at La Española and resent it? Or did they take it out together? We still don't know the answers.

275

All we know is that when I carried Patsy's body down that night, Jessica went completely to pieces, screaming hysterically that she had nothing to do with it, that she hadn't *touched* Patsy. I heard it, and I'll never forget it. That brilliant, half-cracked kid, who'd had a nervous breakdown that summer after whizzing through all her exams, screaming and screaming that she hadn't seen Patsy the afternoon before. Patsy hadn't been in the house. She *shouldn't* have been in the house. On and on it went. And all the things she was denying, we knew had happened. She had known all along Patsy was in the house, but said nothing until she saw the body. Then her nerves cracked. The things she said about Patsy. I wouldn't have believed Jessica even knew words like that, vile words. Tolson got her to her room, but the screaming went on. When Dr. Murray came he gave her an injection. He had treated Jessica when she'd cracked up that summer; he'd no doubt have said she was still in a period of diminished responsibility. So we just told the police and all the searchers that Patsy had been found, and it was all over. . . .

"Later, as Jessica grew better, it was less possible to believe that she really had screamed those things. She couldn't, of course, ever admit it herself. Not that perfect little ice maiden!"

"Nat, what do you honestly think did happen?"

"I *suppose* either Jessica found Patsy up there with La Española or they went there together. Some row blew up, Jessica flew out in a rage, slammed the door, and that was enough to jam the lock."

"So she might not have touched her, just as she said."

He shook his head. "Probably didn't. What she didn't do was *tell* us that Patsy was there. And she reconnected the alarm system so that her grandfather wouldn't think Patsy was in Thirlbeck."

"But why? She couldn't have known Patsy would die. And she'd be in terrible trouble when Patsy did get out."

"You've seen kids do something wrong, haven't you, and try to cover it up as long as possible, even when they know it'll be discovered in the end? When all the searchers started combing the Thirlbeck valley she must have been scared stiff. She might honestly have had a mental blackout. Dr. Murray told me that same night, that he was referring Jessica to a psychiatrist in London. She went away for a while. Had shock treatment I think. Then she went to a man in Carlisle a couple of times a week for two years. And all the time since that night she's been the good little girl she is now. Intelligent, willing, very competent. I almost think she's forgotten what happened, because she doesn't seem to realize I have any reason to hate her."

He carefully squashed his cigarette butt into a rusty tobacco tin. "So, you see, it was for Jessica's sake as well as mine that the Tolsons closed in so tight, making things easier for me, plastering over the cracks in my existence. I've kept quiet, so they probably think I've accepted it. But I haven't forgotten that night, nor do I know how to wipe it all away. I feel, sometimes, I haven't breathed clean air for more than three years."

He sat up then, and I felt his hand hard on my shoulder. "For just these minutes with you I felt I was actually breathing again, Jo, coming out from under. But now I've come to my senses. You don't belong in this world, and I know you're going."

When I left him, there in the shelter, gazing after me, a special warmth still lived in me, a sense of having tasted something for which I would forever after be hungry. I felt, even, that while it might be easier to go away from Thirlbeck, it might not be better.

When I reached the tarn the mist had lifted from the tops of Brantwick and Great Birkeld. Above the crag an eagle soared across the valley and was lost to sight against the bald mountain.

I HAD thought I would find Jessica in the kitchen, and there she was. It was still very early, and she was alone, as I had expected, surrounded by pans and bowls, starting the day's cooking.

She looked up when I came in through the back passage. She was completely calm, not at all disconcerted by the fact that she knew Nat and I had seen her from the shelter. Coffee perked gently on one of the stoves. She jerked her head towards the pot. "It's ready now. Would you like some?"

"Yes, I would." In silence I poured and passed her a cup.

"Thanks." She took a sip and went on measuring ingredients. "It's Bavarian cream for lunch," she said. "Can you cook?"

"Not much."

"No, I didn't think so. I don't know what you do at Hardy's, but you're not terribly useful anywhere else. In a few years, if I keep reading, I'll know as much as you do—much more, probably. And I'll be able to run a house as well."

278

I drew out a chair and sat facing her across the big table. "What's that supposed to mean, Jessica? And why did you hang around the shelter this morning? What were you looking for?"

"Why did *you* go there? Nat Birkett's not the sort for smart London types to amuse themselves with."

"Who does he go for, Jessica? Your type?"

"Why not? Quite soon he'll wake up and know I'm not a child anymore."

While she was talking I had begun fingering a cream-coloured bowl which stood with her mixing basins and measuring cups. It was slightly fluted at the edges, with a thin brown rim, and carved in the centre and sides was a delicate line drawing of flowers and leaves—possibly peony and lotus. A very plain bowl, very beautiful. Jessica probably meant to chill the dessert in it.

"Doesn't Nat already *know* how clever and good you are?"

"Once I'm twenty he'll realize." Her voice was very soft, like a whisper. "He's been too used to thinking of me as a child."

Both of us spoke as if this were an entirely ordinary conversation, our tones level and calm. But I had seen the colour come more strongly to her cheeks, and her china-blue eyes were stony and hard, staring at me with a strange fanatical glow of which I would never have believed her capable. What had Nat accused her of—hate; jealousy; a blind, a possibly murderous rage? I took the bowl in my hands and turned it over, looking at the faint marks, tracing the line carving with my finger. I looked back at Jessica, and I couldn't have told if it was she, so transformed, or the bowl I held that caused the tightening in my throat.

Her voice again, whispery, silky. "Why don't you leave, and we'll have everything back as it used to be."

"Nothing will ever be as it used to be, Jessica. Lord Askew has come home, and *that* has changed things."

"He'll go again. It doesn't really belong to him."

"Who does it belong to, Jessica?"

"To us. To my family and Nat Birkett. Why do old men stay around, making other people wait for what should be theirs?"

I thought she had the blank look of obsession now, the fixed eyes, the voice completely without emotion. I turned and turned the bowl in my hands because she seemed mesmerized by the movement.

279

I spoke very softly to her. "Did Patsy Birkett make you wait too long for what is really yours, Jessica? There was going to be an operation, and she might have gotten well and lived for a long time, mightn't she? She used to come and see La Española. Did *you* take the jewel out that day? Did she find you in the Spanish Woman's room with it? Or was it the other way around? Did you leave her there—alone, frightened? And when she didn't come down you didn't go back to find out what had happened. Not then, nor all the next day, when they were searching."

Incredibly, there was the faintest trace of a smile on her lips. "I did nothing to her. *Caveat raptor:* Who seizes, beware. Patsy held La Española as if it were hers, and she walked around this house as if she already lived here. These rooms—*my* rooms."

"Jessica! No more! You're imagining things again!" Tolson spoke from the doorway. His monumental frame stooped, his shoulders rounded more than before.

And at the sight of him the bowl fell from my suddenly nerveless fingers and smashed in many pieces on the flagstone floor.

CHAPTER SIX

THEN I was driving down the motorway towards London, the pieces of the bowl wrapped in a silk scarf and packed among my clothes in a suitcase. I kept pushing the Mini near seventy, getting frantic and antagonistic blasts from the horns of other cars when I did something especially stupid. It began to rain, and the driving grew harder, but I didn't relax the speed. When, hours later, I was enmeshed in the heavy evening traffic, there was nothing I could do but sit and stare at the lines of cars ahead. It was then I let my thoughts dwell on what had happened at Thirlbeck.

Askew hadn't even wanted to delay his breakfast when I told him. "You don't seem to understand, Lord Askew. It *may* be very valuable, and I've broken it."

Unbelievably he had shrugged. "It's broken. Plenty of things get broken. As well as people."

"But you *do* understand I must go tell my director at Hardy's. I've been unimaginably clumsy. He expects better of me."

"Look," he said, "just sit down and have your breakfast, and let me have mine. There's a good girl." He poured coffee. "I really think you're overdoing this. After all, what need to tell Hardy's if something in my house gets broken?"

"You did say you were considering offering the contents of this house for auction. What I've just done could seriously prejudice that. Whether or not the bowl turns out to be what I suspect it might be, or quite worthless, is hardly the case."

"You *do* take yourself seriously. If it was used in the kitchen, no one had any idea it might be valuable. You could just have kept your mouth shut. Looks like a perfectly ordinary bowl to me."

"Well, not to me. And you'd imagine I'd say nothing?"

He looked at me hard. Then he laughed. "Well, no wonder Gerald sets such store by you. Scout's honour and all the rest of it. But suppose I just say forget it. There was an accident. It was my property. I overlook it. Now do you still have to rush off and confess all to your director?"

"I want to. And I *will*, Lord Askew."

I had left Thirlbeck immediately, and it was after six thirty when I reached Hardy's. I rang the night bell and was routinely examined through a viewer by the security man. "It's you, Jo," he said as he opened up. "Mr. Hudson said you were to go straight to him. Here, want to leave the bag?"

I rummaged around and found the scarf with the pieces in it.

I paused at the top of the stairs, which led on to the salerooms. How long I seemed to have been away, and yet I had left only a few weeks before. Until then I could almost have believed that my whole life had been lived here, would go on being lived here. It wasn't to be quite the same again, ever.

William Hudson rose from his desk when I entered. "Ah, there you are." He paused. "My dear girl, you look terrible! Here—" He went to a beautifully inlaid cabinet and produced a bottle and glasses. "A Scotch, Jo? I expect you've been on the road most of the day. Nasty weather for it, too."

I sipped the Scotch cautiously but gratefully. "Mr. Hudson, I don't think you'll be half as nice when you know what's happened."

His gaze went fondly, as it often did during interviews, to the beautiful glazed pottery figure of a mounted drummer of the Tang dynasty, which stood on top of the writing bureau.

"Jo, I've had a telephone call from Lord Askew. I must confess it made me most curious. He said I was to take notice of absolutely nothing you said. He said he thought you were . . . well, a little *unsettled* still, after your mother's death. Jo, what has happened?"

I brought out the fragments of the bowl. "This is what has happened, Mr. Hudson. I broke it."

He drew the silk scarf towards him gently and examined the pieces. He put a few together, getting an idea of the shape of the bowl, fingering the glaze. His face grew long in concentration, and I saw the dawning of regret.

"Well . . . it looks terribly like that Ting ware basin we had last year. Sung dynasty. Beautiful piece, this—if it were in one piece."

"That's it. I dropped it this morning."

He looked across at me. "And Lord Askew wants me to pay no attention to anything you say. Did you tell him about this?"

"I didn't say what I *thought* it was. I just said I suspected it might be very valuable."

He regarded me bleakly. "He absolved you of any responsibility. Absolutely. But, of course, he didn't know that we sold that other one for forty-nine thousand pounds. That's an awful lot of money to drop, Jo, isn't it?" Again he gently touched the fragments. "And a very beautiful bowl."

"That's why I'm here. I told him I had to come and see you. He didn't understand. He said no one need ever have known."

He sipped his Scotch and seemed to be giving all his attention to the Tang horseman. "*You* would have known. And that, in my mind, is what makes the difference between a person who does a job for what's in it for him, and someone who does it for . . . love, almost. I have to deplore your carelessness and congratulate you on having a good eye for a piece that really is pretty rare. You could go a long way, Jo. I must see if there isn't a place for you in oriental ceramics." He took care not to look at my face, so that I had time to compose it again. "And as for this . . . well, it can be mended, of course, but it can never be the perfect piece it was. I assume Lord Askew was thinking of disposing of it?"

"He didn't know he had it! It's all in such a crazy state up there. He was ready to have us come up and go through the whole house. And then Mr. Stanton got ill! Now Lord Askew seems to have settled in a bit, and he doesn't want to talk business."

We launched into the talk that was close to both of us. For a time, as I described Thirlbeck, the barrier of age and status between us vanished. I told William Hudson about the rooms crammed with furniture, the books, the metal shutters. And, of course, the beauty of La Española. But I found there were things I could not say. I did not talk about the Rembrandt, which gave Gerald so much worry; certainly I said nothing about the Book of Hours, the possibility of an El Greco, or the miniature in my handbag. I didn't even mention Vanessa's ever having been at Thirlbeck; if that part of the story was ever told, it would have to come from Gerald.

I DROVE up a block to an Italian restaurant where I often ate. I was on my way through the bar to the dining section when the voice called to me. "Jo, we hear you've been living it up with the jet set somewhere. How's life? Have a drink."

In the darkened area I recognized two young men from Hardy's, though at the moment it was difficult to put a name to either of them. They were flanked by two young women, neither of whom seemed much enthused by my presence. I didn't think, after all those hours on the motorway, that my appearance posed much threat to their fresh London elegance. I dropped down into a seat beside them, and then my mind began sorting the men out.

"Peter, you speak Spanish, don't you?"

"Yes, a bit. But don't send me to take any exams right now."

"Just hold on—please. I'll be back." A Scotch had been put in front of me. "And don't let them take my drink away."

I returned quickly, bringing from my suitcase what I wanted. I unwrapped it, and Peter Warner examined it closely, a minor variation of William Hudson's behaviour over the Sung bowl. "Jo, where on earth did you come across this?"

"It doesn't matter, Peter. All you have to look at is what's written in the back. Can you make out any of it?"

"Well, the Latin and Spanish is all mixed up, and the spelling is, I'd guess, sixteenth century."

"What does it say?"

"Give me a chance." He sipped his drink. One of the girls at the table looked at the other and gave an exaggerated shrug. I realized then I hadn't even waited to be introduced to them.

"*What*, Peter?"

He fingered the parchment pages. "It says, 'When I am dead, of

283

your charity, offer nine masses for my soul.'" He looked up. "That's typical enough. The Spanish are always brooding about death."

"Thanks, Peter." I finished my drink quickly and fended off questions about Thirlbeck. Then I went and sat alone and ate cannelloni and had a half bottle of wine. Juana Fernández de Córdoba's Book of Hours lay on the banquette beside me, wrapped again. I had no more right to it than to the miniature in my handbag, and I would return it to Thirlbeck. But as I ate, the words of the little exiled Spanish girl came echoing through the centuries. "When I am dead, of your charity, offer nine masses for my soul." No one knew where she was buried or if she had a grave at all. And no one, I thought, had offered nine masses for her soul.

IT WAS probably madness to do what I was doing in this state of fatigue, but it was something I could never manage in the cool calm of an early morning. I needed the feeling of languor as insulation against the shock of visiting Vanessa's flat for the first time since her death.

I drove to Church Street and parked the car. I stared up at her window, the blackness speaking of a terrible emptiness within. My heart ached, and the puzzle of Vanessa's unrevealed presence at Thirlbeck all those years ago nagged and tugged. I suddenly knew why I had come. Somewhere in the labyrinth of Vanessa's personal possessions there might be disclosed the reason for her silence. And now the urgency of that unanswered question became a need to reestablish contact with Vanessa herself, the glowing spirit of the woman, which had not died with her body.

Gerald, who was executor of Vanessa's will, had given me keys to the flat. There was now the absence about the place of the smell of flowers, one of Vanessa's great loves and great extravagances. It was a small flat—just one long room off a hall on the ground floor, which was a combination sitting and dining room with a partly screened-off kitchen at the end, and above it two small bedrooms. One of the bedrooms had been mine when I was growing up; later it was used as an overflow office for the shop, crammed with papers, catalogues of sales—the whole paraphernalia of Vanessa's jumbled existence. It would be there, if anywhere, that I would find some reference to the summer and autumn she had spent at Thirlbeck. But up there was also Vanessa's bedroom,

284

stamped indelibly with her character, her charm, her sensuous nature. I wasn't ready for that yet.

I went into the sitting room. When I closed the curtains on the street side it became the warm and charming room it had been in Vanessa's time—the favourite antiques, the orange carpet, the gold curtains all expressing her vibrant nature.

It was dusted and tidy. I wondered if Gerald had arranged for the cleaning woman to come still. I went into the kitchen and brewed some coffee. I hardly let myself think; it was enough that I had been able to come here. When the coffee was ready I poured a cup and carried it to the chair beside the telephone.

It was a shock to hear Harry answer almost at once. I was so used to the voice of the manservant, telling me that Mr. Peers was elsewhere. "Hello, luv," he said. "Back in London, aren't you?"

"Yes. How did you know?"

"Difference in your voice. Up there you always sounded as if you were off somewhere in cloud-cuckoo-land. A bit absent."

"It's a long way, Harry."

"Sweetheart, you don't know what a long way means. A long way is Australia—or the moon."

"What have you been doing, Harry?"

"This and that. I bought a house, for one thing."

"A house? I thought you were always buying houses."

"Luv, you don't know anything. I buy properties, I don't buy houses. But yesterday I bought a house. A house for *me*."

"You're giving up the flat, then?"

"Well, what do you think? What would I need both for? I'm good at throwing money around, luv, but not absolutely crazy."

"Where is it, Harry? And when are you moving in?"

"When you do."

I was silent a moment. "But Harry, I have a flat."

"Crazy, girl—crazy. Do you expect us to bring up our kids in that two-by-four place? Our kids are going to have nurseries and nannies and the whole razzmatazz. They're going to be wheeled in their prams in St. James's Park and wave at the Palace Guard."

"*Our* kids, Harry?"

"Who else's? The house is in St. James's Place. Nice and convenient for us both. You can get to Hardy's in two minutes—no, three, allowing for the crossing. And I can nip along to St. James's

285

Square and kiss you good-bye on the steps of Hardy's on the way. You can keep on working right up until each kid is born, almost, and then be back again before they've missed you. And you'll end up being a director of Hardy's."

I spoke very deliberately. "I think I need to come and talk to you, Harry."

"What's there to talk about? We're going to get married. And I promise you our honeymoon can be any place in the world you want to go to look at bits and pieces of china. I'll even get you a visa into China itself. All we have to do is arrange to get together in person instead of by telephone. So . . . when will it be?"

"I'll come tonight, Harry. I'm at Vanessa's flat now."

"Not tonight. Tonight—in fact, right this minute—I'm due at a meeting. It's at my office. These guys have come over from New York. It'll be a late session."

"Harry—"

"Sorry, luv. No business meeting, no trip to China. It's that simple. Go and take a look at the house. The one tucked back beside Dukes Hotel. I'll call you. Bye, luv."

I sipped the coffee and noticed my hands shook a little, but a strange calmness was upon me. I had just been handed the world. I could have my job at Hardy's and kids, too—Harry's kids. I could even have China. I was being given the chance to become what I had dreamed of, the one whose name could authenticate almost any piece of ceramic that came to hand. Yet I wasn't feeling the pleasure I should have felt.

I didn't notice how long I sat there, in the quiet room, with just the one lamp lighted on the table beside me. Outside, the traffic took on its late-evening sound, and still I sat, thinking about Harry —about Harry and Vanessa. Strangely I was taking out once more the Hilliard miniature, turning it between my fingers, watching the light play on the tiny features of the woman who suddenly seemed even more to resemble Vanessa.

I don't know when I first became aware of the sound—the slight scraping from the hall. Then there was the murmur of a man's voice. I reached up and switched out the light. I remained in the chair; I couldn't have moved even if I'd known what to do. The door opened, and the light switch beside the door was found. The chandelier over the dining table sprang to life.

"Good evening, Mr. Tolson."

He looked in my direction uncertainly, peering through the pebble glasses, not quite sure of what he saw.

"Dad . . . ?"

"All right, Ted. Just close the door. Miss Roswell and I know each other well enough." Now I recognized one of the Tolson sons.

It was as if something I had been expecting for a long time was beginning to happen. "You seem to know your way, Mr. Tolson."

"Yes, it took a bit of finding, though. I've only been here once before. London's changed since then."

"But you didn't expect to find me here?"

"If I'd known, I'd have waited till you were gone," he answered calmly. "I knew you haven't lived here for a long time."

"I notice you didn't have any difficulty getting in."

He shrugged. "Ordinary locks aren't difficult for Ted."

"Convenient for you to have a son like Ted."

He moved farther into the room. For the first time his movements seemed those of an older man, stiff and cramped.

"I think you'd better sit down, Mr. Tolson. You must be tired. *I* am." I waited in silence while they settled in chairs.

"Why are you here, Mr. Tolson? I shouldn't need to ask, but you don't seem ready to volunteer any information. Does it have anything to do with Jessica this morning? Or the bowl?"

"Nothing directly. But it brought matters to a head, let us say. I've been putting off making this visit. Lord Askew's presence at Thirlbeck compelled me to be there constantly. But your breaking the bowl this morning, and the way you took the pieces to London, made me realize that soon you and others would start asking questions. It is very unfortunate Mrs. Roswell was killed—"

"*Unfortunate!* Mrs. Roswell was my mother. It was more than unfortunate!"

"I beg your pardon. Very clumsy of me. For my wife and me it was a blow as well. We grew quite fond of her over the years."

"Over the years? My mother hadn't been there since 1945."

He sighed. "That isn't quite true. In the last sixteen or seventeen years we'd seen her at Thirlbeck quite frequently. Scouting expeditions, she used to call them."

"Scouting for what—for *what*, Mr. Tolson?"

He took off his glasses and rubbed his eyes. The strength that

287

was implied by the bulk of his body was reinforced by the sight of his eyes, a grey so deep they seemed almost black. He replaced the glasses and answered slowly. "It will be easier if I tell you the whole thing. Any questions you have to ask, I'll answer. Perhaps you will be able to answer one or two for me."

"Try me. I expect I *will* have some questions."

"I sought out your mother when the difficulties first arose at Thirlbeck. Until then—almost seventeen years ago—it is true she had not been back, but in trying to solve my problem I thought of her because I felt I could trust her—"

"*Trust* her! You were the one who called her a gypsy."

"Miss Roswell, when you asked me about her I realized that you must be wondering why your mother had never spoken of Thirlbeck. So I emphasized her—her more raffish qualities, hoping to stop your questions. At that time I hadn't quite given up hope that Lord Askew would grow bored at Thirlbeck and simply go away. It wouldn't have ended my problems, but it might have delayed the exposure of what I had been doing."

"What exactly are your problems, Mr. Tolson? Have you been stealing from Lord Askew?" I felt a kind of deadly cold anger which helped to keep my voice very even. "Are you going to tell me that my mother had been stealing with you?"

"Not that, Miss Roswell. If there's been stealing, I have done it. Your mother was only the means to dispose of items from the estate. It started in a rather small way, but as Lord Askew's demands for money have grown we have had to increase the robbing Peter to pay Paul, so to speak."

"So to speak *nothing*, Mr. Tolson. You were stealing, and you somehow induced my mother to be party to it. And all the time you despised her!"

"I'll try to tell you again, Miss Roswell. I came to your mother seventeen years ago because I *did* trust her. And I trusted her because she loved Thirlbeck—the house, everything that was in it, the valley, the wholeness of it. The summer and autumn she spent there I saw her often enough to know that. The earls of Askew were powerful because of the land they held, land amassed through gifts of the sovereigns they served—Henry the Eighth, Elizabeth. Judicious marriages brought other properties—farms, all the rest of it. I judged, I think rightly, that the land was more

288

important to the future of the Birketts than their other possessions. And I thought, from what I knew of her, that your mother felt the same way. She was a romantic, your mother. She felt strongly about the story of the Spanish Woman, whose death was the price the Birketts had to pay to keep Thirlbeck. The loss of its strength—its land—would have made her death forfeit."

Unbelievably he paused to smile at me. "People like your mother understand such things. So when I had my first important decision to make I traced her in London and asked for her help."

"What sort of help? What could she do for you, Mr. Tolson?"

"I wasn't sure she could or would do anything. I thought she might even get in touch with Lord Askew. But she didn't. She came up to Thirlbeck with a man, a foreigner. They spent the best part of a week there, and when they left they took one small picture with them. Its sale satisfied the earl's requirements for a time. That's how it started, and it went on like that."

"Like *what*? What were you doing?"

He ignored my question. "When the rents from the tenancies failed to reach Lord Askew's demands, he wrote and told me I should start selling off the farms. I was to sell land that was not specifically included in the entail, preferably to those who were already the tenants, and on fair terms. He didn't at all mind the breakup of the estate. He always had some guilt about people being his tenants. He said the time for all that sort of thing was over. He'd become a kind of socialist, but one who could never suppress his own taste for luxury."

He went on calmly. "I chose to disobey Lord Askew's instructions, Miss Roswell. I borrowed money to buy time, and I sought out your mother. I had some idea that the house contained valuable things, but I was no expert. Oh, yes, a list *does* exist of what the earl's grandmother brought to Thirlbeck. And you would have searched till kingdom come before you found it. But I had no idea which of the paintings might be of value, except, of course, the Rembrandt. It was my effort to persuade the earl to sell *that*, instead of the land, which finally made up my mind. I judged it my duty to turn over to the next earl the estate as nearly intact as I could. If it were bits of art which had to go, then that was how it would be. I still think I made the right decision for the Birketts, though I may well end up in jail because of it."

"And suppose my mother ended up in jail with you?"

"That was a risk she seemed prepared to take. And for nothing more than her expenses. I was willing to give her a percentage of whatever we realized, but she refused. It seemed I had judged her feelings well. She had a dedication to Thirlbeck."

"The things—the things she handled—they must have gone to private dealers or clients. They couldn't have passed through Hardy's or anyone who'd demand to know whose property it was. And she couldn't sell the things through her own shop; she was only in the minor league of antique dealers. She would have been suspected almost at once of handling stolen property."

"She pointed this out to me. And since there was not the sort of money we needed among English private buyers, she said she would have to take the items abroad. She had contacts—"

"*Abroad* . . . without an export license? You mean she smuggled art out of this country?"

"She said she had to. Once it was in Switzerland, it could be taken without a licence to America. She said that was where the money was. Museum directors and private collectors asked few questions so long as they were convinced of authenticity."

"How many times did she do this?"

He shrugged helplessly. "I've lost count. The items had to be smallish. There were the Chinese bowls and vases. And the snuff-boxes. She said those were easy."

"What about the pictures?" My voice was very faint. "Did she take more than one?"

"Over the years—I expect she took about twenty."

"Can you remember any of the artists?" I had to ask it, but I was afraid to hear the answer.

"Most I'd never heard of before. There was a van Ruisdael—or was it two? A Seghers, a—a Steen? Would that be right?" I nodded, unable to speak. "There were several small panels by Rubens—"

I gestured to make him stop. "Those are quite enough, Mr. Tolson. It was more than a fine collection. I find it difficult to believe that Lord Askew does not know that they were in his possession."

"He doesn't know, Miss Roswell. He wasn't interested. None of the family had been."

"But my mother would have recognized those pictures and told him, that time she was there."

"She never saw them. Neither did your father. I told you I had made one safe room for them all when the ministry requisitioned the house. They're still there. It was one place I could keep a fairly even temperature—enough heat to keep the damp from getting to them, but not so much that they might crack. I went to the museum in Glasgow to find out about proper care for them—just mentioned that I had charge of a small collection, gave them a false name, and invented a house that didn't exist."

I sat, my stomach churning in a queasy turmoil as I thought of what Vanessa had involved herself with. "What happens when Lord Askew asks for that room to be opened, Mr. Tolson? Even he has to notice that frames are missing."

"The frames are still there, Miss Roswell. What they contain is quite different. We—your mother and I—felt it should appear as if nothing had been changed. They wouldn't deceive an expert, your mother said, but they were very good."

"You mean very good *copies*. Like the Rembrandt?"

He raised his eyebrows. "So Mr. Stanton wasn't deceived? I didn't think he was. We were only planning for the unlikely eventuality that Lord Askew might return. We wanted very good copies of anything *he* might remember."

"The forger, Mr. Tolson. Who was he?"

"I don't know. I think he was a Dutchman. But I never met him, and I wasn't really interested. Mrs. Roswell would carry out a canvas which would fit into her suitcase, and in time back would come a canvas which, to me, looked exactly the same."

"The Rembrandt deceived me, too. But fortunately, to people like Mr. Stanton, it lacks a certain quality. No expert would authenticate that picture, Mr. Tolson."

For a second or two he bowed his head as if in acknowledgment. "We really didn't expect that, Miss Roswell. Your mother warned me often enough. We knew. And I was determined that, if anything was ever called into question, your mother's name should never be connected with it."

"Were you really so naïve, Mr. Tolson? There would have been ways to trace her, the handling of money . . . and so on. If you went to jail, she would have gone with you."

Once more his head went down. There was a restive stirring from behind him. But Ted took his father's silence as a command.

I finally spoke. "So . . . she took out the Rembrandt and many others. You left an awful lot to trust, Mr. Tolson. You couldn't very well verify the price Vanessa got on stolen artworks. How did you know she wasn't taking a cut for herself?"

In my hurt I was deliberately striking out at him, forcing him to recall those things he had said to me about Vanessa when he had virtually denied any knowledge of her.

"In the beginning . . . well, naturally the question was raised by my brother. He didn't know your mother and insisted on checking up on her. There are ways of finding out if someone has more money than they should. We found that she seemed perpetually on the edge of bankruptcy—always big overdrafts and never a sign of money that couldn't be accounted for. No, she wasn't stealing— not from us, not from Thirlbeck. I thought I'd made that quite clear." His tone was not apologetic; he faced my anger and did not turn away from it.

"Thank you—for *that*. She wasn't stealing. But she was taking risks for you. Can you imagine what it would feel like to walk past a customs officer with a Rembrandt in your suitcase?"

"In an odd way it appealed to her. Your mother had quite a lot of daring. And, at any rate, the Rembrandt was to be the last thing we'd take. She had spent almost a year arranging the sale. The painting was lodged in a bank vault in Zurich. The purchaser was going there with two experts for authentication. Your mother never told me his name. She said it was safer not to know. The Dutchman who did the copying went to Zurich, too. He wanted to deposit his fee in a Swiss bank. The buyer was going to pay a million two hundred thousand pounds if the experts agreed the picture was genuine."

"A million two," I repeated. "It could have gone for twice that at public auction. Had you thought of what Lord Askew would have said to selling his property at knockdown prices?"

He gestured to indicate to me that it was a useless question. "I made my decision long ago. This last sale would be big enough to keep pace with Lord Askew's needs for the rest of his life."

While he was talking I wondered about my mother—a stranger who moved quietly, keeping her secret. How often had Gerald or I believed she was spending her weekend with a man, the latest flirtation, when, in fact, she had been at Thirlbeck or had flown

292

to Switzerland? I felt baffled, hurt, as though I'd been shut out.

Tolson continued with his story. "It all blew up, of course, the day I got the cable from Lord Askew asking me to get the house ready for him and the condesa. It came while your mother was in Zurich, and I telephoned her hotel immediately. She had already checked out, so I knew the sale had gone through. And of all the pictures at Thirlbeck, the Rembrandt was the one I needed. I needed it more than I needed the million-odd pounds in a Swiss bank. Now I have neither."

My head jerked up. "You haven't the money? Where is it?"

"I would dearly like to know, Miss Roswell. But it was in a numbered account, opened by your mother especially for this sale. She was to call and give me the name of the bank and the number as soon as she knew it. The account wouldn't be used except to transfer money to Lord Askew. We had done this before, but this time there was a mix-up, and I missed her call. I assumed she would get in touch with me when she returned to London. Then we heard about the plane crash."

"Why have you come *here*? What did you expect to find?"

"I'd the faint hope that she might have left some indication of which bank she intended to use. She might have made notes. A forlorn hope, I know. I have been nearly desperate these last weeks. The whole of my stewardship of Thirlbeck has gone for nothing. Oh, yes, I have the land intact. But now I have defaulted by a million pounds and more." He sighed. "The affairs of the Birketts have never been small. That jewel to guard . . . the estate to hold together. A collection of pictures and furniture, which your mother thought was almost matchless in this country—"

"Stop it! *Stop it, do you hear?* Do you expect me to weep for you? My mother is dead because of you and your insane ideas about the Birketts being something special. I still don't know how you managed to drag her into all this and to keep her in it for almost seventeen years. . . . *Why* did she do it—*why?*"

He breathed deeply before replying. "I thought I hardly needed to explain to you. I can see you going about Thirlbeck almost exactly as she did, falling in love with it."

"Oh, no! Don't try to drag me in, too. Haven't you done enough?"

"I was trying nothing, Miss Roswell. What has happened to you happened of its own accord. But we won't discuss that. I take it that you will not give us permission to look among your mother's belongings. There just may be the faintest chance—"

"No! You'll not touch anything. When someone looks it will be myself. And I'm not going to look now."

He sighed, and struggled heavily to rise. "Then we must be on our way back. I will have to speak to Lord Askew. I can't delay any longer. I'll try to see that your mother gets no blame."

"How good of you—*now*, when she's dead. What a miserable lot you all are up there, hugging your great estate to yourselves. It's really all been for you, hasn't it, Mr. Tolson? You've had steward-ship for so long it really belongs to you—that's what you think. If you can't inherit legally—you or your sons—then you'll have Nat Birkett so brainwashed he'll do exactly as you tell him. And really, didn't you indirectly contribute to the death of his wife? You remained silent, Mr. Tolson. There was no real blame placed on Jessica, although she neglected to tell you where Patsy Birkett was that night she died. Jessica hadn't been well; a lapse like that might be forgiven. She's been a good, quiet, well-behaved girl these past years—cured of all her problems. And so beautiful. You really see no reason why she shouldn't eventually marry Nat Birkett. If you press him hard enough, your stewardship would be justified then, wouldn't it? Nat has two sons, but if the Birkett luck runs its usual course, it's just possible that *your* descendants will inherit the earldom of Askew. You couldn't have been so evil as to plan it that way. But now, as things are, it's possible, isn't it, Mr. Tolson?"

He was at the door, Ted moving with him. "You're very tired, Miss Roswell. So am I. Those are harsh words you have used. I think we had better forget them. Perhaps we won't meet again. It would be better if we didn't. But . . . if you should find anything that might help . . ." He shrugged and half turned away. "Well, you could communicate with me through Ted. Good-bye."

He was in the hall before I called him back. It was something that my years of training at Hardy's had given to me, and it could not be stopped.

He returned, betraying just a shade of eagerness. "Yes?"

"Those pictures—the ones that are left. And the ones my mother took away. Do you remember anything about an El Greco?"

His disappointment was plain. "El Greco?" He shook his head.

The Property of a Gentleman

"No. Strange, though ... your mother once had some such notion. She searched the whole of Thirlbeck, but she never found it."

He waited a while longer, perhaps with hope. But I simply stared at him, my anger giving me a hardness I had never possessed before. They slipped out, and soon I heard a car start. If I measured Tolson rightly, they would drive all night, and he would be there at Thirlbeck by the morning to tell his tale to Robert Birkett.

Vanessa's little Louis XIV clock on the mantel showed a quarter to one. I sat in the chair, and I thought of the smashed and burned wreckage on that mountain slope in Switzerland, the baggage lying broken in the dirty snow. There had been no suitcase I had been able to identify as Vanessa's among those assembled for inspection, no object or article of clothing other than her handbag. And that had contained nothing that would have helped Tolson. I wondered what would happen if Vanessa's true mission in Switzerland came out. There were enough people to say she had been capable of what she had done and much more. Vanessa had had only friends or enemies—hardly anyone in between. Tears of anger and fatigue rolled down my cheeks. They brought, in time, their own sort of relief, temporary but welcome; I felt myself slip towards sleep. When I woke, the clock was striking two.

I DROVE the Mini the short distance to the streets around St. James's Square; it was silent and almost totally deserted, except for a police car on a slow patrol. Over on one side of the square I stopped my car. The top floor of a modern building was still brightly lighted, and Harry's sports car was parked at the kerb. He was still there, on that lighted top floor. I sat and looked up at it for a few minutes. I could sense a restless power which disturbed the quietness of the great square. I started the Mini and drove down into Pall Mall.

When I turned into St. James's Place it was totally deserted, too. I pulled into the tiny yard where Dukes Hotel was, and there stood the house Harry had bought—tall, narrow, elegant, with bay trees in tubs at each side of the door. Hard to think what he must have paid for it. And he was right; even with traffic at its thickest, it was barely a three-minute walk from Hardy's and only a few minutes beyond that to his office in St. James's Square. Harry had made

295

his plans swiftly and with great precision. Yet somehow I knew that, whatever it was he planned for himself and me, I would be waiting, always waiting, for a telephone call from Harry.

It was then that I remembered the last time I had been conscious of lights burning in the early hours of the morning. It had been as we had followed the ambulance to Kesmere, and the lights had shone on Nat Birkett's hill.

I WAS at Hardy's early the next morning, but I didn't go directly down to the ceramics department. I really didn't know if I should be there at all. Probably Gerald was expecting me to return to Thirlbeck, but I was conscious of the need to break with that world, to return to what was familiar and understood. And yet hadn't Tolson's story shaken the foundations of this familiar world? If it became known that Vanessa had smuggled works of art out of this country, would it be possible for me to remain here? The Roswell name might become notorious in the art world, instead of mildly famous, as my father had made it. I stood for a moment at the bottom of the stairs gazing through the inner double glass doors to the street, watching a few people hurry up the steps carrying catalogues of what was on view that day.

Mr. Hudson, my director, had not told me last night whether I should return to Thirlbeck. It was my duty to ask Lord Askew if he wished the Sung bowl mended and offered for auction. Until this was clear and the paper signed, Hardy's insurance did not begin to operate. I was floundering in a state of fatigue and bewilderment, and nothing seemed to sort itself into a decision.

At last I went upstairs to the salerooms. In the central area was a display of English pictures. In two of the side rooms the morning sales of silver and Chinese ceramics had just begun. It was early in the season, and the really important auctions were weeks away; the public attending were mostly dealers and a few interested collectors. I watched the silver sale for a while and listened to the auctioneer make his expert way through the catalogue, knowing most of the dealers by name, recording price and buyer in the day book, and always moving at a deliberate pace, never sounding pleased or disappointed. Some lots were bought back into the house, others went for prices well beyond expectation. Whichever way it went, the little hammer fell at the end of each sale, and the next lot was brought out for display. I went on to the sale of Chinese ceramics.

Here Mr. Hudson was taking the auction. I would have to wait until it was over before I could talk with him. Mr. Arrowsmith, from the front counter, appeared beside the rostrum; he had a bid commissioned for a certain lot, but the price went beyond what he had been authorized to pay, and he made his way from the room, smiling at me as he left. I turned back to look at the rostrum.

I suppose it was fatigue. The night had been too long, and there had been too much to absorb—Harry, Vanessa, Tolson. For a few seconds the room seemed to swim in a blur of faces and voices. A new lot was brought out—a jade carving too small for me to see from my place. The bidding went on—rising, rising as the auctioneer judged his audience and paced the rise to meet the competition. "Against you on the left . . . I'm offered four thousand pounds . . . four thousand five hundred . . . against you . . ." The hammer fell, the record went into the day book. The next lot produced a K'ang Hsi vase. But as I watched, the vase seemed to become the fantasy shape of a great eagle. I saw it—majestic, awesome, fierce, with neck and crown of gold, perched on the ledge of the rostrum. And the auctioneer's voice saying quietly, "What am I bid . . . ?"

Frightened, I turned to leave, but I did look back. Everything was as it should be, the bids being placed for the K'ang Hsi vase. And no golden eagle surveyed the scene. I went then, almost running down the stairs and out into the street.

A YOUNG man in a habit showed me into a reception room with a bare polished floor, four straight-backed chairs, a small table rigidly in the centre of the room. There was a single crucifix on the wall. I had come here because it was the only place I could think of quickly. Sometimes Gerald and I had come to the church to listen to one of the more famous Jesuits preach. Gerald had an intellectual interest in such things, though he wasn't a Catholic.

I stood up when a young priest entered. He held out his hand. "I'm Father Kavanagh. Please sit down." I told him my name, and then I couldn't seem to say anything else.

"Is there some way I can help you?"

They must be used to all kinds, I thought, all sorts of requests, every kind of story. "I'm not a Catholic," I said.

297

He smiled then. "It's still very possible you'll get into heaven."

"Well, I wondered if it's possible to offer masses for someone who's been dead a long time?"

"Of course. Is this person some relation—some friend? Would you like to talk about it?"

"She's been dead a very long time. Almost four hundred years."

"I see." He didn't show any wonder. "No prayer is offered too late, if the intention is right. You would like a mass offered for the repose of the soul of this person, I take it?"

"Yes, that's it," I said eagerly. That was what she had written: "Offer nine masses for my soul." And I added, "But I would like nine masses. Can you do that?"

"We'll offer a novena of masses. Was this person a Catholic? Not that it matters. One can still pray."

"Oh, yes. She probably died because she was a Catholic."

He raised his eyebrows. "A martyr?"

"No, not officially. Just a young girl who died a long time ago." I spelled out the name for him, surprised at how easily it came off my lips without referring to her book. "Juana Fernández de Córdoba, Mendoza, Soto y Alvarez."

He wrote it all down, and then he said, "I expect the Lord will know whom I mean if I just say 'Juana.'"

I didn't know how much money to offer him. "Anything is acceptable," he said. And he smiled again. "I'll say the masses myself. The soul of your young Spanish girl will be comforted by the fact that someone remembered her after nearly four hundred years."

I went and sat in the church, seeking its quietness to still my own racing mind. The little peace I had bought with the request for masses ebbed away. I was back with the bewildering, frightening thoughts of Vanessa and George Tolson. By now he had probably told Lord Askew. I wondered if Gerald knew yet; would he be disappointed that I had not returned? And what would Nat think of someone who had left him so swiftly, almost in flight?

I had the miniature out, and played with it between my fingers. More than ever I saw Vanessa in the features of the third countess. Again I placed the broken piece of the frame where it belonged, making it whole. But I saw something else then, something I had never seen before. Excitement caught in my stomach. I almost didn't want to reason it out; reason might destroy the hope that

had so quickly built. Yes . . . yes, it was possible. It could be tried, at any rate.

At my flat I repacked the big red suitcase, putting the pieces of the Sung bowl and the Book of Hours where they would be best protected by my clothes. I was going back to Thirlbeck. Just as I was leaving, the telephone began to ring. It could be Harry, it could be Gerald or Tolson. I let it ring.

I STOPPED the Mini just before I entered the birch copse on the Thirlbeck estate. I had not thought it would feel so familiar, as if I were returning to a place I had known all my life. I looked up, tracing the outline of Great Birkeld against the sky. I might have lost my life on that mountain if the dogs had not led me down, and yet the sight of it now brought no shiver of fear. It was something known, respected, and loved.

I drove slowly through the birch copse, half expecting to see the white shape of the great hound that had confronted me on that first journey. The valley widened out, the house now was visible. There were no lights anywhere. It was past two, and the valley was utterly still; not a wind stirred the mirror surface of the lake. A silent, enchanted world, frozen in the moonlight.

I drove around to the back of the house. I knew that the dogs had heard the car and come downstairs. I could hear the scrape of their paws against the door leading to the kitchen passage. And yet they did not bark. I felt a prickle of gooseflesh as I pushed the bell at the back door, hoping it would not wake Gerald or Lord Askew. The morning would be time enough for them.

Tolson came very soon, wearing a heavy woollen dressing gown; I guessed he had been sleepless, perhaps sitting before the warmth of the kitchen stove. "You should have told me you were coming," he said. "I could have had a meal ready." For the first time I heard no implied hostility in his tone. He motioned me inside. "I'll make some tea and toast."

I sat at the kitchen table and shovelled the toast into my mouth and gulped the tea. Around me the dogs sat, two circles of them, fanning out like some exotic adornment. Finally the hunger was gone, and the tea had warmed me. I leaned back in the big chair, and my hands went naturally to the heads of the dogs nearest me. I wondered how I had ever lived without dogs before.

I turned then to the waiting Tolson. "I have something to show you. I *hope* . . ." I brought the miniature from my handbag. Tolson bent over it as I explained. Then he drew back, but in that large body I sensed a quiet relief, a release of pain and despair.

"Could be," he offered.

"You've already told Lord Askew?"

"Yes, I have. He acted as you would expect a gentleman to act."

"I'll see him in the morning, then," I said.

"Yes, if it suits you. If that's what you want."

"That's the way it should be."

We sat silently for some time. A strange companionship existed between us, where before there had only been unease. A bridge of compromise had been walked in these two nights.

He spoke at last. "It's late. You'll need some sleep."

The dogs moved ahead of us up the stairs and on to the Spanish Woman's room, as if I had lived there always.

"I didn't have the bed stripped," he said as we entered. He switched on the only electric light. "I had a feeling you'd be back." He put a match under the freshly laid fires in the two fireplaces. "It'll warm up in a bit," he said. "You'll have a good sleep."

I halted him as he was about to leave. "We'll see Lord Askew together in the morning," I said. He nodded. We had entered into some unlikely compact, the two of us.

After I had undressed and washed quietly in Gerald's bathroom I sat in bed watching the light of the two fires thrown up to the ceiling. I had my cigarettes close by, but I realized that I did not really need one now. It hardly even seemed strange that two of the wolfhounds had stayed, their great lengths stretched on the rug before one fire. I thought I could even distinguish them from the rest—two males, the leaders of the pack. "Thor . . . Ulf," I whispered. The big heads raised, and a flicker ran along each tail. After a while I slid between the sheets and slept.

CHAPTER SEVEN

I HAD not thought it possible he could seem so changed. Askew faced me across the desk in the study, Gerald at his side, Tolson, who refused a chair, standing slightly behind him. Askew seemed much older, or perhaps merely his age. The boyish nonchalance was gone. I did not see him now as the natural companion of a much younger woman, but as a rather worn man made suddenly aware of his years and a responsibility he could no longer put aside.

I had told him of Vanessa's part in taking the paintings from Thirlbeck. Then Tolson had produced a notebook, and in Vanessa's hand there were lists and descriptions, rather vague, but good enough to give us an idea of the hundreds of treasures this house once held, which were dispersed forever to nameless buyers.

"The prices Mrs. Roswell got seemed very high to me," Tolson concluded.

Gerald sighed. "They would be much higher now. Most of these were sold quite some time ago." He stabbed the list with his pen. "Oh, heavens! 'Fourteenth-century wine jar. Yüan dynasty, 13½ inches, applied moulded flowering chrysanthemum, tree peony, pomegranate, camellia.' If this is accurate, we might have sold almost a twin of that for two hundred and ten thousand guineas. Robert, do you hear? *Two hundred and ten thousand!* But Vanessa did very, very well for you, considering it had to have been a very private transaction."

Gerald looked at Tolson as if he were going to try to explain the enormity of what had been done, but decided against it. He merely asked, "This list was just for you, so that you could identify the pieces as you remembered them?"

"It was for her own guidance, too. There were so many pieces—saucers, bowls, snuffboxes. Mrs. Roswell didn't pretend to know all about them. She tried to replace some with modern copies, so there shouldn't be too many blank spaces."

Miserably I was remembering the prunus jar in the library. Gerald looked at Askew, who had remained silent and seemingly not very interested. "Did you know about the collection of snuff-boxes, Robert?"

He seemed to drag himself out of a daze. "Of course I knew. We never took any of it seriously. Snuffboxes seemed an odd thing to collect. They came to the family through the marriage of the—I suppose it must have been the thirteenth earl. There's a picture of him somewhere, holding a snuffbox. Snuffbox Johnny, I used to call him. Well, the boxes were all displayed in a glass case—the sort of thing you see in museums. It used to be in the library. One day, when I was about eight, I was practising cricket strokes and the damn bat sailed clean out of my hands and smashed the case. My mother was upset and got it moved out of the library at once, before my father saw it. I don't think he ever missed it. I don't know what happened to the boxes."

"Nor do we, now," Gerald said. "Vanessa did a good job on selling this lot, and why not? They must have been very fine. 'Louis XV gold and enamel rectangular snuffbox—Jean-Marie Tiron. English chased gold snuffbox by George Michael Moser.' The best names of the finest period. Twenty-four in all. At public auction they might have gone at better than two hundred thousand pounds. Vanessa didn't achieve anything like that, but she didn't do badly, considering—"

He stopped as Askew's hand slammed down on the desk. Askew turned a troubled, angry face to each of us. "Can't we stop this?" he said. "Remember, we're talking about someone who didn't steal these things but who ran considerable risks to sell them quietly. We're talking about Vanessa Roswell. Remember that!"

Gerald answered him slowly. "I *am* remembering it, Robert." His voice was firm, and he showed no trace of his recent invalidism. It was as if this news of Vanessa's involvement in the plunder of Thirlbeck had shaken him back to life. Now his tone was thoughtful. "I knew Vanessa as a woman who enjoyed city life, who functioned best surrounded by people and talk, who thrived on the infighting in her business. She had a very quick eye. When she saw the best she always recognized it. If it was doubtful, she also was doubtful. What is taking time to adjust to is the Vanessa I didn't know—the person who recognized the best in ideals, as well as objects, for obviously she believed passionately in what she and Tolson were doing. Well, that's a dimension I have to get used to. In the meantime I must just try to evaluate what exactly was taken from here."

"To what purpose?" Askew said. "It's gone, isn't it? And none of us will ever understand Vanessa's motives. Smuggling must have been so difficult for her."

Gerald tapped the desk with his pen. "Well, we all know that smuggling goes on constantly. There are always buyers ready for what they know must be smuggled and probably has been stolen. And there's always some old family prepared to swear that a work of art has been with them hundreds of years. I would guess that for every painting Vanessa took, her contact in Switzerland had a Hungarian prince or a Prussian count in exile who was willing to give it some sort of provenance. If the article itself is genuine, there's no problem in selling."

He turned sharply to look up at Tolson. "That was why she dared the Rembrandt, wasn't it? You had run out of all the other things small enough to leave this country in a suitcase."

Tolson nodded. "She said we had taken all the really top-class things that could be taken. There was only the Rembrandt left. We hesitated for a long time about that. The man—the one who did the copying—didn't want to take it on. He had doubts about his ability to reproduce such a painting. Mrs. Roswell persuaded him. It was the money, I suppose. He was getting old, he'd been in prison for forgery, and the only employment he'd had after that was with a firm of picture restorers."

"This forger," Gerald said. "Was his name van Hoyt? He's the only copyist I'm aware of good enough to have done that." He nodded towards the shadowed picture on the wall.

Tolson shook his head. "No. I've been trying to remember a name ever since Miss Roswell asked me. I seem to remember something like . . . Lastman. It seemed a sort of made-up name to me."

"Lastman . . . " We all turned. Gerald was staring at us, his brow creased. "I remember encountering that name very recently. I stayed on there in Switzerland for a day after you left with your father, Jo. By that time only one man among the dead had not been claimed. He had a passport, though, and they said his name was Lastman. Taking that name would be just the sort of bitter jest that a man who had been in prison for forging Dutch masters might make. You perhaps remember that one of Rembrandt's early teachers was an artist named Pieter Lastman. It could have been a supreme irony for van—for Lastman to have made his final copy a self-portrait of Rembrandt—" He stopped abruptly. "Are you all right, Robert?"

Askew's face was ashen, but he waved his hand impatiently. "Perfectly all right, Gerald. As well as anyone can be who finds out what other people have been doing for him, at risk."

"My lord—" Tolson began.

Askew cut him off. "Tolson, just one more favour, please. Would you mind bringing me some brandy? Thank you."

Tolson left the room. Askew nodded after him. "It is pretty shameful to come back and find that his stewardship has been so much better than my treatment of him and this place merited. Strange . . . strange to think that he and Vanessa were some kind of superpatriots, in their fashion, determined to keep this little bit of England intact. I agree with you, Gerald. One doesn't see Vanessa that way. Tolson, one understands better. What shames me most is that he had to do it as he did because I was not here where I should have been."

I licked dry lips. "You don't intend to prosecute?"

"Prosecute? Of course not! The man hasn't stolen anything! It's all here, isn't it? Everything is accounted for. As it happens, I think he made the right choice." He shook his head. "And Vanessa's dead now. Directly or indirectly, it happened because of me."

"Don't dwell on it, Robert," Gerald said. "It does no good. What might have been, whose fault it was. You've got to live with the here and now."

Tolson had returned with a tray, three glasses, and a bottle of brandy. Askew's hand trembled as he poised the bottle over the glass, looking at me. I shook my head; then he turned to Gerald, who also declined. He poured a large amount for himself and drank quickly. After he put the glass down he said to Tolson, "For heaven's sake, do sit down! And have some brandy."

Gingerly, Tolson drew up a chair and sat down. He paid no attention to the invitation to pour himself a brandy.

Askew motioned to me. "Like the gentleman he is, Tolson refused to tell me who had managed to dispose of all the things—only that they were gone. I still don't understand why *you* had to come back here and tell us these things about your mother."

"I didn't intend to. Then something happened to change my mind. Mr. Tolson said that the payment for the Rembrandt was lodged in a Swiss bank in a numbered account—which bank and which number, only Vanessa knew."

Gerald leaned forward anxiously. "Have you found something, Jo?" he demanded. "Have you?"

"I think so—I hope so."

I took the miniature from my handbag and passed it to Askew. He tensed visibly as he saw it and seemed reluctant to take it. It was actually Gerald who took it from me. He placed it immediately as the miniature missing from the set of five upstairs.

"It was in the handbag Vanessa was carrying when the plane crashed," I said to Askew. "I had never seen it before."

There was heartbreak now in talking. I had not thought it would be easy, but the agony of sifting through the pathetic possessions of the victims in that mountain village was back in full force. As I spoke I saw Askew's hand go slowly towards the little portrait of the red-haired lady now lying between himself and Gerald. He turned it between his fingers, as I had done so often, and I saw some reflection of my pain on his face. Then he laid the miniature down. "With her, you said? In her handbag?"

"Yes. I assumed she had bought it in Zurich, for there was still what appeared to be a price tag on it." I turned to Gerald. "I haven't really *looked* at it all these weeks. To me it was just the price she had paid in Swiss francs. But it suddenly came to me that it couldn't be. It's all wrong, isn't it?"

Gerald turned the tiny piece of white cardboard on its thin red string. "SF thirteen thousand seven hundred and five," he read. He looked at me inquiringly.

"In Vanessa's handwriting—I don't know why I never wondered about *that* before. It couldn't have been the price marked on it in some shop. And in Swiss francs that price doesn't make sense for a Hilliard miniature."

Askew shook his head. "Vanessa didn't buy it. I gave it to her."

I nodded. "I never could believe that she had stolen it." I reached into the miniature's little leather pouch. "This bit of frame must have broken in the crash." I had almost forgotten what I meant to say as I watched Askew place the broken piece against the whole. Gerald's voice recalled me.

"Jo, what *is* it you're saying?"

I took a deep breath. "It wouldn't have been like Vanessa to trust her own memory on figures. I searched everything in that handbag for some number. And I checked the mail that had arrived in her flat during these past weeks, in case she had sent the number to herself in London. There was nothing."

"It's possible, Jo. It's possible." Gerald's voice was shot with excitement. "The Suisse-Française bank. Almost the largest there is. Hardy's often uses it. The bank—and the number, one three seven oh five." Then his excitement died. "It's possible, but not good enough. What branch? I wonder. It has hundreds of them."

I turned to Tolson. "Where in Zurich did she stay?"

"The St. Gotthard."

"On the Bahnhofstrasse," Gerald said. "And so is the largest branch of the Banque Suisse-Française. It's a starting point. We could produce a death certificate and the passport."

Tolson cleared his throat. "If you really think that is the number, Mr. Stanton, then I might be of help."

"What do you mean?" Gerald said.

"Mrs. Roswell would designate me as the person who had access to the account—on production of the number. She handled the deposits, but wanted nothing to do with the withdrawals or transfers. While my brother was alive his name was also included in the account, and, in fact, it was he who arranged the transfers to Lord Askew's bank. It's been more difficult since he died. I was glad this was going to be the last time. Mrs. Roswell would telephone as soon as the account was opened and tell me the bank, the branch, and the number. But this time it didn't work. This time . . . well, we missed each other."

"Missed each other?" Gerald questioned.

"You see, I'd been trying all day to reach Mrs. Roswell at her hotel, but she wasn't in. I'd just received the cable from Lord Askew that he was returning, and I guessed that the question of the Rembrandt would come up. I was desperate to stop the sale. So I had left an urgent message for Mrs. Roswell to telephone here. I was up in the attic, wondering if Lord Askew would notice the absence of so many items, when I heard the telephone ring, and hurried down. But by then Jessica had answered, and said I wasn't here. The child didn't know where I was. I rang back to her hotel immediately, but they said she had just left for the airport. It must all have been done—the picture sold, the money deposited—more quickly than we judged."

Tolson turned and looked at me, knowing the pain the words must bring. "She must have wanted to get to London quickly to have taken a plane that had a stopover in Paris. My own belief is that she was a standby for that flight. When they reported the crash, there had been no vacant seats."

Askew's face crinkled into a mask of lines. This time, when he motioned to me with the brandy bottle, I nodded. Then I said

307

something that had nothing to do with the chance flight that Vanessa had caught, in a hurry, from Zurich. I was thinking of that telephone call. "Does Jessica know—about all this?"

Tolson sought his words with caution. "Yes, I have to say she knew. I never discussed the details with anyone, but Jessica's so familiar with the house, she knew almost at once when some of the items were taken. And she knew about Mrs. Roswell's visits. She must have guessed a great deal about what we were doing."

It seemed to me that Jessica, with some kind of unhappy genius, had spun a glittering and terrible web between the last two tragedies of Thirlbeck. I thought of Patsy Birkett, dying alone, and of the telephone call that would have given Tolson the information he needed to prove his good faith. And Jessica had hung up before he could reach the phone, probably because she had disliked Vanessa and feared her influence at Thirlbeck. Tolson had paid a cruel price for his love of his granddaughter.

I looked at the three men about me; only Gerald seemed free of anguish, competent to manage what new developments my suggestion had thrust on them. In a fashion, he now took over.

"Well, we have somewhere to begin. Tolson, you must assemble any piece of proof the bank may need."

Gerald was managing, almost enjoying himself.

"As for the rest . . . well, I shall see we don't have any of Hardy's geniuses near the place until it has been gone through thoroughly. I have already looked at the pictures that remain. There's a man I can trust to be discreet, who will come and verify my opinion. And after that, if Robert wishes, Hardy's can do a complete assessment. No need to worry about the bad copies of the ceramics; every family has some of those. But we do have to make sure that not a single copy by van—by Lastman remains. To some people it would be the most delicious scandal of the decade if modern copies, all by the same hand, should turn up among the legitimate treasures. Imagine the anxious calls of collectors to their dealers asking them to verify that what they have is genuine. I must say, Lastman did a splendid job—"

I broke in. "Gerald, you know what you're saying? I mean, you're involving yourself—"

"My dear Jo, there's no need to tell me what I'm doing. A criminal act, an act of smuggling on a grand scale, has taken place. I

308

am assisting in covering it up." He sighed. "Well, what else can I do? Robert is a capable man, but in the art world, an absolute innocent. If I walk away, he'll betray himself and the whole situation. And then someone other than Hardy's will handle the sale. I have a duty to Hardy's, I have a duty to Vanessa, I have a duty to Robert and you, Jo. To discharge those duties I have to step on the other side of the law. Now . . ."

Quickly he began to discuss what we would do. Then to Tolson he added, "I hope all is in order with the tax people as far as Lord Askew is concerned?"

"I believe so, Mr. Stanton. My brother was very careful that all the income and expenditures of the estate were recorded and the usual taxes paid. But the extras paid to Lord Askew from the Swiss accounts—they're another matter. My brother handled all these things."

Gerald frowned. "Pity we don't have him to work on this. But still we must manage. Robert, are you all right?"

"Yes . . . yes." Askew sipped his brandy. "It's so damn complicated, isn't it? I've paid personal taxes, I know, but only when Edward Tolson told me to. Since he died, two years ago, I've not answered an official letter." His eyes took on a glazed, faraway expression; I caught a glimpse of the man who had fled from Thirlbeck and its responsibilities, who, until this morning, had seemed to retain much of the spirit and outlook of a boy.

Gerald looked at him with faintly disguised impatience. "I'll go ahead with all this, Robert?" It was hardly a question at all. "After we've been through the Swiss tangle we'll give our attention up here. We must catalogue the furniture very carefully and see that the right people know about it. And the pictures should be held until the next important old masters' sale."

I looked at Gerald. "Important? But I thought Vanessa had taken all the good ones."

Now a smile of real pleasure broke on Gerald's face. "She only took what was portable, Jo. It's rather difficult to take a Cuyp measuring about three-and-a-half feet by five feet out in a suitcase. You'll love it, Jo. It's a beautiful thing. There are others of very fine quality. The van Huygenses must have acquired all their pictures in the seventeenth century—almost hot off the artists' easels—during that one great period of Dutch painting. I haven't any doubt that this is . . . well, what everyone like myself dreams of—a major art discovery."

"When did you see them? I would have liked—"

"Jo, you weren't here. It was after Tolson told his story yesterday. I must say Tolson was very determined to guard every single picture the house held. We've been through everything—"

I interrupted him. "You said we. Was the condesa there? Does she know?"

"Well, it became quite impossible to conceal from her that the Rembrandt is a copy. She is an intelligent woman; she guessed that if there was this one copy, there were probably others. She understands, and she will not betray what happened here."

"And Jessica," I demanded. "Was she also with you?"

"I thought it was unwise to involve Jessica any further," Tolson said. "So I sent her home to the South Lodge. She must suspect something is stirring, but she doesn't know exactly what."

Gerald and Tolson were two men infinitely capable in their own spheres. Yes, one could leave it to them. But I made one final effort in my daze of fatigue. "You went through all the paintings—*all* of them?"

"Yes, all of them."

I turned to Tolson. "You did say you had gathered up every picture in the house? Every one? There aren't any others—not on staircases or in out-of-the-way places?"

"What is it, Jo?" Gerald asked.

"Just some odd idea I had. I don't suppose you came across anything that looked remotely like an El Greco?"

"Remotely? Jo, you know as well as I do that there is no such thing as a painting that is remotely like an El Greco. It either is El Greco or it isn't. He had no imitators."

"I'm sorry. I know it sounded stupid. So much has happened." I got to my feet. "Do you need me here, Gerald? I thought I'd take a walk. My head feels as if it's packed with cotton wool."

"No, not right now, Jo."

Askew rose, too, and rather unexpectedly addressed himself to me. "Mind if I go with you? My own head could stand a bit of clearing. Things to think over. All right?" His was the face of a desperately lonely man.

"Yes . . . yes, of course. I'll just go upstairs and get my jacket."

I was conscious of a sense of disappointment. I hadn't realized until Askew made his undeniable request that I had been intending to walk to Nat Birkett's house. I had told myself all through the drive up here that I would merely say what I had come to say, offer the miniature, and then go home. I had meant to leave Nat Birkett free of any sense that I was reaching out to hold him, to bind him in the Tolsons' fashion. We would have our memories of that radiant dawn in the shelter by the woods. But now I had to acknowledge that independence had no place in what I remembered of that morning.

UPSTAIRS, in Gerald's bathroom, I splashed cold water into my stinging eyes. Strangely, the face I saw in the mirror seemed to have altered. I looked older. There was a twist to the mouth I never noticed—if it had been there. I did not look at all like Vanessa, maybe never had, although I'd tried to. It almost seemed as if I had stepped out finally from behind her shadow and declared myself. Perhaps it had happened when I stood at the door of my flat and refused to answer the insistent ringing of the telephone, when before I would have flown to it in the hope that it was Harry. Or perhaps when I entered Thirlbeck once again and was greeted by the hounds as if I had been known to them all my life. Or perhaps later, as the sun had risen over Brantwick and the young priest in London had robed himself to say the first of those nine masses. It could have been all of those things, or one.

But when I went back to the Spanish Woman's room to get my parka I was at once aware of an alien presence—something distant, almost warning. I looked around, but everything seemed in its place. My clothes were hanging as I had left them; the suitcase with the pieces of the Sung bowl, and the Book of Hours seemed undisturbed. I turned at the doorway and looked back. I had expected to see her, there in the chair by the fireplace or in the shadow thrown on the floor by the sunlight. But she was my friend, and whatever, whoever had recently entered here, was not. I thought of the spun-sugar fairy who had danced about on that morning I had first wakened at Thirlbeck. No. Jessica had been sent home. But home was only a mile down the valley, and Jessica had inhabited Thirlbeck all her life. No prohibition by her grandfather could keep her out.

311

Either Askew had not intended to take a walk or his resolution had faltered. He was there, where I had seen him before with the condesa and Gerald, on that patch of grass with the long view of the tarn. A bottle of champagne, embedded in an ice bucket, stood ready on the wooden table.

"Thought we might enjoy the sun," he greeted me. "Sheltered here. You'll have a drink?" The words and sentences were cut short, as if he had no strength for unneeded effort.

I thought of the brandy we both had drunk, and now the champagne. It hardly seemed to matter. It was the sort of day I would never live again. "Yes, thank you."

He poured for us and eased himself into the deck chair close to me. We made a slight inclination to each other with our glasses, but exchanged no salutation. As with each situation here, I was beginning to believe that I had been doing it for a long time. I believed it also as Tolson approached, walking purposefully but not hurrying. Always a Tolson come to serve a Birkett.

But it was to me he spoke. "There's a telephone call for you, Miss Roswell. It's Mr. Peers. He said he'd wait."

I started to rise; then I dropped back in the seat. "Thank you, Mr. Tolson. Would you mind telling Mr. Peers that you can't find me but you'll deliver the message?"

He nodded. "Of course, Miss Roswell."

When Tolson had left, Askew said, "You could have gone. I don't mind."

"No. For once, Harry will have to wait. He won't wait very long," I added. "After a while he won't call anymore."

"Isn't that a rather unfair way of getting rid . . . well, I'm sorry, it isn't my business, and it may not be what I think."

"Unfair? Oh, I won't just let him go by default. But I'm too tired now to talk to him. I have to wait until I'll sound as if I'm sure. Harry is used to a rather different person—someone ready to be told what to do." I looked across at Askew. "No, you really don't know much of what it's about. But for the first time I know that I don't want to drift into something just because it's easier than other decisions. It's only fair to tell Harry that I'm not the sort of person I was. Have you got a cigarette?"

He gave me one from the gold case and lighted it before taking one for himself. We sat in silence. The wind from the tarn was gentle and sun-warmed. I sipped the champagne and smoked, and wished that, for some time, life could stay just like this. I needed a little time—time to get used to the creature who had broken from the chrysalis, the wings yet feeble and uncertain. I had just handed back the world on a golden plate that Harry had offered me. I would have been safe with Harry—safe and empty, as over the years I waited for him to come back from his trips. I would have been, like my china figurines, relegated to a shelf until wanted for use or inspection.

What I would have in place of Harry I didn't know. What was important was that the person who had broken out of the mould must stay out. Suddenly I could face anyone now—anyone at all.

I turned to Askew. "What will you do now? Will you let Gerald take over arrangements for the sale? If we recover the million pounds, will you just go off and spend it?"

"I don't see how I can go off, do you? Too many people have paid too high a price because I have refused my responsibilities here. I'm thinking now . . . that I shall stay. Maybe I shall try to make some sort of arrangement for Nat Birkett, to ease the burden of death duties. There are a lot of things I could do . . . should do. I don't know how to live this sort of life, but at least I can try."

I sat silent for a while, thinking about what he had said. "But does it all have to be sold—all the furniture and pictures and books? You could open it to the public. You were born in this house. But when I first saw it I thought it had grown out of a fairy tale. It's very beautiful—all of this valley. England is a very crowded little island, Lord Askew. I wonder if it's right that people like you— and Tolson, I suppose—should be allowed to keep quite so much to themselves. This whole region is one of the few national parks we have. And you own a slice in its very heart."

"You're talking about my going into the stately-homes business. I could never do it—set up souvenir stands, have strangers walking through my house. No, but when Nat Birkett's time comes he can make his own decisions."

"By that time," I said, "the best of the furniture and the pictures will be gone—all the things that help draw people."

"Look," he said wearily, "there has to be a choice. I have to put several hundred thousand pounds into Tolson's hands to do what needs doing about this place. You can see for yourself that it

313

needs a new roof. Tolson and his sons need new farm equipment—yes, even if they're tenants they've a right to some help. There could be a sort of cooperative for tractors and machinery. It's got to be paid for with something. What will Nat Birkett thank me for most? A flourishing estate or a few antiques?"

"Have you suddenly become a farmer yourself?"

He shook his head. "If I stay here, it will be to relieve Tolson of the financial problem of supporting me elsewhere. And he seems to think there's some symbolic value in my actually residing here."

"When did he say this?"

"Last night. After our day of revelations about the pictures and things, he and I had a long talk. I wondered what he would do with the money if he had it. He has a lot of plans. Breeding better beef cattle for the Common Market—but it takes years to do that. We should have a completely automated milking parlour for the dairy herd—and that stock needs improving, too. And he says he could get good, qualified workers if he could build decent cottages for them and pay more than the minimum rate. A model farm, Tolson paints it as—with me, belatedly, as the model landlord."

"Gerald once described you as antiestablishment. And now you'll be living an almost feudal life."

He stubbed out the cigarette and reached for another. "I had some half-baked ideas on socialism. I dashed off to Spain to fight for the common man and his rights. I thought when I told Tolson to sell the farms at fair prices to the tenants I was doing my bit for land reform. It never occurred to me that he would see it all in larger terms—that the Birkett estate should be one big cooperative. He has schemes so grand, I can't even imagine how he'll work them. But then, all he wants of me is that I be here, and let him run the show."

Why should my heart ache for Lord Askew? And yet it did. In these last few hours we had grown rapidly closer. He was a stranger in his own land and struggling, in his sixties, to make it less strange. He would try to stick it out, but I thought he would very often be making the headlong flight down the motorway to London, and then, restless and bored there, would head back north to the strangeness at Thirlbeck.

"I hope you and Gerald will come sometimes," he said. "I'd be glad if you would."

"We'll come, of course."

"Good! It will be very bad indeed once Carlota goes."

"Are you sure she will go?"

He nodded. "Yes, in time. She's a rare and exotic bird. I couldn't expect her to settle down like a little broody hen."

It was hardly a shock to see the miniature come out of his pocket. Often, as we had talked, I had noticed that his hand went there and he touched something, as if for reassurance.

"I didn't think it mattered if I took it. Gerald has the number. He doesn't need this."

"Do you?"

"Perhaps." He sat and looked at it for a moment. "It really belongs to you, but do you mind if I keep it? Just for a while?"

I had the sense that, of all the treasures Thirlbeck possessed, this was perhaps the only thing he really wanted. "Keep it as long as you want. Vanessa might have liked that best, having it go back to you. She must have thought it very special. It was in the zippered compartment of her handbag, as if she rarely were parted from it. And yet I'd never seen it before."

"I wish she had taken much more from me, but she never would. It looks like her, doesn't it? That's why I gave it to her. Red-haired and beautiful, Vanessa was—and a little bit wild. Just the way I imagined the woman in this portrait was. When I was a boy I used to look at this quite often and wish I had known her. When Vanessa came it was like seeing the portrait come to life."

Now it was I who rose and poured the champagne. Was the sensation of being totally relaxed with this man merely what champagne drunk in the sun will do? "Tell me about it. What was it like then, here at Thirlbeck? The three of you—"

"Then? Well, we were all young—that's the first point. At least we *seemed* young. I was in my thirties, Jonathan about twenty-seven. Vanessa was only twenty-one. It was very isolated up here then. At times we felt as if we were the only three people left alive in the world. No doubt we were very selfish. Every fine day was an excuse for a picnic. Mrs. Tolson was a splendid cook, and a baked rabbit was a feast. Funny, how I remember the food. After the army food, I used to look forward to every meal. I used to gather the eggs from the hen run myself, and I used to shoot deer, partridge, and pheasant. Vanessa and Jonathan eventually ate

315

most of their meals here; I wanted their company. Any reason was good enough to bring up the best wine from the cellar. It began to seem like one long party, and we gave Jonathan very little chance to work. It made him angry sometimes, and he'd keep to himself for a day or two. But he wasn't well and he wasn't working well. So he'd be back with us, and the party would go on.

"Then one day it seemed as if we'd come to the last of the wine. It was autumn, and Vanessa and Jonathan went—quite suddenly. So I went, too. Vanessa had left an address in London, but when I went to it I found out that they'd never been there. That was when I knew she didn't want to see me again."

"But you had given her the miniature, and she had taken it. That must have meant something."

"Obviously it didn't mean what I had hoped."

What had seemed difficult before, now was easy. I asked my question directly. "Did you love her? Did she love you?"

"I loved her. I really believed I did. But perhaps she didn't believe it herself. Perhaps she never loved me. She never said she did. I remember . . . she never actually said it."

We looked at each other, and there was knowledge in the look. "And now," I said, "you know that she did love you. *That* was why she was willing to do so much for Thirlbeck and kept so quiet about it. I wonder . . . I wonder if my father knew she loved you."

Askew sighed. "I don't know. I probably was blindly selfish about that, too. She and Jonathan were married during the war. He was captured soon after and was in a POW camp right until the surrender. They'd spent so little time together. Renting the lodge here was an effort to get to know each other again. They tried terribly hard, and without me they might have had a chance."

"They really didn't have much of a chance," I said. "It was a marriage that went wrong, and they both knew it. They stayed together until I was born, and then my father went to Mexico. There seemed to be no bitterness. As soon as he started selling some paintings he sent money. Later Vanessa used to show me his letters. He sounded nice. When I finally did meet him he turned out to be rather more than nice. But I couldn't picture him *married* to Vanessa. She was a bit too much for most people, except in small doses. Perhaps she knew that. Perhaps that was why she went away and never saw you again."

He sighed. "If it was, then she was wiser than I guessed. I pressed her a little before they left. She said she couldn't compete with a ghost. I suppose she meant my wife."

I didn't try to answer him. Who could tell now what ghosts, friendly or not, Vanessa had experienced at Thirlbeck? Or had she used that phrase only as an excuse, so that the independence she had fought for would remain hers? Vanessa had always been supremely her own woman; even so young, she must have known this was how it had to be for her. For this reason, probably, she and my father had parted. They both had been rare spirits, and neither could have long remained subordinate to another.

"There are all sorts of ghosts, aren't there?" I said finally. "Do you think she thought at all about the Spanish Woman? Do you think that's why she called me Joanna?"

Before he could answer, the whole pack of hounds started a joyful rush towards us. As they came close I was aware again of their formidable size and those wise, wistful eyes that seemed to look at me from my own level. They fanned out between myself and Askew, surrounding us with a sea of moving tails.

"Strange, isn't it, how they've taken to you?" Askew said. "All the hounds I remember from my childhood—the ancestors of these dogs—were a bit reserved. This lot seemed no different until you came along. I know it infuriated Tolson. He believed he had quite an invincible force of watchdogs whom no one could cajole. But I almost think for you they'd roll over like spaniels to have their tummies scratched."

"I didn't think so the first time I saw them. I was terrified. If you hadn't come, I couldn't have moved from the car. Especially after what happened at the birch woods."

"At the birch woods?" Askew leaned forward. "What happened at the birch woods?"

"Well, I feel foolish saying it, but I thought I saw one of the dogs. In fact, I was *certain* I saw him. He ran right in front of the car—seemed to spring out of nowhere. I slammed on the brakes, and we went into a bad skid. After I got the car under control I looked back and caught the last of him, just a whitish shape, going through the trees. That wouldn't have been so strange, except that Gerald didn't see him. He didn't *see* him, Lord Askew. And when we got down to the house you said all the dogs were with you at the time—and there were no other wolfhounds around."

Askew reached out and jerked my sleeve. "Are you absolutely *sure* you saw a white hound up there at the birch copse?"

"Yes, but I tell you Gerald saw nothing at all. I could have killed us that evening—"

Askew slumped back in the chair. I had to bend towards him to hear the next words. "I *did* kill my wife and my son. There, at the same place. The day before my father's funeral. That white hound, straight in front of the car. But when I pulled myself out of the wreck and ran for help, they told me that all the dogs had been in the house at that time. No one believed me, you see. I'd been drinking—yes, I'd had some drinks before I could face Thirlbeck again. But I wasn't drunk. *I wasn't!* I couldn't stand up in court and say that a phantom hound had caused the crash. I couldn't say that strange things had happened at that place so many times in the Birketts' history. There are tales that the Spanish Woman used to go to that point in her walks, waiting for news from Spain. I wonder if one of the hounds was her companion."

He brushed a trembling hand across his mouth. "Well, that's no defence in a court of law. But you—*you* saw it. It is something that happens to Birketts—and sometimes to those who threaten them in some way. 'Who seizes, beware.' But you'd never been here in your life, never knew Vanessa had." His hands gripped the arms of the chair. "Jo—you're Vanessa's child. Are you *mine?*"

We looked at each other for a long time, face examining face, eyes suddenly familiar. A terrible weakness struck me, and the beginning of joy.

"I wonder," I said softly. There would be no way to prove it, but that didn't matter. We both knew. Then, above us, there was a far-off but powerful thrust of wings. All the dogs and I raised our faces, and across the sun came the shape of an eagle—one of Nat Birkett's golden eagles in that soaring, heart-stopping flight. For an instant the shadow of the great wings seemed to cross us, but it couldn't have; the bird was far distant and growing more distant with every second. I wanted to cry out to it not to leave us; the moment of grace was precious, and soon gone.

I looked down at the man beside me. He had collapsed in the chair, and a stain of bright red blood had trickled from his mouth and already spread evilly across his shirt and jacket.

318

CHAPTER EIGHT

We didn't wait for the ambulance or for Dr. Murray. Askew had
vomited blood once more before we got him stretched on the back
seat of Gerald's Daimler. The condesa was driving, and I took the
seat beside her, unbidden. Tolson had called the hospital to alert
them; then he called Jessica's mother to tell her to open the gates
at the South Lodge. Gerald stayed behind. "I might be of more use
here. I'll follow in a bit. How awful . . ."

The condesa drove quickly but with great skill. At each junction she managed to get us through without stopping, although the
traffic had begun to thicken with holiday crowds. At one traffic
light we waited three minutes; turning towards Askew I saw him
give a convulsive shudder, and there was more blood. "What . . . ?"
I whispered to the condesa. "What is happening to him?"

Her reply was almost savage. "You saw it happen before. The
pain, but not the bleeding that time. He has been warned. The
duodenal ulcer. Too much drink, too much smoking, the upset
of these last days. And now the massive haemorrhage. Pray God
he does not lose too much blood before they can help him."

We went to the emergency entrance of the hospital, and they
were waiting for us. The condesa took Askew's hand as they
wheeled him inside. After I parked the car I was directed to a glass
corridor connected to a small wing of the main building. Here, on
a long seat, was the condesa. Someone, Jeffries perhaps, had put
her needlework bag into the car, and she was reaching into its
depths for cigarettes. She had none, and snatched, without thanks,
at the packet I offered.

"What are they doing?"

"He has lost a lot of blood. They must make a transfusion."

Her tone was sharp. "He is very ill, they say. In shock. Why
can't they *do* something?" Suddenly her anger and fear seemed to
transfer to me. "*You* don't have to stay. What use for the two of us
to be here?" In her agitation her slight accent became stronger. Her
face, too, had altered, the high cheekbones more pronounced, the
warm olive skin sallow. There was something much more elemental in her now. The sheen of sophistication had slipped from her.

"Let me wait a little, please. I would like to take back some
news to Gerald. I would like to know—"

"To know!" She flung her hands wide. "They tell you nothing. He is closed in there, and I cannot see him!"

As she spoke a young doctor came out of Askew's room with a covered kidney-shaped vessel in his hand. The condesa jumped to her feet. "Please, you will tell me—"

"Later, madam." He half ran along the corridor. A nurse came out of the room, and I had a glimpse of two other nurses. I couldn't see Askew, but I saw the sphygmomanometer being used. Then one of the nurses came out with Askew's clothing.

"Give me those." The condesa snatched the clothes, as if the bloodstained bundle were precious, not to be touched by other hands. We waited for long minutes, and then the young doctor came back and went into Askew's room. He reappeared almost at once. In the doorway he encountered an older doctor who had come down the corridor at that sort of flying march that heralds an emergency.

"Tough one, sir," the young man said. He glanced at the condesa and his voice dropped. We couldn't hear the next words. The older man disappeared into Askew's room; the young man went to an office almost opposite us, whose door stood open. At once he was on the telephone. As eagerly as the condesa I strained to hear his words. The call was to a hospital in Penrith.

" . . . done the group and cross match. Unless I've lost my mind it's . . . Yes, I know. Well, you've got a list of donors, haven't you? I'll hang on. But do hurry!" There followed a long pause. Then the doctor's voice again. "No one at all? Well, damn—to be expected, I suppose. I'll try Carlisle."

He put through another call. The first sentences were calm. Then his voice rose in frustration. "Yes . . . that's what I said. *Yes,* I know it's rare as hen's teeth! *Have you got a donor?* Well look, will you? I'll hold on." While we waited I looked down at my hands, and they were as tense as the condesa's. We heard the doctor's voice again. "Have you? Good. Just pray he's not out at the pub, or something. How long do you think? I don't think *we've* got much time unless we can control the haemorrhaging. Alert the police and they'll give you an escort. Thanks." He hung up, and for a moment his young body sagged. Then a violent rap of his pen on the blotter. "Damn!"

It was as if his expletive suddenly broke through my numbed

320

reflexes. What he had been saying translated itself into the typed symbols on a card I carried with me always. I got up and went to the doorway. I had taken my wallet out of the pocket of my parka, and I was shuffling the few credit cards in it. "My blood is the type you need. Here's my donor's card. I'm registered with St. Giles's in London."

He sprang to his feet and grabbed the card. "God Almighty!" Then he looked at me sharply. "You related to Lord Askew?"

I looked at him very directly and then shook my head. "No, just coincidence that I'm here."

"You're sure about your blood type? I mean absolutely *sure?*"

I was getting angry. "As sure as St. Giles's is. I've been called three times for emergencies. I give blood routinely a few times a year. If you doubt *them*—"

He let out a sort of whistle. "No, I don't. But I'll have to do my own test. It won't take long. I just can't chance a mistake. If you were an incompatible donor, there could be a fatal reaction. Well, let's get going."

In a room off in another wing he took the blood sample and asked me about my general health. Then he said, "O.K. Go back to where you were. I'll be along in a minute."

When I got back to the condesa her angry hand gripped my arm. "What is happening? What have you to do with him?"

I explained about the blood, but she didn't understand. "Why can't I give him *mine?* I'd give him all of it. *All!*"

"He can't take it, Condesa. There'd be a rejection—"

"*Rejection!*" She bent her head, but she did not weep.

The young doctor came back and talked briefly with the older man in Askew's room. Then he came to the door and beckoned me.

Askew's bed was surrounded by screens, but I could see the oxygen tank. "I understand that you know the procedure," the older doctor said. I nodded. I rolled up my sleeve, kicked off my shoes, and lay down on an empty bed. I automatically clenched my fist to give them the vein sharp and clear, and felt the prick of the needle. The tubing was attached to the bottle and the suction started. After that it was a matter of waiting. A half litre was taken from me. They put the next bottle in place.

I had never gone beyond this point. I didn't care. The sounds from a few feet away told me Askew continued to vomit up blood.

The bottle of my own blood was now suspended on a stand above him; I continued to pump more into the vessel next to my bed. The voices at the other bed were low. "One hundred and forty." Was that the pulse? I turned my head and saw that the blood pressure was being monitored constantly. "Sixty," the nurse said.

People came and went. For a few seconds I heard the condesa's voice in the corridor, angry, frantic. They closed the door. I didn't know time anymore. There was a blankness creeping over me. The second half-litre bottle was taken away. Someone came over—took temperature, blood pressure, pulse.

"Can you give any more?" It was a voice I knew, though in the dizziness that seized me his face was a blur. I couldn't remember the name, but it was the doctor who had taken care of Gerald.

"Go on," I said. "I'm all right."

I watched the blood mount in the third bottle they attached to me. When it was almost full they took it away, to suspend above the other bed. The needle and tube were disconnected. I was dimly aware that a blanket was pulled over me.

I tried to cry out, to beg, but my voice was only a whisper. "Go on! For God's sake, go on! I've got more blood."

A voice said gently in my ear, "You've given all you can. Go to sleep. You've done your best."

The face moved away. I heard the soft, measured tone from the other bed. "Blood pressure fifty, Doctor."

He was going to die. I wondered if, through his shock and weakness, he had been aware of my presence in the room, of its being my blood he was receiving. I realized that the real gift I had given him was not just the chance of life but the release from the guilt he had carried through those years for the death of his wife and son. *Two* Birketts, at least, had seen that phantom white hound. The release, and the shock of recognition that Vanessa's child was also his, had started the fatal haemorrhage. I hoped he had known that I had tried to give my blood back to him.

Time passed, and still I held out against sleep, somehow believing that while I kept my senses he would keep his life. They seemed to have forgotten me and moved the screens aside to work more freely. I saw his face, colourless, and very still. "Pressure forty-seven." Then the activity seemed to cease. They remembered me, saw that my eyes were still open, and replaced the screens. The last thing I saw was the empty bottle being unhooked from the stand.

He was dead. My father, Robert Birkett, eighteenth Earl of Askew, was dead. I closed my eyes.

I woke in a private room. Almost at once a nurse came, and there was the routine of temperature, pulse, and blood pressure. The shadows outside were growing longer in the late afternoon.

"How are you feeling?" It wasn't a social inquiry.

"All right. Can I go now?"

"No, of course not. You've given about as much blood as anyone can and still be alive. You've got to rest and make it up a bit. You can probably leave here tomorrow, but it'll take weeks before you're quite fit again. We've been trying to locate that donor in Carlisle, because you really should have a transfusion."

"It didn't save Lord Askew, did it? He's dead."

"I'm sorry—yes. He kept haemorrhaging as fast as we gave it to him. You mustn't fret. You did more than anyone could expect."

I didn't answer her. I just lay there and thought about my father—the father I had discovered in the last hours of his life. I knew quite surely what Askew would have wanted to do if he had learned that Vanessa was bearing his child. And she had known, with equal sureness, that it would have been a useless thing. If they had married, they would not have remained long together. She had chosen the hardest, and the best way. And I knew also that she would have told all this to Jonathan Roswell. I now read things in his attitude which I had not seen before—his gentle protectiveness, the assumption that if we were lucky we would be friends—and we had become friends.

So I had had, in the space of a few weeks, two fathers. And I thought that few people could have that experience and be so lucky as to make friends of both of them.

A dim light flicked on in the small room. The nurse's voice. "Lord Askew is here to see you, Miss Roswell."

I struggled half upright. "Lord Askew? Lord Askew is dead!"

And then the nurse was gone, and Nat was bending over me. "I wanted to come earlier, Jo, but they said you had to rest."

He seemed different, and then I realized I hadn't seen him dressed in a suit before. "Nat, you know all about it?"

323

He pulled up a chair. "I know about the blood transfusion, the rare blood group. Not really a coincidence, is it, Jo? Gerald Stanton told me about your mother having been at Thirlbeck. You're part of the family now. You and I are cousins sixteen times removed, or something stupid like that." His roughened hand lay on mine. "Jo, you look so pale. Are you all right?"

"Yes, I'm all right. But I'm sorry about—about him. He wanted to live, Nat. He was going to do things for Thirlbeck, for you. We were talking about it. He had guessed about me—before the transfusion—and I think he was glad. He seemed so lonely . . . and I was in the room when he died."

"Hush, Jo, hush. You're tiring yourself."

"I'll be all right." I fingered the dark material of his jacket. "Sometime, Nat, I'll tell you everything that happened today."

He smiled. "I'd like to hear it. I don't know what sort of mess I've inherited. There have been shocks already, like the story Gerald Stanton told me about what your mother and Tolson had been doing. The strange thing was that Askew had been here all these weeks and not found out about the land still being his." He shrugged. "Well, suddenly *I've* become the landowner. And young Thomas is now Viscount Birkett. The only thing he asked me was did we *have* to go and live in Thirlbeck, and I said no, we *didn't!*"

In the stillness we heard the Kesmere church clock striking. Nat got to his feet. "I'll have to go. They're moving the body from here to the church this evening. We're keeping it all as quiet and simple as possible. We'll bring Askew back for burial in the private ground at Thirlbeck, but the service tomorrow has to be in the parish church." He was scribbling something on a paper. "This is a phone number. The telephone company's assigned a new unlisted number to Thirlbeck, but still people find a way of getting it. The newspapers have started ringing already. Questions about La Española and the wretched curse. I hope no one on the hospital staff remembers a Roswell renting the North Lodge, or if they do, that they keep their mouths shut about who the blood donor was. The papers would have a field day. Oh, hell—why *now?*"

"Why not now?"

"Because we haven't had a chance. I thought when you rushed off to London that you were running away from me. Then Stanton told me about the bowl, and all. Well, this isn't the place to talk.

Stanton says he'll come to see you when it's over, later this evening."

"No, don't let him! He mustn't come here. Nat, take care of him. I need him now. I've lost—I've lost enough."

"Yes, Jo, I'll take care of him."

As he reached the door I called to him, "Nat, come back and take me home to Thirlbeck. I don't want to stay here."

"Tomorrow, Jo. Tomorrow you'll be stronger."

He was gone. The church clock struck another quarter hour. Tears of frustration and weakness brimmed in my eyes.

THEY brought me clear soup and toast, and a boiled egg. I ate some of it and then got out of bed. I found I could walk quite steadily, with only a slight blurring of vision. I found my clothes and slowly dressed. Then I opened the door. A young nurse was at a desk, writing. She looked up in surprise.

"Oh, you're up! I don't think—"

"Please, I'd like to go. I'm perfectly well. I wonder if I can get a taxi to Thirlbeck?"

"I'm sorry, Miss Roswell. I don't think you should go, and I haven't the authority to let you. I'll have to call a doctor."

"I'd like to sign myself out. I don't need to see a doctor for that." It took some insistence, and another nurse came along and tried to persuade me to go back to bed. But in time they produced the necessary form, and I signed it. Then I asked again about a taxi.

The younger of the two nurses glanced hesitantly at the other, then spoke to me. "I'm going off duty in ten minutes. I live in that direction. It wouldn't be any trouble to take you in my car."

I thanked her, and waited. I fingered the keys to the gates of Thirlbeck, still in the pocket of my parka. I seemed to need to get within those gates, to the quiet there, and the safety.

The young nurse's car was a Mini, just a little older than mine. "I hope it's really no trouble for you," I said.

"Oh, no. The sooner you're back in bed, the better, and since you were determined to go . . . you're sure you'll take proper care? Have some hot tea as soon as you get there, and see that you keep warm."

It was all she said until we reached the South Lodge. She used the key, then drove through the gates, leaving them unlocked for her return. "I confess I've always wanted to come in here," she said as she drove on slowly. "When you're kept out of a place you

325

always want to see what's behind the walls." It was getting dark as we neared the house. The pace became even slower. "It's all right, isn't it?" the girl said. "I mean—there will be *someone* here?"

I felt an impatience rise in me. "It doesn't matter if there isn't."

A single light burned above the front door. Suddenly I realized that I didn't have a key to the house itself. I didn't know what I would do. Then, unexpectedly, the door opened and the dogs streamed down the steps. I felt the girl stiffen beside me. "They're monsters!" And then, "Oh, look—who's that?"

For an instant she seemed hardly different from the first time I had seen her—the slender figure in silhouette against the lighted hall, her face shadowed as it had been then. But now she was wearing pants and a jacket, and there was no languor in her stance.

"She—she is a friend of Lord Askew's. The one who died," I remembered to add.

The condesa came down to help me out of the car, her hands surprisingly gentle after the savagery of that morning. She was almost unnaturally calm. The girl took courage from the silence and apparent friendliness of the dogs, and came around to help, too. I was grateful for support; I hadn't imagined my legs would feel like this. The girl was talking to the condesa. "She insisted on discharging herself from the hospital. I'm a nurse there. She should go to bed at once. . . ." We had reached the top of the steps and entered the hall, and the girl's voice faded as the great extent of the hall and the staircase was revealed. The girl found her voice at last. "Would you . . . would you like me to help see her to bed?"

I expected the condesa to accept, but she shook her head. "You are most kind. But I'm sure I shall manage. The others will be back soon." She addressed herself to me now. "You understand that I could not go to—to *that*."

I felt ashamed. In my own grieving I had not thought too much of hers. "I'll leave then," the girl said, disappointed; she had wanted to see more. "If you'd just see that the dogs . . . ?"

"Of course," I said. I sat on a chair, and the dogs crowded about me. The girl gave a last long look about the hall and walked slowly to the door. The condesa was there before her, the door already open, as if she were impatient for her to be gone. "Can she have brandy?" she asked the nurse.

"I'm not really sure. Giving alcohol is always chancy. Better not, perhaps. Just hot tea and hot-water bottles . . ." She looked back at me. "Well, I hope you feel better soon. Good-bye."

"Thank you so very much." Even as she walked down the steps the condesa had closed the doors and begun thrusting the bolts home. I had a sudden wish that the girl had not gone. The aloofness of the condesa was disconcerting, and the house was so silent.

The condesa came towards me briskly. "I'll help you up the stairs, and then I think some brandy . . ." She cut short my protest. "Ah, what do *they* know? At that hospital they are all fools."

I could feel the athletic strength of her body as she helped me rise; I wondered why I ever thought her slenderness denoted weakness. As we mounted the stairs I thought of something else. I had seen her handbag on a chair in the hall, and the jacket she was wearing was leather, as if she were dressed for travel. All at once I realized that now she was a woman very much alone.

"I tried—" I began.

She cut me short again. "I know you did. The grief for me is that I was not permitted to try." Then her calm broke. "If we had been elsewhere—in London or Paris—Roberto would have lived. I know it! There would have been better people, better treatment."

"I don't think so," I answered. "He just couldn't keep the blood." I wondered if she suspected my relationship with Askew.

"If they could have found that other donor. The fools—they did not try hard enough." Then she cried out in fury, as one of the dogs pressed too close. "I have stood these dogs for Roberto's sake, but they are ugly brutes, always in the way. I have been trying to get into the study to telephone for plane reservations, and they will not let me pass."

I realized that I felt sorry for her, a new experience. She was much more alone than I. "I think—I think there's a telephone extension in Lord Askew's room."

"Yes, so there is." Her tone was curiously flat, as if that information was not what she sought. "But still those dogs, they follow one everywhere." Her tone became harshly nervous.

So I turned on the stairs and said gently to the dogs, "Stay! Thor, Ulf, Odin. Stay!" They halted, and the pleasured wagging of their tails was stilled. I was sorry to leave them behind. But the condesa was trying to be kind, and the dogs annoyed her.

We reached the Spanish Woman's room. I slumped into the chair by the fire. Someone had relaid the kindling and the wood, but it didn't seem to occur to the condesa to set a match. All her life others had been doing such things for her.

"You should get undressed and into bed," she was saying. "I shall bring brandy." She didn't offer to help me. She wasn't the kind of person to handle other people's clothing, and yet I recalled how she had snatched Askew's clothes from the nurse that morning.

"Yes . . . thank you."

She was gone, and I was alone, wishing more than ever that I had asked the nurse to stay. It was easier for the condesa to bring brandy than to fuss with tea and hot-water bottles. I wished the fire had been lighted. I saw matches on the rim of the candlestick, but it was too much of an effort to bend down to the fire. At last I went to the closet, took off my parka, and hung it up carefully. I was like a person drunk, performing each action with great concentration. I was reaching for my nightgown hanging on one of the heavy oak pegs on the back wall of the closet when my balance seemed to desert me. I grabbed at the peg and hung there, swaying, fighting off the blackness that threatened. The strain on my arms became too much. I felt myself falling, and the very back of the closet was no longer there to support my body as I slipped down. I fell into blackness and the smell of ancient dust.

I don't know how long the blackness remained; it could have been minutes, or only seconds. I could open my eyes, but the faint light from the bedside lamp did not reach into this space—a new space, I realized, not part of the closet but an extension of it. Groping, my fingers encountered rough bricks and crumbling mortar. The dust on the floor was a thick, muffling sheet. The smell of the ages was in this recess. I crawled backward out of the space and pulled myself to my feet.

I rested with both hands on the mantelshelf for a few minutes. The fall had knocked the breath out of me, and I waited for a while to recover it. My hand trembled violently as I lit the candle. Then I went inside again, kicking aside the clothes that had fallen with me. I stood there with the candle burning steadily in that draughtless space, and I saw what had survived of the Spanish Woman for almost four hundred years.

That short body, now a skeleton, had been laid with reverence on a carved oak chest. It was dressed in a gown of yellow silk, which might once have been white, as might the lace of the cap that was tied about that narrow little skull. The hair held in place by the cap was black. The gloved skeletal fingers had been intertwined about an elaborately jewelled crucifix. A heavy signet ring had been placed over one finger. Cautiously, afraid that the glove might crumble to dust at my touch, I traced the initials on the ring. J.F.C. Juana Fernández de Córdoba.

I felt no horror at what I saw. That little face might once have been beautiful; she had been only seventeen, they said. Someone—some Catholic sympathizer perhaps—had recovered her body and brought it back here, dressing her tenderly in what might have been her bridal gown. The oak chest on which she lay probably held some of the possessions she had brought from Spain, other gowns and slippers, the baby clothes she would have been stitching for her unborn child. I stood and wondered why she had been brought here. Secret places such as this were no novelty in a house of this period. Had it been intended as a priest hole—to shelter hunted Catholics? Had indeed the first earl remained secretly Catholic, even heard mass in the little room which had become the Spanish Woman's tomb?

If someone had intended eventually to bury her with appropriate ceremony, the chance had never come, and the secret of the Spanish Woman's hiding place had died. But her spirit had spoken with great force over the centuries to some of the people who had inhabited this house, this room, myself among them. "When I am dead, of your charity, offer nine masses for my soul." Today the first of Juana's nine masses *had* been offered.

I raised the candle and looked around me. The rough brick my hand had encountered was probably a chimney flue, part of the huge one that led up from the fireplace in the great hall below. The chamber itself was very dry, which could have accounted for the preservation of the Spanish Woman's clothes. Just the right amount of heat had reached this space to offset the dampness that would have caused those silken and lace garments to rot.

I held the candle higher and saw the only other thing the chamber contained. It was propped against the brick wall at the back of the chest—a smallish rectangle, completely dust-covered, but with elaborate carving on its delicate frame. I reached across the little skeleton to touch this possession of hers. My hand removed some of the heavy dust. A faint reflection glowed back at me. It was a mirror, rare in the days of the Spanish Woman. I put down the candle and stretched out both hands to lift the precious thing.

It was too much for my strength. As I was about to lower it to the floor beside me it slipped and crashed down. The old Venetian glass shattered, and two large fragments fell from the frame. I sighed in agony. Why hadn't I waited until I had help? I had destroyed, once again, something very valuable. Then another thought came, the memory of the translation of that scrap of parchment. "This our likeness, a mirror of conscience." The prickling of excitement ran through my body like warm wine. Where the fragments of glass had fallen away a canvas showed. Frantically I began to pick at what remained. Reason told me to wait, but instinct and emotion overrode it. Piece by piece the glass came out. I knelt down and lifted the candle so that the light fell upon the face of Philip II of Spain, painted, in his own words, "by the hand of Domenico Theotokopoulos." It was unmistakably his unique style. I gazed at it in awe. Priceless. The greatest treasure Thirlbeck contained. A hitherto unknown painting by El Greco.

And then, my body seeming to pulse with the joy of this discovery, I began to feel cold and weak again. I didn't understand the warmth against my hand until I looked down. In picking away the fragments of the mirror, I had gashed my palm. The blood was trickling down my fingers. I grabbed one of my dresses which was lying on the closet floor and wrapped it tightly about my hand. I tried to rise, but the strength wouldn't come. Then I remembered that the condesa would return soon with the brandy. With that thought I let myself lie down beside the Spanish Woman.

I probably had moments of unconsciousness. There was no way to mark the time until I heard the footsteps, saw the shadow fall across the candlelight. For a second I thought it must be Jessica. The sense of hostility was strong. But no, not Jessica this time. Before she spoke I had the scent of her perfume.

"What . . . ?" A long silence followed. No hand attempted to raise my head. But she had picked up the candle; its light was higher. "*You* have found it!" The voice was well-known, a kind of harsh triumph in it now. "And I have searched all these weeks. Even the picture room when they believed I was having the siesta."

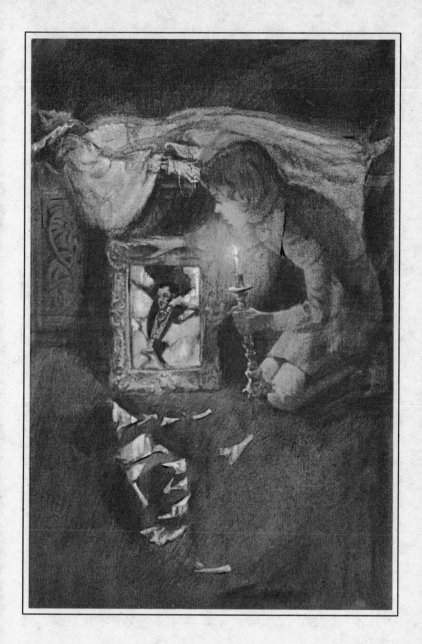

"Please," I whispered. I could feel the blood seeping through the rough bandage; I raised my hand so that she might see it.

"She is ours." Now the tone had softened, as if the condesa spoke to herself. "The Spanish lady and her possessions are ours. For many generations in our family we have known of this painting, as we have always known about the jewel. She was of our family, sent in marriage to England by Felipe. Just when I had begun to believe that it must have been destroyed *you* have found it."

I shifted my head, but nothing came into focus. "Help me!" I whispered. "I'm bleeding again. Please . . ."

If she heard me, it made no difference. Whatever anguish she might have felt at Robert Birkett's death now seemed to be submerged in the triumph of winning what she had come to Thirlbeck to seek. She was no longer a woman alone—a woman who had lost everything. "So, I take it now, since it does not belong to the Birketts but to my family. It will go to the highest bidder. Very private, and for a great deal of money."

I felt the canvas in its elaborate frame removed from my side, and then the candle itself was withdrawn. I made one last feeble attempt to stop her when she tugged at the panel which had sealed the dark little chamber. I had to pull back my fingers as the panel squeezed them. Then I could only lie there and listen to the sound of the closet door being closed. I felt tears of despair prick my eyes, but there was no energy to weep or cry out. My lips formed a word. "Please . . ." But there was no sound.

In the darkness I pulled the rough bandage tighter and clenched my fist around the cloth. Still the gentle ooze of blood continued. The stuffy chamber was suddenly as cold as death. For four hundred years this silent, dusty place had been the tomb of the Spanish Woman. And now I shared it with her.

THE sounds came from very far away; I wondered if, as a prelude to death, sounds came back that were part of life. I heard no voices, but I did hear the dogs, those strangely haunting sounds with which they had called to one another that day in the thick mist on the mountain. Strange, that in a whole lifetime of people's voices to hear and remember, the last thing I should be aware of was the cries of the great hounds of the Birketts.

Then some sense returned, and I knew the sounds were not

imagined, but real—and near. Were they beyond the door of the Spanish Woman's room, setting up that massive chorus? They kept on, insistent, almost frantic. Was there anyone in the house to hear them? Oh, God . . . I prayed for the dogs not to give up until someone should heed the demand of their clamour.

There was another period of blackness, and then the sounds were even nearer. The dogs had been let into the room, and now all eight of them must have taken their stance before the closed door of the closet. "Quickly . . . quickly," I whispered in the darkness. The closet door was open and then came the frantic scraping of claws on the other side of the panel. Whoever was there didn't waste any time. I heard the blessed splintering of wood. Something—a poker, even an axe—was tearing its way to me.

One of the dogs was through first, the great head thrusting into the hole, trying to lick life and warmth back into me. He was forcibly withdrawn, and the chopping recommenced with care. A strong beam of light was now shining on me. I felt myself being lifted with great gentleness. Nat's voice was close to my ear.

"You're going to make a rotten farmer's wife. You know that, don't you?"

Through the drive to the hospital Nat's arms cradled me still. "Hang on, Jo. The hospital telephoned. The donor is on his way there. Where you should have stayed."

Tolson was driving, and I knew that Gerald was in the car with us. They had tied a tourniquet about my arm, but the dizziness persisted. I framed words, but few would come. "Gerald, the condesa . . ." It was the lightest whisper, and Nat caught it.

"Yes, Jo. We know she's gone. Don't try to talk."

I did try again, but it was no use. When we reached the hospital I was aware of the strangeness of staring face up at the lights as I was wheeled along the corridors. The wound was stitched and bound, the tourniquet released, and the transfusion begun. As they prepared to put me to sleep, I summoned the strength to demand that Nat and Gerald return. The nurses brought them in, but once more my strength failed. "The condesa . . . she has . . ."

It was Gerald who put his fingers on my lips. "Please don't try to talk, Jo. We know all about it. The condesa has gone, and so has La Española. Everything is being done, and you are to sleep."

"La Española . . ." I whispered.

"Jo, stop it!" Nat's voice. "What are you bothering about it for? Tolson has told the police. The ports and airports have been alerted to watch for her. For myself, I hope she gets clean away with it. But I don't suppose we'll be that lucky."

"Nat, please." Gerald's voice was cautioning him. "Look, there's the nurse with an injection. You *must* rest, Jo."

I licked my dry lips. "An El Greco . . ." But the words had no form, and no one heard. I could feel my rising panic. Confused thoughts whirled within me. No one knew that the condesa had taken the El Greco as well as La Española, that by telling the police, they were placing themselves in terrible jeopardy. If she were caught now, she could claim that she was merely one more of the couriers who had left Thirlbeck with a precious canvas. And the world would know the secret Vanessa and Tolson had kept so faithfully. She would implicate Gerald, and possibly Nat. But if she did get out of the country and disposed of the jewel and the painting, the danger would recede for all of us. So I didn't try anymore to tell them. It was too difficult.

I felt the jab of the needle. In the last seconds before the blackness, I managed to touch Nat's hand. He bent towards my lips, but I didn't know how the words came out. "You have to get me in the morning. Must be there when they bury him. Promise?"

He had heard. "I promise, Jo. Go to sleep now."

I felt sure that La Española would return to Thirlbeck. What had been the Spanish Woman's would remain hers. And whatever ruin followed, we would have to bear. But still the thought persisted, until the oblivion of the drug took hold, that to me she was a friendly spirit, the Spanish Woman.

CHAPTER NINE

NAT came quite early, but I was dressed and waiting for him. He entered the room with his brows settled into a frown. "Jo, you know this is madness. You should stay at least another day."

I shook my head. "I have to be there, Nat. I'll rest, I promise: But I have to be there."

He accepted the inevitable, but insisted on using a wheelchair to take me to the car—Gerald's car. "It won't shake you around like the Land-Rover," he said. Still he drove with exaggerated care. "All I want is to see you safely back in bed. I don't care how long it takes to get to Thirlbeck."

Through the slow drive I didn't speak to him of the condesa. I had listened to the early news bulletins on the radio, and there had been no mention of her. For the moment it served no purpose to lay further burdens on Nat. We reached the South Lodge, and Jessica's mother was there to open the gate for us. As we drove on, Nat said, "You know, it was Jessica who saved your life."

"*Jessica!* How?"

"She'd seen you pass the South Lodge in a strange car last evening. When it came back again quite soon she got concerned. She knew the condesa was at the house, but doubted that she could do the right things for you—see you to bed, and so on. So she walked to Thirlbeck and was in time to see the condesa drive off in Askew's car—heading over Brantwick. In the house the dogs were kicking up an almighty fuss, trying to get into the Spanish Woman's room. The door was locked, and there was no key—at least not on the outside. She heard no sound inside the room. So she telephoned the vicarage, hoping to get a message to Tolson and me, since we'd accompanied the body to the church. She reached us and said that something seemed very wrong, and we just about burned up the road getting back here."

I was silent, thinking about it. Thirlbeck was in plain view before I spoke. "Then Jessica did the exact opposite of what she did with Patsy. When she could have spoken before, she didn't. This time she took more on herself than she need have. Nat—oh, Nat, this is a bitter sort of twist for you. She could have saved Patsy, but she saved me. I suppose she was ill then, but . . ."

His hand touched mine. "I can't weigh you and Patsy in the same scales, Jo, and don't ever think it. Patsy was sweet and lovely, and I loved her. Now I love you. I have to leave behind what Jess did or didn't do in the past. Last night I think she saved your life. For that I'm in her debt, and always will be. When Tolson realized what Jessica had done he looked like a man who'd had an intolerable burden removed from him. He can face anything now. And so can I."

I had little time to get used to this new knowledge of Jessica. It was she who opened the door at Thirlbeck. She was standing there at the top of the steps as we drove up. Involuntarily I felt myself stiffen at the sight of her. And Nat's voice came gently. "Easy, Jo. We have to give her a chance."

The first greeting was lost in the surge of the dogs, their tails waving in a frenzy of welcome. Jessica had opened the car door before Nat could get around, and stretched out her hand to help me. "I waited until you came to cook breakfast," she said.

There was a blazing fire in the dining room, and a sofa had been placed before it, heaped with cushions. Jessica motioned Nat to take me to it, and I found myself with my legs up and a rug spread over me. She brought a small table, and I watched her as she moved to the sideboard to pour two cups of coffee. She was in some way older; her body did not seem to dance through its tasks, as if they were some graceful game she played. She didn't smile, and the shining blonde hair was not shaken for Nat's admiration. When she had given Nat and me the coffee she said, "There's news, Lord Askew."

"Cut the rubbish, Jess. My name is Nat."

She shook her head. "Oh, no. Not anymore. Everything's changed. No one can help it. It just has changed."

He sighed, and stirred his coffee. "What's the news, Jess?"

"This morning, very early, I went to take your watch at the shelter. I knew you wouldn't be able to go. Well, when it got light I started watching the eagles with the glasses. I looked out over the whole valley, and I saw something up by the birch copse—something I'd never seen before. I went there as quickly as I could. It was Lord Askew's car; it had run off the road, broken through a wall, and crashed down among the trees. The condesa was in it. I was much too late to help her. Dr. Murray thinks she must have died almost at once. He thinks her neck was broken."

Nat looked from Jessica to me. "Dead? She's dead!"

"There wasn't anything I could do," Jessica said softly. "I did try. Honestly, I did. It was . . . it was rather horrible. There's a lot of broken glass. She wasn't wearing a seat belt, and she was jammed against the steering wheel. She had the key of the North Lodge gates in her handbag. And La Española."

Briefly Nat's head sank. "I was hoping La Española would cease to exist for us. But she never even got it out of this valley."

I grasped the coffee cup between both my hands to force still-

336

ness upon them. "Did you find anything else, Jessica?" I asked.

"Yes . . . yes, I did find something else. So that was why . . . yes, *that* was why she shut you in that place with the Spanish Woman. You had found it in there."

"What the hell are you talking about?" Nat demanded.

Jessica turned to him. "In the back of the car I found Miss Roswell's big red suitcase. I decided I'd bring it down—and La Española. It seemed strange that the condesa should have taken that suitcase and left all her own behind. Hers were so expensive."

"But mine was tough. Cheap fiberglass, but tough. Was the painting in it, Jessica?"

She nodded. "It was all packed about with your clothes—a protection, I suppose. My grandfather had never seen it before. We woke Mr. Stanton. He was much more pleased about that being back here than La Española."

Nat interrupted. "Would you mind explaining? I'm beginning to feel even more dense than usual."

I sank back against the pillows, a sense of relief surging through me. "It was a painting by El Greco." I found myself telling him what I had not been able to say last night.

From the doorway, Gerald's voice. He had entered very quietly, had been standing behind us, listening. "How are you, Jo?" He came around to inspect me. "You shouldn't be out of the hospital at all, but I'm glad to see you, my dear. You still look like a ghost— and you nearly died there with the Spanish Woman."

I went on then with what had happened the night before. "The condesa was all ready to leave just with La Española, and I made a gift to her of the El Greco as well. I even helped her take La Española. Until I came the dogs wouldn't move away from the door of the study. I made them stay on the landing, left her free to switch off the alarm and take what she wanted."

"The dogs saved your life," Gerald said. "The dogs and Jessica. Without the dogs we wouldn't have found that little chamber. I don't pretend to know what it is those dogs have bred into them, but it is something that primarily concerns the Birketts."

"What has happened to the painting?" I asked.

"Grandfather kept the suitcase and the painting here," Jessica answered. "We returned La Española to the car. It had to be there when the police came. We're just to say—when it's time to an-

337

nounce it—that the painting was discovered in the little room with the Spanish Woman. No need to bring the condesa into that. . . ."

"It *is* Philip the Second, isn't it, Gerald?"

He nodded his thanks as Jessica handed him a cup of coffee. "I'd say so. El Greco has made him look more spiritual than any picture I've ever seen of him. Strange, how Philip neglected the one artist who truly caught the spirit of Spain. Well, it's a splendid portrait. Almost as moving, in its way, as that wonderful *Portrait of an Unknown Man* in the Prado." He made a little smacking noise with his lips. "What a sensation! What a sale it will make!"

Then he sighed. "That poor woman, the condesa. I wonder if she fastened onto Robert just to make him come here, so that she could search for it? Perhaps not. Perhaps she only decided to take La Española because there was nothing else left for her. With Robert dead her world was collapsing." His tone dropped lower. "I do wonder about that place at the birch copse." He shrugged. "Useless wondering about things like that. . . . Never gets you anywhere."

I shivered, and Nat was quickly beside me. "You cold, Jo?"

"No," I said. "I'm all right." I wasn't going to say, not now or ever, what it might be that the condesa had seen at the beginning of the birch copse. Perhaps she had seen nothing. An accident with no apparent cause. But the dying words of the Spanish Woman had once more proved their potency.

Gerald went to the sideboard for more coffee. "There are nice obituaries about Robert in *The Times* and *Telegraph* this morning. They talk about the Victoria Cross and the Military Cross. The other papers are just treating it as a news story—digging up all the old tales about La Española and about his being in prison."

"I get angry," Jessica said. "They're not even giving Nat—I mean Lord Askew—a chance. They're already making life miserable. It will be much worse when they find out that the condesa died at Thirlbeck, and with La Española in her possession." She turned to Gerald. "Isn't there *any* way to stop it?"

Gerald shook his head. "There's no way to bottle up the news. It's part of the freedom of the press, Jessica."

She turned back to the sideboard and began slicing bread for the toaster. Then she shrugged. "Well, perhaps the publicity won't hurt in the end."

Nat said slowly, "What do you mean, Jessica?"

"Well, I suppose in the end you'll have to open the house to the public. There really isn't any other way to pay for it. People want to see places like Thirlbeck, and *they* provide the money. You could open up the valley just to this point and make the rest of it a nature sanctuary or something. There'll be some pictures left, surely, some furniture to show off." She flung a rather frightened glance at Gerald and myself. "I mean, you won't have to sell *everything*, will you? Miss Roswell would be very good at working it all out. I'm sure Mr. Stanton would help. *I'd* help all I could. I know the history of most of the family, and I'd learn the rest."

She stopped, perhaps because the silence had become too heavy. "Oh, well, it's just an idea. You'll have to do *something*." The finished slices popped from the toaster, and she put more in. "I'll go and do the eggs now."

She paused in the doorway. "We'll just all have to stick together. I've already told the children they're not to talk to the reporters, Nat—Lord Askew. They're going to the service for the earl in Kesmere. Grandfather thought it was right. But I'll stay here with Miss Roswell, and I'll go to the burial ground when you bring the body back. Nat, shall I get the Land-Rover? You could drive Miss Roswell to the burial ground in that; it's too far for her to walk." Then the door closed behind her.

After she had gone we all exchanged glances, but it was on Nat's face that a smile first appeared. "Well, there you are," he said. "Everything laid out nicely. Everything taken care of."

"And the thing is," Gerald said, "the child could be right."

"If I didn't feel so miserable—and so damn bewildered," Nat said, still smiling, "I could almost laugh. Look at them, the Tolsons. Every last one of them, I'm certain, is already planning for Thirlbeck. How we'll all hang together. There's Jessica now, fighting to redeem herself in some way. She'll give her heart and soul to this place. We've got Jessica and the Tolsons—and Thirlbeck, for the rest of our lives. Can you bear it, Jo?" He shook his head impatiently. "Of course you can. You'll bear it because I need you and because you're his daughter. My need—and your inheritance, Jo. It's a formidable combination."

He rose and went to the window, looking up the valley. "I said you'll make a rotten farmer's wife, Jo—that's the truth. But you'll be great for Thirlbeck."

Now he looked quite deliberately between Gerald and myself, perhaps even glad that there was a witness to his next words. "I'm not really asking you, Jo. I'm telling you the way things have to be. I've got to have you with me. If you decide not to stay, then that's the end of Thirlbeck. I'll sell every damn thing that's saleable, and if no one will buy the house, I'll tear it down. It's possible to give up a title, and I'll give up this one. The earldom of Askew will cease to exist. I have no heart and no guts for this job unless you are here."

I saw Gerald give a faint, almost involuntary nod. I felt incredibly weary. "Nat," I said, "you won't tear down Thirlbeck, anymore than you'll give up trying to save the golden eagles. You'll handle both in a different way from the last earl, but you'll handle them, not throw them away. Yes, I know I'll make a rotten farmer's wife. The rest—I'll do what I can."

I looked down at the bandaged hand. "You'll have to go soon and get changed. You have to be at the church and be ready to face the cameras and the questions, and keep your temper. There's an awful lot to learn. We might as well begin properly."

I STOOD at Nat Birkett's side when they brought the body of Robert Birkett, eighteenth Earl of Askew, back to Thirlbeck to be buried. Nat's sons, and the Tolson families, had brought flowers picked from the gardens of the farms and from the lanes and hedgerows. I looked at the faces of those about me, gathered here to witness the end of one era and the beginning of another.

"We brought nothing into this world, and it is certain that we can carry nothing out."

That was what it had all been about, and why it was continuing. We had, all of us standing here by his grave, been concerned with the property of a gentleman known as Robert Birkett. Vanessa had unwittingly died for it; Robert Birkett had died knowing that Vanessa had been willing to serve this legacy because she had borne a child to him; Tolson had endured years of punishing doubt and worry to hold this property intact. Up there, on the mountainside last night, another woman had died because she had sought to take away that property. Gerald and I had come to cast a coldly commercial eye over it and had stayed to become as enmeshed in its saving as any of those standing about us.

And I thought also of Jonathan Roswell, the other man who had loved Vanessa once, who had given me his name. One day he also would be buried in a private family burial ground, not among the English mists and green grass, but in the hard, baked earth of Mexico, and the sun would warm his bones, even in death.

Thinking this, on that bright, rainless morning of the English spring, I was surprised to find the wetness on my face, to see George Tolson's head bowed, as if he did not know how to handle his grief, and then to see on the face of Jessica the tears that would make her whole and human. The full realization of what I must take on with Nat, the responsibility for the lives and loyalties of all these people, came fully to me then. Perhaps I wept for myself as well as for my father, Robert Birkett.

THAT same day the priest came out from the Catholic Church in Kesmere and talked with Nat and myself. "I don't know why it should not be done," he said. "Every Christian soul deserves Christian burial—and she has waited a long time."

In what remained of that day we set the Tolson grandchildren to clearing the floor of the chapel, but we left the young birch tree that had sprung up within its walls. Mrs. Tolson provided a table that could be covered with a white cloth. Jessica brought great masses of flowers in big vases to set about on the ground. At the end of the day young Thomas, Nat's son, brought me white violets wrapped in damp paper. "They're for her," he said. "Dad says it will be very early, and I should not come. He said not to think too much about her—but I do. I'm sorry she's been up there in that place alone all these years." He went off with the calm matter-of-factness of a child, this future earl of Askew.

Nat sat with me late that night as I rested in the bed of the Spanish Woman. All of the dogs were with us, lying before the two fires; they had attached themselves to Nat in the immediate way they had attached themselves to Robert Birkett and to myself. He looked at them now. "We'll have to breed some more of them, Jo, as well as some kids for ourselves."

"Yes."

He was sitting in the chair where so often I had thought I saw the shadowy figure of the Spanish Woman. A candle burned on the mantel above him, and he had been trying, in a dazed and

341

tired fashion, to make some notes of things needing to be done. He was still not completely reconciled to the idea of opening Thirlbeck to the public.

"What can we do with it, Jo? Even if they don't find out what Tolson and your mother were doing, there's still a hell of a lot of things that will be lumped into the estate for taxes. Will we be beggars because of this?"

"The revenue people will be on to you in good time. But they won't put their hands on your shoulder tomorrow. We'll just have to talk to them about it all. But there's that million pounds sitting in a Swiss bank. That's the biggest worry. If we find it, it can be paid into Lord Askew's account. Then you inherit—and pay the tax—and the rest can be spent as it's needed. No Swiss bank is going to give out information about where it came from. I don't quite see yet how it's all to be handled. But Thirlbeck is going to be saved, Nat. If you have to grit your teeth and let the public in, then grit your teeth."

He managed a tired smile. "I've got good strong teeth."

"They'd better be. You'll grind them a lot in the next few years. We might even have to sell the El Greco to the National Gallery."

"Yes, Jo, and what else?"

"A lot of the French furniture could be sold. As beautiful as it is, it doesn't belong in this house. But we should try to keep the Dutch pictures. They're a beautiful collection. We could specialize. Oh, yes . . . and there's La Española."

"What about it? Damn, Jo, can't I just hand that over to the revenue people? Let *them* get killed trying to sell it."

I spoke softly. "It can't leave here, Nat. You know that. The first accident, the first misfortune that strikes anyone who handles it, will half kill you. You'll blame yourself. It stays here. We'll have to make a deal with the revenue people. You'll pay the tax however and whenever you can manage it. And La Española will become the jewel it was always meant to be. If legend belongs to it—if people want to think there's a curse on it—then let them come and see it. Put in the best security system and relieve Tolson finally of this hellish responsibility. Then tell the story, tell it as if the Spanish Woman were telling it. Make them weep, Nat. The little Spanish girl has been neglected too long."

He came and sat on the bed beside me. "I'll do it if you say I

342

must. What a child Robert Birkett has left behind in you! You're still as weak as a kitten, and you've already begun to fight for this place. When you first came you seemed such a quiet type. Now you suddenly seem as tough as old boots. I don't really understand *your* sort of Birkett. *He* didn't want to fight, except when they put him in a war."

"I'm also Vanessa's daughter," I said. "Stop worrying, Nat. Birketts fight when there's something to fight for."

He sighed, and slipped off his shoes, lying back on the piled-up pillows that supported me. "If only we—you and I, Jo—could have started with just my farm. Farming's all a fight, but it's things you understand—the weather, crops, sheep. And what did I get? You and Thirlbeck. . . ." His voice trailed off, and in a few minutes his deeper breathing told me he had fallen asleep. We were not like new lovers then, but people long accustomed to each other, facing our problems together.

Nat's voice came again, sleepily. He spoke with his eyes still closed. "I didn't tell you, did I? The great news. One of the eagle's eggs hatched today. And . . . and I retired the Bentley. It's not to be used again." In a very little while he was asleep again.

THE next morning we were ready very early. Tolson was waiting in the library, where the oak coffin rested—the coffin which contained all that remained of the Spanish Woman.

Nat, George Tolson, and his sons carried the coffin between them. It was so early the mist had not yet lifted from the tarn, and all we could see was the low white swirling blanket over the water, and rising from it, startling in the early sun, the peaks of Brantwick and Great Birkeld were revealed in their bald strength.

The coffin was laid on trestles in the newly tidied chapel. Mrs. Tolson's table was covered by a starched white cloth. The priest was waiting with a young boy as acolyte, both robed for the mass. I noticed that the priest's vestments were the white of joy, not the black of mourning. I had asked him to recite the mass in Latin. "She didn't understand English," I had said.

Afterwards she was buried among the Birketts, and I laid Thomas's white violets on her grave. A sense of peace, of happiness, stole across me. Now that she was at last accepted among us, accorded her due place, the Birketts themselves might know change. Perhaps her spirit would become, for all of us, the benign presence it had always seemed to me. And she was truly among us. Standing in place there above the grave, the results of Nat's labours yesterday with Ted Tolson, was the rough-hewn stone, with the uncertain hand and spelling. Juana, The Spanishe Woman.

The priest was finished; the holy water sprinkled. *"Requiescat in pace."* For Nat and myself there was an additional blessing, perhaps a special grace passed on to us by the Spanish Woman, who lay at last in a hallowed grave. "And may you live in peace."

Catherine Gaskin

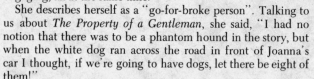

Catherine Gaskin, the best-selling author from the mountains of Wicklow, sparkles like some blue-eyed Irish sprite; and many who marvel at her seemingly magical success could mistake her for exactly that. In fact she is a very dedicated, hard-working woman who happens to be very attractive and very engaging, all at the same time.

She describes herself as a "go-for-broke person". Talking to us about *The Property of a Gentleman*, she said, "I had no notion that there was to be a phantom hound in the story, but when the white dog ran across the road in front of Joanna's car I thought, if we're going to have dogs, let there be eight of them!"

To perfect Joanna's professional background, Cathy spent long hours at Christie's, the famous London auctioneers. "I spent a week at the front counter, trying to pick up all I could. But if you don't know the plot of the book—as I didn't then— you don't know what questions to ask. So I had to go back from time to time to check."

Cathy's capacity for such dedication stems from her desire to excel. "I'm not what is called a serious novelist. I come from a race of storytellers. I *want* people to read me for sheer enjoyment. I'm not going to shoot myself because I'm not Solzhenitzyn. But I believe in giving value for money. I must feel I've done my best. I'll research even a tiny detail."

Now that all the hard work is over, what stands out in Cathy Gaskin's mind about *The Property of a Gentleman*?

"That it turned out to be a ghost story," she replied promptly. "I never expected that. In the beginning I had thought of the Spanish Woman only as decoration for the jewel. Then she began to be a real person. In the little Book of Hours, after I'd put down her name, her ghost quietly took over, and almost as if I didn't write it I put down her prayer."

Cathy Gaskin paused, and then, with the gentle lilt of her soft Irish brogue, recited Juana's plea: "'When I am dead, of your charity, offer nine masses for my soul.'"

Come to think of it, perhaps she is a blue-eyed Irish sprite after all.

Published by Secker & Warburg, London

I Can Jump Puddles

A CONDENSATION OF THE BOOK BY

Alan Marshall

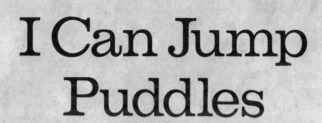

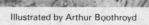

Illustrated by Arthur Boothroyd

As a boy in the Australian bush, author Alan Marshall was stricken by poliomyelitis and lost the use of his legs. And that, for most boys in the early 1900's, would have meant the beginning of a life of frustration and inactivity.

But Alan was no ordinary boy and his bushman father was no ordinary parent. "Forget your legs," said Alan's father, and Alan did. He taught himself to swim and ride and to bound along on his crutches, keeping up with his friends in all the pranks of country boys.

And when he came to write this story he looked back on his childhood with humour and without self-pity. The result is a book acknowledged as a world classic.

Preface

THIS BOOK is the story of my childhood, those influences and incidents that helped to make me what I am. In it, I wanted to do more than record my experiences of a little boy on crutches; I wanted to give a picture of a period that has passed. The influences that made the people of that period self-reliant, forthright and compassionate, have given way to influences that can develop characters just as fine; but the mould has changed and the product is different.

To give a picture of life at that time, I have gone beyond the facts to get at the truth. I have sometimes altered scenes, made composite characters, changed time sequences, added dialogues. A book of this nature demands a treatment that facts do not always supply; the truth it seeks can only be revealed with the help of imagination.

Alan Marshall

Chapter One

When my mother lay in the small front room of the weather-board house in which we lived, awaiting the arrival of the midwife to deliver me, she could see tall gums tossing in the wind, and a green hill, and cloud shadows racing across the paddocks, and she said to my father, "It will be a son; it is a man's day."

My father bent and looked through the window to where the dark green barrier of the bush stood facing the cleared paddocks. "I'll make him a bushman and a runner," he said with determination. He was a lean man with bowed legs and narrow hips, the result of years in the saddle, for he was a horsebreaker who had had to come to Victoria from Queensland because there were no schools in the outback.

Father sat in the kitchen with my sisters while I was being born. Mary and Jane wanted a brother to take to school with them, and father had promised them one called Alan.

When the midwife brought me out for them to see, I was wrapped in red flannelette. She placed me in father's arms.

"It was funny looking down on you there," he said. "*My son . . .* There was a lot of things I wanted you to be able to do. I wanted you to have good hands on a horse. Running, of course . . . They reckoned you had good limbs on you. I kept wondering if you would be like me."

I HAD NOT long started school when I contracted infantile paralysis
—poliomyelitis. The epidemic that began in Victoria in the early
1900's moved into the country districts, striking down children on
isolated farms and in bush homes. I was the only victim in Turalla,
and the people for miles around heard of my illness with a feeling
of dread, wrapped their children up more warmly and gazed at
them anxiously. They associated the word "paralysis" with idiocy,
and the query, "Have you heard if his mind is affected?" was asked
often.

The neighbours drove quickly past our house, looking with a new
interest at the old picket fence, the unbroken colts in the stockyard
and my tricycle lying on its side by the chaff house.

"It hits you like a blow from God," said Mr. Carter, the baker
and superintendent of the Bible Class. "But the back is made for
the burden," he added piously, confident the remark would please
the Almighty. He was always quick to seize any opportunity to
ingratiate himself with God.

Father snorted his contempt of such a philosophy and said, with
some savagery, "That boy's back was never made for the burden,
and, let me tell you, this won't be a burden either."

Later, standing beside my bed, he asked anxiously, "Have you
got any pains in your legs, Alan?"

"No," I told him. "They feel dead."

"Oh, hell!" he exclaimed, his face stricken.

He had a bushman's face, brown and lined, with sharp blue eyes
embedded in the wrinkles that came from the glare of saltbush
plains. A drover mate of his, who called in to see him one day,
exclaimed, as father crossed the yard to greet him. "By cripes,
Bill, you still walk like a bloody emu!"

His walk was light and mincing, and he always looked at the
ground ahead of him as he walked, a habit he attributed to the
fact that he came from "snake country".

Sometimes, when he had a few drinks in, he would ride into the
yard on some half-broken colt and go rearing and plunging amongst
the gig shafts and the remains of old wheels, scattering the squawk-
ing fowls and giving high, larrikin yells.

"Wild cattle and no brands! Let them ring! Ho, there!"

Then he would rein the horse back on its haunches and swing
his hat round in mock acknowledgment of applause, bowing

towards the kitchen door where mother generally stood with a little smile upon her face, a smile that was a mixture of amusement, love and concern.

Father was fond of horses, not because they were the means by which he earned his living, but because of some beauty he saw in them. He thought they were like human beings.

"Yes, it's a fact," he said. "I've seen them. Some horses sulk if you as much as touch 'em with a whip. So do some kids. . . . Box their ears and they won't talk to you for days."

Father was the youngest of four children and inherited the temperament of his Irish mother. He was earning his own living at twelve. His education was limited to a few months' schooling under a drunken teacher to whom each child attending the slab hut that served as a school paid half a crown a week.

After he started work he drifted round from station to station horsebreaking or droving. His youth and early manhood were spent in the saltbush plains and red sandhills of the outback areas of New South Wales and Queensland, and it was these areas that furnished the material for all his yarns. "There's something in the back country," he once told me. "You're satisfied out there. You get on a pine ridge and light a fire . . ." He stopped, looking at me in a troubled way. After a while he said, "We'll have to think up some way to stop your crutches sinking into the sand outback. Yes, we'll get you up there some day."

NOT LONG AFTER I became paralysed the muscles in my legs began to shrink, and my back, once straight and strong, curved to one side. Though my mother massaged my legs with brandy and olive oil, the sinews behind my knees tightened into cords that tugged at my legs till they gradually bent and became locked in a kneeling position. My mother kept calling on Dr. Crawford to prescribe some treatment that would enable me to move them normally again.

Dr. Crawford lived at Balunga, the township four miles from our home, and would only visit patients in outlying districts when the case was an urgent one. Polio was a disease of which he knew very little. He had called in two other doctors for consultation when I became ill, and it was one of these who announced that I had infantile paralysis.

Mother was impressed by this doctor and turned to him for

further information, but all he would say was, "If he were a son of mine I would be very, very worried."

"I'm sure you would," said my mother dryly and never had any faith in him from then on.

She believed in Dr. Crawford, who, when the other two doctors had gone, said, "Mrs. Marshall, no one can tell whether your son will live or die. I believe he will live, but it is in God's hands."

This pronouncement comforted my mother, but my father said, "Once they tell you you're in God's hands you know you're done."

The problem of my contracting legs was one that Dr. Crawford eventually had to face. Troubled and uncertain, he beat his pudgy fingers on the washstand beside my bed while Mother stood tense beside him, like a prisoner awaiting sentence.

"Well, Mrs. Marshall, about these legs . . . I'm afraid there is only one thing we can do. He's a brave boy. Those legs must be forced straight. The best way, I think, would be to lay him on the table each morning then press your weight upon his knees till the legs are flat on the table."

"Will it be very painful?" my mother asked.

"I'm afraid so." Dr. Crawford paused, then added, "You will need all your courage."

Each morning when my mother laid me on my back on the kitchen table, I looked at the picture of horses that hung above the mantelpiece. It was an engraving of a black horse and a white horse crowding together in terror while a jagged streak of lightning projected out of the dark background of storm and rain and hung poised a few feet in front of their distended nostrils.

These frightened horses were important to me. Each morning I fled with them from jagged pain. Our fears merged and became a single fear that bound us together in a common need.

My mother would place her two hands upon my raised knees, then, with her eyes tightly closed so that her tears were held back by her clenched lids, she would lean her weight upon my legs, forcing them down till they lay flat upon the table. As they straightened to her weight my toes would spread apart then curve down and round like the talons of a bird. When the sinews beneath my knees began to stretch I would scream, my eyes wide on the terrified horses above the mantelpiece. I would cry out, "Oh! horses, horses, horses . . . Oh! horses, horses . . ."

Chapter Two

The hospital was in a township over twenty miles from our home. Father drove me there with mother in the brake, the long-shafted, strongly-built gig in which he broke in horses. The warm sun and the noise of the wheels sent me to sleep, and I lay with my head against mother's arm till she woke me three hours later.

When the gig wheels were crunching the gravel in the hospital yard I sat up, looking at the hushed white building with its narrow windows. The quietness frightened me, as my father carried me in. A nurse at a desk asked father a lot of questions and wrote his answers in a book while he watched her as he would have watched an untrustworthy horse that had its ears back.

She left, taking the book with her, and father said to mother, "I never come into one of these places without feeling like telling them all to go to hell. They strip the feelings from a man like you skin a cow; ask questions as if a bloke was trying to put something over them."

The nurse returned with a wardsman who carried me to a cool, clean bed. There I pleaded with mother not to go. My mattress was hard and unyielding and I could not gather the blankets into folds about me. There would be no warm caves beneath these blankets nor pathways for marbles, winding about on the quilt. There were no protecting walls close to me and I could not hear the barking of a dog nor the noise of a horse munching chaff. These belonged to my home and I wanted them desperately.

Father bade me goodbye but mother lingered. Then she suddenly kissed me quickly and walked away, and that she could do this was to me incredible.

The man in the next bed asked, "Why are you crying?"

"I want to go home."

"We all want that," he said, then sighed.

The ward in which we lay had white iron bedsteads facing each other in two rows along the walls. There were fourteen in the ward, and I was the only child. Some of the men called out to me and told me not to worry.

"You'll be all right," a man said, "we'll look after you."

They asked me what was wrong with me and when I told them

infantile paralysis, one man said it was murder, that's what it was. This remark made me feel important and I liked the man who said it. I regarded my illness as a temporary inconvenience. In the days that followed I met the painful periods with resentment and anger that quickly turned to despair when the pain was prolonged; once the pain stopped it was quickly forgotten. I was pleasantly surprised to see the effect my illness had on people who stood beside my bed looking at me with sad faces. It established me as a person of importance and kept me contented.

"You're a brave boy," they said mournfully.

I used to puzzle over this bravery which was attributed to me. It began to embarrass me to accept tributes to my courage, tributes which I knew I had not earned, for the sound of a mouse gnawing behind the skirting boards of my room always frightened me and I was frightened to go out to the tank to get a drink at nights because of the dark.

The patients used me as a butt for their jokes, patronizing me, as adults do children. I believed everything they told me and this amused them. They spoke as if I were deaf and could not hear their words.

"He believes everything you tell him," a youth explained to a newcomer. "You listen. Hey, Smiler," he called to me, "there's a witch down the well near your place, isn't there?"

"Yes," I said.

"There you are," said the youth. "He's a funny little beggar. He'll never walk, they tell me."

I thought the youth was a fool, to imagine I would never walk again. I knew what I was going to do. I was going to break in wild horses and yell "Ho! Ho!" and wave my hat in the air.

I liked the man in the next bed. "We'll be mates," he said to me not long after I arrived. He was Angus McDonald, the tallest and biggest man of the fourteen patients in the ward. He had a flexible, sensitive mouth that easily broke into a smile, but he was suffering from some painful complaint and sometimes he would sigh or swear or give a deep groan that frightened me.

"Why do you take so long to say your prayers?" he asked me once. "I've watched your lips moving."

"I have to ask a lot of things," I explained to him.

"What things? Tell me. We're mates."

355

I repeated my prayers to him while he listened, gazing at the ceiling, his hands clasped on his chest. When I had finished he turned his head and looked at me. "You haven't left anything out. You've given Him the lot. God'll think a hell of a lot of you by the time He's listened to all that."

His comment made me feel happy and I decided I would ask God to make him better too.

The long prayer I repeated each night was the result of an increasing number of requests I was making to God. My needs grew greater each day and as I only dropped requests when they were answered the new pleas were far in excess of those that were answered. Mother had never allowed me to miss Sunday School and from her I had learnt my first prayer which was a little composition beginning with "Gentle Jesus, meek and mild," and ending with the request to bless various people, dad included, though in my heart I always felt he didn't need blessing.

Later, when looking at a perfectly good cat that someone had thrown away, I became frightened at its rigid stillness and was told that it was dead. In bed at nights I thought of mother and father lying still with lifted lip like the cat, and I prayed with anguish that they mightn't die before me. After further consideration I decided to include Meg, my dog, requesting God to preserve her till I was a man and old enough to stand her death. Feeling troubled that I might be demanding too much, I added that I would be satisfied if Meg and my parents lived till I was a man of thirty. At that great age I would be past tears. Men never cry. Then I prayed to be made better, always adding that, if He didn't mind, I would like to be cured before Christmas, two months away.

The pets I kept in enclosures in our backyard also had to be prayed for, since, now that I couldn't feed them or change their water, I prayed that they might never be forgotten. My irascible old cockatoo, Pat, had to be let out of his cage each night for a fly round the trees. On washing days he would land on neighbours' clotheslines and pull out the pegs. Angry women threw sticks and stones at Pat, and I had to pray that they would never hit him.

I also had to pray to be made a good boy. . . .

"What do you think God looks like?" Angus asked.

I always pictured God as a mighty man dressed in a white sheet like an Arab. He sat on a chair with His elbows on His knees looking down at the world, His eyes darting rapidly from person to person. I never associated Him with kindliness, while Jesus, I thought, would be kind like dad. The fact that Jesus only rode donkeys and never horses was disappointing to me.

Angus commented that maybe my picture was closer to it than his was. "My mother always spoke in Gaelic," he said. "I always saw God as a stooped old man with a white beard, surrounded by a lot of old women talking in Gaelic. I couldn't imagine God doing anything without first consulting mother."

Men like father, I thought, were stronger than any God, but men in hospitals were different. Pain robbed them of something I could not define. Some called out to God in the night and I did not like to admit to myself that men could experience fear.

The nurses with their white, starched aprons, pink frocks and flat shoes, smiled at me as they passed, smelling of antiseptics, or stopped to tuck in my blankets, mothering me. Father liked women. He commented to mother that there were some good shafters among the nurses but they were all shod wrong.

Father wrote me saying, "It's keeping dry up here and I've had to start feeding Kate. I want to keep her in good nick for you when you come back."

I told Angus, "I've got a pony called Kate. She's a bit ewe-necked but she's honest."

"Your old man breaks in horses, doesn't he?" he asked me.

"Yes," I said. "He's easy the best rider in Turalla."

"He dresses flash enough," muttered McDonald. "I thought he was out of a buckjump show when I saw him."

I wondered whether this was against father or for him. Father took a pride in his clothes. He liked his moleskin trousers to be white and unmarked and his boots were always shining.

He often talked about a Professor Fenton who ran a buckjump show in Queensland. He wore a white silk shirt and a red sash and could do a double "Sydney Flash" with a stockwhip. Father could crack a whip but not like Professor Fenton.

While I was thinking about these things he came walking down the ward to see me, one arm across his chest where, beneath his white shirt, something bulky was concealed. Standing beside my bed he looked down at me. "How are you, son?"

He brought with him the atmosphere of home and I suddenly

felt like crying. Father tightened his lips. He thrust his hand within his open shirt and suddenly pulled out a struggling thing of soft brown.

"Here, clutch that to you," he said fiercely. "It's one of Meg's pups. We're calling it Alan."

I wrapped my arms around his warm, snuggling softness and held him to me with a surge of pure happiness; and, looking into my father's eyes, I passed it on to him, for he smiled at me. Then I looked down beneath the arch of blankets I had formed with a lifted arm. There it lay with its bright eyes watching me, and, seeing me, it wriggled with a quick friendliness. The eager life of it moved into me, and it smelt of home. I wanted to hold it forever.

McDonald, who had been watching us, called to a patient walking down the ward with a towel across his arm, "Keep the nurses talking out there!" To father, he said, "You know what they are— dogs in here. . . . No understanding. . . ."

"That's so," said father. "Well, five minutes'll do him. It's like a pot to a thirsty man."

EVERY MORNING after breakfast, the nurses hurried from bed to bed replacing the quilts they had removed the previous evening, and patting smooth bedclothes into creaseless bindings in preparation for the matron's tour of inspection.

The matron was a stout woman with three black hairs sprouting from a mole on her chin. Her uniform was always stiffly starched and dictated her way of moving so that sometimes she gave the impression of being animated by strings pulled by the nurse following behind her.

When she reached my bed one morning she assumed the attitude of one about to say amusing and comforting things to a child for the purpose of impressing the adults listening. It made me uncomfortable, as if I were being pushed onto a stage and told to perform.

"Well, how is the brave little man today? Nurse tells me you often sing in the morning. Will you sing for me one day?" I was too confused to answer. "I think you will be a singer one day," matron went on. "Would you like to be a singer?" She did not wait for me to answer. "Now, Alan, tomorrow you'll go to sleep and when you wake up your leg will be in a white cocoon. Won't that be nice?" Then to the nurse, "His operation is at ten thirty."

"What's an operation?" I asked Angus when they had gone.

"Oh, they mess around with your leg . . . fix it up . . . Nothing much . . . They do it while you're asleep."

I could see he did not want to explain it to me and a feeling of fear touched me for a moment.

Once when father had left a young horse standing in the brake, the reins tied to the rim of the strapped wheel while he went in to get a cup of tea, it had plunged, snapped the tightened reins and bolted, leaving the smashed brake piled against a post as it galloped away free. Father, who had dashed out with me at the sound, surveyed the wreckage for a moment, then turned to me and said, "Well, blast it, anyway! Let's go finish our tea."

I thought of this now. "Well, blast it, anyway!" I said.

"That's the spirit," said Angus.

Chapter Three

Dr. Robertson, who attended me, was a tall man who always wore his Sunday suit. I divided clothes into Sunday clothes and those you wore the rest of the week. You could wear your Sunday suit during the week but only on special occasions. My Sunday suit was a coarse, blue serge that came, wrapped in tissue paper, in a brown box. It had a wonderful new smell, but I didn't like wearing it because I had to keep it clean.

I was amazed that Dr. Robertson wore his Sunday suit every day. Not only that, I found he had four Sunday suits, so I concluded he must be very rich and live in a house with a lawn. After that I found it difficult to talk to him. All the people I knew were poor. I knew the names of rich people and saw them drive past our place, but they never looked at poor people or spoke to them.

"Here comes Mrs. Carruthers," my sister would yell, and we would rush to the gate to see her go past, a groom driving her pair of grey horses. It was like seeing the Queen go by. I could understand Dr. Robertson but I could never get used to his speaking to me.

He had pale, sunless skin, and I liked his eyes which were light blue with wrinkles around them that folded when he laughed. His hands smelt of soap and were cool when he touched you.

360

He pressed my back and legs and asked me if it hurt. Then he stood erect and said to the sister, "Severe curvature there already. The muscles on one side of his back are badly affected." He examined my leg, then patted my head and said, "We'll soon straighten that." And to the sister, "A re-alignment of his thigh bone is necessary." His hand moved to my ankle. "The sinews here will have to be shortened and the foot lifted. We'll cut them in front of the ankle." He moved his finger in a slow stroke just above my knee. "We'll do the alignment here."

I always remember the movement of his finger since it marked the line of the scar I was to bear.

After Dr. Robinson had left the ward, mother, who had been waiting, was allowed to come in and see me. I felt shy and embarrassed as she walked towards me. I knew she would kiss me and I regarded displays of affection as sissy. Yet I would have been disappointed if she had not kissed me.

I had not seen her for a few weeks and she looked a new mother to me. Her smile, her comfortable figure, the fair hair that was coiled into a bun at her neck—all these were so familiar to me that I had never noticed them before; now I noted these things with pleasure.

Her mother had been an Irishwoman from Tipperary and her gentle and kindly father a German musician. She must have resembled her father. She had a pleasant expression and wore her character upon her face for all to see. The wind and rain of many a winter's drive in the open brake had left fine lines upon it. Cosmetics had never touched her weathered face, not because she did not believe in them but because she never had the money to buy them.

When she reached my bed she must have noticed my embarrassment because she whispered, "I'd like to kiss you but there are too many looking. So we'll pretend I have." Then she felt in her bag and brought out a parcel tied with string. "Mrs. Carruthers sent it to you," she said. "We're all waiting to see what is in it. She drove up to the front gate and handed it to Mary and told Mary it was for her little sick brother."

I slipped off the wrapping impressively addressed to "Master Alan Marshall" and looked excitedly at the lid of a flat box featuring pictures of windmills and waggons made from perforated strips of metal. I lifted the lid and there lay the strips and, beside them, screws, screwdrivers, spanners and wheels. I could hardly believe it was mine.

The toy was impressive but the fact that it came from Mrs. Carruthers was unbelievable. It could almost be said that Mrs. Carruthers *was* Turalla. She had built the Presbyterian church there, the Sunday School, the new wing of the manse. The annual school prizes were donated by her. All the farmers were deeply in debt to her. She owned Mount Turalla, Lake Turalla, and all the best land along Turalla Creek. She had a specially padded pew in the church with a special hymnbook bound in leather.

Mr. Carruthers was dead but, according to father, when he was alive he was always protesting against something. When he protested he raised a pudgy hand and cleared his throat. He protested against cows on the road and the decline in manners. He also protested against father.

Mr. Carruthers's father, representing an English company, had landed in Melbourne in 1837 and made west from that town in bullock drays laden with stores. He eventually took up hundreds of square miles of rich land that, now divided into scores of farms mortgaged to the estate, brought in a large income in interest alone. The enormous bluestone mansion he built on a picked site eventually became the property of Mrs. Carruthers.

The house stood in the centre of thirty acres of parkland, a large area of which was laid out in gardens designed in English style with formal flowerbeds blooming under strict direction. In the shade of elms and oaks, and sheltered by shrubs brought out from England, pheasants, peacocks, and strange-coloured ducks from China pecked and scratched in the leaf mould. In the spring, snowdrops and daffodils flowered amidst the dark green of Australian bracken and later gardeners wheeled laden barrows between the hollyhocks and phlox.

From the gateway to the homestead a gravelled drive wound between rows of elm trees. Halfway up the drive was a small fenced enclosure. Once tall bluegums had lifted their naked limbs high above the kangaroo grass and emu bush that grew there but now dark pines shaded it. A red deer walked ceaselessly around the enclosure, following a worn track that skirted the fence. Sometimes it raised its head and bellowed hoarsely.

Across from the enclosure were the stables, large, two-storey, bluestone buildings with lofts and stalls and feed bins hollowed from the trunks of trees.

Sometimes a visiting governor or an English gentleman and his lady came up from Melbourne to experience station life and see the "real Australia". On these nights the Carrutherses would hold a ball in the big house and, from a bracken-covered hill behind the mansion where a clump of wattles had escaped destruction, the more daring or wistful of Turalla's residents would stand looking down at the vast, lighted windows behind which women in low-cut gowns and carrying fans bowed to their partners in the opening of the waltz quadrilles. The music would come up to this little group of people and they would not feel the cold. They were listening to a fairy story.

Once when father stood with them holding a half-empty bottle, he began to give a happy whoop at the end of every swing in the set they were dancing behind the lighted windows and he wheeled round the wattles with the bottle as a partner.

After a while a stout man wearing a gold watch chain from which hung a gold-mounted lion's claw, a mounted miniature of the man's mother and several medals, came out to investigate. He ordered father away and when father continued whooping he swung a punch at father. Later, father would say, "I side-stepped him then came in quick and played up and down his ribs with the good old one-two-three like a xylophone. The wind that came out of his mouth nearly blew my hat off."

When father was helping the man to his feet and brushing his clothes, he said to him, "I thought you had too many gee-gaws about you to be any good."

"Yes," said the man vaguely. "Too many. I feel slightly dazed."

"Have a drink," said father handing him the bottle. After the man drank he and father shook hands.

"He was all right," explained father afterwards. "He'd just got in with the wrong mob."

Father broke in most of Carruthers's horses and was friends with Peter Finlay, the head groom. Peter was a remittance man and could talk on anything, but all the Carrutherses were poor talkers. Their reputation for brains was based on their ability to say, "Hm, yes," or "Hm, no," at the right times. When the important people visited the Carrutherses' home, the evenings were full of long, uncomfortable silences, so Mr. Carruthers always sent down to the stables for Peter. When Peter received the message he entered the big house by a back door. In a small room reserved for the purpose was a bed with a damask quilt and upon the bed, neatly folded, was one of Mr. Carruthers's best suits. Peter would put the suit on, then present himself at the drawing room where he would be introduced as a visiting Englishman.

At the dinner table his conversation delighted the guests and gave openings for Mr. Carruthers to say "Hm, yes," or "Hm, no," in an intelligent manner. After the guests had retired Peter would take off the suit and go back to his room behind the stables.

Once he came to father and told him that Mr. Carruthers would like father to put on an exhibition of riding for the benefit of some important visitors. At first father said, "To hell with them," but after a while he reckoned he'd do it for ten bob. "You can't just turn your back on ten bob," he said.

On the day he was to present himself at Carruthers's he tied a red handkerchief around his neck and put a cabbage-tree hat on his head and rode a bay mare called Gay Girl. She was sixteen hands and could jump like a kangaroo, so when the visitors were all nicely seated on the wide veranda, sipping drinks, father galloped through the trees like a bushranger, whooping wildly. "I come round the bend to the five-bar gate flat out," he said, when telling the story. "I steady her till her stride is balanced then put her at it. I always say a grass-fed horse'll give you all you want in a burst. I'd only just brought Gay Girl in and she is fresh as paint. Well, she takes off too soon, being fresh. She's going to clout, I can see that; the gate's swung high.

"When I feel her lift I go up with her to save her as much weight as I can—you could've shoved your head between me and the saddle as she rises. Hell, that horse could jump! S'elp me Bob! she gives a twist and gets another two inches from the air. It don't stop her clouting with her back legs but she's in her stride two bounds from where she lands, and I'm sitting on her as snug as a brand.

"I reef her back on her haunches beside the veranda just in front of the Carruthers mob and they're on their feet shoving back chairs before they've swallowed their last mouthful of grog. Well, I jam my heels into Gay Girl's flanks then, and she tries to brush me off against a tree—she's like that, a dirty bucker. I drag her round, flapping me hat against her ribs and she bounds sideways onto the veranda. She's a twisting bucker and every time she spins she knocks over a chair or a table. There's glasses of grog flying everywhere and women screaming, and some of the blokes jump between me and the women with faces on them like they was heroes, and women hang on to 'em, and the boat's going down, and throw out the lifebelts and God Save the King, and all that sort of thing. Hell! you never saw the like."

When father reached this stage of the story he began laughing and didn't stop till he had wiped his eyes with his handkerchief. "Well, before I quieten her, I knock Sir Frederick Salisbury, or whatever his name is, head over turkey into a clump of peacocks."

"Did all this happen, dad?" I asked him once. "Is it true?"

He screwed up his face and rubbed his chin with his hand. "Well, no son, I suppose it isn't," he decided. "Something like that happened, but after you tell it a few times you keep on making it funnier, see? It's good to make people laugh. There's a hell of a lot of other things making them sad."

"Is it like that about the deer?" I asked him.

"Yes," he said. "It is, a bit. I rode him but that's all."

Why Mr. Carruthers protested against father was because father rode his deer.

"There he was going round and round," father told me. "Poor beggar . . . I was up there with some of the boys and I stood on the fence and as he passed beneath me I jumped onto his back." He paused, a faint smile on his face, then added, "Hell!" in a tone that suggested a terrific reaction from the deer.

He would never tell me more about this escapade, which he seemed to regard as childish, but I asked the Carrutherses' groom, Peter Finlay, about it.

"Did the deer toss father?" I asked him.

"No," he said, "your father tossed the deer."

Apparently, the deer broke a horn on father and this was what annoyed Mr. Carruthers.

After Mr. Carruthers died, Mrs. Carruthers sent the deer away, but you could still see the deep track it had made walking around and around.

Because of the awe in which everyone in Turalla, except father, held Mrs. Carruthers, I looked at this box on the bed before me almost reverently, valuing it more than any other gift I had received. "Mum," I said, my hands still clasped around the box, "when Mrs. Carruthers handed Mary the present, did Mary touch her?"

NEXT MORNING, I was restless and excited and had moments of fear during which I wanted mother. I was wheeled on a trolley into the operating theatre and lifted onto a high table.

Dr. Robertson entered briskly and stood smiling down at me as he massaged his fingers. Then Dr. Clarke, a grey-haired man with a tight-lipped mouth, walked in.

"The Council hasn't filled in that hole near the gate yet," he said, turning to face a sister holding his white gown up. "Can you rely on any man's word these days? This gown seems too big . . . No, it's mine all right."

I looked at the white ceiling and thought of the hole near our gate, with the puddle that always came after rain; I could jump it easily but Mary couldn't. I could jump any puddle.

Dr. Clarke moved around to my head where he stood holding a hollowed, white pad like a shell above my nose. At a sign from Dr. Robertson he saturated the pad with liquid from a little blue bottle and I gasped as I drew a laden breath. I jerked my head from side to side but he followed my nose with the pad and I saw coloured lights, then clouds came and I floated away upon them.

When I woke I fought through haze without comprehending where I was until suddenly, I saw the ceiling of the theatre again and the sister's face. "You mustn't move even the tiniest bit," she said. "The plaster on your leg is still wet."

I became conscious of my heavy leg and the stone-like clasp of the plaster encircling my hips and waist.

"Lie still now," she said. "I'm going out for a minute. Watch him, nurse," she said to a young nurse named Conrad.

"How's my boy?" Nurse Conrad asked.

I had always loved her plump cheeks, flushed like apples, and her twinkling eyes tucked away beneath thick, dark brows. I wanted her to stop with me and not to go away, but I felt sick and I was shy and couldn't tell her these things.

"Don't move, will you?" she cautioned me.

"I think I might have moved my toes a bit," I said.

The repeated warnings not to move made me want to move just to see what would happen. I felt that once I knew I could move I would be satisfied and stop.

I was kept on the operating table until lunch time, then wheeled carefully to my bed where a steel framework held the blankets high above my legs.

"How're you feeling now, Alan?" asked Angus.

My leg was aching and I was lonely. I began to cry. "My leg is aching," I told him.

"It will soon stop," he said to comfort me.

But it didn't stop. When the plaster was still moist and soft, I must have lifted my big toe in some brief spasm but lacked the strength in my paralysed muscles to force it down again to its natural position. Some movement of my hip, too, had lifted the inside plaster bandage, setting it in a ridge that pressed like a blunt knife against my hip bone. Gradually over the next two weeks this ridge ground its way into my flesh till it touched the bone itself. The pain from my lifted toe was unceasing but I got some relief from my torn hip when I lay still with my body twisted a little. Even in the short intervals of sleep that came to me between the waiting period of pain, I had dreams in which I moved through other worlds of suffering.

Dr. Robertson looked frowningly down at me as he pondered on my descriptions of my pains.

"Are you sure it is your toe that is paining you?"

"Yes. All the while," I told him. "It never stops."

"It must be his knee," he said to the matron. "He probably imagines it is his toe." He turned to me, "Does your hip ache all the time too?"

"It hurts when I move."

He pushed at the plaster above my hip. "Does that hurt?"

"Oo!" I exclaimed, trying to move away from him. "Oo, yes!"

"Hm!" he muttered.

A week after the operation, the angry defiance that had enabled me to bear the pain gave way to despair, and the fear I had of being thought a baby did not help me any more. I began to cry more often, silently, gazing open-eyed through my tears at the high, white ceiling above me. I wished I was dead, seeing in death not a frightening absence of life, but a sleeping without pain. I

367

began repeating over and over again in my mind in a jerky rhythm, "I wish I were dead, I wish I were dead, I wish I were dead."

I found that by jerking my head from side to side to the rhythm of the words, I achieved a mental distraction that brought relief from the pain. By keeping my eyes open as I flung my head from side to side the white ceiling became blurred and the bed rose on wings from the floor. I usually sought this relief at night but sometimes, if the pain was bad, I did it in the daytime when the nurses were out of the ward. Angus noticed this. One day he asked, as I began moving my head, "What d'you do that for, Alan?"

"It stops the pain. I get giddy," I explained.

Later I heard him telling Nurse Conrad that something had better be done about me. "He's game," he said. "He wouldn't do that unless he was crook."

That night the sister gave me a needle and I slept without waking, but next day the pain continued and I was given doses of A.P.C. and told to lie quietly and go to sleep.

A local infection now began to develop in my hip where the plaster had cut into the flesh, and in the next few days it reached the stage where I suddenly felt a boil had broken high up somewhere on my leg. The dull ache of my toe had been hard to stand that day and now this burning sensation in my hip . . . As I began sobbing in a hopeless, tired manner, I noticed Angus watching me with a troubled expression. "Mr. McDonald," I said, my voice trembling. "I'm sick of pain. I want it stopped. I think I'm busted."

He sat up, looking towards the ward door. "Where's the bloody nurses?" he called out in a savage voice. "Someone go get them. This kid's had enough."

Soon a nurse came in. She raised my bedclothes, lowered them again without speaking and hurried away.

I remembered being surrounded by the doctor, the matron, and the nurses, and I remember the doctor sawing and hacking the plaster from my leg, but I was burning hot and giddy and I didn't remember father or mother coming that week.

When I again became conscious of the ward, there was a stranger in Angus's bed. Angus had left me three eggs and a half jar of pickles. I missed him.

My leg from the knee to the ankle was now in a splint instead of plaster, and the pain had gone.

"The bone is slow in knitting," I heard Dr. Robertson tell the matron. "The circulation is poor in that leg. He's pale, too. Put him in a wheelchair each day and let him sit in the sun." That afternoon a sister pushed a wheelchair beside my bed. She lifted me gently into it. My feet could not reach the wooden foot support, so my legs dangled uselessly, the feet pointing downward. But my arms were strong, and as we passed through the door into the garden, the fresh open air and the sunshine poured itself over me in one immense torrent and I rose to meet it, sitting upright in my chair, facing the blue and the sparkle and the gentle push of the air against my face, like a diver rising from the sea.

For three months I had not seen a cloud or felt the sun upon me. Now they were returned to me, newly created, perfected, radiant with qualities they never possessed before. The sister left me near some she-oak trees and though there was no wind I could hear them whispering together as father said they always do.

I wondered what had happened to things while I had been away, what had changed them so. I watched a dog trotting along the street on the other side of the high picket fence. I had never seen such a wonderful dog, so pattable, so full of possibilities. A grey thrush called and its note was a gift to me. I looked down at the gravel upon which my chair rested. Each grain had colour and they lay there in their millions, tossed into strange little hills and hollows. Some had escaped into the grass which skirted the pathway and the grass stems leant over them in lovely curves of tenderness. The leaves of the gum trees glittered, throwing off diamonds of sunshine that hurt my eyes, unprepared for such brightness. The sun wrapped itself around me like arms.

After a while I began to experiment with the chair, trying to turn the wheels, but the gravel was too deep and the pathway was flanked with stones.

A boy came walking up the street. He clattered a stick along the pickets as he walked and he was followed by a brown dog. I knew and liked the boy. His name was George and his mother brought him each visiting day to the hospital. He often gave me things— comics, cigarette cards.

The sight of him filled me with joy. "How's it goin', George?" I yelled.

"Not bad. But mum said I gotta come straight home!"

"Aw!" I exclaimed, disappointed.

"I gotta bag of lollies here," he informed me. "Come over to the fence and I'll give you what's left."

After an automatic but futile struggle with the chair, I told him, "I can't walk yet. They're still curing me."

"Well, I'll pitch 'em over," announced George. He stepped back onto the roadway to take a run at it. I watched him approvingly. If ever there was a boy who demonstrated by text-book preliminaries that he was a perfect thrower, that boy was George. "Here she comes!" he cried. He began his run with a graceful skip—the touch of a perfectionist—took three long strides and threw.

Any girl could have thrown better.

"I slipped," George explained in a tone of exasperation.

I looked at the bag of lollies lying some eight yards away and said "How about coming in and getting them for me?"

"I can't," explained George. "Mum's waiting. Leave them there and I'll get them for you tomorrow. See you then. Hurroo."

"Hurroo, George," I called abstractedly. I was looking at the lollies and trying to work out some way of getting them, for eating a lolly was to me a delightful experience. Whenever a man gave me a penny for holding his horse I would run to the shop where lollies were sold, and stand gazing at the display of Rum-rum-go-goes, Milk Poles, Silver Sticks, Cough Sticks, Sherbet Suckers, Liquorice Straps, Aniseed Balls and Snowballs, and stand there a long time quite unable to make up my mind what to buy.

Now I looked at the bag of lollies on the grass. Blow my legs! I would get them. I seized the arm-rests of my chair and began to rock it from side to side till it hung poised on a slanting wheel at the end of each sway; then I gave an extra lift and it crashed to its side, flinging me face downwards on the grass. My splinted leg struck the stone border of the pathway and the sudden pain made me mutter angrily. But I began to drag myself towards the lollies, leaving behind me as I progressed, some pillows, a rug, a comic. . . . I reached the paper bag, grasped it in my hand and smiled.

I opened the bag, and after a moment's pleased inspection, extracted a conversation lolly upon which I read the words, "I love you." I lay on my back looking up at a she-oak and crushed the lolly between my teeth.

I felt very happy, and the consternation of the nurses who found me lying on the grass surprised me. I could not understand the summoning of the matron, the gathering round my bed and the mixture of concern and anger that marked their interrogation. I kept repeating, "I tipped myself over to get the lollies," and the matron answered, "But why didn't you call a nurse?" I answered, "I wanted to get them by myself."

"I can't understand you," she complained.

But father understood. When I told him, he said, "I wouldn't have called a nurse either. She would have got them all right but then it would have been different."

"It would have been different," I said, liking him more than ever.

"But don't tip yourself out for lollies again," he warned me. "Tip yourself out for big things, like a fire."

For the next few weeks I was watched carefully when I sat in the wheelchair. Then one day the doctor brought a pair of crutches.

"Here are your front legs," he told me.

The matron and some of the nurses came to see me attempt my first walk on crutches in the garden. The doctor lifted me from the chair while the matron placed the crutches beneath my armpits.

My right leg, the one I called my "bad" leg, was completely paralysed and swung uselessly from the hip, scarred and deformed. I called my left leg my "good" leg. It was only partially paralysed and could bear my weight. For weeks I had been testing it while sitting on the edge of my bed. The curvature of my spine gave me a decided lean to the left, but resting on the crutches pulled it temporarily straight.

My stomach muscles were partially paralysed, but my chest and arms were unaffected. In the years that were to follow I came to regard my legs as not worth much consideration. They seemed to live a sad life of their own apart from me and I felt sorry for them. My arms and chest were my pride and they were to develop out of all proportion to the rest of my body.

I stood there uncertainly for a moment looking ahead towards where, a few yards away, a bare patch of ground was worn in the grass. I will get there, I thought.

The doctor took his hands away, but held them on each side of me, ready to grab me should I fall. I lifted the crutches and swung them heavily forward, my shoulders jerking upward to the sudden jar as my weight came down on the armpit rests once more. I swung my legs forward, my right leg dragging in the dirt like a broken wing. I paused, breathing deeply.

"Good!" exclaimed the doctor. "Now again."

I went through the same movements three times till at last I stood achingly upon the patch of earth. I had walked.

"That will do for today," said the doctor. "Back into your chair. You can have another try tomorrow."

In a few weeks I could walk around the garden and though I fell a few times I had acquired confidence. When I was told I was going home, I was not as excited as I had thought I would be. The hospital had become a permanent background to my thoughts and activities, and I felt that in leaving it I would lose the security I had acquired there.

When mother arrived for me I was dressed and sitting on the edge of my bed looking at the empty wheelchair I would not be able to ride in again. Father didn't have enough money to buy a wheelchair, but he had made a three-wheeled vehicle out of an old perambulator and mother was wheeling this.

When Nurse Conrad kissed me goodbye, I wanted to cry but I didn't and I gave her some parrot feathers father had once brought me. I had nothing else to give her but she said that was enough. Mother had wrapped me in a rug and I lay in the pram clutching a little lion made of clay that Nurse Conrad had given me.

Mother wheeled me onto the street and pushed me over a kerb. Somehow the pram tipped over into the gutter. Mother's efforts to raise the pram from where it lay half on top of me, and her anxious demands to know whether I was hurt were lost to me. I was too busy searching for my clay lion and there he was, sure enough, underneath the rug with his head broken off as I had expected.

A man dashed forward in answer to mother's call.

"Could you help me lift my little boy back?" she asked him.

"What's wrong with the kid?" exclaimed the man seizing the pram and lifting it with a quick heave.

"I tipped him over. Be careful! Don't hurt him; he's lame!"

This exclamation of mother's shocked me. The word "lame" was associated in my mind with limping horses and suggested complete uselessness. I looked at mother with an expression of astonishment.

"Lame, mum?" I exclaimed with some force. "What did you say I was lame for?"

Chapter Four

The word "crippled" suggested to me a condition that could be applied to some people, but not to myself. But since I now began to hear people refer to me as crippled, I was forced to concede that I must fit this description. Yet I retained a conviction that though being crippled was obviously a distressing state for some people, with me it didn't matter. The crippled child considers his useless legs inconvenient or annoying, but he is confident that they will never prevent him doing what he wants to do. If he considers them a handicap it is because he has been told they are.

Other children make no distinction between one who is lame and one who has full use of his limbs. They will ask a boy on crutches to run here and there for them and complain when he is slow. Moreover, children's sense of humour is not restricted by adult ideas of good taste and tact. They often laughed at the spectacle of me on crutches and shouted with merriment when I fell over. I joined in their laughter, gripped by some sense of absurdity that made a stumble on crutches an hilarious thing.

"Come an' see Alan's funny leg! He can put it over his head!"

The pained mother, hearing her son announce bluntly, "Here's Alan, mum. His leg is all crooked," hastens to stop him saying more, forgetting she is facing two happy little boys, her son proud of his exhibit, Alan happy to be able to provide it.

I had no pain now, and could walk on crutches. But grown-ups who visited our home called my happiness "courage". Most grown-up people talk frankly about children in front of them, as if children were incapable of understanding. "He's a happy kid despite his affliction," they would say as if surprised that this were so.

Why shouldn't I be happy? I thought. Having a normal mind my attitude to life was that of a normal child and my crippled limbs could not alter this attitude. Suffering because of being crippled is not for you in your childhood; it is reserved for those men and women who look at you.

AFTER THE spaciousness of the ward I had to adjust myself to life in a house that suddenly seemed as tiny as a box. When father wheeled me into the kitchen I was astonished how it had shrunk.

The table with its rose-patterned cover seemed to fill the room so completely that there was hardly space for my pram. A strange cat sat licking itself on the hearth.

"Whose cat?" I asked, surprised that this familiar room should contain a cat I had not sponsored.

"It's Blackie's kitten," explained my sister, Mary. "You know— she had them before you went to the hospital."

Mary was excited at my return. She was older than me, a devoted, thoughtful person with dark hair and brown eyes. She sat hunched over a book when she wasn't helping mother but became full of indignant energy when called upon to defend some ill-treated animal, a crusade that took up a lot of her time. Once when a horse-man, leaning from his saddle, flogged a lagging, exhausted calf that was unable to keep up with its mother, Mary stood on the top rail of our gate and screamed at him with tears in her voice. He did not hit it again.

Jane was the eldest in our family and she fed the fowls and kept three lambs a drover had given her when they were too tired to travel. She was tall and walked with her head up. She helped Mrs. Mulvaney, the baker's wife, to look after her babies and she was paid five shillings a week and could buy anything she wanted after she gave mum some.

Mary was anxious to tell me everything of importance that had happened since I left—all about the canaries and Pat, the corella, and my pet possum and the king parrot that hadn't a tail. She had fed them every day and she had put in two new salmon tins for the canaries' water. The bottom of Pat's cage needed scraping but that was all. The possum still scratched you when you held it but not so much.

I sat there in my pram—mother had hidden my crutches as I was only allowed to use them for an hour each day—and watched mother spread the cloth and set the table for dinner. The little things that were now happening around me were re-entering my life with a new vividness, a new magic.

A lamp with a fluted column and a pink Edwardian globe stood on the meatsafe beside me. At night it would be lit and placed in the centre of the table and there would be a circle of bright light beneath it on the cloth.

A big black kettle with a spout like a striking snake steamed on

374

the stove and above the stove the mantelpiece was girded with a drape of brown baize, dulled by smoke. A tea caddy and a coffee tin with a picture of a bearded Turk stood upon it and above was the picture of the frightened horses. It was good to see this picture again.

A door led into my bedroom, a small box-like room with newspaper-covered hessian walls that swelled and subsided when wind buffeted the house, as if the room were breathing.

AFTER LUNCH father wheeled me to the stable where I could hear horses snorting chaff from their nostrils and the sharp sound of their iron shoes striking the rough stone floor as they moved. The stable was sixty years old and seemed as if it would collapse with the weight of its straw thatch. It was walled with upright slabs split from the trunks of trees felled beside it. Ropes tied to iron rings in the wall held the horses as they fed from feed troughs made from heavy logs hollowed with an adze and squared with a broad axe. Under the same thatched roof, now noisy with nesting sparrows, was the chaff house, its rough board floor inches deep with spilt chaff. Next to it was the harness room, which held tins of neatsfoot oil, harness black, bottles of turpentine, Solomon's Solution and drenches. The thatched roof continued over the buggy shed where a three-seated buggy and the brake were kept.

The back door of the stable led into the horse yard, a circular enclosure fenced with rough-hewn seven-foot posts and split rails. This high fence sloped outward so that a bucking horse could not scrape father's legs against the rails or crush him against the post.

Across the dirt roadway was an area of bushland, a refuge for the few kangaroos that still refused to retreat back to less settled areas. The store, post office and school were almost a mile away along the road. A large hill, Mt. Turalla, rose behind the township. At the top was a crater down which the children rolled boulders that went bounding and crashing through ferns till they came to rest on the bottom far below. Father said that horses reared on the slopes of Mt. Turalla were always sure-footed and worth a couple of quid more than those reared on the flats.

"I have a half-draught colt here," father said as he pushed my pram into the stable. "It shows the whites of its eyes and I've never known a horse that showed the whites of its eyes that wouldn't

375

kick the eye out of a mosquito if it got half a chance. It belongs to
Brady. It'll kill him one day, you mark my words. Whoa there!" he
called to the horse that had flinched forward with a flattened rump.
"See! He's ready to lash out now. I've mouthed him, he's not going
to be hard in the mouth, but I'll put a kicking strap on him when
I harness him up."

"Can I go with you when you put him in, dad?" I asked him.

"Well, yes, you could," he said slowly as he began to fill his pipe.
"You could help me break him in by holding him an' that. You
would be a great help to me, but," he tamped the tobacco down
with his finger, "I reckon I better take him for one or two runs first.
I'd like you to watch from the ground and tell me what you think
of his gait when I bring him past you. I want you to do a lot of that
for me. I don't know anybody that's got as good a feel for a horse
as you have."

"I'll tell you what he's like!" I exclaimed, eager to help. "I'll
watch his legs. I'd like doing that, dad."

"I knew you would," he said lighting his pipe. "I was lucky to
get you."

"How did you get me, dad?" I asked him.

"Mother carried you round inside her for a while then you were
born. You grew like a flower beneath her heart, she says."

"Like the kittens Blackie had?" I asked.

"Yes, like that."

"It makes me feel sick, a bit."

"Yes." He paused, looking out through the stable door. "It did
me, too, when I first heard of it, but after a while it seems good
like. You can't beat seeing a foal running beside its mother, pressing
against her—you know." He pushed against the post to show me.
"Well, she carried it before it was born. And it bucks round her like
it wanted to get back. It's better than just being brought to your
mother."

"Yes, I reckon it is." I quickly changed my view. "I wouldn't like
to be just brought," I said.

Father wheeled me out of the stable into the yard and told me to
watch him greasing the buggy.

"Did you know it was the picnic on Saturday?" he asked me as he
jacked up one of the wheels.

"The picnic!" I exclaimed, excited at the thought of this annual

Sunday School gathering. Then a stab of disappointment changed
my expression. "I won't be able to run," I said.

"No," said father abruptly.

He spun the wheel of the buggy and I sat there in my pram
watching him with a rug over my crippled legs.

"You won't be able to run this time," he said at last, "but I want
you to watch them running. You stand near the tape. Run with
them while you watch them. When the first kid breasts the tape
you breast it with him."

"How, dad?" I did not quite understand what he meant.

"Think it," he said.

I thought over what he said while he went into the harness
room for a tin of axle grease. When he came out he placed it on
the ground beside the buggy then wiped his hands on a piece of
rag and said, "I had a black bitch once—a half-bred kangaroo dog.
She could run like the son of a gun. She was the best dog I've ever
had. A bloke offered me a fiver for her once."

"Why didn't you sell her, dad?" I asked.

"Well, you see, I reared her from when she was a pup. I called
her Bessie."

"I wish we had her now, dad," I said.

"Yes, I do, too, but she got staked in the shoulder and put it out
or something. She was never any good after that. But I took her
out just the same and she did all the barking and the other dogs
did all the running. I've never seen a dog get so excited. Well,
you've got to be like her. Fight and run and race and ride and yell
your bloody head off while you're looking on. Forget your legs.
I'm going to forget them from now on."

Chapter Five

The children who lived farther down our road called for me each
morning and pushed me to school in the pram. They liked doing it
because each one had turns riding with me. Those pulling the pram
would prance like horses and I would yell out, "Hup! Hup!" and
wave an imaginary whip. There was Joe Carmichael, who lived
almost opposite us—he was my mate—and Freddie Hawk, who
could do everything better than anyone else and was the hero of

the school, and "Skeeter" Bronson, who always said that he'd "tell on you" when you hit him.

Two girls lived up our road. Alice Barker was one. All the boys wished she was their girl but she liked Freddie Hawk. Maggie Mulligan was the other. She was a big girl and knew three terrible swears and would say the three of them together if you got her wild. She would clip you on the ear as quick as look at you and I liked her wheeling me in the pram better than anyone else because I loved her. Sometimes, when we played "bucking horses" the pram tipped over and Maggie would say the three swears and call to the others, "Here! Help me chuck him back before someone comes."

At school they always left my pram near the door and I walked into the schoolroom on my crutches. The school was a long, stone building with high, narrow windows and you couldn't see out of them when you were sitting down.

Miss Pringle taught the Little Ones and Mr. Tucker taught the Big Ones. Miss Pringle had grey hair and looked at you over her glasses. She wore a high whale-bone collar that made it hard for her to nod her permission for you to go out and I was always wanting to go out because then you could stand in the sun and look at Mt. Turalla and hear magpies.

Mr. Tucker was the head teacher. His eyes were sharp and hard and cold and he used them like a whip. He always washed his hands in an enamel basin in the corner of the room and after he had washed them he would look at the pupils while he dried them on a small, white towel. No one moved while he dried his hands. When he finished he would fold the towel and put it in the desk drawer and then he would smile at us with his teeth and lips. He terrified me as a tiger would.

He had a cane and before he used it on a boy he would swish it twice through the air and then draw it through his closed hand as if to clean it. "Now," he would say, his teeth smiling.

To be able to stand the cuts was evidence of superiority, and boys who cried were thereafter unable to boss any other boy in the playground. My pride demanded I establish myself in some field children valued and since most of these fields were closed to me I developed a disdainful attitude towards being caned. I refused to jerk my outstretched hand back as the cane came down, as some boys did. Though afterwards my numbed fingers could not clasp

the hand-grips of my crutches, I placed the backs of my hands beneath the grips and could get back to my seat in that way.

We rubbed resin in the palms of our hands, believing that this rendered the hand so tough no cut could hurt it.

I gradually became the authority on resin, describing the amount to use, the method of application, the varying qualities of resin, in a tone that showed I was a veteran and could not be contradicted.

Later I turned to wattlebark, soaking my hands in the brown liquid made from pouring hot water over the bark. I claimed this tanned the hands, and displayed my palms, calloused from constant rubbing on the crutch grips, to prove it.

MY CRUTCHES were becoming a part of me. I had developed arms out of proportion to the rest of my body and my armpits were tough and hard. I practised different walking styles, calling them after the gaits of horses. I could trot, pace, canter and gallop. I fell frequently and heavily but learnt to throw myself into positions that saved my bad leg from injury. I was never free of bruises or lumps and each evening found me attending to some injury I had received that day. But they did not distress me. I accepted these annoying inconveniences as being part of normal living.

I began walking to school and became acquainted with exhaustion—a state familiar to cripples, and their constant concern. I always cut corners, always made in as straight a line as I could to where I wanted to go. I walked through clumps of thistles rather than go round them, climbed through fences rather than deviate a few yards to go through a gate.

A normal child expends its surplus energy by cavorting, skipping, spinning in circles, as it walks up the street. I, too, felt the need to do this and I indulged in clumsy caperings as I walked up the road because of a need to express how well I felt. People seeing me expressing my joy in living so clumsily regarded it as pathetic and stared at me with pity. I immediately stopped till they were out of sight then threw myself into my happy world again, free from their sadness and pain.

My values were changing and from having a natural respect for those boys who spent most of their time reading, I became absorbed in physical achievement. I admired a football player far more than those with impressive mental achievements. Yet violence of any kind was abhorrent to me. After seeing a man flog a horse or kick a dog, I would creep home and hold Meg tightly for a moment. It made me feel better, as if her security embraced myself.

Animals and birds were never long out of my mind. Birds in flight affected me like music. I watched dogs running with an almost painful awareness of the beauty of their motion. I was not aware that in this worship of all action that suggested power I was compensating for an inability to indulge in such action myself.

I began walking into the bush in the evenings so that I could smell the earth and the trees. I knelt among the moss and pressed my face against the earth, breathing it into me. I dug among the roots of grass. The fine, hair-like roots seemed magical to me and I began to feel that my head was too far above the earth to appreciate to the fullest the grass and wildflowers. I wanted to be like a dog, running with my nose to the earth so that there would be no fragrance missed, no miracle of stone or plant unobserved. I would crawl through ferns by the swamp's edge, making tunnels of discovery through the undergrowth, or lie prone among the curled fronds of bracken newly emerged from the creative darkness of the earth, gently clasped like babies' hands. Oh! the tenderness of them; the kindness and compassion of them!

After tea, before it was time to go to bed, I would stand at our gate listening to the frogs or a mopoke or the chirr of a possum, and I would launch myself out, in my imagination, into a powerful run through the night, galloping on four legs, my nose to the earth as I followed a rabbit's trail. I was a dingo or a dog living a life of its own in the bush through which I loped in tireless strides. As a dog running through the night I experienced no fatigue, no painful falls. I raced through the bush with my nose to the leaf-strewn earth, animated by an intense and joyful energy.

The world of reality forged me; in the world of dreams I swung the blade.

AFTER SCHOOL hours Joe Carmichael and I were rarely apart. Joe had a fresh, ruddy face and a slow smile that made grown-ups like him. He raised his cap to women and would go messages for anyone. He never quarrelled but always clung stubbornly to an opinion even though he did not defend it. On Saturday afternoons we always went hunting hares and rabbits together and on week nights we set traps which we visited early each morning. We knew the names of all the birds in the bush around our homes, we knew their habits and nesting places, and each of us had a collection of eggs that we kept in cardboard boxes half full of pollard.

Joe's father worked for Mrs. Carruthers. He had a sandy moustache and father said he was the most honest man in the district. Mrs. Carruthers paid him twenty-five shillings a week but she took five shillings back for the rent of his house. Joe's mother, Mrs. Carmichael, was a thin, little woman with her hair drawn back into a bun. She washed clothes in round wooden troughs made from halves of barrels and she always hummed as she washed, on an even key, like an expression of contentment. It greeted me as I came through the trees to their place and I always stood still to listen to it.

Mrs. Carmichael always smiled at me when I came there. "I will give you and Joe a piece of bread and jam in a minute an' I will," she would say.

She never looked at my crutches, only at my face. She spoke to me as if unaware that I couldn't run like other boys. "Run down and get Joe now," she'd say. I always wanted her house to catch fire so I could dash in and save her life.

Joe and I sold the skins of the hares and rabbits we caught to a bearded buyer who used to drive his horse and waggon up to Joe's each week. The money we received for the skins we placed in a tin. We were saving up to buy *Leach's Bird Book* which we regarded as the most wonderful book you could possibly get.

"I suppose the Bible's better," Joe once conceded. Joe was faintly religious at times.

On these hunting excursions Joe adapted his pace to suit mine. He never robbed me of the pleasure of discovery. When he detected, before me, the crouched form of a hare in its seat, he would beckon me with violent gestures and make soundless contortions with his mouth that suggested urgent cries for me to hurry. I would swing towards him on my crutches, raising and lowering them with exaggerated care so that they came to rest in silence between each leap. Then he would watch it as it crouched with its frightened eyes staring at us, its ears flattened along its back.

Each day after school Joe drove his mother's ducks and geese to a pond a quarter of a mile away and each evening he drove them back again. I nearly always accompanied him and we sat by the pond together.

"You never know what's in there," Joe reflected at times.

On windy days we placed crews of ants in empty fish tins and sailed them across the pond, and sometimes we paddled around the edge looking for apus, that strange, shrimp-like creature with its moving gills.

"They're very delicate," Joe told me. "They die if you put them in bottles."

We also wandered in the bush looking for birds, and, in the spring, climbing to their nests. I was fond of climbing trees. Anything in the nature of a challenge always roused me. My bad leg swung uselessly as I drew myself up from limb to limb and my good leg could only be used as a prop while my hands reached to higher branches. I was afraid of heights but managed to overcome this by avoiding looking down unless it was necessary.

When the magpies nested, Joe would stand below yelling a warning just before the birds attacked. If you could watch them making their gliding dive it wasn't so bad because you could strike at them as they came in and they would swerve away with a quick flick of their wings and a furious jab at your hand, but when your back was to them and you needed both hands to hold on with, they often struck you with their bills or wings.

When this happened to me I would hear Joe's voice below, full of quick concern. "Did he get ya?"

"Yes. On the side of the head." When I could free a hand I would feel my head then glance at my hand. "She's bleeding," I'd yell to Joe, both pleased and concerned with the evidence.

Sometimes I fell, but lower limbs generally broke my fall and I was never badly hurt. Joe developed a philosophical attitude towards the falls I had when walking with him. Immediately I plunged forward on my face, or tottered sideways before collapsing, or crashed on my back, he would sit down and continue his conversation knowing that, for a little while, I would lie as I fell. Since I was nearly always tired, a fall offered me an excuse to rest as I lay stretched on the ground. Joe never made the mistake of coming to my aid unless I called him. He would sit on the grass, give one glance at me rolling in pain, then look resolutely away and say, "It's a cow!"

383

THE BIG DROUGHT that struck Australia at this time introduced Joe and me to fear and pain and suffering we had never known. In our experience, the sun was never cruel and God looked after the cows and horses. When an animal suffered it was because of man. We often reflected on what we would do if we were a cow or a horse and we always decided we would leap fence after fence until there was only bush around us and no people whatever, and here we would live in perfect happiness till we died peacefully in the shelter of trees with long, green grass to rest upon.

The drought started with the failure of the autumn rains. When the winter rains came the earth was too cold for growth and seeds did not sprout and the perennial grass was eaten down to the roots by hungry cattle. The spring was dry and when summer came in, dust was blowing across paddocks that in other years were covered in grass.

Farmers, unable to feed aged horses they had retired to their back paddocks, and lacking the courage to shoot the animals, turned them out onto the roads to fend for themselves. Along the roads, bands of horses and cattle could be seen muzzling the dusty earth for roots or standing on the metal eating the dry manure left by chaff-fed horses that had been driven by. As the drought progressed and the burning heat continued, the bands grew smaller and smaller. Each day the weakest stumbled and fell and the others moved away from the rising dust of its struggling, walking slowly on with dragging feet and drooping heads.

From horizon to horizon the haze of bushfire smoke and the smell of burning gum leaves hung disquietingly above the grassless earth.

Entire herds of dairy cattle died in the paddocks of their owners. They lay on their sides, the earth around their hooves kicked into new-moon holes as they struggled to rise.

Joe and I tortured ourselves with harrowing descriptions of the slow deaths taking place in the paddocks and bush around us. For some reason, the death of animals in paddocks did not affect either of us as badly as did the deaths on the road. The road animals, it seemed to us, were friendless, deserted, while the cattle and horses in paddocks had owners who felt for them.

On the hot summer evenings when the sky remained red long after the sun had set Joe and I walked down to the road trough to watch the stock come in to drink. The horses came every second night, being able to survive two days without water. The cattle came every night but they gradually died around the trough, not being able to range as far as the horses.

One day we sat looking at the sunset and waiting for the horses. The road stretched straight through timber, then into open country, disappearing finally over a rise. In a little while the horses came towards us with a clinking of neck chains and the clatter of hooves on stones, twenty or more, their heads drooping, all stumbling a little. As the trough came in sight some neighed, others quickened their pace. One bay mare with each rib showing distinctly on her sides, suddenly crumpled, her legs buckled beneath her, pitching forward so that her nose hit the ground before she rolled to her side. She lay still a moment then made a desperate effort to rise, but her hind legs gave way and she fell back.

"Come on," I cried to Joe. "We've got to raise her. All she needs is a drink and it'll put strength into her." We placed our hands beneath her neck and tried to lift but she did not move. She was breathing deeply.

"Let her have a blow for a bit," Joe advised. "She might be able to get up then."

We stood beside her in the gathering dark, restless and irritable with frustration. We wanted to go home but we were afraid to be alone with the tormenting picture of her lying there dying in the night.

I suddenly grabbed her head. Joe slapped her rump. We yelled at her. For a moment she fought to rise then fell back. We couldn't stand it. "What the hell is everybody doing?" Joe shouted angrily, looking round at the empty roads as if expecting strong men with ropes to dash forward to help us.

"We'll have to get her a drink," I said in desperation. "Go get the bucket from the chaff house."

When Joe came back with the bucket we filled it at the trough. It was too heavy for Joe to carry alone so I helped him lift it a yard at a time. We held the handle together and swung it forward a yard then we would walk ahead of the bucket again and reach back and swing it forward once more until we reached the mare. When we placed the bucket in front of her she thrust her nose deep into the water and sucked so strongly the level fell swiftly around her nose as we watched it. In a minute she had emptied the bucket. We brought her another one and she emptied that, then another one. . . .

But by now I was exhausted. I fell and was too tired to rise. I lay beside the mare, all my strength gone.

"I'll have to be carting you water next," said Joe.

He sat down beside me looking at the stars and he sat there for a long time not moving or talking. All I could hear was the deep, sad breathing of the horse.

Chapter Six

One Saturday Joe and I had arranged to meet Skeeter Bronson and Steve McIntyre at the foot of Mt. Turalla. We were taking the dogs, as foxes were often seen amongst the bracken that covered its sides, but our main object was to roll stones down the crater.

The climb up the mount was an exhausting walk for me. I needed the frequent spells that I always had when Joe was my only companion, but when other boys were with us they complained. ("Cripes! Ya not stoppin' again are ya?") I stole time for resting. I would point to runs through the ferns and exclaim, "I can smell a fox! He musta just passed! Follow him up!" The discussion as to whether it was worth following the trail took time, and I would gain the rest I needed.

We followed a narrow horse-pad that girdled the side of the hill. The ferns that skirted it were high and offered stiff, tangling resistance to my crutches. I had to keep one crutch swinging along the open pathway, my legs and the other crutch forcing their way through the growth. The strategies I used to distract Skeeter and Steve from their intention to reach the top without delay succeeded, and we all walked over the crest together. The unimpeded wind blew strongly against us and we breasted it with delight, sending loud yells echoing round the crater lying like a deep bowl in front of us.

We sent a rock hurtling down its steep slopes, watching it crash into trees in spiralling leaps to the crater floor. I longed to follow it, to see for myself what lay hidden down there amongst the ferns and trees that grew on the bottom.

"There might be a big hole down there with just a bit of earth covering it," I said, "and if you stood on it, you'd go through into boiling mud."

"It's extinct," said Steve with a typical lack of co-operation.

"It might be," Joe said solemnly, "but there's no knowin' what's down there."

"I'm going halfway down," said Steve.

"Come on!" said Skeeter eagerly. "It'll be good fun."

Joe looked at me. "I'll wait for you," I said.

The slopes of the crater were littered with scoria and stones that long ago must have bubbled in some fierce heat before solidifying. They were lumps of froth turned into stone and they were so light they floated on water. My crutches would not grip on the steep, crumbling earth. I sat down, prepared to wait. It did not distress me that I could not go with the others. I believed I was staying because of my *decision* to stay. I *never* felt helpless. I was exasperated, but my exasperation was directed against the Other Boy.

The Other Boy was always with me. He was my shadow-self, weak and full of complaints, apprehensive, always seeking to restrain. I despised him, yet in all moments of decision I had to free myself of his influence. He wore my body and walked on crutches. I strode apart from him on legs as strong as trees. When Joe announced he was going to walk down the crater, the Other Boy spoke quickly to me in urgent tones: "Alan, go easy. I've had enough."

"All right," I assured him, "but there are a lot of things I want to do and you're not going to stop me from doing them."

It was a quarter of a mile to the bottom of the crater. I could see the boys scrambling down the slope, holding on to the trunks of trees when they stood a moment looking around them. I expected them to turn and come climbing back again. When I saw they had made up their minds to continue to the bottom I felt a sense of betrayal. I looked at my crutches, wondering whether they would be safe there; then I turned onto my hands and knees and set off for the bottom where the boys were now exploring the flat area they had reached.

At first I crawled, crashing my way through ferns as I went plunging downward. Sometimes my hands slipped and I fell on my face, skidding on loose earth till I was stopped by some obstruction. Near the bottom the huge stones that once had rested on the top of the mount lay piled amongst the ferns. Ever since the early pioneers had entered this country those who climbed the mount had been levering these heavy rocks from where they had been lying half-buried on the summit, and had watched them hurtling downward. I found it difficult to cross this barrier of tumbled stone. I moved from rock to rock, taking all my weight on my hands to save my knees, but when I reached a less crowded area where I could crawl between them, my knees were scratched and bleeding.

The boys had watched me, and when I came tumbling through a belt of fern onto level ground, Joe was waiting for me. "How in hell are ya goin' to get up?" he asked as he dropped down on the grass beside me. "It must be after three o'clock now and I've got to bring the ducks home."

"I'll get up easy," I told him shortly, then continued, "Is the ground soft down here like what you thought?"

"It's just like on top," said Joe. "Skeeter caught a lizard but he won't let you hold it. Steve and 'im keep talking about us when I'm not there. Look at 'em now."

Skeeter and Steve were standing near a tree talking and glancing towards us with the unmistakable furtiveness of conspirators. "We can hear you," I yelled out. This lie was the traditional opening to acknowledgments of enmity.

Steve replied with undisguised hostility. "Who're *you* talking to?" He took a step towards us.

"Not to you, anyway," called Joe, who regarded this answer as a devastating retort.

"Look, they're off," I said. Skeeter and Steve had turned and were beginning the climb up the side of the crater. "Let 'em go. Who cares for them?" We watched the two boys in silence as they picked their way up through the stones.

Joe chewed a grass stem. "It seems funny down here, don't it? Listen to how it echoes."

"Hullo!" he yelled and round the side of the crater came faint "Hullos" in answer to him.

For a little while we sent echoes tumbling from the slopes, then Joe said, "Let's go. I got to get the ducks yet. And I don't like down here. It's like as if it'll fall in on you."

It did seem as if the enclosing sides would topple over and

down, shutting us off from the sky. From here the sky was no longer a dome that covered the earth but a frail roof resting on walls of stone and gravel. It was pale and thin, rendered insignificant by the mighty slopes that rose to meet it. And the earth was brown, brown . . . The dark green of the ferns was swamped with brown. The still, silent boulders were brown. Even the silence was brown. We felt we were being watched by something huge and unfriendly.

I lowered myself onto the earth and began crawling back on knees that were already inflamed and tender. I had to rest every few yards, sinking down with my face pressed to the ground and my arms lying limp beside me. I could hear the beating of my heart coming from the earth.

High up on the crater's side I stopped to rest again, breathing deeply. From the ground against which my ear was pressed I heard two quick thuds. I looked up towards the top of the crater and there outlined against the sky were Skeeter and Steve, yelling in fear and waving their arms. "Look out! Look out!"

The stone that under a sudden impulse they had sent rolling down on us had not yet gathered speed. Joe saw it at the same time as I did.

"The tree," he yelled, and we floundered towards a towering dead gum. We reached it just before the stone passed us with thuds that shook the ground. Far below us we heard the sharp crack as it struck boulders hidden in bracken. It broke in half and the two pieces separated and shot away from each other at an angle. Steve and Skeeter, frightened by what they had done, were running away over the crest.

"They're gone!" I said. "Wait till we tell the kids at school!"

When finally we reached the top I lay on the ground while all my flesh twitched like that of a kangaroo from which the hide had just been taken. Then I rose to my feet, placed the crutches beneath my arms, and we set off down the mountain.

IT TROUBLED father to see me returning exhausted from such long walks. He said, "Don't walk so far, Alan. Hunt in the bush round the house."

"There are no hares there," I said. "I like going out hunting. All the boys go hunting. Joe stops when I'm tired."

"Anyway, toss it in and lie down when you're done. You have to spell even a champion horse going up a long hill."

Father began looking at the second-hand advertisements in the *Age*. One day he drove to Balunga and brought home an invalid chair that came up in the train. It was standing in the yard when I came home from school.

"It's yours," father said. "Hop into the saddle and give it a fly."

The chair had two over-size bicycle wheels at the back and a small wheel in the front attached to a goose-neck. Two handles attached to rods fitted to cranks on the axle could be worked to and fro, and there was a steering device.

After a few days I could race the chair up the road, my arms working like pistons. I rode it to school and became the envy of my mates who climbed aboard with me sitting on my knee or facing one another on the goose-neck.

The invalid chair brought Turalla Creek within reach for me. It was three miles from our home and I only saw it when father drove that way in the brake. But Joe often walked to the creek to fish for eels and now I could accompany him.

Saturday night was our fishing night and we always left home in the late afternoon, arriving before the sun set at McCallum's Hole, a long, dark stretch of water, deep and still. Redgums lined its banks and threw powerful limbs across the water. Their trunks were gnarled and twisted, charred by bush fires or bearing the long, leaf-like scar left by a blackfellow after he had removed the bark for a canoe.

Joe and I eagerly examined these canoe trees, looking for the marks of the stone axe that had been used to cut the bark from the trunk. Some of the scars were small, and we knew the bark from these had been used to fashion coolamons, the shallow dish in which the lubras placed their piccaninnies to sleep or in which they carried the vegetable food they gathered. One such tree had its huge roots touched by the water of McCallum's Hole. On still nights when our floaters sat motionlessly in a moonlight path on the water, the dark surface at our feet would glitter with ripples then break and for a moment a platypus would be floating there, watching us with sharp eyes before it curved its body and returned to its burrow amongst the submerged roots of the old tree.

Water rats also lived in holes beneath the tree. They brought up mussels from the mud and broke the shells on the flat surface of a huge root. We gathered the pieces to bring home to the fowls.

"It's the best shell grit you can get," Joe told me, but Joe always dealt in superlatives.

One night we had made a "bob". Catching eels with a hook can be exciting but with a bob the catch is much bigger. A bob is made by threading worms onto a strand of wool till you have one tremendous worm several yards long. This is then cast into the water. It sinks to the bottom and is almost immediately seized by an eel whose file-like teeth get caught in the wool. When the one holding the line feels the tug he jerks the eel from the water and it falls with the bob onto the bank beside him. He then has to seize it before it escapes back into the water, cut through the back of its neck with a knife, and thrust it into his bag.

We lit a campfire when we reached the old tree and boiled the billy, in which mother had already placed tea and sugar, while munching corned-beef sandwiches. I threw my crusts into the river and Joe said, "Don't frighten the eels. Eels is terrible nervous and, what's more, there's an east wind tonight and they won't bite with an east wind."

He stood up and wet his finger by thrusting it into his mouth. He held it upright in the still air and waited a moment.

"Yes, it's east all right. It feels cold on the east side."

But the eels bit better than Joe anticipated, and by eleven o'clock we had eight. But Joe wanted ten. "It's better to say, 'we got ten last night' than to say 'we got eight'."

The moon had risen and we decided to stay till twelve. It was cold and we were thinly clad, so Joe gathered more wood for the fire. Then he dropped an armful of wood and ran to grab the rod which had moved to the tug of an eel. He flung the eel out onto the bank where it fell near the fire, glittering black and silver as it writhed away from the heat. It was the biggest eel we had caught and I flung myself at it eagerly. It slipped from my grasp and slithered towards the water. Joe seized it near the edge of the water, but it squeezed through his hands and fell to the ground. He dived at it again as it was entering the water, slipped on the mud and went into the creek up to his waist. He crawled out onto the bank and stood up, his arms curved away from his sides as he looked down at the pool of water gathering at his feet. "I'll get into a row

391

over this," he said with concern. "I'll have to dry my pants if it's the last thing I do."

"Take 'em off and dry 'em at the fire," I suggested.

He began taking off his trousers with great speed as if a bull ant had gone up his leg.

I thrust the end of a forked stick into the ground so that it leant almost over the fire where his trousers would dry quickly in the rising heat.

Joe took a piece of sodden string, a brass door knob and some marbles from his pocket and placed them on the ground, then he hung his trousers on the stick and began dancing up and down before the fire to keep warm.

I flung the bob back into the creek, hoping to catch the eel we had lost and when I finally felt a bite I jerked the rod with the power of one about to lift a heavy weight.

A wriggling eel, clinging to the bob, flashed high in the air above my head, came down in a curve behind me, and crashed into the stick holding Joe's trousers. The trousers fell into the fire.

Joe raced round the fire swearing in an anguished fashion then grabbed the rod from my hands and poked at his flaming trousers in an effort to jerk them out. When at length he got the end of the rod beneath them, he gave such a tremendous heave on the rod that the trousers leapt upward and described a rainbow of fire against the night before sailing free of the rod and dropping with a sizzle and a puff of steam into the waters of the creek. The black patch of the sinking trousers could be seen against the gleam of the moving water before they disappeared, and Joe watched this patch, bending out over the water with the glow of the fire painting his bare behind a rosy pink.

"My God!" he said.

When he had recovered sufficiently to discuss his predicament he announced that we must get home quickly. "It's agin the law to leave your pants off," he told me earnestly. "You can do a stretch quick and lively if you're caught. I wish it wasn't a full moon."

We hurriedly tied our rods to the side of the chair, placed the bag of eels on the footboard and set off, Joe sitting on my knee and complaining of cold. Far ahead of us, we saw the lights of a buggy approaching us, with the clock-clock of a jogging horse. I said, "That sounds like old O'Connor's grey."

"That'll be him," said Joe. "Let me off. I'll hide behind the trees over there."

I stopped the chair and Joe disappeared into a dark clump of trees. When O'Connor came level with my chair he called out, "Whoa." He leant forward in the seat and peered at me. "It beats me what a kid like you wants to go round ridin' in that bloody contraption in the middle of the night for. You'll go and get your-self kilt." He raised his voice. "I'm damned if I can make your old man out and there's a lot more can't make him out either. A kid crippled up like you should be home restin' in bed. Giddup." His horse roused itself and moved off. "Hurroo," he said.

"Goodnight, Mr. O'Connor."

Joe emerged from the clump of trees and ran to the chair, and we set off again, Joe shivering between exclamations of concern and anger at the loss of his trousers. "Mum'll go stone mad. I've only got one other pair and the backside's out of 'em."

I pulled and pushed at the handles with all my strength and the chair bounced along over the rough road. "One thing," said Joe seeking to comfort himself, "I took everything out of the pockets of me pants before they were burnt."

A SWAGMAN sitting near our gate had told me he knew a man who had both legs off and yet he could swim like a fish.

I often thought of this man swimming like a fish in the water. I had never even seen anyone swimming. None of the boys at the school could swim nor could any of the men I knew in Turalla.

I had a large, bound volume of a boys' paper called *Chums* in which there was an article on swimming. It was illustrated with three pictures of a man in a striped bathing suit and a moustache who, in the first picture, stood facing you with his arms stretched above his head; the next picture showed his arms stretched out at right angles to his body, and in the last picture they were by his side. Arrows curving from his hands to his knees suggested he moved his arm downward in what the writer called the "Breast Stroke". I was determined to learn to swim, and on summer even-ings began sneaking off in my chair to a lake three miles away where I began practising.

The lake lay hidden in a hollow with the steep, high bank rising in terraces for two or three hundred yards from the water. These terraces must have continued beneath the surface, for a few yards out from the edge the bottom dropped abruptly into depths where trailing waterweeds grew and the water was cold and still. Only on very hot evenings, and under a strong incentive, were men tempted to go to the lake which was always regarded as dangerous. Children were warned to keep away from it. However, groups of boys sometimes ignored their parents' instructions and splashed in the water round the edge.

Swimming was an achievement upon which the children placed great value and it was the custom to proclaim you could swim when you could lie face downward upon the water and draw yourself forward with your hands on the bottom. But I wanted to be able to swim in deep water.

I left my chair in a wattle clump on the top of the bank, then scrambled down the grass-covered terraces till I reached the shore where I undressed and crawled across the stones and mud till I reached the sand. Here I could sit down with the water no higher than my chest.

The article in *Chums* said nothing about bending your arms and thrusting them forward in a way that offered no resistance to the water. My interpretation of the drawings was that you merely moved your straightened arms up and down.

I reached the stage where I could keep myself afloat with a mighty threshing but could not go forward and it was not until the second year, when I discussed swimming with another swagman at our gate, that I learnt how to move my arms.

I learnt very quickly after that until there came a day when I decided to test myself in the deep water. It was a hot summer evening and the lake was as blue as the sky. I sat naked on the bank watching the black swans far out on the water, rising and falling as they rode the tiny waves, while I argued with the Other Boy who wanted me to go home.

"You swam easily a hundred yards along the edge," he reasoned. "No other boy at school could do that."

But I would not listen to him until he said, "See how lonely it is." The loneliness frightened me. No trees grew around the lake. It lay open to the sky and there was always a still silence above it.

After a while I crawled into the water and continued on, keeping erect by moving my arms in a swimming stroke on the surface, till

I reached the edge of the drop into the dark blue and the cold. I stood there moving my arms and looking down into the clear water where I could see the long, pale stems of weeds swaying like snakes as they stretched out from the steep side of the submerged terrace.

I was alone in the world and I was afraid.

I stood there a little while then drew a breath and struck out over the drop. As I moved forward a cold tendril of leaves clung for a moment to my trailing legs then slipped away and I was swimming in water that I felt went down beneath me for ever. I wanted to turn back but I kept on, repeating over and over in my mind, "Don't be frightened now; don't be frightened now. . . ."

I turned gradually and when I was facing the shore again and saw how far away it seemed to be I panicked for a moment and churned up the water with my arms, but the voice within me kept on and I recovered myself and swam slowly again.

I crawled out onto the shore as if I were an explorer returning home from a long journey of danger and privation. The lakeside was no longer a lonely place of fear but a very lovely place of sunshine and grass. I whistled as I dressed.

I could swim!

OUR GATEWAY was shaded by huge redgums. Swagmen passing along the road often slipped their swags off their shoulders and stood looking speculatively at the house and the wood heap before coming in to beg some tucker. Mother was well known to those swaggies whose beat passed our home. She always gave them bread, meat and tea without asking them to chop wood in return.

Father had humped his bluey in Queensland and was familiar with the ways of swagmen. He always called them "travellers". The bearded men who kept to the bush he called "Scrub Turkeys" and those who came from the plains he called "Plain Turkeys". He could tell the difference between them and whether they were broke or not.

When a swaggie camped at our gate for the night father knew he was broke. "If he were holding well, he'd keep on to the pub," he told me. From the stockyard he often watched them carrying billies to our door and if they clung to the lid of the billy and didn't hand it to mother he would smile and say "old-timer".

I asked him what it meant when they held on to the lid while mother took the billy and he said, "When you're on the track there's some people as wouldn't give you the smell of an oilrag. You've gotta work 'em like you was a sheep dog. Say you want tea and sugar—that's what you always want. You put a few leaves of tea in the bottom of the billy—not many, enough so she knows you're light on the tea. When she comes to the door, you ask for a drop of hot water to make some tea and you say, 'The tea's in the billy, lady.' She takes the billy and then you say, as if you'd just thought of it see, 'You could stick in a bit of sugar if you don't mind, lady!' Now when she goes to put the hot water in the billy she sees there's not enough tea in it to colour a spit. She don't like handing it back to a bloke weak as dishwater, so she shoves in more tea. Then she chucks in the sugar and he's got the lot."

"But why does he hold on to the lid?" I persisted.

"Well, you never get as much if they can cover it up. When there's no lid to hide what they give you they don't like facing you unless the billy is full."

"Mum's not like that, is she, dad?"

"Hell, no!" he said. "She'd give you the boots off her feet if you let her. But it's not old clothes they want, but tucker, especially meat. Giving tucker costs money. A lot of people'd sooner give 'em a pair of old pants their old man won't wear no more."

Sometimes a swagman slept in our chaff house. Mary was feeding the ducks one frosty morning and saw a swaggie covered in a blanket as stiff as a board. He had frost on his beard and eyebrows and when he got up he walked around in a stooped position till the sun warmed him. After that, when Mary saw a swagman camped at the gate, she sent me down to tell him he could sleep in the chaff house. I always followed him into the chaff house and when mother sent Mary out with his dinner she would send me out my dinner too. She knew I liked to hear swagmen talking about the places they had seen. Father said they pulled my leg but I didn't think so.

When I showed one old man my rabbit skins, he told me that where he came from the rabbits were so thick you had to sweep them aside to set the traps.

It was a dusty night and I told him if he put the *Age* over his face it would keep the dust off him. I slept out on the back veranda then and I always did it.

"How much dust would it keep off?" he asked me as he raised his billy to his mouth. "Would it keep off a pound now?"

"I think so," I said doubtfully.

"Do you think it would keep off a ton of dust?" he asked, wiping his beard with the back of his hand.

"No," I said, "it wouldn't."

"I been crossing outback stations where you got to sleep with a pick and shovel beside you when a dust storm's coming on, so's you can dig yourself out in the morning." He looked at me with his strange little black eyes that had lights in them.

Sometimes a swaggie would sit over his campfire and shout at the trees or mumble to himself as he looked at the flames; then I knew he was drunk. Sometimes he would be drinking wine and sometimes methylated spirits.

There was a metho drinker called "The Fiddler" who always held his head a little to one side as if he were playing a fiddle. He was tall and thin and was a three-strap man. Father had told me that one strap around the swag meant a newchum who had never been on the track before; two straps meant you were looking for work; three straps showed you didn't want to find it; and four straps was a travelling delegate.

When The Fiddler was sober he talked to me in a high-pitched voice. He said once, "What's wrong with your leg?"

"I got infantile paralysis," I told him.

"Fancy that now!" he said, clucking his tongue. "Well, you've got a roof over your head, anyway." He looked at me, "And a bloody good head it is; like a Romney Marsh lamb."

I liked these men because they never pitied me. They gave me confidence. In the world they travelled, being on crutches was not as bad as sleeping out in the rain or walking with your toes on the ground. They saw nothing but the track ahead of them; they saw brighter things ahead of me.

Once, when I said to The Fiddler, "This is a good place to camp, isn't it?" he glanced round and said, "Yes, I suppose it is—to a bloke who hasn't got to camp here." He gave a scornful laugh. "A cocky said to me once, 'You blokes are never satisfied. If a bloke gives you cheese you'll want to fry it.' I've seen the time when I've thought if I only had tea and sugar I'd be right. Then when I've got tea and sugar I want a smoke, and when I've got a smoke I

399

want a good camp, and when I've got a good camp I want something to read."

The Fiddler was the only swagman I met who carried a frying pan. He took it from his tucker bag and looked at it with satisfaction. "A solid pan, this," he said. "I picked it up near Mildura." He took some liver wrapped in newspaper from his tucker bag and frowned at it for a moment. "Liver is the worst meat in the world to spoil your pan," he said, pursing his lips. "It sticks like a plaster."

Like all swagmen, he was always studying the sky and speculating as to whether it was going to rain. He did not carry a tent, just the usual two blue blankets rolled around a few tattered possessions. "A hundred and sixty points of rain fell on me one night near Elmore," he told me. "It was too bloody dark to move and I sat there with me back to a post just thinkin'."

I told him he could sleep in the chaff house and I took him up there. Father, having seen me talking to him, had already thrown in some armfuls of clean straw.

The Fiddler looked at it for a few moments in silence then he said, "You don't know how lucky you are."

"It's good to be lucky, isn't it," I said, liking him a lot. I stood watching him unroll his swag.

"S'elp me!" he exclaimed, looking around at me. "You hang round like a drover's dog. Hadn't you better go and have tea?"

"Yes," I said. "I'd better. Goodnight, Mr. Fiddler."

A fortnight later he was burnt to death in his campfire eight miles from our place. The man who told father about it said, "He'd been on the metho for a couple of days, they say. He rolled into the fire in the night. I was sayin' to Alec Simpson, 'It was his breath that caught fire, that's what it was'."

Father was silent a moment then said, "Well, that's the end of The Fiddler, poor beggar; he's dead and gone now."

Chapter Seven

Most men patronized me, their usual attitude towards children. When other adults were listening it pleased them to raise a laugh at my expense, not because they wished to hurt me but because my ingenuousness tempted them.

400

"Been riding any buckjumpers lately, Alan?" they would ask, a question I considered a serious one.

"No," I would say. "I will be soon, though." And this was considered worthy of a laugh.

On the other hand I discovered that swagmen and bushmen, lonely men, were often awkward and unsure of themselves when a child spoke to them; but when met with uncritical friendliness they were eager to continue the conversation.

One old bushman I knew was Peter McLeod, a teamster who carted wooden posts from deep in the bush, forty miles below our place. Each week he came out with his laden waggon, spent Sunday with his wife, then returned again, striding beside his team or standing upright in the empty waggon whistling some Scotch air. When I called out, "Good day, Mr. McLeod," he would stop and talk to me as if I were a man.

"What's the bush like where you go, Mr. McLeod?" I asked.

"As thick as the hairs on a dog," he answered. "Yes, she's thick all right. By hell, she's thick!"

He was a tall man with a shining black beard and long legs. His big arms hung down a little in front of him. Father said he unfolded like a three-foot rule, but father liked him and told me he was an honest man and could fight like a tiger cat.

"There's none round here could beat him at his best," he said. "He's a tough, hard man with a soft heart, but when he hits a man, the man stays hit."

Peter hadn't gone to church for twenty years. Father said, "then he went to vote against the Presbyterians joining up with the Methodists."

Once a Mission came to Turalla and Peter decided to become converted. But he backed out when he found they expected him to knock off drinking and smoking. "I've been drinking and smoking to the Glory of God for forty years," he told father, "and I'll keep on for the Glory of God."

"That about sums up how he stands with God," father said.

The bush Peter described to me seemed a magical place where kangaroos hopped quietly through the trees and possums chirred at night. Peter called it "maiden bush"—bush that had never known an axe. It took Peter two and a half days to reach the post-splitters' camp and he slept beside his waggon for a week.

"I wish I were you," I said. "Then I could see the maiden bush."

It was September and my school was closed for a week. I had followed Peter's team in my chair, wanting to see his five horses drink from the trough. He carried a bucket to the two shafters as I watched him.

"I'll take you there," he said, "I want a good bloke to help me. You ask your old man if you can come."

"When are you going?"

"I leave at five tomorrow morning, from the house."

"Thank you, Mr. McLeod," I said. "I'll be there."

I set off for home as fast as my arms would take me. When I told father and mother that Mr. McLeod said he would take me to the bush, father looked surprised and mother asked, "Are you sure he meant it, Alan?"

"He wants me to help him," I said quickly. "We're mates." Mother looked questioningly at father. "It's not the trip so much," she said. "It's the drink and the bad language. You know what it's like when men are shut up in the bush."

"There'll be grog and bad language all right," father agreed. "But that won't hurt him. It's the kid who never sees men grogging up or swearing who takes to it when he grows up."

Mother looked at me and smiled. "Did Mr. McLeod mention anything about tucker?"

"No," I said.

"Well, I've got that round of corned beef for tonight's tea."

"Toss it into a bag with a couple of loaves of bread. That'll do him. Peter'll have tea."

"Help Peter as much as you can, son," said father. "Show him the breed holds good. Light his campfire for him while he feeds the horses. There's lots of jobs you can do."

"I'll work," I said, "My word, I will!"

Next morning I heard the creak of a board as mother came out of her bedroom. I jumped out of bed and lit the candle. It was dark and cold and for some reason I felt depressed. When I joined her she had lit the fire in the stove and had scrambled me an egg. I began eating it with haste.

"Alan," mother said, "did you wash properly? Behind the ears?"

"Yes, all round my neck."

"I've put some things in this little bag for you. Don't forget to

402

clean your teeth with salt every morning." She looked down at my boots. "Your boots aren't clean. Take them off and I'll black them."

She broke a piece off a stick of blacking and mixed it with water in a saucer. I stood fidgeting, impatient to be gone, while she rubbed the black liquid over my boots. She carried the two sugar bags out to my chair and struck a match while I stacked them on the footboard and tied my crutches to the side.

The darkness had a bite of frost in it. I could hear a willy wagtail whistling from a redgum. I had never been up so early and I was excited with this new day that was unspoilt by people, silent with sleep. "No one in the world is up yet, are they?" I said.

"No, you're the first up in the world," mother said.

She opened the gate and I passed through almost at top speed. Beneath the trees the darkness was like a wall and I slowed down. It was good to be alone and free to do as I wished. No grown-up was guiding me now.

Once I had left the lane and passed onto the main road I could go faster again and my arms were beginning to ache by the time I reached Peter's gate.

As I came down the track towards his house I could hear the iron shoes of the horses striking the cobblestoned floor of the stable. Peter was yoking up the horses in his waggon when I pulled up in front of the stable. He dropped the trace chain he was holding and stepped over to the chair.

"It's you, Alan. Cripes, you're not coming with me, are you?"

"You asked me," I replied uncertainly.

"'Course I asked you. Your old man said you could come, did he?"

"Yes. So did mum. I've got my tucker. Here it is." I lifted the bag to show him.

He grinned at me through his beard. "I'll hop into that tonight. Shove your cart in the shed. We'll be on the road at five."

The waggon was a heavy wood-waggon with broad iron tyres and brake blocks of redgum. Its woodwork was bleached and cracked with sun and rain. There were no sides but at the four corners a heavy iron standard with a looped top was thrust into a socket. It had a floor of heavy, loose planks that clattered loudly on bumpy roads.

After Peter had yoked the horses he threw the nosebags and

some bags of chaff onto the waggon, then turned to me and said, "Hop up! Here, I'll take your bags."

I swung over to the front of the waggon, and, holding onto the shafts with one hand, I threw my crutches up into the waggon with the other. Mr. McLeod walked to the leaders' heads and stood there until I lifted myself with my hands, got the knee of my good leg on the shaft, then reached up and grasped the crupper of the shafter beside me. I pulled myself up till I was resting on his rump. It was warm and firm and divided by the shallow valley of his back into two powerful mounds of muscle. "Rest your hand on a good horse and the strength of him goes through you," father had told me. From the shafter's rump I swung over into the waggon and sat down on the tucker box.

Peter gathered the reins and clambered up beside me. "There's a hell of a lot of men can't get into a waggon as good as you," he said. "But I can't make your old man out."

Dawn had broken and there was a pink glow in the east. From every clump of trees the magpies were carolling. I felt there could be nothing in the world more lovely than this—sitting behind a team of horses in the early morning and listening to magpies. Soon we were following a track winding between timber that gradually grew thicker till only the bush was around us and the fences had gone. The dust from the horses' hooves rose into the air and settled softly on our hair and clothes.

I wanted Peter to tell me stories of his adventures. He was the hero of so many tales. In hotel bars, so father said, men would say, "You talk about fights! I saw Peter McLeod fight Long John Anderson behind the hall at Turalla." And everyone would listen to his tale of the fight that lasted two hours. "Yes," the man would say, "they carried Long John away on a hurdle."

I said now, "Father told me you could fight like a thrashin' machine, Mr. McLeod."

"Did he!" he exclaimed, a pleased expression on his face. "Your old man thinks a lot of me. They tell me he was a great runner once." He changed his tone. "An' he said I could fight, did he?"

"Yes," I said, then added, "I wish I could fight."

"Aw, you'll be a good fighter some day. You can take punishment. If you want to be any good you've got to be able to take punishment. Your old man could scrap, and you're like him."

We were passing through a clearing in the bush. A decayed dog-leg fence encircled a paddock in which scrub marked the return of the bush. A grass-grown track led from some sliprails to a deserted bark hut where thin saplings swept their leaves against the walls. Peter roused himself from his thoughts and said, "This is Jackson's place. I'll show you the stump where Young Bob Jackson broke his neck. His horse bolted and threw him. Two months later Old Jackson wrapped a bullock chain round himself and walked into the dam. He went queer after his son's death. He wasn't exactly cranky. He was just like he'd gone broke—sad all the time."

When we came to the dam Peter reined in the horses and said, "Well, there is where it was, near the far bank. He walked straight in and never came up. His old woman and the other boy cleared out after that. She felt it terrible. I brought in the cart and shifted her bits of furniture to Balunga. I told her Old Jackson was a white man if ever there was one. But maybe that makes it worse. I dunno. . . ." He started the horses then said, "Old Jackson was a good bloke. All he wanted was a mate to say, 'Give it another go,' and he would have been all right. The trouble was I was getting the horses shod that day."

THAT NIGHT we camped in a deserted shingle-splitter's hut. Peter unharnessed the team, then took a pair of hobbles and a horsebell from a bran bag. I lifted the bell from the ground. It was a heavy bell with a deep musical note. I rang it, listening to the sound that I would always associate with clear mornings in the bush, when leaves were wet with dew and the magpies were singing. I dropped it a few inches to the ground and Peter, who had been rubbing some neatsfoot oil on the hobbles, exclaimed sharply, "Don't do that! You mustn't drop a bell. It ruins 'em." He held out his hand for the bell and I handed it to him.

"This is a Mongan bell, the best bell in Australia." He examined it carefully. "You can hear it eight miles on a clear day."

"Dad said the Condamine bell is the best."

"Well, he comes from Queensland. The Condamine sends a horse deaf. It's too high a note. There's only two bells—the Mennicke and the Mongan, and the Mongan's the best. That bell's made out of a pit saw, one with a good ring in it."

"What horse are you going to put it on?" I asked.

"Kate," he said. "She's my bell horse. She's got a long gait and shakes her head. The others can't ring it properly. I bell her and hobble Nugget. He's the boss. They all stop with him."

When he came into the hut later I had the billy boiling. He threw a handful of tea into the bubbling water and placed the billy on the hearth. "Where's your corned beef?" he asked.

I took the round of beef in its newspaper wrapping from one of my bags and handed it to him. He pressed it with a dirt-blackened finger and commented, "It's prime beef, this—a piece of silverside." He cut me a thick slice and placed it between two huge pieces of bread. "This'll stick to your ribs." He filled two tin pannikins with strong, black tea and handed me one. "I've never seen the woman yet who can make tea. You can always see the bottom of the cup when a woman makes it."

We sat before the fire eating. After Peter had finished the last pannikin of tea he tossed the dregs into the fire and said, "Now, how's this leg of yours at night? Do you have to tie it up?"

"No," I said. "I don't know it's there."

"If you were my kid I'd take you up to Wang at Ballarat."

I had heard of this Chinese herbalist. Most people round Turalla regarded him as the man to go to when doctors failed. But father always called him a "weed merchant".

"This Wang never asks you what's wrong with you," Peter went on. "He just looks at you and tells you. I wouldn't've believed it, mind you, but Steve Ramsay told me all about him. Ramsay was a bloke that couldn't hold nothing on his stomach. Well, Wang cured him. Steve says to me, when I had the crook back, 'You go to Wang. He'll hold your hand and tell you things that'll stagger you.' I took a week off and drove up and he held my hand like Steve said, and he says, 'You've had an accident?' 'No,' I tells him. 'Think again,' he says. 'Aw, well, about a year ago I was thrown out of a gig and the wheel ran over me,' I says, 'but I wasn't hurt.' 'Oh yes you were!' he reckons. 'Your side is out of position.' Then he give me a packet of herbs for two quid and mum boils 'em up for me—terrible taste it was. I never got a pain after."

"But that's your stomach," I said. "I want my legs back."

"It all comes from the stomach." Peter spoke with conviction. "Doctors know nothing when it comes to these Chinese herbalist

blokes." He rose to his feet and looked out the hut door. "I'll hobble
Kate and let 'em out, then we'll turn in." He looked up at the stars.
"The Milky Way's running north and south. It's gonna be fine. It's
when she's east and west you get the rain. Well, I won't be long."

When he returned he said, "Now, what about a bed for you?"

He looked carefully round the earth floor of the hut then walked
over to a small hole beneath the wall. He took the paper in which
the corned beef had been wrapped and stuffed it into the hole
with his fingers.

"Might be a snake hole," he muttered. "We'll hear that paper
rattle if he comes out." He laid two half-filled chaff bags on the
floor and flattened them till they formed a mattress.

"There you are," he said, "that should do you. Lie down there
and I'll chuck this rug over you."

I took my boots off and lay upon the bags with my head resting
on my arm. I thought it was a beautiful bed. Peter lay down upon
some bags he had prepared for himself, yawned noisily, and pulled
a horse rug over himself.

I lay awake listening to the sounds of the bush. It was so good
to be there I didn't want to sleep. Through the open door of the hut
the smell of gum and wattle released by the night came moving
across my bed. The wild cries of plovers going over, the call of a
mopoke, the rustles and squeaks—these created a presence in the
darkness. Then, softly through the other sounds, came the notes of
the horsebell and I sank back relaxed into the chaff mattress,
seeing, as I fell asleep, the long striding gait and swinging head of
Kate ringing her Mongan bell.

Next day the bush through which we travelled became more
stately, more aloof. As the trees increased in height, isolation from
them became greater. They thrust their pure, limbless trunks two
hundred feet above the earth before crowning themselves with
leaves. No struggling scrub cluttered their feet; beneath them
was a strange silence.

Our tiny waggon with its tiny horses moved slowly, sometimes
scraping some huge root-spur as we followed a turn in the track.
The jingle of trace chains and the soft thud of hooves on the
springy earth were small sounds that did not venture beyond the
nearest tree. Even the creak of the waggon took on a plaintive note.
In open spaces where the thin, wild grasses scarcely hid the earth,

mobs of kangaroos stood watching us, raising twitching nostrils to get our scent before bounding away.

"I've shot 'em," Peter declared, "but it's like shooting a horse; it gives you a crook feeling." He lit his pipe and added mildly, "I don't say as it's wrong, but a lotta things that ain't wrong ain't right either."

That night we camped on the bank of a creek. I slept beneath a bluegum and as I lay on my chaff bags I could see the stars beyond its branches. The horsebell sounded a clearer note. Sometimes it rang with sudden vigour when Kate clambered up a bank or descended to the creek, but it was never silent.

"We'll reach the camp today," Peter told me in the morning.

The post-splitters' camp lay on the side of a hill. It came into view as we rounded a spur—an open patch shorn from a fleece of trees. In the centre of the clearing were two tents with a campfire burning in front of them. Blackened billies hung from a tripod over the fire and four men were approaching it from where they had been working on a fallen tree lower down. A team of bullocks stood at rest beside a stack of split posts, while the bullock driver sat on his tucker box beside the waggon eating his lunch.

Peter had told me about the men who were camped here. He liked Ted Wilson, a man with stooped shoulders, a wispy, tobacco-stained moustache, and merry blue eyes embedded in wrinkles. Ted had put up a slab house about half a mile from the camp and lived there with Mrs. Wilson and his three children. Peter's opinion of Mrs. Wilson was divided. He considered her a good cook but complained she liked "howling about people who died".

Stewart Prescott, one of three other men who camped on the site, was a young man of twenty-two, with wavy hair. He had a huckaback waistcoat with round, red buttons like marbles, and he sang "Save My Mother's Picture from the Sale" in a nasally voice. He accompanied himself on the concertina and Peter regarded him as a great singer, but "a proper darn mug with horses". People called Stewart Prescott "The Prince" because of his flash clothes, and he had gradually become known as Prince Prescott.

He had once worked in the bush below our home. Father rode into Balunga with him one day. When father returned he told me, "I knew that fellow couldn't ride; every time he got off the horse he did his hair."

Arthur Robins, the bullocky, came from Queensland. When Peter asked him why he left that state, he explained, "Me wife lives up there." Arthur was a little man with stiff, wiry whiskers in the midst of which a large, red, pitted nose stood naked to the weather. Peter thought Arthur looked like a wombat. "Every time I see him I feel like hiding the spuds," he told me.

Arthur did not mind comments on his appearance but he resented any reflection on his bullocks. He once told the barman at the Turalla pub, in explaining why he had just been fighting a mate, "I stood him abusing me, but I wasn't going to stand him running down me bullocks."

When Peter reined in near the tents and climbed down the men were already filling their pannikins from the billies on the fire. When I followed him, each man in the group looked at me with surprise. I hesitated, momentarily confused. Then anger stirred in me and I swung towards them with quick, determined thrusts of my arms.

"That's Alan Marshall," Peter informed the others. "He's a mate of mine. We'll bot some tucker off these blokes, Alan."

"Good day, Alan," said Prince Prescott, feeling satisfaction at knowing me. He turned to the others. "He's the kid that got infantile paralysis. They say he'll never walk again."

Peter turned on him angrily. "What the hell are you talkin' about?" he demanded. "What's wrong with you?"

This outburst astonished Prince. "What's wrong with what I said?" asked Prince, appealing to his mates.

Peter grunted. He took my pannikin and filled it with tea. "Nothing wrong," he said, "but don't say it again."

"So you've gone in the fetlocks, is that it?" asked Ted Wilson, smiling at me. At his words all the men smiled.

"I tell you," declared Peter, "if you could sole your boots with this kid's guts they'd last for ever."

I had felt lost and alone amongst these men even with Ted Wilson. I wished I were home. Then Peter's final remark burst upon me, and I experienced a feeling of elation. He had ensured the respect of these men for me. I felt so grateful to Peter that I wanted to express it in some way. I stood as close to him as I could and when I cut slices from the mutton he had cooked the night before I gave him the best piece.

PETER ALWAYS brought a case of beer down with him each trip, and it was the custom for the men to gather at Ted Wilson's house the night he loaded up, to drink and yarn and sing songs.

Arthur, the bullocky, always camped within walking distance on this night and two sleeper cutters, the Ferguson brothers, came over from their camp to have a drink and a yarn. Prince Prescott and the two other splitters were frequent visitors to the home, and on this night Prince brought his concertina and wore his huckaback waistcoat.

The house was built of upright slabs, the gaps packed with clay. A bark chimney filled one end and beside the chimney an iron tank was fed from a curled piece of bark that caught some of the rainwater shed by the bark roof. There was neither fence nor garden to shield it from the encroaching bush. A thin, stringy bark sapling bowed over it in the wind, and ferns grew thickly before the unused front door. Near the back door an upright log formed a stand for a chipped enamel basin. Back from the house four sapling posts, supporting a bark roof, formed a shelter for a gig, the harness for which was hanging on the dashboard.

Peter pulled his team up in front of the shelter and I climbed down. Two children stood watching me as I placed my crutches beneath my armpits. One little boy, about three years old, was completely naked. Peter, tossing the reins on Kate's back, looked down at him with a pleased smile on his face. "Well!" he exclaimed. He reached out his rough, horny hand and stroked the little boy's back with his fingers. "What a smooth little fella, eh! What a smooth little fella!"

The other boy was about five. He was wearing long cotton stockings, but his garters had broken and the stockings hung around the tops of his boots like shackles. Braces made of rope supported the patched trousers, and his buttonless shirt only had one arm. His hair looked as if it had never been brushed. It stood straight out from his head like the hair on the back of a frightened dog.

Ted shouted at him, "Frank, pull up yer socks! Pull up yer socks! Peter'll think you're some new breed of fowl." The boy bent and pulled up his stockings. "Now take Alan here inside while we take out the horses."

The woman who turned from the open fireplace to look at me

410

as I entered the house wore an expression that suggested she was wagging a tail. Her face was fat and placating and she wiped her soft, damp hands hurriedly on a black apron patched with flour as she came over to me.

"Oh, you pore boy!" she exclaimed. "You're the cripple from Turalla, are you? Would you like to sit down now? I'll get a cushion for your pore back."

I sank into a chair feeling confused and unhappy, wishing I were outside amongst the men, while Mrs. Wilson began questioning me on the "terrible disease" I had. She wanted to know did my leg hurt, my back ache, and did my mother rub me down with goanna oil.

"It's so penetrating it will go through a bottle," she informed me. She also thought I might have a lot of acid in me and it might be as well for me to carry a potato in my pocket wherever I went. "As it withers it sucks the acid out of ya," she explained.

I began to like her after she forgot me and talked of her own diseases. She busied herself around the kitchen as she talked, placing steaming mutton on a large plate on the table and mashing potatoes she had tipped from another saucepan. Straightening her back as if it hurt she told me in the confidential way of one imparting a secret that she would never make old bones. I asked her why, and she replied darkly that her organs were all out of place. "I can't never have no more children," she informed me, then added after a moment's thought, "Thank God!"

"Run and get Georgie's pants and shirt," she said suddenly to Frank. "They'll be dry now." Frank brought them in and she dressed Georgie, warning him, "You come and tell me when you want to go anywhere next time or I'll smack you if you don't."

When Ted came in with Peter he slapped Mrs. Wilson so boisterously on the rump that I felt a sudden concern for her organs. "How's the old woman?" he cried happily. He looked at the table to see what was for tea, then said to Peter, "This is a prime bit of mutton I got. Wait till you taste it."

When the table was cleared after tea and the Miller lamp hanging by a chain from the ceiling was lit, Peter brought in the case of beer and he and Ted worked out on a piece of paper what each visitor was to pay for "the grog".

Mrs. Wilson put the two boys to bed in the other room where I

411

could hear a baby crying. After a while it stopped and she came out fastening her blouse. The two sleeper cutters arrived and their greeting showed they liked her. Then Arthur Robins and the three post-splitters arrived and Ted began filling the pannikins lined up on the table. Each man had brought his own, and though the pannikins varied in size Ted poured the same quantity of beer into each of them.

After a few rounds Prince Prescott began playing his concertina. He swayed his shoulders in an exaggerated fashion, sometimes throwing his head back and flinging his arms above him where, for a moment, the concertina jigged in and out before being swept down again.

Arthur Robins had sat beside me on a box near the fire. A gentle smile of anticipation never left his face. He was fond of songs with a kick in them, as he described it, and kept asking Prince to sing "The Wild Colonial Boy".

"What's wrong with the fella!" he exclaimed testily when Prince, absorbed in the "Valetta", failed to hear him.

The concertina stopped with a wheeze. "Righto," said Prince. "Here we go."

As he began to sing Arthur leant forward on his box, his lips moving to the words and his eyes bright with pleasure.

> *"There was a wild Colonial boy, Jack Doolan was his name,*
> *Of poor but honest parents, he was born in Castlemaine;*
> *He was his father's only hope, his mother's only joy,*
> *The pride of both his parents was the wild Colonial boy."*

This was father's favourite song and when there were men at our place and he had a few drinks in he would sing it, and when he came to the chorus he would shout, "Stand up when you sing this!" When Prince broke into the chorus I took my crutches from against the wall and stood up, and said with quick urgency to Arthur, "Stand up!"

"By God, I will, boy!" he said, and he rose to his feet and crashed his tin pannikin on the table and he lifted his whiskery face and bellowed the chorus. And I sang with him in high, unbroken tones and Peter and Ted and the sleeper cutters rose to their feet and sang too:

> *"Come, all my hearties, we'll roam the mountains high,*
> *Together we will plunder, together we will die;*
> *We'll wander over valleys, and gallop over plains,*
> *And we'll scorn to live in slavery, bound down with iron*
>   *chains."*

"Ah, there's a song now!" said Arthur huskily as he sat down and held out his pannikin for more beer. "It puts great heart into a man when he can see no end to his labourin'."

The song infected Peter with a desire to contribute something stirring. He was too busy drinking to waste time singing, but he knew two lines of an Adam Lindsay Gordon poem that, throughout the evening, he repeated almost reverently.

> *"Between sky and water, the Clown came and caught her,*
> *Our stirrups clashed loud as we lit."*

For a moment after he finished he continued staring at the wall, then he felt impelled to explain the quotation.

"You know what it means, don't ya? Some blokes miss it. This Clown is a fast jumper. He takes off well back, see, and he fairly flies over the waterjump. Now the other horse takes off first but the Clown, coming up fast, takes off behind him and catches him fair over the jump. That's what it means when it says 'between sky and water'. They land together. The other horse bores in as they land—you can bet that—and their stirrups clash. The Clown must have been a well-sprung horse, good bone with plenty of daylight under him. I'd like to meet the bloke that wrote it."

After a time it was hard to stop Prince singing. He sang "The Face on the Bar-room Floor", "The Luggage Van Ahead", "What Will You Take for Me, Papa"?

Each song made tears run down the face of Mrs. Wilson. "Aren't they beautiful?" she sobbed. "Do you know 'There's Another Picture in my mamma's Frame'?"

"I know two verses of it," Prince said. "Now, how's it go . . .?" His eyes closed, he listened to the notes he squeezed from the concertina, then smiled and nodded. "I've got it."

"Quiet over there." Mrs. Wilson looked at Peter and Ted who were talking together but not listening to each other.

413

"This saddle was a bit knocked about—the girth was no good —but I put it in the back of the cart . . ."

"I bought the grey for a fiver," Peter broke in, "I rode him twenty miles that night . . . ."

"It was a Queensland saddle," Ted interrupted, filling his pannikin. "He never turned a hair . . ." said Peter. "I bought a new girth . . ." Ted went on. "Never raised a sweat . . ." Peter addressed the wall.

"Shut up, you two," said Arthur, and Prince began singing:

> *"Come, my baby, tell me why you're crying,*
> *Don't you see it pains your papa so?*
> *Every day for you nice things I'm buying,*
> *And I'd like to see you smile, you know,*
> *Then she said, I know you are the dearest*
> *And the sweetest papa of them all,*
> *If you love me truly, you will tell me surely*
> *Who's the lady's picture on the wall?"*

Prince had the attention of all of us. Even Peter turned to look at him. He broke into the chorus with great confidence.

> *"There's another picture in my mamma's frame,*
> *It's some other lady, her smile is not the same;*
> *My mamma was sweeter, I think it is a shame,*
> *There's another picture in my mamma's frame."*

Mrs. Wilson wept quietly as Prince began the second verse.

> *"Yes, my darling, it's a pretty lady,*
> *And she's going to be your new mamma,*
> *She'll be good and kind to you, and, maybe,*
> *You will love her, so 'twill please papa."*

Arthur drank two pannikins of beer while Prince was singing, and when Prince was finished he informed me darkly, "Any man who marries twice wants his head read."

I was tired and I fell asleep in the chair while the singing continued. When Peter woke me up the party was over.

416

"Arise," he said in the tone of a minister beginning a sermon. "Arise, and come with me." We went out to the gig shelter and Peter suddenly addressed the night:

"*Between sky and water, the Clown came and caught her,*
Our stirrups clashed loud as we lit."

Chapter Eight

Father wanted to know all that had happened to me on my trip with Peter. He was pleased when I spoke excitedly about the staunch horses and how they pulled the laden waggon home with never a slackened trace.

He asked, "Did he let you take the reins?"

He looked away when he asked me this, awaiting my answer with his hands suddenly still on the table.

"Yes," I told him.

He was pleased and nodded, smiling to himself. "A pair of hands is the thing . . ." he murmured, following a train of thought of his own. "You never want to worry over not being able to ride," he added. "I like a good driver, myself."

It was the first time for some years that he had mentioned my not being able to ride. After I returned from the hospital I talked about riding as if it were only a matter of weeks before I would be in the saddle riding buckjumpers. It was a subject father did not like discussing. He was always silent and uncomfortable when I pleaded with him to lift me onto a horse, but at last he must have felt compelled to explain his attitude.

"When you ride," he said, "you grip the horse with your legs, see. When you rise to the trot you take your weight on the stirrups. Your legs can't grip, Alan. There's often things a bloke wants to do but can't."

I did not believe what he said was true. He was always right; now for the first time he was wrong. Even as he spoke it pleased me to think how happy he would be when, one day, I galloped past our house on some arched-necked horse fighting my hold on the reins. One of the boys at school rode an Arab pony called Starlight. Starlight was white with a thin, sweeping tail and a

417

quick swinging walk. He had fine, sinewy fetlocks and trod the ground as if to spare the earth his weight.

Starlight became a symbol of perfection to me. Bob Carlton, who owned him, was a thin boy with red hair. Each lunch time he rode Starlight down to the road-trough a quarter of a mile away to give him a drink. It was a task that took him away from the games in the school ground and he would have avoided it if he had not been trained never to neglect his horse.

One day I offered to do it for him, an offer he quickly accepted. He always rode Starlight bareback down to the trough, but he saddled him for me and legged me onto his back with instructions to let him have his head and he would take me there and back even if I never touched the reins.

When I was seated in the saddle Bob shortened the stirrups and I bent down and lifted my bad leg, thrusting the foot into the iron as far as the instep where it rested, taking the weight of the useless limb. I did the same for my good leg, but since it was not as badly paralysed I found I could put some pressure on it. I gathered the reins in my hands then grasped the pommel of the saddle. I could not pull upon the reins or guide the pony, but I could feel the tug of his mouth upon my hands and this gave me an impression of control.

Starlight walked briskly through the gate then turned along the track towards the trough. I did not feel as secure as I had thought I would. My fingers began to ache from my grip on the pommel, but I could not relax and sit loosely in the saddle believing that, if I did, I would fall. I felt ashamed of myself, but I was angry too— angry with my body.

When we reached the trough, Starlight thrust his muzzle deep in the water. He drank with a sucking sound, but in a minute he lifted his muzzle just above the surface, with water running from his mouth, and gazed with pricked ears across the paddock behind the trough.

Everything he did was impressed upon me with a sharp vividness. I was sitting on a pony with no one to direct me and this was how a pony drank when you were on its back alone with it; this was how it felt to be riding. I looked down at the ground at the scattered stones against which a crutch would strike, at the mud around the trough in which a crutch would slip. They presented

418

no problems to me here. I need never consider them when on a pony's back.

Starlight began to drink again. I leant forward, bending down and touching the lower part of his neck where I could feel the pulsing passage of the water he swallowed. His flesh was firm and he was strong and fleet and had a great heart. I suddenly loved him with a passion and a fierce hunger.

Each day after that I took Starlight to water. I bridled and saddled him myself then led him round to Bob who legged me on and placed my crutches against the school wall. In a few weeks I could ride him without concentrating on keeping my seat, but I still could not rein him in or direct him. I pondered this problem. Before dropping off to sleep at night I designed saddles with sliding grips on them, with backs like chairs, with straps to bind my legs to the horse, but when on Starlight's back I realized these saddles would not help me. I had to learn to balance myself without the aid of my legs, to ride without holding on.

I began urging Starlight into a jog trot the last few yards to the trough, and gradually increased this distance till I was jogging over the last hundred yards, though it was not a pleasant gait. I bumped violently up and down on the saddle, unable to control my bouncing body by taking some of the shock with my legs. Now my mind kept demanding results that my body was incapable of producing. For a year I had to be satisfied with walking and jog trotting to the trough. Then I made up my mind to canter even if I did fall off.

There was a slight rise approaching the trough and when I reached it I leant forward quickly and touched him with the heel of my good foot. He broke into an easy canter and I found myself swinging along in curves of motion, with a new wind upon my face and an urge to shout within me. After that I cantered each day until I felt secure, even when he turned sharply at the school gates.

But I was still clinging with both hands to the pommel of the saddle. I often tried to ride with only one hand on the pommel but the curvature of my spine made me lean to the left and one hand did not prevent a tendency for me to fall in that direction.

One day, while Starlight was walking, I began gripping the saddle in various places, searching for a more secure position on which to hold. My left hand, owing to my lean in that direction could reach far lower than my right while I was still relaxed. I

420

moved my seat a little to the right in the saddle then thrust my left hand under the saddle flap beneath my leg. Here I could grasp the surcingle just where it entered the flap after crossing the saddle. I could bear down upon the inner saddle pad to counter a sway to the right or pull on the surcingle to counter a sway to the left.

For the first time I felt completely safe.

Now I could guide him. With a twist of my hand I could turn him to the right or the left and as he turned I could lean with him and swing back again as he straightened to an even stride. My grip on the surcingle braced me to the saddle, a brace that could immediately adjust itself to a demand for a steadying push or pull.

I cantered Starlight for a little while, then on a sudden impulse I yelled him into greater speed. I felt his body flatten as he moved from a canter into a gallop. The undulating swing gave way to a smooth run and the quick tattoo of his pounding hooves came up to me like music. I kept thinking about father and how pleased he would be when I could prove to him I could ride. I wanted to ride Starlight down next day and show him, but I knew the questions he would ask me, and I felt that I could not truthfully say I could ride until I could mount and dismount without help.

I would soon learn to get off, I reflected. If I got off beside my crutches I could cling to the saddle with one hand till I got hold of them and put them beneath my arms. But getting on was another matter. Strong legs were needed to rise from the ground with one foot in the stirrup. I would have to think of another way.

Sometimes when romping at home I would place one hand on top of our gate and one on the armpit rest of a crutch, then raise myself slowly till I was high above the gate. It was a feat of strength I often practised, and I decided to try it with Starlight in place of the gate. If he stood I could do it.

I tried it next day but Starlight kept moving and I fell several times. I got Joe to hold him, then placed one hand on the pommel and the other on the top of the two crutches standing together. I drew a breath, then swung myself up and onto the saddle with one heave. I slung the crutches on my right arm, deciding to carry them, but they frightened Starlight and I had to hand them to Joe.

Each day Joe held Starlight while I mounted but in a fortnight the pony became so used to me swinging onto the saddle in this fashion that he made no attempt to move till I was seated. I never asked Joe to hold him after that, but I still could not carry my crutches. I showed Bob how I wanted to carry them, slung on my right arm, and asked if he would ride Starlight round while he carried my crutches in this fashion. He did so and Starlight lost his fear of them.

Starlight never shied. I did not realize that normal legs were needed to sit a sudden shy. I was confident that only a bucking horse could throw me and I began riding more recklessly than the boys at school.

One day I came around a corner at a hand gallop. It was beginning to rain and I wanted to reach the school before I got wet. A woman walking along the pathway in front of the church suddenly put up her umbrella and Starlight swerved away from it.

I felt myself falling and I tried to will my bad leg to pull the foot from the stirrup. I had a horror of being dragged. Father had seen a man dragged with his foot caught in the stirrup and I could never forget his description of the galloping horse and the bouncing body. When I hit the metal and knew I was free of the saddle I only felt relief. I lay there a moment wondering whether any bones were broken then sat up and felt my legs and arms which were painful from bruises.

Starlight had galloped back to the school and I knew that Bob and Joe would soon be along with my crutches. I sat there dusting my trousers when I noticed the woman who had opened the umbrella. She was running towards me.

"Oh!" she cried. "Oh! You fell! I saw you. You poor boy! Are you hurt? I'll never forget it!"

I recognized her as a Mrs. Conlon and thought, "She'll tell mum I fell. I'll have to show dad I can ride tomorrow."

"You should never ride ponies, Alan," Mrs. Conlon said while she dusted my shoulders. "It'll be the death of you, see if it isn't." Her voice took on a tender, kindly note and she knelt beside me and bent her head till her face was close to mine. "You're different from other boys. You can't do what they do. If your poor father and mother knew you were riding ponies it would break their hearts. Promise you won't ride again."

Bob and Joe came running up, Joe carrying my crutches. Mrs. Conlon rose, looking at me with tragic eyes as Joe helped me up and thrust my crutches beneath my arms.

422

"Now we'll all shut up about this," whispered Joe, looking sideways at Mrs. Conlon, "or they'll never let you on a horse again." He looked me up and down as we set off for the school. "There's one thing. There's no damage done; you're walking just as good as ever."

Next day I rode Starlight home during lunch hour. I did not hurry. I wanted to enjoy my picture of father seeing me ride. I thought he would place his hand on my shoulder and say, "I knew you could do it."

He was bending over a saddle near the chaff house door when I rode up. I stopped at the gate and called out, "Hi!"

He stood up quietly and gazed at me for a moment. "You, Alan!" he said, his tone restrained as if I were riding a horse a voice could frighten into bolting.

"Yes," I called. "Watch me. Remember when you said I'd never ride? Yahoo!" I gave the yell he sometimes gave when on a spirited horse and leant forward in the saddle with a quick lift and a sharp clap of my good heel on Starlight's side.

The white pony sprang forward with short, eager bounds, gathering himself until, balanced, he flattened into a run. I followed our fence to the wattle clump then reefed him back and round. Stones scattered as he finished the turn; he doubled himself to regain speed: then I was racing back again while father ran desperately towards the gate. I passed him, my hand on the reins moving forward and back to the pull of Starlight's extended head. Round again and back to a skidding halt with Starlight tossing his head.

I looked down at father, noticing with concern that he was pale. Mother came out of the house and was hurrying towards us. She reached out her hand to father as she came up to the gate.

"I saw it," she said, and they looked into each other's eyes a moment. "He's you all over again." She turned to me. "You learnt to ride yourself, Alan, did you?"

"Yes," I said, leaning on Starlight's neck so that my head was closer to theirs. "For years I've been learning. I've only had one buster; that was yesterday."

"Listen, son," father said, looking up at me with a serious face. "We know you can ride now. You went past that gate like a bat out of hell. But you don't want to ride like that. If you do people will think you don't understand a horse. A good rider hasn't got to be rip-snorting about like a pup off the chain just to show he can ride. A good rider don't have to prove nothing. You take it quietly. Don't be a show-off. A gallop's all right on a straight track but the way you're riding, you'll tear the guts out of a horse in no time. Now, walk Starlight back to school and give him a rub down before you let him go." He paused, then added, "You're a good bloke, Alan. I like you. And I reckon you're a good rider."

Chapter Nine

Cars were appearing on the roads, in streamers of dust speeding along highways designed for the iron-shod wheels of buggies. They sent stinging pellets of gravel clattering against the dashboards of gigs they passed and honked their way through groups of road cattle, scattering them in fear. They had great brass acetylene lamps, and upright, dignified windscreens behind which men in dustcoats and goggles leant forward, clutching wheels they sometimes tugged at like reins. Startled horses wheeled and plunged and angry drivers stood erect in buggies brought to a halt far out on the areas of grass that skirted the roadways, and cursed. Farmers left their paddock gates open so that frightened horses could be guided through into areas away from the road where they were held trembling and prancing till the cars had passed.

Peter Finlay was no longer a groom for Mrs. Carruthers; he was her chauffeur and wore a peaked cap and a uniform.

"What do you hug the road for?" father demanded of him. "Everybody's got to get off on the grass when you come along. It's getting so I'm frightened to take a young horse out on the roads. If I could get a horse that would face that car I'd drive straight at you."

After that Peter always stopped when father wanted to pass him with a young horse. Father hated cars, but he told me they were here to stay. He was getting fewer horses to break in now. I was riding ponies he had quietened and was having frequent falls. Ponies, newly-broken, shied readily and I could never learn to sit a shier. But father began teaching me how to fall—relaxed and limp so that the blow was cushioned.

He was quick with solutions to the problems presented by my crutches, but what I was to do when I left school—this he could not answer. Finally, it was only two months to my last day at school. Mr. Simmons, the storekeeper at Turalla, had promised to give me five shillings a week to keep his books after I left school, but though it pleased me to think I would be earning money, I wanted work that would test that part of my mind that was my possession alone. "I want to write books," I told father.

"You can do that," he said, "but how are you going to earn your living while you learn? Anyway, it's no good writing a book just for money. I'd sooner break in horses. When you break in horses you make something good out of something that could be bad. It's easy to turn out an outlaw but it's hard to give a horse— well, sort of . . . you know . . . character, say—make him work with you instead of against you."

We were sitting on the top rail of the horseyard looking at a colt he was mouthing. The horse champed at the heavy mouthing bit. The corners of its mouth were red and raw.

"That colt's too long in the back," he said suddenly, then went on, "If a bloke gave you a hundred quid for a book you can bet your life it's his way, but if all the poor and suffering people raise their hats to you for writing it—that's different; it makes it worth while then. But you'll have to mix it with people first. . . . Write books. But take this job at Simmons's till you find your feet."

Mr. Simmons showed me an advertisement a few days later. A Business College in Melbourne was offering a scholarship in Accountancy to those who could pass an examination in History, Geography, Arithmetic and English. The papers would be sent to local schoolmasters, on application.

I wrote away for these papers and a week later our teacher, Mr. Tucker, told me they had arrived. "You will notice, Marshall," he told me severely, as if I had made an accusation against him, "that the seal on these examination papers is intact. It is therefore impossible to tamper with the papers in any way, I have told William Foster about this examination and he will also be sitting for the scholarship. I'd like you to present yourself at the school at ten o'clock sharp on Saturday morning."

William Foster was Tucker's pet and his star pupil. He could name all the Victorian rivers without drawing a breath and could do mental arithmetic with both hands on his head to show he didn't count with his fingers.

When I met him at school on Saturday morning he was stiff and unfriendly, so I sat by the window, looking at Mt. Turalla, green and vivid in the sunshine. I was thinking of Joe and what a great day it was for rabbiting when Mr. Tucker rapped the desk.

"I am now about to break the seal securing the examination paper's of Poulter's Business College," he said. "You will note that the seal is intact."

He snapped the string and withdrew the papers from the wrapping, keeping his cruel eyes on me as he did so.

For the next twenty minutes he sat reading the papers, sometimes raising his head and looking approvingly at William Foster who lowered his head in acknowledgment.

Then Tucker handed us our papers. He glanced at the clock and said crisply, "It is now ten thirty; you have till eleven thirty to finish this paper."

I looked at the printed yellow sheet in front of me. "Work out the compound interest on . . ." Huh, this was easy . . .

"If ten men took . . ." Cripes, proportion! This was a soda.

"A piece containing four acres three rods two perches . . ." This was harder—hm!

When I compared my answers with William Foster after we left the schoolroom I concluded that most of my answers were wrong, since they didn't agree with his. When I reached home I told father I had failed and he replied, "Never mind. You had a crack at it; that's the main thing."

A week before school broke up a long, brown envelope addressed to me came in the mail. It had been delivered to father and he was waiting in the kitchen with Mary and mother, for me to open it when I returned from school.

They gathered around me as I broke the flap and pulled out the folded paper.

We take pleasure in announcing that you have been awarded a full scholarship . . .

"I've got it!" I exclaimed unbelievingly, looking at them as if for an explanation. Father clapped my back. "Good on ya, son.

426

You're a champion." Then to mother, "What's it for, again? What does it make him?"

"An accountant," said Mary. "An accountant has an office to himself and everything."

"Who's an accountant round here?" asked father. "Would the bookkeeper be an accountant, now?"

"No, but Mr. Bryan would be," said Mary. "He's the secretary of the butter factory. Someone said he gets six pounds a week."

"If he gets that someone's a liar," said father decidedly. "I don't think the *manager* gets that. I'll go find out. But it sounds like our troubles are over, anyway. If Alan ever makes six quid a week he needn't call the king his uncle."

Father saddled a horse and made for the butter factory. When he returned he had further astounding news—William Foster had failed. "And I saw Bryan, too," he went on. "You're right, Mary. He's an accountant, and he told me that top-ranking accountants can get *over* six quid a week. And when blokes become accountants they have letters after their name." He fumbled in his pocket and found a paper. "L.I.C.A. and that means—I've got it here—Licentiate of the Institute of Commonwealth Accountants." He looked at me approvingly. "I never thought I'd live to see the day that Alan has letters after his name." On a sudden impulse he lifted me in his arms, big as I was, and gave me a hug.

For the next week he and mother sat up late at night, working out figures on paper. "Mum and I have decided that we all shift to Melbourne, Alan," father told me one day. "It'll take us a while to fix things up, but when we do we'll pack up our swags and beat it. Your future is down there, not here. I'll get work; that'll be easy enough. And you can take a job in an office while you're learning how to be an accountant." Then he added, "How do you feel about leaving here?"

"Good," I said. "I'll learn to be a writer the same time as I learn to be an accountant. It'll be great, I reckon."

But when, alone, I thought it over, I suddenly felt that I could never leave the bush from which, in some strange way, I gained my strength. I had never seen a city. Now I saw it as some vast complex machine attended by hosts of L.I.C.A.'s with their ledgers and sunless faces. The thought depressed me and I sought out Joe who was setting traps behind his house.

When I told him we would soon be going away to live in Melbourne, he said, "You're a lucky cow, there's no doubt about it. But you always been lucky. Remember when you caught two rabbits in the one trap?"

"Yes," I answered, pleased with the memory.

We sat down together on the grass and talked about Melbourne and of how I would earn six pounds a week.

"You'll have to give up riding," said Joe. "A horse'll come down in Melbourne quicker than anywhere."

"Yes, that's the crook part about it," I said, depressed again.

"I wonder how you'll get on with your crutches down there?" Joe mused. "The crowds an' that . . .?"

"Crutches!" I exclaimed, dismissing the inference contemptuously. "Crutches are nothing!"

Alan Marshall

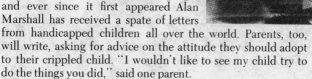

To meet Alan Marshall is an intensely rewarding experience. One is immediately conscious of his aura of power and wisdom, of a raging vitality of spirit and a deep fund of loving kindness.

I Can Jump Puddles has already sold a million copies in fourteen languages and ever since it first appeared Alan Marshall has received a spate of letters from handicapped children all over the world. Parents, too, will write, asking for advice on the attitude they should adopt to their crippled child. "I wouldn't like to see my child try to do the things you did," said one parent.

"Then you are turning him into a cripple," replied Alan Marshall, "for a child is hardly aware of being one. The greatest handicap of the handicapped is the attitude of people towards us, and this problem is the same all over the world."

Though trained as an accountant, Alan Marshall found difficulty in getting work because of his handicap. In the long struggle through the Depression years he had a series of curious and make-shift jobs—nightwatchman in a coffin factory, boarding-house keeper, side-show fortune-teller (which incidentally led to his magazine column of advice for women, *Alan Marshall Says*, which ran for fifteen years) and wanderer of country roads. It was tough going, but furnished him with splendid material, feeding his compulsion to write.

Now in his early seventies and with fifteen published books to his credit, his zest is undiminished. Recently he careered around Europe in his wheelchair attended by one of his daughters and a nephew. His itinerary was characteristically colourful. First to Russia for the launching of his fairy tale, *Whispering in the Wind*, then on to Arctic regions to observe Eskimos and caribou, a visit to a Bactrian camel stud-farm near Samarkand, and to Czechoslovakia for the filming of parts II and III of his autobiographical trilogy, *This is the Grass* and *In Mine Own Heart*. *I Can Jump Puddles* has already been filmed. Finally, he came to London where he received an O.B.E. from the Queen at Buckingham Palace.

Alan Marshall now lives with his sister at Black Rock, a seaside suburb of Melbourne.

GO IN AND SINK !

A CONDENSATION OF THE BOOK BY

Douglas Reeman

Published by Hutchinson, London

ILLUSTRATED BY

Lieutenant Commander Steven Marshall, weary
and tense after months of sea duty, is given his
new command—a captured German
submarine—and ordered to sail her into
dangerous waters on a top secret mission. In
British hands but flying the German flag, *U-192*
is to create havoc—destroy German supply ships,
sink their floating docks. enter seas *verboten*
to all other British ships. even land a beautiful
French spy on the enemy shore. But *U-192* is also
open to attack from friend as well as foe. . . .

This is one of Douglas Reeman's finest tales—
one that will further reinforce his reputation as
the best living writer about fighting men and
the sea, a worthy successor to the great
C. S. Forester.

Chapter 1

IT was nine o'clock on a February morning in 1943 when His Majesty's Submarine *Tristram* edged against the greasy piles at Fort Blockhouse, Portsmouth, and her lines were taken by the waiting shore party.

In the forepart of her conning tower Lieutenant Commander Steven Marshall watched the cables being dragged to the bollards along the pier. In the early morning, while they had idled outside the harbour until the tide was right to enter the submarine base, he had searched his thoughts for some sensation of achievement. Now, as he glanced briefly at the curious faces below on the pier, he could sense little but anticlimax.

For fourteen months he and his men had lived together in their own confined world within this hull, going from one end of the Mediterranean to the other, with each day bringing some fresh threat to their existence. These men, his company of fifty officers and enlisted men, would soon be scattered to the corners of the British Isles to share their leave with wives and girl friends, parents and children, merging for just a few weeks in that other side of World War II; the world of rationing and shortages.

When the leave was over they would be sent to other boats to form a hard core among men like the recruits being trained at this base. They would crew new boats which were being built to replace those strewn across the beds of a dozen disputed seas.

He shivered, feeling the wind cold and clammy across his face. The year was now a month old. What, when his own leave was over, would it have for him?

"All secure aft, sir."

Marshall turned and glanced at his first lieutenant, Robert Gerrard, tall and thin, with the slight stoop brought about by service in this and other boats. He seemed strangely alien in his blue uniform reefer and best cap. For months they had seen each other in almost anything but regulation dress. Old flannel trousers and discarded cricket shirts. Shorts and sandals on mild days.

"Thank you, Bob. Ring off main motors."

From the periscope standards above his head flew their Skull and Crossbones, which the coxswain had cared for so proudly. Sewn around the grinning death's-head were their recorded battle honours —bars for vessels sunk, crossed guns for those hair-raising attacks on ships and coastal installations.

The deck gave a quick shudder and lay still. They had officially arrived. Soon the boat would be stripped and refitted from bow to stern. He sighed. She needed it. There was hardly a square yard without a dent or a scar of some sort. Splinters from shellbursts, buckled plates below from depth charges. The deep furrow across the bridge was from Italian cannon fire outside Taranto.

A wooden gangway had been hauled out from the pier. He saw the captain of the base and some other officers coming aboard to go through the formalities. He did not recognize many of them. He climbed out of the bridge and down the casing.

The base captain was genuinely welcoming, his handshake hearty. "Good to see you, Marshall," he said. "It's a tonic to read what you've done out there. Let's go to my office."

Marshall was tired, and despite a clean shirt and his best uniform he felt dirty and unkempt. You did not shake off submarines merely by the prospect of walking ashore. The smells, diesel and wet metal, seemed to get right inside you. But he was not too weary to notice a sense of urgency.

The captain returned the sentry's salute and led the officers who had come with him to greet Marshall back to the dock. Marshall walked through the familiar gates, allowing the conversation to flow around him. He saw young officers marching to instruction, others sitting in classrooms where he had once sat. Fort

Blockhouse seemed to have altered little. Only he felt different.

They came to a large office, where a fire burned invitingly. A steward was busying himself with glasses, and the captain said cheerfully, "Early in the morning, I know. But *this* is special."

Glasses filled, everyone turned towards him as the captain said, "Welcome home. You and your people have done a fine job." His eyes dropped to the breast of Marshall's reefer. "A Distinguished Service Cross and bar, and damn well earned."

They all raised their glasses, and it was then that Marshall caught sight of himself in a wall mirror. No wonder he felt different. He *was* different. His dark hair, unruly at the best of times, had grown too long over his ears, and he noticed tiny flecks of grey in it. And he was twenty-eight years old.

Marshall could feel the whisky searing his throat, stirring his insides. *Tristram*'s return was special, all right. Five other boats of the same class had left Portsmouth for the Mediterranean. They now littered the seabed, their companies sealed inside them.

The captain said, "I was sorry to hear about young Wade."

"Yes, sir, he was due to come home the week after it happened." The others fell silent as he continued. "We did our commanding-officers' course together, and when I got *Tristram* he was given *Tryphon*. We were always running into each other."

A new voice asked, "How did it happen?"

"We were taking food and ammunition to Malta," Marshall replied. He gestured vaguely. "Nothing but a sub could get in. *Tryphon* left Malta before dawn that particular day. She was never heard of again." He nodded slowly. "A mine, I expect. There were enough of them about!"

As he spoke he recalled his last meeting with Wade. Bill Wade with his black beard and huge grin. The drinks and the áncient Maltese playing a piano in the next room. Almost his last words had been, "Never thought we'd make it, old man. I guess we were just meant to survive." Poor Bill. He had been mistaken about that.

The base captain glanced at his watch. "I think we'd better get things moving. I'll just put Lieutenant Commander Marshall in the picture." The other officers filed out of the room, each pausing to murmur a word of congratulation or welcome.

"Sit down." The captain moved to his desk and leaned comfortably on one corner. "Did you have any plans for leave?"

"Not really, sir." No plans. His mother had died before the war. His father had been commodore of a westbound Atlantic convoy. His ship and several others were sunk by a U-boat pack.

The captain seemed to be hesitating over something. "Fact is, there's a job waiting for you, if you'll take it. I'd not be so blunt about it, if there were more time. But there isn't. It could be dangerous, but you're no stranger to that. The appointment demands every ounce of the experience and skill you have."

Marshall watched him gravely as he went on.

"Ever heard of Captain Giles Browning? Buster Browning they called him in the last war. Got the Victoria Cross for taking his submarine into the Dardanelles during the Gallipoli fiasco."

Marshall nodded. "I read about him somewhere."

"He was out of the service soon after the war. Now he's come back to do various jobs, and has a special appointment in Combined Ops. It's all very vague, but it has to be." The captain was studying Marshall intently. "If you accept, I'll have you whistled up to Scotland tomorrow morning, where you'll meet Captain Browning." He grinned. *"Buster."*

Outside the thick walls a tug hooted mournfully. Why not? thought Marshall. There was no point in spending a whole leave going from one hotel to another. He stood up. His limbs felt strangely light. He nodded. "I'll have a go at it, sir."

"Thank you. I know what you've been through. So do all those concerned. But you are what we need."

A staff officer peered around the door. "Sir?"

"Lieutenant Commander Marshall has agreed." The captain added, "You'd better send for Lieutenant Gerrard and brief him."

The door closed again.

Marshall turned sharply. "What has my first lieutenant got to do with this?"

"He will be *asked* to volunteer to go with you. We must have a perfect team at the top."

Marshall said, "He can't be pitchforked straight into another boat after fourteen months in the Med. He's married, sir. And he's due for a commanding-officers' course at the end of his leave."

"I'll let him have a couple of days at home before he follows you up north." The captain smiled sadly. "Can't be helped. This is important."

436

Marshall thought of Gerrard's face that morning as they had docked. Like a child seeing a Christmas tree for the first time.

A telephone started to ring. "Take yourself off and relax for a bit," said the captain. "I'll see you before you go tomorrow."

Marshall picked up his cap and left.

AT FIRST light Marshall was taken in a staff car to a naval air station a few miles inland. Once strapped into a seat aboard a noisy transport plane, he considered his experiences of the previous day. For the most part they had been disappointing. Embarrassment at showing true feelings had marred his farewells to *Tristram*'s company. It was often so in the service.

Marshall was still not sure what Gerrard had thought about the sudden change of plans. He had seemed more worried about what his wife would think than anything. Of his proposed command course he had said nothing.

When the last of his men had hurried off, Marshall had gone ashore. A taxi had carried him to the house on the outskirts of Southampton, and over each mile of the journey he had wondered what he was going to say to Bill's widow, the girl his best friend had married just two months before they had sailed for the Med. He remembered her well. And so he should! Small and dark, with the vitality and wildness of a young colt.

But his trip was fruitless. She had moved away. No, the present occupants of the house did not know where.

He had returned to the base feeling tired and depressed. He had bought a bottle of gin, and now that was not helping him face the bumpy flight to Scotland. He was grateful for the coffee and sandwiches brought by one of the aircraft's crew.

They flew to Cape Wrath, the northwesterly tip of the British Isles. He could not imagine what they could have up there. The landing field proved to be little more than a strip of tarmac surrounded by mud. Some oilskinned figures emerged reluctantly from a prefabricated hut and ran towards the plane, their bodies bowed to a steady drizzle.

As they gathered up Marshall's luggage a burly marine sergeant squelched across to meet him, gave a stiff salute and gestured towards a dripping car. Marshall climbed in and held to a strap as the car churned noisily across the furrowed ground.

The sergeant squinted through the windshield and said, "Loch Cairnbawn, sir. That's where we're 'eading." He swore as a sheep ambled across the narrow track. "If we're spared!"

It was all but dark by the time they reached the loch. There were barbed wire and armed sentries, and Marshall's identity card was scrutinized. A lieutenant said apologetically, "I'm sorry about all this, sir. Security's pretty tight here."

Marshall nodded. He could see no sign of any ship.

The lieutenant waved towards a small motorboat. "The old *Guernsey* is moored out in the loch, sir. This launch will take you out."

The *Guernsey* was not unknown to Marshall. An old depot ship, coal-fired and extremely uncomfortable, she rarely appeared anywhere these days, except as a temporary accommodation vessel.

It did not take long to reach the moored ship. As the boat plunged and dipped around her outdated stern Marshall saw two submarines tethered alongside.

At the entry port the officer of the day saluted smartly and said, "Nice to have you aboard, sir. Captain Browning is expecting you."

Like much of the ship, the captain's office had an air of shabby opulence. When Marshall entered, Captain Giles Browning stood and thrust out a large hand. "Glad to have you, Marshall." His voice was thick and resonant, his grasp hard. He gestured to a chair. Browning's face was interesting, crumpled and uneven; Marshall guessed he had once been a boxer or rugby player.

The captain's blue, very clear eyes fixed on Marshall's. "I know a lot about you," he said. He seated himself carefully in a big chair. "You've been damn good to achieve your record. But it doesn't follow that you're any use for what I want!"

Marshall came up in the chair with a jerk.

But Browning held up one of his massive hands. "Keep calm. I speak my mind. And as I'm far senior to you, I can speak mine first, right?" A grin spread slowly across his battered features.

Like sunlight on some old ruin, Marshall thought. But he found himself smiling. *Buster!* "*Right,* sir."

"Good. This job is very hush-hush. Has to be. You've been a long time in the Med. You know the picture out there. It's been a hard struggle, but now the Germans in North Africa are on the run. The next thing will be an Allied invasion of Europe." Browning spoke

438

with such calm assurance that it was fascinating. He asked sharply, "Do you know what a milch cow is?"

Marshall started. "Yes, sir. A German submarine that supplies other U-boats. Well over two thousand tons each, or so I hear."

"You probably know that the average U-boat can cover seven thousand miles on an operational cruise. They lose four thousand miles just getting out to mid-Atlantic and back home again. That only leaves three thousand miles to do any damage, right?"

Marshall nodded. He could find no connection between events in North Africa and U-boat operations in the Atlantic.

"So these milch cows can meet their U-boats at prearranged billets. Supply 'em with food and fuel, torpedoes, almost anything they need. They can treble the time that each boat can stay at sea and attack our convoys, and so far we've not been able to track down any of 'em." He took a deep breath. "In the next month or so we can expect huge troop convoys from the States, if we are to exploit the North African successes. If we could bag a couple of their milch cows, or even one, it would make all the difference. It might take weeks for the Germans to realize what happened. Valuable weeks when half of their U-boats are creeping home or running out of fuel and supplies before more aid can be sent to them."

Marshall understood. His new command was to try to run a milch cow to earth. He said, "How can we hope to find one, sir?"

Browning smiled. He was enjoying himself. "Last month a U-boat outward bound from Kiel to the Atlantic developed trouble in her motors. She was not new, but her crew were. Green as grass. The weather was foul at the time, blowing a whole gale, and the U-boat's skipper decided to run for shelter. He chose a fjord on the east coast of Iceland. He took a risk but it probably seemed a good idea—the Icelanders have no love for us and the Americans since we occupied their country." He studied Marshall for several seconds. "Fortunately, the skipper of one of our sonar-equipped trawlers had had the same idea. They met eye to eye, so to speak!"

Marshall stared at him. "And you've captured the codes showing where she'll rendezvous with her supply submarine?"

"Better'n that, boy. We've got the bloody U-boat! She's out there now." Browning's eyes were dancing. "And now we've got a captain for her, right?"

Marshall forced a smile. *"Right,* sir."

Browning beamed. "Thought you'd like the idea." He seized a decanter. "Have some port, *Herr Kapitän!"*

MARSHALL stayed with Browning long into the night, listening to the other man. Capturing the U-boat had been a series of lucky incidents. Once faced by the armed trawler, the German commander had tried to scuttle his boat, only to discover that the strong gale had driven him farther into the fjord than he had intended. The U-boat had come to rest on a hard shoulder, her periscope standards still awash. Caught in the trawler's searchlight, and with a few warning cannon shells whining dangerously overhead, the submarine's crew decided to surrender without further trouble.

The news had been flashed to the Admiralty in London, and within hours an expert salvage team was on its way by air to Reykjavik. At the isolated fjord they raised the U-boat and at the first easing of the weather had her in tow, en route for Scotland.

Browning kept a ceaseless radio and intelligence watch, trying to ascertain if the U-boat had been able to signal her predicament before capture. But as the days wore on he gained confidence that no message had, in fact, been sent.

AFTER a hasty breakfast the next morning Marshall hurried on deck, where he found Captain Browning and two of the ship's officers in conversation by the guardrail.

Browning turned to Marshall and grinned. "Morning!" Then he introduced his two companions. Both were commanders who had been responsible for preparing the U-boat for sea.

One, a bearded man, said cheerfully, "We've had a lot of the gear relabelled. Metres into feet and so on, but most of the technical equipment is as before, so don't forget the fact if you go into a crash dive." Then he added gravely, "Naturally we're not in the habit of stocking spare parts for German subs. You'll have to make do with what you've got. In the meantime I'll get my people to rummage discreetly around. We may need the parts later."

During their long discussion Browning had hinted as much. If Marshall was successful, they might be able to use the U-boat in another unorthodox operation—the kind Combined Operations was set up for.

440

Marshall leaned over the guardrail and stared down at the boats tethered alongside. The inner one was a small submarine—H-class. Browning murmured, "We use her for training and as a guinea pig. She also helps to make inquisitive eyes ashore think we're just doing normal instruction."

Marshall did not hear him. He ran his gaze slowly along the outer craft, feeling a strange sensation in his stomach, a mixture of excitement and uncertainty. Although her conning tower was crudely masked by painted canvas as an additional precaution against prying eyes, there was no mistaking the U-boat's outline and design.

Browning said, "Vicious-looking beast, eh? Her skipper got the Iron Cross after his last cruise." He added bitterly, "Put down twenty-two ships."

Marshall followed Browning and the two commanders down a steep catwalk and across the H-boat to the deck of the U-boat. He looked up at its conning tower, where a seaman was putting finishing touches to a newly painted insignia, a prancing black bull with steam shooting from flared nostrils. The bearded commander said, "Thought it best to invent a new badge for the boat. Just in case Jerry knows he's lost her."

Browning turned. "Your new company has been training for two weeks. It was all the time we could afford. But you can rub off the rough edges while you're on passage to the rendezvous area. After all, I'm not expecting you to start looking for trouble. Just the target we talked about." The blue eyes hardened. "No heroics beyond the job."

Marshall nodded. His teeth were chattering so badly he imagined the others must have noticed. Cold, nerves, or just the apprehension of going straight back into the fire without a break.

They climbed up the straight ladder to the U-boat's bridge. It was narrower and longer than *Tristram*'s bridge, and mounted on a bandstand just behind the conning tower he saw a deadly-looking Vierling gun. Four-barrelled, eighty-eight millimetre cannon with a tremendous rate of fire. He knew that much already.

Then they climbed down into the well-lit control room, which was more spacious than he had expected. Marshall saw the printed instructions that had been pasted over German wording on many of the gauges and dials. One brass plate remained on the bulkhead:

441

U-192. KRUPP—GERMANIA, KIEL—1941. Despite his excitement he felt a chill on his spine.

He asked, "Can we have the main periscope raised?" As he stooped to seize the handles, watching the great periscope as it hissed from its well, he had a sudden picture of those who had gone before him. He could imagine the scream of the klaxon, the commander's eye glittering in the periscope lens as it broke surface. All the world of attack and target being drawn through the small aperture for translation into action, and death. But now, when he swung the periscope slowly in a small arc, he saw only a cluster of houses across the choppy waters of the loch.

Browning said, "She mounts four tubes forward and one aft. She carries fourteen spare torpedoes in pressure-tight compartments. A total of nineteen tin fish! Excellent diesels. Will give you eighteen knots on the surface. The electric motors can do eight submerged."

Marshall looked at him gravely. It was all there on the captain's battered face. Pleasure, pride. But most of all, envy.

Poor old Buster, he thought. He's been left behind.

Browning continued. "You will have one officer who speaks fluent German. Two of your telegraphists are also handpicked for their work with enemy codes and transmissions."

Occasionally men squeezed past them as they carried on with their inspection. Marshall saw their glances. The word would soon get around. The new CO was aboard. What's he like? Wait and see. You never know with officers. And so on.

And here was the wardroom, where he would meet his officers, then the petty officers' mess and, beyond that, the refrigerator compartment, where a supply officer was checking his lists. Forward into the torpedo stowage compartment, the long gleaming fish in their racks. A glance above to the forward escape hatch, a quick look down into the sonar compartment and through the watertight door to the torpedo tubes, four gleaming breeches.

Once or twice Marshall made quick notes on his pad, allowing the submarine's shape and area to form in his mind. Finally he said, "I think that does it."

When they went back aboard the depot ship *Guernsey,* Browning asked, "D'you know a chap called Roger Simeon, by the way?"

Marshall frowned. "Slightly. He was first lieutenant of a sub last time I saw him." He got a brief mental picture of a square, reckless face, short fair hair. A man who would excite any woman's attention.

"He's promoted to commander now, of course."

Marshall waited. *Of course?* What did that mean?

"Bright lad. He's heavily involved in Combined Operations, too. First-class brain, and a real goer. You'll be meeting him shortly."

Marshall darted a quick glance at him, thinking, You hate his guts, don't you? Aloud he said, "I never knew him other than casually at Fort Blockhouse."

"Er, yes." Browning waited for the other officers to move away. "Lieutenant Commander Wade was a good friend of yours, I believe? Damn bad luck about his being lost."

Marshall watched him warily. "We were pretty close."

"You'd better hear it from me then," the captain said. "Wade's widow married Commander Simeon last month."

Marshall turned to stare through a nearby scuttle. He tried to recall exactly what Bill had said in those last days. Had he just discovered about his wife? It was bad in any sense to con a submarine out of Malta through those minefields. If Bill had had that on his mind, it would have been more than enough. It needed only seconds, a few precious moments, for a lack of vigilance to bring oblivion.

He controlled himself with an effort, but when he spoke his voice was flat. "Thank you, sir. I'm glad you told me."

For the next three days Marshall thought of little but the job in hand. He absorbed himself completely in putting his command through every test and trial he could envisage.

During the forenoon of the fourth day he was sitting in his cabin aboard the U-boat, rereading his notes. Gerrard was due to arrive that afternoon, and he would need to have every last detail at his fingertips when he began briefing him.

He found himself thinking about his officers. Apart from himself and Gerrard, there were four of them. A mixed bunch, and still hard to see as a team.

Lieutenant Adrian Devereaux, the navigator, was handsome and well-bred, with the easy drawling tone of one who could be slightly contemptuous of those around him. Lieutenant Victor Frenzel, the chief engineer, was the complete opposite. He had worked his way from lowly junior stoker to commissioned rank by the hardest route. He had dark curly hair, a broad grin, and seemed totally unimpressed by the job he had been given.

Lieutenant Colin Buck, the torpedo officer, had been a garage manager and used-car dealer. Sharp-featured, cold-eyed, he would be a difficult man to know. Unless he wanted you to, Marshall thought. The wardroom's junior member was Sub-Lieutenant David Warwick. He was fresh-faced and outwardly had the innocence of a child. He was gunnery officer and the one picked to deal with German translations. He had passed his submarine and gunnery courses at the top of the list. So there had to be more to him than met the eye.

There was a tap at the door, and Lieutenant Devereaux, officer of the day, announced, "Captain Browning is coming aboard, sir, and Lieutenant Gerrard has landed at the field."

"Thank you, Pilot." Marshall stretched his arms and stood up. "Your department all buttoned up?"

Devereaux shrugged elegantly. "Quite, sir."

Together they climbed to the bridge and met Browning as he heaved himself over the rim of the conning tower.

He looked at Devereaux. "Are you O.O.D?"

"Yes, sir."

"Good. Go aboard *Guernsey* and get all your people back here. I want 'em mustered within the hour."

As Devereaux hurried down the ladder Browning murmured, "Pompous prig. Still, he has a good record." Once in Marshall's cabin he shut the door and said, "You'll be sailing sooner than we expected." He shook his head gravely. "I *know* what you're about to say, and I agree. But something's happened. I've had a signal from Iceland. One of this boat's original crew has escaped from prison camp. He may be dead, frozen stiff, or he could be hiding out or searching for a neutral ship to carry him off the island. But we have to assume that he might be able to blow our secret to the winds."

"I see, sir."

Marshall went to his cupboard and took out a bottle. It would be pointless to mention that Gerrard would arrive shortly with no knowledge of this boat in which he would be first lieutenant—

Number One. Browning watched as he poured two full glasses of Scotch. Then he said, "By God, I wish you were taking me with you!"

"So do I." Marshall was surprised to find that he meant it.

Feet clattered on the casing, and Browning said abruptly, "You can slip at sixteen thirty. It'll be all but dark then. I've laid on the armed yacht *Lima* to guide you out. She'll stand by for your test dive." He sounded tired. "After that, you'll be on your own."

There was a tap at the door, and Lieutenant Frenzel poked his head inside the cabin. "We were wondering if you would join us in the wardroom before we get busy, sir?" He grinned at Browning. "And you, of course, sir."

Marshall nodded. "Thanks, Chief. That would be fine."

Surprisingly, Browning stood up and said, "Sorry. Lot to do. But I'll watch you leave, and I wish you all the luck in the world."

Frenzel nodded. "I'll pass it on, sir." He vanished.

As the door closed Browning said harshly, "I couldn't sit there drinking with Frenzel as if nothing had happened." He thrust one hand into his pocket and pulled out a crumpled telegram. "Came an hour ago. His wife and kid were killed in an air raid last night. If I told him now, it could do no good and might put the whole mission in jeopardy."

Marshall watched his despair. "It *is* the only way."

They shook hands gravely, and Browning said, "I'll tell him when you get back. My responsibility."

They walked up to the bridge, and Marshall watched until Browning had disappeared aboard the depot ship.

It was all his now.

Chapter 2

AFTER the tension brought about by last-minute preparations the actual moment of getting under way was a relief. The weather had worsened, and a stiff wind lashed the waters of the loch into short, vicious whitecaps. Close by, the armed yacht *Lima* lay hove-to to guide them out to the open sea.

Lieutenant Buck climbed up through the hatch to the bridge and groped his way forward to the steel gratings where Marshall stood. "All ready, sir." He had a faint South London accent.

445

Marshall waved his hand. "Let go forward!" He felt the deck lift slightly as the submarine's bows edged away from the H-boat. "Let go aft! Steer two nine zero." He added, "Tell the first lieutenant to con the boat on *Lima*'s stern light."

He watched the rakish armed yacht turning steeply to lead them clear. She was beautiful. A millionaire's plaything in happier times. Probably kept in the Med. Warm nights, tanned bodies, soft wine.

Warwick's boyish face appeared above the bridge screen, shining with spray. "All cables secured and stowed, sir!"

Marshall smiled. Perhaps he had been like Warwick once. It hardly seemed possible. "Right. You can go below."

Warwick asked shyly, "Can I stay here, sir?"

"Of course." Marshall watched the yacht stagger across the first of the inshore swells. "But hold tight."

Somewhere above, an aircraft droned faintly. Marshall thought suddenly of Frenzel. Over the engineer's bunk Marshall had seen a picture of his wife and small son. That had been a bad moment.

Warwick asked, "Do you think we'll get close to them, sir?"

"The Jerries, you mean?" He shrugged. "Could be. You'll have to be all about, if that happens."

Warwick murmured, "I'll try, sir."

Colin Buck said, "He'll look a right little Kraut when he gets his gear on!"

Marshall nodded. They had a selection of German uniforms on board. If they got close enough to need them, the gunnery officer would have to be good indeed.

Buck added, suddenly changing his attitude, "You'll be O.K., David, don't you sweat!"

Warwick relaxed slightly. "It's all right for you. Torpedoes don't need to speak German or *any* language."

The bridge lurched steeply and brought a curtain of spray dousing over the periscope standards. It was getting wilder.

"Able Seaman Churchill requests permission to come to the bridge, sir." The lookout could not restrain a grin.

Churchill was a torpedoman who also acted as wardroom steward. His was a difficult name to have in this particular war.

He squeezed through the hatch carrying a jug and mugs against his chest. He poured thick cocoa into a mug and squinted outboard at the tossing whitecaps. Marshall held the hot mug against his face and watched Churchill slither back into the open hatchway.

A lookout whispered, "Give our love to the war cabinet!"

Churchill's head quivered in the hatchway. "Get lost!"

Buck said, "I hope the torpedoes won't let us down. I hear Jerry has a fair share of duds." He added, "I'll go forward now, with your permission, sir."

When he had gone, Warwick asked, "Was that right, sir?"

"We have our share of duds, too. Nothing you can explain. It just happens sometimes." He called over the speaking tube to Gerrard. "Watch your revolutions. The yacht is making hard going of it. We'll overtake her, if we're not careful."

As the submarine pushed farther and farther from the land the motion increased in steep, dizzy plunges. It would be better once they could clap on more speed. A U-boat was designed to run faster on the surface than they were now going. To chase her quarry and overreach it. Then dive for the kill. Marshall could feel his stomach tightening and guessed that many of the new hands would be in real torment.

At long last they arrived at the arranged position, and as the *Lima* rolled drunkenly in the steep troughs Marshall said, "This is it." He spoke into the tube. "Signal the *Lima*. 'Am about to carry out trim dive.'" To the lookouts he added, "Clear the bridge." He felt strangely calm.

The others hurried to the hatch as Marshall snapped shut the cocks on the two speaking tubes and took a last glance around. Then he lowered himself through the hatch and spun the locking wheel into place. He went down the polished ladder, where a seaman waited to close the lower hatch.

After the stinging wind and spray his cheeks felt flushed in the ordered world of the control room. He ran his gaze over the men around him. Starkie, the coxswain, small and intent at his wheel. The two planesmen, heads tilted to watch their dials. Gerrard, arms folded, standing just behind the coxswain. Devereaux by the chart table. Frenzel leaning on his control panel.

"All set, Number One?" Marshall asked the first lieutenant.

Gerrard turned towards him. "Ready, sir."

Marshall crossed to the forward periscope and swung it gently until he had found the *Lima*'s vague outline about two hundred yards away.

447

"Test fore and aft planes, Number One."

He watched the hydroplanes moving from rise to dive positions, before returning to their horizontal trim. Beyond the periscope he caught a glimpse of a young stoker watching him like a mesmerized rabbit. He gave him a brief smile, but the youth showed no change of expression.

"Hydroplanes tested and found correct, sir."

"Ready, Chief?" He saw Frenzel nod.

He turned back to the periscope. The moment had come. How quiet it was now that the diesels had given way to the electric motors. "Group up. Slow ahead together," he ordered. "Open main vents. Take her down to fourteen metres!"

He depressed the periscope lens and concentrated his gaze on the foreplanes as they tilted downward like fins. It was a sight that never failed to excite him. The bow dropping, the sea surging up towards him while the deck tilted below his feet. He saw spray leaping at him, and as always he was tempted to hold his breath as if to avoid drowning. "Down periscope."

He stood back, bracing his body as he looked quickly over the depth gauges and hydroplane telltales. Gerrard was doing well. Nice and smooth. He watched the big needle edging around, steadying.

"Fourteen metres, sir. Periscope depth." Gerrard sounded hoarse.

"Up periscope."

Again a quick circling inspection. No sign of *Lima*, but he could hear her ragged engine beat without difficulty.

"Down periscope." He clapped home the handles. "Twenty metres." He waited.

Gerrard said, "Twenty metres, sir." They maintained that depth and the same speed for the prescribed half hour. The hull felt as steady as a barrack square.

"She seems fine," Gerrard said.

Marshall looked at the men around him. "Well then, *U-192* is in business." He smiled gravely. "Under entirely new management!"

MARSHALL opened his eyes and stared at the curved deckhead above his bunk. He knew by the silence that the submarine was still dived, that breakfast had not yet begun. He looked at his watch. It was six in the morning. Since leaving the loch eight days ago they had spent most days submerged and most nights running on the surface, charging batteries and checking the inflow of signals.

He licked his lips, tasting the diesel in his throat. It was a pity they had been made to dive overnight, but safety came first. They had driven westward into the Atlantic, avoiding the main convoy routes, avoiding friend and foe alike. The submarine was now about a thousand miles south of Cape Farewell, Greenland, and a similar distance east of Newfoundland. Out here the enemy was not only made up of men. There could be ice, and it was best to run deep.

He twisted his head to look at the German cap which hung behind his door. The one he might have to wear, if every other ruse failed. It had a white top, the mark of a U-boat commander. He had tried it on just once. The effect had been startling.

The passage to the rendezvous area where the milch cows were known to meet the U-boats they tended had been busy with all the usual teething troubles. Faulty valves and inexplicable failures in wiring which had to be traced with the aid of Warwick's translation from the German handbooks.

They had also done their first deep practice dive. It was always a tense moment in any boat, let alone this one. As they had sunk deeper and deeper, to three hundred and fifty feet, with Frenzel and his engine-room hands creeping about the hull in search of faults and leaks, several men must have considered the fact that the boat's skin was less than an inch thick.

Gerrard had been busy with his slide rule and calculations before the actual moment of taking her down. The boat's trim had to be constantly watched and checked. As fuel was consumed the weight had to be compensated. Food and fresh water, even the movement of numbers of men at any one time, such as going to diving stations, had to be allowed for. A bad first lieutenant had been known to let his submarine's bows flounder above the surface at the moment of firing torpedoes, merely because he had not compensated for the sudden loss of their weight.

Every so often there had been a sharp squeak or groan, with gasps from the inexperienced men aboard. For even at one hundred feet there was a weight of twenty-five tons of water on every square yard of the hull. Marshall had listened calmly to the reports coming through the intercom. The Kiel dockyard workers had done a good job.

But everyone had to trust him and the boat. "Three hundred and eighty feet, Number One," he had snapped.

Gerrard had nodded. "Very good, sir."

More groans, and a few flakes of paint which had drifted down like snow as the hull had taken the increasing strain. As she had levelled off, the surface was the height of St. Paul's Cathedral above their heads. But nothing happened, and Frenzel was quite satisfied with both hull and machinery. The dive had given them all more confidence.

Now feet padded past Marshall's cabin and he heard the clink of breakfast cups. He sighed and stretched. Encased in heavy jersey and seaboots, he would have given anything for a hot bath, a shave and a change of clothes. But outward bound it was too wasteful.

"ALL right, make yourselves comfortable," Marshall said as he entered the wardroom. He waited for Gerrard, Devereaux and Frenzel to seat themselves and for Warwick to lay the chart on the table. Beneath the solitary deckhead lamp their faces looked strained and tense. They had now had twenty-nine days of being completely severed from the rest of the world, shut off from reality.

For the past three days they had remained submerged, watching and listening in vain for the milch cow's brief signal as they made their way across the rendezvous area. They had heard only the constant flow of distress calls from merchant ships under attack, instructions from German submarine headquarters, and garbled snatches from warships and aircraft. Marshall found himself wondering if the Germans had changed their plans for refueling U-boats at sea, or had discovered that there was an enemy in their midst. There might even now be U-boats hunting them, changing their role to that of victim.

He looked down at the chart. The submarine's present position was some two hundred miles south of Bermuda, a thousand miles east of the Florida coast. An hour earlier, when they had gone up to periscope depth, he had seen a glistening panorama of pale green sea, catching the sunlight like a million bright diamonds. But Marshall didn't dare risk surfacing anywhere in the rendezvous area until he was sure of a contact with the milch cow.

Reports had been picked up of a heavy enemy attack on a convoy to the east, and Marshall had guessed that the milch cow had taken herself to the position where she would be most greatly needed—to *this* area. Now he was no longer so optimistic.

He said, "I've called this conference to hear your views."

Frenzel leaned forward. "I'm not happy about this enforced diving, sir. We need to ventilate the boat and charge batteries. Later, if we run into trouble, we'll need all the power we can get." He looked bleakly at the solitary lamp. "I've shut down all the heaters, lights and fans I can without driving our lads berserk."

Marshall straightened his back. He said, "We'll surface tonight, Chief. It's the best I can do. I know we're pretty safe from Allied patrols out here, but—"

Buck's voice through the intercom cut him off. "Captain in the control room!"

With the others close on his heels Marshall ran for the brightly lit compartment. Buck said crisply, "Sonar reports HE at two five zero, sir." Hydrophone effect was reported whenever the listening devices picked up sounds, possibly propeller noises or the like.

Marshall strode to the shielded compartment where Speke, the senior sonar operator, was crouching over his controls. "Well?"

The seaman shrugged but kept his eyes on the dial. "Very faint, sir. Single screw. Diesel."

Marshall said, "Keep listening." He tried to hide his disappointment. Whatever it was, it was certainly not the big supply submarine.

He heard Warwick say, "I'll bet it's a damaged U-boat. Coming to another for help."

Marshall swung around and touched Warwick's arm. "You could just be right, Sub!" He looked at Buck. "Bring her around to intercept. Then sound the alarm. Complete silence throughout the boat after that." He held up one hand. "But remember, if this is a damaged U-boat making a rendezvous, we will have to act fast. The attack team must be perfect."

"Steady on two five zero, sir."

"Very well. Klaxon, please."

As the men came running Marshall could feel his weariness falling away. "Periscope depth, Number One," he said, and crouched beside the periscope well.

"Fourteen metres, sir."

"Up periscope." He glanced at the stoker. "Slowly."

He bent double, his forehead pressed against the rubber pad, watching the swirl of silver bubbles, the sudden blinding flash as the lens broke surface. "Hold it there!"

He edged around the well, watching the misty sunlight playing across a long green swell. He could almost feel the warmth across his face, taste the clean salt air. His eye still on the lens, he said, "How is the bearing now?"

"As before, sir, but still very faint," said Speke.

"Full extent." He straightened his body as the periscope slid smoothly from its well. He brought it to full power, but the haze, like steam, was too thick.

"Down periscope." He stood back. "Increase to seven knots, Chief. We'll miss this chap, if we're not careful."

As the periscope hissed into its well Warwick shouted, "Radio operator reports milch cow's signal, sir!" He had his handset to his ear. "Bearing approximately the same as the other boat."

Marshall crossed to the chart. We must make more speed, he thought. The milch cow was probably lying directly ahead of their own course, with the damaged boat somewhere in between.

He snapped, "Group up. Full ahead together. Twenty metres." He was thinking aloud. "We'll get as close as we can to the first boat. Then we'll surface. The supply boat would be suspicious of any of her brood approaching submerged. She'd dive and be away, no matter how much trouble the other chap's in."

Speke said, "The range must be about six thousand yards, sir. It's hard to tell. The one diesel sounds pretty dicey."

Only three miles. But he must not think of this one, limping target. One salvo would send her to the bottom. The other submarine was something else entirely. They must be sure.

"Diesel's stopped, sir."

"*Blast!*"

The damaged boat probably had the milch cow in sight. He could picture it in his mind. The weary lookouts numb with relief as the massive hull heaved in sight. And aboard the supply boat all the busy preparations to pipe fuel across to the battered survivor of some attack. Food and fresh clothing; there would even be a surgeon aboard to care for the sick and wounded.

He said, "Stand by to surface. Continue on batteries, but be ready to switch to main engines as soon as we're spotted."

He looked around at their intent faces. "Sub, you can muster your gun crew. See that they're rigged out in German caps and life jackets." He saw Churchill hovering by the attack table. "Fetch my cap." He knew his words had sunk in. That it was going to be close and quick.

As Churchill scurried away he added quietly to Gerrard, "If we catch it on the surface, Bob, take her deep. Don't try and save the deck party. Just get the hell out of it."

Gerrard nodded, his eyes grave. "Right."

Marshall took the white cap from Churchill, touching the salt-stained eagle, the swastika in its claws. "We'll do a surface attack with four tubes. Gun action as a last resort."

Feet clattered below the conning-tower hatch and he saw Warwick and his gun crew, some of them grinning sheepishly as they adjusted their German caps and slipped into the bright orange life jackets which were always worn by U-boat deck parties.

"Prepare your gun as soon as we surface," Marshall told Warwick. "After that keep your people hanging around. Casual, but ready to move like quicksilver."

They were all staring at him, suddenly moulded together, the strain showing on each unshaven face.

He said, "Periscope depth again," and waited as the deck tilted slightly, the compressed air pulsing into the ballast tanks.

"Fourteen metres, sir."

He licked his lips. Thank God the Germans had perfected the fan method of firing. A British boat had to be aimed at her target or swung at the moment of releasing each of her torpedoes. Every German boat was fitted with a device which allowed each shot to be fired on varying bearings while the boat's course remained constant.

"Up periscope."

He let his breath exhale very slowly. There she was.

He heard Buck intone, "Range four thousand yards, sir."

Marshall ignored him, watching the other U-boat's conning tower as it lifted in the drifting haze. Smaller than this one. Dirty grey in the filtered sunlight. He could see a length of broken guard-rail, evidence of her earlier encounters.

"Down periscope." He strode to the ladder. "Open the lower hatch." He started up the smooth rungs, the gun crew crowding

453

up behind him. Someone had hold of his feet. It was not unknown for a captain to be plucked out of the hatch before the buildup of pressure adjusted itself.

He took a deep breath. "*Surface!*" It had started.

Seconds later he heard Gerrard's voice far below, and with all his strength he swung the locking wheel, feeling the ice-cold water dash into his face as he opened the hatch and dragged himself onto the bridge. The gratings were only just free of water as, with her hydroplanes at full elevation, the boat lurched into the sunlight. He ran to the forepart of the bridge, and saw the other U-boat almost broadside on to their approach.

He trained his glasses on the conning tower and saw a flash of sunlight as someone levelled binoculars on them. He could imagine the Germans' panic at their rapid surfacing, then fear giving way to relief at the realization it was one of their own.

The damaged U-boat was rolling heavily in the swell, her after-casing awash where some seamen gathered below the conning tower. She had not stopped merely because she was awaiting help. Her last diesel must have packed up.

Marshall moved his glasses very slowly. The supply boat might be visible to the damaged one, but not to him. He snapped, "Tell the chief to switch to main engines. Slow ahead together." They were rapidly closing with the other boat, but they must hold back until the milch cow showed herself. The diesels would help make conversation with the damaged boat difficult and ease any remaining suspicion of their arrival.

A light stabbed across the water and Petty Officer Blythe, the yeoman of signals, acknowledged it with his hand lamp. At Marshall's side one of the telegraphists translated breathlessly. "He's asking your number, sir."

"Reply, Yeoman. 'One nine two.'" He added, "Make the coded challenge."

He gripped the screen. Down below Gerrard would be peering through the small attack periscope, ready to dive the instant things went wrong. The wrong code, a false acknowledgment, and . . .

Blythe murmured, "Reply, sir. 'U-one five four.' Requests that we take her in tow, sir. Has too much drift to—"

He broke off as a lookout said sharply, "There she is! Fine on the port bow!"

Almost simultaneously Marshall heard Gerrard on the speaking tube. "Target in sight, sir. Bearing red one five. Range five thousand yards. Closing."

At first Marshall could see nothing, and he cursed as he wiped moisture from his glasses. Then he saw the great supply boat edging out of the haze like some vast nightmare creation. She bore little resemblance to a normal submarine and her upper hull was like that of a partially completed surface craft.

Blythe hissed, "Blimey, she's a big un!"

Warwick, leaning on the guardrail, was waving his cap towards the damaged boat while some of his men pointed and gestured like old comrades.

Gerrard's voice again. "All tubes ready, sir."

Marshall replied slowly, "You must carry out the attack from the control room. If they see me using the bridge sights—"

"What shall I reply, sir?"

Marshall glanced at the yeoman. He had almost forgotten the Germans' request for aid.

"Make to them that we are going to cross their port bow. Stand by on the forecasing with heaving lines." He shouted to Warwick, "Make it look as if we're trying, Sub!" He saw Warwick wave, and Petty Officer Cain dragging a spare cable and fastening it to a heaving line.

"Range now four thousand five hundred yards, sir." Gerrard sounded very cool. "Tubes one to four ready."

Marshall bit his lip. The damaged boat was barely four hundred yards away now. It would have to be soon. At any moment the Germans might notice something.

Gerrard called, "We can't torpedo the damaged boat, sir. The explosion would finish us, too."

"Yes." He beckoned to a lookout. "Pass the word to the gun crews. Rapid fire on the damaged boat when I give the word."

The other lookout said, "The Jerry's got a megaphone, sir! He's gettin' ready to chat when we gets a bit closer!"

Marshall's eyes were again on the milch cow. She was moving very slowly, like some great slab of grey pier, her upper deck alive with tiny figures.

A voice echoed tinnily across the heaving water, almost drowned by the mutter of diesels and the hiss of spray.

Slowly he removed his cap and waved it towards the damaged U-boat. It seemed to do the trick. The other captain spread his arms and pretended to hurl the megaphone overboard in disgust.

"*Sir!*" The lookout's voice made him freeze. "Smoke! On the starboard quarter."

"Control room! This is the captain. Smoke on the starboard quarter. Check it with the main periscope."

An agonizing pause, and then a voice called, "One ship, sir. On the horizon."

He barked, "Start the attack!"

The speaking tube went dead; then he heard Buck's orders being passed across the intercom. "Fire one!"

Marshall felt the steel screen kick gently against his chest. Pictured the first torpedo as it shot towards the milch cow.

"Fire two!"

On the forecasing one of the seamen was whirling a heaving line around his head, playing out the long, dragging seconds.

"Fire three!"

Marshall snapped, "Get *ready!*" Again the little kick. Like a conspiratorial nudge.

"Torpedoes running, sir!" The last one was to have been for the damaged boat, but she was too near now.

The lookout called, "Ship on the starboard quarter is closing, sir. One funnel. American destroyer, probably."

Marshall nodded, unable to drag his eyes from the outline of his target. He pictured the torpedoes streaking through the water.

The first explosion was like a thunderclap. In a split second Marshall saw the forward portion of the enemy's hull burst open and upward in one great searing orange ball of fire. The remaining torpedoes' detonations were all but lost in the devastation.

On the damaged U-boat the first stricken horror had changed to a wild scramble of running figures, some of whom had already reached the deck gun, where an officer was firing his pistol blindly across the narrow strip of water. Marshall ducked as a bullet clanged into the tower and shrieked away over the sea. He could see nothing of the milch cow. Just a huge pall of drifting smoke against the sky, a spreading pattern of oil and bobbing flotsam to mark her last dive.

He yelled, "Full ahead together. Port ten!"

456

He watched as Warwick's crew brought the Vierling's long muzzle around across the rail, following the other boat as it appeared to career drunkenly on their mounting bow wave.

"*Shoot!*" The gun bucked back on its springs, and a savage glare lit up the bridge. Marshall saw the other boat's periscope standards and radio antennae reel apart as Warwick's gunners found their mark. Another shell slammed into the exposed ballast tank, and it was possible to hear the surge of inrushing water. Some of the German gunners were running aft towards the tower. It was futile, for without engine power the U-boat was helpless.

The Vierling crackled viciously, the four barrels cutting down these same running men with the ease of a reaper in a field. The officer, isolated and alone, was reloading his pistol when a shell smashed him into oblivion.

U-192's conning tower shook violently, and a waterspout rocketed skyward a hundred yards from her side. Marshall knew the answer even as the lookout yelled, "Destroyer has opened fire, sir!"

Marshall spoke steadily into the speaking tube. "Secure the gun! Clear the bridge!"

Men tumbled into the hatch, dragging with them the machine guns, one still smoking as it vanished. Wild eyes and breathless voices, until only Marshall remained. The destroyer was approaching, her skipper probably imagining he had caught two U-boats in the act of sinking an unidentified ship.

Marshall crouched over the speaking tube as a shell screamed low overhead, the shock wave hitting his shoulders. "Dive! Dive! Dive! Ninety metres! Shut off for depth-charging!"

He closed the cock and paused to peer abeam. The stern of the stricken U-boat was just poking out of the seething bubbles and escaping oil.

Then he jumped into the hatch, feeling the hull falling steeply as Gerrard took her into a crash dive. He slammed the hatch and locked the wheel. Down into the control room. The lower hatch banged shut and he turned to meet Gerrard's gaze. "Done it, sir."

Marshall clung to the ladder, his chest heaving. He managed to nod. Then he replied, "Not too much time in hand." He felt completely spent and sick. Two submarines and some hundred and fifty men. Wiped out just like that. He swallowed hard. He hoped that Browning would be satisfied. Mission accomplished.

Overhead he heard the thrumming beat of the destroyer's racing screws, and then a depth charge exploded some distance away, like a muffled drum in a tunnel. The destroyer's detection gear had probably homed onto the sinking submarine.

He glanced at the men all around him as they listened and then understood. They were safe.

Chapter 3

Two days after her successful attack *U-192* had received a brief signal in her own top secret code. "Return to base forthwith."

The first part of the return passage had gathered something like a holiday atmosphere, as the boat had headed northeast, avoiding shipping lanes and spending most of the time on the surface. The men took turns on deck, sunning, and once even swimming.

When they had drawn nearer to the convoy routes and into the range of patrolling aircraft they had twice been faced with disaster. The first occasion had been while they were surfaced, charging batteries. A fat Sunderland flying boat had plunged out of low clouds, machine guns hammering, depth charges dropping from either wing, as the U-boat dived frantically for safety. Off the coast of Ireland they had been caught again, this time by a twin-engined fighter streaking out of the mist barely feet above the water. The bullets had clanged across casing and bridge.

For two days they had idled back and forth west of the Outer Hebrides, awaiting the right moment to meet their guide, the armed yacht *Lima*. During those last days Marshall had had plenty of time to watch his companions. Daily he had found it harder to meet Frenzel's eye or to join him in casual conversation. Soon Browning would break the news about his wife and child. And Gerrard seemed to grow more restless as hour by hour they crawled back and forth.

Marshall had spent less time than he would have liked with young Warwick. In the two months they had been at sea he had altered from a boy to a hollow-eyed stranger. Marshall was fully aware of the reason. He had seen him in the control room when they had heard the damaged submarine breaking up as she plunged to the seabed. Warwick had been shaking uncontrollably, his face like chalk. Marshall had heard Buck saying quietly to Gerrard one

459

night, "What can you expect, Number One? He's just a kid, seen nothing, knows nothing but what he's got from books. Then it all became real. And nasty."

It was to be hoped that some shore leave would make a difference. Otherwise, he would have to recommend that Warwick be transferred out of submarines. Too much depended on each of them. They needed one another's strength.

At the arranged time, as dusk was falling, they had turned towards the land. The sound of a small charge detonated underwater had told them their guide had arrived, and they had gone to periscope depth again, and followed *Lima*'s blue stern light in to the shore. When they surfaced, Loch Cairnbawn seemed exactly as before. It was April now, but the air was as keen as a knife, the choppy water just as dark as when they had left the place.

When he saw the tall side of the depot ship Marshall touched his face, thinking of a bath and change of clothes. He saw the lines snaking across a beam of light, heard the shouts from the waiting seaman, the grate of mooring cables.

"Stop together." He felt the bridge begin to roll as the loch's uneasy waters took charge.

He lowered his face to the speaking tube. "Ring off main motors. Send some extra hands up to help rig the awnings around the conning tower, just in case we're still on the secret list."

Feet clattered on the casing and a head appeared over the rim of the bridge. It was one of Browning's aides. He thrust out his hand and said, "Glad to see you! Captain Browning is waiting for you, but he wants to see your engineer officer first. What a rotten welcome for him."

Summoned, Frenzel thrust himself through the hatch. "What's all this, sir? I've a lot to do."

Marshall said quietly, "Get along over to Captain Browning. Your chief petty officer will watch things for you."

After a pause Frenzel replied, "Very well." He looked at the commander but did not seem to see him.

He knows, Marshall thought. He's guessed already.

WHEN Marshall walked into the big cabin below the *Guernsey*'s bridge, Browning strode across the carpet, both hands outstretched. "I can't say what it means to see you back safely."

Browning moved to the decanter and glasses, saying, "I saw Lieutenant Frenzel. He didn't say much. I think he knew why I'd sent for him." He handed a glass to Marshall and raised his own. "Well, here's to you, anyway. You've done damn well. I'm bloody proud of you." It was whisky, neat and fiery. After two months without any, Marshall could feel it going to his head.

They sat down opposite each other. Browning swallowed some whisky. "You bagged the milch cow, which the enemy'll be relying on still. We've heard nothing to suggest they know you sunk her." He shook his head. "And you caught another U-boat for good measure. Marvellous."

Marshall listened to the wind sighing against the hull. Despite the cabin's steamy heat he felt cold. He needed to bathe and change. Adjust his mind to an absence of danger.

Browning said suddenly, "The Admiralty has required us to hand over the captured codes. Escort group commanders, hunter-killer frigates and the rest will use 'em to full advantage. They insist that it will do far more good than individual operations like yours."

Marshall let the whisky burn across his tongue. "I expected that, sir. But of course it will mean that the enemy will realize what's happened just that much sooner. The codes will be changed. And what of us? Do we become His Majesty's U-boat and take a conventional place in things?"

Browning did not smile. "Well, not exactly. It is felt that you can do a lot to help in the same unorthodox way as before."

The door opened and a crisp voice asked, "All right to join the party, sir?" He did not wait for permission but strode in, a briefcase under one arm.

Marshall made to rise, but the newcomer waved him down. "Not to bother. You look bushed." He smiled, but without warmth.

"This is Commander Simeon." Browning sounded unusually formal. "He's been running our liaison with Intelligence."

Marshall eyed Simeon thoughtfully. Well-pressed and impeccable. The man who had married Gail, Bill's widow.

Simeon turned to Browning. "I'll take a glass, if there's one going, sir."

Marshall darted a quick glance at the elderly captain. It was sickening to see the way he shambled over to get a drink for his subordinate.

461

Simeon removed a pink file from his briefcase and opened it, one hand outstretched for the whisky. "Cheers," he said.

Marshall watched him coldly. No wonder Browning was in awe of him. This man was going somewhere, no matter who got in his way.

Simeon frowned and ran a finger down the file. "Strange how luck comes into even the best-laid plans. That Jerry who escaped from the Icelandic camp, for instance. He was found half-dead with cold less than a quarter of a mile from the place. But the fear of his escape was enough to get things *moving*, to send you off to sea double-quick. Without that, you'd have been rotting here in the loch for weeks." He looked at Browning. "By the way, sir, Operations has *U-192*'s report. I think they'd like your opinion." He walked to the table and picked up the decanter. "About now, I think, sir."

Browning walked to Marshall's chair. "I'll see you later." He did not turn towards Simeon as he added hotly, "Damn good to see a real submariner again." He slammed the door behind him.

Simeon shook his head. "Pathetic. Four years of war and we're still bogged down with old-age pensioners like him."

Marshall replied evenly, "Not too many pensioners about with Victoria Crosses, I'd have thought?" He smiled. "Sir."

"Possibly, but I'm not here to discuss him. The important thing is that I, that is *we*, have another job lined up." He leaned on the desk, his eyes very bright. "The Atlantic battle is on the turn. More U-boats sunk, more convoys getting through. In North Africa the Germans will be forced to surrender or get out. After that the Allies will have to mount an invasion in Europe." He lowered his voice slightly. "The top secret label is on this, of course, but we're going into Sicily and up through Italy. Our people will try to make a secret pact with the Eyeties, so that as we advance they will come over to our side."

Marshall watched Simeon. He could not see what Gail had found in him, what had made her turn her back on Bill.

"For years we've had agents in every occupied country, supplying anyone who can pull a trigger or place a dagger in Jerry's ribs. These partisans, patriots or bloody bandits, call them what you will, are the ones who can help us."

Marshall asked, "Where do I come in?"

"Where you have the best chances of continuing to use deception. In the Med. You know the stamping ground well. You will operate whenever and wherever you can do the most good. Cloak-and-dagger operations. Later, landing raiding parties. That sort of thing."

Marshall eyed him coolly. How much time had Simeon put in at sea? he wondered. "I can see the possibilities," he said. "But this last job taught me that it's no fun being hunted by your own ships and aircraft. It's a double strain on my crew to be an enemy of both sides. And what about leave?"

"Leave? You have to be joking. It's asking a helluva lot from you. I know it. But we simply can't afford to allow the grass to grow under our feet."

Marshall stood up, seeing himself in the bulkhead mirror, tousled hair and oil-stained sweater against Simeon's sleek image. "I'd like to tell my officers in my own way, sir."

"Certainly. Might be able to wangle a couple of days' leave for a few special cases." He was groping vaguely through his briefcase when he asked, "I believe you knew my wife at one time?"

Marshall watched him. "Yes."

"Splendid." He was being very casual. "I've got a commandeered house a few miles from the loch. You must drop in and have a bite to eat." He swung around. "How about it?"

"Thanks." Marshall paused. "It was bad luck about Bill Wade."

"Wade?" Simeon smiled distantly. "Oh, yes, it was. Hardly any of the old crowd left now. Frightful waste." He snapped the briefcase shut quickly. "See you tomorrow." He strode to the door.

For a few quick seconds Marshall had seen through Simeon's façade of efficiency and self-control. It could have been resentment harboured because he had known Gail even before Bill.

He picked up his cap and left the cabin. When he reached *U-192* he found his engineer officer alone in the wardroom, staring at the glass between his fingers.

"All right, Chief?" Marshall's voice was soft.

Frenzel stared up at him. "You *knew*, didn't you, sir?"

Marshall nodded. "Yes. I'm sorry. I had to agree."

Frenzel pulled another glass from a locker. "I'd have done the same in your shoes." His hand shook as he slopped gin into the glass. "Join me?"

463

Marshall sat down slowly. "I think I can arrange leave for you, Chief. Before we shove off again."

Frenzel drained his glass, some of the gin running down his chin like tears. "Leave? Thanks, but no. What I like about the sea. You get lost in it. You forget."

He stood up and carefully removed two photographs from his bunk. As he laid them in his wallet something dropped across them. This time it was not gin. He said quietly, "Don't worry about me. I'll be all right."

Marshall moved towards the door. "I never doubted it."

WITHIN two days of her return to Loch Cairnbawn things had started to move rapidly for *U-192*. Almost hourly, or so it appeared to Marshall, mysterious experts arrived to whisk the submariners away to some new instruction. Shooting with pistols and automatic weapons. Hauling each other up and down gullies and cliffs. After the first grumbles they had settled down to their training with enthusiasm. It was different, and they had soon become hardened to the exercises and the Scottish weather. They discovered, too, that they had drawn closer together as a unit.

On the last full day of training Browning had come to Marshall and said, "Thought you ought to know. The Germans will learn today that we have the crew of *U-192* as prisoners of war. We couldn't keep it secret forever. It's not humane."

"They'll know about us then, sir."

Browning had shaken his head. "Not as far as I can discover. The German crewmen were taken away before our people got to the fjord. As far as they know, their boat is lying on the bottom where they left her. But when you go on your next mission you'll be without your cover. *U-192* has ceased to exist. Your guise for each operation will be as you think fit. Visual, rather than having false papers, so to speak."

Browning had had a bit of good news, too. Some leave had been granted. Local liberty for the bulk of the company. Forty-eight hours' home leave for a handful of others. Gerrard had gone south to see his wife. But most of the men remained on the *Guernsey* while *U-192* got a going over. They restricted their runs ashore to the naval canteen and nearby pubs.

A twenty-year-old stoker named John Willard went ashore on

local leave with no intention of returning at all. His desertion cast a pall of gloom over the rest of the company, spoiling their well-justified pride in what they had achieved.

Simeon said of the deserter, "He must be caught and brought back. I don't care if some MP blows his stupid brains out!"

It was never healthy to keep a man aboard a submarine who tried to desert. There was too much scope for willful damage when a man hung under a cloud like that. But it was equally unsafe to let the man pass through court-martial and punishment, where he might blurt out the secret of *U-192*.

The young stoker was picked up within fifty miles of the loch and brought back to the *Guernsey*. As Marshall sat that afternoon in his borrowed cabin wondering what he should say to the man, Simeon stepped in and slid the door shut behind him.

"You going to see this chap now?" He threw his oak-leaved cap onto a chair. Marshall nodded. "By the way," Simeon said, "you'll be shoving off in about two days' time. Your orders will be arriving later this afternoon. I'll fill you in on details."

Marshall was about to answer when there was a tap at the door and Devereaux stepped over the coaming, his features urbane as he reported, "Prisoner and escort, sir."

The stoker was duly marched in and stood between his escort and Starkie, the coxswain. Willard was small and round-faced, looking even younger than his years. In his best uniform, he presented the perfect picture of innocence and vulnerability.

"What do you want to tell me, Willard?" Marshall kept his voice calm.

"Say, sir?" Willard looked about to crack. He shuffled his feet.

Devereaux said, "Tell the captain why you tried to desert."

"I dunno what to say, sir." Willard's chin trembled slightly as he added, "It's me mother, sir."

Marshall dropped his gaze to the desk. "If your mother is sick, you should have come to one of your officers."

Willard spoke very quietly. "Me dad's a prisoner of war, sir. Only heard last year. We all thought he was dead. When I was on me last long leave I went home." He swallowed hard. "She was—" He tried again. "She was with this bloke."

Marshall said, "All right, Cox'n, you and the escort can fall out." He looked at Devereaux. "You, too."

The door closed behind them. Marshall wished Simeon had gone with the others. He asked, "Is that why you headed for home?"

The stoker nodded jerkily. "She wrote to me, sir. This bloke had been knocking her about. Threatened to carve her. He's been living off her, you see. *Put her on the street.*"

Marshall looked up, seeing the agony on Willard's face. He asked gently, "What did you hope to do?"

"All this training we've had, sir. I've never been no good in a scrap, but those commando blokes taught me *how*, sir. How to fight dirty, to win."

The telephone jangled on the desk, and Marshall snatched it up. "I said no calls!"

It was Browning. He was speaking very quietly. "Sorry about this. Is Simeon still with you?"

Marshall said, "Yes, sir."

Browning coughed. "Bit awkward. I've got a call on the ship's line from the base. Personal. For you." A pause. "Can you take it? I'm afraid she says it must be now."

The phone crackled as Browning transferred the call. Then a woman's voice said, "Lieutenant Commander Marshall, please."

"This is Marshall." He heard her quick intake of breath.

"Steven, this is Gail."

"Well?"

"Roger's going to ask you to come over to the house." She spoke quickly, as if afraid he would hang up. "I knew you'd make some excuse not to come, so I thought if I—if I said I *wanted* you to . . ."

Marshall cleared his throat. "Right." What the hell was he saying? "That will be fine." He put down the phone.

Simeon said sourly, "Browning? Couldn't it wait?"

Marshall looked at the stoker. "You've been a fool, do you know that? You were going to pick a fight with some tough and probably cut his throat into the bargain. What good would that do for your mother?"

Willard said in a whisper, "Had to do something, sir."

"Right now I'm depending on you, Willard. Your place is among your friends, people who rely on you."

He was only half listening to his own words. Why had she called him like that? Taking the risk of rousing Simeon's suspicion.

He continued. "I'll get the welfare people to check up on your story. If it's true, I'll do what I can. If not, I'll see you stand trial. But either way, I want you *here*, under my command."

"Yes, sir. Thank you very much, sir."

"Fall out." The stoker turned and almost tripped over the coaming as he stumbled through the doorway.

Simeon opened his cigarette case. "Hell, his mother's on the street and he wants to save her!"

Marshall stood up, suddenly sick of Simeon. "What would *you* have felt?" he said.

Simeon raised his hands. "Keep your hair on!" Then he said in a matter-of-fact tone, "Come to dinner tonight."

Marshall's answer came out firmly. "Thanks, sir. I will."

MARSHALL studied himself in the mirror for several seconds. Despite a steward's efforts, his best uniform still showed a few creases in the wrong places.

"All set?" Simeon appeared swinging his cap. "Now you look a proper hero, or as Buster would have it, a *real* submariner!"

Marshall smiled dryly. "Two a penny around here, I imagine."

Together they made their way to the upper deck and then into a waiting motorboat. Their shoes rang hollowly as they walked to a well-polished car, and a seaman stepped out, holding the door for Simeon to enter the driver's seat. Simeon waited for Marshall to get in and then called to the seaman, "Give her a good polish again tomorrow." He spoke as if the man were a personal servant.

Once past the gates Simeon pressed on speed with a practised recklessness. Marshall wondered if the importance he attached to his driving skill meant he secretly envied a man who had seen close combat. The car was a good one. Expensive.

In about half an hour they shot through a wide gateway and slithered to a halt. Simeon glanced quickly at Marshall. "It's not much of a house. But I got the admiral to lend me one of his chefs, so the food's palatable."

It was a very pleasant house, comfortably furnished. A log fire burned cheerfully in an open grate, and the room to which Simeon guided Marshall gave off an air of rural prosperity.

"A few others for dinner, I'm afraid. Can't be helped." He gestured to a cabinet. "Mix yourself something. I'm going to wash." He

467

added, "Not like you. Didn't get time before I left the *Guernsey.*"

Marshall smiled. Simeon always had to prove that he was the busy one. A man in constant demand.

He opened the cabinet and regarded the bottles with surprise. No shortages here. He selected some malt whisky and half filled a glass. It could turn out to be a tense evening. A door opened behind him and he turned, the words ready on his lips. But it was not Gail.

The young woman was dressed in a tweed skirt and plain black jersey. In the soft lamplight Marshall thought she looked tired.

He said, "I'm Steven Marshall."

He watched her as she moved to a chair. Very easily and lightly. Like a cat. She had short dark hair, and her eyes, which were large and partly in shadow, seemed very steady.

She said with a faint French accent, "Chantal Travis." Then she smiled. "My home was in Nantes."

"Are you staying here?"

She smiled again, but she did not answer his question. "I see you have many decorations. More than I expected."

Simeon must have told her about him. "There's a war on."

"So I believe." She sounded distant. "A war."

He said quietly, "That was a damn stupid thing to say. I was forgetting. Is your family still in France?"

She nodded slowly. "My father and mother are in Nantes."

Marshall remembered her name. Travis. "You're married?"

Again the slow nod. "An Englishman." She looked at the glass in his hand. "If I may have a choice, I would rather have a drink than any more questions." She smiled at his confusion. "Pardon me. That was unforgivable."

Marshall held up some sherry and she nodded. As he poured it she said, "Commander Simeon's wife told me about what you did in the Mediterranean."

He handed her the glass. "Have you known her long?" He groaned. "God, I'm doing it again."

She laughed. "It is all right. No, I met her recently."

Marshall sat down opposite her. It was like some invisible force between them. Holding him back. If only he had more time, he would like to stay with her. Just to hear her voice, watch the stillness in her.

468

Voices murmured outside and Simeon strode in with two army officers. One Marshall recognized as a medical corps major. They shook hands all around and the conversation became general.

Marshall tensed as a voice said, "Hello, Steven. After all this time." Gail was wearing a flowered dress which left her arms bare. She was exactly as he remembered her.

He rose. "You look marvellous."

Her hand felt ice-cold despite the blazing fire, and he thought it was trembling slightly.

Simeon called, "New dress? Bit bare, old girl, what?"

The major murmured approvingly. "You make a sight to remember. Don't listen to him."

The dinner was excellent—plentiful food and ample wine. As the steward poured the brandy he bent down and whispered in Simeon's ear. Simeon stood up. "Dispatch rider outside. Better go and see what's he's brought." He looked around the table. "Make yourselves comfortable."

The two army officers escorted the French girl to the adjoining room. Marshall looked at Gail. They were alone.

She said quickly, "I had to see you. To tell you about Bill."

"I *know* about Bill." He could not hide his bitterness. "Saw him before he was killed."

"You don't understand," she said. "How can you?"

"Perhaps I don't. All I know is that while Bill was in the Med you decided to leave him to marry Simeon. What else is there?"

She stood up and walked to the fireplace.

"Why did you ever marry Bill?"

"You know why." She met his eyes steadily. "I wanted you, but you were so sure you were going to be killed, remember? So damned sure."

Marshall stared at her. "D'you know what you're saying?"

She nodded. "I've had plenty of time to think about those days we had together. I've never regretted one of them." She swallowed. "Not one. But I wanted to marry, to have a home."

He said, "I'm sorry. I was very fond of Bill."

She moved towards him, her eyes searching his face. "Be honest, won't you! When I married him you felt guilt, too, didn't you? Because you remembered how it was before."

She was almost touching him. "Oh, Steven, you've changed so

469

much." She reached out and took his hands. "The war has turned you into a machine!"

He looked down at her, his defences crumbling. Then his arms were around her and her face was against his chest. The words burst out like a flood. "I *have* to be the way I am. You don't know what it's like. Always telling others to keep going, to remember the ship, the fight, the target, *anything* to hold the whole show together! I couldn't have let you share that sort of life."

She said, "I would have. Willingly."

His hands were on her bare shoulders. "What about Simeon?"

She did not lower her eyes. "He gives me assurance. In his own strange way he needs me." She shook her head. "But *we* had something else again."

The door creaked and Marshall saw her eyes fill with alarm. He turned quickly. But it was Chantal Travis.

She stood very still, looking at them. Then she said, "Sorry. The wrong room, I think."

When the door closed behind her Gail said, "One day, Steven. If we could meet somewhere. No recriminations. No comparisons." She was pleading.

Perhaps his anger at her marrying Simeon had been caused by his own loss, as well as by Bill's. Whatever the true reason, it was too late now. "It's no use," he said. "It's over."

"Only if you want it to be, Steven."

The door swung open again. Simeon looked at them blandly. Then he strode over and put his arm around her shoulder. "Old confidences, eh? Ah well, the party's over, children."

Marshall nodded. In more ways than one, he thought.

Chapter 4

THE day after Simeon's dinner party Marshall received a sudden change of orders. The time had been brought forward twenty-four hours. He would slip from the depot ship at 20:00 that evening.

As the sides of the loch dipped into shadow he sat in his cabin making a last-minute check. Gerrard, who had arrived back that forenoon, waited in the doorway as Marshall signed his readiness report. Marshall said, "Can't think of anything else. Have you inspected the new gear?"

Gerrard nodded. He looked tired. "Yes, sir." He smiled sadly. "Back to the Med. Would you believe it."

Buck peered in. "Commander Simeon is coming aboard, sir."

"Very well. We'll be slipping in about thirty minutes."

Gerrard moved away as Simeon appeared in the doorway. He said crisply, "Buttoned up. Ready for business. Last mail ashore and censored. Twice. I don't think we've forgotten anything."

"Why was the sailing time brought forward, sir?"

"There's a westbound convoy gathering at Greenock. Don't want you to get bogged under with that lot. *Or* with this boat's previous masters, if they're hanging around after that convoy."

"Captain Browning's not back from London yet?"

"What's that got to do with it?" Simeon frowned.

Edgy. It was as Marshall had suspected. Simeon had brought the time forward so that Browning, called to a meeting at the Admiralty, would not be here to see them go. It would be *his* show.

Simeon said, "You will be picking up three agents from one of our launches. I've already had their gear sent aboard, but their presence must be kept secret to the last minute."

Marshall stood up and they walked into the passageway and on to the control room, where Frenzel was leaning over his panel in close conversation with his chief petty officer. If it were possible, Frenzel had given even more energy and time to his engines since Browning had told him about his family.

Marshall led the way up the ladder, and they stood on the bridge watching the men slacking off cables. A voice rattled up one of the tubes. "Captain, sir. Radio operator reports ten minutes to go. *Lima* is on station to lead us out."

"Acknowledge."

Simeon said, "I'd better get over to *Guernsey*'s radio department, in case anything goes wrong at the last minute and I have to make new decisions." He held out his hand. "Good luck, then." He swung over the side of the bridge and dropped to the deck below.

Marshall moved to the speaking tube. "Control room. This is the captain. Prepare to get under way. Main motors ready."

Yeoman Blythe said, "There's *Lima*, sir. Just coming around *Guernsey*'s bows."

"Good."

He thought suddenly of Gail. The feel of her skin. The smell of

471

her hair. "The war's turned you into a machine," she'd said. Damn her. What could he do about it?

A light stabbed from the *Guernsey*'s bridge, and Blythe shuttered his acknowledgment with the hand lamp.

" 'Proceed when ready,' sir."

"Very good. Inform the control room." He hesitated, knowing Blythe was waiting. It was expected. The thing to do. "Make to *Guernsey*, Yeoman. 'Thanks for your help.' " He doubted they would ever tie up alongside her again.

"Let go aft!" He waited. "Slow astern together." He waved to Buck. "Let go forward!"

Stern first, they edged clear of the towering depot ship, the water sluicing along the saddle tanks.

"*Lima*'s gathered way, sir."

"Very well." He crossed to the speaking tube. "Stop together." He watched the pale blue stern light. "Slow ahead together. Port twenty."

"First lieutenant here, sir. Follow the light again?"

"Yes." He heard the periscope shift in its sleeve. "We will be taking on passengers in an hour's time."

He felt the hull steady as the rudder came around, and knew that Gerrard had her under control. "Fall out casing party."

The seamen came swarming onto the bridge and down through the open hatch. Then Warwick, dragging his feet, his head towards the dark slab of land.

"Keep a good lookout." Marshall glanced at Blythe's outline. "The launch will signal. But check the code." He turned to Warwick. "Not like our other departure, Sub."

"It seems no time since we got back, sir. And now—" He did not finish it.

"I know. Can't be helped." Marshall watched the last of the light fading above some hills. "I wasn't expecting to go back to the Med." The words just seemed to come out. "Not after fourteen bloody months of it." He clenched his fists. Saying it was enough. Fourteen months. How long would it be this time?

Warwick asked, "Was it that bad, sir?"

"No." He felt the sweat under his cap. Ice-cold. "Nothing we couldn't handle." Liar. Liar. Why don't you tell him?

He added harshly, "Tell the helmsman he's too far on *Lima*'s port quarter! And, Sub, you're supposed to be able to stand a watch, so *do* it!"

"Yes, sir. I'm sorry." Warwick groped for the speaking tube.

Blythe watched them and sucked his teeth. Warwick was a good kid but wet behind the ears. Thank the Lord it wasn't one of the other officers on the bridge, he thought. That tough egg, Buck, or old "Snooty" Devereaux. They would have recognized the skipper's trouble in a flash. Poor bastard. He's got to carry the whole lot of us. But it's him who needs help.

On and on down the loch, following the light, with only a gentle swish of water to break the stillness.

Then, "Control room to captain." It was Gerrard. "Should be making the pickup at any minute now, sir."

"Very good, Number One. Tell Petty Officer Cain to get his cable-handling party on deck at the double."

Blythe called, "Signal from *Lima*, sir. 'Boat to starboard.'"

There it was. On the button. A black blob across the loch.

"Stop together." He climbed onto the starboard gratings to watch the little launch as it chugged towards the idling submarine. Then the jolting groan of timber against steel, and scrambling figures were hauled onto the casing. He heard the seamen and their passengers groping and stumbling through the hatch, and wondered what sort of men volunteered for such dangerous missions.

He said to Warwick, "Tell Lieutenant Buck to come up and relieve me. I'd better greet our visitors."

Warwick said quietly, "I can do it, sir."

Marshall could feel the intensity of Warwick's eagerness. He said, "Of course, Sub. She's all yours."

He hurried down to the wardroom and almost cannoned into Churchill, who was carrying a coffee pot. The three passengers were unbuttoning their hooded windproof jackets. One, sharp-featured and tall, turned and thrust out his hand. "I'm Carter. We'll try to keep out of your way, Captain."

Marshall smiled. "Good to have you aboard."

The man added, "This is Toby Moss, and I think you know our third member. Mrs. Travis." She was watching his face with an expression of tired gravity.

"Yes. We have met," he said quietly. He added, "We've two spare bunks in here for the men. Mrs. Travis will have my cabin."

Carter removed his jacket and sat down. He said, "I expect Commander Simeon has told you your part in things."

Marshall nodded slowly, his eyes on the girl. She was sipping coffee, holding the thick mug with both hands. "Yes, he did. Your equipment is stowed forward."

She looked up and saw him watching her. "I hope you enjoyed the party last night, Captain?" Her eyes were mocking or accusing, it was hard to tell.

He replied flatly, "Some of it." He left the wardroom and when he reached the bridge he took several deep breaths. He wondered about this girl. Perhaps she was a friend of Simeon's. And now she was here, penned up with the rest of them until . . . He thought suddenly of her tenseness. Her way of watching and listening. She was, like him, going back to something and hating it.

DURING the first two days of the passage south towards the Bay of Biscay, Marshall saw the girl only a few times. Each time it seemed as if she had not moved. Always sitting in the cabin chair, wide-awake.

On the third day he sat in the wardroom drowsing over a cup of coffee. The motion was sickening, for the boat was running on the surface, and the sea was rough. When he looked up he saw her standing in the doorway, clutching the swaying curtains. He got up and piloted her to one of the bench seats.

She said, "It's terrible. I've just been sick."

Marshall said, "I'm sorry. The bay is often like this, I'm afraid."

She stared at him. "Biscay? Are we there already?"

"We're about two hundred miles southwest of Brest. We're pretty safe out here, if we keep our guard up."

"Brest. I've been there several times."

He asked carefully, "Your husband? Is he in France?"

She shook her head. "Italy. We were working together. But I cannot talk about it."

"I hope my lads are looking after you?"

"Thank you, yes. It is like being with friends." She shivered. "I will miss this security."

He said gently, "They'll miss you, too. As I will."

The girl stood up, her features alert again. "I imagine that you will have much to fill your daily lives, Captain."

474

He watched her as she moved unsteadily around the table. "You were wrong about Gail and me, you know. It was something which happened a long while ago. It's over now."

"It's not my concern!" She swung around and looked at him with something like anger. "I don't care what you do!"

In the doorway she encountered Gerrard. "Would it be possible to go on deck?" she asked him. "The air might help."

Gerrard looked at Marshall, his eyes questioning.

Marshall nodded. "Very well. Tell the bridge. Warwick's on watch now. Ask him to fit her with a harness."

"Thank you, Captain. I appreciate it."

After they had left, Marshall went to the control room. He swung the forward periscope in a full circle, watching the spray bursting over the hull and lifting high above the bridge in long tattered streamers. Visibility was very poor. He could picture Warwick and the lookouts with the girl, standing just below the periscope standards. Warwick would hear the periscope moving and joke that the captain was trying to watch them. He swung the lens towards the sky, then froze. There was a brief flash between the clouds. He stared, mesmerized. There it was again.

"Klaxon! Aircraft on the port bow!" He clawed his way up the ladder, his mind blank to everything but that menacing shadow. It might not have seen the submarine in such turbulent waters, but one thing was certain, nobody on the bridge had seen it.

As the klaxon screamed out from below, Marshall hauled himself through the hatch, yelling, "Aircraft! Port bow!" The girl was holding on to the screen, and he tore at her harness. "Clear the bridge! Diving stations!"

As the diesels cut out, Marshall heard the plane's approaching roar. He pulled the girl towards the hatch. A lookout guided her down. A great wave burst over the conning tower, and he heard the sharp rattle of machine guns, the clang and whine of metal on metal all around them. A huge shadow swept across the bridge. The plane was barely a hundred feet overhead.

Despite the urge to get below, Marshall could only stare at the seaman on the edge of the hatch. His hands were like claws as they dug at his chest, his blood mingling with the spray. Someone pulled the man below, and Warwick almost fell after him.

Marshall jumped onto the ladder, the sea spurting up over the

475

screen even as he slammed the hatch and spun the locking wheel. He had to shut his ears to the man's terrible cries, to everything but the need to get the boat away.

"One hundred metres! Group up, full ahead together! Shut off for depth-charging!" He saw Gerrard watching him. "Liberator. Must have extra fuel tanks."

They looked at the depth gauges and then at the telltales as the planesmen fought to pull her out of the dive.

"Hundred metres, sir," Gerrard reported.

Something creaked violently as the hull took the pressure. A seaman jerked with alarm, as if it were a depth charge. But none came. The airmen had been as surprised as they had been with the sudden encounter.

It was very quiet when Buck said, "He's dead, Captain."

Marshall turned and stared at the little group below the conning-tower hatch. The dead lookout flat on his back, Buck and the girl on their knees beside him. Warwick was standing slightly apart.

The girl said huskily, "It was my fault. I shouldn't have gone up there." She reached out and touched Warwick's hand. "You couldn't help it." There were bright tears in her eyes.

Marshall's voice was flat. "You must always anticipate enemy bombers." What was he saying? It had been a Liberator. One of their own. Probably winging back to base now to report they had jumped a U-boat and gunned down some of the deck party.

He continued, "Take the body to the torpedo space. We'll bury him tonight." He heard the girl sobbing quietly and took her arm. "Come on. We need some coffee."

It was a week after their nerve-jarring confrontation with the patrolling bomber that they had again had a most testing moment, this time while getting through the Strait of Gibraltar. Two British destroyers had been sweeping back and forth, carrying out a patrol. Fortunately an ancient, rusty Turkish freighter had come to their rescue, albeit unknowingly. She had steamed towards the destroyers with careless indifference.

Submerged, the submarine had followed her past the destroyers, keeping so close that any sign on the British sonar would be attributed to the freighter.

Unseen past Gibraltar and along the Spanish coast, past the

Balearic Islands and Corsica. Several times they had been made to run deep, as fast-moving vessels had pounded overhead, or some suspicious ship had been sighted. Now they were in enemy territory, patrolled by aircraft from Italy and Sardinia.

Marshall stood by the chart table watching as Devereaux skillfully managed parallel rulers and dividers. Devereaux straightened up. "That's it, sir. We will be at the rendezvous point in thirty minutes."

"Captain, sir?" A messenger hovered by his elbow. "Major Carter asked if you'd mind joining him in the wardroom."

He had hardly seen any of the passengers since the bay. They had been getting all the rest they could and going over their plans for their mission. For *now*.

He strode to the wardroom and paused in the doorway studying the three. The girl was wearing a black coat and sat on one of the bench seats, a suitcase on her lap. Moss had changed into a leather jacket and wore a jaunty beret. As for Major Carter, he could have been any European businessman.

Carter asked, "What d'you think, Captain? Good enough for first night at the Duchess Theatre?" He grinned. "Take care of my army clothes, won't you? Or I'll have it docked from my pay."

Marshall nodded. "I've told Petty Officer Cain to have your gear taken to the forehatch."

Carter said, "Come on, Moss. We'd better check it before we leave." They strolled out of the wardroom.

Marshall said quietly, "I hope everything goes well for you."

She stood up. "Thank you. So we are at the proper place?"

He watched the shadows below her eyes, wanting to touch her.

"Yes. Midway between Corsica and the island of Elba." He hesitated. "Will it be difficult?"

"Once we have left you we will be taken to Elba. When the time is right we shall cross to the mainland." She made it sound so simple. Yet it was over ten miles from Elba to the Italian coast. She continued quietly, "We will pick up the train and make our way south. To Naples. Then we shall see."

"The major seems a pretty competent chap."

"Yes, he's good. We will travel together, but separately, if you understand me. If one gets—" She looked away. "You know what I mean. If that happens, the others keep going."

478

He moved closer and took her hand in his. "I wish to God you were staying here."

"So you said earlier, Captain." But she did not remove her hand.

"Or that I were coming with you."

She smiled. "They would sniff you out in five minutes! But thank you all the same." She gave a small shrug. "I am sorry for some of the things I said."

He said, "I hope we can meet again."

"You'll soon forget about me. That is good." Then she said quickly, "But maybe we *will* meet someday." She picked up her suitcase and he followed her into the control room.

Gerrard said, "All ready, sir."

He glanced at the clock. It was two o'clock in the morning. "Very well. Pass the word. Silent routine in the boat."

He hung on the moment, watching the girl as she waited for a seaman to guide her towards the rest of her party. She turned as if to watch the transformation. From a man who wanted, needed her to stay. To being a captain again.

He said, "Slow ahead together. Group down." A look through the periscope showed the lights of a small fishing fleet some miles away. "Stand by to surface."

It was surprisingly warm on the open bridge. Marshall heard a swishing sound as the rubber dinghy was hauled through the big forehatch. It was always a bad time. With the hull surfaced and the hatch open. Unable to dive if the worst happened.

He held his breath and then steadied his glasses on a small shadow moving on the water.

A lookout confirmed it. "Boat, sir. Starboard beam."

He snapped, "Stop together. Make the signal!"

Buck flashed a shaded flashlight towards the shadow and Marshall waited. He could almost feel the tracer bullets which could come shrieking out of the darkness. Instead he saw a brief stab of light. He let out his breath and called, "Cast off the dinghy!"

A splash and then spurts of phosphorescence from the paddles. The dinghy was merging with the night and with the fishing boat, which had slued around to meet them. He thought of the girl who would be going south to Naples, over two hundred miles, and of the many checkpoints, examinations of passes, questions to which she must have the perfect answers.

"Dinghy's returned and secured, sir!"

"Very well. Close the forehatch." He moved to the speaking tube. "Slow ahead together." He was still thinking about her, the immensity of her loneliness. Of his own.

For six days they continued on a southerly course, skirting the Sicilian coast before turning northeast towards the heel of Italy. It was maddening to see the dazzling sunlight whenever they crept up to periscope depth, then to turn and see the men with their worn faces, their bodies starved of fresh air and the sun's warmth.

Marshall sat at his small desk, which was strewn with papers. "We're going into the Adriatic," he said to Gerrard. "It looks as if the enemy will throw in the towel in North Africa anytime now. The Allies will be getting ready to invade their territory for a change, and Captain Browning seems confident that the Germans have been fooled into believing we're going to invade through Greece and up into the Balkans. Our job is to add to that impression. Intelligence reports that a floating dock is being moved down the Adriatic to Bari. So it looks as if they're sold on the idea."

"The dock would be ready to repair any of their large units which might get damaged in our invasion, eh?"

"Right. We're going to blow up the dock with a big bang. Make it look as if we're desperately doing everything we can to make it easier for our side when the big day dawns."

"I see," Gerrard said. "If we have to show ourselves, our future prospects are a bit grim. But it's not a bad scheme. The Jerries will probably move more naval units to the area, and might even send more troops to Yugoslavia and Greece on the strength of it."

"That's the idea." Marshall thrust his hands into his pockets. "Well, like it or not, we're going through the Otranto Strait tonight. After that we'll find the dock."

Thirty-six hours later they were creeping around the Monte Gargano peninsula, one hundred and twenty miles up the Adriatic, keeping close to the Italian shore. It had been easier than Marshall had dared hope to slip through the Otranto Strait, between Italy's heel and the coast of Albania. They had sighted one patrolling destroyer, and had picked up some fast-moving hydrophone effect on the sonar, which had suggested the enemy had some torpedo boats in the area.

Marshall stood by the conning-tower ladder as Devereaux worked on his chart. They had moved past Bari the previous day, but there had been no sign of the floating dock. If they did not meet it in the next few hours, what would he do? Keep going all the way to Trieste, where it was supposed to have started from?

Speke, the senior sonar operator, said sharply, "HE bearing three one zero." A pause. "Slow reciprocating, sir. Still very faint."

Marshall said, "Periscope depth." It did not sound like the target, but they might have to alter course.

"Fourteen metres, sir."

Marshall waited for the periscope to hiss smoothly from its well. A quick look around and overhead, and then on to the bearing, where he saw the other vessel. He said, "A grey motor yacht." It was just possible to see the tiny flag on her mast. "Italian. Antisubmarine patrol."

Behind him he heard somebody murmur, "Thought it was the old *Lima* coming to look for us!" Someone laughed.

Speke called, "Getting more HE, sir, same bearing. Heavier but very faint. Too slow for a warship."

Gerrard said quietly, "One of the dock's tugs—"

The sonar operator interrupted. "Getting jumbled HE now, sir. Might be another ship."

Marshall brought the periscope lens to full power, and he felt his heart thump against his ribs. The dock loomed through the mist, half-shrouded in haze and the smoke from a tug. It was like looking at a giant building which had somehow got swept out to sea.

"Action stations, Number One." He straightened his back. "Down periscope." He shut his ears to the grating klaxon as he said, "Tell Warwick to get ready. We're going in surfaced."

AFTER the cool damp of the enclosed hull the heat on the bridge was fierce. Marshall lifted the glasses and held them on the yacht. She was zigzagging slowly, her raked stem making a show of spray in the bright sunlight. He said, "The escort's skipper's not even seen us yet. When he does, be ready."

Beside him Buck was adjusting the torpedo sights. In his German cap and leather coat he was like a stranger. Marshall shifted his gaze to the casing below. There, too, it seemed as if the boat had been returned to her original owners. Warwick in his cap and

481

shorts, a Luger hanging prominently from one hip, and beside him the gun crew attired in their bright life jackets.

When he looked again at the yacht he saw the towering shape of the dock looming astern of her, its outline still hazy. Heavy smoke beyond the slow-moving huddle betrayed the presence of another tug.

Buck glanced at Marshall. "What d'you think, sir? Shall we fire a full salvo right away?"

Marshall shook his head. "No. If we fire now, we might only hit the yacht. We'll need minimum depth settings on all torpedoes. Otherwise they might pass right under the dock."

He heard the yeoman snap, "They've seen us, sir!" as a light blinked from the yacht's bridge.

Blythe lifted his hand lamp. "Reply?"

"Not yet. Let 'em sweat for a bit."

Marshall tried to picture his boat as she would look to the on-coming vessels. The U-boat's number had been replaced by a large Iron Cross. It had been badly scored by sea and slime, but should appear authentic enough.

"There it is again, sir."

"Very well. Make the reply."

Through a speaking tube he heard one of Buck's team intone, "All tubes standing by, sir."

Marshall licked his lips. "Depth setting of three metres. But we must close the range still farther."

The yacht's course was bringing her slowly towards the sub-marine's starboard bow. He could see a few figures in white uni-forms on her deck and more grouped around a businesslike-looking gun just forward of the bridge.

Blythe asked, "Shall I hoist the colours, sir?"

Marshall nodded. "Yes. We'll go the whole way." He heard the squeak of halyards and saw the big scarlet flag with its black cross and swastika rise to the periscope standards.

Blythe said, "Damn! They've got some lighters tied to the side of the dock, sir." It seemed likely that the enemy had lashed the lighters to the dock's sides as protection. A single torpedo, even a pair, might explode against the lighters without real damage to the dock itself.

Marshall leaned over the bridge screen. "Sub! Get ready to do

482

your stuff in German if they draw closer!" When he looked again he saw the dock fully for the first time. It rode above its reflection like a pale cliff, with a spidery upperworks of derricks and gantries. He saw the lighters, long low craft, four of them. The towing tug was a great brute of a thing. The second one was still hidden astern.

The armed yacht was less than a thousand yards away now and would soon lead the slow procession across the submarine's starboard quarter. The range of the target would be just right.

"Get ready." He lowered his eyes to the sights and held his breath as first the yacht, then the towing tug and then the mass of dock moved ponderously into the sights. "Stand by one to four." He could feel tension all around him. Now or never.

"Fire one!" He felt the hull buck.

"Torpedo running, sir!" Buck held his stopwatch, his sharp features contorted against the glare.

"Fire two!"

Marshall heard the sudden shriek of a siren and knew they had been discovered. He snapped, "Gun crews get ready. *Open fire!*"

The Vierling settled its four muzzles on the yacht. Four lines of tracer ripped across the water with the sound of a band saw. Pieces of wood, steel and rigging were hurled in all directions.

Marshall moved towards the speaking tube and then felt himself hurled backward as a deafening explosion shook the bridge, followed instantly by a blinding blue flash directly below the bows.

Buck was yelling, "Bloody fish must have nose-dived and hit the bottom!" He ducked wildly as a stream of red tracer ripped over the bridge and hammered against the steel.

Marshall was almost unable to speak. If that faulty torpedo had damaged their hull, they might as well surrender right now. But he dragged himself to the speaking tube. "Carry on with the torpedo attack!" The yacht was swinging across their line of advance, with two machine guns firing from the bridge while the deck gun groped steadily towards them.

A dull boom echoed across the water. He swung his glasses on the dock and saw smoke drifting above the lighters, or where two of them had been. Another explosion slammed over the calm water, marking the arrival of their second torpedo.

"All torpedoes fired, sir!"

Marshall cowered against the steel plates as more bullets whined viciously nearby, striking sparks from the metal.

"Bloody hell! We're not hurting it." Buck wiped his eyes and peered at the dock's smoky silhouette.

Blythe called, "Two men wounded on the casing, sir!" Without waiting he bellowed, "Stretcher party to the bridge!"

The yacht was in a bad way. Her slender hull was a pitted shambles, with smoke and darting flames showing from scores of holes. An internal explosion flung a complete length of the deck into the air, and the yacht started to roll over.

"Aircraft, sir!" the lookout was yelling. "Port beam!"

Marshall tried to control his reeling mind. The aircraft was far away, probably over the land which was now hidden by smoke.

Buck yelled, "Another hit!" He was waving his cap in the air.

The torpedo had struck the dock some two-thirds along its tall side. A column of smoke stood frozen against the sky.

A figure blundered through the bridge, carrying a bag with a red cross on it. It was the young stoker, Willard, the one whose mother was "on the street". The boy looked at him and grinned, then leaped over the side and down the ladder to the casing.

The last torpedo hit the dock within yards of the previous one. Another tall column of smoke, but no flames. Marshall stared at the dock's square outline, unable to believe that anything could survive such a battering.

"Aircraft's turning, sir!"

Marshall swung the glasses abeam, seeing it alter its course towards the battle far below.

Buck was shouting, "Shall I clear the bridge?"

Marshall gripped his arm. "No! We must make sure of the dock! Tell the Vierling gunners to stand by to repel aircraft!"

"Aircraft closing, sir!"

He turned as a low, sullen rumble came across the water from the dock. It went on and on like some piece of massive undersea machinery.

Buck gasped. "We got her! She's done for!"

The dock was tilting towards them, very slowly. A tall derrick fell outboard and hung downward above the sea like a dead stork, and other fragments could be seen splashing along the full length of the side. The towing tug was burning fiercely.

Marshall snapped, "That's it! Clear the casing! Prepare to dive!"

He heard the klaxon screaming as the guns fell silent. Men clambered over the bridge, some dragging wounded with them.

The aircraft burst into view just four hundred yards abeam. Marshall saw the stabbing flashes from its guns, the hail of bullets plowing across the water, over the casing and away to the opposite beam. The Vierling followed around, the sharp explosions and darting tracer making some of the running seamen falter.

Buck shouted, "Get below! Move your bloody selves!"

More bangs, and the attendant clang of steel on steel, before the plane streaked out of range to begin another turn. One more attack like that and they might be crippled and unable to dive.

Marshall thrust his mouth against the speaking tube. "Hard astarboard! Full ahead, group up!"

Buck hung over the screen calling, "There's the last of 'em!" It was the stoker, Willard, his round face as white as a sheet. Trying to save a wounded gunner. Trying as he stood alone on the casing to show Marshall what he could do. What it meant to him.

Buck swore savagely and then croaked, "Get below, you fool!"

The plane had turned and now burst out of the smoke, the machine guns firing as before, some whipping through the German flag overhead, some straddling the casing. Marshall saw the stoker, who had reached the wounded man, stagger sideways and then jerk violently through the safety rail to roll over the side.

Marshall shouted, "Take her *down*, Number One!" He saw the stoker's body being washed along the saddle tank, arms and legs moving languidly. The deck was tilting and the air full of noise. The sea was surging up and over the casing. Somehow Marshall's feet were on the ladder. Then he was in the control room as the boat glided down as deep as she dared. He watched the depth gauges, listened to the regular reports from the echo sounder. He knew exactly what was happening, yet felt no part of it.

A deep echo rumbled against the hull. The dock coming to rest on the bottom.

Gerrard crossed to his side. "I've seen to the damage, sir."

He removed his cap and stared at it. The German eagle clutching the swastika in its claws. He walked up and down. Finally he said, "You can fall out diving stations. And tell the cook to prepare a meal." It was as if he had to keep giving instructions.

485

As he walked to the door, Gerrard walked with him. "I'll call you if anything happens, sir." He tried to smile. "You get some rest."

Marshall did not fight back. He replied quietly, "That was a bad one. It seems to get worse every time."

Chapter 5

FOR over a week after sending the great floating dock and its escort to the bottom they had endured the frustration of uncertainty, while Frenzel's fuel levels had dropped and food supplies had become exhausted. It was like being forgotten by that other world to which they listened on the busy radio waves. Then at last the signal had come. When it had been decoded and the references marked on Devereaux's charts, Marshall had headed towards the North African coastline. Someone at last had remembered them and with any sort of luck would have the fuel and supplies waiting to be loaded. And there would be a chance to rest.

They had been on the surface for nearly half an hour, but everything was wet and icy to the touch. Marshall steadied his glasses across the bridge screen.

Gerrard's voice echoed up the tube. "Should have made a sighting by now, sir. We're ten minutes overdue."

"Yes." He moved his glasses slightly to starboard again. Nothing. Nor was there a sound above their own stealthy approach. "Maybe something's gone wrong."

Buck said, "I was thinking. Suppose the Jerries have made a comeback? We might run smack into one of their patrols."

Marshall smiled. "I'm getting so that I can't remember which side I'm really on."

How could he chat, when every second dragged at his nerves and even the placid sea appeared to be full of menacing outlines?

"Sir!" Buck was leaning over the screen. "Boat! Port bow!"

Marshall pushed past him, his heart beating urgently. The boat was little more than a darker blob against the sea. He said harshly, "No wonder we couldn't hear them. They're drifting." He saw the quick stab of a lamp. "Reply, Yeoman."

Blythe shuttered off their recognition code. Instantly a boat's engine coughed into life and a dark shadow edged closer to the submarine's hull. It was a very old boat with the high bow and stern

486

posts of a Portuguese fisherman. But the voice which boomed through a megaphone was British enough. "Just follow me, Captain! The Jerries were thoughtful enough to make a bit of a breakwater with some sunken ships when they were last here."

A bobbing stern light presented itself beyond the U-boat's bows, and they set off towards the invisible shore. Marshall saw something loom past the starboard side. A ship, or part of one, like a buckled, rusting reef, man-made, and left by men to rot. When the war ended, would they ever be able to clean up the debris?

A bright beam of light probed from the darkness and moved slowly along the submarine's hull. Marshall saw a heaving line snaking into the lights, and figures hurrying with fenders to ease the first contact. The hull lurched and the deck party secured the boat against a motionless wreck. A figure was helped over the saddle tank, and even as Marshall ordered Frenzel to ring off the motors a head rose above the bridge screen and said calmly, "So you made it, old son. Good show." It was Simeon.

To Marshall it was unreal and vaguely absurd. Two men meeting out here in the black wilderness. Simeon said, "Let's go below, eh? It's a bit snappy. I'm not dressed for it."

Down in the brightly lit control room Marshall made comparisons. His own men, tired-eyed and in filthy sweaters as they hurried about their business. Simeon, on the other hand, was perfect, wearing pale khaki drill. He followed Marshall into the wardroom and stared around at the untidy interior with ill-disguised amusement. "Really, you chaps have been roughing it!"

Marshall took out a bottle and two glasses. He said shortly, "We sank the dock. Cost us two men—" He faltered, remembering Willard. "I'm still not sure about our damage. A faulty torpedo—" He broke off, seeing the emptiness in Simeon's eyes. He didn't care.

Simeon took his glass and replied, "We heard about the dock from other sources. Good show. The enemy still doesn't seem to know about *you* though." He lifted the glass. "Cheers."

Marshall swallowed the whisky in one mouthful.

Simeon said, "Now don't you worry about a thing. I'll give you your full capacity of diesel fuel before daylight. Water, too, and almost anything else you want."

"Thanks." Marshall could not help feeling admiration.

Gerrard appeared in the doorway. "Could I let some of our hands ashore, sir? They can start taking our gear to wherever Commander Simeon has earmarked for us while we're here."

Simeon eyed him coolly. "Look after the lads first, eh?" He smiled. "But it's not on, I'm afraid. This boat will be out of here by dawn, or I'll want to know why."

Gerrard stared at Marshall. "Is this true, sir?"

Simeon snapped, "Look, I don't intend to discuss my arrangement with everyone. I will tell your captain. He will tell you." He eyed Gerrard for several seconds. "If he feels like it."

Marshall stood up slowly. "Carry on, Number One." He waited until Gerrard had left and then said, "Didn't you see my people when you came aboard, sir? Some of them have been on their bloody feet for days and nights on end!" He could feel his limbs shaking. "What the hell are you asking of them now?"

"*Do* sit down and I'll explain." Simeon regarded him calmly. "The war out here has reached a climax. The Germans are almost gone from North Africa. Everything's geared for an invasion through Sicily. It's a vital time. I don't feel inclined to order a halt while you and your company sit on your backsides!"

Marshall stared at his empty glass. "What is it you want?"

"That's more like it, old son." Simeon took out a fat notebook and flicked through the pages. "The Intelligence people have got word that the Germans have invented a new weapon. A radio-controlled bomb. Once dropped from an aircraft it can be homed by radio onto any large target. No big ships would be safe or capable of maintaining a bombardment for the invasion. The army would have to hit the beaches on their own."

Marshall asked, "Where do we come in?"

"I want you to lift off some agents," Simeon said. "They'll know, if anyone does, what the Germans are up to. If this invasion is to work, we must know for sure what we've got against us."

"A sea pickup?" Marshall looked away.

"No. You must lift them off the Italian mainland. There's an alert out for them. Even now, we might be too late."

Marshall stood quite still, listening to a motor chugging busily as fuel was pumped into the U-boat. Fill her up and get her away by dawn. That was all that mattered to the men onshore. It was unfair. More than that, it was dangerous to push the boat and her crew beyond their limits.

He heard Simeon say quietly, "One of the agents is that French girl. You brought her out here, remember?"

Marshall swung around. "Of course I remember."

"I could ask for a conventional submarine, of course. But under the circumstances, I think this is best."

"Yes. I understand."

"I knew you'd see it my way." Simeon stood up. "There'll be a few Intelligence chaps coming with you."

Marshall followed him out of the wardroom and saw Warwick standing by the conning-tower hatch. "Officers' conference in the wardroom in one hour, Sub." He watched Simeon vanish up the ladder and walked to his cabin. He stared at the bunk, fighting back the urge to lie down and let darkness sweep over him. Then he remembered that she was somewhere on the enemy coast. Waiting for help. For him.

An hour later the assembled officers listened to him in silence. Buck lolled against the bulkhead, his eyes red-rimmed and almost closed. Devereaux was little better, and young Warwick could not stop himself from yawning repeatedly. Frenzel stared at his logbook, his eyes blank and unseeing. Only Gerrard seemed to be holding on.

When Marshall had finished, Buck lurched to his feet. "I'm going to get the spare torpedoes shifted from their containers on the aftercasing while we're still tied up to something steady."

Frenzel also stood up. He looked at Marshall and smiled. "Pity Commander Simeon's not coming along for the ride." He followed Buck through the door.

Devereaux rubbed his eyes and murmured, "Just tell me where, sir. I'll find the right chart for it."

Gerrard said simply, "Good bunch, sir."

Marshall touched his arm, unable to face him. "Best yet, Bob."

"CAPTAIN in the control room!"

Marshall threw himself out of the bunk and hurried from his cabin. He could not recall whether he had been asleep. One second he was lying on his blankets, the next he was at Gerrard's elbow.

Gerrard grimaced. "Just picked up some fast-moving HE at two six zero, sir. Might mean we're getting near trouble."

Marshall nodded and walked to the chart. It had been three

days since they had left their makeshift harbour. Three days of unnatural quiet, as if the whole Mediterranean were taking a brief rest after the months of battle. The strain had been all the greater because of it, he thought. Impossible to relax.

They were now heading towards the well-known bottleneck between Sicily and Cape Bon on the Tunisian shore. Eighty-odd miles over which the struggle for mastery had swayed back and forth without letup, where submarines of both sides hunted ceaselessly. They did not want any trouble now. Not from either side. It would take another two days to reach the pickup point on Italy's west coast and more valuable time to get into position.

He thought of the three Intelligence men in the wardroom, no doubt sleeping while they still had the time. The senior one was a Major Mark Cowan. Slightly built, with a matter-of-fact manner, he looked anything but a regular soldier. From the little he had said, he did not seem too hopeful for the success of the mission.

A radio message had been sent to the agents to tell them the pickup time and rendezvous point. But no acknowledgment was expected. Cowan had said that the Germans had discovered the agents' hiding place, and any radio message from them would certainly kill their last chance of rescue.

"We'll take a look," Marshall said to Gerrard. "Up periscope." He crouched down, his fingers on the twin handles, locking the periscope on to the last bearing, then edging it around. Hold it. Even at full power the ship was indistinct. Probably a destroyer.

"Down periscope." He looked at Gerrard. "Steer three two zero. Take her down to thirty metres."

He turned and saw Major Cowan by the bulkhead door. "A destroyer on patrol," he said. "Well away from us."

Cowan replied, "Not what I imagined. Thought there'd be bells ringing, men dashing about. That sort of thing."

Marshall smiled. Stick around a bit longer, my friend. Aloud he said, "I'm just going to have some coffee. Join me?"

In the wardroom he said, "Will you fill me in on some details?"

Cowan smiled. "What exactly do you want to know?"

"Mrs. Travis. What is her part in all this?"

Cowan sighed. "I was against her getting involved again. She worked in Paris the last time. Being French, her services were invaluable. But her cover broke and she was caught."

Marshall thought of the way she moved. Like a hunted animal.

"Our people managed to get her out of it just in time. A close thing." Cowan shrugged. "But when she was asked to do this job, she agreed without hesitation. Her husband's in Italy."

"I see. So he's working for you, too?"

Cowan watched him sadly. "Actually, no. He's working for the other side. A collaborator. An engineer. Doing the same sort of construction job he was doing in France."

Marshall felt dazed. "And she agreed to see him?"

The major put down his cup. "Did she mention her parents? Well, her father works for the Resistance. He's with the French railways. Very useful contact. And we heard that Travis is getting cold feet. Wants to change sides again. Come home and be forgiven. She is the only one he might listen to. She despises him, but he trusts her."

Marshall looked at his cup, suddenly sick. "And your people let her go back to him. Knowing the Germans might suspect her."

Cowan said, "It is a risk of course, but she is his wife, she has the right papers, and she knows her job." He added quietly, "Travis knows about those new bombs. If we can get him out alive, we might save countless of our own people later on."

"And if she's failed to convince him?"

"Then we'll just have to get what we can from the other agents. We can't know for sure until—"

The rest of his words were lost as the deck gave a sudden lurch, and from the control room came a cry of alarm.

Marshall staggered and almost fell as the hull jerked violently, and he heard a new sound, like a saw on metal, screeching along the submarine's casing. He ran to the control room. Gerrard was clinging to the periscopes, his face like chalk as he yelled, "Blow all main ballast! *Surface!*"

Marshall gripped his arm. "Belay that order! Klaxon!" He could hardly think because of the screeching around him. "What happened?" He had to shake Gerrard's wrist to make him react.

Gerrard stared at him. "The hull plunged. Then that noise!" He looked around as the sound stopped. "I thought we'd hit a wreck."

Marshall said, "Check the trim." To Frenzel he added, "Report damage to hull."

One of the planesmen said hoarsely, "Can't hold her, sir! The afterplanes are jamming. We must have picked up something."

Marshall nodded, seeing Cowan and his two companions in the bulkhead doorway, yet not seeing them.

Frenzel reported, "No hull damage, sir."

Marshall made himself wait for several agonizing seconds. When he spoke he expected to hear a break in his voice. "Take her up slowly, Number One. Periscope depth. If she starts to dive, blow everything."

The sound came suddenly as before, like a jarring whine, ending just as abruptly with a violent clang across the casing.

"Fourteen metres, sir." Gerrard sounded very tense.

"Up periscope." Marshall brought the lens towards the stern and depressed it slightly. There, bobbing close astern, was a mine.

It was covered with green slime, and had probably broken adrift from a field months ago. But it was as deadly as the day it had left Germany. Or England.

To the control room at large Marshall said, "It's a mine. We are towing it about fifty feet astern of us." He saw their stunned expressions. He crossed to the chart. "How about it, Pilot?"

Devereaux wiped his mouth with the back of his hand. "It's a bad place to surface, sir."

"I didn't choose it." He leaned over the table. "Smack in the middle of the strait. Alter course and steer due north." He warned them sharply. "Take your time. The cable is caught around the afterplanes. I don't want that mine veering into the screws!"

Cowan asked quietly, "Couldn't we wait until dark, Captain? If you surface, you might be spotted."

"If we tried it in the dark, we would most likely get blown up, Major." Marshall thrust his hands into his pockets. "Chief, get your men and all the gear you need. As few hands on deck as possible."

Buck said, "I'll take charge, if I may, sir." He forced a grin. "I reckon I've cut up more bloody cars in my garage than the chief's had hot dinners. This is right up my street."

Marshall nodded. "That makes sense." He sought out Warwick. "Automatic-weapon crews stand by."

Tools clanked in the background, and then he heard Buck say, "I'll want that, and that big cutter over there." He sounded satisfied. "Ready when you are, sir."

Gerrard said, "I'm sorry, sir. I should have kept my head."

492

Marshall eyed him thoughtfully. "Not to worry," he said.

Men pushed towards the ladder. Deck party in life jackets and carrying Buck's tools. Gun crews with their ammunition belts.

Marshall said to Gerrard, "Shut off the boat once we're on the surface. If this thing explodes, do your best to get our lads out the escape hatches." He paused. "If you get clear and we don't, Major Cowan will tell you where to go and what to do. It'll be up to you to get those people off." He gripped his arm. "All right, Bob?"

"Yes." Gerrard nodded jerkily. "But watch out."

The lower hatch clanged open and Marshall began to pull himself up the ladder. His voice rang hollowly in the tower. "Surface!"

Lieutenant Colin Buck tugged his cap down over his eyes and stared at the mine, a slime-covered sphere with bobbing horns. He watched a petty officer, naked but for a pair of shorts, crawl along the edge of the casing above the hydroplanes. Despite the dangers of being on the surface in sunlight, Buck felt quite calm.

"Well, Rigby, what d'you make of it?"

The petty officer leaned over the edge and pointed into the U-boat's gentle wake. "The cable seems to be wrapped tightly around the port hydroplane." He squinted up at Buck.

"I see." Buck turned and looked at Marshall's silhouette on the bridge. "Cable's fouled around the plane, sir," he shouted. "It will have to be cut underwater."

Rigby muttered, "Don't fancy that job. Not with a bloody screw spinning around me."

Buck shouted, "If you stop the motors, sir, the weight of the cable will pull the mine into our stern."

Marshall called, "Any ideas?"

Buck looked at his small group of helpers. "My lads will shove that mine clear if it comes any closer." He was stripping off his shirt. "I'll do the cutting."

Rigby grimaced. "Watch out for the undertow, sir. There's always a nasty tug under these boats."

Buck nodded. He fixed some goggles over his eyes and eased himself outboard over the slimy casing, a bowline tied around his waist. The sea was like ice. A shock after the sun's warmth.

He ducked under the water, peering at the cable. It was jagged and coated with rust and growth. He dragged himself into the

warm air again. "Never do it with this wire cutter. Tell the chief to rig a power cutter and be bloody quick about it."

Buck heard Marshall questioning the man who had gone forward with his message. He was a good bloke, this Marshall. Not a bit like some of the stuck-up sods he had encountered when he had enlisted. Men like Marshall made it all worthwhile.

Buck leaned out to watch the screw. One slip. Just one, and it would be his lot.

Rigby said, "Here comes the cutter, sir."

Two seamen were dragging the electric cable aft, the powerful cutter between them. It was a useful piece of gear. Most U-boats carried one, so that a diver could hack through antisubmarine nets and harbour booms while the hull was submerged.

From their position on the bridge Marshall and Warwick saw Buck vanish below the surface with the cutter. Warwick asked Marshall, "How long will it take, sir?"

Marshall shrugged. "Half an hour. Hard to tell."

He swung around as Warwick said, "From control room, sir. Fast-moving HE at one five zero. Closing."

Marshall ran to the rear of the bridge and levelled his glasses. Haze masked the dark line of the horizon. "Keep a good lookout. Maybe it'll go away."

Warwick said, "Lieutenant Buck, sir. Shall I tell him?"

"Negative. I don't want him to get flustered."

Minutes later he saw Buck emerge gasping beside the hull.

This unknown ship was almost certain to be British or American. But he could not dive with the mine still in tow. It would hamper their movements, and even a badly aimed depth charge would explode it and rip off their stern.

"HE steady on same bearing, sir. Range approximately twelve thousand yards." Warwick added quietly, "*Two* ships, sir. Speke thinks they may be destroyers."

A lookout said, "Lieutenant Buck's gone under again, sir. That's five times."

Marshall peered up at the main periscope. It was raised to full extent. Soon now, it had to be.

Another lookout yelled, "Ship's in sight, sir!"

Warwick said between his teeth, "Coming out of the sun. We'll be sitting ducks!"

495

Marshall knew that Rigby was staring at him from right aft. It did not take a genius to know something was happening. He said to Warwick, "Go and find out how Buck's managing."

"They've opened fire, sir!"

Marshall heard the crash of gunfire and saw twin waterspouts burst skyward directly in line with the hull, but well clear.

"Out of range, but not for long." He pictured the other captains as the reports started to come in. A U-boat on the surface. Hasn't dived, therefore damaged. The chance of a lifetime.

Two more columns shot up from the blue water, hanging in the sunlight like glittering crystal curtains before dropping reluctantly. Closer—a bare half mile clear. The destroyers would be charging through the sea like the thoroughbreds they were.

Warwick came back. "Nearly through, sir. Just a few strands more." Two more shells burst. Wider apart. Getting the range.

A lookout muttered, "To think they're our own blokes out there!" Another pair of shells exploded. This time the hull gave a sharp jerk. The destroyers were clearly visible now, the leader almost dead astern. There were more flashes and abbreviated whistles as her shells smashed down into the sea.

"Aircraft, sir! Starboard bow! German. Dornier 17Z. Turning towards us."

Marshall watched as the twin-engined bomber roared overhead, its bomb doors open. The pilot had weighed the situation. A German submarine pinned down by two destroyers. He would do what he could. But even now, as he started to climb, the air around the plane erupted in several blobs of dirty brown smoke. Any destroyer which hoped to survive in the Mediterranean was a floating gun platform. The plane wouldn't have a chance, Marshall thought grimly. But it could give him valuable time.

There was a hoarse cry from aft. "Cable's cut, sir!"

Marshall saw the mine spiralling away and Buck being hauled aboard, his slime-covered hands and body running blood. Cuts from the rough wire and plating.

"Diving stations!" Men tumbled down the ladder hurling tools and equipment through the hatch.

The bomber was rocking dangerously, and Marshall imagined it had been hit by shell fragments. The German pilot *had* given them time to get rid of the mine, but the destroyers would still close in for a depth-charge attack. He stared as a bomb detached itself from the Dornier's belly and plummeted into the sunlight.

"Clear the bridge! *Dive, dive, dive!*"

But Warwick clutched at him, yelling, "That bomb, sir! It can't be! It's *tracking* the destroyer, *following her around!*"

Even as he found the bomb with his glasses, Marshall saw it hit the destroyer just abaft her bridge. There was a tremendous flash, followed by a mounting pall of smoke, and with stunned surprise he saw the destroyer begin to turn turtle, the impetus of her speed thrusting the raked stem into the sea like a ploughshare.

Then he was dragging the hatch over his head, as he heard the sea surge hungrily over the conning tower.

He said sharply, "Hold her at periscope depth, Number One!"

He blinked to accustom his eyes to the control room, and saw Major Cowan by the chart table. "It was a British ship, Major." He let the words drop like stones. "Sunk by one of those radio-controlled bombs that were *supposed* to be secret!"

He turned to the periscope and took a long look astern. One ship where there had been a pair, and it had stopped to lower boats. No sign of the bomber that had saved them.

"Down periscope. Resume course and depth." He nodded to Gerrard and walked quickly to the wardroom. Buck was slumped on a seat, eyes closed, as Churchill dabbed at dozens of grazes and cuts with a wad of dressing. Marshall opened the cabinet and said, "Whisky for the torpedo officer." He held up the all-but-filled glass. "I'll see you get recognition for what you did back there."

Buck gaped at him. "Whisky will do for me," he said.

Marshall said, "Stay with him, Churchill." Then he left the wardroom and walked to Devereaux's table. As he studied the Italian coastline he kept seeing the destroyer as she had staggered brokenly onto her side. Simeon had stressed the importance of the mission, but he did not know the half of it. The enemy not only had invented a new weapon, he was already using it.

Chapter 6

THE air in the wardroom was clammy and unmoving as they crowded around Marshall's chart. He tapped it with his dividers. "This is where we are. Naples is about sixty miles to the southeast

497

of our position. We are about three miles south of this cape."

Major Cowan nodded. "Seems all right to me." He jabbed the chart with his finger. "Our people will be here. All being well."

Marshall asked, "Anything we ought to know?"

"Nearest place of any size is Terracina, about ten miles east of where we'll be." He shrugged. "Mostly Italian guardposts in the past. But now . . . we'll just have to see."

Marshall straightened. Just have to see. It sounded so easy. He said to the major, "Number One will give you your landing instructions." Then he glanced at Gerrard. "We will surface in fifteen minutes. If it all seems quiet, I shall get close inshore and watch for the signal. Then we'll open the forehatch and launch the boat. Questions?"

Cowan shook his head. "None from me."

Buck stood up. "I'll get forward and check the dinghy."

Marshall turned to the three passengers. "Good luck. I hope you get them safely."

They followed him to the control room. Marshall looked at the bulkhead clock. "Ready, Number One?"

Gerrard's eyes glittered in the dimmed lights. "Yes, sir."

Marshall nodded gravely. "If we get a hot welcome, we'll head out to sea. Fast." He walked to the ladder. "Surface!"

As usual, the noise seemed deafening, and as Marshall, Warwick and the two lookouts clambered out onto the bridge he found it hard to believe that nobody heard. Yet he knew that a submarine breaking surface was barely audible a hundred yards away.

He moved his glasses very slowly to port. It was very dark. But the air was like wine. Cool and sweet.

Warwick whispered, "Control room says five minutes, sir."

How quiet it was. Just the easy murmur along the saddle tanks, the gentle pulsing of the motors. He could distinguish the land now. It was an uneven edge below the stars.

A lookout said, "*There*, sir! Starboard bow!"

In the pitch-darkness the signal seemed incredibly bright. Marshall relaxed as the light went out. "Open forehatch. Gun crews close up."

Warwick said, "Pilot says we're about one thousand yards offshore, sir." He hesitated. "Suggests you start your turn now."

"No. Must get closer. We have to give them a chance, Sub.

Imagine paddling that damn dinghy there and back." He tensed. "There's the signal again!" He touched Warwick's arm. "Get down to your gun and train it on the light. Be ready for anything."

There was a brief clank of steel, and Marshall saw figures hauling the dinghy onto the casing.

"Ten fathoms, sir."

"Stop both motors. Slip the dinghy." Marshall watched the little boat bobbing clear. He looked at his luminous watch. Wait for the major's own signal and then get under way. By the time they had made a full circle and arrived here again, the dinghy should be back and waiting. He found he was clenching his fists with sudden desperation. Chantal had to be safe.

"Signal, sir," the lookout reported. "The major's made contact."

Marshall lowered his mouth to the speaking tube. "Slow ahead both motors. Take her around again, Pilot."

"Aye, aye, sir." The submarine swung towards open sea, the gun pivoting to cover the land until it was masked by the conning tower.

"THERE's the dinghy, sir!" Blythe pointed over the screen, his voice hoarse with excitement.

Marshall held his glasses very steady while the submarine lifted and plunged. He could just make it out. "Are they all there?"

The yeoman did not reply immediately. "Hard to be sure."

"Stop both motors."

Marshall saw the dinghy slue around as the first line was made fast, heard Warwick shouting to a seaman to assist the passengers aboard. A figure was lifted onto the casing. He felt his heart thumping against his ribs. Dead or injured? It was impossible to say.

Then Major Cowan came running aft. He said tersely, "They've had a bit of bother, Captain." He gestured towards the shore. "Been running and hiding for days. The whole place is swarming with patrols." He sucked in long gulps of air. "But we've got Travis."

"What about the others?"

"We lifted off some of our chaps. A paratroop lieutenant who has been working with an Italian sabotage group. And Moss, the only one of the original party."

"And the rest?"

"Major Carter and Mrs. Travis went inland. It was the only way

499

they could draw off the search party. Moss was shot in the thigh, so he couldn't help."

Marshall said, "Do you think they've been caught, Major?"

Cowan nodded. "They intended to be. Nothing else would have convinced the enemy and given us the chance to get Travis off."

Marshall said to a seaman, "Get the first lieutenant up here immediately. I'm going forward." He flung himself over the side of the bridge and hurried along the wet casing, Warwick and the major close behind him. The dinghy was still in the water.

Marshall sought out the paratroop officer, whose name was Smith. "Do you know this area well?"

"Fairly well. I wasn't involved with *this* affair." Smith added bitterly, "I'm afraid I'd have shot that Travis character."

Marshall's thoughts raced. "I'm going ashore." He continued sharply, "Do you think we could find them? Get them away?"

Smith shrugged. "Not much chance. But . . ." He nodded slowly. "I'll come with you." He turned. "How about it, Major?"

Cowan replied, "I'm sorry. My orders are to start the investigation on Travis."

Gerrard appeared on the casing, groping along the guardrail.

Marshall said, "I'm going ashore, Number One. You will assume command. Stand well offshore and rendezvous here in four hours."

Gerrard exclaimed, "It's madness! You'll never stand a chance."

Petty Officer Cain called, "Five volunteers be enough, sir?"

Marshall looked at him. "Thank you. Submachine guns and grenades. Just like they taught us in Scotland."

He and Smith followed Cain and his men into the dinghy. "Shove off." He gripped a paddle. "Let's see how fast we can move this thing!" When he turned his head he saw the submarine looming above him, and felt a sharp sense of loneliness.

Smith said, "I know the only likely place where the Eyeties would hold prisoners until the Gestapo arrives. But if I'm wrong, we can forget it. It'll be dawn in four hours."

As the shoreline took on a more definite shape nobody spoke, and Marshall was conscious of their tension. Cain said suddenly, "'Ere's a bit of beach, sir. We'll 'ave to wade the last part."

They scrambled into the water, and Marshall felt the undertow pulling at his feet. He said, "Two stay with the dinghy. If we don't come back, you will rendezvous with Lieutenant Gerrard."

500

Smith held a wrist compass to his eyes. "Follow me. Keep quiet, and freeze when I do. If you have to fight, then fight. No fancy stuff, just kill." He turned on his heel and strode up a steep bank.

Only once did he pause, and that was to whisper in Marshall's ear, "You know, Captain, it might just come off. After all, nobody but a raving lunatic would attempt this sort of caper."

SMITH guided them inland through rough and deserted country-side. They had been on the move for over an hour when suddenly he rolled onto his side and they all dived into the grass, hearing the rumble of vehicles growing and then fading into the stillness.

Smith said calmly, "Probably troops called off from the hunt." He stood up. "About two miles farther on there's a police post on the road junction. Used to belong to the carabinieri. Now they have a permanent squad of soldiers."

They moved forward cautiously, each man holding himself low, as if to avoid a sudden burst of gunfire. Finally Cain whispered, "There's a light, sir." He sounded excited.

Smith nodded. "That's it." The police post was very easy to see, white-walled, with double gates. He gestured to Marshall. "One sentry. Just inside. See his cigarette? The guardroom is directly opposite the gates. Usually about ten men and a lieutenant."

"Car coming, sir!"

"*Down!*"

They flopped into the long, coarse grass as the engine grew louder along the road. Marshall saw headlights sweeping across the white wall, heard a string of angry German words.

Smith murmured, "Bad. The Krauts are here now."

Doors slammed. The solitary cigarette reappeared by the gates.

Smith snapped at the men nearest him, "One of you at each end of the wall, but this side of the road. That'll give good cross fire." He handed something to the third seaman. "Up that telephone pole and cut the cable."

Cain whispered uneasily, "That leaves us then, sir."

"Right." Smith was examining his grenades. "We just go in and let rip." He reached down to pull a commando dagger from his boot and vanished across the road. His figure was etched against the wall. There was not even the slightest sound. But the glowing cigarette was moving very slowly to the ground.

With Cain beside him Marshall ran across the road. Smith wiped his knife on the dead sentry's coat and stood up. They followed him towards the main building.

Smith's head showed briefly against a lighted slit in a shutter. Then he whispered, "A good dozen in there. Swilling vino." He reached up and gently tested a corner of the shutter. "Careless." He added, "Two grenades each. Pull out the pins, release the levers, count two and then pop them into the window."

Marshall and Cain pulled the pins from their grenades as Smith dragged back the shutter with all his strength. "Ready? *Now!*"

They barely had time to throw themselves down before the front of the building erupted in one great burst of fire and noise. Glass, woodwork and stones flew across the yard, and from above came a deluge of tiles and plaster.

Smith yelled, "Inside!"

He kicked open the sagging door and dashed into the room. In a dark corner someone was screaming and choking. He aimed a short burst of automatic fire, and the screaming stopped.

Smith ran into the passageway, his gun cutting down a terrified man in a cook's apron who had come careering around the corner. Smith reached another door and threw his weight against it, falling almost flat as the catch collapsed.

A single shot came from the room, cutting plaster from the wall by Marshall's shoulder. He saw an Italian officer staring at him wildly, an automatic in his hand. Smith screamed, *"Get him!"*

Marshall felt his gun jump, and saw the officer spin around like a puppet, the wall beyond him splashed with scarlet.

Cain shouted, "'Ere's the major's body, sir!" Carter had been shot several times, and his face was barely recognizable.

The door at the other side of the room, narrow and heavily studded, opened very slowly and a hand appeared, holding a white handkerchief. Marshall could feel himself gritting his teeth and panting like a wild animal.

Smith yelled, "Come out with your hands up!" There were two Gestapo men. Smith gestured to the floor. "Down! Hands behind your heads!"

Then he said quietly, "Watch 'em, Cain." Very gently he pushed the door wide open.

Marshall followed, the gun almost slipping from his fingers as he saw the girl. She was lying naked on a heavy table, her arms and legs tied to its corners. She looked like a small broken statue.

Smith snapped, "Don't touch her!"

He moved swiftly to the table, while Marshall stood motionless. There were wires connected to the girl's breasts and thighs; they in turn were attached to a humming metal box.

Smith ran his fingers over a line of controls. The humming stopped, and he said quietly, "Now give me a hand."

Marshall took her head in his hands, his eyes smarting as he saw the raw marks on her body, the blood on her mouth. Smith unclipped the wires one by one. Only then did she open her eyes, her stomach contracting as if to resist some new torture. Marshall whispered, "It's all right. *It's all right.*"

Smith took off his long leather coat. "Here. Get her into this."

Marshall eased the girl from the table. Just one movement made her cry out, and then she fell limply against him.

"Let's move." Smith jammed a fresh magazine into his gun.

As Marshall carried the girl through the adjoining room, Smith called, "You two. In here. *Schnell!*"

The two Gestapo men scrambled to their feet. As Smith backed from the cell he threw his last grenade at their feet, then leaped outside and dragged the heavy door shut. He heard their screams, their frantic fists against the door before the grenade exploded. "Sleep well, you bastards!" he said.

Outside on the road he snapped to the sailors, "Give your captain a hand."

Cain stumbled after them, the gun dangling at his side. It was not real. He thought of Major Carter, all bloody and broken. And that poor girl, what they had been doing to her. He thought of the way Marshall had carried her. No sign of weariness. He had marched as if he were carrying the most precious thing in the whole world.

Chapter 7

"IF YOU'LL wait in here, sir." The orderly held open a door. "The captain will see you in just a moment."

Marshall walked slowly to the one wide window which overlooked the harbour of Alexandria. Outside it was blazing hot, the

503

glare throwing up shimmering reflections from the many anchored ships and the broad expanse of blue water.

The room's fine mosaic floor and domèd ceiling gave it an air of calm, and after the passage from the depot ship where the U-boat had secured just an hour earlier it felt as cool as a tomb.

Marshall looked at the huge murals of voluptuous dancing girls and turned away, recalling with sickening clarity the girl strapped to the table a week ago. He remembered her twisting in his arms, fighting him without strength or purpose.

Once on board, with the submarine heading into open waters, he had made sure she was comfortable in his cabin.

Major Cowan had protested. "But I'm trying to interrogate Travis in there!"

Marshall had snapped, "Do it somewhere else. Stick him in a torpedo tube, for all I care!"

For by then he had discovered that Travis had not come willingly to help his own country. The Paris office of the Gestapo had sent details of his wife's suspected connections with the Resistance to the Italians at the site where Travis worked. Her arrival had sprung the odds against him, and with moments to spare, he had been smuggled through a tightening cordon. As the small party had moved through "safe" houses in the countryside, Travis had seen his wife as the main cause of his own destruction. But for her he would have been working safely for the Germans.

Over and over again Marshall had tried to imagine the sort of man who would knowingly let his wife go straight into the hands of the Gestapo. Just to give him time to get away.

On board, Marshall had done all he could to make her feel safe. He recalled the first time she had spoken to him. He had been standing just inside the cabin, watching Churchill hold a cup of soup to her lips. How small she had looked. Lost in a submarine sweater and somebody's best bell-bottom trousers. She had suddenly pushed the cup away and had said huskily, "Where *were* you? You didn't come!" Then she had fallen back on the pillows.

Churchill had said, "She ain't makin' sense yet, sir."

Once in Alexandria, alongside the depot ship, things had moved swiftly. Grim-faced officers had come for Travis and the three agents. Medical staff had looked after the girl and the wounded agent, Moss. Smith had been the last to leave. "I wish you well,

Captain. You are a brave man." He had tapped his heart. "But too much of this, I think."

The door opened silently. "The captain will see you now, sir."

Marshall followed the orderly to a room where Captain Browning was silhouetted against the window. He turned and said, "Marshall, you never fail to astound me!" He gripped his hand. "You look well, despite what you've been doing."

Marshall placed his cap on a table and sat down.

"I've read your report, of course. About the destroyer being sunk by a guided bomb." He shook his massive head. "Terrible."

"Which ship was she, sir?"

"The *Dundee.*" Browning turned to look out of the window, his swivel chair creaking. "My son David was midshipman in her."

Marshall stared at him. "Were there any survivors, sir?"

Browning took a deep breath. "A few. He wasn't one of them."

"I'm very sorry, sir," Marshall said.

Browning cleared his throat and turned over some papers on his desk. "I'm afraid there'll be no leave for your people. I've told the depot ship to make 'em comfortable. Baths, a few film shows, that sort of thing. I'm sorry I can't do more. Security."

"I was wondering about the girl, sir." Marshall watched for some reaction. "What will become of her now?"

"Back home, I imagine. Her department will deal with it. Brave girl. I'd like to have met her." A smile puckered his mouth. "That was a fine thing you did. Some people take a different view." He shrugged.

The door opened. "Commander Simeon is here, sir."

Simeon strode into the room and threw his cap onto a chair. "Damn it, Marshall, I've had just about all I can take from you!"

Browning said, "Sit down. I'm not having a row in my room!"

Simeon sat down and continued in a quieter tone. "When I heard how you jeopardized the mission, the submarine, *everything*, for your own amusement, I could hardly credit it."

Marshall replied, "The submarine stayed to the precise moment laid down in your instructions." He studied him calmly. "Sir."

"I didn't tell you to go off like a madman on your own!" Simeon's face was flushed. "Mrs. Travis had her job to do. We all have."

Marshall was on his feet. "She was being tortured. Not sitting behind a desk. She and Major Carter went inland alone, knowing they would be caught. Just to save that gutless traitor you've been talking to." His eyes were cold.

Browning stood up and said, "Now I'll have my say, gentlemen. I've been with the chiefs of staff for the last few days."

Simeon momentarily forgot Marshall. "What's this, sir? I've not been told."

Browning eyed him blandly. "I'm telling you now, aren't I? We're going into Sicily in the first two weeks of July."

"Oh that, sir. I know about *that*."

"Good." Browning smiled. "But before then, there is something more we in this section must do."

Simeon sat bolt upright but said nothing.

Browning continued. "These radio-controlled bombs are assembled at the site where Travis was employed. From there they go by rail and road to the various airfields. Mostly to the east and the Adriatic coast. A good supply is in Sicily, though nowhere near the amount there would be if the enemy knew our real intentions. The storage point there is under the command of a certain Italian general. I knew him well during the last war. But for the present circumstances we would still be firm friends."

"Well, I shouldn't talk too much about *that*, sir!" Simeon laughed.

"Oh, but I did. To the chiefs of staff, as a matter of fact. They all agree that we will get the Italians on our side once we invade. The general I spoke of is shrewd enough to know that if he cooperates *before* the invasion, his future will be secure."

Simeon half rose. "*Before* the invasion, sir?"

"That is what I said. Given a solemn promise, he would be able to take over all the bunkers where the bombs are stored and seal 'em off. By the time the Jerries got more supplies of bombs brought from elsewhere—" He swept a beefy hand across the desk. "Bang! John Bull and Yankee Doodle will be there!"

Simeon exploded. "And who would be entrusted to make him such a promise, if I might be told *that*, sir?"

Browning smiled. "Me."

"But, but—" Simeon looked around the room wildly. "You have no experience in this sort of work, sir!"

"No? Too old, eh?" Browning sighed contentedly. "Well, some think otherwise. If you hop over to the commander-in-chief's office, you'd be filled in on details. Because you'll be coming, too."

Simeon stood up very stiffly. "Very well, sir. If it's all settled, then—"

"It is." Browning smiled again. "Definitely."

As the door closed, Browning hurried to a cupboard and produced a bottle. "I've waited a long while for this. Just to see his face, damn his impertinence!"

"You'll be needing my boat, sir?"

He nodded. "I'm fond of you. You're very like David might have become. Or so I like to think."

Marshall said, "Thank you. I appreciate that, sir."

Browning said, "I'm glad. After this I think we can give this boat a proper name and allow her more conventional work to do."

"What about you, sir?"

"Well, I am getting on a bit." He sounded very casual. "There has been talk, just talk, that I will be made a rear-admiral and put in charge of a submarine base somewhere."

"I'm pleased for you, sir. You've more than earned it."

"I'll need a good chap to run the base for me until it's just as I want it. An *operational* man, not some stuffed shirt from the Admiralty. Think about it."

Marshall felt dazed. "I will, sir."

"It'll be a while yet before I can get my little scheme moving, so I've arranged for you and your first lieutenant to be quartered ashore. How is he, by the way?"

Marshall wrenched his mind back to Gerrard. "He's fine."

"Good. He did a fine job in getting you off. I've put him in for a decoration." He grinned. "Too." Before Marshall could speak he added, "Now be off with you. I'm going to have another drink and bask in my petty victory."

THE army truck jerked to a halt. The driver, a bronzed youngster, gestured towards a white-walled building at the roadside. "That's the place you want, sir."

Marshall climbed down and the truck roared away.

At the gateway an army sentry saluted. "Can I help, sir?"

Marshall held out a pass. "I have permission to visit a patient in the hospital."

It was no ordinary hospital. It was for those who had been hurt, physically or mentally, in espionage work. Inside, a messenger examined Marshall's pass. He picked up a telephone. "The room at the far end. Number twenty."

Marshall walked to the end of the corridor, but as he hesitated outside the door it was opened by a nurse.

"I'm Lieutenant Commander Marshall," he began.

She nodded. "We've been informed." She looked at her watch. "Don't stay long. She may want you to go immediately. They do sometimes." She stood aside and closed the door behind him.

Chantal was lying on a white cot, her head and shoulders propped up on pillows. She turned slowly towards him, her eyes completely hidden by dark sunglasses. "It's you." One hand moved upward, pulling the sheet closer to her throat. "They told me you had come." There was no emotion in her voice.

Marshall moved to the bedside and sat down on a chair.

"I wish I'd had time to buy something for you." He wanted to reach out and hold her hand. "How are you?"

"I can watch the window from here." She lapsed into silence.

He leaned forward slightly and saw her flinch.

He said, "You look marvellous. Even in service pyjamas." But she did not smile. "It's like an oven outside." He felt the despair crowding through him. He was useless. Clumsy and useless.

She turned towards him. "How is that nice sailor? From London."

"Churchill?" He forced a smile. "Fine. He misses having you to look after." Then he said quickly, "I wish I could take you out of here. Right now."

She shrugged. "And where would you take me?"

"Where you could be free of war. We could see the pyramids at Giza. Have dinner by the Nile. You could ride on a camel. Be like tourists." He laid his hand on hers. "It might help. . . ."

She pulled her hand away and thrust it under the sheet. "The pyramids." She seemed very drowsy. "You have seen them?"

"Only in the films."

Fascinated, he watched her hand emerge from the sheet. Like an animal coming from its hiding place.

She whispered, "But they would never allow it." Her hand lay beside his. "Regulations."

"I could try." Her wedding ring was gone. "I know I'm not much in the way of company, Chantal, but—"

She fastened her fingers on his hand, gripping it hard. "Do not

508

say that! You are a fine person. When I think how I once treated you. What you did for me—"

Two tears ran from beneath the sunglasses and she said, "No, it is all right! I find I cry a lot here." She did not draw back as he dabbed her cheeks with his handkerchief.

He said, "I'll speak with the doctor." He stood up.

"You called me by my name just then." Her lip quivered.

"Of course." He smiled. "It's a beautiful name."

"And you are Steven." She nodded. "Nice."

"Is SHE going to be all right?" Marshall asked Dr. Williams.

"To be frank, I don't know. She might rally. Or she could slip right under."

After he listened in silence to Marshall's request, he said, "How long have you got?"

"I'm not certain. A few days."

"It might work. I don't see too much against it. Unless . . ."

"Unless what?"

"If you try to force a recovery, she might crack up completely. Any real human contact is a risk at the moment. But a worthwhile one. Fix it at your end. Leave the rest to us."

CAPTAIN Browning dabbed the back of his neck with his handkerchief. "Bloody hot." He gestured vaguely at the litter of folders and telegrams. "I'm just waiting to tie up a few loose ends. After that, I'll expect you to give me a ride." He grinned. "A meeting with my Italian friend has been arranged."

Marshall nodded. He was thinking of his visit to the hospital yesterday. He had spoken to Browning about his idea, but the captain obviously had a lot on his mind.

"I can get you four days. If that's what you want?" Browning said suddenly.

Marshall stared at him. "Four days, sir?"

Browning beamed. "Dr. Williams has fixed it from his end. He has a house in Cairo. He and his wife started off with Mrs. Travis about an hour ago." He rose and propelled Marshall to the door. "I've wangled the chief of staff's driver for you. If he gets a move on, you'll be in Cairo before dusk." He cocked his head to one side. "Four days. Make the most of 'em!"

It was a small but very pleasant-looking house on the outskirts of Cairo, close enough to the Nile to see the crowded masts of the local craft. Dr. Williams came down some steps to greet him.

"Here, let my houseboy take your bag. He'll get a bath ready, but first, a drink." He led the way to a cool, book-lined room. "Gin suit you?"

Marshall nodded and sat down, feeling strangely relaxed.

Williams gave him a glass and said, "Cheers. Fact is, I want to put you in the picture, as you naval chaps say. She's upstairs, by the way, with Megan, my wife."

He seemed to be assembling his thoughts. Then he said, "Chantal met her husband in England just before the war. She was a student, and he, too, was at the university. He's a first-rate engineer. I can imagine he would seem very attractive to any girl. Anyway, they got married and went straight to France. He was working there when the collapse came. Chantal had by that time gone home to Nantes, to her family."

Marshall started. "Left him?"

"Yes. She had discovered he was not the man she thought he was. He acted like a dyed-in-the-wool Nazi, and the German military authorities were damn glad to get him."

Marshall asked, "Then why did she go back to him in Paris?"

"Partly because she was afraid for her father. He is a Resistance chief in Nantes. I think she thought Travis would get at her through him. Give his name to the Germans." He sighed. "She started to work for Intelligence herself when Travis betrayed ten Frenchmen to the Gestapo. They were tortured, and the lucky ones were shot. From that moment Chantal was determined to find out what she could and warn the Resistance, or inform them if any chance of sabotage was likely.

"She was smuggled to England when the Gestapo were almost on her neck. Travis thought she was visiting her parents. When the department heard of these new radio-controlled bombs, and that Travis was in charge of the construction work in Italy, she was an obvious choice for making contact. A terrible risk to her, of course." Williams stood up. "I hear them coming."

The two women entered the room, and Marshall caught his breath. The girl was in a plain white dress which made her skin seem gold by comparison. She was wearing the same sunglasses.

The doctor's wife beamed at Marshall. The girl held out her hand. "I'm glad you could come. I expect you can do with some leave after—" Then she stiffened. "I am sorry. No *shoptalk*."

He replied, "Just four days, I'm afraid. But far better than I'd dared to hope."

She smiled for the first time. "You sound as if you mean that."

"He does." Williams strode to his cabinet. "Now we'll have a couple of drinks while *he* hops off to a bath and some dust-free clothes."

As Marshall followed the houseboy towards the stairs, the doctor's wife said, "What a nice fellow, but he looks so tired."

He heard the girl say simply, "We must try to make his leave a happy one."

He made his way up the stairs. We must try. For *his* sake. It was a beginning.

THE first two days were crammed with incident and colour, with cheerful companionship and only a few moments of tension. Williams took them to Giza and the pyramids. Panting after a nimble-footed guide, they climbed the Great Pyramid of Cheops, all four hundred and fifty feet of it. Williams and his wife had stopped half-way, protesting it was too much at their time of life.

Once at the summit they looked at the spectacular view with pleasure and awe. She said, "I feel free up here. I really do." She added, "Are you happy?"

He touched her arm. "Very."

She did not draw away, but looked down at his hand, as if to test her own reactions.

At the foot of the pyramid Marshall had a camel ride. He could appreciate why they were called ships of the desert. When the beast rose to its feet in four separate lurches, it was all he could do to hold on. Chantal stood watching him, clapping her hands like a delighted schoolgirl.

On the third day Williams and his wife went into the city, and as Marshall sat opposite the girl at lunch he could feel an uncertainty growing between them.

She looked at him searchingly. "What will you do next?"

"Another job." He found he could hardly bear to face it. He hesitated. "I want to see you again. Very much."

511

"You hardly know me."

He watched her gravely. Was she pleased? "I want to know you, Chantal. I need to."

She stood up and walked to the window. "I might bring you unhappiness, as I have done to others."

He moved quickly to her side. "You must not say that. Any man would give his life for you. I know I would."

His hand was on her shoulder, but she pushed herself away. "But don't you understand, Steven?" Her voice was shaking. "I might hurt you! Perhaps I will never be able to—to *feel* anything."

"I can wait as long as you like."

She relaxed slightly. "I know that, too." She touched his mouth with her fingers. "But it would be cruel. I would never hurt you willingly."

"Well, then." He forced a smile. "Trust me."

He pulled her very gently against his chest. He could feel his heart pounding, matching hers. "I mustn't lose you, Chantal. I don't think I could go on."

She whispered, "Oh, Steven, I never thought this would happen."

Williams's car rattled past the window and then the doctor came into the room.

Marshall said, "It's all right, Doc. We've not been up to anything." He and the girl laughed like two conspirators.

Williams bit his lip. Marshall saw the paper in his hand and asked dully, "Recall?"

"I'm afraid so. They're sending a car for you." He added, "I'll go and tell Megan."

Alone again, they looked at each other. She said quietly, "Oh, Steven, your face. I hadn't realized. I am so full of my own troubles." She shook her head. "You have to go back. And I cannot even begin to share it with you." She dropped her forehead against his chest. "It's not fair. One more day would not have hurt them!"

He lifted her chin with his fingers. "I'll be back. There will be more than one day then."

She was studying him, the tears pouring down her face quite unheeded. "I will remember everything—the Great Pyramid, how you looked on that camel, *everything*."

Marshall heard a car outside. He stooped and kissed her gently on the forehead. Then he turned and walked out into the sunlight.

Frenzel waited in the cabin doorway until Marshall finished signing some papers and looked up. "All ready to go, Chief?" he asked.

"The depot ship's engineers have just gone, sir," Frenzel said. "They made a pretty fair job, considering the lack of time."

It was seven in the evening. Sailing time had been set for nine. Browning had informed Marshall that the Italian general had been given Browning's personal message by British Intelligence agents. Phase two would be this rendezvous at sea.

Gerrard edged around the door and said, "I've made arrangements for our passengers, sir. Captain Browning would like to bunk in the wardroom."

"Yes." Marshall smiled. "I offered him this cabin, but he'd rather get the full treatment, apparently."

Frenzel chuckled. "He'll be one of the boys again."

A boatswain's mate peered over Gerrard's shoulder. "Beg pardon, sir, but Commander Simeon's comin' aboard."

Marshall said, "I'd better go and meet him." He found Simeon in the wardroom, staring at a cup of coffee. "Has your gear been stowed, sir?" He was careful to be formal.

Simeon looked at him calmly. "Yes. Captain Browning will be aboard in about an hour with the others."

"Who will they be?"

Simeon eyed him without expression. "An Intelligence chap from HQ, and of course, er, Travis."

"Travis." Marshall stared at him. "What the hell for?"

"Browning got his way over meeting this Italian *friend* of his. But apart from the old-comrades association, we need something else to bargain with. Insurance. If this wavering Eyetie brass hat is to understand what might happen if he goes against us on *the day,* Travis is the man to tell him. With his knowledge of the bombs' potential and how the Jerries intend to use 'em, who better?"

"I see." It made Marshall feel sick that Travis was to be aboard his ship again. "Will he be under guard, sir?"

Simeon smiled. "*Watched.*" He gestured vaguely. "But he will mess with us. Give him a sense of belonging again."

Marshall regarded him gravely. You know. About Chantal. You're enjoying it. Getting your own back. Aloud he said, "As far as I'm concerned, he can go to hell."

514

Simeon nodded, his face very serious. "Of course, old chap. You run the boat, and leave the diplomacy to us, eh?"

Marshall walked past him. By the time he had reached the bridge he was feeling calmer. A seaman climbed up the ladder from the casing and saluted. "The mail, sir." He held out an envelope. "For you. By hand, from a Dr. Williams."

Marshall almost tore it from the man's fingers. There was a photograph inside and a short note: "Got it developed as fast as I could. Thought it might help."

She looked just as she had when they were alone together. Sad, happy, wistful. He stared at it fixedly, remembering her voice when she had said, "I would never hurt you. . . ." He put the picture carefully in his wallet. The doctor had done far more than he knew.

Warwick called, "Prisoner and escort coming aboard, sir!"

Marshall shook his head. "Not a prisoner, Sub. Mr. Travis is to be treated as a passenger."

Warwick stared at him with astonishment. "Aye, aye, sir."

Travis climbed up the ladder and greeted Marshall with a curt nod. "We meet again," he said.

The army captain who accompanied him said, "I'm not much of a one for ships, sir."

Marshall replied, "It should be calm enough."

He turned his back on them as Captain Browning arrived, obviously excited by the prospect of his trip in a submarine.

Marshall saluted. "You're very welcome, sir."

Browning beamed. "I have a feeling we're going to be lucky on this mission."

Soon the deck picked up the steady quiver of Frenzel's motors. Marshall saw the blink of a light from the depot ship, heard Blythe say, "Proceed, sir."

"Let go forward."

He could feel Browning just behind him, hear his heavy breathing as he lived each separate function and movement. Marshall saluted and said, "She's all yours, sir. If you'd like to take her out." Browning stared at him. Then he stepped up onto the foregratings and tugged his cap firmly over his eyes.

Marshall stood aside, and was glad he had made the offer.

A voice called, "Control room to bridge."

The massive head moved very slightly. "Bridge."

The other voice sounded surprised. "Commander Simeon requests permission to come up, sir."

Browning glanced at Marshall. Then he bent over the speaking tube. "Denied," was all he said.

Chapter 8

It HAD taken six days to reach their present position off the northwest coast of Sicily. A careful, steady run, surfacing only briefly to charge batteries at night.

All day they had prowled back and forth, well clear of the land, but as evening had drawn near Marshall had ordered a change of course, one which would take the submarine directly south to the rendezvous. General Cappello was to meet them in a launch, then come aboard the U-boat.

Marshall and Browning entered the wardroom and found Simeon making notes on his personal chart. Captain Hart of Intelligence, who had moaned and retched through most of the passage, was drooped at the table, his face the colour of cheese. Travis was slumped in a corner, staring fixedly at nothing.

Simeon asked, "Satisfied, sir?"

"Quite, thanks." Browning sat down. "Tonight, God willing."

Travis remarked, "Not too soon for me."

Simeon looked at him. "What'll you do after the war?"

"Go back to work, I expect," Travis replied. "Why?"

"Just wondered."

Travis said curtly, "I know what you think. I couldn't care less. Your bosses appear to know my real value."

Simeon smiled. "What about your *wife?*"

"None of your damned business." Travis's composure was fading. There was something frightening and unbalanced about him.

Simeon glanced at Marshall. "How was she when you saw her in Cairo? Pretty fit?"

Browning interrupted. "That'll do."

Simeon held up both hands apologetically. "Sorry, sir, if I put my big foot in something." He looked at Marshall. "Didn't realize it was like that, old boy."

Marshall felt anger rising inside him like a flood. "Well, now you know, don't you, sir?"

So Simeon was using Travis to get at him. To needle him into saying or doing something stupid. It was Gail. Simeon was brooding over the fact that long ago he and Gail had been lovers. It hurt his pride.

MARSHALL waited beside the periscope well and watched the busy preparations around him. According to all the reports they did not have too much to fear. There was no regular antisubmarine patrol in the rendezvous area, and though by day there were plenty of aircraft on the lookout for intruders, the Italians seemed loath to do anything at night. He looked at the clock. Nearly midnight.

Browning came in dressed in fresh khaki drill. He grinned and said, "Mustn't let the side down. Want to look my best, eh?"

The seamen by the ladder smiled broadly. They all seemed to like Browning.

"Ready when you are, sir," Marshall said.

Browning said, "Let's get it over with."

Marshall nodded. "Take her up, Number One. Periscope depth."

Through the periscope he was pleased to see the sky clouded over. He said, "Surface," and then, "Try not to let the general fall in the drink. It would be a bad start."

The responding laughter was lost in the roar of air into the tanks, and Marshall was up the ladder and spinning the locking wheel. The night air struck him in the face like a wet towel, and he had to grip the streaming metal to stop himself from falling.

Blythe struggled up beside him, opening the speaking tubes.

Marshall moved his night glasses across the screen, wondering how good the agents' report had been about this Italian general. Then he saw a small stab of light, almost lost in spray.

Blythe called, "It's the right signal."

"Good. Acknowledge. And get Captain Hart up here to interpret for me."

Hart appeared on the pitching bridge. "You all right?" Marshall asked.

The soldier nodded. "I feel better in the open."

The other craft was lifting and rolling on a cautious diagonal approach. Someone was shouting through a megaphone, and Hart said angrily, "The general won't come over to us, sir. He wants us to go aboard the launch."

517

"Ask him why the change of plan."

"He says there have been two fast patrol boats from the mainland poking about to the north of this area, sir."

Marshall could hardly blame the general for not wanting to be caught in an enemy submarine. He said to Blythe, "Yeoman, tell Captain Browning what's happening."

A line was thrown across, and as the launch surged and groaned into the fenders that had been rigged, Marshall saw the helmsman glowing faintly in a compass light. There were several other figures, but not many. The general was taking no chances.

Browning reached the bridge, panting fiercely. "Seems I'll have to go over. I'm taking Travis and Hart with me."

Marshall said, "I'll send an armed party with you, sir."

"You won't," Browning said. "I'm not even taking Simeon. It takes long enough to get out of trouble without having half the bloody navy in the launch!"

Marshall guided him to the ladder. It made sense of course. And in any case the launch was now firmly lashed alongside. It was just that he disliked the idea of Browning going with only Hart and Travis for company.

Browning lifted his leg over the coaming and muttered, "In any case, I've got my revolver with me. And thanks, my boy. You know what for." Then he was gone.

Marshall held his breath as the three men made their way across the treacherous pattern of spray between the hulls.

On the speaking tube he heard, "Control room to bridge. Fast HE to the north of us, sir. But it's very faint. Nothing to worry about yet."

Blythe, who had returned to the bridge, said, "Probably those patrol boats, sir."

Gerrard's voice came again. "Control room to bridge. Torpedo officer wants to come up, sir."

"Trouble?"

Gerrard hesitated. "I'd rather he told you, sir."

"Very well."

Buck pounded up the ladder. "The Very pistol, sir. Missing from the wardroom." He was breathing fast.

A lookout yelled, "Sir! They're fighting aboard the launch!"

Marshall climbed up to the screen. He saw several figures reeling about in the wheelhouse, and then a man burst out and ran aft waving his arm in the air. There was a dull crack, and seconds later a flare burst.

"It's Travis!" Marshall yelled. "Shoot him down, Cain!"

Marshall saw Browning's bald head shining in the glare as he groped his way towards Travis, who was bent double, reloading the flare pistol, his hair blowing wildly in the wind.

Cain yelled, "Can't shoot, sir! The others are in the way!"

Browning steadied himself against a ventilator, dragging the revolver from his pocket. Travis raised the pistol once more, his teeth bared as if he were laughing or screaming.

"Control room to bridge! HE at zero one zero. Closing!"

Blythe said desperately, "They'd be blind to miss that flare!"

Travis pulled his trigger even as Browning dropped on one knee and fired. Then, as Browning's bullet smashed the other man down, the second flare exploded into the rear of the small wheelhouse in a searing ball of fire.

In the next instant the whole of the launch's deck seemed to be on fire. Blazing petrol ran down the scuppers, and Marshall saw two men leap screaming into the sea.

Gerrard was yelling, "HE closing fast, sir! *We must get out of it!*"

Marshall watched the launch helplessly as more petrol burst into flames, the fire licking towards the submarine until the mooring lines parted like cotton.

Blythe gasped, "The cap'n's had it, sir!" Browning had lurched to his feet, hesitated, and then toppled backward into the flames.

The wind and sea were carrying the burning launch clear. Then with a great spluttering sound it sank under the surface.

Marshall heard himself say, "Casing party below. Clear the bridge." As soon as he heard the distant roar of engines he shouted into the speaking tube, "Dive, dive, dive!"

Men dashed past him, then he himself ran to the hatch. As his boots thudded onto the control-room deck he said, "One hundred and eighty metres."

The hull gave a sharp creak as the boat went into her dive. Down, down, the depth needles crept around remorselessly.

"One hundred and eighty metres, sir."

Marshall clenched his fists, thinking of Browning, fighting back the sense of loss and the anger. He swung around as Simeon shouted in his ear, "Why did Travis do it?" He was almost screaming. "Why?"

Marshall brushed him aside. "Probably because you triggered him off. *Sir!*"

THREE minutes later the first charges exploded. Several seamen exchanged quick glances, but Marshall kept his eyes on the depth needles. She was going down, deeper than she ever had in his hands, and metal groaned as the pressure mounted.

"HE closing from astern, sir. Two vessels."

The first attack had been made by one vessel. The second had no doubt stopped, to keep her sonar unimpaired by the attacker's propeller noises, but would join the attack any moment.

Marshall tightened his grip on the support, picturing the depth charges rolling off their little rails, falling slowly, ten feet a second.

The charges exploded, the echoing detonation booming against the hull. The boat rocked to one side, shook herself and came back again. Flakes of paint drifted through the lamplight.

Marshall listened to the subdued roar of engines as the attacking vessel tore away to prepare another sortie. He snapped, "Group up. Full ahead."

Simeon asked harshly, "What are you doing? Wouldn't it be better to lie low until they give up?"

Marshall replied, "I think not, sir. The real job of these patrol boats is to pin us down until dawn. By then they'll have plenty of help." He looked at Simeon impassively. "I'm not waiting."

Blythe murmured, "Here we go again."

The engine noises grew louder, rattled high overhead and then faded again. The charges exploded much nearer, making the hull tilt and yaw. Marshall said, "Take her up to ninety metres. Slow ahead."

Gerrard glanced at him quickly. "Take her *up*, sir?"

"Yes. They're getting us fixed." He waited, listening to the compressed air as it drowned out the enemy's engines.

"Ninety metres, sir."

"Hold her so."

The deck rocked gently as a charge exploded. It seemed a long way off, and somebody gave a disbelieving whistle.

Marshall looked at the chart. "Starboard twenty. Steer three zero zero. Must get more sea room." He turned to Gerrard. "What d'you think, Number One? How many charges do they carry?"

"They've not room for more than a dozen each, sir." He swung around at a scratching sound, the echo from the patrol boats' sonar.

Marshall said, "One hundred and eighty metres again!"

A pattern of six charges exploded in a long and ragged bombardment. The last pair burst with such a roar that the hull tilted its stern too steeply for Gerrard's men to restrain the dive. On every side the boat seemed to be jerking and groaning in agony. More paint flaked down, and when a signalman grasped the conning-tower ladder for support he shouted, "It's *bending!*"

When the telltales flickered into line, the depth gauges read two hundred metres. Even the air felt different, as if it were being squeezed solid by the tremendous pressure around the hull. Marshall smiled at Gerrard. "Makes our first deep dive seem a bit trivial, eh?" It was all he could do to speak so lightly.

Devereaux cleared his throat. "We are in six hundred fathoms, sir. As far as I can see, we've plenty of sea room now."

Marshall looked at Simeon, and was surprised to see him sitting on the deck, his back against the main bulkhead. He was staring at a space between his feet, like a man under a spell.

"HE closing from astern, sir." The monotonous *thrum-thrum-thrum* seemed endless.

They all looked at the deckhead, visualizing the great depth of water above, the crushing darkness below.

"HE's speeding up, sir!"

Marshall glanced quickly around the control room. His men would all know why the engines were increasing speed. The charges were coming down . . . *now.* The enemy was haring away to avoid having his own tail blown off.

There were three, and to those who crouched and clung to the wildly bucking hull it was like an avalanche crashing about their ears. Lights shattered, glass flew in all directions and pieces of loose equipment rained down on the sobbing, gasping men.

"Emergency lights!"

Marshall skidded on broken glass and heard someone calling for help. He watched, fascinated, as the depth gauges took another

521

slow turn. They were over seven hundred feet beneath the surface. It was incredible that they had withstood the pressures of both sea and explosions. He peered at the clock. After three in the morning. The attack had gone on for over two hours.

Gerrard croaked, "She's steady, sir."

"Hold her." Marshall touched his arm. "You can do it, Bob!"

Gerrard nodded dumbly, and turned back to his gauges as Marshall added, "Check all departments now."

No damage or casualties were reported. But they heard the distant revolutions again as the enemy began another slow sweep somewhere to starboard.

Simeon crossed to Marshall's side. In a fierce whisper he said, "Get us out of this! Increase speed, do what you like, but get me out of it!"

Marshall regarded him coldly. "You said *us* the first time, sir."

"HE still closing from starboard, sir."

Marshall did not turn. "I'm going to increase speed very soon now. When I surface, not before."

"HE's stopped, sir."

Even the operator turned in his seat as Simeon exclaimed, "*Surface?* Are you bloody mad? You'll kill the lot of us!"

Marshall replied quietly, "The enemy's stopped. They're probably looking for flotsam and oil slicks, or bodies maybe. So we'll stay down here. Silent routine until they go away."

Simeon was shouting. "And if they don't go?"

"Then we'll have to stick it out till tomorrow night."

Simeon gaped. "Tomorrow night. Another day of this?"

Frenzel said flatly, "By then they'll have whistled up the heavy mob." He was watching Simeon with disgust. "We'll have plenty of company."

Marshall said to Simeon, "Get a grip on yourself and I'll—"

Gerrard shouted, "They've started up their engines!"

The even thrumming beat grew and then began to fade until it was lost completely. Marshall breathed out very slowly. "Ten minutes and then we'll go up for a look."

The ten minutes seemed twenty times as long as the attack. Nobody spoke, and apart from the motors' purring hum and the occasional creak of protesting steel, they stuck it out in silence.

Marshall thought of Browning's face above the screen before

he had gone aboard the launch. "Thanks, my boy. You know what for." What had he meant? For replacing his dead son perhaps. Marshall hoped it was that.

He said, "Stand by to take her up, Number One. But first warn all departments. In case we're jumped as we pop up."

But when they rose to periscope depth Marshall found the sea devoid of movement. He told Buck to take over the periscope and then walked to the intercom beside the wheel. He paused, not knowing what to say.

"This is the captain. It's been a noisy night." That would make someone smile. "Some of you still don't know about Captain Browning." He bit his lip. "Well, he died back there. Doing something he thought was worthwhile, as I did, and still do." He turned to hide his face from the others. "If he could, I'm sure he'd be the first to compliment you on the way you've behaved. I'm trying to do it for him. Thank you all." He tried again. "Very much."

He released the button and said quietly, "Open the lower hatch. We'll switch over to the diesels and begin charging as soon as I've had another look around."

He saw Frenzel blocking his way to the ladder. "What's wrong, Chief?"

Frenzel faced him gravely. "I just wanted to say thanks to you, sir. From us."

Chapter 9

THE room in Alexandria looked just the same, yet without Browning behind his big desk it seemed totally different. Marshall tried to relax in a cane chair, surprised that he felt no tiredness. He had berthed his submarine alongside the depot ship in the early morning. Now it was evening.

There were four others in the room. The chief of staff, two lieutenants and Rear Admiral Dundas, the top liaison officer with British and American Intelligence. In a lightweight grey suit he looked rather like a retired schoolmaster. The rear admiral pressed his fingertips together and regarded Marshall through heavy-framed glasses. "We've had a lot more information since the last time you were here. The Germans are building up stocks of radio-controlled bombs, some even larger and better than the one you saw at work." He added, "If our invasion of Sicily is to have a chance of succeeding, we *must* minimize the use of this weapon."

Marshall replied, "Captain Browning believed that, sir!"

Dundas went on. "The invasion is timed to take place three weeks and four days from tomorrow. We can forget about the bombs already in Sicily. The first wave of commandos will have to neutralize them. The dump on the mainland is the real headache. It's a port called Nestore in the Gulf of Policastro. It has good rail and road links to carry the bombs to different military sectors."

Marshall stood up and walked to the nearest wall chart. Nestore. It was shown as a small fishing village.

The chief of staff crossed to his side. "The Jerries have made the place into a strongbox. They have an antisubmarine net across the harbour and several observation towers, and the Italians are supplying an around-the-clock antisubmarine patrol."

"What about a bombing attack, sir?"

"Out of the question, I'm afraid. It would be too difficult to make a real impression. And it would tell the enemy what we were really afraid of, and why. Just as if we'd given him the time and place of the invasion."

Marshall said, "I think we could do it, sir." He had spoken almost without realizing it.

Dundas regarded him gravely. "Do you really know what you're saying?"

Marshall did not reply directly. "We've had my submarine for months now, and yet perhaps none of us has properly understood how to use her to full advantage." He began to move restlessly back and forth in front of the desk. Browning's desk. "This one last job would prove our worth."

Dundas added, "And prove Browning's faith was justified from the beginning."

"Yes, sir. Something like that. But I'd want a free hand. Once we reach the place. My decision whether we go in, or turn and pull out if the situation's hopeless."

The chief of staff's eyebrows rose very slightly, but dropped again as Dundas snapped, "Agreed. It's quite an idea! You'll carry a landing party, Marshall, about thirty Royal Marine commandos. You'll have to cram 'em in where you can." He rose and held out his hand. "I thought I'd seen every sort of bravery. Yours is a new kind.

525

I'm proud to have met you." Then he turned to the chief of staff. "I'll want maximum effort, Charles!"

"Yes, sir." The chief of staff looked at Marshall. "My men will get on with running repairs. I understand from your engineer that the starboard screw is a bit damaged after that last attack?"

"A flaw in one of the blades, sir. Could be awkward."

The admiral waved his hand. "Do what you can, Charles." To Marshall he said, "I want you right out of it. I can't give you more than three days, I'm afraid. But if I let you remain here, you'll be poking around the boat, and I want you *fresh* when you put to sea again."

"Thank you, sir." Marshall felt confused. She would know by now about her husband. Would she blame him?

"One other thing." The admiral was smiling broadly. "Your promotion to commander has come through. Congratulations. So be off with you. I'm grateful. As many others will be when you've pulled this one off."

At least he had not said "if."

Marshall picked up his cap and walked out the door.

In the room a lieutenant said, "Surely, sir, it's not possible, is it?"

Dundas said, "An hour ago I'd have said it was completely *im*possible. But after meeting that young man, I'm not certain." His eyes sharpened. "If anyone can make a go of it, *he* will!"

IT WAS one in the morning when Marshall reached Dr. Williams's house beside the river. All the way from Alexandria in the chief of staff's car he had been thinking about this moment. How she would accept him. What she might say.

The door swung open as he reached for it. It was Chantal. His heart beat painfully just to see her. With the light behind her she looked very slim. He could smell the scent of her hair and wanted to hold her and not let go for a long time. Instead he said quietly, "You shouldn't have waited up."

She took his arm. Her eyes looked very bright. "The others have gone to bed." She smiled. "Tact, I think."

There were cold meat and salad on a small table. A bottle of wine stood in a bucket of ice beside it. She said, "I will pour you some wine now, yes?"

He sat down. "About your husband, Chantal. I . . ."

He saw her fingers tighten on the bottle. "They explained. I was so afraid this might happen. Right from the moment I heard, I began to worry."

He replied, "I'm sorry. I thought you might feel like this."

She turned very quickly. "No!" The bottle fell back into the bucket and she ran across the room. "I was afraid for *you!*" She dropped on her knees beside him, her eyes searching his face. "When I learned they had sent him with you . . ." She touched his hand. "But you are back. I have been praying for that."

Marshall felt the strain giving way to a peace he had never known. He said quietly, "To hear you say that. To know . . ."

She tried to smile. "Do not look so sad, *please*. You are back. It is all I care about. When Dr. Williams told me it was over, I . . ." Her hand gripped his wrist. "Steven, it *is* over? Tell me!"

He replied dully, "It didn't work, Chantal."

Then she said very softly, "You're going to do another mission? Is that what you are telling me?"

He nodded. "Yes."

"But why must it be *you?* You have done enough. Let someone else take over."

He ran his fingers through her hair. "I must do it, my darling. You, of all people, must know that I have to."

"Yes, Steven, I do. That only makes it worse."

"I've got three days. They want me out from under their feet."

"Three days. Why do the British always think three days is just the right amount?" She smiled, tears running down her cheeks.

She went to the table and poured wine, and they drank in silence until Marshall said suddenly, "When I get back will you please marry me?"

She stared at him for several moments. As if she had misheard. He said, "You must know how I feel."

"You do not have to ask, Steven." She touched his hair. "If *you* are sure. I am so worried that—"

The rest was lost as he pulled her against him. It was all he wanted. To know she felt as he did.

They walked up the stairs and she left him by his door, saying, "I am glad I waited up for you. Perhaps you would have changed your mind otherwise?" She moved away before he could answer.

Later, as he lay in bed half listening to a breeze against the shut-

527

ters, he stiffened, hearing the door open and close very softly. The girl stood motionless beside the bed, her figure a pale ghost.

She said, "Please. I had to come." She sounded as if she were shaking. "But do not touch me, my darling. Try to understand."

He lay beside her, hardly daring to breathe. He could sense her desperate uncertainty, and he wanted more than anything to help her. He listened to her breathing until it became steadier.

She reached out impulsively and took his hand. She slowly laid it on her breast. "Steven." She kept repeating his name. Then she said, "Love me, Steven. *Love me.*"

IN THE depot ship's operations room Marshall followed Rear Admiral Dundas to the chart table and nodded to his own officers.

There were others, too. The Royal Marine commando officers, the senior operations officer, Intelligence experts, the chief of staff and, he was surprised to see, the paratroop lieutenant called Smith, who had so recently led them to find Chantal.

Dundas stood looking down at the chart and then said, "You have been given details of the mission. To enter the port of Nestore and destroy the enemy's bombing capability. This job is the big one. The grand slam. Captain Lambert is in charge of a detachment of thirty marines and their equipment. Including their canoes"—he shot the captain a quick smile—"or cockles, as I understand they are known. Lieutenant Smith will be in charge of demolition and act as general adviser on local matters. The submarine's fuel and fresh water will be reduced to a minimum to help compensate for the extra load." He looked at Marshall. "You want to add anything?"

Marshall shook his head.

Dundas consulted his watch. "You slip from the depot ship in approximately eight hours. You will embark the marines as soon as it is dark." He looked at Frenzel. "You want something?"

"The damaged screw, sir. Can't it be repaired?"

"The base engineer said it would take too long." He smiled thinly. "The Allies will invade Sicily three weeks from tomorrow. If you fail to destroy the enemy's supply of radio bombs, there may be no invasion . . . period." Dundas was closing his briefcase. He said suddenly, "I should add that Commander Simeon will be accompanying this mission, to take overall control of land operations."

Marshall remained impassive. He already knew about this. He also knew why Simeon was absent from the briefing.

He had been unpacking his grip in a borrowed cabin aboard the depot ship when Simeon strode in, his face cold with anger. "So you're the admiral's bright boy at last!" he had said.

Marshall had stayed silent.

Simeon had gone on, "Well, I've had your number for some time. I knew what you'd been up to with my wife—".

Marshall had interrupted, "Before you knew her."

Simeon's face had been pink with rage. "And now you've stepped into Travis's shoes, and no doubt his bed as well!"

Marshall said quietly, "Oh, I forgot to mention my promotion. Now, *old chap*, I can't be accused of striking a superior officer!"

The pain had lanced up his arm, and he had seen Simeon sprawled on the bunk, blood running down his chin and over his impeccable white shirt.

MARSHALL stepped over a sleeping marine and walked into the control room. The boat was crammed with marines and seamen, struggling to sleep, eat and work in some semblance of order. They had had over a full week of it.

Frenzel was standing by his control panel. "Still bothered, Chief?" Marshall asked.

"A bit." Frenzel cocked his head. "That flaw in the screw. We can't do more than six knots submerged without making a bad vibration. Any good sonar would pick us up in no time."

"Then six knots it must be, Chief." He smiled. "If there's a real emergency, we'll have to take to the cockles!"

He entered the packed wardroom and waited while the others eased into position to see his large-scale plan. With all but essential fans and machinery shut down, the air was greasy and humid, and everyone was showing signs of wear. But their eyes were lit by that old excitement. Anxiety, tension, fear, the need to get it over with. He said, "Most of you know that the weather report is bad. Strong winds from the southwest and a rough sea."

He looked at them slowly. The marine officers and Smith, his own small team, except for Gerrard and Frenzel, who were on watch. And Simeon, sitting at the opposite end of the table, arms folded, his face devoid of expression.

He continued. "So this is how we'll handle it."

They all craned forward. On the chart the port of Nestore looked like a large pouch, with the entrance barely a quarter of a mile across. Marshall said, "We know there's an antisubmarine boom here"—he reached out with some brass dividers—"controlled by a single vessel which pulls it open and closed as required. The left side of the port is an almost sheer cliff, and to the right, where the main fishing village.once stood, the land has been cleared and pill-boxes have been constructed to give a good field of fire." He tapped the small coloured circles.

Devereaux asked, "What about the coastal patrols, sir?"

"Yesterday we were able to time one of the boats. They are regular and precise, and therefore predictable." He added sharply, "However, we shall take nothing for granted when we surface and lower the cockles."

They had had a brief run-through of the method of unloading the cockles two days earlier, and one unpleasant fact had come to light. On their own the cockles were very light and easy to handle. But loaded with weapons and demolition gear they would break up, if an attempt to slide them outboard was made in bad weather. Buck had come up with a simple solution. The submarine's deck gun would be used as a derrick to sway them over the side.

Marshall looked at Simeon. "Over to you."

Simeon took the dividers. "Here is a railway which runs from the port. Captain Lambert will lead half the landing force and carry out demolition. I will take the other party, and with Lieutenant Smith will do our bit above the village itself." His eyes flickered towards Marshall. "And our commander here will carry out a torpedo attack on the main loading jetty at the top of the harbour. It is a concrete bunker which enables the bombs to be loaded aboard ship without appearing aboveground." He added, "The engineer, Travis, stated that the construction is formidable, but once brought down, it would block the whole installation for weeks."

Lambert said, "Should be interesting."

Marshall said, "It's mostly a matter of timing. The nearest German garrison of any size is sixteen miles northeast of the port. So, bearing that in mind, we have three vital points." He ticked them off on his fingers. "First, the coastal patrols. Second, the boom and the inner harbour patrol. Finally, how soon or late the port defenders

530

will be alerted and thereby call for inland support." He smiled at their strained faces. "Any comments?"

Warwick asked, "Couldn't we cut the boom and slip through undetected, sir?"

"Afraid not, Sub. The port is only about six fathoms deep. It was dredged for coasters and medium-sized ships. We will approach the boom at the arranged time. Fire our fish into the top of the harbour, and then lift off the landing parties, who with luck will have created their own sort of pandemonium by then." He looked at his watch. "We'll go to action stations in four hours. German uniforms and equipment will then be issued, but first I want everyone to have a good meal."

MARSHALL wedged his elbows painfully against the bridge screen and levelled his glasses towards the land while the conning tower swayed dizzily through a steep arc. The weather was bad, and with a following sea it felt as if the boat were out of control.

Blythe shouted above the tumult of spray and wind, "All clear on sonar, sir!" He spluttered as a wave exploded over the bridge. "*Hell*, what a night!"

Marshall said, "Open the main hatch."

They had been surfaced for ten minutes. It seemed like an hour. He peered across the bows. If they could get the cockles in the water without mishap, the wind might help them reach shore. He made up his mind. "First landing party prepare to move off."

The forward hatch scraped noisily, and the first of the little boats was hauled towards the makeshift crane. Marshall watched as Warwick's crew swung the gun slowly over the side, one small cockle, complete with occupants and weapons, dangling from the tackle like an overloaded basket.

Buck yelled, "Lower away, lads!" and the cockle touched the tossing water almost shyly. In a second it was free and away, its paddles glinting.

"Next!" Buck was clinging to the guardrail. "Lower away!"

Finally all five canoes were off, and Blythe gave a great sigh. "There they go, paddles flying like bottles in the fleet canteen."

"Good. Close the forehatch. Gun crew below." Marshall wiped his streaming face. "Clear the bridge."

He groped for the speaking tube. "Bring her around onto the

new course. Then take her down. Ninety metres." He scrambled down the ladder with Blythe.

It was a relief to run in deeper water again. The motion steadied, and he felt his cheeks tingling from wind and sea.

Simeon was watching from the chart space, his eyes in shadow as he asked, "How long now?"

Marshall moved to the chart. "It'll take Lambert's party all of three hours to get ashore." He could picture the tiny cockles bobbing over the waves, Lambert and his men peering through the darkness for a first glimpse of land. And then . . .

He walked over to join Lieutenant Smith. "I will get close to the boom and drop your party. You shouldn't have too much bother."

Smith grinned. "I've briefed 'em, sir. I know this part of the coast from way back, when the good people of Nestore caught fish."

Marshall smiled and said, "Just remember the arrangements for pickup, even if you forget everything else."

The hands on the control-room clock moved slowly. One hour. Then two.

"Getting close, sir." Devereaux's fingers were twisting a pencil over and over in short nervous jerks.

"*Sir!*" It was Speke, the senior sonar operator. "I'm getting some strange echoes at green four five."

Marshall put a hydrophone headset to his ear and heard it, like water tinkling in a fountain or someone tapping a delicate glass at regular intervals. He thrust his hands into his pockets to stop their shaking. Then he said quietly, "They must have laid a complete detection grid on the seabed. As much as two miles out."

To reach any sort of position for attacking the harbour installations they would have to be right up to the boom. He felt anger and despair squeezing his brain like a vice. He looked at the clock. "What time is first light?"

Devereaux said dully, "Couple of hours' time, sir."

Marshall said, "We will go in *on the surface*. We will retain Lieutenant Smith's landing party until we are inside the harbour."

It seemed an age before anyone spoke. Then Devereaux said, "But they'll never open the boom for us, sir!"

"You'll talk your way inside, eh?" Simeon could not hide his amusement. "I think you're deluding yourself!"

"Perhaps. But that is how we will do it, so pass the word to all sections." He looked at Gerrard. "The enemy will most likely keep the boom shut while they send a boat to investigate."

In his mind he could see it. The submarine lying surfaced and naked under the eyes of a coastal battery. The boom vessel's skipper being called to his bridge. It would all take time. He said in an expressionless tone, "It's too late to execute another raid, even if we had the means. It's this boat and our lives balanced against what is at stake in ten days' time." He paused, watching their faces. "We have to succeed. That's my decision."

Smith whistled. "Right up to the front door!"

Simeon came forward and stood almost touching Marshall, his face tense and pale. "If you wreck this one, my friend, I'll see that you never even command a ferryboat for the *rest of your life!*"

Marshall met his stare. "If *we* wreck this one, I don't imagine anyone will be left, do you?"

As MARSHALL, with the lookouts and Blythe at his heels, burst through the hatch and climbed to the bridge, he realized that the weather had eased. Warwick climbed up beside him and adjusted his binoculars against the small patch of paling sky.

"Control room, sir. Commander Simeon wants to come up."

"Granted." Marshall looked at Warwick and Blythe. "We have intelligence reports that U-178 is one of several U-boats working with the Italian navy. She's not supposed to be in this area, but when we're challenged to identify ourselves we'll claim her number and hope for the best."

Simeon's voice came through the gloom. "My, we are getting cunning."

"If you wish to remain on the bridge, just remember, one more crack like that and down you go."

"Five thousand yards to the detection grid, sir." The muzzles of the Vierling were shining in the first faint daylight.

The machine gunners were standing by their weapons, their heads encased in German coal-scuttle helmets. Warwick, too, was in his enemy uniform.

Marshall consulted his watch. Getting close.

"Tell the chief to switch to main engines. No friendly boat would come sneaking inshore using battery power."

He jumped as the clutches brought the heavy diesels into use, the exhaust spluttering and coughing throatily. Out there, dozing over his radio set in some shore bunker, the enemy operator would hear it soon enough. Probably long before the detector on the seabed made any direct contact. The uneven swish of their damaged screw. The fault might yet be used to their advantage.

He snapped, "Run up the German ensign, Yeoman."

Simeon was crouched almost double, fumbling with a submachine gun. He said irritably, "I hope this thing works!"

The scarlet flag flapped in the wind above their heads. Marshall glanced at it. Hating it. Depending on it.

"Sonar reports echoes from dead ahead, sir."

Marshall sucked in a long breath. "Tell your deck gunners to prepare, Sub."

"Your cap, sir."

Marshall took it and pulled it over his unruly hair. He said, "Any second now, I should think."

The light seemed to grow with each turn of the screws, laying them bare and vulnerable. Across the sharp stem he saw the first blunt outline of land. In half an hour there would be no room to manoeuvre, if the plan misfired.

Suddenly a piercing blue light blinked over the undulating water. "The challenge, sir." Blythe licked his lips. "I'd better get ready." He seemed unable to hold his lamp firmly.

Marshall turned deliberately. "Now don't get jumpy. We've had a bad time of it and we're trying to get into the first available *friendly* port, right?"

All but Simeon nodded in time to his quiet voice.

He touched Warwick's hand. "You've got the signal ready. Read it to the yeoman." He hoped Warwick had made a proper translation. The signal read, "We require assistance." Nothing more. What any submarine commander might send, if he were at last within sight of safety.

The blue light blinked again. Warwick said, "They're asking our number, sir."

"Then make it. *U-178*."

This was the vital moment. He bit his lip. Someone out there was trying to make a decision.

When he raised his glasses again he saw the full breadth of the

535

harbour mouth and, poised just to starboard, the boom vessel, her bridge windows glinting faintly. He moved the glasses slowly, noting the lines of dots, the buoys which held the antisubmarine boom in position.

"Tell Lieutenant Buck to stand by. Tubes one to five."

Gerrard's voice came up the tube. "There's a freighter moored in the harbour, sir. I just saw it on the main periscope." He was almost shouting. "We won't be able to hit the installations!"

Simeon crossed the bridge in three strides. He spoke in a savage whisper. "Well, you can't fire now, can you? That ship will take the salvo, and the Jerries will have the wreck moved within a week!"

"Signal, sir." Warwick was listening to Blythe. "They want us to heave to. They're sending someone out."

"Slow ahead both engines. But retain course."

Soon a small harbour boat could be seen crossing the boom.

Simeon said fiercely, "Let's get out while we still can!"

Warwick said, "Captain Lambert's party will be coming back by now, sir, if they've not been caught. We can't leave them."

Marshall said to Simeon, "He's right." He looked at Warwick and added, "Thanks, Sub." He turned away. "Tell Smith I want him on the forecasing."

Blythe had glasses trained on the approaching boat. He said, "Eyetie launch, sir. But there's a Jerry officer in charge!"

Some of the seamen on the casing were waving at the launch, and Marshall saw an unfamiliar sailor just below the bridge. It was Smith, who had stripped to his shorts and wore a German forage cap rakishly over one ear. He, too, was waving, and he shouted something in German.

Clinging to the launch's small wheelhouse was a white-clad lieutenant, a megaphone in one hand. *"Was ist los, Herr Kapitän?"*

Marshall took Warwick's arm. "Tell him we've got engine trouble." He licked his lips as Smith climbed down to the saddle tank. "And ask him aboard for a drink. He'll like that."

Simeon muttered, "It'll never work."

But it did.

As hands took the launch's lines, the German lieutenant clambered up the slippery bulge of the tank. He was met by Smith, who wrapped his arms around the surprised German and drove a knife

536

into his stomach. Other figures scrambled down into the launch, and in minutes it was over.

Marshall said, "Quickly now. Smith's landing party in the launch. Make the Italian seamen understand that they'll live only if they do as we say."

Simeon stared at him and then said, "I will take the launch. We'll move that moored freighter and get clear as best we can."

Their eyes held.

"I'll pick you up when the job's done." Without conscious thought Marshall thrust out his hand. "Good luck."

Simeon stared at his hand but made no effort to take it. Instead he said, *"Go to hell!"*

As the launch idled clear Marshall had to shake himself. The boom vessel lay unmoving as before. The launch, with two or three Italian seamen on deck, was steering towards the harbour. He waited, hardly daring to blink, as the boom vessel slowly began to winch open the antisubmarine net.

"Half ahead together. Follow the guard boat."

Nearer and nearer, until all at once the boom vessel was gliding abeam, an officer coming out to the bridge to salute as the U-boat entered harbour.

"He's closing the boom behind us, sir."

But Marshall was watching the little launch as it increased speed and dashed towards the moored freighter.

"Launch is alongside the freighter, sir."

"Slow ahead together."

Marshall tried not to think about the pillboxes on the hillside. He watched Cain and the casing party making a great pretense of preparing lines for mooring, and on the little jetty he saw a handful of yawning Italians.

Warwick was saying hoarsely, "Come on! Come on!"

Marshall snapped, "Watch the freighter. As soon as Simeon's party casts off we've got to move fast." He looked at his watch. Surely something would break soon.

Warwick gripped his arm. "The freighter's moving, sir!"

Marshall sprang to the speaking tube. "Full ahead! Port ten." He felt the hull lurch forward, the bow sluicing past the jetty and the mesmerized Italians.

"We've got to take the freighter's tow rope and warp her clear," he shouted. He conned the submarine around in one huge arc, while high in the freighter's bows he saw the marines lowering a hawser. Others held their submachine guns trained on the shore.

Somewhere in the distance a klaxon blared, and within seconds tracer ripped above the harbour, although it was obvious the garrison had been caught completely unprepared.

"Stop the port engine!"

He gritted his teeth as the freighter loomed over the conning tower. There was no time to rig fenders. No more time for anything. A bullet smashed into the tower and whimpered away over the water.

More machine-gun fire probed into the harbour, and Warwick yelled, "Open fire, sir?"

"Yes," he replied. "Stop starboard!"

The submarine's starboard bow shuddered and lurched below the freighter's great anchor, metal screaming in protest as both hulls ground together. Hands hauled on lines, dragging the hawser down onto the casing and to the forward mooring bollards.

The air seemed to split apart as Warwick's gun crews fired long bursts of cannon shells and tracer towards the nearest pillboxes. From one came an answering volley, and someone fell thrashing wildly in a pattern of blood. Against the dull steel it looked like black paint.

"Hawser secured, sir!"

"Tell the boarding party to get back here on the double!"

He winced as the deck gun crashed out. The shell exploded beside a pillbox and the firing stopped instantly.

There was a short whistle and a violent explosion. Devereaux was shouting, "Mortar! Above the bunker!"

Blythe yelled, "Chief reports he's ready to tow, sir!"

Marshall shouted, "Slow astern together!"

He saw the hawser tauten, felt the towering hull alongside shudder violently as a mortar shell exploded on the upper deck. But she was answering. Slowly and painfully, as the U-boat pulled astern, the freighter began to swing away from her original moorings. Another mortar shell shrieked down and burst on the ship, hurling splinters and fragments of steel in all directions.

Farther around and still farther, with gunfire blasting from

538

every side, although there was so much smoke it was hard to tell friend from enemy.

"She's sinking!" Warwick was waving his cap like a madman. "Simeon has opened her cocks!"

It was true, and with the damage caused by the mortar, it would not take long before she settled on the bottom. A rope ladder had been thrown over, and Marshall saw some of the marines clambering down and being dragged bodily onto the casing.

A savage burst of bullets swept from the land, and when Marshall looked again he saw several of his men sprawled on the deck and others dragging themselves towards the conning tower.

A dull boom echoed and re-echoed around the hills, and Blythe yelled, "Captain Lambert's charges have blown, sir!"

"That'll get 'em out of bed!" The lookout who had spoken clutched his chest and toppled with an amazed gasp. He was dead before he hit the deck.

Marshall snapped, "Prepare to cast off. Stop both motors." He could not wait another second.

Blythe shouted, "Here comes Lambert's mob!"

The returning raiding party were scampering behind the pill-boxes, and the air shook and crashed to their grenades. It must have been a nightmare for the Germans in the pillboxes. The grenades, the lethal clatter of submachine guns. Oblivion.

Cain cupped his hands and shouted, "Two more men to come from the freighter, sir!" Marshall ducked as more tracer slashed overhead. One of them had to be Simeon. He shaded his eyes and peered at the listing ship.

Then he saw them. Smith clambering down the ladder, with Simeon clutching his body like a drowning man.

Warwick gasped, "Simeon's bought it, sir."

Marshall shouted, "Open the forehatch." To Cain, "Help those two across!"

But just as they reached the casing a groan went up. A bullet had found Smith. He lost his hold and fell to the water, the foam around him turning crimson.

Marshall saw Simeon being dragged towards the hatch and shouted, "*Cast off!*"

When he looked again the forecasing was almost empty but for a cluster of dead sailors. Devereaux was struggling to get the heavy eye of the hawser off the bollard, while Cain tried to help him, one arm bloody and useless at his side.

Simeon was halfway through the hatch, his shoulder shining where a splinter had cut him down on the freighter's deck. He pushed someone away who was trying to aid him and lurched back onto the casing. Devereaux turned and saw him; then he, too, was down, his life splashed across the buckled plating. Simeon pushed Cain towards the hatch and then threw himself on the heavy hawser. Once, twice, and then it was free, splashing into the harbour.

He turned and stared towards the bridge, and seemed to grin. Or perhaps it was a grimace, for even as Simeon made to follow Cain he dropped to his knees and toppled slowly over the side.

Marshall said hoarsely, "Full astern. We'll pick up Lambert's party *now*."

The submarine hardly paused as she slid stern first past the small jetty where they had first seen the waiting Italians. It did not take long for the breathless marines to leap aboard. Lambert was with them, but he had less than half his men intact.

"Help those men below," Marshall shouted. "Then clear the deck. We must finish what we came for."

The stern was edging out into the harbour again. "Stern tube *ready*." He rested his forehead on the sights, watching the boom vessel through the crosswires. "Fire." He winced as more metal crashed into the hull, and saw Warwick pulling a wounded marine through the hatch like a sack.

The hull kicked very slightly as the torpedo burst from its tube. When the spray and fragments began to fall he saw the boom vessel toppling onto her side in a welter of smoke and flames. She would soon sink, and with her the boom.

He staggered to the forepart of the bridge again and saw what they had come all this way to destroy. With the freighter leaning at a steep angle on the opposite side of the harbour, the towering wall of concrete and the cavernous mouth of the bunker stood out as they had on Travis's neat diagrams.

"Standing by, one to four, sir."

Marshall shouted a reply. "Fire one. Carry on firing. Three-second intervals."

He concentrated on the pier at the entrance of the bunker. A

540

powerful mobile derrick, and some big metal cases beyond. Bombs which would have been in the freighter tomorrow morning, en route to some German airfield.

The fourth torpedo had left the tube when the first exploded against the pier. After that it was impossible to tell one from the next, or night from day.

The torpedoes must have touched off some of the stacked bombs, and in an instant a massive explosion rocked the harbour, sending a small tidal wave creaming wildly towards the submarine. The noise went on and on, fading and then mounting again as the piled explosives detonated far inside the bunker, into the hillside itself.

Marshall coughed in the smoke which had almost blotted out the harbour. "Full ahead starboard. Wheel hard astarboard!"

Metal cracked into the bridge, and he found himself on the gratings, a terrible pain in his side. He felt Blythe pulling him towards the hatch, but managed to haul himself back to the speaking tube.

"Full ahead port. Wheel amidships." He moaned with pain.

Then he heard Gerrard's voice and saw him clinging to the screen at his side. "It's all right, sir. I've got her now."

Marshall stared at him. "Clear the boom area, Bob. Then get her down and run for it."

Gerrard said, "I can cope. You get below and have that gash cleaned." Blythe half carried Marshall to the hatch.

Then Gerrard crouched over the tube and snapped, "Steer one five zero. Maximum revolutions!" He glanced astern, but there was only smoke and the intermittent sound of underground explosions.

He thought of Marshall and what he had seen him do. What he had done for all of them. The victors.

THREE days later, surfaced, and with both diesels damaged almost beyond repair, the U-boat was steering west for Gibraltar. Marshall stood on the battered bridge, watching the sea.

They had done all they set out to do, and now there was nothing left but to reach Gibraltar before some new failure left them at the mercy of an enemy attack.

Two destroyers found them on the morning of the third day, and as they ploughed towards the crawling submarine Blythe muttered, "I hope they've been *told*, that's all, sir."

They had. As the lights stammered back and forth Blythe asked thickly, "Their senior officer wants to know, sir. Do you wish to abandon or shall he take you in tow?"

Marshall turned and looked up at the flag overhead. The proper one, for once. Then at the full length of his ship. "We've come this far," he said. "I'll not leave her now." He touched the ache in his side. "Tell him neither. Tell him His Majesty's U-boat is rejoining the fleet."

"Signal from escort, sir. 'Congratulations.'"

Marshall smiled. "Thanks. I think we've earned them!"

Douglas Reeman

Douglas Reeman lives in the style one might expect, surrounded by trophies of his life-long love of the sea. In the hall—a watercolour of the motor torpedo boat on which he served in the North Sea during World War II. On the drawing-room wall—his own ceremonial Royal Navy sword and a painting depicting a dozen of the heroines of his modern sea stories—ships, every one. Guarding the front door of his cottage, but not at all out of place, is a nineteenth-century naval swivel gun.

Go In and Sink! is his fifteenth "Reeman", and much of the background is authentic. A German submarine, *U-570*, was in fact captured by the British, rechristened the H.M.S. *Graph* and then used against her previous owners. In 1943 the Germans did have a secret weapon in the form of a radio-controlled bomb which could be launched and directed by one of their aircraft. After the Italian invasion, the Allied navies often took part in the kind of cloak-and-dagger operation that "Buster" Browning attempted with the Italian general. In real life one of the Allied officers to undertake such a mission was American General Mark Clark.

Reeman, who served in all the major theatres of war, learned about much of this background firsthand. "I firmly believe that an author should have some experiences to offer his readers," Reeman says, "In my case the experience of war at sea came swiftly. I entered the navy straight from school, and my mind was bare, like an unused canvas. I took part in sea-borne invasions, sailed in convoys and learned what it was like to feel a ship sinking under me and to see others destroyed in a dozen different ways. Good friends lost, sights too awesome to understand—they all left their mark on me."

When peacetime came, Reeman became a policeman and then a welfare worker. Eventually he bought a twenty-five-ton yacht, aboard which he and his wife cruised for seven years, and on which he decided to write his first books.

That was sixteen years ago and he has never had to search for a subject. For Douglas Reeman it has always been fighting men and the sea.